THE
HARBRACE
ANTHOLOGY
OF
SHORT FICTION

THE HARBRACE ANTHOLOGY OF SHORT FICTION

THIRD EDITION

SENIOR EDITORS

Jon C. Stott, emeritus, University of Alberta
Raymond E. Jones, University of Alberta
Rick Bowers, University of Alberta

CONTRIBUTING EDITORS

William Connor, University of Alberta
Sara Marie Jones, University of Western Ontario
Glennis Stephenson, Sterling University
Bruce Stovel, University of Alberta

NELSON
™
THOMSON LEARNING

Australia • Canada • Mexico • Singapore • Spain • United Kingdom • United States

NELSON

™

THOMSON LEARNING

**The Harbrace Anthology of Short Fiction
Third Edition**

by Jon C. Stott, Raymond E. Jones,
and Rick Bowers

Editorial Director and Publisher:
Evelyn Veitch

Acquisitions Editor:
Anne Williams

Marketing Manager:
Cara Yarzab

Developmental Editors:
Shefali Mehta and
Martina van de Velde

Production Editor:
Gil Adamson

Production Coordinators:
Hedy Sellers and Cheri Westra

Copy Editor/Proofreader:
Faith Gildenhuys

Proofreader:
Mary Dickie

Creative Director:
Angela Cluer

Cover and Interior Design:
The Brookview Group Inc.

Cover Image:
The Illuminated Tree by Brian
Kipping. Oil on wood, 8.25 by
8.25". Copyright 1992 Brian
Kipping. Reproduced with
permission of the artist and Bau-Xi
Gallery, Toronto.

Compositor:
Carolyn Sebestyen

Printer:
Transcontinental Printing Inc.

**National Library of Canada
Cataloguing in Publication Data**

Main entry under title:

The Harbrace anthology of short
fiction

3rd ed.
Includes bibliographical references
and indexes.
ISBN 0-7747-3725-5

1. Short stories, English. 2. College
readers.   I. Stott, Jon C., 1939-   .
II. Jones, Raymond E. III. Bowers,
Rick.

PN6120.2.H37 2001   823.0108
C2001-930673-3

PREFACE

"We imagine ourselves, we create ourselves, we touch ourselves into being with words, words that are important to us," writes Native North American author Gerald Vizenor. One means by which we imagine or create ourselves is through the reading of literature.

The Harbrace Anthology of Short Fiction uses three approaches to encourage its readers in this activity. First, it presents significant and representative works from the increasingly widening canon of stories in English. Second, it provides strategies to assist readers in their appreciation of works of literature. Third, by introducing readers to the language of literature, both simple and complex, and by suggesting methods for articulating responses, it provides opportunities to explore stories and to respond to language in its rich and varied forms.

Although no anthology can include all of its readers' favourite works, the editors have attempted to make their selections as varied and diverse as possible. Thus, *The Harbrace Anthology of Short Fiction* offers many contemporary short stories, by men and women alike, from a variety of cultures and backgrounds, in addition to many of those works that have always formed an integral part of the accepted stories of literature in English. It also includes a large sampling of English-Canadian literature in the belief that Canadian students should have the opportunity to experience the major works of their literary tradition both on their own terms and within the larger context of literature written in English.

Individual works in *The Harbrace Anthology of Short Fiction* mirror the diversity of backgrounds and interests of Canadian students as well as reflecting an expanded canon. The short stories reveal many of the characteristic themes and artistic techniques of their authors; they also reflect the cultural and social contexts in which they were written. In particular, they embody, as the eighteenth-century poet Alexander Pope observed, "what oft was thought but ne'er so well expressed." Most readers of this anthology will find its works speaking directly to them and addressing their most deeply felt concerns.

The Harbrace Anthology of Short Fiction is organized chronologically, according to the birth dates of the authors. Following a selection, its date of publication is printed in parentheses on the right. Such an organizational pattern, based on chronology rather than on pedagogical or theoretical concerns, invites a broad range of responses to a work, unencumbered by artificial or purely technical groupings based on content or theme. It does, of course, implicitly suggest a historical continuity in literature: that works from a specific period often have technical and thematic similarities; and that earlier works and authors can influence later ones.

The book's Introduction considers the reading of literature both as a personal, necessary lifelong activity and as a discipline. It explores how reading poems, plays, and short stories allows individuals to understand their own lives and responses to literature in relation to those of other people. It also demonstrates how readers can engage more deeply with a text, experiencing it more fully and relating it more completely to their own lives.

The introduction to the genre focusses directly on the characteristics and conventions of stories, using examples from the literature presented in *The Harbrace Anthology of Short Fiction*. Discussions of individual characteristics are intended not to offer explanations or explications, but to indicate ways in which authors have used the various elements of the genre. For the reader, an awareness of these characteristics may assist in engagement with the text and lead to a broader range of responses.

Each work is prefaced by a brief headnote establishing a biographical and literary context. The headnote may also touch on technique or theme. Explanatory footnotes identify historical, fictional, and mythological personages; literary and artistic works; real and fictional places; and terms not usually found in standard dictionaries. This material provides resources to assist readers in the personal creation of meaning — not to impose a critical viewpoint or to force interpretation in a specific, narrow direction.

Reading literature invites writing about it. The chapter entitled "Writing Essays about Literature" explores some of the challenges that writing about literature poses, without prescribing a recipe or rigid format for writing. It offers constructive suggestions to assist readers and writers in articulating responses — intellectual, aesthetic, or emotional — to works of literature.

ACKNOWLEDGEMENTS

The compilation of this anthology was a co-operative venture of the seven colleagues whose names appear on the title page; however, no book, even one developed by seven people, is ever created in a vacuum. During the planning, compiling, writing, and editing stages of *The Harbrace Anthology of Short Fiction*, many people offered suggestions and made valuable comments. We wish to acknowledge the contributions and suggestions of reviewers from universities across Canada.

As well, we thank Anne Williams, Martina van de Velde, Shefali Mehta, Gil Adamson, Faith Gildenhuys, and Cindy Howard. These people have made this a better anthology; the responsibility for its limitations is our own.

A Note from the Publisher

Thank you for selecting *The Harbrace Anthology of Short Fiction*, Third Edition, edited by Jon C. Stott, Raymond E. Jones, and Rick Bowers. The editors and publisher have devoted considerable time and care to the development of this book. We appreciate your recognition of this effort and accomplishment.

CONTENTS

INTRODUCTION

"Part of the beauty of all literature," commented novelist and short story writer F. Scott Fitzgerald, is that "you discover that your longings are universal longings, that you're not lonely and isolated from anyone. You belong." Sharing experience through the creation and reception of stories, poems, and plays is a very old, basic, and necessary human activity, as necessary to human existence as food, shelter, and clothing. The literary critic Northrop Frye further emphasized the importance of literature, observing that "whenever a society is reduced to the barest primary requirements of food and sex and shelter, the arts, including poetry, stand out sharply in relief as ranking with those primary requirements." The need to bring order, through language and stories, to human experience seems to be fundamental to all societies and cultures.

While some literature may simply entertain or allow escape from everyday lives, the works that ultimately stay with their readers are those that challenge, engage, or make demands. Well-crafted literature invites its readers to laugh, to cry, to wonder, to analyze, to explore, to understand.

Throughout our lives, we seek to understand ourselves, our emotions, our experiences, and our relationships with others. We also attempt to define our connections to larger social and cultural institutions. One way that we can do so is through literature, for works of literature are the records of individual response to the world in which we live.

Because of our own experiences, we are able to understand the self-doubts and uncertainties expressed in T.S. Eliot's "The Love Song of J. Alfred Prufrock," the wonder of first love experienced by Ferdinand and Miranda in William Shakespeare's *The Tempest*, the disillusionment and disappointment of returning to a family home after a prolonged absence in Greg Hollingshead's "The Naked Man," and the anguish of Phyllis Webb's "Treblinka Gas Chamber." The specific experiences may be different from our own, but we recognize similarities in the thoughts and emotions of the characters; examination and reflection may lead to clearer insights into our own lives.

Because works of literature are often demanding, they offer great rewards. Readers come to fuller awareness of themselves and others. They discover both the uniqueness and the universality of human experience; they explore both their own world and worlds they may never otherwise see. Through critical response to literature, readers question a work, examine their relationship to the author, consider the author's role, and develop an appreciation of the work, both on its own terms and as an expression of the author's vision of life. Readers may also explore a work in the context of its times, whether social, historical, or ideological.

Until fairly recently, much of the literature studied in English courses was chosen from a list of works deemed important by a majority of critics and scholars, a list referred to as the canon of English literature. Like most of these

1

critics and scholars, most of the writers were white, male, and British or of British descent. The list usually began with the anonymous creator of the Anglo-Saxon epic "Beowulf" and ended with such earlier twentieth-century writers as T.S. Eliot, W.H. Auden, and Dylan Thomas. Because it included very few works by women, members of ethnic minorities, or writers from the British colonies, however, it could not be said to reflect the diversity of writing in English.

The past 30 years have seen a remarkable change in our society as a whole: the recognition of the equal place of all people in it, regardless of gender or ethnic origin. As a consequence, many literary scholars and critics have vigorously sought to expand the canon so that it speaks to everyone. They have demanded the inclusion of the many voices whose stories, poems, and dramas are worthy of study, both on their own merits and because of the insights they offer into a very large segment of the population of the English-speaking world. Such critics have argued that literature should certainly present universal human concerns but should also help readers understand how gender, cultural background, and social position influence responses to life. The works in this anthology reflect this expanded canon.

Reading and reflecting on works of literature reveal human similarities as well as differences. Aphra Behn's drama *The Rover* makes us aware of the position of women in the male-dominated upper-class English society of the late seventeenth century. Tennessee Williams's *Cat on a Hot Tin Roof* presents intense family conflicts as these take place within the culture of the rural American south in the middle of the twentieth century. The poetry of Oodgeroo Noonuccal (Kath Walker) reveals a modern Australian aboriginal woman examining her people's past and its troubled relationships with both government and newcomers.

Readers who come actively to such works with an open, questioning mind will be able to join with their authors in making explicit the implicit. They will appreciate that an author has used language connotatively, choosing words that, in addition to their dictionary meanings, suggest a range of emotions, ideas, or associations. They will recognize the symbolic nature of actions, characters, and objects. As the German literary critic Wolfgang Iser has commented, literary texts are incomplete; they contain gaps that readers fill in or bridge to create meaning. Readers anticipate, make inferences, draw conclusions; in short, they actively work with the language of a piece of literature to arrive at meaning.

Reading for meaning is a very personal act. It is not simply a matter of paraphrasing or summarizing a story or play, of transforming poetry into prose, or of examining literary technique or metaphorical language. Each reader is unique and will, therefore, respond differently — perhaps slightly, perhaps dramatically — to a work. A Dubliner will no doubt react differently to James Joyce's "Araby" than will a Winnipegger; a man about to retire will react differently to Shakespeare's *The Tempest* than will a young woman who has just left home for first-year college or university; a woman will react differently to Margaret Atwood's "The Resplendent Quetzal" than will a man. People who have read widely in each of these three authors or who have a well-developed knowledge of literature would likely have a different and broader interpretation of these three works than someone who seldom reads. Readers draw on personal experience, knowledge, and awareness of both specific literature and literary techniques to appreciate and interpret a literary work.

There is no one simple process for interpreting literature; different readers develop different approaches, some of which will be more useful for some works than for others. That said, interpretation of a literary work begins with the words of the text themselves. Readers question the choice and arrangement of details and ponder their significance. Such active inquiry may commence on reading the title or during a first reading. Individual interpretation will change with each rereading as readers observe more details, acquire more information about them, and perceive new relationships among them.

Readers bring their own experiences to their interpretation of literature. Basing interpretation on the words of the text, they can compare and contrast their own responses to life with those of authors and characters. Readers who have had intense family conflicts will be able to make inferences about the domestic arguments in Eudora Welty's "Why I Live at the P.O." Reciprocally, interpretation of literature can enrich experiences of life. Younger readers will not have had the experiences of the middle-aged women in Jane Rule's "Inland Passage," but a reading of that story may bring empathy for problems different from theirs. Recalling personal experience while reading a work for the first time can assist in its interpretation.

Readers also bring considerable literary experience to their reading of literature: an understanding of the ways in which authors use language and the general patterns of the major literary genres (poetry, drama, and fiction), awareness of important themes, and, frequently, familiarity with other works by the same writer. For example, knowledge of Shakespeare's use of blank verse, his creation of patterns of imagery, and the structure of his earlier comedies will make a study of *The Tempest* more rewarding. Reflection on the myths surrounding men and women will aid in the interpretation of Adrienne Rich's "Diving into the Wreck." Readers draw on what they already know and on critical literature to expand their interpretation of a literary work.

While readers bring considerable knowledge and experience to a literary work, they must also be conscious of the creative intelligence behind the selection and arrangement of its elements. General techniques and genre characteristics, as well as cultural or other forces at play during the writing, may influence some of the selection and arrangement, but most choices arise from the author's purpose in writing the work. Although readers may not find this purpose apparent on first reading, speculation on purpose, based on attention to details and their sequence, may reveal potentially deeper meanings in a work.

Understanding is enhanced as readers acquire more relevant background information and apply it to the text. Knowledge of the actual people and literary or mythological characters mentioned in the text, of allusions to historical events and episodes in other works, and of geographical or architectural settings will clarify their function in a work. In "Fogbound in Avalon," for example, Annie, the narrator, reads a magazine article about the painter Edvard Munch. Examining that artist's works may reveal a clearer picture of Annie's state of mind.

Literary works often reflect events and conflicts in the lives of their authors; awareness of such personal details can enhance a reader's understanding of how and why authors have written as they have. For example, James Joyce, in "Araby," William Wordsworth, in "Lines Composed a Few Miles Above Tintern Abbey," and Amy Tan, in "Two Kinds," drew on facts from their own lives. What is perhaps most interesting is the way in which an author has taken such raw materials of life and shaped them to meet the needs of the work.

Literary works are also products of the times in which they were written, for nearly all writers have been sensitive to and influenced by the literary, intellectual, political, and social forces around them. Ernest Hemingway's attitude toward the rejection by many of traditional moral and religious values during and after World War I helps to explain the actions of the two waiters and the elderly man in "A Clean, Well-Lighted Place." Familiarity with Margaret Atwood's musings on being a woman writer will enrich interpretations of her poetry and such short stories as "The Resplendent Quetzal."

Finally, readers should remember that just as it is impossible to understand completely another person or even oneself, so there is no such thing as a final, complete, or totally correct interpretation of a work of literature. To successive readings of a work readers bring different frames of mind, other personal experiences, new literary or other factual knowledge, and greater familiarity with the work. Thus, with each reading, fuller, more rewarding, and potentially new interpretations are possible.

To assist readers in the creation of meaning, the introductions to the three genres in this anthology — poetry, drama, and short stories — discuss technical aspects of literary works. Headnotes and footnotes provide information about authors and their works and about names, places, and obscure terms mentioned in the texts. The Glossary defines terms frequently used in discussing literature.

Critical response to literature often involves writing about poems, stories, and dramas. Through writing, readers explore the parts and the whole of a work, examine their previous interpretations and test their validity, evaluate the significance of relationships among parts of a work, and create new meanings. Of course, new interpretations may not be final ones; indeed, they may be modified several times during the writing process. Exploration of apparently contradictory information may provide fresh insights into a work. If, in creating an interpretation, the writer has based the statements on the text, has provided evidence and not ignored contradictory evidence, and has argued logically and clearly, then the interpretation is valid. For those seeking assistance in the writing of interpretive essays, the chapter entitled "Writing Essays about Literature" offers a number of suggestions and guidelines.

What are the rewards of becoming active readers and interpreters? An answer can be found by returning to this introduction's opening discussion of essential human needs. Poems, plays, and short stories are artistic and articulate responses to life that offer emotional, intellectual, and imaginative nourishment to their readers. Anthologies such as this provide exposure to literature that enhances the readers' knowledge of themselves and the world outside of themselves. Such experiences can lead to self-discovery and a lifelong love of reading.

SHORT FICTION

INTRODUCTION TO SHORT FICTION

The daily lives of most people are full of stories, sometimes written down but, more often, not. People imagine, develop plans for a successful day, relate accounts (sometimes true and sometimes embroidered) about what they have done, or gossip about other people. They personalize, modify, and extend stories they have heard or read; retell and sometimes add variations to jokes and anecdotes; read newspaper stories; listen to country and western ballads; watch movies, television programs, and commercials (which are often mini-dramas). They receive some of their religious and political messages in the form of stories included in sermons and election speeches.

The processes of creating, transmitting, and receiving stories are among the most basic human activities. "One wants to tell a story, like Scheherazade," novelist Carlos Fuentes wrote, "in order not to die. It's one of the oldest urges of mankind. It's a way of stalling death." Like eating, sleeping, and breathing, it is a necessary human activity, and like breathing, so natural that we are often unaware that it is occurring. In *Tellers and Listeners: The Narrative Imagination*, the noted British critic Barbara Hardy has written:

> Nature, not art, makes us all story-tellers. Daily and nightly we devise fictions and chronicles, calling some of them daydreams or dreams, some of them nightmares, some of them truths, records, reports, and plans. Some of them we call, or refuse to call lies. Narrative imagination is a common human possession, differentiating us ... from the animals.

The creation of all stories involves the selection and structuring of details that assist the storytellers in achieving their intended purposes. While in the types of stories described by Hardy these activities may be casual and haphazard, in those written as short stories and novels they are usually very deliberate and precise. Authors include only those characters, events, objects, and details that they consider to be necessary for their stories, and they arrange them in artistically satisfying and meaningful patterns. As an example, we know that in their day-to-day lives people spend much time on routine activities such as obtaining, preparing, and eating food. Although some people have transformed them into highly entertaining events, authors describe these only when they are important to their stories in some way: to development of plot and conflict, perhaps, or to portray character.

Some stories make few demands on their readers, offering light entertainment. Others require attentive readers, not only because their characters and themes are more complex and involved, but also because their authors frequently imply, rather than explain, elements of character and theme. Authors may, for example, leave the significance of actions, dialogue, and objects for readers to discover. They may create narrators who are not reliable reporters or interpreters. Moreover, they may present events in other than chronological order or may not supply clear links or bridges between sections of a story.

Readers easily recognize the basic elements of most stories — characters, actions, and settings — and the basic organizing pattern, which is the introduction, development, and resolution of one or more conflicts. An understanding of the varied and complex ways in which both these elements and the pattern of conflict are used by authors, along with an awareness of the significance of such techniques as narrative point of view, symbolism, and irony will bring to readers fuller, richer comprehension of the stories they encounter. Careful attention to these elements is especially important in the reading of short stories, in which authors must achieve their purposes within a limited space, generally a few thousand words. Like lyric poets, to whom they have been frequently compared, they cannot waste words and must make each word contribute to their stories' total effect and meaning.

PLOT AND CONFLICT

Key to many stories are the incidents they contain; readers want to know what happens next and how a story ends. Authors select and organize events and then add details that contribute to the **plot** and lead toward a satisfying conclusion. The plot of a story provides more than factual information about who did what and when; it helps readers understand why these events occurred.

In most short stories, the plot begins with an **exposition** and then is organized around the introduction, development, and **resolution** of one or more **conflicts**. The exposition provides necessary background about characters, settings, and events. Those stories told or narrated in the same order in which the events occurred, or chronological order, usually introduce the conflict near the beginning. The events that follow form the **rising action**, or sequence of actions, leading to the **climax** or turning point, which is the most significant moment in the story. The **dénouement**, or final outcome or consequence of events, and the resolution of the conflict usually follow quickly. "The Naked Man," "Rappaccini's Daughter," and "Bliss" present events in chronological order, helping to reveal both the relationships between actions and the nature of the characters' responses to them.

Many writers use **flashbacks**, interrupting the chronological presentation of events to introduce earlier actions that clarify the immediate present of the narrative. For example, during a Christmas vacation in Mexico, Sarah and Edward, the childless couple in "The Resplendent Quetzal," think about their courtship and unhappy married life in Toronto. By presenting these thoughts, which neither communicates to the other, the author clarifies the significance of their actions during an excursion to some Aztec ruins. While she sits in a bar, the central character in "Too Much to Explain" has several brief, but painful memories of the past while she is trying to extricate herself from a destructive relationship. Other writers use **foreshadowing**, providing clues which hint at significant events that occur later in the story. In "A Rose for Emily," the reasons for the title character's purchase of arsenic are not explained. Only at the conclusion are her motivations and the ironic significance of the notation on the package, "For rats," made clear.

Most readers demand more than an exciting plot to stimulate their imaginations or develop their understanding of themselves and the world around them. This is particularly the case in many modern short stories, where the plot is minimal, there are few, if any, physical actions, and the events may initially appear to be almost trivial. Interest in the motivations of characters and their responses frequently leads to a rereading of such stories. Do they develop during the course of a plot? Do they gain clearer understandings of themselves and their situations? What are the causes of the changes or insights, or the failure to achieve them?

When they change, the central characters, or **protagonists**, often do so as a result of conflicts with one or more of three kinds of opposing characters or forces, often referred to as **antagonists**. First, individuals may be in conflict with themselves. In "Rappacini's Daughter," Giovanni must wrestle with his conflicting opinions about Beatrice, attitudes that reveal more about different sides of his own nature than they do about the young woman. In contrast, the narrator's mother in "Borders" is in conflict with the immigration officials who demand that she declare herself either a Canadian or an American citizen. Her struggle symbolizes that between Native peoples and colonial powers that, will not allow the subjects to define themselves in their own terms.

Second, characters find themselves in conflict with those around them — quite often brothers and sisters, parents and children, husbands and wives. Because family conflicts are among the most intense and intimate that most people experience, the frequency with which these occur in stories is not surprising. Often, in quarrelling with those closest to them, individuals are trying to define themselves and to define their positions in the relationships. In "The Naked Man," the members of a family are reunited when the son returns from a year-long trip to Australia. From the parents' surprise over his call from the airport, to the mother's anxiety to get to her hair appointment, to the welcome-home party at which the young man considers himself an outsider, the lack of family cohesiveness becomes increasingly apparent. The reclusive heroine of "A Rose for Emily," the last member of a once-proud and wealthy Southern family, asserts her own status by defying the townspeople, refusing to pay taxes, and flaunting her Northern lover before them. In both "Squatter" and "The Motor Car," young immigrants to Canada find themselves in conflict with the cultures of their new country.

Third, conflict may place the central characters in opposition to natural or supernatural forces. In "The Open Boat," four men attempt to survive a violent storm, while in "The Lamp at Noon," a husband and wife are virtually helpless in the face of drought and dust storms that are destroying their farm. In both stories, characters respond differently to the struggle with nature. While they have little chance of success against the elements, those who display courage and determination, like the Oiler in "The Open Boat," achieve a kind of moral victory.

Most stories present conflicts of more than one type and usually examine the interrelationships between them. In "The Conversion of the Jews," for example, Ozzie seeks to define himself while attempting to deal with the conflicting expectations of his mother, the rabbi, and his peers. The narrator of "Bartleby, the Scrivener," while attempting to understand the motives behind Bartleby's behaviour, is also wrestling with his own opposing attitudes and with the dehumanizing effect of life in New York.

Not all stories conclude with conflicts resolved. In some, the characters confront forces or realities they cannot alter, as is the case in "A Clean, Well-Lighted Place." In others, their own inner flaws do not permit resolution. The narrator of "Why I Live at the P.O." believes she has triumphed over her family by leaving home. Although she does not appear to realize it, it is she who has created many of the situations that have made conditions intolerable at the house, and, in her account of events, she unconsciously reveals that her anger and hostility, the sources of much of the conflict, remain.

CHARACTER AND CHARACTERIZATION

Short stories generally focus on one or two major **characters**. These are almost always **rounded**; that is, they possess the complexities, contradictions, and depths of personality associated with actual human beings. They are distinguished from **flat characters**, whose personalities are presented briefly and in little depth. They may also be **dynamic**, changing during the course of a story. The change may be positive, as it is for Fido in "Inside Passage." At first suspicious and resentful of her cabin mate, Fido reveals her own insecurities and vulnerabilities. However, she is able both to understand and accept the other woman's weakness and to control her own vulnerability sufficiently to declare her new-found love. Character change may also be negative, as in the case of Giovanni in "Rappaccini's Daughter." At first he is merely a naïve young man in a strange city. But the uncertainties he develops about Beatrice are based on his own self-centred concerns, and he must bear a great deal of responsibility for the disastrous outcome of the events.

In some modern short stories, characters are **static**, undergoing no development. Lack of change may be a result of the brevity of a story; there simply may not be the space to portray development. It may also be a reflection of the characters' inability to grow or to develop, or it may represent a thematic and philosophical position that views people as subject to outside forces that they can neither understand nor control. In "A Clean, Well-Lighted Place," for example, the older waiter, who is sympathetic to the old man who frequents the café, does not change as a result of his knowledge of the meaninglessness of life, a condition he cannot change. He merely accepts what is.

At the conclusion of many short stories, one or more of the major characters may experience what James Joyce called an "**epiphany**," a moment of revelation that brings understanding of a character's situation in life. In "Araby," the boy, while standing in the darkness, perceives the truth of his motivations for coming to the bazaar and the nature of his feelings for his friend's older sister. Annie, the narrator of "Fogbound in Avalon," finally realizes that returning to her home town has not helped her to overcome the unhappiness of her adult life.

In presenting characters confronting the conflicts in their lives, authors seldom engage in direct character analysis. Instead, they employ a variety of devices, especially **dialogue** and **action**, that reveal character implicitly. The conversation of the two waiters in "A Clean, Well-Lighted Place" consists of short, often abrupt phrases and sentences that seem very similar in style;

however, the younger man asks a number of questions that reveal his lack of understanding of either his fellow worker or their customer. His partner gives simple answers without elaboration; these are the facts he accepts without questioning or resistance. In "The Naked Man," Dennis's and his parents' attitudes toward his Studebaker car indicate his new and somewhat awkward relationship in his family.

In these stories, the contrasting actions of people in the same situations reveal character. "Bartleby, the Scrivener" and "The Boat" also use this method, and there are many other examples. In the former story, the work patterns of Turkey and Nippers, two copyists for a New York lawyer, represent contrasts that the cautious narrator is able to keep in balance. While each exhibits some extreme behaviours, the fact that their personalities complement each other allows the lawyer to maintain the calmness of his daily routine. However, the arrival of the title character upsets both his routine and peace of mind. The lives of the mother and father in "The Boat" have been tied to the sea since their youth, but each views the attachment and their children's attitude to the sea differently. The father seems to have sacrificed his love of literature to the necessity of fishing; the mother, who has never read a book since high school, sees making a living on the water the natural and honourable thing to do. Not surprisingly, the father is more sympathetic to his daughters' desires to leave; the mother sees their departures as almost a desertion.

Characters' thoughts and statements about themselves and other people also cast light on their own personalities. Their analyses and judgements should not necessarily be taken at face value. Rather, the reasons for them should be analyzed to discover what there is about particular characters that makes them view themselves and other people the way they do. For example, the narrator of "Why I Live at the P.O.," in expressing her negative opinion of her sister, reveals her own insecurity and resentment. In "Bartleby, the Scrivener," the narrator's satisfaction with his occupation and his position in New York legal circles may help to explain why he reacts to Bartleby as he does.

Physical objects, such as possessions or clothing, can reveal character. The items belonging to the dead priest in "Araby" reveal a great deal about both him and the young narrator. The two women sharing a cabin in "Inland Passage" dress differently, a reflection of how they are coping with the events of their pasts. By wearing her best silk dress to travel into the United States to visit her daughter, the mother of the narrator in "Borders" is indicating elements of her character that will become more evident in her confrontation with the officials.

Finally, authors' descriptions of the physical appearance of individuals assist in the delineation of character. Melville carefully describes not only the clothing, but also the faces of the three scriveners in "Bartleby." While Turkey and Nippers are obvious, simple contrasts in looks and behaviour, Bartleby, considered in relation to them, is far more ambiguous. Hawthorne makes careful use of physical description in "Rappaccini's Daughter." Rappaccini's "sickly and sallow hue," his "stooping posture," and his fixity of gaze are all intended to symbolize the negative effects of his intense, almost total preoccupation with his scientific pursuits.

SETTING

Settings of stories, the locations and times in which the actions occur, can be specific social or cultural contexts, such as a character's home, neighbourhood, or place of work; larger, more generalized geographical regions, such as the Canadian Prairies, or the coastline of eastern Florida; specific times of the day or of the year; and historical periods. Even weather conditions may be an important part of setting. In addition to assisting readers in visualizing events, settings provide contexts for the actions and contribute to the delineation of character, the creation of mood, and the development of theme. Settings are frequently symbolic, representing internal emotional states of characters. Readers who interpret settings rather than simply read them literally, who question why authors have selected particular times and places for their stories, will gain fuller understanding of the works they encounter.

In Sinclair Ross's "The Lamp at Noon," set on a Saskatchewan farm during the drought of the 1930s, the use made of buildings, landscape, and weather contributes to the development of the theme. Although the summer season and the time of day should bring both brightness and hope, a three-day dust storm has obscured the sun and blown away the precious topsoil needed to grow crops. The dust settling over everything in the dimly lit kitchen symbolizes the hopelessness the farm wife experiences. In "When Twilight Falls on the Stump Lots," the semi-cleared land midway between forest and farm underscores the implicit clash between the natural and human worlds.

A major setting in many stories is the home of the central character, a place that should represent security, stability, and nurturance. Frequently, characters leave homes that do not possess these qualities. In "The Motor Car," Calvin departs from Barbados because his life there seems unfulfilling compared with the lives of the Canadian tourists who visit the island. He believes that Toronto will be everything for him that his home is not. In "The Naked Man," Dennis expects to return to a place that is emotionally, as well as physically, the same as when he left it. However, not only is his prized car missing, he is displaced from his own bedroom by a stranger, and his parents seem to resent his return as an intrusion into the new routines of their lives. The decaying condition of the House of Usher, which is described in detail by Poe's narrator, parallels the psychological state of the man for whom it is home. Introverted and melancholy, his withdrawal from the larger world leads to his destruction, just as the instability of the house leads to its collapsing in on itself.

Even though the characters in many stories have dwellings to which they can return, these places do not always offer them security. In "The Resplendent Quetzal," the fact that Sarah and Edward spend Christmas, a time associated with home and family, on vacation in Mexico implies much about their lives back in Canada. Unlike his younger colleague, the older waiter in "A Clean, Well-Lighted Place" is not anxious to return to his lodgings, preferring to stay until dawn in a bar where he can better endure his life.

POINT OF VIEW

The narrator of a story, the person reporting on the characters, actions, and settings of a story, is as important as these elements themselves. While authors write their stories, they do not tell them directly; they create **narrators**, through whose voices the stories are related. By the choice of narrative **point of view**, the perspective from which a story is told, an author influences its interpretation. Third-person narrators are not characters in the stories they tell. They may be objective, reporting only the observable facts of the story without direct comment; omniscient, delving into the minds of several or all of the characters; or limited, delving only into the mind of the central character. First-person narrators are present in the stories they tell, either as observers or minor participants, or as major characters. It is interesting, after reading a story, to speculate how its meaning might have been altered had the author selected a different point of view or narrator.

Each type of narrator provides specific advantages to an author. Immediately observable in objective third-person narrators is their detachment from the scenes they recount. During most of Hemingway's "A Clean, Well-Lighted Place," the narrator describes, without comment, the bar and café, the actions of the old man, and the conversations between the two waiters. Only at the conclusion of the story does the narrator present the thoughts of the older waiter. This shift from objective to limited third-person narration casts light on the "facts" of the earlier part of the narration. Knowing the attitude of the waiter, readers can perceive that the apparently objective reporting earlier in the story consisted of elements carefully selected to reveal the characters' attitudes toward life.

Choosing a third-person omniscient narrator who reports on the emotions and thoughts of several characters allows an author to develop comparisons between individuals and to portray more fully the nature of the relationships between them. Atwood's "The Resplendent Quetzal" consists of five sections. In the first four, the narrator reports alternately on the thoughts of Sarah and her husband, Edward, each of whom is in a different part of the Aztec ruins they are touring. Even in the concluding section, when Edward returns to his wife, the narrator presents the thoughts first of one and then the other. The abruptly shifting point of view indicates the nature of the couple's relationship.

Although able to enter into the mind of only one character, a limited third-person narrator is able to explore that character fully, often exposing the character's failure to perceive the nature of the situations in which she finds herself, as is the case in "Bliss," or presenting aspects of the character not understood by those around her, as in "The Story of an Hour." In the latter story, other people attribute the heroine's death to her shock of joy on discovering that her husband, presumed dead, is still alive. The narrator, in presenting the woman's thoughts as she sits alone after receiving the news of her husband's supposed death, provides readers with information that explains the true cause of her death.

Because they are characters in the stories they report on, first-person narrators usually have access to less information than do third-person narrators. The words of first-person narrators raise such questions as: "How reliably does the narrator interpret events, his or her own character, and the characters of other people?" The observer narrator, a representative of the townspeople in "A Rose for Emily," recounts incidents he has heard of or seen from a distance. Using such phrases as "we believed," "we said," and "we were sure," he also presents hypotheses about the recluse. Only after her death, when he, along with other townsmen, has entered her bedroom, does he make a discovery that provides an explanation of the elderly woman's life and casts light on the accuracy of her neighbours' suppositions about it. Through the use of this type of narrator, Faulkner creates a story that is as much about the townspeople who interpret and judge Emily Grierson as it is about her life itself.

First-person narrators who are the main characters in a story are also limited by the extent of the knowledge they possess. Moreover, qualities of their personalities may cause them to ignore, overlook, or misinterpret the significance of the actions in which they are involved and the characters with whom they interact as in the case in "Why I Live at the P.O." Other narrators may be more aware of themselves, and their narratives may present their consciousness of character change, as in "Bartleby, the Scrivener," in which the narrator seems to be as interested in explaining how the young man influenced him as he is in analyzing Bartleby himself. For the mature narrators of "What I Learned from Caesar" and "The Boat," their remembrance of their boyhood relationships with their fathers provides them with fuller understanding of important aspects of their childhood and adolescence.

SYMBOLISM

Through an author's careful employment of **symbols** — objects, characters, or actions that stand for something beyond themselves — specific elements of many stories assume greater significance. Universal symbols, often called **archetypes**, are interpreted in much the same way in many different cultures. The use of the cycles of day and night and of the seasons to present the phases of human life is a familiar example. Cultural symbols hold special meanings for a specific group. For example, the cross embodies a number of complex spiritual beliefs for Christians. **Contextual symbols** are given or take on meaning only within the stories that contain them.

When employing universal or cultural symbols, authors usually assume their readers' general knowledge of the relationship between the literal objects, events, and characters and their symbolic meanings. Readers use this knowledge to interpret the symbols and hence to understand the stories they read more fully. For example, early in "Rappaccini's Daughter," Giovanni looks at the enclosed garden outside his window. Considering the garden in relation to the biblical Garden of Eden, readers may come to a fuller understanding of the theme of the fall from innocence and of the author's view of the character of the young man.

In "The Resplendent Quetzal," a cultural symbol takes on contextual meanings unique to the story. A sacred bird, whose feathers symbolize the souls of unborn babies to the Aztecs, it is the only bird Sarah decides she wishes to see. Edward, who "felt he was allowed to see birds only when they wanted him to," does not think there are any in the area they are visiting. He is correct: neither one sees a quetzal. An understanding of what the bird symbolizes for each of them illuminates aspects of their characters. Atwood also draws on the fact that male quetzals play an important role in the hatching and raising of offspring, staying close to and assisting their mates during the entire process.

In "Borders" and "The Loons," the titles introduce the major contextual symbols, which acquire additional meanings each time they appear. In the former story, the international boundary between Canada and the United States, the "border," comes to represent divisions, not only between countries, but also between cultures and even between members of a family. In "The Loons," the calls of the shy, elusive birds were "plaintive, and yet with a quality of chilling mockery...[and] belonged to a world separated by aeons from our neat world of summer cottages and the lighted lamps of home." To the teenage narrator of the story, they stand for Piquette, a young, lonely Métis woman whom she had tried unsuccessfully to befriend.

IRONY

Irony, one of the most frequently used techniques in stories, is of three types. Verbal irony is created when there is a difference between the apparent and actual meanings of a speaker's words. In "Rappaccini's Daughter," Baglioni offers Giovanni a cure for the sickness affecting him, heartily announcing, "Be of good cheer, son of my friend! It is not yet too late for the rescue." However, to himself he admits his true motivation: "We will thwart Rappaccini yet!" In dramatic irony, readers have clearer perceptions of situations than do the characters involved in them. In "Araby," the narrator is so involved in his emotions about Mangin's sister that he does not see how his thoughts and actions are indications of infatuation and sexual arousal, emotions that Joyce makes clear to the reader. Again, "Rappaccini's Daughter" provides an example. Giovanni offers Beatrice what he believes will be an antidote and thinks that, once cured of her toxic qualities, the two will live happily together. What results is not what he expected.

In some stories, the situational irony is of cosmic dimensions, as characters struggle against natural or supernatural forces that frequently defeat them. In "The Open Boat," the Oiler, who has been presented as the strongest and most courageous of the four men in the lifeboat, is the only person to die. Merit is of no importance in a harsh and impersonal universe, one that may have no guiding powers, as the Correspondent has vaguely realized during the ordeal.

Katherine Mansfield's "Bliss" contains all three types of irony. Harry practises verbal irony when speaking of Miss Fulton, a dinner guest, in terms that conceal his true attitude about her. The situational irony is introduced in the title, "Bliss," which refers to the emotion Bertha experiences for the first time. Because of it, she is "waiting for something...divine to happen...that she knew must happen...infallibly." However, the events of the evening result in her feeling far from blissful. Bertha perceives the blossoming pear tree as a visual embodiment of her emotion and believes that Miss Fulton does as well. She is correct, but does not realize the cause of the other woman's feelings. On first reading, an attentive reader may notice in "Bliss" several instances of dramatic irony that subtly foreshadow the story's conclusion. These hints provide an undercurrent that contrasts Bertha's perceptions and anticipations with the realities of her situation.

INTERPRETATION AND PERSONAL RESPONSE

Because of differences in gender, age, cultural backgrounds, and personal experiences, readers respond individually to short stories. Their interpretation begins with the words of the works themselves, for as creations of other individuals, these are influenced by their authors' gender, age, cultural and literary background, and personal experience. Full, informed response to a work requires that readers initially relinquish freedom of response, giving consideration to the contexts out of which a story emerged and the technical aspects of language used in writing it. Careful, analytical attention to a story will lead to speculation on an author's purpose in writing. Based on such inquiry, readers can engage in more informed evaluation of a work, considering how clearly and artistically the author has communicated and judging the validity of the work's theme. Then, having responded to it on its own terms, they can respond to it personally, relating it to their own lives, identifying with or reacting against the characters, accepting or rejecting the author's attitudes toward or interpretation of life, or modifying their own views in the light of those presented. In making informed personal responses, readers achieve a new freedom, one that helps them to enjoy stories more fully and to make the creating, telling, and reading of stories an integral part of their lives.

Nathaniel Hawthorne (1804–1864)

A native of Salem, Massachusetts, where an ancestor was a judge in the seventeenth-century witch trials, Nathaniel Hawthorne set many of his short stories and *The Scarlet Letter*, his best-known novel, in colonial New England. He was more than a creator of historical fiction, however, describing himself as a writer who delved into "the depths of our common human nature." "Rappaccini's Daughter," for example, is set in sixteenth-century Italy, but does not deal with Renaissance history. Instead, it presents a common plot structure and theme: a young man's journey from country to city, symbolic of his coming of age. Hawthorne uses the garden as his central setting, introducing into the story the idea of a moral fall from innocence to experience. In addition to presenting Giovanni's ambiguous response to adult sexuality, as seen in the youth's shifting reactions to Beatrice and the garden, Hawthorne examines the profound effect that professional jealousies between the older authority figures, Baglioni and Rappaccini, have on the lives of Giovanni and Beatrice.

RAPPACCINI'S DAUGHTER
From the Writings of Aubépine [1]

A young man, named Giovanni Guasconti, came, very long ago, from the more southern region of Italy, to pursue his studies at the University of Padua. Giovanni, who had but a scanty supply of gold ducats in his pocket, took lodgings in a high and gloomy chamber of an old edifice, which looked not unworthy to have been the palace of a Paduan noble, and which, in fact, exhibited over its entrance the armorial bearings of a family long since extinct. The young stranger, who was not unstudied in the great poem of his country,[2] recollected that one of the ancestors of this family, and perhaps an occupant of this very mansion, had been pictured by Dante as a partaker of the immortal agonies of his Inferno. These reminiscences and associations, together with the tendency to heart-break natural to a young man for the first time out of his native sphere, caused Giovanni to sigh heavily, as he looked around the desolate and ill-furnished apartment.

"Holy Virgin, Signor," cried old dame Lisabetta, who, won by the youth's remarkable beauty of person, was kindly endeavoring to give the chamber a habitable air, "what a sigh was that to come out of a young man's heart! Do you find this old mansion gloomy? For the love of heaven, then, put your head out of the window, and you will see as bright sunshine as you have in Naples."

Guasconti mechanically did as the old woman advised, but could not quite agree with her that the Paduan sunshine was as cheerful as that of southern Italy. Such as it was, however, it fell upon a garden beneath the window, and expended its fostering influences on a variety of plants, which seemed to have been cultivated with exceeding care.

---

1 French for Hawthorn (tree). 2 *The Divine Comedy*, by Dante Alighieri. In this early-fourteenth-century Italian poem, the narrator is guided in a dream vision through Hell and Purgatory by the classical Roman poet Virgil, and through Heaven by a young maiden, Beatrice.

"Does this garden belong to the house?" asked Giovanni.

"Heaven forbid, Signor! — unless it were fruitful of better pot-herbs than any that grow there now," answered old Lisabetta. "No; that garden is cultivated by the own hands of Signor Giacomo Rappaccini, the famous Doctor, who, I warrant him, has been heard of as far as Naples. It is said that he distils these plants into medicines that are as potent as a charm. Oftentimes you may see the Signor Doctor at work, and perchance the Signora his daughter, too, gathering the strange flowers that grow in the garden."

The old woman had now done what she could for the aspect of the chamber, and, commending the young man to the protection of the saints, took her departure.

Giovanni still found no better occupation than to look down into the garden beneath his window. From its appearance, he judged it to be one of those botanic gardens, which were of earlier date in Padua than elsewhere in Italy, or in the world. Or, not improbably, it might once have been the pleasure-place of an opulent family; for there was the ruin of a marble fountain in the centre, sculptured with rare art, but so wofully shattered that it was impossible to trace the original design from the chaos of remaining fragments. The water, however, continued to gush and sparkle into the sunbeams as cheerfully as ever. A little gurgling sound ascended to the young man's window, and made him feel as if the fountain were an immortal spirit, that sung its song unceasingly, and without heeding the vicissitudes around it; while one century embodied it in marble, and another scattered the perishable garniture on the soil. All about the pool into which the water subsided, grew various plants, that seemed to require a plentiful supply of moisture for the nourishment of gigantic leaves, and, in some instances, flowers gorgeously magnificent. There was one shrub in particular, set in a marble vase in the midst of the pool, that bore a profusion of purple blossoms, each of which had the lustre and richness of a gem; and the whole together made a show so resplendent that it seemed enough to illuminate the garden, even had there been no sunshine. Every portion of the soil was peopled with plants and herbs, which, if less beautiful, still bore tokens of assiduous care; as if all had their individual virtues, known to the scientific mind that fostered them. Some were placed in urns, rich with old carving, and others in common garden-pots; some crept serpent-like along the ground, or climbed on high, using whatever means of ascent was offered them. One plant had wreathed itself round a statue of Vertumnus,[3] which was thus quite veiled and shrouded in a drapery of hanging foliage, so happily arranged that it might have served a sculptor for a study.

While Giovanni stood at the window, he heard a rustling behind a screen of leaves, and became aware that a person was at work in the garden. His figure soon emerged into view, and showed itself to be that of no common laborer, but a tall, emaciated, sallow, and sickly-looking man, dressed in a scholar's garb of black. He was beyond the middle term of life, with grey hair, a thin grey beard, and a face singularly marked with intellect and cultivation, but which could never, even in his more youthful days, have expressed much warmth of heart.

---

3 the Roman god of vegetation who seduced Pomona, goddess of fruits.

Nothing could exceed the intentness with which this scientific gardener examined every shrub which grew in his path; it seemed as if he was looking into their inmost nature, making observations in regard to their creative essence, and discovering why one leaf grew in this shape, and another in that, and wherefore such and such flowers differed among themselves in hue and perfume. Nevertheless, in spite of this deep intelligence on his part, there was no approach to intimacy between himself and these vegetable existences. On the contrary, he avoided their actual touch, or the direct inhaling of their odors, with a caution that impressed Giovanni most disagreeably; for the man's demeanor was that of one walking among malignant influences, such as savage beasts, or deadly snakes, or evil spirits, which, should he allow them one moment of license, would wreak upon him some terrible fatality. It was strangely frightful to the young man's imagination, to see this air of insecurity in a person cultivating a garden, that most simple and innocent of human toils, and which had been alike the joy and labor of the unfallen parents of the race. Was this garden, then, the Eden of the present world?— and this man, with such a perception of harm in what his own hands caused to grow, was he the Adam?

10   The distrustful gardener, while plucking away the dead leaves or pruning the too luxuriant growth of the shrubs, defended his hands with a pair of thick gloves. Nor were these his only armor. When, in his walk through the garden, he came to the magnificent plant that hung its purple gems beside the marble fountain, he placed a kind of mask over his mouth and nostrils, as if all this beauty did but conceal a deadlier malice. But finding his task still too dangerous, he drew back, removed the mask, and called loudly, but in the infirm voice of a person affected with inward disease:

"Beatrice! — Beatrice!"

"Here am I, my father! What would you?" cried a rich and youthful voice from the window of the opposite house; a voice as rich as a tropical sunset, and which made Giovanni, though he knew not why, think of deep hues of purple or crimson, and of perfumes heavily delectable. — "Are you in the garden?"

"Yes, Beatrice," answered the gardener, "and I need your help."

Soon there emerged from under a sculptured portal the figure of a young girl, arrayed with as much richness of taste as the most splendid of the flowers, beautiful as the day, and with a bloom so deep and vivid that one shade more would have been too much. She looked redundant with life, health, and energy; all of which attributes were bound down and compressed, as it were, and girdled tensely, in their luxuriance, by her virgin zone.[4] Yet Giovanni's fancy must have grown morbid, while he looked down into the garden; for the impression which the fair stranger made upon him was as if here were another flower, the human sister of those vegetable ones, as beautiful as they — more beautiful than the richest of them — but still to be touched only with a glove, nor to be approached without a mask. As Beatrice came down the garden path, it was observable that she handled and inhaled the odor of several of the plants, which her father had most sedulously avoided.

15   "Here, Beatrice," said the latter, — "see how many needful offices require to be done to our chief treasure. Yet, shattered as I am, my life might pay the

---

4 outer girdle-type garment worn on a woman's lower hips.

penalty of approaching it so closely as circumstances demand. Henceforth, I fear, this plant must be consigned to your sole charge."

"And gladly will I undertake it," cried again the rich tones of the young lady, as she bent towards the magnificent plant, and opened her arms as if to embrace it. "Yes, my sister, my splendor, it shall be Beatrice's task to nurse and serve thee; and thou shalt reward her with thy kisses and perfumed breath, which to her is as the breath of life!"

Then, with all the tenderness in her manner that was so strikingly expressed in her words, she busied herself with such attentions as the plant seemed to require; and Giovanni, at his lofty window, rubbed his eyes, and almost doubted whether it were a girl tending her favorite flower, or one sister performing the duties of affection to another. The scene soon terminated. Whether Doctor Rappaccini had finished his labors in the garden, or that his watchful eye had caught the stranger's face, he now took his daughter's arm and retired. Night was already closing in; oppressive exhalations seemed to proceed from the plants, and steal upward past the open window; and Giovanni, closing the lattice, went to his couch, and dreamed of a rich flower and beautiful girl. Flower and maiden were different and yet the same, and fraught with some strange peril in either shape.

But there is an influence in the light of morning that tends to rectify whatever errors of fancy, or even of judgment, we may have incurred during the sun's decline, or among the shadows of the night, or in the less wholesome glow of moonshine. Giovanni's first movement on starting from sleep, was to throw open the window, and gaze down into the garden which his dreams had made so fertile of mysteries. He was surprised, and a little ashamed, to find how real and matter-of-fact an affair it proved to be, in the first rays of the sun, which gilded the dew-drops that hung upon leaf and blossom, and, while giving a brighter beauty to each rare flower, brought everything within the limits of ordinary experience. The young man rejoiced, that, in the heart of the barren city, he had the privilege of overlooking this spot of lovely and luxuriant vegetation. It would serve, he said to himself, as a symbolic language, to keep him in communion with Nature. Neither the sickly and thought-worn Doctor Giacomo Rappaccini, it is true, nor his brilliant daughter, were now visible; so that Giovanni could not determine how much of the singularity which he attributed to both, was due to their own qualities, and how much to his wonder-working fancy. But he was inclined to take a most rational view of the whole matter.

In the course of the day, he paid his respects to Signor Pietro Baglioni, professor of medicine in the University, a physician of eminent repute, to whom Giovanni had brought a letter of introduction. The Professor was an elderly personage, apparently of genial nature, and habits that might almost be called jovial; he kept the young man to dinner, and made himself very agreeable by the freedom and liveliness of his conversation, especially when warmed by a flask or two of Tuscan wine. Giovanni, conceiving that men of science, inhabitants of the same city, must needs be on familiar terms with one another, took an opportunity to mention the name of Doctor Rappaccini. But the Professor did not respond with so much cordiality as he had anticipated.

"Ill would it become a teacher of the divine art of medicine," said Professor Pietro Baglioni, in answer to a question of Giovanni, "to withhold due and well-considered praise of a physician so eminently skilled as Rappaccini. But, on the other hand, I should answer it but scantily to my conscience, were I to permit a worthy youth like yourself, Signor Giovanni, the son of an ancient friend, to imbibe erroneous ideas respecting a man who might hereafter chance to hold your life and death in his hands. The truth is, our worshipful Doctor Rappaccini has as much science as any member of the faculty — with perhaps one single exception — in Padua, or all Italy. But there are certain grave objections to his professional character."

"And what are they?" asked the young man.

"Has my friend Giovanni any disease of body or heart, that he is so inquisitive about physicians?" said the Professor, with a smile. "But as for Rappaccini, it is said of him — and I, who know the man well, can answer for its truth — that he cares infinitely more for science than for mankind. His patients are interesting to him only as subjects for some new experiment. He would sacrifice human life, his own among the rest, or whatever else was dearest to him, for the sake of adding so much as a grain of mustard-seed to the great heap of his accumulated knowledge."

"Methinks he is an awful man, indeed," remarked Guasconti, mentally recalling the cold and purely intellectual aspect of Rappaccini. "And yet, worshipful Professor, is it not a noble spirit? Are there many men capable of so spiritual a love of science?"

"God forbid," answered the Professor, somewhat testily — "at least, unless they take sounder views of the healing art than those adopted by Rappaccini. It is his theory, that all medicinal virtues are comprised within those substances which we term vegetable poisons. These he cultivates with his own hands, and is said even to have produced new varieties of poison, more horribly deleterious than Nature, without the assistance of this learned person, would ever have plagued the world withal. That the Signor Doctor does less mischief than might be expected, with such dangerous substances, is undeniable. Now and then, it must be owned, he has effected — or seemed to effect — a marvellous cure. But, to tell you my private mind, Signor Giovanni, he should receive little credit for such instances of success — they being probably the work of chance — but should be held strictly accountable for his failures, which may justly be considered his own work."

25   The youth might have taken Baglioni's opinions with many grains of allowance, had he known that there was a professional warfare of long continuance between him and Doctor Rappaccini, in which the latter was generally thought to have gained the advantage. If the reader be inclined to judge for himself, we refer him to certain black-letter tracts on both sides, preserved in the medical department of the University of Padua.

"I know not, most learned Professor," returned Giovanni, after musing on what had been said of Rappaccini's exclusive zeal for science — "I know not how dearly this physician may love his art; but surely there is one object more dear to him. He has a daughter."

"Aha!" cried the Professor with a laugh. "So now our friend Giovanni's secret is out. You have heard of this daughter, whom all the young men in Padua are wild about, though not half a dozen have ever had the good hap to see her face. I know little of the Signora Beatrice, save that Rappaccini is said to have instructed her deeply in his science, and that, young and beautiful as fame reports her, she is already qualified to fill a professor's chair. Perchance her father destines her for mine! Other absurd rumors there be, not worth talking about, or listening to. So now, Signor Giovanni, drink off your glass of Lacryma."[5]

Guasconti returned to his lodgings somewhat heated with the wine he had quaffed, and which caused his brain to swim with strange fantasies in reference to Doctor Rappaccini and the beautiful Beatrice. On his way, happening to pass by a florist's, he bought a fresh bouquet of flowers.

Ascending to his chamber, he seated himself near the window, but within the shadow thrown by the depth of the wall, so that he could look down into the garden with little risk of being discovered. All beneath his eye was a solitude. The strange plants were basking in the sunshine, and now and then nodding gently to one another, as if in acknowledgment of sympathy and kindred. In the midst, by the shattered fountain, grew the magnificent shrub, with its purple gems clustering all over it; they glowed in the air, and gleamed back again out of the depths of the pool, which thus seemed to overflow with colored radiance from the rich reflection that was steeped in it. At first, as we have said, the garden was a solitude. Soon, however, — as Giovanni had half-hoped, half-feared, would be the case, — a figure appeared beneath the antique sculptured portal, and came down between the rows of plants, inhaling their various perfumes, as if she were one of those beings of old classic fable, that lived upon sweet odors. On again beholding Beatrice, the young man was even startled to perceive how much her beauty exceeded his recollection of it; so brilliant, so vivid was its character, that she glowed amid the sunlight, and, as Giovanni whispered to himself, positively illuminated the more shadowy intervals of the garden path. Her face being now more revealed than on the former occasion, he was struck by its expression of simplicity and sweetness; qualities that had not entered into his idea of her character, and which made him ask anew, what manner of mortal she might be. Nor did he fail again to observe, or imagine, an analogy between the beautiful girl and the gorgeous shrub that hung its gem-like flowers over the fountain; a resemblance which Beatrice seemed to have indulged a fantastic humor in heightening, both by the arrangement of her dress and the selection of its hues.

30   Approaching the shrub, she threw open her arms, as with a passionate ardor, and drew its branches into an intimate embrace; so intimate, that her features were hidden in its leafy bosom, and her glistening ringlets all intermingled with the flowers.

"Give me thy breath, my sister," exclaimed Beatrice; "for I am faint with common air! And give me this flower of thine, which I separate with gentlest fingers from the stem, and place it close beside my heart."

With these words, the beautiful daughter of Rappaccini plucked one of the richest blossoms of the shrub, and was about to fasten it in her bosom. But now, unless Giovanni's draughts of wine had bewildered his senses, a singular incident occurred. A small orange-colored reptile, of the lizard or chameleon species, chanced to be creeping along the path, just at the feet of Beatrice. It appeared to Giovanni — but, at the distance from which he gazed, he could

---

5 strong, sweet red wine named after the tears of Christ.

scarcely have seen anything so minute — it appeared to him, however, that a drop or two of moisture from the broken stem of the flower descended upon the lizard's head. For an instant, the reptile contorted itself violently, and then lay motionless in the sunshine. Beatrice observed this remarkable phenomenon, and crossed herself, sadly, but without surprise; nor did she therefore hesitate to arrange the fatal flower in her bosom. There it blushed, and almost glimmered with the dazzling effect of a precious stone, adding to her dress and aspect the one appropriate charm, which nothing else in the world could have supplied. But Giovanni, out of the shadow of his window, bent forward and shrank back, and murmured and trembled.

"Am I awake? Have I my senses?" said he to himself. "What is this being?— beautiful, shall I call her?— or inexpressibly terrible?"

Beatrice now strayed carelessly through the garden, approaching closer beneath Giovanni's window, so that he was compelled to thrust his head quite out of its concealment in order to gratify the intense and painful curiosity which she excited. At this moment, there came a beautiful insect over the garden wall; it had perhaps wandered through the city and found no flowers nor verdure among those antique haunts of men, until the heavy perfumes of Doctor Rappaccini's shrubs had lured it from afar. Without alighting on the flowers, this winged brightness seemed to be attracted by Beatrice, and lingered in the air and fluttered about her head. Now, here it could not be but that Giovanni Guasconti's eyes deceived him. Be that as it might, he fancied that while Beatrice was gazing at the insect with childish delight, it grew faint and fell at her feet; — its bright wings shivered; it was dead — from no cause that he could discern, unless it were the atmosphere of her breath. Again Beatrice crossed herself and sighed heavily, as she bent over the dead insect.

35 An impulsive movement of Giovanni drew her eyes to the window. There she beheld the beautiful head of the young man — rather a Grecian than an Italian head, with fair, regular features, and a glistening of gold among his ringlets — gazing down upon her like a being that hovered in mid-air. Scarcely knowing what he did, Giovanni threw down the bouquet which he had hitherto held in his hand.

"Signora," said he, "there are pure and healthful flowers. Wear them for the sake of Giovanni Guasconti!"

"Thanks, Signor," replied Beatrice, with her rich voice, that came forth as it were like a gush of music; and with a mirthful expression half childish and half woman-like. "I accept your gift, and would fain recompense it with this precious purple flower; but if I toss it into the air, it will not reach you. So Signor Guasconti must even content himself with my thanks."

She lifted the bouquet from the ground, and then as if inwardly ashamed at having stepped aside from her maidenly reserve to respond to a stranger's greeting, passed swiftly homeward through the garden. But, few as the moments were, it seemed to Giovanni when she was on the point of vanishing beneath the sculptured portal, that his beautiful bouquet was already beginning to wither in her grasp. It was an idle thought; there could be no possibility of distinguishing a faded flower from a fresh one at so great a distance.

For many days after this incident, the young man avoided the window that looked into Doctor Rappaccini's garden, as if something ugly and monstrous would have blasted his eye-sight, had he been betrayed into a glance. He felt conscious of having put himself, to a certain extent, within the influence of an unintelligible power, by the communication which he had opened with Beatrice. The wisest course would have been, if his heart were in any real danger, to quit his lodgings and Padua itself, at once; the next wiser, to have accustomed himself, as far as possible, to the familiar and day-light view of Beatrice; thus bringing her rigidly and systematically within the limits of ordinary experience. Least of all, while avoiding her sight, ought Giovanni to have remained so near this extraordinary being, that the proximity and possibility even of intercourse, should give a kind of substance and reality to the wild vagaries which his imagination ran riot continually in producing. Guasconti had not a deep heart — or at all events, its depths were not sounded now — but he had a quick fancy, and an ardent southern temperament, which rose every instant to a higher fever-pitch. Whether or no Beatrice possessed those terrible attributes — that fatal breath — the affinity with those so beautiful and deadly flowers — which were indicated by what Giovanni had witnessed, she had at least instilled a fierce and subtle poison into his system. It was not love, although her rich beauty was a madness to him; nor horror, even while he fancied her spirit to be imbued with the same baneful essence that seemed to pervade her physical frame; but a wild offspring of both love and horror that had each parent in it, and burned like one and shivered like the other. Giovanni knew not what to dread; still less did he know what to hope; yet hope and dread kept a continual warfare in his breast, alternately vanquishing one another and starting up afresh to renew the contest. Blessed are all simple emotions, be they dark or bright! It is the lurid intermixture of the two that produces the illuminating blaze of the infernal regions.

40   Sometimes he endeavored to assuage the fever of his spirit by a rapid walk through the streets of Padua, or beyond its gates; his footsteps kept time with the throbbings of his brain, so that the walk was apt to accelerate itself to a race. One day, he found himself arrested; his arm was seized by a portly personage who had turned back on recognizing the young man, and expended much breath in overtaking him.

"Signor Giovanni! — stay, my young friend!" cried he. "Have you forgotten me? That might well be the case, if I were as much altered as yourself."

It was Baglioni, whom Giovanni had avoided, ever since their first meeting, from a doubt that the Professor's sagacity would look too deeply into his secrets. Endeavoring to recover himself, he stared forth wildly from his inner world into the outer one, and spoke like a man in a dream:

"Yes; I am Giovanni Guasconti. You are Professor Pietro Baglioni. Now let me pass!"

"Not yet — not yet, Signor Giovanni Guasconti," said the Professor, smiling, but at the same time scrutinizing the youth with an earnest glance. — "What; did I grow up side by side with your father, and shall his son pass me like a stranger, in these old streets of Padua? Stand still, Signor Giovanni; for we must have a word or two, before we part."

45   "Speedily, then, most worshipful Professor, speedily!" said Giovanni, with feverish impatience. "Does not your worship see that I am in haste?"

Now, while he was speaking, there came a man in black along the street, stooping and moving feebly, like a person in inferior health. His face was all overspread with a most sickly and sallow hue, but yet so pervaded with an expression of piercing and active intellect, that an observer might easily have overlooked the merely physical attributes, and have seen only this wonderful energy. As he passed, this person exchanged a cold and distant salutation with Baglioni, but fixed his eyes upon Giovanni with an intentness that seemed to bring out whatever was within him worthy of notice. Nevertheless, there was a peculiar quietness in the look, as if taking merely a speculative, not a human, interest in the young man.

"It is Doctor Rappaccini!" whispered the Professor, when the stranger had passed. — "Has he ever seen your face before?"

"Not that I know," answered Giovanni, starting at the name.

"He *has* seen you! — he must have seen you!" said Baglioni, hastily. "For some purpose or other, this man of science is making a study of you. I know that look of his! It is the same that coldly illuminates his face, as he bends over a bird, a mouse, or a butterfly, which, in pursuance of some experiment, he has killed by the perfume of a flower; — a look as deep as Nature itself, but without Nature's warmth of love. Signor Giovanni, I will stake my life upon it, you are the subject of one of Rappaccini's experiments!"

50 "Will you make a fool of me?" cried Giovanni, passionately. "*That*, Signor Professor, were an untoward experiment."

"Patience, patience!" replied the imperturbable Professor. — "I tell thee, my poor Giovanni, that Rappaccini has a scientific interest in thee. Thou hast fallen into fearful hands! And the Signora Beatrice? What part does she act in this mystery?"

But Guasconti, finding Baglioni's pertinacity intolerable, here broke away, and was gone before the Professor could again seize his arm. He looked after the young man intently, and shook his head.

"This must not be," said Baglioni to himself. "The youth is the son of my old friend, and shall not come to any harm from which the arcana of medical science can preserve him. Besides, it is too insufferable an impertinence in Rappaccini, thus to snatch the lad out of my own hands, as I may say, and make use of him for his infernal experiments. This daughter of his! It shall be looked to. Perchance, most learned Rappaccini, I may foil you where you little dream of it!"

Meanwhile, Giovanni had pursued a circuitous route, and at length found himself at the door of his lodgings. As he crossed the threshold, he was met by old Lisabetta, who smirked and smiled, and was evidently desirous to attract his attention; vainly, however, as the ebullition of his feelings had momentarily subsided into a cold and dull vacuity. He turned his eyes full upon the withered face that was puckering itself into a smile, but seemed to behold it not. The old dame, therefore, laid her grasp upon his cloak.

55 "Signor! — Signor!" whispered she, still with a smile over the whole breadth of her visage, so that it looked not unlike a grotesque carving in wood, darkened by centuries — "Listen, Signor! There is a private entrance into the garden!"

"What do you say?" exclaimed Giovanni, turning quickly about, as if an inanimate thing should start into feverish life. — "A private entrance into Doctor Rappaccini's garden!"

"Hush! hush! — not so loud!" whispered Lisabetta, putting her hand over his mouth. "Yes; into the worshipful Doctor's garden, where you may see all his fine shrubbery. Many a young man in Padua would give gold to be admitted among those flowers."

Giovanni put a piece of gold into her hand.

"Show me the way," said he.

60   A surmise, probably excited by his conversation with Baglioni, crossed his mind, that this interposition of old Lisabetta might perchance be connected with the intrigue, whatever were its nature, in which the Professor seemed to suppose that Doctor Rappaccini was involving him. But such a suspicion, though it disturbed Giovanni, was inadequate to restrain him. The instant that he was aware of the possibility of approaching Beatrice, it seemed an absolute necessity of his existence to do so. It mattered not whether she were angel or demon; he was irrevocably within her sphere, and must obey the law that whirled him onward, in ever lessening circles, towards a result which he did not attempt to foreshadow. And yet, strange to say, there came across him a sudden doubt, whether this intense interest on his part were not delusory — whether it were really of so deep and positive a nature as to justify him in now thrusting himself into an incalculable position — whether it were not merely the fantasy of a young man's brain, only slightly, or not at all, connected with his heart!

He paused — hesitated — turned half about — but again went on. His withered guide led him along several obscure passages, and finally undid a door, through which, as it was opened, there came the sight and sound of rustling leaves, with the broken sunshine glimmering among them. Giovanni stepped forth, and forcing himself through the entanglement of a shrub that wreathed its tendrils over the hidden entrance, he stood beneath his own window, in the open area of Doctor Rappaccini's garden.

How often is it the case, that, when impossibilities have come to pass, and dreams have condensed their misty substance into tangible realities, we find ourselves calm, and even coldly self-possessed, amid circumstances which it would have been a delirium of joy or agony to anticipate! Fate delights to thwart us thus. Passion will choose his own time to rush upon the scene, and lingers sluggishly behind, when an appropriate adjustment of events would seem to summon his appearance. So was it now with Giovanni. Day after day, his pulses had throbbed with feverish blood, at the improbable idea of an interview with Beatrice, and of standing with her, face to face, in this very garden, basking in the Oriental sunshine of her beauty, and snatching from her full gaze the mystery which he deemed the riddle of his own existence. But now there was a singular and untimely equanimity within his breast. He threw a glance around the garden to discover if Beatrice or her father were present, and perceiving that he was alone, began a critical observation of the plants.

The aspect of one and all of them dissatisfied him; their gorgeousness seemed fierce, passionate, and even unnatural. There was hardly an individual shrub which a wanderer, straying by himself through a forest, would not have been startled to find growing wild, as if an unearthly face had glared at him out of the thicket. Several, also, would have shocked a delicate instinct by an appearance of artificialness, indicating that there had been such commixture, and, as it were, adultery of various vegetable species, that the production was no longer of God's making, but the monstrous offspring of man's depraved fancy, glowing with only an evil mockery of beauty. They were probably the result of experiment, which, in one or two cases, had succeeded in mingling plants individually lovely into a compound possessing the questionable and ominous character that distinguished the whole growth of the garden. In fine, Giovanni recognized but two or three plants in the collection, and those of a kind that he well knew to be poisonous. While busy with these contemplations, he heard the rustling of a silken garment, and turning, beheld Beatrice emerging from beneath the sculptured portal.

Giovanni had not considered with himself what should be his deportment; whether he should apologize for his intrusion into the garden, or assume that he was there with the privity, at least, if not by the desire, of Doctor Rappaccini or his daughter. But Beatrice's manner placed him at his ease, though leaving him still in doubt by what agency he had gained admittance. She came lightly along the path, and met him near the broken fountain. There was surprise in her face, but brightened by a simple and kind expression of pleasure.

65   "You are a connoisseur in flowers, Signor," said Beatrice with a smile, alluding to the bouquet which he had flung her from the window. "It is no marvel, therefore, if the sight of my father's rare collection has tempted you to take a nearer view. If he were here, he could tell you many strange and interesting facts as to the nature and habits of these shrubs, for he has spent a lifetime in such studies, and this garden is his world."

"And yourself, lady" — observed Giovanni — "if fame says true — you, likewise, are deeply skilled in the virtues indicated by these rich blossoms, and these spicy perfumes. Would you deign to be my instructress, I should prove an apter scholar than if taught by Signor Rappaccini himself."

"Are there such idle rumors?" asked Beatrice, with the music of a pleasant laugh. "Do people say that I am skilled in my father's science of plants? What a jest is there! No; though I have grown up among these flowers, I know no more of them than their hues and perfume; and sometimes, methinks I would fain rid myself of even that small knowledge. There are many flowers here, and those not the least brilliant, that shock and offend me, when they meet my eye. But, pray, Signor, do not believe these stories about my science. Believe nothing of me save what you see with your own eyes."

"And must I believe all that I have seen with my own eyes?" asked Giovanni pointedly, while the recollection of former scenes made him shrink. "No, Signora, you demand too little of me. Bid me believe nothing, save what comes from your own lips."

It would appear that Beatrice understood him. There came a deep flush to her cheek; but she looked full into Giovanni's eyes, and responded to his gaze of uneasy suspicion with a queen-like haughtiness.

70   "I do so bid you, Signor!" she replied. "Forget whatever you may have fancied in regard to me. If true to the outward senses, still it may be false in its

essence. But the words of Beatrice Rappaccini's lips are true from the depths of the heart outward. Those you may believe!"

A fervor glowed in her whole aspect, and beamed upon Giovanni's consciousness like the light of truth itself. But while she spoke, there was a fragrance in the atmosphere around her, rich and delightful, though evanescent, yet which the young man, from an indefinable reluctance, scarcely dared to draw into his lungs. It might be the odor of the flowers. Could it be Beatrice's breath, which thus embalmed her words with a strange richness, as if by steeping them in her heart? A faintness passed like a shadow over Giovanni, and flitted away; he seemed to gaze through the beautiful girl's eyes into her transparent soul, and felt no more doubt or fear.

The tinge of passion that had colored Beatrice's manner vanished; she became gay, and appeared to derive a pure delight from her communion with the youth, not unlike what the maiden of a lonely island might have felt, conversing with a voyager from the civilized world.[6] Evidently her experience of life had been confined within the limits of that garden. She talked now about matters as simple as the daylight or summer-clouds, and now asked questions in reference to the city, or Giovanni's distant home, his friends, his mother, and his sisters; questions indicating such seclusion, and such lack of familiarity with modes and forms, that Giovanni responded as if to an infant. Her spirit gushed out before him like a fresh rill, that was just catching its first glimpse of the sunlight, and wondering at the reflections of earth and sky which were flung into its bosom. There came thoughts, too, from a deep source, and fantasies of a gem-like brilliancy, as if diamonds and rubies sparkled upward among the bubbles of the fountain. Ever and anon, there gleamed across the young man's mind a sense of wonder, that he should be walking side by side with the being who had so wrought upon his imagination — whom he had idealized in such hues of terror — in whom he had positively witnessed such manifestations of dreadful attributes — that he should be conversing with Beatrice like a brother, and should find her so human and so maiden-like. But such reflections were only momentary; the effect of her character was too real, not to make itself familiar at once.

In this free intercourse, they had strayed through the garden, and now, after many turns among its avenues, were come to the shattered fountain, beside which grew the magnificent shrub with its treasury of glowing blossoms. A fragrance was diffused from it, which Giovanni recognized as identical with that which he had attributed to Beatrice's breath, but incomparably more powerful. As her eyes fell upon it, Giovanni beheld her press her hand to her bosom, as if her heart were throbbing suddenly and painfully.

"For the first time in my life," murmured she, addressing the shrub, "I had forgotten thee!"

75

"I remember, Signora," said Giovanni, "that you once promised to reward me with one of these living gems for the bouquet, which I had the happy boldness to fling to your feet. Permit me now to pluck it as a memorial of this interview."

---

6 implicit reference to the meeting of Miranda and Ferdinand in William Shakespeare's *The Tempest*

He made a step towards the shrub, with extended hand. But Beatrice darted forward, uttering a shriek that went through his heart like a dagger. She caught his hand, and drew it back with the whole force of her slender figure. Giovanni felt her touch thrilling through his fibres.

"Touch it not!" exclaimed she, in a voice of agony. "Not for thy life! It is fatal!"

Then, hiding her face, she fled from him, and vanished beneath the sculptured portal. As Giovanni followed her with his eyes, he beheld the emaciated figure and pale intelligence of Doctor Rappaccini, who had been watching the scene, he knew not how long, within the shadow of the entrance.

No sooner was Guasconti alone in his chamber, than the image of Beatrice came back to his passionate musings, invested with all the witchery that had been gathering around it ever since his first glimpse of her, and now likewise imbued with a tender warmth of girlish womanhood. She was human: her nature was endowed with all gentle and feminine qualities; she was worthiest to be worshipped; she was capable, surely, on her part, of the height and heroism of love. Those tokens, which he had hitherto considered as proofs of a frightful peculiarity in her physical and moral system, were now either forgotten, or, by the subtle sophistry of passion, transmuted into a golden crown of enchantment, rendering Beatrice the more admirable, by so much as she was the more unique. Whatever had looked ugly, was now beautiful; or, if incapable of such a change, it stole away and hid itself among those shapeless half-ideas, which throng the dim region beyond the daylight of our perfect consciousness. Thus did he spend the night, nor fell asleep, until the dawn had begun to awake the slumbering flowers in Doctor Rappaccini's garden, whither Giovanni's dreams doubtless led him. Up rose the sun in his due season, and flinging his beams upon the young man's eyelids, awoke him to a sense of pain. When thoroughly aroused, he became sensible of a burning and tingling agony in his hand — in his right hand — the very hand which Beatrice had grasped in her own, when he was on the point of plucking one of the gem-like flowers. On the back of that hand there was now a purple print, like that of four small fingers, and the likeness of a slender thumb upon his wrist.

Oh, how stubbornly does love — or even that cunning semblance of love which flourishes in the imagination, but strikes no depth of root into the heart — how stubbornly does it hold its faith, until the moment come, when it is doomed to vanish into thin mist! Giovanni wrapt a handkerchief about his hand, and wondered what evil thing had stung him, and soon forgot his pain in a reverie of Beatrice.

After the first interview, a second was in the inevitable course of what we call fate. A third; a fourth; and a meeting with Beatrice in the garden was no longer an incident in Giovanni's daily life, but the whole space in which he might be said to live; for the anticipation and memory of that ecstatic hour made up the remainder. Nor was it otherwise with the daughter of Rappaccini. She watched for the youth's appearance, and flew to his side with confidence as unreserved as if they had been playmates from early infancy — as if they were such playmates still. If, by any unwonted chance, he failed to come at the appointed moment, she stood beneath the window, and sent up the rich sweetness of her tones to float around him in his chamber, and echo and reverberate throughout his heart — "Giovanni! Giovanni! Why tarriest thou? Come down!" — And down he hastened into that Eden of poisonous flowers.

But, with all this intimate familiarity, there was still a reserve in Beatrice's demeanor, so rigidly and invariably sustained, that the idea of infringing it scarcely occurred to his imagination. By all appreciable signs, they loved; they had looked love, with eyes that conveyed the holy secret from the depths of one soul into the depths of the other, as if it were too sacred to be whispered by the way; they had even spoken love, in those gushes of passion when their spirits darted forth in articulated breath, like tongues of long-hidden flame; and yet there had been no seal of lips, no clasp of hands, nor any slightest caress, such as love claims and hallows. He had never touched one of the gleaming ringlets of her hair; her garment — so marked was the physical barrier between them — had never been waved against him by a breeze. On the few occasions when Giovanni had seemed tempted to overstep the limit, Beatrice grew so sad, so stern, and withal wore such a look of desolate separation, shuddering at itself, that not a spoken word was requisite to repel him. At such times, he was startled at the horrible suspicions that rose, monster-like, out of the caverns of his heart, and stared him in the face; his love grew thin and faint as the morning-mist; his doubts alone had substance. But when Beatrice's face brightened again, after the momentary shadow, she was transformed at once from the mysterious, questionable being, whom he had watched with so much awe and horror; she was now the beautiful and unsophisticated girl, whom he felt that his spirit knew with a certainty beyond all other knowledge.

A considerable time had now passed since Giovanni's last meeting with Baglioni. One morning, however, he was disagreeably surprised by a visit from the Professor, whom he had scarcely thought of for whole weeks, and would willingly have forgotten still longer. Given up, as he had long been, to a pervading excitement, he could tolerate no companions, except upon condition of their perfect sympathy with his present state of feeling. Such sympathy was not to be expected from Professor Baglioni.

The visitor chatted carelessly, for a few moments, about the gossip of the city and the University, and then took up another topic.

"I have been reading an old classic author lately," said he, "and met with a story that strangely interested me. Possibly you may remember it. It is of an Indian prince, who sent a beautiful woman as a present to Alexander the Great. She was as lovely as the dawn, and gorgeous as the sunset; but what especially distinguished her was a certain rich perfume in her breath — richer than a garden of Persian roses. Alexander, as was natural to a youthful conqueror, fell in love at first sight with this magnificent stranger. But a certain sage physician, happening to be present, discovered a terrible secret in regard to her."

"And what was that?" asked Giovanni, turning his eyes downward to avoid those of the Professor.

"That this lovely woman," continued Baglioni, with emphasis, "had been nourished with poisons from her birth upward, until her whole nature was so imbued with them, that she herself had become the deadliest poison in existence. Poison was her element of life. With that rich perfume of her breath, she blasted the very air. Her love would have been poison! — her embrace death! Is not this a marvelous tale?"

"A childish fable," answered Giovanni, nervously starting from his chair. "I marvel how your worship finds time to read such nonsense, among your graver studies."

"By the bye," said the Professor, looking uneasily about him, "what singular fragrance is this in your apartment? Is it the perfume of your gloves? It is faint, but delicious, and yet, after all, by no means agreeable. Were I to breathe it long, methinks it would make me ill. It is like the breath of a flower — but I see no flowers in the chamber."

90   "Nor are there any," replied Giovanni, who had turned pale as the Professor spoke; "nor, I think, is there any fragrance, except in your worship's imagination. Odors, being a sort of element combined of the sensual and the spiritual, are apt to deceive us in this manner. The recollection of a perfume — the bare idea of it — may easily be mistaken for a present reality."

"Aye; but my sober imagination does not often play such tricks," said Baglioni; "and were I to fancy any kind of odor, it would be that of some vile apothecary drug, wherewith my fingers are likely enough to be imbued. Our worshipful friend Rappaccini, as I have heard, tinctures his medicaments with odors richer than those of Araby.[7] Doubtless, likewise, the fair and learned Signora Beatrice would minister to her patients with draughts as sweet as a maiden's breath. But woe to him that sips them!"

Giovanni's face evinced many contending emotions. The tone in which the Professor alluded to the pure and lovely daughter of Rappaccini was a torture to his soul; and yet, the intimation of a view of her character, opposite to his own, gave instantaneous distinctness to a thousand dim suspicions, which now grinned at him like so many demons. But he strove hard to quell them, and to respond to Baglioni with a true lover's perfect faith.

"Signor Professor," said he, "you were my father's friend — perchance, too, it is your purpose to act a friendly part towards his son. I would fain feel nothing towards you, save respect and deference. But I pray you to observe, Signor, that there is one subject on which we must not speak. You know not the Signora Beatrice. You cannot, therefore, estimate the wrong — the blasphemy, I may even say — that is offered to her character by a light or injurious word."

"Giovanni! — my poor Giovanni!" answered the Professor, with a calm expression of pity, "I know this wretched girl far better than yourself. You shall hear the truth in respect to the poisoner Rappaccini, and his poisonous daughter. Yes; poisonous as she is beautiful! Listen; for even should you do violence to my grey hairs, it shall not silence me. That old fable of the Indian woman has become a truth, by the deep and deadly science of Rappaccini, and in the person of the lovely Beatrice!"

95   Giovanni groaned and hid his face.

"Her father," continued Baglioni, "was not restrained by natural affection from offering up his child, in this horrible manner, as the victim of his insane zeal for science. For — let us do him justice — he is as true a man of science as ever distilled his own heart in an alembic. What, then, will be your fate? Beyond a doubt, you are selected as the material of some new experiment. Perhaps the

---

7 the Middle East, a source of perfumes and spices popular in Europe.

result is to be death — perhaps a fate more awful still! Rappaccini, with what he calls the interest of science before his eyes, will hesitate at nothing."

"It is a dream!" muttered Giovanni to himself, "surely it is a dream!"

"But," resumed the Professor, "be of good cheer, son of my friend! It is not yet too late for the rescue. Possibly, we may even succeed in bringing back this miserable child within the limits of ordinary nature, from which her father's madness has estranged her. Behold this little silver vase! It was wrought by the hands of the renowned Benvenuto Cellini,[8] and is well worthy to be a love-gift to the fairest dame in Italy. But its contents are invaluable. One little sip of this antidote would have rendered the most virulent poisons of the Borgias innocuous. Doubt not that it will be as efficacious against those of Rappaccini. Bestow the vase, and the precious liquid within it, on your Beatrice, and hopefully await the result."

Baglioni laid a small, exquisitely wrought silver phial on the table, and withdrew, leaving what he had said to produce its effect upon the young man's mind.

100   "We will thwart Rappaccini yet!" thought he, chuckling to himself, as he descended the stairs. "But, let us confess the truth of him, he is a wonderful man! — a wonderful man indeed! A vile empiric, however, in his practice, and therefore not to be tolerated by those who respect the good old rules of the medical profession!"

Throughout Giovanni's whole acquaintance with Beatrice, he had occasionally, as we have said, been haunted by dark surmises as to her character. Yet, so thoroughly had she made herself felt by him as a simple, natural, most affectionate and guileless creature, that the image now held up by Professor Baglioni, looked as strange and incredible, as if it were not in accordance with his own original conception. True, there were ugly recollections connected with his first glimpses of the beautiful girl; he could not quite forget the bouquet that withered in her grasp, and the insect that perished amid the sunny air, by no ostensible agency, save the fragrance of her breath. These incidents, however, dissolving in the pure light of her character, had no longer the efficacy of facts, but were acknowledged as mistaken fantasies, by whatever testimony of the senses they might appear to be substantiated. There is something truer and more real, than what we can see with the eyes, and touch with the finger. On such better evidence, had Giovanni founded his confidence in Beatrice, though rather by the necessary force of her high attributes, than by any deep and generous faith, on his part. But, now, his spirit was incapable of sustaining itself at the height to which the early enthusiasm of passion had exalted it; he fell down, grovelling among earthly doubts, and defiled therewith the pure whiteness of Beatrice's image. Not that he gave her up; he did but distrust. He resolved to institute some decisive test that should satisfy him, once for all, whether there were those dreadful peculiarities in her physical nature, which could not be supposed to exist without some corresponding monstrosity of soul. His eyes, gazing down afar, might have deceived him as to the lizard, the insect, and the flowers. But if he could witness, at the distance of a few paces, the sudden blight of one fresh and healthful flower in Beatrice's

---

8 sixteenth-century Italian sculptor and goldsmith.

hand, there would be room for no further question. With this idea, he hastened to the florist's, and purchased a bouquet that was still gemmed with the morning dew-drops.

It was now the customary hour of his daily interview with Beatrice. Before descending into the garden, Giovanni failed not to look at his figure in the mirror; a vanity to be expected in a beautiful young man, yet, as displaying itself at that troubled and feverish moment, the token of a certain shallowness of feeling and insincerity of character. He did gaze, however, and said to himself, that his features had never before possessed so rich a grace, nor his eyes such vivacity, nor his cheeks so warm a hue of superabundant life.

"At least," thought he, "her poison has not yet insinuated itself into my system. I am no flower to perish in her grasp!"

With that thought, he turned his eyes on the bouquet, which he had never once laid aside from his hand. A thrill of indefinable horror shot through his frame, on perceiving that those dewy flowers were already beginning to droop; they wore the aspect of things that had been fresh and lovely, yesterday. Giovanni grew white as marble, and stood motionless before the mirror, staring at his own reflection there, as at the likeness of something frightful. He remembered Baglioni's remark about the fragrance that seemed to pervade the chamber. It must have been the poison in his breath! Then he shuddered — shuddered at himself! Recovering from his stupor, he began to watch, with curious eye, a spider that was busily at work, hanging its web from the antique cornice of the apartment, crossing and re-crossing the artful system of interwoven lines, as vigorous and active a spider as ever dangled from an old ceiling. Giovanni bent towards the insect, and emitted a deep, long breath. The spider suddenly ceased its toil; the web vibrated with a tremor originating in the body of the small artizan. Again Giovanni sent forth a breath, deeper, longer, and imbued with a venomous feeling out of his heart; he knew not whether he were wicked or only desperate. The spider made a convulsive gripe with his limbs, and hung dead across the window.

105

"Accursed! Accursed!" muttered Giovanni, addressing himself. "Hast thou grown so poisonous, that this deadly insect perishes by thy breath?"

At that moment, a rich, sweet voice came floating up from the garden:—

"Giovanni! Giovanni! It is past the hour! Why tarriest thou! Come down!"

"Yes," muttered Giovanni again. "She is the only being whom my breath may not slay! Would that it might!"

He rushed down, and in an instant, was standing before the bright and loving eyes of Beatrice. A moment ago, his wrath and despair had been so fierce that he could have desired nothing so much as to wither her by a glance. But, with her actual presence, there came influences which had too real an existence to be at once shaken off; recollections of the delicate and benign power of her feminine nature, which had so often enveloped him in a religious calm; recollections of many a holy and passionate outgush of her heart, when the pure fountain had been unsealed from its depths, and made visible in its transparency to his mental eye; recollections which, had Giovanni known how to estimate them, would have assured him that all this ugly mystery was but an earthly illusion, and that, whatever mist of evil might seem to have gathered over her, the real Beatrice was a heavenly angel. Incapable as he was of such high faith, still her presence had not utterly lost its magic. Giovanni's rage was quelled into an aspect of sullen insensibility. Beatrice, with a quick spiritual sense, immediately felt that there was a gulf of blackness between them, which neither he nor she could pass. They walked on together, sad and silent, and came thus to the marble fountain, and to its pool of water on the ground, in the midst of which grew the shrub that bore gem-like blossoms. Giovanni was affrighted at the eager enjoyment — the appetite, as it were — with which he found himself inhaling the fragrance of the flowers.

110   "Beatrice," asked he abruptly, "whence came this shrub?"

"My father created it," answered she, with simplicity.

"Created it! created it!" repeated Giovanni. "What mean you, Beatrice?"

"He is a man fearfully acquainted with the secrets of nature," replied Beatrice; "and, at the hour when I first drew breath, this plant sprang from the soil, the offspring of his science, of his intellect, while I was but his earthly child. Approach it not!" continued she, observing with terror that Giovanni was drawing nearer to the shrub. "It has qualities that you little dream of. But I, dearest Giovanni, — I grew up and blossomed with the plant, and was nourished with its breath. It was my sister, and I loved it with a human affection: for — alas! hast thou not suspected it? there was an awful doom."

Here Giovanni frowned so darkly upon her that Beatrice paused and trembled. But her faith in his tenderness reassured her, and made her blush that she had doubted for an instant.

115   "There was an awful doom," she continued, — "the effect of my father's fatal love of science — which estranged me from all society of my kind. Until Heaven sent thee, dearest Giovanni, Oh! how lonely was thy poor Beatrice!"

"Was it a hard doom?" asked Giovanni, fixing his eyes upon her.

"Only of late have I known how hard it was," answered she tenderly. "Oh, yes; but my heart was torpid, and therefore quiet."

Giovanni's rage broke forth from his sullen gloom like a lightning-flash out of a dark cloud.

"Accursed one!" cried he, with venomous scorn and anger. "And finding thy solitude wearisome, thou hast severed me, likewise, from all the warmth of life, and enticed me into thy region of unspeakable horror!"

120   "Giovanni!" exclaimed Beatrice, turning her large bright eyes upon his face. The force of his words had not found its way into her mind; she was merely thunder-struck.

"Yes, poisonous thing!" repeated Giovanni, beside himself with passion. "Thou hast done it! Thou hast blasted me! Thou hast filled my veins with poison! Thou hast made me as hateful, as ugly, as loathsome and deadly a creature as thyself, — a world's wonder of hideous monstrosity! Now — if our breath be happily as fatal to ourselves as to all others — let us join our lips in one kiss of unutterable hatred, and so die!"

"What has befallen me?" murmured Beatrice, with a low moan out of her heart. "Holy Virgin pity me, a poor heart-broken child!"

"Thou! Dost thou pray?" cried Giovanni, still with the same fiendish scorn. "Thy very prayers, as they come from thy lips, taint the atmosphere with death. Yes, yes; let us pray! Let us to church, and dip our fingers in the holy water at the portal! They that come after us will perish as by a pestilence. Let us sign crosses in the air! It will be scattering curses abroad in the likeness of holy symbols!"

"Giovanni," said Beatrice calmly, for her grief was beyond passion, "why dost thou join thyself with me thus in those terrible words? I, it is true, am the horrible thing thou namest me. But thou! — what hast thou to do, save with one other shudder at my hideous misery, to go forth out of the garden and mingle with thy race, and forget that there ever crawled on earth such a monster as poor Beatrice?"

125 "Dost thou pretend ignorance?" asked Giovanni, scowling upon her. "Behold! This power have I gained from the pure daughter of Rappaccini!"

There was a swarm of summer-insects flitting through the air, in search of the food promised by the flower-odors of the fatal garden. They circled round Giovanni's head, and were evidently attracted towards him by the same influence which had drawn them, for an instant, within the sphere of several of the shrubs. He sent forth a breath among them, and smiled bitterly at Beatrice, as at least a score of the insects fell dead upon the ground.

"I see it! I see it!" shrieked Beatrice. "It is my father's fatal science! No, no, Giovanni; it was not I! Never, never! I dreamed only to love thee, and be with thee a little time, and so to let thee pass away, leaving but thine image in mine heart. For, Giovanni — believe it — though my body be nourished with poison, my spirit is God's creature, and craves love as its daily food. But my father! — he has united us in this fearful sympathy. Yes; spurn me! — tread upon me! — kill me! Oh, what is death, after such words as thine? But it was not I! Not for a world of bliss would I have done it!"

Giovanni's passion had exhausted itself in its outburst from his lips. There now came across him a sense, mournful, and not without tenderness, of the intimate and peculiar relationship between Beatrice and himself. They stood, as it were, in an utter solitude, which would be made none the less solitary by the densest throng of human life. Ought not, then, the desert of humanity around them to press this insulated pair closer together? If they should be cruel to one another, who was there to be kind to them? Besides, thought Giovanni, might there not still be a hope of his returning within the limits of ordinary nature, and leading Beatrice — the redeemed Beatrice — by the hand? Oh, weak, and selfish, and unworthy spirit, that could dream of an earthly union and earthly happiness as possible, after such deep love had been so bitterly wronged as was Beatrice's love by Giovanni's blighting words! No, no; there could be no such hope. She must pass heavily, with that broken heart, across the borders of Time — she must bathe her hurts in some fount of Paradise, and forget her grief in the light of immortality — and *there* be well!

But Giovanni did not know it.

130 "Dear Beatrice," said he, approaching her, while she shrank away, as always at his approach, but now with a different impulse — "dearest Beatrice, our fate is not yet so desperate. Behold! There is a medicine, potent, as a wise physician has assured me, and almost divine in its efficacy. It is composed of ingredients the most opposite to those by which thy awful father has brought this calamity upon thee and me. It is distilled of blessed herbs. Shall we not quaff it together, and thus be purified from evil?"

"Give it me!" said Beatrice, extending her hand to receive the little silver phial which Giovanni took from his bosom. She added, with a peculiar emphasis: "I will drink — but do thou await the result."

She put Baglioni's antidote to her lips; and, at the same moment, the figure of Rappaccini emerged from the portal, and came slowly towards the marble fountain. As he drew near, the pale man of science seemed to gaze with a triumphant expression at the beautiful youth and maiden, as might an artist who should spend his life in achieving a picture or a group of statuary, and finally be satisfied with his success. He paused — his bent form grew erect with conscious power, he spread out his hands over them, in the attitude of a father imploring a blessing upon his children. But those were the same hands that had thrown poison into the stream of their lives! Giovanni trembled. Beatrice shuddered nervously, and pressed her hand upon her heart.

"My daughter," said Rappaccini, "thou art no longer lonely in the world! Pluck one of those precious gems from thy sister shrub, and bid thy bridegroom wear it in his bosom. It will not harm him now! My science, and the sympathy between thee and him, have so wrought within his system, that he now stands apart from common men, as thou dost, daughter of my pride and triumph, from ordinary women. Pass on, then, through the world, most dear to one another, and dreadful to all besides!"

"My father," said Beatrice, feebly — and still, as she spoke, she kept her hand upon her heart — "wherefore didst thou inflict this miserable doom upon thy child?"

135 "Miserable!" exclaimed Rappaccini. "What mean you, foolish girl? Dost thou deem it misery to be endowed with marvellous gifts, against which no power nor strength could avail an enemy? Misery, to be able to quell the mightiest with a breath? Misery, to be as terrible as thou art beautiful? Wouldst thou, then, have preferred the condition of a weak woman, exposed to all evil, and capable of none?"

"I would fain have been loved, not feared," murmured Beatrice, sinking down upon the ground. — "But now it matters not; I am going, father, where the evil, which thou hast striven to mingle with my being, will pass away like a dream — like the fragrance of these poisonous flowers, which will no longer taint my breath among the flowers of Eden. Farewell, Giovanni! Thy words of hatred are like lead within my heart — but they, too, will fall away as I ascend. Oh, was there not, from the first, more poison in thy nature than in mine?"

To Beatrice — so radically had her earthly part been wrought upon by Rappaccini's skill — as poison had been life, so the powerful antidote was death. And thus the poor victim of man's ingenuity and of thwarted nature, and of the fatality that attends all such efforts of perverted wisdom, perished there, at the feet of her father and Giovanni. Just at that moment, Professor Pietro Baglioni looked forth from the window, and called loudly, in a tone of triumph mixed with horror, to the thunder-stricken man of science:

"Rappaccini! Rappaccini! And is *this* the upshot of your experiment?"

(1844)

Edgar Allan Poe   (1809–1849)

Born in Boston and raised by foster parents in Richmond, Virginia, Edgar Allan Poe struggled all his adult life to earn a living as a professional author, serving as a magazine editor and writing poetry, short stories, and reviews. A controversial figure before and after his death, he is remembered as a poet whose works influenced late-nineteenth- and early-twentieth-century French, British, and American poets, and as one of the first major writers of the short story. He developed a theory of the short story as a brief prose piece, capable of being read in no more than an hour, in which all details are selected and arranged to create a unified effect. Poe applied this theory skillfully in his story "The Fall of the House of Usher." The narrator's response to the setting, the Usher twins, and the events communicates a sense of increasing horror. Not only does he witness Roderick Usher's increasing madness, he seems drawn into the unnatural atmosphere and barely escapes with his sanity and his life.

THE FALL OF THE HOUSE OF USHER

Son coeur est un luth suspendu;
Sitôt qu'on le touché il résonne.
              — De Béranger.[1]

During the whole of a dull, dark, and soundless day in the autumn of the year, when the clouds hung oppressively low in the heavens, I had been passing alone, on horseback, through a singularly dreary tract of country; and at length found myself, as the shades of the evening drew on, within view of the melancholy House of Usher. I know not how it was — but, with the first glimpse of the building, a sense of insufferable gloom pervaded my spirit. I say insufferable; for the feeling was unrelieved by any of that half-pleasurable, because poetic, sentiment, with which the mind usually receives even the sternest natural images of the desolate or terrible. I looked upon the scene before me — upon the mere house, and the simple landscape features of the domain — upon the bleak walls — upon the vacant eye-like windows — upon a few rank sedges — and upon a few white trunks of decayed trees — with an utter depression of soul which I can compare to no earthly sensation more properly than to the after-dream of the reveller upon opium — the bitter lapse into everyday life — the hideous dropping off of the veil. There was an iciness, a sinking, a sickening of the heart — an unredeemed dreariness of thought which no goading of the imagination could torture into aught of the sublime. What was it — I paused to think — what was it that so unnerved me in the contemplation of the House of Usher? It was a mystery all insoluble; nor could I grapple with the shadowy fancies that crowded upon me as I pondered. I was forced to fall back upon the unsatisfactory conclusion, that while, beyond

---

1 "His heart is a tightly stringed lute; as soon as one touches it, it resonates" — based on eighteenth-century French poet Pierre-Jean de Béranger's "Le Rufus."

doubt, there are combinations of very simple natural objects which have the power of thus affecting us, still the analysis of this power lies among considerations beyond our depth. It was possible, I reflected, that a mere different arrangement of the particulars of the scene, of the details of the picture, would be sufficient to modify, or perhaps to annihilate its capacity for sorrowful impression; and, acting upon this idea, I reined my horse to the precipitous brink of a black and lurid tarn that lay in unruffled lustre by the dwelling, and gazed down — but with a shudder even more thrilling than before — upon the remodelled and inverted images of the gray sedge, and the ghastly tree-stems, and the vacant and eye-like windows.

Nevertheless, in this mansion of gloom I now proposed to myself a sojourn of some weeks. Its proprietor, Roderick Usher, had been one of my boon companions in boyhood; but many years had elapsed since our last meeting. A letter, however, had lately reached me in a distant part of the country — a letter from him — which, in its wildly importunate nature, had admitted of no other than a personal reply. The MS. gave evidence of nervous agitation. The writer spoke of acute bodily illness — of a mental disorder which oppressed him — and of an earnest desire to see me, as his best, and indeed his only personal friend, with a view of attempting, by the cheerfulness of my society, some alleviation of his malady. It was the manner in which all this, and much more, was said — it was the apparent *heart* that went with his request — which allowed me no room for hesitation; and I accordingly obeyed forthwith what I still considered a very singular summons.

Although, as boys, we had been even intimate associates, yet I really knew little of my friend. His reserve had been always excessive and habitual. I was aware, however, that his very ancient family had been noted, time out of mind, for a peculiar sensibility of temperament, displaying itself, through long ages, in many works of exalted art, and manifested, of late, in repeated deeds of munificent yet unobtrusive charity, as well as in a passionate devotion to the intricacies, perhaps even more than to the orthodox and easily recognisable beauties, of musical science. I had learned, too, the very remarkable fact, that the stem of the Usher race, all time-honoured as it was, had put forth, at no period, any enduring branch; in other words, that the entire family lay in the direct line of descent, and had always, with very trifling and very temporary variation, so lain. It was this deficiency, I considered, while running over in thought the perfect keeping of the character of the premises with the accredited character of the people, and while speculating upon the possible influence which the one, in the long lapse of centuries, might have exercised upon the other — it was this deficiency, perhaps, of collateral issue, and the consequent undeviating transmission, from sire to son, of the patrimony with the name, which had, at length, so identified the two as to merge the original title of the estate in the quaint and equivocal appellation of the "House of Usher" — an appellation which seemed to include, in the minds of the peasantry who used it, both the family and the family mansion.

I have said that the sole effect of my somewhat childish experiment — that of looking down within the tarn — had been to deepen the first singular impression. There can be no doubt that the consciousness of the rapid increase of my superstition — for why should I not so term it? — served mainly to accelerate the increase itself. Such, I have long known, is the paradoxical law of all sentiments having terror as a basis. And it might have been for this reason only, that, when I again uplifted my eyes to the house itself, from its image in the pool, there grew in my mind a strange fancy — a fancy so ridiculous, indeed, that I but mention it to show the vivid force of the sensations which oppressed me. I had so worked upon my imagination as really to believe that about the whole mansion and domain there hung an atmosphere peculiar to themselves and their immediate vicinity — an atmosphere which had no affinity with the air of heaven, but which had reeked up from the decayed trees, and the gray wall, and the silent tarn — a pestilent and mystic vapour, dull, sluggish, faintly discernible, and leaden-hued.

Shaking off from my spirit what *must* have been a dream, I scanned more narrowly the real aspect of the building. Its principal feature seemed to be that of an excessive antiquity. The discoloration of ages had been great. Minute fungi overspread the whole exterior, hanging in a fine tangled web-work from the eaves. Yet all this was apart from any extraordinary dilapidation. No portion of the masonry had fallen; and there appeared to be a wild inconsistency between its still perfect adaptation of parts, and the crumbling condition of the individual stones. In this there was much that reminded me of the specious totality of old wood-work which has rotted for long years in some neglected vault, with no disturbance from the breath of the external air. Beyond this indication of extensive decay, however, the fabric gave little token of instability. Perhaps the eye of a scrutinizing observer might have discovered a barely perceptible fissure, which, extending from the roof of the building in front, made its way down the wall in a zigzag direction, until it became lost in the sullen waters of the tarn.

5   Noticing these things, I rode over a short causeway to the house. A servant in waiting took my horse, and I entered the Gothic archway of the hall. A valet, of stealthy step, thence conducted me, in silence, through many dark and intricate passages in my progress to the *studio* of his master. Much that I encountered on the way contributed, I know not how, to heighten the vague sentiments of which I have already spoken. While the objects around me — while the carvings of the ceilings, the sombre tapestries of the walls, the ebon blackness of the floors, and the phantasmagoric armorial trophies which rattled as I strode, were but matters to which, or to such as which, I had been accustomed from my infancy — while I hesitated not to acknowledge how familiar was all this — I still wondered to find how unfamiliar were the fancies which ordinary images were stirring up. On one of the staircases, I met the physician of the family. His countenance, I thought, wore a mingled expression of low cunning and perplexity. He accosted me with trepidation and passed on. The valet now threw open a door and ushered me into the presence of his master.

The room in which I found myself was very large and lofty. The windows were long, narrow, and pointed, and at so vast a distance from the black oaken floor as to be altogether inaccessible from within. Feeble gleams of encrimsoned light made their way through the trellised panes, and served to render sufficiently distinct the more prominent objects around; the eye, however, struggled in vain to reach the remoter angles of the chamber, or the recesses of the vaulted and fretted ceiling. Dark draperies hung upon the walls. The general furniture was profuse, comfortless, antique, and tattered. Many books and musical instruments lay scattered about, but failed to give any vitality to the scene. I felt that I breathed an atmosphere of sorrow. An air of stern, deep, and irredeemable gloom hung over and pervaded all.

Upon my entrance, Usher arose from a sofa on which he had been lying at full length, and greeted me with a vivacious warmth which had much in it, I at first thought, of an overdone cordiality — of the constrained effort of the *ennuyé* man of the world. A glance, however, at his countenance, convinced me of his perfect sincerity. We sat down; and for some moments, while he spoke not, I gazed upon him with a feeling half of pity, half of awe. Surely, man had never before so terribly altered, in so brief a period, as had Roderick Usher! It was with difficulty that I could bring myself to admit the identity of the wan being before me with the companion of my early boyhood. Yet the character of his face had been at all time remarkable. A cadaverousness of complexion; an eye large, liquid, and luminous beyond comparison; lips somewhat thin and very pallid, but of a surpassingly beautiful curve; a nose of a delicate Hebrew model, but with a breadth of nostril unusual in similar formations; a finely moulded chin, speaking, in its want of prominence, of a want of moral energy; hair of a more than web-like softness and tenuity; these features, with an inordinate expansion above the regions of the temple, made up altogether a countenance not easily to be forgotten. And now in the mere exaggeration of the prevailing character of these features, and of the expression they were wont to convey, lay so much of change that I doubted to whom I spoke. The now ghastly pallor of the skin, and the now miraculous lustre of the eye, above all things startled and even awed me. The silken hair, took, had been suffered to grow all unheeded, and as, in its wild gossamer texture, it floated rather than fell about the fact, I could not, even with effort, connect its Arabesque expression with any idea of simple humanity.

In the manner of my friend I was at once struck with an incoherence — an inconsistency; and I soon found this to arise from a series of feeble and futile struggles to overcome an habitual trepidancy — an excessive nervous agitation. For something of this nature I had indeed been prepared, no less by his letter, than by reminiscences of certain boyish traits, and by conclusions deduced from his peculiar physical conformation and temperament. His action was alternately vivacious and sullen. His voice varied rapidly from a tremulous indecision (when the animal spirits seemed utterly in abeyance) to that species of energetic concision — that abrupt, weighty, unhurried, and hollow-sounding enunciation — that leaden, self-balanced and perfectly modulated guttural utterance, which may be observed in the lost drunkard, or the irreclaimable eater of opium, during the periods of his most intense excitement.

It was thus that he spoke of the object of my visit, of his earnest desire to see me, and of the solace he expected me to afford him. He entered, at some length, into what he conceived to be the nature of his malady. It was, he said, a constitutional and a family evil, and one for which he despaired to find a remedy — a mere nervous affection, he immediately added, which would undoubtedly soon pass off. It displayed itself in a host of unnatural sensations. Some of these, as he detailed them, interested and bewildered me; although, perhaps, the terms, and the general manner of the narration had their weight.

He suffered much from a morbid acuteness of the senses; the most insipid food was alone endurable; he could wear only garments of certain texture; the odours of all flowers were oppressive; his eyes were tortured by even a faint light; and there were but peculiar sounds, and these from stringed instruments, which did not inspire him with horror.

10   To an anomalous species of terror I found him a bounden slave. "I shall perish," said he, "I *must* perish in this deplorable folly. Thus, thus, and not otherwise, shall I be lost. I dread the events of the future, not in themselves, but in their results. I shudder at the thought of any, even the most trivial, incident, which may operate upon this intolerable agitation of soul. I have, indeed, no abhorrence of danger, except in its absolute effect — in terror. In this unnerved — in this pitiable condition — I feel that the period will sooner or later arrive when I must abandon life and reason together, in some struggle with the grim phantasm, Fear."

I learned, moreover, at intervals, and through broken and equivocal hints, another singular feature of his mental condition. He was enchained by certain superstitious impressions in regard to the dwelling which he tenanted, and whence, for many years, he had never ventured forth — in regard to an influence whose supposititious force was conveyed in terms too shadowy here to be re-stated — an influence which some peculiarities in the mere form and substance of his family mansion, had, by dint of long sufferance, he said, obtained over his spirit — an effect which the *physique* of the gray walls and turrets, and of the dim tarn into which they all looked down, had, at length, brought about upon the *morale* of his existence.

He admitted, however, although with hesitation, that much of the peculiar gloom which thus afflicted him could be traced to a more natural and far more palpable origin — to the severe and long-continued illness — indeed to the evidently approaching dissolution — of a tenderly beloved sister — his sole companion for long years — his last and only relative on earth. "Her decease," he said, with a bitterness which I can never forget, "would leave him (him the hopeless and the frail) the last of the ancient race of the Ushers." While he spoke, the lady Madeline (for so was she called) passed slowly through a remote portion of the apartment, and, without having noticed my presence, disappeared. I regarded her with an utter astonishment not unmingled with dread — and yet I found it impossible to account for such feelings. A sensation of stupor oppressed me, as my eyes followed her retreating steps. When a door, at length, closed upon her, my glance sought instinctively and eagerly the countenance of the brother — but he had buried his face in his hands, and I could only perceive that a far more than ordinary wanness had overspread the emaciated fingers through which trickled many passionate tears.

The disease of the lady Madeline had long baffled the skill of her physicians. A settled apathy, a gradual wasting away of the person, and frequent although transient affections of a partially cataleptical character, were the unusual diagnosis. Hitherto she had steadily borne up against the pressure of her malady, and had not betaken herself finally to bed; but, on the closing in of the evening of my arrival at the house, she succumbed (as her brother told me at night with inexpressible agitation) to the prostrating power of the destroyer; and I learned that the glimpse I had obtained of her person would thus probably be the last I should obtain — that the lady, at least while living, would be seen by me no more.

For several days ensuing, her name was unmentioned by either Usher or myself: and during this period I was busied in earnest endeavours to alleviate the melancholy of my friend. We painted and read together; or I listened, as if in a dream, to the wild improvisations of his speaking guitar. And thus, as a closer and still closer intimacy admitted me more unreservedly into the recesses of his spirit, the more bitterly did I perceive the futility of all attempt at cheering a mind from which darkness, as if an inherent positive quality, poured forth upon all objects of the moral and physical universe, in one unceasing radiation of gloom.

15

I shall ever bear about me a memory of the many solemn hours I thus spent alone with the master of the House of Usher. Yet I should fail in any attempt to convey an idea of the exact character of the studies, or of the occupations, in which he involved me, or led me the way. An excited and highly distempered ideality threw a sulphureous lustre over all. His long improvised dirges will ring forever in my ears. Among other things, I hold painfully in mind a certain singular perversion and amplification of the wild air of the last waltz of Von Weber.[2] From the paintings over which his elaborate fancy brooded, and which grew, touch by touch, into vaguenesses at which I shuddered the more thrillingly, because I shuddered knowing not why; — from these paintings (vivid as their images now are before me) I would in vain endeavour to educe more than a small portion which should lie within the compass of merely written words. By the utter simplicity, by the nakedness of his designs, he arrested and overawed attention. If ever mortal painted an idea, that mortal was Roderick Usher. For me at least — in the circumstances then surrounding me — there arose out of the pure abstractions which the hypochondriac contrived to throw upon his canvas, an intensity of intolerable awe, no shadow of which felt I ever yet in the contemplation of the certainly glowing yet too concrete reveries of Fuseli.[3]

One of the phantasmagoric conceptions of my friend, partaking not so rigidly of the spirit of abstraction, may be shadowed forth, although feebly, in words. A small picture presented the interior of an immensely long and rectangular vault or tunnel, with low walls, smooth, white, and without interruption or device. Certain accessory points of the design served well to convey the idea that this excavation lay at an exceeding depth below the surface of the earth. No outlet was observed in any portion of its vast extent, and no torch, or other artificial source of light was discernible; yet a flood of intense rays rolled throughout, and bathed the whole in a ghastly and inappropriate splendour.

I have just spoken of that morbid condition of the auditory nerve which rendered all music intolerable to the sufferer, with the exception of certain effects of stringed instruments. It was, perhaps, the narrow limits to which he thus confined himself upon the guitar, which gave birth, in great measure, to the fantastic character of his performances. But the fervid *facility* of his *impromptus* could not be so accounted for. They must have been, and were, in

---

2 Composed by Karl Gottlieb Reissiger in honour of Karl Maria Von Weber, nineteenth-century German composer of operas. 3 late eighteenth- early nineteenth-century Swiss painter interested in psychological horror and the supernatural.

the notes, as well as in the words of his wild fantasias (for he not unfrequently accompanied himself with rhymed verbal improvisations), the result of that intense mental collectedness and concentration to which I have previously alluded as observable only in particular moments of the highest artificial excitement. The words of one of these rhapsodies I have easily remembered. I was, perhaps, the more forcibly impressed with it, as he gave it, because, in the under or mystic current of its meaning, I fancied that I perceived, and for the first time, a full consciousness on the part of Usher, of the tottering of his lofty reason upon her throne. The verses, which were entitled "The Haunted Palace," ran very nearly, if not accurately, thus:

I.

In the greenest of our valleys,
     By good angels tenanted,
Once a fair and stately palace —
     Radiant palace — reared its head.
In the monarch Thought's dominion —
     It stood there!
Never seraph spread a pinion
     Over fabric half so fair.

II.

Banners yellow, glorious, golden,
     On its roof did float and flow;
(This — all this — was in the olden
     Time long ago)
And every gentle air that dallied,
     In that sweet day,
Along the ramparts plumed and pallid,
     A winged odour went away.

III.

20   Wanderers in that happy valley
     Through two luminous windows saw
Spirits moving musically
     To a lute's well-tuned law,
Round about a throne, where sitting
     (Porphyrogene!)[4]
In state his glory well befitting,
     The ruler of the realm was seen.

IV.

And all with pearl and ruby glowing
     Was the fair palace door,
Through which came flowing, flowing, flowing
     And sparkling evermore,
A troop of Echoes whose sweet duty
     Was but to sing,

4 of royal birth.

In voices of surpassing beauty,
    The wit and wisdom of their king.

V.

But evil things, in robes of sorrow,
    Assailed the monarch's high estate;
(Ah, let us mourn, for never morrow
    Shall dawn upon him, desolate!)
And, round about his home, the glory
    That blushed and bloomed
Is but a dim-remembered story
    Of the old time entombed.

VI.

And travellers now within that valley,
    Through the red-litten windows, see
Vast forms that move fantastically
    To a discordant melody;
While, like a rapid ghastly river,
    Through the pale door,
A hideous throng rush out forever,
    And laugh — but smile no more.

I well remember that suggestions arising from this ballad, led us into a train of thought wherein there became manifest an opinion of Usher's which I mention not so much on account of its novelty, (for other men have thought thus,) as on account of the pertinacity with which he maintained it. This opinion, in its general form, was that of the sentience of all vegetable things. But, in his disordered fancy, the idea had assumed a more daring character, and trespassed, under certain conditions, upon the kingdom of inorganization. I lack words to express the full extent, or the earnest *abandon* of his persuasion. The belief, however, was connected (as I have previously hinted) with the gray stones of the home of his forefathers. The conditions of the sentience had been here, he imagined, fulfilled in the method of collocation of these stones — in the order of their arrangement, as well as in that of the many *fungi* which overspread them, and of the decayed trees which stood around — above all, in the long undisturbed endurance of this arrangement, and in its reduplication in the still waters of the tarn. Its evidence — the evidence of the sentience — was to be seen, he said (and I here started as he spoke,) in the gradual yet certain condensation of an atmosphere of their own about the waters and the walls. The result was discoverable, he added, in that silent, yet importunate and terrible influence which for centuries had moulded the destinies of his family, and which made *him* what I now saw him — what he was. Such opinions need no comment, and I will make none.

25   Our books[5] — the books which, for years, had formed no small portion of the mental existence of the invalid — were, as might be supposed, in strict keeping with this character of phantasm. We pored together over such works

5   these obscure books deal with supernatural occurrences, death, and damnation.

as the Ververt et Chartreuse of Gresset; the Belphegor of Machiavelli; the Heaven and Hell of Swedenborg; the Subterranean Voyage of Nicholas Klimm by Holberg; the Chiromancy of Robert Flud, of Jean D'Indaginé, and of De la Chambre; the Journey into the Blue Distance of Tieck; and the City of the Sun of Campanella. One favourite volume was a small octavo edition of the *Directorium Inquisitorum*, by the Dominican Eymeric de Gironne; and there were passages in Pomponius Mela, about the old African Satyrs and Ægipans, over which Usher would sit dreaming for hours. His chief delight, however, was found in the perusal of an exceedingly rare and curious book in quarto Gothic — the manual of a forgotten church — the *Vigiliae Mortuorum secundum Chorum Ecclesiae Maguntinæ*.

I could not help thinking of the wild ritual of this work, and of its probable influence upon the hypochondriac, when, one evening, having informed me abruptly that the lady Madeline was no more, he stated his intention of preserving her corpse for a fortnight, (previously to its final interment,) in one of the numerous vaults within the main walls of the building. The worldly reason, however, assigned for this singular proceeding, was one which I did not feel at liberty to dispute. The brother had been led to his resolution (so he told me) by consideration of the unusual character of the malady of the deceased, of certain obtrusive and eager inquiries on the part of her medical men, and of the remote and exposed situation of the burial-ground of the family. I will not deny that when I called to mind the sinister countenance of the person whom I met upon the staircase, on the day of my arrival at the house, I had no desire to oppose what I regarded as at best but a harmless, and by no means an unnatural, precaution.

At the request of Usher, I personally aided him in the arrangements for the temporary entombment. The body having been encoffined, we two alone bore it to its rest. The vault in which we placed it (and which had been so long unopened that our torches, half smothered in its oppressive atmosphere, gave us little opportunity for investigation) was small, damp, and entirely without means of admission for light; lying, at great depth, immediately beneath that portion of the building in which was my own sleeping apartment. It had been used, apparently, in remote feudal times, for the worst purposes of a donjon-keep, and, in later days, as a place of deposit for powder, or some other highly combustible substance, as a portion of its floor, and the whole interior of a long archway through which we reached it, were carefully sheathed with copper. The door, of massive iron, had been, also, similarly protected. Its immense weight caused an unusually sharp grating sound, as it moved upon its hinges.

Having deposited our mournful burden upon tressels within this region of horror, we partially turned aside the yet unscrewed lid of the coffin, and looked upon the face of the tenant. A striking similitude between the brother and sister now first arrested my attention; and Usher, divining, perhaps, my thoughts, murmured out some few words from which I learned that the deceased and himself had been twins, and that sympathies of a scarcely intelligible nature had always existed between them. Our glances, however, rested not long upon the dead — for we could not regard her unawed. The disease which had thus entombed the lady in the maturity of youth, had left, as usual in all maladies of a strictly cataleptical character, the mockery of a faint blush upon the bosom and the face, and that suspiciously lingering smile upon the lip which is so terrible in death. We replaced and screwed down the lid, and, having secured the door of iron, made our way, with toil, into the scarcely less gloomy apartments of the upper portion of the house.

And now, some days of bitter grief having elapsed, an observable change came over the features of the mental disorder of my friend. His ordinary manner had vanished. His ordinary occupations were neglected or forgotten. He roamed from chamber to chamber with hurried, unequal, and objectless step. The pallor of his countenance had assumed, if possible, a more ghastly hue — but the luminousness of his eye had utterly gone out. The once occasional huskiness of his tone was heard no more; and a tremulous quaver, as if of extreme terror, habitually characterized his utterance. There were times, indeed, when I thought his unceasingly agitated mind was labouring with some oppressive secret, to divulge which he struggled for the necessary courage. At times, again, I was obliged to resolve all into the mere inexplicable vagaries of madness, for I beheld him gazing upon vacancy for long hours, in an attitude of the profoundest attention, as if listening to some imaginary sound. It was no wonder that his condition terrified — that it infected me. I felt creeping upon me, by slow yet certain degrees, the wild influences of his own fantastic yet impressive superstitions.

30   It was, especially, upon retiring to bed late in the night of the seventh or eighth day after the placing of the lady Madeline within the donjon, that I experienced the full power of such feelings. Sleep came not near my couch — while the hours waned and waned away. I struggled to reason off the nervousness which had dominion over me. I endeavoured to believe that much, if not all of what I felt, was due to the bewildering influence of the gloomy furniture of the room — of the dark and tattered draperies, which, tortured into motion by the breath of a rising tempest, swayed fitfully to and fro upon the walls, and rustled uneasily about the decorations of the bed. But my efforts were fruitless. An irrepressible tremour gradually pervaded my frame; and, at length, there sat upon my very heart an incubus of utterly causeless alarm. Shaking this off with a gasp and a struggle, I uplifted myself upon the pillows, and, peering earnestly within the intense darkness of the chamber, hearkened — I know not why, except that an instinctive spirit prompted me — to certain low and indefinite sounds which came, through the pauses of the storm, at long intervals, I knew not whence. Overpowered by an intense sentiment of horror, unaccountable yet unendurable, I threw on my clothes with haste (for I felt that I should sleep no more during the night), and endeavoured to arouse myself from the pitiable condition into which I had fallen, by pacing rapidly to and fro through the apartment.

I had taken but few turns in this manner, when a light step on an adjoining staircase arrested my attention. I presently recognised it as that of Usher. In an instant afterward he rapped, with a gentle touch, at my door, and entered, bearing a lamp. His countenance was, as usual, cadaverously wan — but, moreover, there was a species of mad hilarity in his eyes — an evidently restrained *hysteria* in his whole demeanour. His air appalled me — but anything was preferable to the solitude which I had so long endured, and I even welcomed his presence as a relief.

"And you have not seen it?" he said abruptly, after having stared about him for some moments in silence — "you have not then seen it? — but, stay! you shall." Thus speaking, and having carefully shaded his lamp, he hurried to one of the casements, and threw it freely open to the storm.

The impetuous fury of the entering gust nearly lifted us from our feet. It was, indeed, a tempestuous yet sternly beautiful night, and one wildly singular in its terror and its beauty. A whirlwind had apparently collected its force in our vicinity; for there were frequent and violent alterations in the direction of the wind; and the exceeding density of the clouds (which hung so low as to press upon the turrets of the house) did not prevent our perceiving the life-like velocity with which they flew careering from all points against each other, without passing away into the distance. I say that even their exceeding density did not prevent our perceiving this — yet we had no glimpse of the moon or stars — nor was there any flashing forth of the lightning. But the under surfaces of the huge masses of agitated vapour, as well as all terrestrial objects immediately around us, were glowing in the unnatural light of a faintly luminous and distinctly visible gaseous exhalation which hung about and enshrouded the mansion.

"You must not — you shall not behold this!" said I, shudderingly, to Usher, as I led him, with a gentle violence, from the window to a seat. "These appearances, which bewilder you, are merely electrical phenomena not uncommon — or it may be that they have their ghastly origin in the rank miasma of the tarn. Let us close this casement; — the air is chilling and dangerous to your frame. Here is one of your favourite romances. I will read, and you shall listen; — and so we will pass away this terrible night together."

35   The antique volume which I had taken up was the "Mad Trist" of Sir Launcelot Canning;[6] but I had called it a favourite of Usher's more in sad jest than in earnest; for, in trust, there is little in its uncouth and unimaginative prolixity which could have had interest for the lofty and spiritual ideality of my friend. It was, however, the only book immediately at hand; and I indulged a vague hope that the excitement which now agitated the hypochondriac, might find relief (for the history of mental disorder is full of similar anomalies) even in the extremeness of the folly which I should read. Could I have judged, indeed, by the wild overstrained air of vivacity with which he hearkened, or apparently hearkened, to the words of the tale, I might well have congratulated myself upon the success of my design.

I had arrived at that well-known portion of the story where Ethelred, the hero of the Trist, having sought in vain for peaceable admission into the dwelling of the hermit, proceeds to make good an entrance by force. Here, it will be remembered, the words of the narrative runs thus:

"And Ethelred, who was by nature of a doughty heart, and who was now mighty withal, on account of the powerfulness of the wine which he had drunken, waited no longer to hold parley with the hermit, who, in sooth, was of an obstinate and maliceful turn, but, feeling the rain upon his shoulders, and fearing the rising of the tempest, uplifted his mace outright, and, with blows, made quickly room in the plankings of the door for his gauntleted hand; and now pulling therewith sturdily, he so cracked, and ripped, and tore all asunder, that the noise of the dry and hollow-sounding wood alarmed and reverberated throughout the forest."

At the termination of this sentence I started, and for a moment, paused; for it appeared to me (although I at once concluded that my excited fancy had

6   the author and book are imaginary; Poe wrote the descriptions to fit this story.

deceived me) — it appeared to me that, from some very remote portion of the mansion, there came, indistinctly, to my ears, what might have been, in its exact similarity of character, the echo (but a stifled and full one certainly) of the very cracking and ripping sound which Sir Launcelot had so particularly described. It was, beyond doubt, the coincidence alone which had arrested my attention; for, amid the rattling of the sashes of the casements, and the ordinary commingled noises of the still increasing storm, the sound, in itself, had nothing, surely, which should have interested or disturbed me. I continued the story:

"But the good champion Ethelred, now entering within the door, was sore enraged and amazed to perceive no signal of the maliceful hermit; but, in the stead thereof, a dragon of a scaly and prodigious demeanour, and of a fiery tongue, which sate in guard before a palace of gold, with a floor of silver; and upon the wall there hung a shield of shining brass with this legend enwritten —

40   Who entereth herein, a conqueror hath bin;
           Who slayeth the dragon, the shield he shall win;

And Ethelred uplifted his mace, and struck upon the head of the dragon, which fell before him, and gave up his pesty breath, with a shriek so horrid and harsh, and withal so piercing, that Ethelred had fain to close his ears with his hands against the dreadful noise of it, the like whereof was never before heard."

Here again I paused abruptly, and now with a feeling of wild amazement — for there could be no doubt whatever that, in this instance, I did actually hear (although from what direction it proceeded I found it impossible to say) a low and apparently distant, but harsh, protracted, and most unusual screaming or grating sound — the exact counterpart of what my fancy had already conjured up for the dragon's unnatural shriek as described by the romancer.

Oppressed, as I certainly was, upon the occurrence of the second and most extraordinary coincidence, by a thousand conflicting sensations, in which wonder and extreme terror were predominant, I still retained sufficient presence of mind to avoid exciting, by any observation, the sensitive nervousness of my companion. I was by no means certain that he had noticed the sounds in question; although, assuredly, a strange alteration had, during the last few minutes, taken place in his demeanour. From a position fronting my own, he had gradually brought round his chair, so as to sit with his face to the door of the chamber; and thus I could but partially perceive his features, although I saw that his lips trembled as if he were murmuring inaudibly. His head had dropped upon his breast — yet I knew that he was not asleep, from the wide and rigid opening of the eye as I caught a glance of it in profile. The motion of his body, too, was at variance with this idea — for he rocked from side to side with a gentle yet constant and uniform sway. Having rapidly taken notice of all this, I resumed the narrative of Sir Launcelot, which thus proceeded:

"And now, the champion, having escaped from the terrible fury of the dragon, bethinking himself of the brazen shield, and of the breaking up of the enchantment which was upon it, removed the carcass from out of the way before him, and approached valorously over the silver pavement of the castle to where the shield was upon the wall; which in sooth tarried not for his full coming, but fell down at his feet upon the silver floor, with a mighty great and terrible ringing sound."

No sooner had these syllables passed my lips, than — as if a shield of brass had indeed, at the moment, fallen heavily upon a floor of silver — I became aware of a distinct, hollow, metallic, and clangorous, yet apparently muffled reverberation. Completely unnerved, I leaped to my feet; but the measured rocking movement of Usher was undisturbed. I rushed to the chair in which he sat. His eyes were bent fixedly before him, and throughout his whole countenance there reigned a stony rigidity. But, as I placed my hand upon his shoulder, there came a strong shudder over his whole person; a sickly smile quivered about his lips; and I saw that he spoke in a low, hurried, and gibbering murmur, as if unconscious of my presence. Bending closely over him, I at length drank in the hideous import of his words.

45 "Not hear it? — yes, I hear it, and *have* heard it. Long — long — long — many minutes, many hours, many days, have I heard it — yet I dared not — oh, pity me, miserable wretch that I am! — I dared not — I *dared* not speak! *We have put her living in the tomb!* Said I not that my senses were acute? I *now* tell you that I heard her first feeble movements in the hollow coffin. I heard them, many, many days ago — yet I dared not — *I dared not speak!* And now — tonight — Ethelred — ha! ha! — the breaking of the hermit's door, and the death-cry of the dragon, and the clangour of the shield! — say, rather, the rending of her coffin, and the grating of the iron hinges of her prison, and her struggles within the coppered archway of the vault! Oh whither shall I fly? Will she not be here anon? Is she not hurrying to upbraid me for my haste? Have I not heard her footstep on the stair? Do I not distinguish that heavy and horrible beating of her heart? MADMAN!" here he sprang furiously to his feet, and shrieked out his syllables, as if in the effort he were giving up his soul — "MADMAN! I TELL YOU THAT SHE NOW STANDS WITHOUT THE DOOR!"

As if in the superhuman energy of his utterance there had been found the potency of a spell — the huge antique panels to which the speaker pointed, threw slowly back, upon the instant, their ponderous and ebony jaws. It was the work of the rushing gust — but then without those doors there DID stand the lofty and enshrouded figure of the lady Madeline of Usher. There was blood upon her white robes, and the evidence of some bitter struggle upon every portion of her emaciated frame. For a moment she remained trembling and reeling to and fro upon the threshold, then, with a low moaning cry, fell heavily inward upon the person of her brother, and in her violent and now final death-agonies, bore him to the floor a corpse, and a victim to the terrors he had anticipated.

From that chamber, and from that mansion, I fled aghast. The storm was still abroad in all its wrath as I found myself crossing the old causeway. Suddenly there shot along the path a wild light, and I turned to see whence a gleam so unusual could have issued; for the vast house and its shadows were alone behind me. The radiance was that of the full, setting, and blood-red moon which now shone vividly through that once barely discernible fissure of which I have before spoken as extending from the roof of the building, in a zigzag direction, to the base. While I gazed, this fissure rapidly widened — there came a fierce breath of the whirlwind — the entire orb of the satellite burst at once upon my sight — my brain reeled as I saw the mighty walls rushing asunder — there was a long tumultuous shouting sound like the voice of a thousand waters — and the deep and dank tarn at my feet closed sullenly and silently over the fragments of the "HOUSE OF USHER."

(1839)

Herman Melville   (1819–1891)

Born in New York City, Herman Melville spent many years as a sailor, including a cruise on a whaling ship, before becoming a writer. His most famous book, *Moby-Dick*, combined factual details about whaling with a symbolic examination about the nature of reality, particularly the conflict between good and evil. It is narrated by Ishmael, a quiet, thoughtful crew member, and presents the monomaniacal quest of Captain Ahab to slay a great white whale. Although "Bartleby, the Scrivener," written shortly after the novel, is much shorter and is set in a large city, it bears many similarities to *Moby-Dick*. The unnamed narrator is fascinated by a character who is much different from him, as Ishmael was fascinated by Ahab. The realistic and mundane details of a law office are given symbolic meanings, particularly the blank wall at which Bartleby stares. The lonely scrivener represents the condition of many human beings, orphans and "isolatoes," as Melville termed them, in a world where the significance of life, if there is any, cannot usually be understood. The short story also satirizes nineteenth-century Americans' preoccupation with the acquisition of wealth.

BARTLEBY, THE SCRIVENER
A Story of Wall-Street

I am a rather elderly man. The nature of my avocations for the last thirty years has brought me into more than ordinary contact with what would seem an interesting and somewhat singular set of men, of whom as yet nothing that I know of has ever been written:— I mean the law-copyists or scriveners. I have known very many of them, professionally and privately, and if I pleased, could relate divers histories, at which good-natured gentlemen might smile, and sentimental souls might weep. But I waive the biographies of all other scriveners for a few passages in the life of Bartleby, who was a scrivener the strangest I ever saw or heard of. While of other law-copyists I might write the complete life, of Bartleby nothing of that sort can be done. I believe that no materials exist for a full and satisfactory biography of this man. It is an irreparable loss to literature. Bartleby was one of those beings of whom nothing is ascertainable, except from the original sources, and in his case those are very small. What my own astonished eyes saw of Bartleby, *that* is all I know of him, except, indeed, one vague report which will appear in the sequel.

Ere introducing the scrivener, as he first appeared to me, it is fit I make some mention of myself, my *employés*, my business, my chambers, and general surroundings; because some such description is indispensable to an adequate understanding of the chief character about to be presented.

Imprimis: I am a man who, from his youth upwards, has been filled with a profound conviction that the easiest way of life is the best. Hence, though I belong to a profession proverbially energetic and nervous, even to turbulence, at times, yet nothing of that sort have I ever suffered to invade my peace. I am one of those unambitious lawyers who never addresses a jury, or in any way draws down public applause; but in the cool tranquillity of a snug retreat, do a snug business among rich men's bonds and mortgages and title-deeds. All who know me, consider me an eminently *safe* man. The late John Jacob Astor,[1] a personage little given to poetic enthusiasm, had no hesitation in pronouncing my first grand point to be prudence; my next, method. I do not speak it in vanity, but simply record the fact, that I was not unemployed in my profession by the late John Jacob Astor; a name which, I admit, I love to repeat, for it hath a rounded and orbicular sound to it, and rings like unto bullion. I will freely add, that I was not insensible to the late John Jacob Astor's good opinion.

Some time prior to the period at which this little history begins, my avocations had been largely increased. The good old office, now extinct in the State of New-York, of a Master in Chancery,[2] had been conferred upon me. It was not a very arduous office, but very pleasantly remunerative. I seldom lose my temper; much more seldom indulge in dangerous indignation at wrongs and outrages; but I must be permitted to be rash here and declare, that I consider the sudden and violent abrogation of the office of Master in Chancery, by the new Constitution, as a — premature act; inasmuch as I had counted upon a life-lease of the profits, whereas I only received those of a few short years. But this is by the way.

5 My chambers were up stairs at No. — Wall-street.[3] At one end they looked upon the white wall of the interior of a spacious sky-light shaft, penetrating the building from top to bottom. This view might have been considered rather tame than otherwise, deficient in what landscape painters call "life." But if so, the view from the other end of my chambers offered, at least, a contrast, if nothing more. In that direction my windows commanded an unobstructed view of a lofty brick wall, black by age and everlasting shade; which wall required no spy-glass to bring out its lurking beauties, but for the benefit of all near-sighted spectators, was pushed up to within ten feet of my window panes. Owing to the great height of the surrounding buildings, and my chambers being on the second floor, the interval between this wall and mine not a little resembled a huge square cistern.

At the period just preceding the advent of Bartleby, I had two persons as copyists in my employment, and a promising lad as an office-boy. First, Turkey; second, Nippers; third, Ginger Nut. These may seem names, the like of which are not usually found in the Directory. In truth they were nicknames, mutually conferred upon each other by my three clerks, and were deemed expressive of their respective persons or characters. Turkey was a short, pursy Englishman of about my own age, that is, somewhere not far from sixty. In the morning, one might say, his face was of a fine florid hue, but after twelve o'clock, meridian — his dinner hour — it blazed like a grate full of Christmas coals; and continued blazing — but, as it were, with a gradual wane — till 6 o'clock, P.M. or thereabouts, after which I saw no more of the proprietor of the face, which gaining its meridian with the sun, seemed to set with it, to rise, culminate, and decline the following day, with the like regularity and undiminished glory.

---

1 at the time of his death in 1848, Astor was the richest man in the United States. 2 officer of the court whose duties included taking testimonies, administering oaths, and acknowledging deeds. 3 located in New York City, the financial centre of the United States.

There are many singular coincidences I have known in the course of my life, not the least among which was the fact, that exactly when Turkey displayed his fullest beams from his red and radiant countenance, just then, too, at that critical moment, began the daily period when I considered his business capacities as seriously disturbed for the remainder of the twenty-four hours. Not that he was absolutely idle, or averse to business then; far from it. The difficulty was, he was apt to be altogether too energetic. There was a strange, inflamed, flurried, flighty recklessness of activity about him. He would be incautious in dipping his pen into his inkstand. All his blots upon my documents, were dropped there after twelve o'clock, meridian. Indeed, not only would he be reckless and sadly given to making blots in the afternoon, but some days he went further, and was rather noisy. At such times, too, his face flamed with augmented blazonry, as if cannel coal had been heaped on anthracite. He made an unpleasant racket with his chair; spilled his sandbox; in mending his pens, impatiently split them all to pieces, and threw them on the floor in a sudden passion; stood up and leaned over his table, boxing his papers about in a most indecorous manner, very sad to behold in an elderly man like him. Nevertheless, as he was in many ways a most valuable person to me, and all the time before twelve o'clock, meridian, was the quickest, steadiest creature too, accomplishing a great deal of work in a style not easy to be matched — for these reasons, I was willing to overlook his eccentricities, though indeed, occasionally, I remonstrated with him. I did this very gently, however, because, though the civilest, nay, the blandest and most reverential of men in the morning, yet in the afternoon he was disposed, upon provocation, to be slightly rash with his tongue, in fact, insolent. Now, valuing his morning services as I did, and resolved not to lose them; yet, at the same time made uncomfortable by his inflamed ways after twelve o'clock; and being a man of peace, unwilling by my admonitions to call forth unseemly retorts from him; I took upon me, one Saturday noon (he was always worse on Saturdays), to hint to him, very kindly, that perhaps now that he was growing old, it might be well to abridge his labors; in short, he need not come to my chambers after twelve o'clock, but, dinner over, had best go home to his lodgings and rest himself till tea-time. But no; he insisted upon his afternoon devotions. His countenance became intolerably fervid, as he oratorically assured me — gesticulating with a long ruler at the other end of the room — that if his services in the morning were useful, how indispensable, then, in the afternoon?

"With submission, sir," said Turkey on this occasion, "I consider myself your right-hand man. In the morning I but marshal and deploy my columns; but in the afternoon I put myself at their head, and gallantly charge the foe, thus!" — and he made a violent thrust with the ruler.

"But the blots, Turkey," intimated I.

"True, — but, with submission, sir, behold these hairs! I am getting old. Surely, sir, a blot or two of a warm afternoon is not to be severely urged against gray hairs. Old age — even if it blot the page — is honorable. With submission, sir, we *both* are getting old."

This appeal to my fellow-feeling was hardly to be resisted. At all events, I saw that go he would not. So I made up my mind to let him stay, resolving, nevertheless, to see to it, that during the afternoon he had to do with my less important papers.

Nippers, the second on my list, was a whiskered, sallow, and, upon the whole, rather piratical-looking young man of about five and twenty. I always deemed him the victim of two evil powers — ambition and indigestion. The ambition was evinced by a certain impatience of the duties of a mere copyist, an unwarrantable usurpation of strictly professional affairs, such as the original drawing up of legal documents. The indigestion seemed betokened in an occasional nervous testiness and grinning irritability, causing the teeth to audibly grind together over mistakes committed in copying; unnecessary maledictions, hissed, rather than spoken, in the heat of business; and especially by a continual discontent with the height of the table where he worked. Though of a very ingenious mechanical turn, Nippers could never get this table to suit him. He put chips under it, blocks of various sorts, bits of pasteboard, and at last went so far as to attempt an exquisite adjustment by final pieces of folded blotting-paper. But no invention would answer. If, for the sake of easing his back, he brought the table lid at a sharp angle well up towards his chin, and wrote there like a man using the steep roof of a Dutch house for his desk:— then he declared that it stopped the circulation in his arms. If now he lowered the table to his waistbands, and stooped over it in writing, then there was a sore aching in his back. In short, the truth of the matter was, Nippers knew not what he wanted. Or, if he wanted any thing, it was to be rid of a scrivener's table altogether. Among the manifestations of his diseased ambition was a fondness he had for receiving visits from certain ambiguous-looking fellows in seedy coats, whom he called his clients. Indeed I was aware that not only was he, at times, considerable of a ward-politician,[4] but he occasionally did a little business at the Justices' courts, and was not unknown on the steps of the Tombs.[5] I have good reason to believe, however, that one individual who called upon him at my chambers, and who, with a grand air, he insisted was his client, was no other than a dun, and the alleged title-deed, a bill. But with all his failings, and the annoyances he caused me, Nippers, like his compatriot Turkey, was a very useful man to me; wrote a neat, swift hand; and, when he chose, was not deficient in a gentlemanly sort of deportment. Added to this, he always dressed in a gentlemanly sort of way; and so, incidentally, reflected credit upon my chambers. Whereas with respect to Turkey, I had much ado to keep him from being a reproach to me. His clothes were apt to look oily and smell of eating-houses. He wore his pantaloons very loose and baggy in summer. His coats were execrable; his hat not to be handled. But while the hat was a thing of indifference to me, inasmuch as his natural civility and deference, as a dependent Englishman, always led him to doff it the moment he entered the room, yet his coat was another matter. Concerning his coats, I reasoned with him; but with no effect. The truth was, I suppose, that a man with so small an income, could not afford to sport such a lustrous face and a lustrous coat at one and the same time. As Nippers once observed, Turkey's money went chiefly for red ink. One winter day I presented Turkey with a highly-respectable looking coat of my own, a padded gray coat, of a most comfortable warmth, and which buttoned straight up from the knee to the neck. I thought Turkey would appreciate the favor, and abate his rashness and

4 similar to an alderman or town-councillor. 5 New York City prison.

obstreperousness of afternoons. But no. I verily believe that buttoning himself up in so downy and blanket-like a coat had a pernicious effect upon him; upon the same principle that too much oats are bad for horses. In fact, precisely as a rash, restive horse is said to feel his oats, so Turkey felt his coat. It made him insolent. He was a man whom prosperity harmed.

Though concerning the self-indulgent habits of Turkey I had my own private surmises, yet touching Nippers I was well persuaded that whatever might be his faults in other respects, he was, at least, a temperate young man. But indeed, nature herself seemed to have been his vintner, and at his birth charged him so thoroughly with an irritable, brandy-like disposition, that all subsequent potations were needless. When I consider how, amid the stillness of my chambers, Nippers would sometimes impatiently rise from his seat, and stooping over his table, spread his arms wide apart, seize the whole desk, and move it, and jerk it, with a grim, grinding motion on the floor, as if the table were a perverse voluntary agent, intent on thwarting and vexing him; I plainly perceive that for Nippers, brandy and water were altogether superfluous.

It was fortunate for me that, owing to its peculiar cause — indigestion — the irritability and consequent nervousness of Nippers, were mainly observable in the morning, while in the afternoon he was comparatively mild. So that Turkey's paroxysms only coming on about twelve o'clock, I never had to do with their eccentricities at one time. Their fits relieved each other like guards. When Nippers' was on, Turkey's was off; and *vice versa*. This was a good natural arrangement under the circumstances.

Ginger Nut, the third on my list, was a lad some twelve years old. His father was a carman,[6] ambitious of seeing his son on the bench instead of a cart, before he died. So he sent him to my office as student at law, errand boy, and cleaner and sweeper, at the rate of one dollar a week. He had a little desk to himself, but he did not use it much. Upon inspection, the drawer exhibited a great array of the shells of various sorts of nuts. Indeed, to this quick-witted youth the whole noble science of the law was contained in a nut-shell. Not the least among the employments of Ginger Nut, as well as one which he discharged with the most alacrity, was his duty as cake and apple purveyor for Turkey and Nippers. Copying law papers being proverbially a dry, husky sort of business, my two scriveners were fain to moisten their mouths very often with Spitzenbergs[7] to be had at the numerous stalls nigh the Custom House and Post Office. Also, they sent Ginger Nut very frequently for that peculiar cake — small, flat, round, and very spicy — after which he had been named by them. Of a cold morning when business was but dull, Turkey would gobble up scores of these cakes, as if they were mere wafers — indeed they sell them at the rate of six or eight for a penny — the scrape of his pen blending with the crunching of the crisp particles in his mouth. Of all the fiery afternoon blunders and flurried rashnesses of Turkey, was his once moistening a ginger-cake between his lips, and clapping it on to a mortgage for a seal. I came within an ace of dismissing him then. But he mollified me by making an oriental bow, and saying — "With submission, sir, it was generous of me to find you in stationery on my own account."

6 driver of a cart. 7 variety of apple.

15   Now my original business — that of a conveyancer[8] and title hunter, and drawer-up of recondite documents of all sorts — was considerably increased by receiving the master's office. There was now great work for scriveners. Not only must I push the clerks already with me, but I must have additional help. In answer to my advertisement, a motionless young man one morning, stood upon my office threshold, the door being open, for it was summer. I can see that figure now — pallidly neat, pitiably respectable, incurably forlorn! It was Bartleby.

     After a few words touching his qualifications, I engaged him, glad to have among my corps of copyists a man of so singularly sedate an aspect, which I thought might operate beneficially upon the flighty temper of Turkey, and the fiery one of Nippers.

     I should have stated before that ground glass folding-doors divided my premises into two parts, one of which was occupied by my scriveners, the other by myself. According to my humor I threw open these doors, or closed them. I resolved to assign Bartleby a corner by the folding-doors, but on my side of them, so as to have this quiet man within easy call, in case any trifling thing was to be done. I placed his desk close up to a small side-window in that part of the room, a window which originally had afforded a lateral view of certain grimy back-yards and bricks, but which, owing to subsequent erections, commanded at present no view at all, though it gave some light. Within three feet of the panes was a wall, and the light came down from far above, between two lofty buildings, as from a very small opening in a dome. Still further to a satisfactory arrangement, I procured a high green folding screen, which might entirely isolate Bartleby from my sight, though not remove him from my voice. And thus, in a manner, privacy and society were conjoined.

     At first Bartleby did an extraordinary quantity of writing. As if long famishing for something to copy, he seemed to gorge himself on my documents. There was no pause for digestion. He ran a day and night line, copying by sun-light and by candle-light. I should have been quite delighted with his application, had he been cheerfully industrious. But he wrote on silently, palely, mechanically.

     It is, of course, an indispensable part of a scrivener's business to verify the accuracy of his copy, word by word. Where there are two or more scriveners in an office, they assist each other in this examination, one reading from the copy, the other holding the original. It is a very dull, wearisome, and lethargic affair. I can readily imagine that to some sanguine temperaments it would be altogether intolerable. For example, I cannot credit that the mettlesome poet Byron[9] would have contentedly sat down with Bartleby to examine a law document of, say five hundred pages, closely written in a crimpy hand.

20   Now and then, in the haste of business, it had been my habit to assist in comparing some brief document myself, calling Turkey or Nippers for this purpose. One object I had in placing Bartleby so handy to me behind the screen, was to avail myself of his services on such trivial occasions. It was on the third day, I think, of his being with me, and before any necessity had arisen for having his own writing examined, that, being much hurried to complete a

---

8 person who prepares documents for property transfers. 9 an English poet of the early nineteenth century, Byron was known for his flamboyant temperament.

small affair I had in hand, I abruptly called to Bartleby. In my haste and natural expectancy of instant compliance, I sat with my head bent over the original on my desk, and my right hand sideways, and somewhat nervously extended with the copy, so that immediately upon emerging from his retreat, Bartleby might snatch it and proceed to business without the least delay.

In this very attitude did I sit when I called to him, rapidly stating what it was I wanted him to do — namely, to examine a small paper with me. Imagine my surprise, nay, my consternation, when without moving from his privacy, Bartleby in a singularly mild, firm voice, replied, "I would prefer not to."

I sat awhile in perfect silence, rallying my stunned faculties. Immediately it occurred to me that my ears had deceived me, or Bartleby had entirely misunderstood my meaning. I repeated my request in the clearest tone I could assume. But in quite as clear a one came the previous reply, "I would prefer not to."

"Prefer not to," echoed I, rising in high excitement, and crossing the room with a stride. "What do you mean? Are you moon-struck? I want you to help me compare this sheet here — take it," and I thrust it towards him.

"I would prefer not to," said he.

25   I looked at him steadfastly. His face was leanly composed; his gray eye dimly calm. Not a wrinkle of agitation rippled him. Had there been the least uneasiness, anger, impatience or impertinence in his manner; in other words, had there been any thing ordinarily human about him, doubtless I should have violently dismissed him from the premises. But as it was, I should have as soon thought of turning my pale plaster-of-paris bust of Cicero out of doors. I stood gazing at him awhile, as he went on with his own writing, and then reseated myself at my desk. This is very strange, thought I. What had one best do? But my business hurried me. I concluded to forget the matter for the present, reserving it for my future leisure. So calling Nippers from the other room, the paper was speedily examined.

A few days after this, Bartleby concluded four lengthy documents, being quadruplicates of a week's testimony taken before me in my High Court of Chancery. It became necessary to examine them. It was an important suit, and great accuracy was imperative. Having all things arranged I called Turkey, Nippers and Ginger Nut from the next room, meaning to place the four copies in the hands of my four clerks, while I should read from the original. Accordingly Turkey, Nippers and Ginger Nut had taken their seats in a row, each with his document in hand, when I called to Bartleby to join this interesting group.

"Bartleby! quick, I am waiting."

I heard a slow scrape of his chair legs on the uncarpeted floor, and soon he appeared standing at the entrance of his hermitage.

"What is wanted?" said he mildly.

30   "The copies, the copies," said I hurriedly. "We are going to examine them. There" — and I held towards him the fourth quadruplicate.

"I would prefer not to," he said, and gently disappeared behind the screen.

For a few moments I was turned into a pillar of salt,[10] standing at the head of my seated column of clerks. Recovering myself, I advanced towards the screen, and demanded the reason for such extraordinary conduct.

---

10 in Genesis 19, Lot's wife was turned into a pillar of salt for disobeying God's orders not to look at the evil city of Sodom, which He was destroying.

"*Why* do you refuse?"

"I would prefer not to."

35   With any other man I should have flown outright into a dreadful passion, scorned all further words, and thrust him ignominiously from my presence. But there was something about Bartleby that not only strangely disarmed me, but in a wonderful manner touched and disconcerted me. I began to reason with him.

"These are your own copies we are about to examine. It is labor saving to you, because one examination will answer for your four papers. It is common usage. Every copyist is bound to help examine his copy. Is it not so? Will you not speak? Answer!"

"I prefer not to," he replied in a flute-like tone. It seemed to me that while I had been addressing him, he carefully revolved every statement that I made; fully comprehended the meaning; could not gainsay the irresistible conclusion; but, at the same time, some paramount consideration prevailed with him to reply as he did.

"You are decided, then, not to comply with my request — a request made according to common usage and common sense?"

He briefly gave me to understand that on that point my judgment was sound. Yes: his decision was irreversible.

40   It is not seldom the case that when a man is browbeaten in some unprecedented and violently unreasonable way, he begins to stagger in his own plainest faith. He begins, as it were, vaguely to surmise that, wonderful as it may be, all the justice and all the reason is on the other side. Accordingly, if any distinterested persons are present, he turns to them for some reinforcement for his own faltering mind.

"Turkey," said I, "what do you think of this? Am I not right?"

"With submission, sir," said Turkey, with his blandest tone, "I think that you are."

"Nippers," said I, "what do *you* think of it?"

"I think I should kick him out of the office."

45   (The reader of nice perceptions will here perceive that, it being morning, Turkey's answer is couched in polite and tranquil terms, but Nippers replies in ill-tempered ones. Or, to repeat a previous sentence, Nippers's ugly mood was on duty, and Turkey's off.)

"Ginger Nut," said I, willing to enlist the smallest suffrage in my behalf, "what do *you* think of it?"

"I think, sir, he's a little *luny*," replied Ginger Nut, with a grin.

"You hear what they say," said I, turning towards the screen, "come forth and do your duty."

But he vouchsafed no reply. I pondered a moment in sore perplexity. But once more business hurried me. I determined again to postpone the consideration of this dilemma to my future leisure. With a little trouble we made out to examine the papers without Bartleby, though at every page or two, Turkey deferentially dropped his opinion that this proceeding was quite out of the common; while Nippers, twitching in his chair with a dyspeptic nervousness, ground out between his set teeth occasional hissing maledictions against the stubborn oaf behind the screen. And for his (Nippers's) part, this was the first and the last time he would do another man's business without pay.

50   Meanwhile Bartleby sat in his hermitage, oblivious to every thing but his own peculiar business there.

Some days passed, the scrivener being employed upon another lengthy work. His late remarkable conduct led me to regard his ways narrowly. I observed that he never went to dinner; indeed that he never went any where. As yet I had never of my personal knowledge known him to be outside of my office. He was a perpetual sentry in the corner. At about eleven o'clock though, in the morning, I noticed that Ginger Nut would advance toward the opening in Bartleby's screen, as if silently beckoned thither by a gesture invisible to me where I sat. The boy would then leave the office jingling a few pence, and reappear with a handful of ginger-nuts which he delivered in the hermitage, receiving two of the cakes for his trouble.

He lives, then, on ginger-nuts, thought I; never eats a dinner, properly speaking; he must be a vegetarian then; but no; he never eats even vegetables, he eats nothing but ginger-nuts. My mind then ran on in reveries concerning the probable effects upon the human constitution of living entirely on ginger-nuts. Ginger-nuts are so called because they contain ginger as one of their peculiar constituents, and the final flavoring one. Now what was ginger? A hot, spicy thing. Was Bartleby hot and spicy? Not at all. Ginger, then, had no effect upon Bartleby. Probably he preferred it should have none.

Nothing so aggravates an earnest person as a passive resistance. If the individual so resisted be of a not inhumane temper, and the resisting one perfectly harmless in his passivity; then, in the better moods of the former, he will endeavor charitably to construe to his imagination what proves impossible to be solved by his judgment. Even so, for the most part, I regarded Bartleby and his ways. Poor fellow! thought I, he means no mischief; it is plain he intends no insolence; his aspect sufficiently evinces that his eccentricities are involuntary. He is useful to me. I can get along with him. If I turn him away, the chances are he will fall in with some less indulgent employer, and then he will be rudely treated, and perhaps driven forth miserably to starve. Yes. Here I can cheaply purchase a delicious self-approval. To befriend Bartleby; to humor him in his strange wilfulness, will cost me little or nothing, while I lay up in my soul what will eventually prove a sweet morsel for my conscience. But this mood was not invariable with me. The passiveness of Bartleby sometimes irritated me. I felt strangely goaded on to encounter him in new opposition, to elicit some angry spark from him answerable to my own. But indeed I might as well have essayed to strike fire with my knuckles against a bit of Windsor soap.[11] But one afternoon the evil impulse in me mastered me, and the following little scene ensued:

"Bartleby," said I, "when those papers are all copied, I will compare them with you."

55   "I would prefer not to."

"How? Surely you do not mean to persist in that mulish vagary?"

No answer.

I threw open the folding-doors near by, and turning upon Turkey and Nippers, exclaimed:

11 brown-coloured, scented soap.

"Bartleby a second time says, he won't examine his papers. What do you think of it, Turkey?"

It was afternoon, be it remembered. Turkey sat glowing like a brass boiler, his bald head steaming, his hands reeling among his blotted papers.

"Think of it?" roared Turkey; "I think I'll just step behind his screen, and black his eyes for him!"

So saying, Turkey rose to his feet and threw his arms into a pugilistic position. He was hurrying away to make good his promise, when I detained him, alarmed at the effect of incautiously rousing Turkey's combativeness after dinner.

"Sit down, Turkey," said I, "and hear what Nippers has to say. What do you think of it, Nippers? Would I not be justified in immediately dismissing Bartleby?"

"Excuse me, that is for you to decide, sir. I think his conduct quite unusual, and indeed unjust, as regards Turkey and myself. But it may only be a passing whim."

"Ah," exclaimed I, "you have strangely changed your mind then — you speak very gently of him now."

"All beer," cried Turkey; "gentleness is effects of beer — Nippers and I dined together to-day. You see how gentle *I* am, sir. Shall I go and black his eyes?"

"You refer to Bartleby, I suppose. No, not to-day, Turkey," I replied; "pray, put up your fists."

I closed the doors, and again advanced towards Bartleby. I felt additional incentives tempting me to my fate. I burned to be rebelled against again. I remembered that Bartleby never left the office.

"Bartleby," said I, "Ginger Nut is away; just step round to the Post Office, won't you? (it was but a three minutes walk,) and see if there is any thing for me."

"I would prefer not to."

"You *will* not?"

"I *prefer* not."

I staggered to my desk, and sat there in a deep study. My blind inveteracy returned. Was there any other thing in which I could procure myself to be ignominiously repulsed by this lean, penniless wight?— my hired clerk? What added thing is there, perfectly reasonable, that he will be sure to refuse to do?

"Bartleby!"

No answer.

"Bartleby," in a louder tone.

No answer.

"Bartleby," I roared.

Like a very ghost, agreeably to the laws of magical invocation, at the third summons, he appeared at the entrance of his hermitage.

"Go to the next room, and tell Nippers to come to me."

"I prefer not to," he respectfully and slowly said, and mildly disappeared.

"Very good, Bartleby," said I, in a quiet sort of serenely severe self-possessed tone, intimating the unalterable purpose of some terrible retribution very close at hand. At the moment I half intended something of the kind. But upon the whole, as it was drawing towards my dinner-hour, I thought it best to put on my hat and walk home for the day, suffering much from perplexity and distress of mind.

Shall I acknowledge it? The conclusion of this whole business was, that it soon became a fixed fact of my chambers, that a pale young scrivener, by the name of Bartleby, had a desk there; that he copied for me at the usual rate of four cents a folio (one hundred words); but he was permanently exempt from examining the work done by him, that duty being transferred to Turkey and Nippers, out of compliment doubtless to their superior acuteness; moreover, said Bartleby was never on any account to be dispatched on the most trivial errand of any sort; and that even if entreated to take upon him such a matter, it was generally understood that he would prefer not to — in other words, that he would refuse point-blank.

As days passed on, I became considerably reconciled to Bartleby. His steadiness, his freedom from all dissipation, his incessant industry (except when he chose to throw himself into a standing revery behind his screen), his great stillness, his unalterableness of demeanor under all circumstances, made him a valuable acquisition. One prime thing was this, — *he was always there;* — first in the morning, continually through the day, and the last at night. I had a singular confidence in his honesty. I felt my most precious papers perfectly safe in his hands. Sometimes to be sure I could not, for the very soul of me, avoid falling into sudden spasmodic passions with him. For it was exceeding difficult to bear in mind all the time those strange peculiarities, privileges, and unheard of exemptions, forming the tacit stipulations on Bartleby's part under which he remained in my office. Now and then, in the eagerness of dispatching pressing business, I would inadvertently summon Bartleby, in a short, rapid tone, to put his finger, say, on the incipient tie of a bit of red tape with which I was about compressing some papers. Of course, from behind the screen the usual answer, "I prefer not to," was sure to come; and then, how could a human creature with the common infirmities of our nature, refrain from bitterly exclaiming upon such perverseness — such unreasonableness. However, every added repulse of this sort which I received only tended to lessen the probability of my repeating the inadvertence.

85   Here it must be said, that according to the custom of most legal gentlemen occupying chambers in densely populated law buildings, there were several keys to my door. One was kept by a woman residing in the attic, which person weekly scrubbed and daily swept and dusted my apartments. Another was kept by Turkey for convenience sake. The third I sometimes carried in my own pocket. The fourth I knew not who had.

Now, one Sunday morning I happened to go to Trinity Church, to hear a celebrated preacher, and finding myself rather early on the ground, I thought I would walk round to my chambers for a while. Luckily I had my key with me; but upon applying it to the lock, I found it resisted by something inserted from the inside. Quite surprised, I called out; when to my consternation a key was turned from within; and thrusting his lean visage at me, and holding the door ajar, the apparition of Bartleby appeared, in his shirt sleeves, and otherwise in a strangely tattered dishabille, saying quietly that he was sorry, but he was deeply engaged just then, and — preferred not admitting me at present.

In a brief word or two, he moreover added, that perhaps I had better walk round the block two or three times, and by that time he would probably have concluded his affairs.

Now, the utterly unsurmised appearance of Bartleby, tenanting my law-chambers of a Sunday morning, with his cadaverously gentlemanly *nonchalance*, yet withal firm and self-possessed, had such a strange effect upon me, that incontinently I slunk away from my own door, and did as desired. But not without sundry twinges of impotent rebellion against the mild effrontery of this unaccountable scrivener. Indeed, it was his wonderful mildness chiefly, which not only disarmed me, but unmanned me, as it were. For I consider that one, for the time, is a sort of unmanned when he tranquilly permits his hired clerk to dictate to him, and order him away from his own premises. Furthermore, I was full of uneasiness as to what Bartleby could possibly be doing in my office in his shirt sleeves, and in an otherwise dismantled condition of a Sunday morning. Was any thing amiss going on? Nay, that was out of the question. It was not to be thought of for a moment that Bartleby was an immoral person. But what could he be doing there?— copying? Nay again, whatever might be his eccentricities, Bartleby was an eminently decorous person. He would be the last man to sit down to his desk in any state approaching to nudity. Besides, it was Sunday; and there was something about Bartleby that forbade the supposition that he would by any secular occupation violate the proprieties of the day.

Nevertheless, my mind was not pacified; and full of a restless curiosity, at last I returned to the door. Without hindrance I inserted my key, opened it, and entered. Bartleby was not to be seen. I looked round anxiously, peeped behind his screen; but it was very plain that he was gone. Upon more closely examining the place, I surmised that for an indefinite period Bartleby must have ate, dressed, and slept in my office, and that too without plate, mirror, or bed. The cushioned seat of a ricketty old sofa in one corner bore the faint impress of a lean, reclining form. Rolled away under his desk, I found a blanket; under the empty grate, a blacking box and brush; on a chair, a tin basin, with soap and a ragged towel; in a newspaper a few crumbs of ginger-nuts and a morsel of cheese. Yes, thought I, it is evident enough that Bartleby has been making his home here, keeping bachelor's hall all by himself. Immediately then the thought came sweeping across me, What miserable friendlessness and loneliness are here revealed! His poverty is great; but his solitude, how horrible! Think of it. Of a Sunday, Wall-street is deserted as Petra;[12] and every night of every day it is an emptiness. This building too, which of week-days hums with industry and life, at nightfall echoes with sheer vacancy, and all through Sunday is forlorn. And here Bartleby makes his home; sole spectator of a solitude which he has seen all populous — a sort of innocent and transformed Marius[13] brooding among the ruins of Carthage![14]

For the first time in my life a feeling of overpowering stinging melancholy seized me. Before, I had never experienced aught but a not-unpleasing sadness. The bond of a common humanity now drew me irresistibly to gloom.

---

12 destroyed and abandoned city in north Africa.   13 Roman military commander who fled to Africa in the first century B.C.   14 north African city destroyed by the Romans in the second century B.C.

A fraternal melancholy! For both I and Bartleby were sons of Adam. I remembered the bright silks and sparkling faces I had seen that day, in gala trim, swan-like sailing down the Mississippi of Broadway; and I contrasted them with the pallid copyist, and thought to myself, Ah, happiness courts the light, so we deem the world is gay; but misery hides aloof, so we deem that misery there is none. These sad fancyings — chimeras, doubtless, of a sick and silly brain — led on to other and more special thoughts, concerning the eccentricities of Bartleby. Presentiments of strange discoveries hovered round me. The scrivener's pale form appeared to me laid out, among uncaring strangers, in its shivering winding sheet.

90   Suddenly I was attracted by Bartleby's closed desk, the key in open sight left in the lock.

I mean no mischief, seek the gratification of no heartless curiosity, thought I; besides, the desk is mine, and its contents too, so I will make bold to look within. Every thing was methodically arranged, the papers smoothly placed. The pigeon holes were deep, and removing the files of documents, I groped into their recesses. Presently I felt something there, and dragged it out. It was an old bandanna handkerchief, heavy and knotted. I opened it, and saw it was a savings' bank.

I now recalled all the quiet mysteries which I had noted in the man. I remembered that he never spoke but to answer; that though at intervals he had considerable time to himself, yet I had never seen him reading — no, not even a newspaper; that for long periods he would stand looking out, at his pale window behind the screen, upon the dead brick wall; I was quite sure he never visited any refectory or eating house; while his pale face clearly indicated that he never drank beer like Turkey, or tea and coffee even, like other men; that he never went any where in particular that I could learn; never went out for a walk, unless indeed that was the case at present; that he had declined telling who he was, or whence he came, or whether he had any relatives in the world; that though so thin and pale, he never complained of ill health. And more than all, I remembered a certain unconscious air of pallid — how shall I call it? — of pallid haughtiness, say, or rather an austere reserve about him, which had positively awed me into my tame compliance with his eccentricities, when I had feared to ask him to do the slightest incidental thing for me, even though I might know, from his long-continued motionlessness, that behind his screen he must be standing in one of those dead-wall reveries of his.

Revolving all these things, and coupling them with the recently discovered fact that he made my office his constant abiding place and home, and not forgetful of his morbid moodiness; revolving all these things, a prudential feeling began to steal over me. My first emotions had been those of pure melancholy and sincerest pity; but just in proportion as the forlornness of Bartleby grew and grew to my imagination, did that same melancholy merge into fear, that pity into repulsion. So true it is, and so terrible too, that up to a certain point the thought or sight of misery enlists our best affections; but, in certain special cases, beyond that point it does not. They err who would assert that invariably this is owing to the inherent selfishness of the human heart. It rather proceeds from a certain hopelessness of remedying excessive and organic ill. To a sensitive being, pity is not seldom pain. And when at last it is perceived that such pity cannot lead to effectual succor, common sense bids the soul be rid of it. What I saw that morning persuaded me that the scrivener was the victim of innate and incurable disorder. I might give alms to his body; but his body did not pain him; it was his soul that suffered, and his soul I could not reach.

I did not accomplish the purpose of going to Trinity Church that morning. Somehow, the things I had seen disqualified me for the time from church-going. I walked homeward, thinking what I would do with Bartleby. Finally, I resolved upon this; — I would put certain calm questions to him the next morning, touching his history, &c., and if he declined to answer them openly and unreservedly (and I supposed he would prefer not), then to give him a twenty dollar bill over and above whatever I might owe him, and tell him his services were no longer required; but that if in any other way I could assist him, I would be happy to do so, especially if he desired to return to his native place, wherever that might be, I would willingly help to defray the expenses. Moreover, if, after reaching home, he found himself at any time in want of aid, a letter from him would be sure of a reply.

95 The next morning came.

"Bartleby," said I, gently calling to him behind his screen.

No reply.

"Bartleby," said I, in a still gentler tone, "come here; I am not going to ask you to do any thing you would prefer not to do — I simply wish to speak to you."

Upon this he noiselessly slid into view.

100 "Will you tell me, Bartleby, where you were born?"

"I would prefer not to."

"Will you tell me *any thing* about yourself?"

"I would prefer not to."

"But what reasonable objection can you have to speak to me? I feel friendly towards you."

105 He did not look at me while I spoke, but kept his glance fixed upon my bust of Cicero,[15] which as I then sat, was directly behind me, some six inches above my head.

"What is your answer, Bartleby?" said I, after waiting a considerable time for a reply, during which his countenance remained immovable, only there was the faintest conceivable tremor of the white attenuated mouth.

"At present I prefer to give no answer," he said, and retired into his hermitage.

It was rather weak in me I confess, but his manner on this occasion nettled me. Not only did there seem to lurk in it a certain calm disdain, but his perverseness seemed ungrateful, considering the undeniable good usage and indulgence he had received from me.

Again I sat ruminating what I should do. Mortified as I was at his behavior, and resolved as I had been to dismiss him when I entered my office, nevertheless I strangely felt something superstitious knocking at my heart, and forbidding me to carry out my purpose, and denouncing me for a villain if I dared to breathe one bitter word against this forlornest of mankind. At last,

---

15 renowned Roman orator of the first century B.C.

familiarly drawing my chair behind his screen, I sat down and said: "Bartleby, never mind then about revealing your history; but let me entreat you as a friend, to comply as far as may be with the usages of this office. Say now you will help to examine papers to-morrow or next day: in short, say now that in a day or two you will begin to be a little reasonable:— say so, Bartleby."

110   "At present I would prefer not to be a little reasonable," was his mildly cadaverous reply.

Just then the folding-doors opened, and Nippers approached. He seemed suffering from an unusually bad night's rest, induced by severer indigestion than common. He overheard those final words of Bartleby.

"*Prefer not*, eh?" gritted Nippers — "I'd *prefer* him, if I were you, sir," addressing me — "I'd *prefer* him; I'd give him preferences, the stubborn mule! What is it, sir, pray, that he *prefers* not to do now?"

Bartleby moved not a limb.

"Mr. Nippers," said I, "I'd prefer that you would withdraw for the present."

115   Somehow, of late I had got into the way of involuntarily using this word "prefer" upon all sorts of not exactly suitable occasions. And I trembled to think that my contact with the scrivener had already and seriously affected me in a mental way. And what further and deeper aberration might it not yet produce? This apprehension had not been without efficacy in determining me to summary measures.

As Nippers, looking very sour and sulky, was departing, Turkey blandly and deferentially approached.

"With submission, sir," said he, "yesterday I was thinking about Bartleby here, and I think that if he would but prefer to take a quart of good ale every day, it would do much towards mending him, and enabling him to assist in examining his papers."

"So you have got the word too," said I, slightly excited.

"With submission, what word, sir," asked Turkey, respectfully crowding himself into the contracted space behind the screen, and by so doing, making me jostle the scrivener. "What word, sir?"

120   "I would prefer to be left alone here," said Bartleby, as if offended at being mobbed in his privacy.

"*That's* the word, Turkey," said I — "*that's* it."

"Oh, *prefer*? oh yes — queer word. I never use it myself. But, sir, as I was saying, if he would but prefer —"

"Turkey," interrupted I, "you will please withdraw."

"Oh certainly, sir, if you prefer that I should."

125   As he opened the folding-doors to retire, Nippers at his desk caught a glimpse of me, and asked whether I would prefer to have a certain paper copied on blue paper or white. He did not in the least roguishly accent the word prefer. It was plain that it involuntarily rolled from his tongue. I thought to myself, surely I must get rid of a demented man, who already has in some degree turned the tongues, if not the heads of myself and clerks. But I thought it prudent not to break the dismission at once.

The next day I noticed that Bartleby did nothing but stand at his window in his dead-wall revery. Upon asking him why he did not write, he said that he had decided upon doing no more writing.

"Why, how now? what next?" exclaimed I, "do no more writing?"

"No more."

"And what is the reason?"

130 "Do you not see the reason for yourself," he indifferently replied.

I looked steadfastly at him, and perceived that his eyes looked dull and glazed. Instantly it occurred to me, that his unexampled diligence in copying by his dim window for the first few weeks of his stay with me might have temporarily impaired his vision.

I was touched. I said something in condolence with him. I hinted that of course he did wisely in abstaining from writing for a while; and urged him to embrace that opportunity of taking wholesome exercise in the open air. This, however, he did not do. A few days after this, my other clerks being absent, and being in a great hurry to dispatch certain letters by the mail, I thought that, having nothing else earthly to do, Bartleby would surely be less inflexible than usual, and carry these letters to the post-office. But he blankly declined. So, much to my inconvenience, I went myself.

Still added days went by. Whether Bartleby's eyes improved or not, I could not say. To all appearance, I thought they did. But when I asked him if they did, he vouchsafed no answer. At all events, he would do no copying. At last, in reply to my urgings, he informed me that he had permanently given up copying.

"What!" exclaimed I; "suppose your eyes should get entirely well — better than ever before — would you not copy then?"

135 "I have given up copying," he answered, and slid aside.

He remained as ever, a fixture in my chamber. Nay — if that were possible — he became still more of a fixture than before. What was to be done? He would do nothing in the office: why should he stay there? In plain fact, he had now become a millstone to me, not only useless as a necklace, but afflictive to bear. Yet I was sorry for him. I speak less than truth when I say that, on his own account, he occasioned me uneasiness. If he would but have named a single relative or friend, I would instantly have written, and urged their taking the poor fellow away to some convenient retreat. But he seemed alone, absolutely alone in the universe. A bit of wreck in the mid Atlantic. At length, necessities connected with my business tyrannized over all other considerations. Decently as I could, I told Bartleby that in six days' time he must unconditionally leave the office. I warned him to take measures, in the interval, for procuring some other abode. I offered to assist him in this endeavor, if he himself would but take the first step towards a removal. "And when you finally quit me, Bartleby," added I, "I shall see that you go not away entirely unprovided. Six days from this hour, remember."

At the expiration of that period, I peeped behind the screen, and lo! Bartleby was there.

I buttoned up my coat, balanced myself; advanced slowly towards him, touched his shoulder, and said, "The time has come; you must quit this place; I am sorry for you; here is money, but you must go."

"I would prefer not," he replied, with his back still towards me.

140 "You *must*."

He remained silent.

Now I had an unbounded confidence in this man's common honesty. He had frequently restored to me sixpences and shillings carelessly dropped upon the floor, for I am apt to be very reckless in such shirt-button affairs. The proceeding then which followed will not be deemed extraordinary.

"Bartleby," said I, "I owe you twelve dollars on account; here are thirty-two; the odd twenty are yours. — Will you take it?" and I handed the bills towards him.

But he made no motion.

"I will leave them here then," putting them under a weight on the table. Then taking my hat and cane and going to the door I tranquilly turned and added — "After you have removed your things from these offices, Bartleby, you will of course lock the door — since every one is now gone for the day but you — and if you please, slip your key underneath the mat, so that I may have it in the morning. I shall not see you again; so good-bye to you. If hereafter in your new place of abode I can be of any service to you, do not fail to advise me by letter. Good-bye, Bartleby, and fare you well."

But he answered not a word; like the last column of some ruined temple, he remained standing mute and solitary in the middle of the otherwise deserted room.

As I walked home in a pensive mood, my vanity got the better of my pity. I could not but highly plume myself on my masterly management in getting rid of Bartleby. Masterly I call it, and such it must appear to any dispassionate thinker. The beauty of my procedure seemed to consist in its perfect quietness. There was no vulgar bullying, no bravado of any sort, no choleric hectoring, and striding to and fro across the apartment, jerking out vehement commands for Bartleby to bundle himself off with his beggarly traps. Nothing of the kind. Without loudly bidding Bartleby depart — as an inferior genius might have done — I *assumed* the ground that depart he must; and upon that assumption built all I had to say. The more I thought over my procedure, the more I was charmed with it. Nevertheless, next morning, upon awakening, I had my doubts, — I had somehow slept off the fumes of vanity. One of the coolest and wisest hours a man has, is just after he wakes in the morning. My procedure seemed as sagacious as ever, — but only in theory. How it would prove in practice — there was the rub. It was truly a beautiful thought to have assumed Bartleby's departure; but, after all, that assumption was simply my own, and none of Bartleby's. The great point was, not whether I had assumed that he would quit me, but whether he would prefer so to do. He was more a man of preferences than assumptions.

After breakfast, I walked down town, arguing the probabilities *pro* and *con*. One moment I thought it would prove a miserable failure, and Bartleby would be found all alive at my office as usual; the next moment it seemed certain that I should find his chair empty. And so I kept veering about. At the corner of Broadway and Canal-street, I saw quite an excited group of people standing in earnest conversation.

"I'll take odds he doesn't," said a voice as I passed.

"Doesn't go? — done!" said I, "put up your money."

I was instinctively putting my hand in my pocket to produce my own, when I remembered that this was an election day. The words I had overheard bore no reference to Bartleby, but to the success or non-success of some candidate for the mayoralty. In my intent frame of mind, I had, as it were, imagined that all Broadway shared in my excitement, and were debating the same question with me. I passed on, very thankful that the uproar of the street screened my momentary absent-mindedness.

As I had intended, I was earlier than usual at my office door. I stood listening for a moment. All was still. He must be gone. I tried the knob. The door was locked. Yes, my procedure had worked to a charm; he indeed must be vanished. Yet a certain melancholy mixed with this: I was almost sorry for my brilliant success. I was fumbling under the door mat for the key, which Bartleby was to have left there for me, when accidentally my knee knocked against a panel, producing a summoning sound, and in response a voice came to me from within — "Not yet; I am occupied."

It was Bartleby.

I was thunderstruck. For an instant I stood like the man who, pipe in mouth, was killed one cloudless afternoon long ago in Virginia, by summer lightning; at his own warm open window he was killed, and remained leaning out there upon the dreamy afternoon, till some one touched him, when he fell.

155 "Not gone!" I murmured at last. But again obeying that wondrous ascendancy which the inscrutable scrivener had over me, and from which ascendancy, for all my chafing, I could not completely escape, I slowly went down stairs and out into the street, and while walking round the block, considered what I should next do in this unheard-of perplexity. Turn the man out by an actual thrusting I could not; to drive him away by calling him hard names would not do; calling in the police was an unpleasant idea; and yet, permit him to enjoy his cadaverous triumph over me, — this too I could not think of. What was to be done? or, if nothing could be done, was there any thing further that I could *assume* in the matter? Yes, as before I had prospectively assumed that Bartleby would depart, so now I might retrospectively assume that departed he was. In the legitimate carrying out of this assumption, I might enter my office in a great hurry, and pretending not to see Bartleby at all, walk straight against him as if he were air. Such a proceeding would in a singular degree have the appearance of a home-thrust. It was hardly possible that Bartleby could withstand such an application of the doctrine of assumptions. But upon second thoughts the success of the plan seemed rather dubious. I resolved to argue the matter over with him again.

"Bartleby," said I, entering the office, with a quietly severe expression, "I am seriously displeased. I am pained, Bartleby. I had thought better of you. I had imagined you of such a gentlemanly organization, that in any delicate dilemma a slight hint would suffice — in short, an assumption. But it appears I am deceived. Why," I added, unaffectedly starting, "you have not even touched that money yet," pointing to it, just where I had left it the evening previous.

He answered nothing.

"Will you, or will you not, quit me?" I now demanded in a sudden passion, advancing close to him.

"I would prefer *not* to quit you," he replied, gently emphasizing the *not.*

160 "What earthly right have you to stay here? Do you pay any rent? Do you pay my taxes? Or is this property yours?"

He answered nothing.

"Are you ready to go on and write now? Are your eyes recovered? Could you copy a small paper for me this morning? or help examine a few lines? or step round to the post-office? In a word, will you do any thing at all, to give a coloring to your refusal to depart the premises?"

He silently retired into his hermitage.

I was now in such a state of nervous resentment that I thought it but prudent to check myself at present from further demonstrations. Bartleby and I were alone. I remembered the tragedy of the unfortunate Adams and the still more unfortunate Colt[16] in the solitary office of the latter; and how poor Colt, being dreadfully incensed by Adams, and imprudently permitting himself to get wildly excited, was at unawares hurried into his fatal act — an act which certainly no man could possibly deplore more than the actor himself. Often it had occurred to me in my ponderings upon the subject, that had that altercation taken place in the public street, or at a private residence, it would not have terminated as it did. It was the circumstance of being alone in a solitary office, up stairs, of a building entirely unhallowed by humanizing domestic associations — an uncarpeted office, doubtless, of a dusty, haggard sort of appearance; — this it must have been, which greatly helped to enhance the irritable desperation of the hapless Colt.

165   But when this old Adam[17] of resentment rose in me and tempted me concerning Bartleby, I grappled him and threw him. How? Why, simply by recalling the divine injunction: "A new commandment give I unto you, that ye love one another." Yes, this it was that saved me. Aside from higher considerations, charity often operates as a vastly wise and prudent principle — a great safeguard to its possessor. Men have committed murder for jealousy's sake, and anger's sake, and hatred's sake, and selfishness' sake, and spiritual pride's sake; but no man that ever I heard of, ever committed a diabolical murder for sweet charity's sake. Mere self-interest, then, if no better motive can be enlisted, should, especially with high-tempered men, prompt all beings to charity and philanthropy. At any rate, upon the occasion in question, I strove to drown my exasperated feelings towards the scrivener by benevolently construing his conduct. Poor fellow, poor fellow! thought I, he don't mean any thing; and besides, he has seen hard times, and ought to be indulged.

I endeavored also immediately to occupy myself, and at the same time to comfort my despondency. I tried to fancy that in the course of the morning, at such time as might prove agreeable to him, Bartleby, of his own free accord, would emerge from his hermitage, and take up some decided line of march in the direction of the door. But no. Half-past twelve o'clock came; Turkey began to glow in the face, overturn his inkstand, and become generally obstreperous; Nippers abated down into quietude and courtesy; Ginger Nut munched his noon apple; and Bartleby remained standing at his window in one of his profoundest dead-wall reveries. Will it be credited? Ought I to acknowledge it? That afternoon I left the office without saying one further word to him.

16 Samuel Adams was killed in 1841 in a fight with John Colt, a brother of the manufacturer of guns.
17 reference to the biblical first man, whose temperament was believed to have been passed on to all the human race.

Some days now passed, during which, at leisure intervals I looked a little into "Edwards on the Will,"[18] and "Priestley on Necessity."[19] Under the circumstances, those books induced a salutary feeling. Gradually I slid into the persuasion that these troubles of mine touching the scrivener, had been all predestinated from eternity, and Bartleby was billeted upon me for some mysterious purpose of an all-wise Providence, which it was not for a mere mortal like me to fathom. Yes, Bartleby, stay there behind your screen, thought I; I shall persecute you no more; you are harmless and noiseless as any of these old chairs; in short, I never feel so private as when I know you are here. At last I see it, I feel it; I penetrate to the predestinated purpose of my life. I am content. Others may have loftier parts to enact; but my mission in this world, Bartleby, is to furnish you with office-room for such period as you may see fit to remain.

I believe that this wise and blessed frame of mind would have continued with me, had it not been for the unsolicited and uncharitable remarks obtruded upon me by my professional friends who visited the rooms. But thus it often is, that the constant friction of illiberal minds wears out at last the best resolves of the more generous. Though to be sure, when I reflected upon it, it was not strange that people entering my office should be struck by the peculiar aspect of the unaccountable Bartleby, and so be tempted to throw out some sinister observations concerning him. Sometimes an attorney having business with me, and calling at my office, and finding no one but the scrivener there, would undertake to obtain some sort of precise information from him touching my whereabouts; but without heeding his idle talk, Bartleby would remain standing immovable in the middle of the room. So after contemplating him in that position for a time, the attorney would depart, no wiser than he came.

Also, when a Reference[20] was going on, and the room full of lawyers and witnesses and business was driving fast; some deeply occupied legal gentleman present, seeing Bartleby wholly unemployed, would request him to run round to his (the legal gentleman's) office and fetch some papers for him. Thereupon, Bartleby would tranquilly decline, and yet remain idle as before. Then the lawyer would give a great stare, and turn to me. And what could I say? At last I was made aware that all through the circle of my professional acquaintance, a whisper of wonder was running round, having reference to the strange creature I kept at my office. This worried me very much. And as the idea came upon me of his possibly turning out a long-lived man, and keep occupying my chambers, and denying my authority; and perplexing my visitors; and scandalizing my professional reputation; and casting a general gloom over the premises; keeping soul and body together to the last upon his savings (for doubtless he spent but half a dime a day), and in the end perhaps outlive me, and claim possession of my office by right of his perpetual occupancy: as all these dark anticipations crowded upon me more and more, and my friends continually intruded their relentless remarks upon the apparition in my room;

18 eighteenth-century American philosopher who believed that human beings' will was controlled by God. 19 eighteenth-century English philosopher who believed that, to prevent revolution, rulers should act in the interests of those they govern. 20 legal hearing in which two parties submit their differences to an arbitrator.

a great change was wrought in me. I resolved to gather all my faculties together, and for ever rid me of this intolerable incubus.

170   Ere revolving any complicated project, however, adapted to this end, I first simply suggested to Bartleby the propriety of his permanent departure. In a calm and serious tone, I commended the idea to his careful and mature consideration. But having taken three days to meditate upon it, he apprised me that his original determination remained the same; in short, that he still preferred to abide with me.

What shall I do? I now said to myself, buttoning up my coat to the last button. What shall I do? what ought I to do? what does conscience say I *should* do with this man, or rather ghost? Rid myself of him, I must; go, he shall. But how? You will not thrust him, the poor, pale, passive mortal, — you will not thrust such a helpless creature out of your door? you will not dishonor yourself by such cruelty? No, I will not, I cannot do that. Rather would I let him live and die here, and then mason up his remains in the wall. What then will you do? For all your coaxing, he will not budge. Bribes he leaves under your own paper-weight on your table; in short, it is quite plain that he prefers to cling to you.

Then something severe, something unusual must be done. What! surely you will not have him collared by a constable, and commit his innocent pallor to the common jail? And upon what ground could you procure such a thing to be done? — a vagrant, is he? What! he a vagrant, a wanderer, who refuses to budge? It is because he will *not* be a vagrant, then, that you seek to count him *as a* vagrant. That is too absurd. No visible means of support: there I have him. Wrong again: for undubitably he *does* support himself, and that is the only unanswerable proof that any man can show of his possessing the means so to do. No more then. Since he will not quit me, I must quit him. I will change my offices; I will move elsewhere; and give him fair notice, that if I find him on my new premises I will then proceed against him as a common trespasser.

Acting accordingly, next day I thus addressed him: "I find these chambers too far from the City Hall; the air is unwholesome. In a word, I propose to remove my offices next week, and shall no longer require your services. I tell you this now, in order that you may seek another place."

He made no reply, and nothing more was said.

175   On the appointed day I engaged carts and men, proceeded to my chambers, and having but little furniture, every thing was removed in a few hours. Throughout, the scrivener remained standing behind the screen, which I directed to be removed the last thing. It was withdrawn; and being folded up like a huge folio, left him the motionless occupant of a naked room. I stood in the entry watching him a moment, while something from within me upbraided me.

I re-entered, with my hand in my pocket — and — and my heart in my mouth.

"Good-bye, Bartleby; I am going — good-bye, and God some way bless you; and take that," slipping something in his hand. But it dropped upon the floor, and then, — strange to say — I tore myself from him whom I had so longed to be rid of.

Established in my new quarters, for a day or two I kept the door locked, and started at every footfall in the passages. When I returned to my rooms after any little absence, I would pause at the threshold for an instant, and attentively listen, ere applying my key. But these fears were needless. Bartleby never came nigh me.

I thought all was going well, when a perturbed looking stranger visited me, inquiring whether I was the person who had recently occupied rooms at No.— Wall-street.

180   Full of forebodings, I replied that I was.

"Then sir," said the stranger, who proved a lawyer, "you are responsible for the man you left there. He refuses to do any copying; he refuses to do any thing; he says he prefers not to; and he refuses to quit the premises."

"I am very sorry, sir" said I, with assumed tranquillity, but an inward tremor, "but, really, the man you allude to is nothing to me — he is no relation or apprentice of mine, that you should hold me responsible for him."

"In mercy's name, who is he?"

"I certainly cannot inform you. I know nothing about him. Formerly I employed him as a copyist; but he has done nothing for me now for some time past."

185   "I shall settle him then, — good morning, sir."

Several days passed, and I heard nothing more; and though I often felt a charitable prompting to call at the place and see poor Bartleby, yet a certain squeamishness of I know not what withheld me.

All is over with him, by this time, thought I at last, when through another week no further intelligence reached me. But coming to my room the day after, I found several persons waiting at my door in a high state of nervous excitement.

"That's the man — here he comes," cried the foremost one, whom I recognized as the lawyer who had previously called upon me alone.

"You must take him away, sir, at once," cried a portly person among them, advancing upon me, and whom I knew to be the landlord of No.— Wall-street. "These gentlemen, my tenants, cannot stand it any longer; Mr. B——" pointing to the lawyer, "has turned him out of his room, and he now persists in haunting the building generally, sitting upon the banisters of the stairs by day, and sleeping in the entry by night. Every body is concerned; clients are leaving the offices; some fears are entertained of a mob; something you must do, and that without delay."

190   Aghast at this torrent, I fell back before it, and would fain have locked myself in my new quarters. In vain I persisted that Bartleby was nothing to me — no more than to any one else. In vain:— I was the last person known to have any thing to do with him, and they held me to the terrible account. Fearful then of being exposed in the papers (as one person present obscurely threatened) I considered the matter, and at length said, that if the lawyer would give me a confidential interview with the scrivener, in his (the lawyer's) own room, I would that afternoon strive my best to rid them of the nuisance they complained of.

Going up stairs to my old haunt, there was Bartleby silently sitting upon the banister at the landing.

"What are you doing here, Bartleby?" said I.

"Sitting upon the banister," he mildly replied.

I motioned him into the lawyer's room, who then left us.

195 "Bartleby," said I, "are you aware that you are the cause of great tribulation to me, by persisting in occupying the entry after being dismissed from the office?"

No answer.

"Now one of two things must take place. Either you must do something, or something must be done to you. Now what sort of business would you like to engage in? Would you like to re-engage in copying for some one?"

"No; I would prefer not to make any change."

"Would you like a clerkship in a dry-goods store?"

200 "There is too much confinement about that. No, I would not like a clerkship; but I am not particular."

"Too much confinement," I cried, "why you keep yourself confined all the time!"

"I would prefer not to take a clerkship," he rejoined, as if to settle that little item at once.

"How would a bar-tender's business suit you? There is no trying of the eyesight in that."

"I would not like it at all; though, as I said before, I am not particular."

205 His unwonted wordiness inspirited me. I returned to the charge.

"Well then, would you like to travel through the country collecting bills for the merchants? That would improve your health."

"No, I would prefer to be something else."

"How then would going as a companion to Europe, to entertain some young gentleman with your conversation,—how would that suit you?"

"Not at all. It does not strike me that there is any thing definite about that. I like to be stationary. But I am not particular."

210 "Stationary you shall be then," I cried, now losing all patience, and for the first time in all my exasperating connection with him fairly flying into a passion. "If you do not go away from these premises before night, I shall feel bound—indeed I *am* bound—to—to—to quit the premises myself!" I rather absurdly concluded, knowing not with what possible threat to try to frighten his immobility into compliance. Despairing of all further efforts, I was precipitately leaving him, when a final thought occurred to me—one which had not been wholly unindulged before.

"Bartleby," said I, in the kindest tone I could assume under such exciting circumstances, "will you go home with me now—not to my office, but my dwelling—and remain there till we can conclude upon some convenient arrangement for you at our leisure? Come, let us start now, right away."

"No: at present I would prefer not to make any change at all."

I answered nothing; but effectually dodging every one by the suddenness and rapidity of my flight, rushed from the building, ran up Wall-street towards Broadway, and jumping into the first omnibus was soon removed from pursuit. As soon as tranquillity returned I distinctly perceived that I had now done all that I possibly could, both in respect to the demands of the landlord and his tenants, and with regard to my own desire and sense of duty, to benefit Bartleby, and shield him from rude persecution. I now strove to be entirely care-free and quiescent; and my conscience justified me in the attempt; though indeed it was not so successful as I could have wished. So fearful was I of being again hunted out by the incensed landlord and his exasperated tenants, that, surrendering my business to Nippers, for a few days I drove about the upper part of the town and through the suburbs, in my rockaway;[21] crossed over to Jersey City and Hoboken, and paid fugitive visits to Manhattanville and Astoria. In fact I almost lived in my rockaway for the time.

When again I entered my office, lo, a note from the landlord lay upon the desk. I opened it with trembling hands. It informed me that the writer had sent to the police, and had Bartleby removed to the Tombs as a vagrant. Moreover, since I knew more about him than any one else, he wished me to appear at that place, and make a suitable statement of the facts. These tidings had a conflicting effect upon me. At first I was indignant; but at last almost approved. The landlord's energetic, summary disposition, had led him to adopt a procedure which I do not think I would have decided upon myself; and yet as a last resort, under such peculiar circumstances, it seemed the only plan.

215   As I afterwards learned, the poor scrivener, when told that he must be conducted to the Tombs, offered not the slightest obstacle, but in his pale unmoving way, silently acquiesced.

Some of the compassionate and curious bystanders joined the party; and headed by one of the constables arm in arm with Bartleby, the silent procession filed its way through all the noise, and heat, and joy of the roaring thoroughfares at noon.

The same day I received the note I went to the Tombs, or to speak more properly, the Halls of Justice. Seeking the right officer, I stated the purpose of my call, and was informed that the individual I described was indeed within. I then assured the functionary that Bartleby was a perfectly honest man, and greatly to be compassionated, however unaccountably eccentric. I narrated all I knew, and closed by suggesting the idea of letting him remain in as indulgent confinement as possible till something less harsh might be done — though indeed I hardly knew what. At all events, if nothing else could be decided upon, the alms-house must receive him. I then begged to have an interview.

Being under no disgraceful charge, and quite serene and harmless in all his ways, they had permitted him freely to wander about the prison, and especially in the inclosed grass-platted yards thereof. And so I found him there, standing all alone in the quietest of the yards, his face towards a high wall, while all around, from the narrow slits of the jail windows, I thought I saw peering out upon him the eyes of murderers and thieves.

"Bartleby!"

220   "I know you," he said, without looking round, — "and I want nothing to say to you."

"It was not I that brought you here, Bartleby," said I, keenly pained at his implied suspicion. "And to you, this should not be so vile a place. Nothing reproachful attaches to you by being here. And see, it is not so sad a place as one might think. Look, there is the sky, and here is the grass."

"I know where I am," he replied, but would say nothing more, and so I left him.

As I entered the corridor again, a broad meat-like man, in an apron, accosted me, and jerking his thumb over his shoulder said — "Is that your friend?"

---

21 luxury carriage.

"Yes."

225 "Does he want to starve? If he does, let him live on the prison fare, that's all."

"Who are you?" asked I, not knowing what to make of such an unofficially speaking person in such a place.

"I am the grub-man. Such gentlemen as have friends here, hire me to provide them with something good to eat."

"Is this so?" said I, turning to the turnkey.

He said it was.

230 "Well then," said I, slipping some silver into the grub-man's hands (for so they called him). "I want you to give particular attention to my friend there; let him have the best dinner you can get. And you must be as polite to him as possible."

"Introduce me, will you?" said the grub-man, looking at me with an expression which seemed to say he was all impatience for an opportunity to give a specimen of his breeding.

Thinking it would prove of benefit to the scrivener, I acquiesced; and asking the grub-man his name, went up with him to Bartleby.

"Bartleby, this is Mr. Cutlets; you will find him very useful to you."

"Your sarvant, sir, your sarvant," said the grub-man, making a low salutation behind his apron. "Hope you find it pleasant here, sir; nice grounds — cool apartments, sir — hope you'll stay with us some time — try to make it agreeable. May Mrs. Cutlets and I have the pleasure of your company to dinner, sir, in Mrs. Cutlet's private room?"

235 "I prefer not to dine to-day," said Bartleby, turning away. "It would disagree with me; I am unused to dinners." So saying he slowly moved to the other side of the inclosure, and took up a position fronting the dead-wall.

"How's this?" said the grub-man, addressing me with a stare of astonishment. "He's odd, aint he?"

"I think he is a little deranged," said I, sadly.

"Deranged? deranged is it? Well now, upon my word, I thought that friend of yourn was a gentleman forger; they are always pale and genteel-like, them forgers. I can't help pity 'em — can't help it, sir. Did you know Monroe Edwards?" he added touchingly, and paused. Then, laying his hand pityingly on my shoulder, sighed, "he died of consumption at Sing-Sing.[22] So you weren't acquainted with Monroe?"

"No, I was never socially acquainted with any forgers. But I cannot stop longer. Look to my friend yonder. You will not lose by it. I will see you again."

240 Some few days after this, I again obtained admission to the Tombs, and went through the corridors in quest of Bartleby; but without finding him.

"I saw him coming from his cell not long ago," said a turnkey, "may be he's gone to loiter in the yards."

So I went in that direction.

"Are you looking for the silent man?" said another turnkey passing me. "Yonder he lies — sleeping in the yard there. 'Tis not twenty minutes since I saw him lie down."

22 state prison north of New York City.

The yard was entirely quiet. It was not accessible to the common prisoners. The surrounding walls, of amazing thickness, kept off all sounds behind them. The Egyptian character of the masonry weighed upon me with its gloom. But a soft imprisoned turf grew under foot. The heart of the eternal pyramids, it seemed, wherein, by some strange magic, through the clefts, grass-seed, dropped by birds, had sprung.

245 Strangely huddled at the base of the wall, his knees drawn up, and lying on his side, his head touching the cold stones, I saw the wasted Bartleby. But nothing stirred. I paused; then went close up to him; stooped over, and saw that his dim eyes were open; otherwise he seemed profoundly sleeping. Something prompted me to touch him. I felt his hand, when a tingling shiver ran up my arm and down my spine to my feet.

The round face of the grub-man peered upon me now. "His dinner is ready. Won't he dine to-day, either? Or does he live without dining?"

"Lives without dining," said I, and closed the eyes.

"Eh! — He's asleep, aint he?"

"With kings and counsellors,"[23] murmured I.

*****

250 There would seem little need for proceeding further in this history. Imagination will readily supply the meagre recital of poor Bartleby's interment. But ere parting with the reader, let me say, that if this little narrative has sufficiently interested him, to awaken curiosity as to who Bartleby was, and what manner of life he led prior to the present narrator's making his acquaintance, I can only reply, that in such curiosity I fully share, but am wholly unable to gratify it. Yet here I hardly know whether I should divulge one little item of rumor, which came to my ear a few months after the scrivener's decease. Upon what basis it rested, I could never ascertain; and hence, how true it is I cannot now tell. But inasmuch as this vague report has not been without a certain strange suggestive interest to me, however sad, it may prove the same with some others; and so I will briefly mention it. The report was this: that Bartleby had been a subordinate clerk in the Dead Letter Office at Washington, from which he had been suddenly removed by a change in the administration. When I think over this rumor, hardly can I express the emotions which seize me. Dead letters! does it not sound like dead men? Conceive a man by nature and misfortune prone to a pallid hopelessness, can any business seem more fitted to heighten it than that of continually handling these dead letters, and assorting them for the flames? For by the cart-load they are annually burned. Sometimes from out the folded paper the pale clerk takes a ring: — the finger it was meant for, perhaps, moulders in the grave; a bank-note sent in swiftest charity: — he whom it would relieve, nor eats nor hungers any more; pardon for those who died despairing; hope for those who died unhoping; good tidings for those who died stifled by unrelieved calamities. On errands of life, these letters speed to death.

Ah Bartleby! Ah humanity!

(1853)

23 see Job 3:14. A reference to death as a condition of tranquillity.

Kate Chopin (1851–1904)

Kate Chopin, who received a traditional Catholic upbringing and moved in the society circles of her native city, St. Louis, Missouri, began a career as an author after the death of her husband. She stated that she strove to present "human existence in its subtle, complex, true meaning, stripped of the veil with which ethical and conventional standards have draped it." Her novel *The Awakening* (1899), now considered a classic, is the story of a young mother's escape from her socially imposed roles; it was condemned as immoral and was mostly ignored until the 1960s, as were such stories as "A Shameful Affair" and "The Storm." "The Story of an Hour," which is praised for its conciseness and its presentation of "daring" themes, focuses on the surface and the secret life of the central character. Chopin's use of the limited third-person narrator and the surprise ending enables readers to understand the conventional attitudes of the other characters and Mrs. Mallard's own, unspoken views.

THE STORY OF AN HOUR

Knowing that Mrs. Mallard was afflicted with a heart trouble, great care was taken to break to her as gently as possible the news of her husband's death.

It was her sister Josephine who told her, in broken sentences; veiled hints that revealed in half concealing. Her husband's friend Richards was there, too, near her. It was he who had been in the newspaper office when intelligence of the railroad disaster was received, with Brently Mallard's name leading the list of "killed." He had only taken the time to assure himself of its truth by a second telegram, and had hastened to forestall any less careful, less tender friend in bearing the sad message.

She did not hear the story as many women have heard the same, with a paralyzed inability to accept its significance. She wept at once, with sudden, wild abandonment, in her sister's arms. When the storm of grief had spent itself she went away to her room alone. She would have no one follow her.

There stood, facing the open window, a comfortable, roomy armchair. Into this she sank, pressed down by a physical exhaustion that haunted her body and seemed to reach into her soul.

5   She could see in the open square before her house the tops of trees that were all aquiver with the new spring life. The delicious breath of rain was in the air. In the street below a peddler was crying his wares. The notes of a distant song which some one was singing reached her faintly, and countless sparrows were twittering in the eaves.

There were patches of blue sky showing here and there through the clouds that had met and piled one above the other in the west facing her window.

She sat with her head thrown back upon the cushion of the chair, quite motionless, except when a sob came up into her throat and shook her, as a child who has cried itself to sleep continues to sob in its dreams.

She was young, with a fair, calm face, whose lines bespoke repression and even a certain strength. But now there was a dull stare in her eyes, whose gaze was fixed away off yonder on one of those patches of blue sky. It was not a glance of reflection, but rather indicated a suspension of intelligent thought.

There was something coming to her and she was waiting for it, fearfully. What was it? She did not know; it was too subtle and elusive to name. But she felt it, creeping out of the sky, reaching toward her through the sounds, the scents, the color that filled the air.

10   Now her bosom rose and fell tumultuously. She was beginning to recognize this thing that was approaching to possess her, and she was striving to beat it back with her will — as powerless as her two white slender hands would have been.

When she abandoned herself a little whispered word escaped her slightly parted lips. She said it over and over under her breath: "free, free, free!" The vacant stare and the look of terror that had followed it went from her eyes. They stayed keen and bright. Her pulses beat fast, and the coursing blood warmed and relaxed every inch of her body.

She did not stop to ask if it were or were not a monstrous joy that held her. A clear and exalted perception enabled her to dismiss the suggestion as trivial.

She knew that she would weep again when she saw the kind, tender hands folded in death; the face that had never looked save with love upon her, fixed and gray and dead. But she saw beyond that bitter moment a long procession of years to come that would belong to her absolutely. And she opened and spread her arms out to them in welcome.

There would be no one to live for her during those coming years; she would live for herself. There would be no powerful will bending hers in that blind persistence with which men and women believe they have a right to impose a private will upon a fellow-creature. A kind intention or a cruel intention made the act seem no less a crime as she looked upon it in that brief moment of illumination.

15   And yet she had loved him — sometimes. Often she had not. What did it matter! What could love, the unsolved mystery, count for in face of this possession of self-assertion which she suddenly recognized as the strongest impulse of her being!

"Free! Body and soul free!" she kept whispering.

Josephine was kneeling before the closed door with her lips to the keyhole, imploring for admission. "Louise, open the door! I beg; open the door — you will make yourself ill. What are you doing, Louise? For heaven's sake open the door."

"Go away. I am not making myself ill." No; she was drinking in a very elixir of life through that open window.

Her fancy was running riot along those days ahead of her. Spring days, and summer days, and all sorts of days that would be her own. She breathed a quick prayer that life might be long. It was only yesterday she had thought with a shudder that life might be long.

20   She arose at length and opened the door to her sister's importunities. There was a feverish triumph in her eyes, and she carried herself unwittingly like a goddess of Victory. She clasped her sister's waist, and together they descended the stairs. Richards stood waiting for them at the bottom.

Some one was opening the front door with a latchkey. It was Brently Mallard who entered, a little travel-stained, composedly carrying his grip-sack and umbrella. He had been far from the scene of accident, and did not even know there had been one. He stood amazed at Josephine's piercing cry; at Richards' quick motion to screen him from the view of his wife.

But Richards was too late.

When the doctors came they said she had died of heart disease — of joy that kills.

(1894)

Joseph Conrad (1857–1924)

Born in the Ukraine of Polish parents, Joseph Conrad worked at sea for twenty years before settling in England. There he began writing novels and short stories, all in his third language, English, which he did not learn until he was an adult. His novels, such as *Lord Jim* and *Nostromo*, are dominated by a concern with the complexities of character and motivation, and focus on the degeneration and corruption of the human spirit. Like *Heart of Darkness* (1902), his best-known short novel, the story "An Outpost of Progress" presents a bleak view of civilization in its portrayal of the two white administrators of an isolated African trading post. Without the support of their own familiar world, Kayerts and Carlier are defeated by their own weaknesses.

AN OUTPOST OF PROGRESS

I

There were two white men in charge of the trading station. Kayerts, the chief, was short and fat; Carlier, the assistant, was tall, with a large head and a very broad trunk perched upon a long pair of thin legs. The third man on the staff was a Sierra Leone nigger, who maintained that his name was Henry Price. However, for some reason or other, the natives down the river had given him the name of Makola, and it stuck to him through all his wanderings about the country. He spoke English and French with a warbling accent, wrote a beautiful hand, understood bookkeeping, and cherished in his innermost heart the worship of evil spirits. His wife was a negress from Loanda, very large and very noisy. Three children rolled about in sunshine before the door of his low, shed-like dwelling. Makola, taciturn and impenetrable, despised the two white men. He had charge of a small clay storehouse with a dried-grass roof, and pretended to keep a correct account of beads, cotton cloth, red kerchiefs, brass wire, and other trade goods it contained. Besides the storehouse and Makola's hut, there was only one large building in the cleared ground of the station. It was built neatly of reeds, with a verandah on all the four sides. There were three rooms in it. The one in the middle was the living-room, and had two rough tables and a few stools in it. The other two were the bedrooms for the white men. Each had a bedstead and a mosquito net for all furniture. The plank floor was littered with the belongings of the white men; open half-empty boxes, town wearing apparel, old boots; all the things dirty, and all the things broken, that accumulate mysteriously round untidy men. There was also another dwelling-place some distance away from the buildings. In it, under a tall cross much out of the perpendicular, slept the man who had seen the beginning of all this; who had planned and had watched the construction of this outpost of progress. He had been, at home, an unsuccessful painter who, weary of pursuing fame on an empty stomach, had gone out there through high protections. He had been the first chief of that station. Makola had watched the energetic artist die of fever in the just finished house with his usual kind of "I told you so" indifference. Then, for a time, he dwelt alone with his family, his account books, and the Evil Spirit that rules the lands under the equator. He got on very well with his god. Perhaps he had propitiated him by a promise of more white men to play with, by and by. At any rate the director of the Great Trading Company, coming up in a steamer that resembled an enormous sardine box with a flat-roofed shed erected on it, found the station in good order, and Makola as usual quietly diligent. The director had the cross put up over the first agent's grave, and appointed Kayerts to the post. Carlier was told off as second in charge. The director was a man ruthless and efficient, who at times, but very imperceptibly, indulged in grim humour. He made a speech to Kayerts and Carlier, pointing out to them the promising aspect of their station. The nearest trading-post was about three hundred miles away. It was an exceptional opportunity for them to distinguish themselves and to earn percentages on the trade. This appointment was a favour done to beginners. Kayerts was moved almost to tears by his director's kindness. He would, he said, by doing his best, try to justify the flattering confidence, &c., &c. Kayerts had been in the Administration of the Telegraphs, and knew how to express himself correctly. Carlier, an ex-non-commissioned officer of cavalry in an army guaranteed from harm by several European Powers, was less impressed. If there were commissions to get, so much the better; and, trailing a sulky glance over the river, the forests, the impenetrable bush that seemed to cut off the station from the rest of the world, he muttered between his teeth, "We shall see, very soon."

Next day, some bales of cotton goods and a few cases of provisions having been thrown on shore, the sardine-box steamer went off, not to return for another six months. On the deck the director touched his cap to the two agents, who stood on the bank waving their hats, and turning to an old servant of the Company on his passage to headquarters, said, "Look at those two imbeciles. They must be mad at home to send me such specimens. I told those fellows to plant a vegetable garden, build new storehouses and fences, and construct a landing-stage. I bet nothing will be done! They won't know how to begin. I always thought the station on this river useless, and they just fit the station!"

"They will form themselves there," said the old stager with a quiet smile.

"At any rate, I am rid of them for six months," retorted the director.

The two men watched the steamer round the bend, then, ascending arm in arm the slope of the bank, returned to the station. They had been in this vast and dark country only a very short time, and as yet always in the midst of other white men, under the eye and guidance of their superiors. And now, dull as they were to the subtle influences of surroundings, they felt themselves very much alone, when suddenly left unassisted to face the wilderness; a wilderness rendered more strange, more incomprehensible by the mysterious glimpses of the vigorous life it contained. They were two perfectly insignificant and incapable individuals, whose existence is only rendered possible through the high organization of civilized crowds. Few men realize that their life, the very essence of their character, their capabilities and their audacities, are only the expression of their belief in the safety of their surroundings. The courage, the composure, the confidence; the emotions and principles; every great and every insignificant thought belongs not to the individual but to the crowd: to the crowd that believes blindly in the irresistible force of its institutions and of its morals, in the power of its police and of its opinion. But the contact with pure unmitigated savagery, with primitive nature and primitive man, brings sudden and profound trouble into the heart. To the sentiment of being alone of one's kind, to the clear perception of the loneliness of one's thoughts, of one's sensations — to the negation of the habitual, which is safe, there is added the affirmation of the unusual, which is dangerous; a suggestion of things vague, uncontrollable, and repulsive, whose discomposing intrusion excites the imagination and tries the civilized nerves of the foolish and the wise alike.

Kayerts and Carlier walked arm in arm, drawing close to one another as children do in the dark; and they had the same, not altogether unpleasant, sense of danger which one half suspects to be imaginary. They chatted persistently in familiar tones. "Our station is prettily situated," said one. The other assented with enthusiasm, enlarging volubly on the beauties of the situation. Then they passed near the grave. "Poor devil!" said Kayerts. "He died of fever, didn't he?" muttered Carlier, stopping short. "Why," retorted Kayerts, with indignation, "I've been told that the fellow exposed himself recklessly to the sun. The climate here, everybody says, is not at all worse than at home, as long as you keep out of the sun. Do you hear that, Carlier? I am chief here, and my orders are that you should not expose yourself to the sun!" He assumed his superiority jocularly, but his meaning was serious. The idea that he would, perhaps, have to bury Carlier and remain alone, gave him an inward shiver. He felt suddenly that this Carlier was more precious to him here, in the centre of Africa, than a brother could be anywhere else. Carlier, entering into the spirit of the thing, made a military salute and answered in a brisk tone, "Your orders shall be attended to, chief!" Then he burst out laughing, slapped Kayerts on the back and shouted, "We shall let life run easily here! Just sit still and gather in the ivory those savages will bring. This country has its good points, after all!" They both laughed loudly while Carlier thought: That poor Kayerts; he is so fat and unhealthy. It would be awful if I had to bury him here. He is a man I respect. . . . Before they reached the verandah of their house they called one another "my dear fellow."

The first day they were very active, pottering about with hammers and nails and red calico, to put up curtains, make their house habitable and pretty; resolved to settle down comfortably to their new life. For them an impossible task. To grapple effectually with even purely material problems requires more serenity of mind and more lofty courage than people generally imagine. No two beings could have been more unfitted for such a struggle. Society, not from any tenderness, but because of its strange needs, had taken care of those two men, forbidding them all independent thought, all initiative, all departure from routine; and forbidding it under pain of death. They could only live on condition of being machines. And now, released from the fostering care of men with pens behind the ears, or of men with gold lace on the sleeves, they were like those lifelong prisoners who, liberated after many years, do not know what use to make of their freedom. They did not know what use to make of their faculties, being both, through want of practice, incapable of independent thought.

At the end of two months Kayerts often would say, "If it was not for my Melie, you wouldn't catch me here." Melie was his daughter. He had thrown up his post in the Administration of the Telegraphs, though he had been for seventeen years perfectly happy there, to earn a dowry for his girl. His wife was dead, and the child was being brought up by his sisters. He regretted the streets, the pavements, the cafés, his friends of many years; all the things he used to see, day after day; all the thoughts suggested by familiar things — the thoughts effortless, monotonous, and soothing of a Government clerk; he regretted all the gossip, the small enmities, the mild venom, and the little jokes of Government offices. "If I had had a decent brother-in-law," Carlier would remark, "a fellow with a heart, I would not be here." He had left the army and had made himself so obnoxious to his family by his laziness and impudence, that an exasperated brother-in-law had made superhuman efforts to procure him an appointment in the Company as a second-class agent. Having not a penny in the world he was compelled to accept this means of livelihood as soon as it became quite clear to him that there was nothing more to squeeze out of his relations. He, like Kayerts, regretted his old life. He regretted the clink of sabre and spurs on a fine afternoon, the barrack-room witticisms, the girls of garrison towns; but, besides, he had also a sense of grievance. He was evidently a much ill-used man. This made him moody, at times. But the two men got on well together in the fellowship of their stupidity and laziness. Together they did nothing, absolutely nothing, and enjoyed the sense of idleness for which they were paid. And in time they came to feel something resembling affection for one another.

They lived like blind men in a large room, aware only of what came in contact with them (and of that only imperfectly), but unable to see the general aspect of things. The river, the forest, all the great land throbbing with life, were like a great emptiness. Even the brilliant sunshine disclosed nothing intelligible. Things appeared and disappeared before their eyes in an unconnected and aimless kind of way. The river seemed to come from nowhere and flow nowhither. It flowed through a void. Out of that void, at times, came canoes, and men with spears in their hands would suddenly crowd the yard of the station. They were naked, glossy black, ornamented with snowy shells and glistening brass wire, perfect of limb. They made an uncouth babbling noise when they spoke, moved in a stately manner, and sent quick, wild glances out of their startled, never-resting eyes. Those warriors would squat in long rows, four or more deep, before the verandah, while their chiefs bargained for hours with Makola over an elephant tusk. Kayerts sat on his chair and looked down on the proceedings, understanding nothing. He stared at them with his round blue eyes, called out to Carlier, "Here, look! look at that fellow there — and that other one, to the left. Did you ever see such a face? Oh, the funny brute!"

Carlier, smoking native tobacco in a short wooden pipe, would swagger up twirling his moustaches, and surveying the warriors with haughty indulgence, would say —

"Fine animals. Brought any bone? Yes? It's not any too soon. Look at the muscles of that fellow — third from the end. I wouldn't care to get a punch on the nose from him. Fine arms, but legs no good below the knee. Couldn't make cavalry men of them." And after glancing down complacently at his own shanks, he always concluded: "Pah! Don't they stink! You, Makola! Take that herd over to the fetish" (the storehouse was in every station called the fetish, perhaps because of the spirit of civilization it contained) "and give them up some of the rubbish you keep there. I'd rather see it full of bone than full of rags."

Kayerts approved.

"Yes, yes! Go and finish that palaver over there, Mr. Makola. I will come round when you are ready, to weigh the tusk. We must be careful." Then turning to his companion: "This is the tribe that lives down the river; they are rather aromatic. I remember, they had been once before here. D'ye hear that row? What a fellow has got to put up with in this dog of a country! My head is split."

Such profitable visits were rare. For days the two pioneers of trade and progress would look on their empty courtyard in the vibrating brilliance of vertical sunshine. Below the high bank, the silent river flowed on glittering and steady. On the sands in the middle of the stream, hippos and alligators sunned themselves side by side. And stretching away in all directions, surrounding the insignificant cleared spot of the trading post, immense forests, hiding fateful complications of fantastic life, lay in the eloquent silence of mute greatness. The two men understood nothing, cared for nothing but for the passage of days that separated them from the steamer's return. Their predecessor had left some torn books. They took up these wrecks of novels, and, as they had never read anything of the kind before, they were surprised and amused. Then during long days there were interminable and silly discussions about plots and personages. In the centre of Africa they made acquaintance of Richelieu and of d'Artagnan, of Hawk's Eye and of Father Goriot, and of many other people.[1] All these imaginary personages became subjects for gossip as if they had been living friends. They discounted their virtues, suspected their motives, decried their successes; were scandalized at their duplicity or were doubtful about their courage. The accounts of crimes filled them with indignation, while tender or pathetic passages moved them deeply. Carlier cleared his throat and said in a soldierly voice, "What nonsense!" Kayerts, his round eyes suffused with tears, his fat cheeks quivering, rubbed his bald head, and declared, "This is a splendid book. I had no idea there were such clever fellows in the world." They also found some old copies of a home paper. That print discussed what it was pleased to call "Our Colonial Expansion" in high-flown language. It spoke much of the rights and duties of civilization, of the sacredness of the civilizing work, and extolled the merits of those who went about bringing light, and faith and commerce to the dark places of the earth. Carlier and Kayerts read, wondered, and began to think better of themselves. Carlier said one evening, waving his hand about, "In a hundred years, there will be perhaps a town here. Quays, and warehouses, and barracks, and — and — billiard-rooms. Civilization, my boy, and virtue — and all. And then, chaps will read that two good fellows, Kayerts and Carlier, were the first civilized men to live in this very spot!" Kayerts nodded, "Yes, it is a consolation to think of that." They seemed to forget their dead predecessor; but, early one day, Carlier went out and replanted the cross firmly. "It used to make me squint whenever I walked that way," he explained to Kayerts over the morning coffee. "It made me squint,

1 heroes in popular adventure novels by Alexandre Dumas, James Fenimore Cooper, and Honoré de Balzac, respectively.

leaning over so much. So I just planted it upright. And solid, I promise you! I suspended myself with both hands to the cross-piece. Not a move. Oh, I did that properly."

15   At times Gobila came to see them. Gobila was the chief of the neighbouring villages. He was a gray-headed savage, thin and black, with a white cloth round his loins and a mangy panther skin hanging over his back. He came up with long strides of his skeleton legs, swinging a staff as tall as himself, and, entering the common room of the station, would squat on his heels to the left of the door. There he sat, watching Kayerts, and now and then making a speech which the other did not understand. Kayerts, without interrupting his occupation, would from time to time say in a friendly manner: "How goes it, you old image?" and they would smile at one another. The two whites had a liking for that old and incomprehensible creature, and called him Father Gobila. Gobila's manner was paternal, and he seemed really to love all white men. They all appeared to him very young, indistinguishably alike (except for stature), and he knew that they were all brothers, and also immortal. The death of the artist, who was the first white man whom he knew intimately, did not disturb this belief, because he was firmly convinced that the white stranger had pretended to die and got himself buried for some mysterious purpose of his own, into which it was useless to inquire. Perhaps it was his way of going home to his own country? At any rate, these were his brothers, and he transferred his absurd affection to them. They returned it in a way. Carlier slapped him on the back, and recklessly struck off matches for his amusement. Kayerts was always ready to let him have a sniff at the ammonia bottle. In short, they behaved just like that other white creature that had hidden itself in a hole in the ground. Gobila considered them attentively. Perhaps they were the same being with the other — or one of them was. He couldn't decide — clear up that mystery; but he remained always very friendly. In consequence of that friendship the women of Gobila's village walked in single file through the reedy grass, bringing every morning to the station, fowls, and sweet potatoes, and palm wine, and sometimes a goat. The Company never provisions the stations fully, and the agents required those local supplies to live. They had them through the good-will of Gobila, and lived well. Now and then one of them had a bout of fever, and the other nursed him with gentle devotion. They did not think much of it. It left them weaker, and their appearance changed for the worse. Carlier was hollow-eyed and irritable. Kayerts showed a drawn, flabby face above the rotundity of his stomach, which gave him a weird aspect. But being constantly together, they did not notice the change that took place gradually in their appearance, and also in their dispositions.

Five months passed in that way.

Then, one morning, as Kayerts and Carlier, lounging in their chairs under the verandah, talked about the approaching visit of the steamer, a knot of armed men came out of the forest and advanced towards the station. They were strangers to that part of the country. They were tall, slight, draped classically from neck to heel in blue fringed cloths, and carried percussion muskets over their bare right shoulders. Makola showed signs of excitement, and ran out of the storehouse (where he spent all his days) to meet these visitors. They came into the courtyard and looked about them with steady, scornful glances. Their leader, a powerful and determined-looking negro with bloodshot eyes, stood in front of the verandah and made a long speech. He gesticulated much, and ceased very suddenly.

There was something in his intonation, in the sounds of the long sentences he used, that startled the two whites. It was like a reminiscence of something not exactly familiar, and yet resembling the speech of civilized men. It sounded like one of those impossible languages which sometimes we hear in our dreams.

"What lingo is that?" said the amazed Carlier. "In the first moment I fancied the fellow was going to speak French. Anyway, it is a different kind of gibberish to what we ever heard."

"Yes," replied Kayerts. "Hey, Makola, what does he say? Where do they come from? Who are they?

But Makola, who seemed to be standing on hot bricks, answered hurriedly, "I don't know. They come from very far. Perhaps Mrs. Price will understand. They are perhaps bad men."

The leader, after waiting for a while, said something sharply to Makola, who shook his head. Then the man, after looking round, noticed Makola's hut and walked over there. The next moment Mrs. Makola was heard speaking with great volubility. The other strangers — they were six in all — strolled about with an air of ease, put their heads through the door of the storeroom, congregated round the grave, pointed understandingly at the cross, and generally made themselves at home.

"I don't like those chaps — and, I say, Kayerts, they must be from the coast; they've got firearms," observed the sagacious Carlier.

Kayerts also did not like those chaps. They both, for the first time, became aware that they lived in conditions where the unusual may be dangerous, and that there was no power on earth outside of themselves to stand between them and the unusual. They became uneasy, went in and loaded their revolvers. Kayerts said, "We must order Makola to tell them to go away before dark."

The strangers left in the afternoon, after eating a meal prepared for them by Mrs. Makola. The immense woman was excited, and talked much with the visitors. She rattled away shrilly, pointing here and there at the forests and at the river. Makola sat apart and watched. At times he got up and whispered to his wife. He accompanied the strangers across the ravine at the back of the station-ground, and returned slowly looking very thoughtful. When questioned by the white men he was very strange, seemed not to understand, seemed to have forgotten French — seemed to have forgotten how to speak altogether. Kayerts and Carlier agreed that the nigger had had too much palm wine.

There was some talk about keeping a watch in turn, but in the evening everything seemed so quiet and peaceful that they retired as usual. All night they were disturbed by a lot of drumming in the villages. A deep, rapid roll near by would be followed by another far off — then all ceased. Soon short appeals would rattle out here and there, then all mingle together, increase, become vigorous and sustained, would spread out over the forest, roll through the night, unbroken and ceaseless, near and far, as if the whole land had been one immense drum booming out steadily an appeal to heaven. And through the deep and tremendous noise sudden yells that resembled snatches of songs from a madhouse darted shrill and high in discordant jets of sound which seemed to rush far above the earth and drive all peace from under the stars.

Carlier and Kayerts slept badly. They both thought they had heard shots fired during the night — but they could not agree as to the direction. In the morning Makola was gone somewhere. He returned about noon with one of yesterday's strangers, and eluded all Kayerts' attempts to close with him: had become deaf apparently. Kayerts wondered. Carlier, who had been fishing off the bank, came back and remarked while he showed his catch, "The niggers seem to be in a deuce of a stir; I wonder what's up. I saw about fifteen canoes cross the river during the two hours I was there fishing." Kayerts, worried, said, "Isn't this Makola very queer to-day?" Carlier advised, "Keep all our men together in case of some trouble."

II

There were ten station men who had been left by the Director. Those fellows, having engaged themselves to the Company for six months (without having any idea of a month in particular and only a very faint notion of time in general), had been serving the cause of progress for upwards of two years. Belonging to a tribe from a very distant part of the land of darkness and sorrow, they did not run away, naturally supposing that as wandering strangers they would be killed by the inhabitants of the country; in which they were right. They lived in straw huts on the slope of a ravine overgrown with reedy grass, just behind the station buildings. They were not happy, regretting the festive incantations, the sorceries, the human sacrifices of their own land; where they also had parents, brothers, sisters, admired chiefs, respected magicians, loved friends, and other ties supposed generally to be human. Besides, the rice rations served out by the Company did not agree with them, being a food unknown to their land, and to which they could not get used. Consequently they were unhealthy and miserable. Had they been of any other tribe they would have made up their minds to die — for nothing is easier to certain savages than suicide — and so have escaped from the puzzling difficulties of existence. But belonging, as they did, to a warlike tribe with filed teeth, they had more grit, and went on stupidly living through disease and sorrow. They did very little work, and had lost their splendid physique. Carlier and Kayerts doctored them assiduously without being able to bring them back into condition again. They were mustered every morning and told off to different tasks — grass-cutting, fence-building, tree-felling, &c., &c., which no power on earth could induce them to execute efficiently. The two whites had practically very little control over them.

In the afternoon Makola came over to the big house and found Kayerts watching three heavy columns of smoke rising above the forests. "What is that?" asked Kayerts. "Some villages burn," answered Makola, who seemed to have regained his wits. Then he said abruptly: "We have got very little ivory; bad six months' trading. Do you like get a little more ivory?"

"Yes," said Kayerts, eagerly. He thought of percentages which were low.

"Those men who came yesterday are traders from Loanda who have got more ivory than they can carry home. Shall I buy? I know their camp."

30

"Certainly," said Kayerts. "What are those traders?"

"Bad fellows," said Makola, indifferently. "They fight with people, and catch women and children. They are bad men, and got guns. There is a great disturbance in the country. Do you want ivory?"

"Yes," said Kayerts. Makola said nothing for a while. Then: "Those workmen of ours are no good at all," he muttered, looking round. "Station in very bad order, sir. Director will growl. Better get a fine lot of ivory, then he say nothing."

"I can't help it; the men won't work," said Kayerts. "When will you get that ivory?"

"Very soon," said Makola. "Perhaps to-night. You leave it to me, and keep indoors, sir. I think you had better give some palm wine to our men to make a dance this evening. Enjoy themselves. Work better to-morrow. There's plenty palm wine — gone a little sour."

Kayerts said yes, and Makola, with his own hands, carried big calabashes to the door of his hut. They stood there till the evening, and Mrs. Makola looked into every one. The men got them at sunset. When Kayerts and Carlier retired, a big bonfire was flaring before the men's huts. They could hear their shouts and drumming. Some men from Gobila's village had joined the station hands, and the entertainment was a great success.

In the middle of the night, Carlier waking suddenly, heard a man shout loudly; then a shot was fired. Only one. Carlier ran out and met Kayerts on the verandah. They were both startled. As they went across the yard to call Makola, they saw shadows moving in the night. One of them cried, "Don't shoot! It's me, Price." Then Makola appeared close to them. "Go back, go back, please," he urged, "you spoil all." "There are strange men about," said Carlier. "Never mind; I know," said Makola. Then he whispered, "All right. Bring ivory. Say nothing! I know my business." The two white men reluctantly went back to the house, but did not sleep. They heard footsteps, whispers, some groans. It seemed as if a lot of men came in, dumped heavy things on the ground, squabbled a long time, then went away. They lay on their hard beds and thought: "This Makola is invaluable." In the morning Carlier came out, very sleepy, and pulled at the cord of the big bell. The station hands mustered every morning to the sound of the bell. That morning nobody came. Kayerts turned out also, yawning. Across the yard they saw Makola come out of his hut, a tin basin of soapy water in his hand. Makola, a civilized nigger, was very neat in his person. He threw the soapsuds skilfully over a wretched little yellow cur he had, then turning his face to the agent's house, he shouted from the distance, "All the men gone last night!"

They heard him plainly, but in their surprise they both yelled out together: "What!" Then they stared at one another. "We are in a proper fix now," growled Carlier. "It's incredible!" muttered Kayerts. "I will go to the huts and see," said Carlier, striding off. Makola coming up found Kayerts standing alone.

"I can hardly believe it," said Kayerts, tearfully. "We took care of them as if they had been our children."

"They went with the coast people," said Makola after a moment of hesitation.

"What do I care with whom they went — the ungrateful brutes!" exclaimed the other. Then with sudden suspicion, and looking hard at Makola, he added: "What do you know about it?"

Makola moved his shoulders, looking down on the ground. "What do I know? I think only. Will you come and look at the ivory I've got there? It is a fine lot. You never saw such."

He moved towards the store. Kayerts followed him mechanically, thinking about the incredible desertion of the men. On the ground before the door of the fetish lay six splendid tusks.

45 "What did you give for it?" asked Kayerts, after surveying the lot with satisfaction.

"No regular trade," said Makola. "They brought the ivory and gave it to me. I told them to take what they most wanted in the station. It is a beautiful lot. No station can show such tusks. Those traders wanted carriers badly, and our men were no good here. No trade, no entry in books; all correct."

Kayerts nearly burst with indignation. "Why!" he shouted, "I believe you have sold our men for these tusks!" Makola stood impassive and silent. "I — I — will — I," stuttered Kayerts. "You fiend!" he yelled out.

"I did the best for you and the Company," said Makola, imperturbably. "Why you shout so much? Look at this tusk."

"I dismiss you! I will report you — I won't look at the tusk. I forbid you to touch them. I order you to throw them into the river. You — you!"

50 "You very red, Mr. Kayerts. If you are so irritable in the sun, you will get fever and die — like the first chief!" pronounced Makola impressively.

They stood still, contemplating one another with intense eyes, as if they had been looking with effort across immense distances. Kayerts shivered. Makola had meant no more than he said, but his words seemed to Kayerts full of ominous menace! He turned sharply and went away to the house. Makola retired into the bosom of his family; and the tusks, left lying before the store, looked very large and valuable in the sunshine.

Carlier came back on the verandah. "They're all gone, hey?" asked Kayerts from the far end of the common room in a muffled voice. "You did not find anybody?"

"Oh, yes," said Carlier, "I found one of Gobila's people lying dead before the huts — shot through the body. We heard that shot last night."

Kayerts came out quickly. He found his companion staring grimly over the yard at the tusks, away by the store. They both sat in silence for a while. Then Kayerts related his conversation with Makola. Carlier said nothing. At the midday meal they ate very little. They hardly exchanged a word that day. A great silence seemed to lie heavily over the station and press on their lips. Makola did not open the store; he spent the day playing with his children. He lay full-length on a mat outside his door, and the youngsters sat on his chest and clambered all over him. It was a touching picture. Mrs. Makola was busy cooking all day as usual. The white men made a somewhat better meal in the evening. Afterwards, Carlier smoking his pipe strolled over to the store; he stood for a long time over the tusks, touched one or two with his foot, even tried to lift the largest one by its small end. He came back to his chief, who had not stirred from the verandah, threw himself in the chair and said —

55 "I can see it! They were pounced upon while they slept heavily after drinking all that palm wine you've allowed Makola to give them. A put-up job! See? The worst is, some of Gobila's people went there, and got carried off too, no doubt. The least drunk woke up, and got shot for his sobriety. This is a funny country. What will you do now?"

"We can't touch it, of course," said Kayerts.

"Of course not," assented Carlier.

"Slavery is an awful thing," stammered out Kayerts in an unsteady voice.

"Frightful — the sufferings," grunted Carlier with conviction.

60 They believed their words. Everybody shows a respectful deference to certain sounds that he and his fellows can make. But about feelings people really know nothing. We talk with indignation or enthusiasm; we talk about oppression, cruelty, crime, devotion, self-sacrifice, virtue, and we know nothing real beyond the words. Nobody knows what suffering or sacrifice mean — except, perhaps the victims of the mysterious purpose of these illusions.

Next morning they saw Makola very busy setting up in the yard the big scales used for weighing ivory. By and by Carlier said: "What's that filthy scoundrel up to?" and lounged out into the yard. Kayerts followed. They stood watching. Makola took no notice. When the balance was swung true, he tried to lift a tusk into the scale. It was too heavy. He looked up helplessly without a word, and for a minute they stood round that balance as mute and still as three statues. Suddenly Carlier said: "Catch hold of the other end, Makola — you beast!" and together they swung the tusk up. Kayerts trembled in every limb. He muttered, "I say! O! I say!" and putting his hand in his pocket found there a dirty bit of paper and the stump of a pencil. He turned his back on the others, as if about to do something tricky, and noted stealthily the weights which Carlier shouted out to him with unnecessary loudness. When all was over Makola whispered to himself: "The sun's very strong here for the tusks." Carlier said to Kayerts in a careless tone: "I say, chief, I might just as well give him a lift with this lot into the store."

As they were going back to the house Kayerts observed with a sigh: "It had to be done." And Carlier said: "It's deplorable, but, the men being Company's men the ivory is Company's ivory. We must look after it." "I will report to the Director, of course," said Kayerts. "Of course; let him decide," approved Carlier.

At midday they made a hearty meal. Kayerts sighed from time to time. Whenever they mentioned Makola's name they always added to it an opprobrious epithet. It eased their conscience. Makola gave himself a half-holiday, and bathed his children in the river. No one from Gobila's villages came near the station that day. No one came the next day, and the next, nor for a whole week. Gobila's people might have been dead and buried for any sign of life they gave. But they were only mourning for those they had lost by the witchcraft of white men, who had brought wicked people into their country. The wicked people were gone, but fear remained. Fear always remains. A man may destroy everything within himself, love and hate and belief, and even doubt; but as long as he clings to life he cannot destroy fear: the fear, subtle, indestructible, and terrible, that pervades his being; that tinges his thoughts; that lurks in his heart; that watches on his lips the struggle of his last breath. In his fear, the mild old Gobila offered extra human sacrifices to all the Evil Spirits that had taken possession of his white friends. His heart was heavy. Some warriors spoke about burning and killing, but the cautious old savage dissuaded them. Who could foresee the woe those mysterious creatures, if irritated, might bring? They should be left alone. Perhaps in time they would disappear into the earth as the first one had disappeared. His people must keep away from them, and hope for the best.

Kayerts and Carlier did not disappear, but remained above on this earth, that, somehow, they fancied had become bigger and very empty. It was not the absolute and dumb solitude of the post that impressed them so much as an inarticulate feeling that something from within them was gone, something that worked for their safety, and had kept the wilderness from interfering with their hearts. The images of home; the memory of people like them, of men that thought and felt as they used to think and feel, receded into distances made indistinct by the glare of unclouded sunshine. And out of the great silence of the surrounding wilderness, its very hopelessness and savagery seemed to approach them nearer, to draw them gently, to look upon them, to envelop them with a solicitude irresistible, familiar, and disgusting.

65

Days lengthened into weeks, then into months. Gobila's people drummed and yelled to every new moon, as of yore, but kept away from the station. Makola and Carlier tried once in a canoe to open communications, but were received with a shower of arrows, and had to fly back to the station for dear life. That attempt set the country up and down the river into an uproar that could be very distinctly heard for days. The steamer was late. At first they spoke of delay jauntily, then anxiously, then gloomily. The matter was becoming serious. Stores were running short. Carlier cast his lines off the bank, but the river was low, and the fish kept out in the stream. They dared not stroll far away from the station to shoot. Moreover, there was no game in the impenetrable forest. Once Carlier shot a hippo in the river. They had no boat to secure it, and it sank. When it floated up it drifted away, and Gobila's people secured the carcase. It was the occasion for a national holiday, but Carlier had a fit of rage over it and talked about the necessity of exterminating all the niggers before the country could be made habitable. Kayerts mooned about silently; spent hours looking at the portrait of his Melie. It represented a little girl with long bleached tresses and a rather sour face. His legs were much swollen, and he could hardly walk. Carlier, undermined by fever, could not swagger any more, but kept tottering about, still with a devil-may-care air, as became a man who remembered his crack regiment. He had become hoarse, sarcastic, and inclined to say unpleasant things. He called it "being frank with you." They had long ago reckoned their percentages on trade, including in them that last deal of "this infamous Makola." They had also concluded not to say anything about it. Kayerts hesitated at first — was afraid of the Director.

"He has seen worse things done on the quiet," maintained Carlier, with a hoarse laugh. "Trust him! He won't thank you if you blab. He is no better than you or me. Who will talk if we hold our tongues? There is nobody here."

That was the root of the trouble! There was nobody there; and being left there alone with their weakness, they became daily more like a pair of accomplices than like a couple of devoted friends. They had heard nothing from home for eight months. Every evening they said, "To-morrow we shall see the steamer." But one of the Company's steamers had been wrecked, and the Director was busy with the other, relieving very distant and important stations on the main river. He thought that the useless station, and the useless men, could wait. Meantime Kayerts and Carlier lived on rice boiled without salt, and cursed the Company, all Africa, and the day they were born. One must have lived on such diet to discover what ghastly trouble the necessity of swallowing one's food may become. There was literally nothing else in the station but rice and coffee; they drank the coffee without sugar. The last fifteen lumps Kayerts had solemnly locked away in his box, together with a half-bottle of Cognâc, "in case of sickness," he explained. Carlier approved. "When one is sick," he said, "any little extra like that is cheering."

They waited. Rank grass began to sprout over the courtyard. The bell never rang now. Days passed, silent, exasperating, and slow. When the two men spoke, they snarled; and their silences were bitter, as if tinged by the bitterness of their thoughts.

One day after a lunch of boiled rice, Carlier put down his cup untasted, and said: "Hang it all! Let's have a decent cup of coffee for once. Bring out that sugar, Kayerts!"

70   "For the sick," muttered Kayerts, without looking up.

"For the sick," mocked Carlier. "Bosh! . . . Well! I am sick."

"You are no more sick than I am, and I go without," said Kayerts in a peaceful tone.

"Come! out with that sugar, you stingy old slave-dealer."

Kayerts looked up quickly. Carlier was smiling with marked insolence. And suddenly it seemed to Kayerts that he had never seen that man before. Who was he? He knew nothing about him. What was he capable of? There was a surprising flash of violent emotion within him, as if in the presence of something undreamt-of, dangerous, and final. But he managed to pronounce with composure —

75   "That joke is in very bad taste. Don't repeat it."

"Joke!" said Carlier, hitching himself forward on his seat. "I am hungry — I am sick — I don't joke! I hate hypocrites. You are a hypocrite. You are a slave-dealer. I am a slave-dealer. There's nothing but slave-dealers in this cursed country. I mean to have sugar in my coffee to-day, anyhow!"

"I forbid you to speak to me in that way," said Kayerts with a fair show of resolution.

"You! — What?" shouted Carlier, jumping up.

Kayerts stood up also. "I am your chief," he began, trying to master the shakiness of his voice.

80   "What?" yelled the other. "Who's chief? There's no chief here. There's nothing here: there's nothing but you and I. Fetch the sugar — you potbellied ass."

"Hold your tongue. Go out of this room," screamed Kayerts. "I dismiss you — you scoundrel!"

Carlier swung a stool. All at once he looked dangerously in earnest. "You flabby, good-for-nothing civilian — take that!" he howled.

Kayerts dropped under the table, and the stool struck the grass inner wall of the room. Then, as Carlier was trying to upset the table, Kayerts in desperation made a blind rush, head low, like a cornered pig would do, and over-turning his friend, bolted along the verandah, and into his room. He locked the door, snatched his revolver, and stood panting. In less than a minute, Carlier was kicking at the door furiously, howling, "If you don't bring out that sugar, I will shoot you at sight, like a dog. Now then — one — two — three. You won't? I will show you who's the master."

Kayerts thought the door would fall in, and scrambled through the square hole that served for a window in his room. There was then the whole breadth of the house between them. But the other was apparently not strong enough to break in the door, and Kayerts heard him running round. Then he also began to run laboriously on his swollen legs. He ran as quickly as he could, grasping the revolver, and unable yet to understand what was happening to him. He saw in succession Makola's house, the store, the river, the ravine, and the low bushes; and he saw all those things again as he ran for the second time round the house. Then again they flashed past him. That morning he could not have walked a yard without a groan.

85 And now he ran. He ran fast enough to keep out of sight of the other man.

Then as, weak and desperate, he thought, "Before I finish the next round I shall die," he heard the other man stumble heavily, then stop. He stopped also. He had the back and Carlier the front of the house, as before. He heard him drop into a chair cursing, and suddenly his own legs gave way, and he slid down into a sitting posture with his back to the wall. His mouth was as dry as a cinder, and his face was wet with perspiration — and tears. What was it all about? He thought it must be a horrible illusion; he thought he was dreaming; he thought he was going mad! After a while he collected his senses. What did they quarrel about? That sugar! How absurd! He would give it to him — didn't want it himself. And he began scrambling to his feet with a sudden feeling of security. But before he had fairly stood upright, a common-sense reflection occurred to him and drove him back into despair. He thought: If I give way now to that brute of a soldier, he will begin this horror again to-morrow — and the day after — every day — raise other pretensions, trample on me, torture me, make me his slave — and I will be lost! Lost! The steamer may not come for days — may never come. He shook so that he had to sit down on the floor again. He shivered forlornly. He felt he could not, would not move any more. He was completely distracted by the sudden perception that the position was without issue — that death and life had in a moment become equally difficult and terrible.

All at once he heard the other push his chair back; and he leaped to his feet with extreme facility. He listened and got confused. Must run again! Right or left? He heard footsteps. He darted to the left, grasping his revolver, and at the very same instant, as it seemed to him, they came into violent collision. Both shouted with surprise. A loud explosion took place between them; a roar of red fire, thick smoke; and Kayerts, deafened and blinded, rushed back thinking: I am hit — it's all over. He expected the other to come round — to gloat over his agony. He caught hold of an upright of the roof — "All over!" Then he heard a crashing fall on the other side of the house, as if somebody had tumbled headlong over a chair — then silence. Nothing more happened. He did not die. Only his shoulder felt as if it had been badly wrenched, and he had lost his revolver. He was disarmed and helpless! He waited for his fate. The other man made no sound. It was a stratagem. He was stalking him now! Along what side? Perhaps he was taking aim this very minute!

After a few moments of an agony frightful and absurd, he decided to go and meet his doom. He was prepared for every surrender. He turned the corner, steadying himself with one hand on the wall; made a few paces, and nearly swooned. He had seen on the floor, protruding past the other corner, a pair of turned-up feet. A pair of white naked feet in red slippers. He felt deadly sick, and stood for a time in profound darkness. Then Makola appeared before him, saying quietly: "Come along, Mr. Kayerts. He is dead." He burst into tears of gratitude; a loud, sobbing fit of crying. After a time he found himself sitting in a chair and looking at Carlier, who lay stretched on his back. Makola was kneeling over the body.

"Is this your revolver?" asked Makola, getting up.

"Yes," said Kayerts; then he added very quickly, "He ran after me to shoot me — you saw!"

"Yes, I saw," said Makola. "There is only one revolver; where's his?"

"Don't know," whispered Kayerts in a voice that had become suddenly very faint.

"I will go and look for it," said the other, gently. He made the round along the verandah, while Kayerts sat still and looked at the corpse. Makola came back empty-handed, stood in deep thought, then stepped quietly into the dead man's room, and came out directly with a revolver, which he held up before Kayerts. Kayerts shut his eyes. Everything was going round. He found life more terrible and difficult than death. He had shot an unarmed man.

After meditating for a while, Makola said softly, pointing at the dead man who lay there with his right eye blown out —

"He died of fever." Kayerts looked at him with a stony stare. "Yes," repeated Makola, thoughtfully, stepping over the corpse, "I think he died of fever. Bury him to-morrow."

And he went away slowly to his expectant wife, leaving the two white men alone on the verandah.

Night came, and Kayerts sat unmoving on his chair. He sat quiet as if he had taken a dose of opium. The violence of the emotions he had passed through produced a feeling of exhausted serenity. He had plumbed in one short afternoon the depths of horror and despair, and now found repose in the conviction that life had no more secrets for him: neither had death! He sat by the corpse thinking; thinking very actively, thinking very new thoughts. He seemed to have broken loose from himself altogether. His old thoughts, convictions, likes and dislikes, things he respected and things he abhorred, appeared in their true light at last! Appeared contemptible and childish, false and ridiculous. He revelled in his new wisdom while he sat by the man he had killed. He argued with himself about all things under heaven with that kind of wrong-headed lucidity which may be observed in some lunatics. Incidentally he reflected that the fellow dead there had been a noxious beast anyway; that men died every day in thousands; perhaps in hundreds of thousands — who could tell?— and that in the number, that one death could not possibly make any difference; couldn't have any importance, at least to a thinking creature.

He, Kayerts, was a thinking creature. He had been all his life, till that moment, a believer in a lot of nonsense like the rest of mankind — who are fools; but now he thought! He knew! He was at peace; he was familiar with the highest wisdom! Then he tried to imagine himself dead, and Carlier sitting in his chair watching him; and his attempt met with such unexpected success, that in a very few moments he became not at all sure who was dead and who was alive. This extraordinary achievement of his fancy startled him, however, and by a clever and timely effort of mind he saved himself just in time from becoming Carlier. His heart thumped, and he felt hot all over at the thought of that danger. Carlier! What a beastly thing! To compose his now disturbed nerves — and no wonder! — he tried to whistle a little. Then, suddenly, he fell asleep, or thought he had slept; but at any rate there was a fog, and somebody had whistled in the fog.

He stood up. The day had come, and a heavy mist had descended upon the land: the mist penetrating, enveloping, and silent; the morning mist of tropical lands; the mist that clings and kills; the mist white and deadly, immaculate and poisonous. He stood up, saw the body, and threw his arms above his head with a cry like that of a man who, waking from a trance, finds himself immured forever in a tomb. "*Help! . . . My God!*"

A shriek inhuman, vibrating and sudden, pierced like a sharp dart the white shroud of that land of sorrow. Three short, impatient screeches followed, and then, for a time, the fog-wreaths rolled on, undisturbed, through a formidable silence. Then many more shrieks, rapid and piercing, like the yells of some exasperated and ruthless creature, rent the air. Progress was calling to Kayerts from the river. Progress and civilization and all the virtues. Society was calling to its accomplished child to come, to be taken care of, to be instructed, to be judged, to be condemned; it called him to return to that rubbish heap from which he had wandered away, so that justice could be done.

100   Kayerts heard and understood. He stumbled out of the verandah, leaving the other man quite alone for the first time since they had been thrown there together. He groped his way through the fog, calling in his ignorance upon the invisible heaven to undo its work. Makola flitted by in the mist, shouting as he ran —

"Steamer! Steamer! They can't see. They whistle for the station. I go ring the bell. Go down to the landing, sir. I ring."

He disappeared. Kayerts stood still. He looked upwards; the fog rolled low over his head. He looked round like a man who has lost his way; and he saw a dark smudge, a cross-shaped stain, upon the shifting purity of the mist. As he began to stumble towards it, the station bell rang in a tumultuous peal its answer to the impatient clamour of the steamer.

The Managing Director of the Great Civilizing Company (since we know that civilization follows trade) landed first, and incontinently lost sight of the steamer. The fog down by the river was exceedingly dense; above, at the station, the bell rang unceasing and brazen.

The Director shouted loudly to the steamer:

105   "There is nobody down to meet us; there may be something wrong, though they are ringing. You had better come, too!"

And he began to toil up the steep bank. The captain and the engine-driver of the boat followed behind. As they scrambled up the fog thinned, and they could see their Director a good way ahead. Suddenly they saw him start forward, calling to them over his shoulder:—"Run! Run to the house! I've found one of them. Run, look for the other!"

He had found one of them! And even he, the man of varied and startling experience, was somewhat discomposed by the manner of this finding. He stood and fumbled in his pockets (for a knife) while he faced Kayerts, who was hanging by a leather strap from the cross. He had evidently climbed the grave, which was high and narrow, and after tying the end of the strap to the arm, had swung himself off. His toes were only a couple of inches above the ground; his arms hung stiffly down; he seemed to be standing rigidly at attention, but with one purple cheek playfully posed on the shoulder. And, irreverently, he was putting out a swollen tongue at his Managing Director.

(1897)

Charlotte Perkins Gilman (1860–1935)

Although "The Yellow Wallpaper" has recently been praised as a major feminist short story, it was virtually unknown until the early 1960s, and its author, a native of Hartford, Connecticut, was remembered chiefly as an important theorist in the women's movement during the early decades of this century. In such book-length tracts as *Women and Economics* (1898) and short stories as "If I Were a Man" and "The Widow's Might," she studied the nature of women's lives and their relationships with men. "The Yellow Wallpaper," one of her first short stories, was based on the extreme mental depression she suffered in part as the result of psychiatric treatments prescribed after the birth of her daughter. It was written, she later stated, "not...to drive people crazy, but to save people from being driven crazy...." Often compared to Edgar Allan Poe's tales that examine the narrator's descent into madness, the story, with its depiction of the prison-like room and its grotesquely designed wallpaper, is often interpreted as a presentation of the destructive effects on women of the repressive patriarchal society of the nineteenth century.

THE YELLOW WALLPAPER

It is very seldom that mere ordinary people like John and myself secure ancestral halls for the summer.

A colonial mansion, a hereditary estate, I would say a haunted house and reach the height of romantic felicity — but that would be asking too much of fate!

Still I will proudly declare that there is something queer about it.

Else, why should it be let so cheaply? And why have stood so long untenanted?

5   John laughs at me, of course, but one expects that.

John is practical in the extreme. He has no patience with faith, an intense horror of superstition, and he scoffs openly at any talk of things not to be felt and seen and put down in figures.

John is a physician, and *perhaps*— (I would not say it to a living soul, of course, but this is dead paper and a great relief to my mind) —*perhaps* that is one reason I do not get well faster.

You see, he does not believe I am sick! And what can one do?

If a physician of high standing, and one's own husband, assures friends and relatives that there is really nothing the matter with one but temporary nervous depression — a slight hysterical tendency — what is one to do?

10   My brother is also a physician, and also of high standing, and he says the same thing.

So I take phosphates or phosphites — whichever it is — and tonics, and air and exercise, and journeys, and am absolutely forbidden to "work" until I am well again.

Personally, I disagree with their ideas.

Personally, I believe that congenial work, with excitement and change, would do me good.

But what is one to do?

15   I did write for a while in spite of them; but it *does* exhaust me a good deal — having to be so sly about it, or else meet with heavy opposition.

I sometimes fancy that in my condition, if I had less opposition and more society and stimulus — but John says the very worst thing I can do is to think about my condition, and I confess it always makes me feel bad.

So I will let it alone and talk about the house.

The most beautiful place! It is quite alone, standing well back from the road, quite three miles from the village. It makes me think of English places that you read about, for there are hedges and walls and gates that lock, and lots of separate little houses for the gardeners and people.

There is a *delicious* garden! I never saw such a garden — large and shady, full of box-bordered paths, and lined with long grape-covered arbors with seats under them.

20   There were greenhouses, but they are all broken now.

There was some legal trouble, I believe, something about the heirs and co-heirs; anyhow, the place has been empty for years.

That spoils my ghostliness, I am afraid, but I don't care — there is something strange about the house — I can feel it.

I even said so to John one moonlight evening, but he said what I felt was a draught, and shut the window.

I get unreasonably angry with John sometimes. I'm sure I never used to be so sensitive. I think it is due to this nervous condition.

25   But John says if I feel so I shall neglect proper self-control; so I take pains to control myself — before him, at least, and that makes me very tired.

I don't like our room a bit. I wanted one downstairs that opened onto the piazza and had roses all over the window, and such pretty old-fashioned chintz hangings! But John would not hear of it.

He said there was only one window and not room for two beds, and no near room for him if he took another.

He is very careful and loving, and hardly lets me stir without special direction.

I have a schedule prescription for each hour in the day; he takes all care from me, and so I feel basely ungrateful not to value it more.

30   He said he came here solely on my account, that I was to have perfect rest and all the air I could get. "Your exercise depends on your strength, my dear," said he, "and your food somewhat on your appetite; but air you can absorb all the time." So we took the nursery at the top of the house.

It is a big, airy room, the whole floor nearly, with windows that look all ways, and air and sunshine galore. It was nursery first, and then playroom and gymnasium, I should judge, for the windows are barred for little children, and there are rings and things in the walls.

The paint and paper look as if a boys' school had used it. It is stripped off — the paper — in great patches all around the head of my bed, about as far as I can reach, and in a great place on the other side of the room low down. I never saw a worse paper in my life. One of those sprawling, flamboyant patterns committing every artistic sin.

It is dull enough to confuse the eye in following, pronounced enough constantly to irritate and provoke study, and when you follow the lame uncertain curves for a little distance they suddenly commit suicide — plunge off at outrageous angles, destroy themselves in unheard-of contradictions.

The color is repellent, almost revolting: a smouldering unclean yellow, strangely faded by the slow-turning sunlight. It is a dull yet lurid orange in some places, a sickly sulphur tint in others.

35 No wonder the children hated it! I should hate it myself if I had to live in this room long.

There comes John, and I must put this away — he hates to have me write a word.

We have been here two weeks, and I haven't felt like writing before, since that first day.

I am sitting by the window now, up in this atrocious nursery, and there is nothing to hinder my writing as much as I please, save lack of strength.

John is away all day, and even some nights when his cases are serious.

40 I am glad my case is not serious!

But these nervous troubles are dreadfully depressing.

John does not know how much I really suffer. He knows there is no reason to suffer, and that satisfies him.

Of course it is only nervousness. It does weigh on me so not to do my duty in any way!

I meant to be such a help to John, such a real rest and comfort, and here I am a comparative burden already!

45 Nobody would believe what an effort it is to do what little I am able — to dress and entertain, and order things.

It is fortunate Mary is so good with the baby. Such a dear baby!

And yet I *cannot* be with him, it makes me so nervous.

I suppose John never was nervous in his life. He laughs at me so about this wallpaper!

At first he meant to repaper the room, but afterward he said that I was letting it get the better of me, and that nothing was worse for a nervous patient than to give way to such fancies.

50 He said that after the wallpaper was changed it would be the heavy bedstead, and then the barred windows, and then that gate at the head of the stairs, and so on.

"You know the place is doing you good," he said, "and really, dear, I don't care to renovate the house just for a three months' rental."

"Then do let us go downstairs," I said. "There are such pretty rooms there."

Then he took me in his arms and called me a blessed little goose, and said he would go down cellar, if I wished, and have it whitewashed into the bargain.

But he is right enough about the beds and windows and things.

55 It is as airy and comfortable a room as anyone need wish, and, of course, I would not be so silly as to make him uncomfortable just for a whim.

I'm really getting quite fond of the big room, all but that horrid paper.

Out of one window I can see the garden — those mysterious deep-shaded arbors, the riotous old-fashioned flowers, and bushes and gnarly trees.

Out of another I get a lovely view of the bay and a little private wharf belonging to the estate. There is a beautiful shaded lane that runs down there from the house. I always fancy I see people walking in these numerous paths and arbors, but John has cautioned me not to give way to fancy in the least. He says that with my imaginative power and habit of story-making, a nervous weakness like mine is sure to lead to all manner of excited fancies, and that I ought to use my will and good sense to check the tendency. So I try.

I think sometimes that if I were only well enough to write a little it would relieve the press of ideas and rest me.

But I find I get pretty tired when I try.

It is so discouraging not to have any advice and companionship about my work. When I get really well, John says we will ask Cousin Henry and Julia down for a long visit; but he says he would as soon put fireworks in my pillow-case as to let me have those stimulating people about now.

I wish I could get well faster.

But I must not think about that. This paper looks to me as if it *knew* what a vicious influence it had!

There is a recurrent spot where the pattern lolls like a broken neck and two bulbous eyes stare at you upside down.

I get positively angry with the impertinence of it and the everlastingness. Up and down and sideways they crawl, and those absurd unblinking eyes are everywhere. There is one place where two breadths didn't match, and the eyes go all up and down the line, one a little higher than the other.

I never saw so much expression in an inanimate thing before, and we all know how much expression they have! I used to lie awake as a child and get more entertainment and terror out of blank walls and plain furniture than most children could find in a toy-store.

I remember what a kindly wink the knobs of our big old bureau used to have, and there was one chair that always seemed like a strong friend.

I used to feel that if any of the other things looked too fierce I could always hop into that chair and be safe.

The furniture in this room is no worse than inharmonious, however, for we had to bring it all from downstairs. I suppose when this was used as a play-room they had to take the nursery things out, and no wonder! I never saw such ravages as the children have made here.

The wallpaper, as I said before, is torn off in spots, and it sticketh closer than a brother — they must have had perseverance as well as hatred.

Then the floor is scratched and gouged and splintered, the plaster itself is dug out here and there, and this great heavy bed, which is all we found in the room, looks as if it had been through the wars.

But I don't mind it a bit — only the paper.

There comes John's sister. Such a dear girl as she is, and so careful of me! I must not let her find me writing.

She is a perfect and enthusiastic housekeeper, and hopes for no better profession. I verily believe she thinks it is the writing which made me sick!

But I can write when she is out, and see her a long way off from these windows.

There is one that commands the road, a lovely shaded winding road, and one that just looks off over the country. A lovely country, too, full of great elms and velvet meadows.

This wallpaper has a kind of sub-pattern in a different shade, a particularly irritating one, for you can only see it in certain lights, and not clearly then.

But in the places where it isn't faded and where the sun is just so — I can see a strange, provoking, formless sort of figure that seems to skulk about behind that silly and conspicuous front design.

There's sister on the stairs!

80   Well, the Fourth of July[1] is over! The people are all gone, and I am tired out. John thought it might do me good to see a little company, so we just had Mother and Nellie and the children down for a week.

Of course I didn't do a thing. Jennie sees to everything now.

But it tired me all the same.

John says if I don't pick up faster he shall send me to Weir Mitchell[2] in the fall.

But I don't want to go there at all. I had a friend who was in his hands once, and she says he is just like John and my brother, only more so!

85   Besides, it is such an undertaking to go so far.

I don't feel as if it was worthwhile to turn my hand over for anything, and I'm getting dreadfully fretful and querulous.

I cry at nothing, and cry most of the time.

Of course I don't when John is here, or anybody else, but when I am alone.

And I am alone a good deal just now. John is kept in town very often by serious cases, and Jennie is good and lets me alone when I want her to.

90   So I walk a little in the garden or down that lovely lane, sit on the porch under the roses, and lie down up here a good deal.

I'm getting really fond of the room in spite of the wallpaper. Perhaps *because* of the wallpaper.

It dwells in my mind so!

I lie here on this great immovable bed — it is nailed down, I believe — and follow that pattern about by the hour. It is as good as gymnastics, I assure you. I start, we'll say, at the bottom, down in the corner over there where it has not been touched, and I determine for the thousandth time that I *will* follow that pointless pattern to some sort of a conclusion.

I know a little of the principle of design, and I know this thing was not arranged on any laws of radiation, or alternation, or repetition, or symmetry, or anything else that I ever heard of.

95   It is repeated, of course, by the breadths, but not otherwise.

Looked at in one way, each breadth stands alone; the bloated curves and flourishes — a kind of "debased Romanesque"[3] with delirium tremens — go waddling up and down in isolated columns of fatuity.

---

1 American Independence Day. 2 Gilman's own physician, Silas Weir Mitchell, popularized the "rest cure" for people suffering from nervous disorders. 3 style of architecture prevalent from the ninth to the twelfth century in Europe, when the Gothic style began to replace it. It is characterized by thick walls and plain, rounded arches supported by columns.

But, on the other hand, they connect diagonally, and the sprawling out-lines run off in great slanting waves of optic horror, like a lot of wallowing sea-weeds in full chase.

The whole thing goes horizontally, too, at least it seems so, and I exhaust myself trying to distinguish the order of its going in that direction.

They have used a horizontal breadth for a frieze, and that adds wonderfully to the confusion.

100 There is one end of the room where it is almost intact, and there, when the crosslights fade and the low sun shines directly upon it, I can almost fancy radiation after all — the interminable grotesque seems to form around a common center and rush off in headlong plunges of equal distraction.

It makes me tired to follow it. I will take a nap, I guess.

I don't know why I should write this.

I don't want to.

I don't feel able.

105 And I know John would think it absurd. But I *must* say what I feel and think in some way — it is such a relief!

But the effort is getting to be greater than the relief.

Half the time now I am awfully lazy, and lie down ever so much. John says I mustn't lose my strength, and has me take cod liver oil and lots of tonics and things, to say nothing of ale and wine and rare meat.

Dear John! He loves me very dearly, and hates to have me sick. I tried to have a real earnest reasonable talk with him the other day, and tell him how I wish he would let me go and make a visit to Cousin Henry and Julia.

But he said I wasn't able to go, nor able to stand it after I got there; and I did not make out a very good case for myself, for I was crying before I had finished.

110 It is getting to be a great effort for me to think straight. Just this nervous weakness, I suppose.

And dear John gathered me up in his arms, and just carried me upstairs and laid me on the bed, and sat by me and read to me till it tired my head.

He said I was his darling and his comfort and all he had, and that I must take care of myself for his sake, and keep well.

He says no one but myself can help me out of it, that I must use my will and self-control and not let any silly fancies run away with me.

There's one comfort — the baby is well and happy, and does not have to occupy this nursery with the horrid wallpaper.

115 If we had not used it, that blessed child would have! What a fortunate escape! Why, I wouldn't have a child of mine, an impressionable little thing, live in such a room for worlds.

I never thought of it before, but it is lucky that John kept me here after all; I can stand it so much easier than a baby, you see.

Of course I never mention it to them any more — I am too wise — but I keep watch for it all the same.

There are things in that wallpaper that nobody knows about but me, or ever will.

Behind that outside pattern the dim shapes get clearer every day.

120 It is always the same shape, only very numerous.

And it is like a woman stooping down and creeping about behind that pattern. I don't like it a bit. I wonder — I begin to think — I wish John would take me away from here!

It is so hard to talk with John about my case, because he is so wise, and because he loves me so.

But I tried it last night.

It was moonlight. The moon shines in all around just as the sun does.

I hate to see it sometimes, it creeps so slowly, and always comes in by one window or another.

John was asleep and I hated to waken him, so I kept still and watched the moonlight on that undulating wallpaper till I felt creepy.

The faint figure behind seemed to shake the pattern, just as if she wanted to get out.

I got up softly and went to feel and see if the paper *did* move, and when I came back John was awake.

"What is it, little girl?" he said. "Don't go walking about like that — you'll get cold."

I thought it was a good time to talk, so I told him that I really was not gaining here, and that I wished he would take me away.

"Why, darling!" said he. "Our lease will be up in three weeks, and I can't see how to leave before.

"The repairs are not done at home, and I cannot possibly leave town just now. Of course, if you were in any danger, I could and would, but you really are better, dear, whether you can see it or not. I am a doctor, dear, and I know. You are gaining flesh and color, you appetite is better, I feel really much easier about you."

"I don't weigh a bit more," said I, "nor as much; and my appetite may be better in the evening when you are here but it is worse in the morning when you are away!"

"Bless her little heart!" said he with a big hug. "She shall be as sick as she pleases! But now let's improve the shining hours by going to sleep, and talk about it in the morning!"

"And you won't go away?" I asked gloomily.

"Why, how can I, dear? It is only three weeks more and then we will take a nice little trip of a few days while Jennie is getting the house ready. Really, dear, you are better!"

"Better in body perhaps —" I began, and stopped short, for he sat up straight and looked at me with such a stern, reproachful look that I could not say another word.

"My darling," said he, "I beg of you, for my sake and for our child's sake, as well as for your own, that you will never for one instant let that idea enter your mind! There is nothing so dangerous, so fascinating, to a temperament like yours. It is a false and foolish fancy. Can you not trust me as a physician when I tell you so?"

So of course I said no more on that score, and we went to sleep before long. He thought I was asleep first, but I wasn't, and lay there for hours trying to decide whether that front pattern and the back pattern really did move together or separately.

140   On a pattern like this, by daylight, there is a lack of sequence, a defiance of law, that is a constant irritant to a normal mind.

The color is hideous enough, and unreliable enough, and infuriating enough, but the pattern is torturing.

You think you have mastered it, but just as you get well under way in following, it turns a back-somersault and there you are. It slaps you in the face, knocks you down, and tramples upon you. It is like a bad dream.

The outside pattern is a florid arabesque,[4] reminding one of a fungus. If you can imagine a toadstool in joints, an interminable string of toadstools, budding and sprouting in endless convolutions — why, that is something like it.

That is, sometimes!

145   There is one marked peculiarity about this paper, a thing nobody seems to notice but myself, and that is that it changes as the light changes.

When the sun shoots in through the east window — I always watch for that first long, straight ray — it changes so quickly that I never can quite believe it.

That is why I watch it always.

By moonlight — the moon shines in all night when there is a moon — I wouldn't know it was the same paper.

At night in any kind of light, in twilight, candlelight, lamplight, and worst of all by moonlight, it becomes bars! The outside pattern, I mean, and the woman behind it is as plain as can be.

150   I didn't realize for a long time what the thing was that showed behind, that dim sub-pattern, but now I am quite sure it is a woman.

By daylight she is subdued, quiet. I fancy it is the pattern that keeps her so still. It is so puzzling. It keeps me quiet by the hour.

I lie down ever so much now. John says it is good for me, and to sleep all I can.

Indeed he started the habit by making me lie down for an hour after each meal.

It is a very bad habit, I am convinced, for you see, I don't sleep.

155   And that cultivates deceit, for I don't tell them I'm awake — oh, no!

The fact is I am getting a little afraid of John.

He seems very queer sometimes, and even Jennie has an inexplicable look.

It strikes me occasionally, just as a scientific hypothesis, that perhaps it is the paper!

I have watched John when he did not know I was looking, and come into the room suddenly on the most innocent excuses, and I've caught him several times *looking at the paper*! And Jennie too. I caught Jennie with her hand on it once.

160   She didn't know I was in the room, and when I asked her in a quiet, a very quiet voice, with the most restrained manner possible, what she was doing with the paper, she turned around as if she had been caught stealing, and looked quite angry — asked me why I should frighten her so!

4 interwoven pattern of flowers and designs.

Then she said that the paper stained everything it touched, that she had found yellow smooches on all my clothes and John's and she wished we would be more careful!

Did not that sound innocent? But I know she was studying that pattern, and I am determined that nobody shall find it out but myself!

Life is very much more exciting now than it used to be. You see, I have something more to expect, to look forward to, to watch. I really do eat better, and am more quiet than I was.

John is so pleased to see me improve! He laughed a little the other day, and said I seemed to be flourishing in spite of my wallpaper.

165   I turned it off with a laugh. I had no intention of telling him it was *because* of the wallpaper — he would make fun of me. He might even want to take me away.

I don't want to leave now until I have found it out. There is a week more, and I think that will be enough.

I'm feeling so much better!

I don't sleep much at night, for it is so interesting to watch developments; but I sleep a good deal during the daytime.

In the daytime it is tiresome and perplexing.

170   There are always new shoots on the fungus, and new shades of yellow all over it. I cannot keep count of them, though I have tried conscientiously.

It is the strangest yellow, that wallpaper! It makes me think of all the yellow things I ever saw — not beautiful ones like buttercups, but old, foul, bad yellow things.

But there is something else about that paper — the smell! I noticed it the moment we came into the room, but with so much air and sun it was not bad. Now we have had a week of fog and rain, and whether the windows are open or not, the smell is here.

It creeps all over the house.

I find it hovering in the dining-room, skulking in the parlor, hiding in the hall, lying in wait for me on the stairs.

175   It gets into my hair.

Even when I go to ride, if I turn my head suddenly and surprise it — there is that smell!

Such a peculiar odor, too! I have spent hours in trying to analyze it, to find what it smelled like.

It is not bad — at first — and very gentle, but quite the subtlest, most enduring odor I ever met.

In this damp weather it is awful. I wake up in the night and find it hanging over me.

180   It used to disturb me at first. I thought seriously of burning the house — to reach the smell.

But now I am used to it. The only thing I can think of that it is like is the *color* of the paper! A yellow smell.

There is a very funny mark on this wall, low down, near the mopboard. A streak that runs round the room. It goes behind every piece of furniture, except the bed, a long, straight, even *smooch*, as if it had been rubbed over and over.

I wonder how it was done and who did it, and what they did it for. Round and round and round — round and round and round — it makes me dizzy!

I really have discovered something at last.

185 Through watching so much at night, when it changes so, I have finally found out.

The front pattern *does* move — and no wonder! The woman behind shakes it!

Sometimes I think there are a great many women behind, and sometimes only one, and she crawls around fast, and her crawling shakes it all over.

Then in the very bright spots she keeps still, and in the very shady spots she just takes hold of the bars and shakes them hard.

And she is all the time trying to climb through. But nobody could climb through that pattern — it strangles so; I think that is why it has so many heads.

190 They get through, and then the pattern strangles them off and turns them upside down, and makes their eyes white!

If those heads were covered or taken off it would not be half so bad.

I think that woman gets out in the daytime!

And I'll tell you why — privately — I've seen her!

I can see her out of every one of my windows!

195 It is the same woman, I know, for she is always creeping, and most women do not creep by daylight.

I see her in that long shaded lane, creeping up and down. I see her in those dark grape arbors, creeping all around the garden.

I see her on that long road under the trees, creeping along, and when a carriage comes she hides under the blackberry vines.

I don't blame her a bit. It must be very humiliating to be caught creeping by daylight!

I always lock the door when I creep by daylight. I can't do it at night, for I know John would suspect something at once.

200 And John is so queer now that I don't want to irritate him. I wish he would take another room! Besides, I don't want anybody to get that woman out at night but myself.

I often wonder if I could see her out of all the windows at once.

But, turn as fast as I can, I can only see out of one at one time.

And though I always see her, she *may* be able to creep faster than I can turn! I have watched her sometimes away off in the open country, creeping as fast as a cloud shadow in a wind.

If only that top pattern could be gotten off from the under one! I mean to try it, little by little.

205 I have found out another funny thing, but I shan't tell it this time! It does not do to trust people too much.

There are only two more days to get this paper off, and I believe John is beginning to notice. I don't like the look in his eyes.

And I heard him ask Jennie a lot of professional questions about me. She had a very good report to give.

She said I slept a good deal in the daytime.

John knows I don't sleep very well at night, for all I'm so quiet!

He asked me all sorts of questions, too, and pretended to be very loving and kind.

As if I couldn't see through him!

Still, I don't wonder he acts so, sleeping under this paper for three months.

It only interests me, but I feel sure John and Jennie are affected by it.

Hurrah! This is the last day, but it is enough. John is to stay in town over night, and won't be out until this evening.

Jennie wanted to sleep with me — the sly thing; but I told her I should undoubtedly rest better for a night all alone.

That was clever, for really I wasn't alone a bit! As soon as it was moonlight and that poor thing began to crawl and shake the pattern, I got up and ran to help her.

I pulled and she shook. I shook and she pulled, and before morning we had peeled off yards of that paper.

A strip about as high as my head and half around the room.

And then when the sun came and that awful pattern began to laugh at me, I declared I would finish it today!

We go away tomorrow, and they are moving all my furniture down again to leave things as they were before.

Jennie looked at the wall in amazement, but I told her merrily that I did it out of pure spite at the vicious thing.

She laughed and said she wouldn't mind doing it herself, but I must not get tired.

How she betrayed herself that time!

But I am here, and no person touches this paper but Me — not *alive*!

She tried to get me out of the room — it was too patent! But I said it was so quiet and empty and clean now that I believed I would lie down again and sleep all I could, and not to wake me even for dinner — I would call when I woke.

So now she is gone, and the servants are gone, and the things are gone, and there is nothing left but that great bedstead nailed down, with the canvas mattress we found on it.

We shall sleep downstairs tonight, and take the boat home tomorrow.

I quite enjoy the room, now it is bare again.

How those children did tear about here!

This bedstead is fairly gnawed!

But I must get to work.

I have locked the door and thrown the key down into the front path.

I don't want to go out, and I don't want to have anybody come in, till John comes.

I want to astonish him.

I've got a rope up here that even Jennie did not find. If that woman does get out, and tries to get away, I can tie her!

But I forgot I could not reach far without anything to stand on!

This bed will *not* move!

I tried to lift and push it until I was lame, and then I got so angry I bit off a little piece at one corner — but it hurt my teeth.

Then I peeled off all the paper I could reach standing on the floor. It sticks horribly and the pattern just enjoys it! All those strangled heads and bulbous eyes and waddling fungus growths just shriek with derision!

I am getting angry enough to do something desperate. To jump out of the window would be admirable exercise, but the bars are too strong even to try.

Besides I wouldn't do it. Of course not. I know well enough that a step like that is improper and might be misconstrued.

I don't like to *look* out of the windows even — there are so many of those creeping women, and they creep so fast.

I wonder if they all come out of that wallpaper as I did?

But I am securely fastened now by my well-hidden rope — you don't get *me* out in the road there!

I suppose I shall have to get back behind the pattern when it comes night, and that is hard!

It is so pleasant to be out in this great room and creep around as I please!

I don't want to go outside. I won't, even if Jennie asks me to.

For outside you have to creep on the ground, and everything is green instead of yellow.

But here I can creep smoothly on the floor, and my shoulder just fits in that long smooch around the wall, so I cannot lose my way.

Why, there's John at the door!

It is no use, young man, you can't open it!

How he does call and pound!

Now he's crying to Jennie for an axe.

It would be a shame to break down that beautiful door!

"John, dear!" said I in the gentlest voice. "The key is down by the front steps, under a plantain leaf!"

That silenced him for a few moments.

Then he said, very quietly indeed, "Open the door, my darling!"

"I can't," said I. "The key is down by the front door under a plantain leaf!" And then I said it again, several times, very gently and slowly, and said it so often that he had to go and see, and he got it of course, and came in. He stopped short by the door.

"What is the matter?" he cried. "For God's sake, what are you doing!"

I kept on creeping just the same, but I looked at him over my shoulder.

"I've got out at last," said I, "in spite of you and Jane. And I've pulled off most of the paper, so you can't put me back!"

Now why should that man have fainted? But he did, and right across my path by the wall, so that I had to creep over him every time!

(1892)

Sir Charles G. D. Roberts (1860–1943)

Along with fellow Canadian Ernest Thompson Seton, Roberts is considered one of the foremost writers of realistic animal stories. Among his best-known works are the novel *Red Fox* (1905) and several collections of short animal stories, including *The Kindred of the Wild* (1902), from which "When Twilight Falls on the Stump Lots" is taken. He was a careful observer of the habits of wild creatures; however, he went far beyond presenting accurate descriptions of his animal characters. "Having got one's facts right," he once commented, "enough of them to generalize from safely, — the exciting adventure lies in the effort to 'get under the skins' ... to discern their motives, to understand and chart their simple mental processes." In "When Twilight Falls," the animals are given human characteristics through the use of such terms as "rapturously," "ecstatic," and "coveted." The story is structured around a series of contrasts such as life and death, children and parents, civilization and nature, human beings and animals. The main setting, a semi-cleared rural area, is the place in which the opposites clash. Although human beings are not directly present, they have profound impact on the lives of the central characters.

WHEN TWILIGHT FALLS ON THE STUMP LOTS

The wet, chill first of the spring, its blackness made tender by the lilac wash of the afterglow, lay upon the high, open stretches of the stump lots. The winter-whitened stumps, the sparse patches of juniper and bay just budding, the rough-mossed hillocks, the harsh boulders here and there up-thrusting from the soil, the swampy hollows wherein a coarse grass began to show green, all seemed anointed, as it were, to an ecstasy of peace by the chrism of that paradisal colour. Against the lucid immensity of the April sky the thin tops of five or six soaring ram-pikes aspired like violet flames. Along the skirts of the stump lots a fir wood reared a ragged-crested wall of black against the red amber of the horizon.

Late that afternoon, beside a juniper thicket not far from the centre of the stump lots, a young black and white cow had given birth to her first calf. The little animal had been licked assiduously by the mother's caressing tongue till its colour began to show a rich dark red. Now it had struggled to its feet, and, with its disproportionately long, thick legs braced wide apart, was beginning to nurse. Its blunt wet muzzle and thick lips tugged eagerly, but somewhat blunderingly as yet, at the unaccustomed teats; and its tail lifted, twitching with delight, as the first warm streams of mother milk went down its throat. It was a pathetically awkward, unlovely little figure, not yet advanced to that youngling winsomeness which is the heritage, to some degree and at some period, of the infancy of all the kindreds that breathe upon the earth. But to the young mother's eyes it was the most beautiful of things. With her head twisted far around, she nosed and licked its heaving flanks as it nursed; and between deep, ecstatic breathings she uttered in her throat low murmurs, unspeakably tender, of encouragement and caress. The delicate but pervading flood of sunset colour had the effect of blending the ruddy-hued calf into the tones of the landscape; but the cow's insistent blotches of black and white stood out sharply, refusing to harmonise. The drench of violet light was of no avail to soften their staring contrasts. They made her vividly conspicuous across the whole breadth of the stump lots, to eyes that watched her from the forest coverts.

The eyes that watched her — long, fixedly, hungrily — were small and red. They belonged to a lank she-bear, whose gaunt flanks and rusty coat proclaimed a season of famine in the wilderness. She could not see the calf, which was hidden by a hillock and some juniper scrub; but its presence was very legibly conveyed to her by the mother's solicitous watchfulness. After a motionless scrutiny from behind the screen of fir branches, the lean bear stole noiselessly forth from the shadows into the great wash of violet light. Step by step, and very slowly, with the patience that endures because confident of its object, she crept toward that oasis of mothering joy in the vast emptiness of the stump lots. Now crouching, now crawling, turning to this side and to that, taking advantage of every hollow, every thicket, every hillock, every aggressive stump, her craft succeeded in eluding even the wild and menacing watchfulness of the young mother's eyes.

The spring had been a trying one for the lank she-bear. Her den, in a dry tract of hemlock wood some furlongs back from the stump lots, was a snug little cave under the uprooted base of a lone pine, which had somehow grown up among the alien hemlocks only to draw down upon itself at last, by its superior height, the fury of a passing hurricane. The winter had contributed but scanty snowfall to cover the bear in her sleep; and the March thaws, unseasonably early and ardent, had called her forth to activity weeks too soon. Then frosts had come with belated severity, sealing away the budding tubers, which are the bear's chief dependence for spring diet; and worst of all, a long stretch of intervale meadow by the neighbouring river, which had once been rich in ground-nuts, had been ploughed up the previous spring and subjected to the producing of oats and corn. When she was feeling the pinch of meagre rations, and when the fat which a liberal autumn of blueberries had laid up about her ribs was getting as shrunken as the last snow in the thickets, she gave birth to two hairless and hungry little cubs. They were very blind, and ridiculously small to be born of so big a mother; and having so much growth to make during the next few months, their appetites were immeasurable. They tumbled, and squealed, and tugged at their mother's teats, and grew astonishingly, and made huge haste to cover their bodies with fur of a soft and silken black; and all this vitality of theirs made a strenuous demand upon their mother's milk. There were no more bee-trees left in the neighbourhood. The long wanderings which she was forced to take in her search for roots and tubers were in themselves a drain upon her nursing powers. At last, reluctant though she was to attract the hostile notice of the settlement, she found herself forced to hunt on the borders of the sheep pastures. Before all else in life was it important to her that these two tumbling little ones in the den should not go hungry. Their eyes were open now — small and dark and whimsical, their ears quaintly large and inquiring for their roguish little faces. Had she not been driven by the unkind season to so much hunting and foraging, she would have passed near all her time rapturously in the den under the pine root, fondling those two soft miracles of her world.

With the killing of three lambs — at widely scattered points, so as to mislead retaliation — things grew a little easier for the harassed bear; and presently she grew bolder in tampering with the creatures under man's protection. With one swift, secret blow of her mighty paw she struck down a young ewe which had strayed within reach of her hiding-place. Dragging her prey deep into the wood, she fared well upon it for some days, and was happy with her growing cubs. It was just when she had begun to feel the fasting which came upon the exhaustion of this store that, in a hungry hour, she sighed the conspicuous markings of the black-and-white cow.

It is altogether unusual for the black bear of the eastern woods to attack any quarry so large as a cow, unless under the spur of fierce hunger or fierce rage. The she-bear was powerful beyond her fellows. She had the strongest possible incentive to bold hunting, and she had lately grown confident beyond her wont. Nevertheless, when she began her careful stalking of this big game which she coveted, she had no definite intention of forcing a battle with the cow. She had observed that cows, accustomed to the protection of man, would at times leave their calves asleep and stray off some distance in their pasturing. She had even seen calves left all by themselves in a field, from morning till night, and had wondered at such negligence in their mothers. Now she had a confident idea that sooner or later the calf would lie down to sleep, and the young mother roam a little wide in search of the scant young grass. Very softly, very self-effacingly, she crept nearer step by step, following up the wind, till at last, undiscovered, she was crouching behind a thick patch of juniper, on the slope of a little hollow not ten paces distant from the cow and the calf.

By this time the tender violet light was fading to a grayness over hillock and hollow; and with the deepening of the twilight the faint breeze, which had been breathing from the northward, shifted suddenly and came in slow, warm pulsations out of the south. At the same time the calf, having nursed sufficiently, and feeling his baby legs tired of the weight they had not yet learned to carry, laid himself down. On this the cow shifted her position. She turned half round, and lifted her head high. As she did so a scent of peril was borne in upon her fine nostrils. She recognised it instantly. With a snort of anger she sniffed again; then stamped a challenge with her fore hoofs, and levelled the lance-points of her horns toward the menace. The next moment her eyes, made keen by the fear of love, detected the black outline of the bear's head through the coarse screen of the juniper. Without a second's hesitation, she flung up her tail, gave a short bellow, and charged.

The moment she saw herself detected, the bear rose upon her hindquarters; nevertheless she was in a measure surprised by the sudden blind fury of the attack. Nimbly she swerved to avoid it, aiming at the same time a stroke with her mighty forearm, which, if it had found its mark, would have smashed her adversary's neck. But as she struck out, in the act of shifting her position, a depression of the ground threw her off her balance. The next instant one sharp horn caught her slantingly in the flank, ripping its way upward and inward, while the mad impact threw her upon her back.

Grappling, she had her assailant's head and shoulders in a trap, and her gigantic claws cut through the flesh and sinew like knives; but at the desperate disadvantage of her position she could inflict no disabling blow. The cow, on the other hand, though mutilated and streaming with blood, kept pounding with her whole massive weight, and with short tremendous shocks crushing the breath from her foe's ribs.

10   Presently, wrenching herself free, the cow drew off for another battering charge; and as she did so the bear hurled herself violently down the slope, and gained her feet behind a dense thicket of bay shrub. The cow, with one eye blinded and the other obscured by blood, glared around for her in vain, then, in a panic of mother terror, plunged back to her calf.

Snatching at the respite, the bear crouched down, craving that invisibility which is the most faithful shield of the furtive kindred. Painfully, and leaving a drenched red trail behind her, she crept off from the disastrous neighbourhood. Soon the deepening twilight sheltered her. But she could not make haste; and she knew that death was close upon her.

Once within the woods, she struggled straight toward the den that held her young. She hungered to die licking them. But destiny is as implacable as iron to the wilderness people, and even this was denied her. Just a half score of paces from the lair in the pine root, her hour descended upon her. There was a sudden redder and fuller gush upon the trail; the last light of longing faded out of her eyes; and she lay down upon her side.

The merry little cubs within the den were beginning to expect her, and getting restless. As the night wore on, and no mother came, they ceased to be merry. By morning they were shivering with hunger and desolate fear. But the doom of the ancient wood was less harsh than its wont, and spared them some days of starving anguish; for about noon a pair of foxes discovered the dead mother, astutely estimated the situation, and then, with the boldness of good appetite, made their way into the unguarded den.

As for the red calf, its fortune was ordinary. Its mother, for all her wounds, was able to nurse and cherish it through the night; and with morning came a searcher from the farm and took it, with the bleeding mother, safely back to the settlement. There it was tended and fattened, and within a few weeks found its way to the cool marble slabs of a city market.

(1902)

Stephen Crane (1871–1900)

Before his death from tuberculosis at age 28, New Jersey–born Stephen Crane had published short stories, poetry, and a novel, *The Red Badge of Courage* (1896). One of a group of authors now known as naturalists, who rejected traditional social and religious beliefs as invalid, Crane examined the courage of individuals living in a world in which victory or defeat in struggles was a matter of chance. "The Open Boat," which was highly praised by both Joseph Conrad and Ernest Hemingway, is based on personal experience. Travelling to Cuba as a newspaper correspondent, Crane had been one of three survivors of a shipwreck off the Atlantic coast of Florida. In a newspaper account published a few days after his rescue, Crane focussed on the events leading to the sinking of the vessel, giving only a few sentences in the final paragraph to the time spent in the lifeboat and the rescue. Subtitled "A Tale Intended to Be after the Fact," "The Open Boat" explores the four men's 30 hours in the three-metre dinghy, examining their growing camaraderie and the correspondent's developing awareness of the impersonality of nature.

THE OPEN BOAT

A Tale Intended to Be after the Fact. Being the Experience of Four Men from the Sunk Steamer 'Commodore'

I

None of them knew the colour of the sky. Their eyes glanced level, and were fastened upon the waves that swept toward them. These waves were of the hue of slate, save for the tops, which were of foaming white, and all of the men knew the colours of the sea. The horizon narrowed and widened, and dipped and rose, and at all times its edge was jagged with waves that seemed thrust up in points like rocks.

Many a man ought to have a bath-tub larger than the boat which here rode upon the sea. These waves were most wrongfully and barbarously abrupt and tall, and each froth-top was a problem in small boat navigation.

The cook squatted in the bottom and looked with both eyes at the six inches of gunwale which separated him from the ocean. His sleeves were rolled over his fat forearms, and the two flaps of his unbuttoned vest dangled as he bent to bail out the boat. Often he said: "Gawd! That was a narrow clip." As he remarked it he invariably gazed eastward over the broken sea.

The oiler, steering with one of the two oars in the boat, sometimes raised himself suddenly to keep clear of water that swirled in over the stern. It was a thin little oar and it seemed often ready to snap.

5   The correspondent, pulling at the other oar, watched the waves and wondered why he was there.

The injured captain, lying in the bow, was at this time buried in that profound dejection and indifference which comes, temporarily at least, to even the bravest and most enduring when, willy nilly, the firm fails, the army loses, the ship goes down. The mind of the master of a vessel is rooted deep in the timbers of her, though he commanded for a day or a decade, and this captain had on him the stern impression of a scene in the greys of dawn of seven turned faces, and later a stump of a top-mast with a white ball on it that slashed to and fro at the waves, went low and lower, and down. Thereafter there was something strange in his voice. Although steady, it was deep with mourning, and of a quality beyond oration or tears.

"Keep 'er a little more south, Billie," said he.

"'A little more south,' sir," said the oiler in the stern.

A seat in this boat was not unlike a seat upon a bucking broncho, and, by the same token, a broncho is not much smaller. The craft pranced and reared, and plunged like an animal. As each wave came, and she rose for it, she seemed like a horse making at a fence outrageously high. The manner of her scramble over these walls of water is a mystic thing, and, moreover, at the top of them were ordinarily these problems in white water, the foam racing down from the summit of each wave, requiring a new leap, and a leap from the air. Then, after scornfully bumping a crest, she would slide, and race, and splash down a long incline, and arrive bobbing and nodding in front of the next menace.

A singular disadvantage of the sea lies in the fact that after successfully surmounting one wave you discover that there is another behind it just as important and just as nervously anxious to do something effective in the way of swamping boats. In a ten-foot dingey one can get an idea of the resources of the sea in the line of waves that is not probable to the average experience, which is never at sea in a dingey. As each salty wall of water approached, it shut all else from the view of the men in the boat, and it was not difficult to imagine that this particular wave was the final outburst of the ocean, the last effort of the grim water. There was a terrible grace in the move of the waves, and they came in silence, save for the snarling of the crests.

In the wan light, the faces of the men must have been grey. Their eyes must have glinted in strange ways as they gazed steadily astern. Viewed from a balcony, the whole thing would doubtlessly have been weirdly picturesque. But the men in the boat had no time to see it, and if they had had leisure there were other things to occupy their minds. The sun swung steadily up the sky, and they knew it was broad day because the colour of the sea changed from slate to emerald-green, streaked with amber lights, and the foam was like tumbling snow. The process of the breaking day was unknown to them. They were aware only of this effect upon the colour of the waves that rolled toward them.

In disjointed sentences the cook and the correspondent argued as to the difference between a life-saving station and a house of refuge. The cook had said: "There's a house of refuge just north of the Mosquito Inlet Light,[1] and as soon as they see us, they'll come off in their boat and pick us up."

"As soon as who see us?" said the correspondent.

"The crew," said the cook.

10

1 located on the Atlantic coast of northern Florida.

15 "Houses of refuge don't have crews," said the correspondent. "As I understand them, they are only places where clothes and grub are stored for the
benefit of shipwrecked people. They don't carry crews."

"Oh, yes, they do," said the cook.

"No, they don't," said the correspondent.

"Well, we're not there yet, anyhow," said the oiler, in the stern.

"Well," said the cook, "perhaps it's not a house of refuge that I'm thinking of as being near Mosquito Inlet Light. Perhaps it's a life-saving station."

20 "We're not there yet," said the oiler, in the stern.

II

As the boat bounced from the top of each wave, the wind tore through the hair
of the hatless men, and as the craft plopped her stern down again the spray
slashed past them. The crest of each of these waves was a hill, from the top of
which the men surveyed, for a moment, a broad tumultuous expanse, shining
and wind-riven. It was probably splendid. It was probably glorious, this play of
the free sea, wild with lights of emerald and white and amber.

"Bully good thing it's an on-shore wind," said the cook. "If not, where
would we be? Wouldn't have a show."

"That's right," said the correspondent.

The busy oiler nodded his assent.

25 Then the captain, in the bow, chuckled in a way that expressed humour,
contempt, tragedy, all in one. "Do you think we've got much of a show now,
boys?" said he.

Whereupon the three were silent, save for a trifle of hemming and hawing.
To express any particular optimism at this time they felt to be childish and
stupid, but they all doubtless possessed this sense of the situation in their
mind. A young man thinks doggedly at such times. On the other hand, the
ethics of their condition was decidedly against any open suggestion of hopelessness. So they were silent.

"Oh, well," said the captain, soothing his children, "we'll get ashore all
right."

But there was that in his tone which made them think, so the oiler quoth:
"Yes! If this wind holds!"

The cook was bailing: "Yes! If we don't catch hell in the surf."

30 Canton flannel gulls flew near and far. Sometimes they sat down on the
sea, near patches of brown seaweed that rolled over the waves with a movement
like carpets on a line in a gale. The birds sat comfortably in groups, and they
were envied by some in the dingey, for the wrath of the sea was no more to
them than it was to a covey of prairie chickens a thousand miles inland. Often
they came very close and stared at the men with black bead-like eyes. At
these times they were uncanny and sinister in their unblinking scrutiny, and
the men hooted angrily at them, telling them to be gone. One came, and evidently decided to alight on the top of the captain's head. The bird flew parallel
to the boat and did not circle, but made short sidelong jumps in the air in

chicken-fashion. His black eyes were wistfully fixed upon the captain's head. "Ugly brute," said the oiler to the bird. "You look as if you were made with a jack-knife." The cook and the correspondent swore darkly at the creature. The captain naturally wished to knock it away with the end of the heavy painter; but he did not dare do it, because anything resembling an emphatic gesture would have capsized this freighted boat, and so with his open hand, the captain gently and carefully waved the gull away. After it had been discouraged from the pursuit the captain breathed easier on account of his hair, and others breathed easier because the bird struck their minds at this time as being somehow grewsome and ominous.

In the meantime the oiler and the correspondent rowed. And also they rowed.

They sat together in the same seat, and each rowed an oar. Then the oiler took both oars; then the correspondent took both oars; then the oiler; then the correspondent. They rowed and they rowed. The very ticklish part of the business was when the time came for the reclining one in the stern to take his turn at the oars. By the very last star of truth, it is easier to steal eggs from under a hen than it was to change seats in the dingey. First the man in the stern slid his hand along the thwart and moved with care, as if he were of Sèvres.[2] Then the man in the rowing seat slid his hand along the other thwart. It was all done with the most extraordinary care. As the two sidled past each other, the whole party kept watchful eyes on the coming wave, and the captain cried: "Look out now! Steady there!"

The brown mats of sea-weed that appeared from time to time were like islands, bits of earth. They were travelling, apparently, neither one way nor the other. They were, to all intents, stationary. They informed the men in the boat that it was making progress slowly toward the land.

The captain, rearing cautiously in the bow, after the dingey soared on a great swell, said that he had seen the lighthouse at Mosquito Inlet. Presently the cook remarked that he had seen it. The correspondent was at the oars then, and for some reason he too wished to look at the lighthouse, but his back was toward the far shore and the waves were important, and for some time he could not seize an opportunity to turn his head. But at last there came a wave more gentle than the others, and when at the crest of it he swiftly scoured the western horizon.

35   "See it?" said the captain.

"No," said the correspondent slowly, "I didn't see anything."

"Look again," said the captain. He pointed. "It's exactly in that direction."

At the top of another wave, the correspondent did as he was bid, and this time his eyes chanced on a small still thing on the edge of the swaying horizon. It was precisely like the point of a pin. It took an anxious eye to find a lighthouse so tiny.

"Think we'll make it, captain?"

40   "If this wind holds and the boat don't swamp, we can't do much else," said the captain.

---

2 beautiful, delicate porcelain made in the commune of the same name on the Seine River in northern France.

The little boat, lifted by each towering sea, and splashed viciously by the crests, made progress that in the absence of seaweed was not apparent to those in her. She seemed just a wee thing wallowing, miraculously top-up, at the mercy of five oceans. Occasionally, a great spread of water, like white flames, swarmed into her.

"Bail her, cook," said the captain serenely.

"All right, captain," said the cheerful cook.

III

It would be difficult to describe the subtle brotherhood of men that was here established on the seas. No one said that it was so. No one mentioned it. But it dwelt in the boat, and each man felt it warm him. They were a captain, an oiler, a cook, and a correspondent, and they were friends, friends in a more curiously iron-bound degree than may be common. The hurt captain, lying against the water-jar in the bow, spoke always in a low voice and calmly, but he could never command a more ready and swiftly obedient crew than the motley three of the dingey. It was more than a mere recognition of what was best for the common safety. There was surely in it a quality that was personal and heart-felt. And after this devotion to the commander of the boat there was this comradeship that the correspondent, for instance, who had been taught to be cynical of men, knew even at the time was the best experience of his life. But no one said that it was so. No one mentioned it.

45   "I wish we had a sail," remarked the captain. "We might try my overcoat on the end of an oar and give you two boys a chance to rest." So the cook and the correspondent held the mast and spread wide the overcoat. The oiler steered, and the little boat made good way with her new rig. Sometimes the oiler had to scull sharply to keep a sea from breaking into the boat, but otherwise sailing was a success.

Meanwhile the lighthouse had been growing slowly larger. It had now almost assumed colour, and appeared like a little grey shadow on the sky. The man at the oars could not be prevented from turning his head rather often to try for a glimpse of this little grey shadow.

At last, from the top of each wave the men in the tossing boat could see land. Even as the lighthouse was an upright shadow on the sky, this land seemed but a long black shadow on the sea. It certainly was thinner than paper. "We must be about opposite New Smyrna,"[3] said the cook, who had coasted this shore often in schooners. "Captain, by the way, I believe they abandoned that life-saving station there about a year ago."

"Did they?" said the captain.

The wind slowly died away. The cook and the correspondent were not now obliged to slave in order to hold high the oar. But the waves continued their old impetuous swooping at the dingey, and the little craft, no longer under way, struggled woundily over them. The oiler or the correspondent took the oars again.

3 located 25 kilometres south of Daytona Beach.

50 Shipwrecks are *à propos* of nothing. If men could only train for them and have them occur when the men had reached pink condition, there would be less drowning at sea. Of the four in the dingey none had slept any time worth mentioning for two days and two nights previous to embarking in the dingey, and in the excitement of clambering about the deck of a foundering ship they had also forgotten to eat heartily.

For these reasons, and for others, neither the oiler nor the correspondent was fond of rowing at this time. The correspondent wondered ingenuously how in the name of all that was sane could there be people who thought it amusing to row a boat. It was not an amusement; it was a diabolical punishment, and even a genius of mental aberrations could never conclude that it was anything but a horror to the muscles and a crime against the back. He mentioned to the boat in general how the amusement of rowing struck him, and the weary-faced oiler smiled in full sympathy. Previously to the foundering, by the way, the oiler had worked double-watch in the engine-room of the ship.

"Take her easy, now, boys," said the captain. "Don't spend yourselves. If we have to run a surf you'll need all your strength, because we'll sure have to swim for it. Take your time."

Slowly the land arose from the sea. From a black line it became a line of black and a line of white, trees and sand. Finally, the captain said that he could make out a house on the shore. "That's the house of refuge, sure," said the cook. "They'll see us before long, and come out after us."

The distant lighthouse reared high. "The keeper ought to be able to make us out now, if he's looking through a glass," said the captain. "He'll notify the life-saving people."

55 "None of those other boats could have got ashore to give word of the wreck," said the oiler, in a low voice. "Else the lifeboat would be out hunting us."

Slowly and beautifully the land loomed out of the sea. The wind came again. It had veered from the north-east to the south-east. Finally, a new sound struck the ears of the men in the boat. It was the low thunder of the surf on the shore. "We'll never be able to make the lighthouse now," said the captain. "Swing her head a little more north, Billie," said he.

"'A little more north,' sir," said the oiler.

Whereupon the little boat turned her nose once more down the wind, and all but the oarsman watched the shore grow. Under the influence of this expansion doubt and direful apprehension was leaving the minds of the men. The management of the boat was still most absorbing, but it could not prevent a quiet cheerfulness. In an hour, perhaps, they would be ashore.

Their backbones had become thoroughly used to balancing in the boat, and they now rode this wild colt of a dingey like circus men. The correspondent thought that he had been drenched to the skin, but happening to feel in the top pocket of his coat, he found therein eight cigars. Four of them were soaked with sea-water; four were perfectly scatheless. After a search, somebody produced three dry matches, and thereupon the four waifs rode impudently in their little boat, and with an assurance of an impending rescue shining in their eyes, puffed at the big cigars and judged well and ill of all men. Everybody took a drink of water.

IV

60 "Cook," remarked the captain, "there don't seem to be any signs of life about your house of refuge."

"No," replied the cook. "Funny they don't see us!"

A broad stretch of lowly coast lay before the eyes of the men. It was of dunes topped with dark vegetation. The roar of the surf was plain, and sometimes they could see the white lip of a wave as it spun up the beach. A tiny house was blocked out black upon the sky. Southward, the slim lighthouse lifted its little grey length.

Tide, wind, and waves were swinging the dingey northward. "Funny they don't see us," said the men.

The surf's roar was here dulled, but its tone was, nevertheless, thunderous and mighty. As the boat swam over the great rollers, the men sat listening to this roar. "We'll swamp sure," said everybody.

65 It is fair to say here that there was not a life-saving station within twenty miles in either direction, but the men did not know this fact, and in consequence they made dark and opprobrious remarks concerning the eyesight of the nation's life-savers. Four scowling men sat in the dingey and surpassed records in the invention of epithets.

"Funny they don't see us."

The light-heartedness of a former time had completely failed. To their sharpened minds it was easy to conjure pictures of all kinds of incompetency and blindness and, indeed, cowardice. There was the shore of the populous land, and it was bitter and bitter to them that from it came no sign.

"Well," said the captain, ultimately, "I suppose we'll have to make a try for ourselves. If we stay out here too long, we'll none of us have strength left to swim after the boat swamps."

And so the oiler, who was at the oars, turned the boat straight for the shore. There was a sudden tightening of muscles. There was some thinking.

70 "If we don't all get ashore —" said the captain. "If we don't all get ashore, I suppose you fellows know where to send news of my finish?"

They then briefly exchanged some addresses and admonitions. As for the reflections of the men, there was a great deal of rage in them. Perchance they might be formulated thus: "If I am going to be drowned — if I am going to be drowned — if I am going to be drowned, why, in the name of the seven mad gods who rule the sea, was I allowed to come thus far and contemplate sand and trees? Was I brought here merely to have my nose dragged away as I was about to nibble the sacred cheese of life? It is preposterous. If this old ninny-woman, Fate, cannot do better than this, she should be deprived of the management of men's fortunes. She is an old hen who knows not her intention. If she has decided to drown me, why did she not do it in the beginning and save me all this trouble? The whole affair is absurd. . . . But no, she cannot mean to drown me. She dare not drown me. She cannot drown me. Not after all this work." Afterward the man might have had an impulse to shake his fist at the clouds: "Just you drown me, now, and then hear what I call you!"

The billows that came at this time were more formidable. They seemed always just about to break and roll over the little boat in a turmoil of foam.

There was a preparatory and long growl in the speech of them. No mind unused to the sea would have concluded that the dingey could ascend these sheer heights in time. The shore was still afar. The oiler was a wily surfman. "Boys," he said swiftly, "she won't live three minutes more, and we're too far out to swim. Shall I take her to sea again, captain?"

"Yes! Go ahead!" said the captain.

This oiler, by a series of quick miracles, and fast and steady oarsmanship, turned the boat in the middle of the surf and took her safely to sea again.

75 There was a considerable silence as the boat bumped over the furrowed sea to deeper water. Then somebody in gloom spoke. "Well, anyhow, they must have seen us from the shore by now."

The gulls went in slanting flight up the wind toward the grey desolate east. A squall, marked by dingy clouds, and clouds brick-red, like smoke from a burning building, appeared from the south-east.

"What do you think of those life-saving people? Ain't they peaches?"

"Funny they haven't seen us."

"Maybe they think we're out here for sport! Maybe they think we're fishin'. Maybe they think we're damned fools."

80 It was a long afternoon. A changed tide tried to force them southward, but wind and wave said northward. Far ahead, where coast-line, sea, and sky formed their mighty angle, there were little dots which seemed to indicate a city on the shore.

"St. Augustine?"[4]

The captain shook his head. "Too near Mosquito Inlet."

And the oiler rowed, and then the correspondent rowed. Then the oiler rowed. It was a weary business. The human back can become the seat of more aches and pains than are registered in books for the composite anatomy of a regiment. It is a limited area, but it can become the theatre of innumerable muscular conflicts, tangles, wrenches, knots, and other comforts.

"Did you ever like to row, Billie?" asked the correspondent.

85 "No," said the oiler. "Hang it."

When one exchanged the rowing-seat for a place in the bottom of the boat, he suffered a bodily depression that caused him to be careless of everything save an obligation to wiggle one finger. There was cold sea-water swashing to and fro in the boat, and he lay in it. His head, pillowed on a thwart, was within an inch of the swirl of a wave crest, and sometimes a particularly obstreperous sea came in-board and drenched him once more. But these matters did not annoy him. It is almost certain that if the boat had capsized he would have tumbled comfortably out upon the ocean as if he felt sure that it was a great soft mattress.

"Look! There's a man on the shore!"

"Where?"

"There! See 'im? See 'im?"

90 "Yes, sure! He's walking along."

"Now he's stopped. Look! He's facing us!"

"He's waving at us!"

4 city on the Atlantic coast of northern Florida.

"So he is! By thunder!"

"Ah, now we're all right! Now we're all right! There'll be a boat out here for us in half-an-hour."

95 "He's going on. He's running. He's going up to that house there."

The remote beach seemed lower than the sea, and it required a searching glance to discern the little black figure. The captain saw a floating stick and they rowed to it. A bath-towel was by some weird chance in the boat, and, tying this on the stick, the captain waved it. The oarsman did not dare turn his head, so he was obliged to ask questions.

"What's he doing now?"

"He's standing still again. He's looking, I think.... There he goes again. Towards the house.... Now he's stopped again."

"Is he waving at us?"

100 "No, not now! he was, though."

"Look! There comes another man!"

"He's running."

"Look at him go, would you."

"Why, he's on a bicycle. Now he's met the other man. They're both waving at us. Look!"

105 "There comes something up the beach."

"What the devil is that thing?"

"Why, it looks like a boat."

"Why, certainly it's a boat."

"No, it's on wheels."

110 "Yes, so it is. Well, that must be the life-boat. They drag them along shore on a wagon."

"That's the life-boat, sure."

"No, by —, it's — it's an omnibus."

"I tell you it's a life-boat."

"It is not! It's an omnibus. I can see it plain. See? One of these big hotel omnibuses."

115 "By thunder, you're right. It's an omnibus, sure as fate. What do you suppose they are doing with an omnibus? Maybe they are going around collecting the life-crew, hey?"

"That's it, likely. Look! There's a fellow waving a little black flag. He's standing on the steps of the omnibus. There come those other two fellows. Now they're all talking together. Look at the fellow with the flag. Maybe he ain't waving it."

"That ain't a flag, is it? That's his coat. Why certainly, that's his coat."

"So it is. It's his coat. He's taken it off and is waving it around his head. But would you look at him swing it."

"Oh, say, there isn't any life-saving station there. That's just a winter resort hotel omnibus that has brought over some of the boarders to see us drown."

120 "What's that idiot with the coat mean? What's he signaling, anyhow?"

"It looks as if he were trying to tell us to go north. There must be a life-saving station up there."

"No! He thinks we're fishing. Just giving us a merry hand. See? Ah, there, Willie."

"Well, I wish I could make something out of those signals. What do you suppose he means?"

"He don't mean anything. He's just playing."

"Well, if he'd just signal us to try the surf again, or to go to sea and wait, or go north, or go south, or go to hell — there would be some reason in it. But look at him. He just stands there and keeps his coat revolving like a wheel. The ass!"

"There come more people."

"Now there's quite a mob. Look! Isn't that a boat?"

"Where? Oh, I see where you mean. No, that's no boat."

"That fellow is still waving his coat."

"He must think we like to see him do that. Why don't he quit it? It don't mean anything."

"I don't know. I think he is trying to make us go north. It must be that there's a life-saving station there somewhere."

"Say, he ain't tired yet. Look at 'im wave."

"Wonder how long he can keep that up. He's been revolving his coat ever since he caught sight of us. He's an idiot. Why aren't they getting men to bring a boat out? A fishing boat — one of those big yawls — could come out here all right. Why don't he do something?"

"Oh, it's all right, now."

"They'll have a boat out here for us in less than no time, now that they've seen us."

A faint yellow tone came into the sky over the low land. The shadows on the sea slowly deepened. The wind bore coldness with it, and the men began to shiver.

"Holy smoke!" said one, allowing his voice to express his impious mood, "if we keep on monkeying out here! If we've got to flounder out here all night!"

"Oh, we'll never have to stay here all night! Don't you worry. They've seen us now, and it won't be long before they'll come chasing out after us."

The shore grew dusky. The man waving a coat blended gradually into this gloom, and it swallowed in the same manner the omnibus and the group of people. The spray, when it dashed uproariously over the side, made the voyagers shrink and swear like men who were being branded.

"I'd like to catch the chump who waved the coat. I feel like soaking him one, just for luck."

"Why? What did he do?"

"Oh, nothing, but then he seemed so damned cheerful."

In the meantime the oiler rowed, and then the correspondent rowed, and then the oiler rowed. Grey-faced and bowed forward, they mechanically, turn by turn, plied the leaden oars. The form of the lighthouse had vanished from the southern horizon, but finally a pale star appeared, just lifting from the sea. The streaked saffron in the west passed before the all-merging darkness, and the sea to the east was black. The land had vanished, and was expressed only by the low and drear thunder of the surf.

"If I am going to be drowned — if I am going to be drowned — if I am going to be drowned, why, in the name of the seven mad gods who rule the sea, was I allowed to come thus far and contemplate sand and trees? Was I brought here merely to have my nose dragged away as I was about to nibble the sacred cheese of life?"

145   The patient captain, drooped over the water-jar, was sometimes obliged to speak to the oarsman.

"Keep her head up! Keep her head up!"

"'Keep her head up,' sir." The voices were weary and low.

This was surely a quiet evening. All save the oarsman lay heavily and listlessly in the boat's bottom. As for him, his eyes were just capable of noting the tall black waves that swept forward in a most sinister silence, save for an occasional subdued growl of a crest.

The cook's head was on a thwart, and he looked without interest at the water under his nose. He was deep in other scenes. Finally he spoke. "Billie," he murmured, dreamfully, "what kind of pie do you like best?"

V

150   "Pie," said the oiler and the correspondent, agitatedly. "Don't talk about those things, blast you!"

"Well," said the cook, "I was just thinking about ham sandwiches, and —"

A night on the sea in an open boat is a long night. As darkness settled finally, the shine of the light, lifting from the sea in the south, changed to full gold. On the northern horizon a new light appeared, a small bluish gleam on the edge of the waters. These two lights were the furniture of the world. Otherwise there was nothing but waves.

Two men huddled in the stern, and distances were so magnificent in the dingey that the rower was enabled to keep his feet partly warmed by thrusting them under his companions. Their legs indeed extended far under the rowing-seat until they touched the feet of the captain forward. Sometimes, despite the efforts of the tired oarsman, a wave came piling into the boat, an icy wave of the night, and the chilling water soaked them anew. They would twist their bodies for a moment and groan, and sleep the dead sleep once more, while the water in the boat gurgled about them as the craft rocked.

The plan of the oiler and the correspondent was for one to row until he lost the ability, and then arouse the other from his sea-water couch in the bottom of the boat.

155   The oiler plied the oars until his head drooped forward, and the over-powering sleep blinded him. And he rowed yet afterward. Then he touched a man in the bottom of the boat, and called his name. "Will you spell me for a little while?" he said, meekly.

"Sure, Billie," said the correspondent, awakening and dragging himself to a sitting position. They exchanged places carefully, and the oiler, cuddling down in the sea-water at the cook's side, seemed to go to sleep instantly.

The particular violence of the sea had ceased. The waves came without snarling. The obligation of the man at the oars was to keep the boat headed so that the tilt of the rollers would not capsize her, and to preserve her from filling when the crests rushed past. The black waves were silent and hard to be seen in the darkness. Often one was almost upon the boat before the oarsman was aware.

In a low voice the correspondent addressed the captain. He was not sure that the captain was awake, although this iron man seemed to be always awake. "Captain, shall I keep her making for that light north, sir?"

The same steady voice answered him. "Yes. Keep it about two points off the port bow."

160 The cook had tied a life-belt around himself in order to get even the warmth which this clumsy cork contrivance could donate, and he seemed almost stove-like when a rower, whose teeth invariably chattered wildly as soon as he ceased his labour, dropped down to sleep.

The correspondent, as he rowed, looked down at the two men sleeping under-foot. The cook's arm was around the oiler's shoulders, and, with their fragmentary clothing and haggard faces, they were the babes of the sea, a grotesque rendering of the old babes in the wood.[5]

Later he must have grown stupid at his work, for suddenly there was a growling of water, and a crest came with a roar and a swash into the boat, and it was a wonder that it did not set the cook afloat in his life-belt. The cook continued to sleep, but the oiler sat up, blinking his eyes and shaking with the new cold.

"Oh, I'm awful sorry, Billie," said the correspondent contritely.

"That's all right, old boy," said the oiler, and lay down again and was asleep.

165 Presently it seemed that even the captain dozed, and the correspondent thought that he was the one man afloat on all the oceans. The wind had a voice as it came over the waves, and it was sadder than the end.

There was a long, loud swishing astern of the boat, and a gleaming trail of phosphorescence, like blue flame, was furrowed on the black waters. It might have been made by a monstrous knife.

Then there came a stillness, while the correspondent breathed with the open mouth and looked at the sea.

Suddenly there was another swish and another long flash of bluish light, and this time it was alongside the boat, and might almost have been reached with an oar. The correspondent saw an enormous fin speed like a shadow through the water, hurling the crystalline spray and leaving the long glowing trail.

The correspondent looked over his shoulder at the captain. His face was hidden, and he seemed to be asleep. He looked at the babes of the sea. They certainly were asleep. So, being bereft of sympathy, he leaned a little way to one side and swore softly into the sea.

170 But the thing did not then leave the vicinity of the boat. Ahead or astern, on one side or the other, at intervals long or short, fled the long sparkling streak, and there was to be heard the whiroo of the dark fin. The speed and power of the thing was greatly to be admired. It cut the water like a gigantic and keen projectile.

---

5 popular nineteenth-century children's story about children who become lost and die in a forest.

The presence of this biding thing did not affect the man with the same horror that it would if he had been a picnicker. He simply looked at the sea dully and swore in an undertone.

Nevertheless, it is true that he did not wish to be alone. He wished one of his companions to awaken by chance and keep him company with it. But the captain hung motionless over the water-jar, and the oiler and the cook in the bottom of the boat were plunged in slumber.

VI

"If I am going to be drowned — if I am going to be drowned — if I am going to be drowned, why, in the name of the seven mad gods who rule the sea, was I allowed to come thus far and contemplate sand and trees?"

During this dismal night, it may be remarked that a man would conclude that it was really the intention of the seven mad gods to drown him, despite the abominable injustice of it. For it was certainly an abominable injustice to drown a man who had worked so hard, so hard. The man felt it would be a crime most unnatural. Other people had drowned at sea since galleys swarmed with painted sails, but still —

175　When it occurs to a man that nature does not regard him as important, and that she feels she would not maim the universe by disposing of him, he at first wishes to throw bricks at the temple, and he hates deeply the fact that there are no bricks and no temples. Any visible expression of nature would surely be pelleted with his jeers.

Then, if there be no tangible thing to hoot he feels, perhaps, the desire to confront a personification and indulge in pleas, bowed to one knee, and with hands supplicant, saying: "Yes, but I love myself."

A high cold star on a winter's night is the word he feels that she says to him. Thereafter he knows the pathos of his situation.

The men in the dingey had not discussed these matters, but each had, no doubt, reflected upon them in silence and according to his mind. There was seldom any expression upon their faces save the general one of complete weariness. Speech was devoted to the business of the boat.

To chime the notes of his emotion, a verse mysteriously entered the correspondent's head. He had even forgotten that he had forgotten this verse, but it suddenly was in his mind.

> A soldier of the Legion lay dying in Algiers,
> There was lack of woman's nursing, there was dearth of woman's tears;
> But a comrade stood beside him, and he took that comrade's hand,
> And he said: "I shall never see my own, my native land."[6]

180　In his childhood, the correspondent had been made acquainted with the fact that a soldier of the Legion lay dying in Algiers, but he had never regarded the fact as important. Myriads of his school-fellows had informed him of the soldier's plight, but the dinning had naturally ended by making him perfectly indifferent. He had never considered it his affair that a soldier of the Legion

6 these are the opening lines, somewhat inexactly quoted, from "Bingen on the Rhine" by Caroline Norton (1808–1877).

lay dying in Algiers, nor had it appeared to him as a matter for sorrow. It was less to him than the breaking of a pencil's point.

Now, however, it quaintly came to him as a human, living thing. It was no longer merely a picture of a few throes in the breast of a poet, meanwhile drinking tea and warming his feet at the grate; it was an actuality — stern, mournful, and fine.

The correspondent plainly saw the soldier. He lay on the sand with his feet out straight and still. While his pale left hand was upon his chest in an attempt to thwart the going of his life, the blood came between his fingers. In the far Algerian distance, a city of low square forms was set against a sky that was faint with the last sunset hues. The correspondent, plying the oars and dreaming of the slow and slower movements of the lips of the soldier, was moved by a profound and perfectly impersonal comprehension. He was sorry for the soldier of the Legion who lay dying in Algiers.

The thing which had followed the boat and waited, had evidently grown bored at the delay. There was no longer to be heard the slash of the cut-water, and there was no longer the flame of the long trail. The light in the north still glimmered, but it was apparently no nearer to the boat. Sometimes the boom of the surf rang in the correspondent's ears, and he turned the craft seaward then and rowed harder. Southward, some one had evidently built a watch-fire on the beach. It was too low and too far to be seen, but it made a shimmering, roseate reflection upon the bluff back of it, and this could be discerned from the boat. The wind came stronger, and sometimes a wave suddenly raged out like a mountain-cat, and there was to be seen the sheen and sparkle of a broken crest.

The captain, in the bow, moved on his water-jar and sat erect. "Pretty long night," he observed to the correspondent. He looked at the shore. "Those life-saving people take their time."

185   "Did you see that shark playing around?"

"Yes, I saw him. He was a big fellow, all right."

"Wish I had known you were awake."

Later the correspondent spoke into the bottom of the boat.

"Billie!" There was a slow and gradual disentanglement. "Billie, will you spell me?"

190   "Sure," said the oiler.

As soon as the correspondent touched the cold comfortable sea-water in the bottom of the boat, and had huddled close to the cook's life-belt he was deep in sleep, despite the fact that his teeth played all the popular airs. This sleep was so good to him that it was but a moment before he heard a voice call his name in a tone that demonstrated the last stages of exhaustion. "Will you spell me?"

"Sure, Billie."

The light in the north had mysteriously vanished, but the correspondent took his course from the wide-awake captain.

Later in the night they took the boat farther out to sea, and the captain directed the cook to take one oar at the stern and keep the boat facing the seas. He was to call out if he should hear the thunder of the surf. This plan enabled the oiler and the correspondent to get respite together. "We'll give those boys a chance to get into shape again," said the captain. They curled down and, after a few preliminary chatterings and trembles, slept once more the dead sleep. Neither knew they had bequeathed to the cook the company of another shark, or perhaps the same shark.

195 As the boat caroused on the waves, spray occasionally bumped over the side and gave them a fresh soaking, but this had no power to break their repose. The ominous slash of the wind and the water affected them as it would have affected mummies.

"Boys," said the cook, with the notes of every reluctance in his voice, "she's drifted in pretty close. I guess one of you had better take her to sea again." The correspondent, aroused, heard the crash of the toppled crests.

As he was rowing, the captain gave him some whisky-and-water, and this steadied the chills out of him. "If I ever get ashore and anybody shows me even a photograph of an oar —"

At last there was a short conversation.

"Billie.... Billie, will you spell me?"

200 "Sure," said the oiler.

VII

When the correspondent again opened his eyes, the sea and the sky were each of the grey hue of the dawning. Later, carmine and gold was painted upon the waters. The morning appeared finally, in its splendour, with a sky of pure blue, and the sunlight flamed on the tips of the waves.

On the distant dunes were set many little black cottages, and a tall white windmill reared above them. No man, nor dog, nor bicycle appeared on the beach. The cottages might have formed a deserted village.

The voyagers scanned the shore. A conference was held in the boat. "Well," said the captain, "if no help is coming we might better try a run through the surf right away. If we stay out here much longer we will be too weak to do anything for ourselves at all." The others silently acquiesced in this reasoning. The boat was headed for the beach. The correspondent wondered if none ever ascended the tall wind-tower, and if then they never looked seaward. This tower was a giant, standing with its back to the plight of the ants. It represented in a degree, to the correspondent, the serenity of nature amid the struggles of the individual — nature in the wind, and nature in the vision of men. She did not seem cruel to him then, nor beneficent, nor treacherous, nor wise. But she was indifferent, flatly indifferent. It is, perhaps, plausible that a man in this situation, impressed with the unconcern of the universe, should see the innumerable flaws of his life, and have them taste wickedly in his mind and wish for another chance. A distinction between right and wrong seems absurdly clear to him, then, in this new ignorance of the grave-edge, and he understands that if he were given another opportunity he would mend his conduct and his words, and be better and brighter during an introduction or at a tea.

"Now, boys," said the captain, "she is going to swamp, sure. All we can do is to work her in as far as possible, and then when she swamps, pile out and scramble for the beach. Keep cool now, and don't jump until she swamps sure."

205 The oiler took the oars. Over his shoulders he scanned the surf. "Captain," he said, "I think I'd better bring her about, and keep her head-on to the seas and back her in."

"All right, Billie," said the captain. "Back her in." The oiler swung the boat then and, seated in the stern, the cook and the correspondent were obliged to look over their shoulders to contemplate the lonely and indifferent shore.

The monstrous in-shore rollers heaved the boat high until the men were again enabled to see the white sheets of water scudding up the slanted beach. "We won't get in very close," said the captain. Each time a man could wrest his attention from the rollers, he turned his glance toward the shore, and in the expression of the eyes during this contemplation there was a singular quality. The correspondent, observing the others, knew that they were not afraid, but the full meaning of their glances was shrouded.

As for himself, he was too tired to grapple fundamentally with the fact. He tried to coerce his mind into thinking of it, but the mind was dominated at this time by the muscles, and the muscles said they did not care. It merely occurred to him that if he should drown it would be a shame.

There were no hurried words, no pallor, no plain agitation. The men simply looked at the shore. "Now, remember to get well clear of the boat when you jump," said the captain.

210 Seaward the crest of a roller suddenly fell with a thunderous crash, and the long white comber came roaring down upon the boat.

"Steady now," said the captain. The men were silent. They turned their eyes from the shore to the comber and waited. The boat slid up the incline, leaped at the furious top, bounced over it, and swung down the long back of the wave. Some water had been shipped and the cook bailed it out.

But the next crest crashed also. The tumbling boiling flood of white water caught the boat and whirled it almost perpendicular. Water swarmed in from all sides. The correspondent had his hands on the gunwale at this time, and when the water entered at that place he swiftly withdrew his fingers, as if he objected to wetting them.

The little boat, drunken with this weight of water, reeled and snuggled deeper into the sea.

"Bail her out, cook! Bail her out," said the captain.

215 "All right, captain," said the cook.

"Now, boys, the next one will do for us, sure," said the oiler. "Mind to jump clear of the boat."

The third wave moved forward, huge, furious, implacable. It fairly swallowed the dingey, and almost simultaneously the men tumbled into the sea. A piece of lifebelt had lain in the bottom of the boat, and as the correspondent went overboard he held this to his chest with his left hand.

The January water was icy, and he reflected immediately that it was colder than he had expected to find it off the coast of Florida. This appeared to his dazed mind as a fact important enough to be noted at the time. The coldness of the water was sad; it was tragic. This fact was somehow so mixed and confused with his opinion of his own situation that it seemed almost a proper reason for tears. The water was cold.

When he came to the surface he was conscious of little but the noisy water. Afterward he saw his companions in the sea. The oiler was ahead in the race. He was swimming strongly and rapidly. Off to the correspondent's left, the cook's great white and corked back bulged out of the water, and in the rear the captain was hanging with his one good hand to the keel of the overturned dingey.

220   There is a certain immovable quality to a shore, and the correspondent wondered at it amid the confusion of the sea.

It seemed also very attractive, but the correspondent knew that it was a long journey, and he paddled leisurely. The piece of life-preserver lay under him, and sometimes he whirled down the incline of a wave as if he were on a hand-sled.

But finally he arrived at a place in the sea where travel was beset with difficulty. He did not pause swimming to inquire what manner of current had caught him, but there his progress ceased. The shore was set before him like a bit of scenery on a stage, and he looked at it and understood with his eyes each detail of it.

As the cook passed, much farther to the left, the captain was calling to him, "Turn over on your back, cook! Turn over on your back and use the oar."

"All right, sir." The cook turned on his back, and, paddling with an oar, went ahead as if he were a canoe.

225   Presently the boat also passed to the left of the correspondent with the captain clinging with one hand to the keel. He would have appeared like a man raising himself to look over a board fence, if it were not for the extraordinary gymnastics of the boat. The correspondent marvelled that the captain could still hold to it.

They passed on, nearer to shore — the oiler, the cook, the captain — and following them went the water-jar, bouncing gaily over the seas.

The correspondent remained in the grip of this strange new enemy — a current. The shore, with its white slope of sand and its green bluff, topped with little silent cottages, was spread like a picture before him. It was very near to him then, but he was impressed as one who in a gallery looks at a scene from Brittany[7] or Holland.

He thought: "Am I going to drown? Can it be possible? Can it be possible? Can it be possible?" Perhaps an individual must consider his own death to be the final phenomenon of nature.

But later a wave perhaps whirled him out of this small deadly current, for he found suddenly that he could again make progress toward the shore. Later still, he was aware that the captain, clinging with one hand to the keel of the dingey, had his face turned away from the shore and toward him, and was calling his name. "Come to the boat! Come to the boat!"

230   In his struggle to reach the captain and the boat, he reflected that when one gets properly wearied, drowning must really be a comfortable arrangement, a cessation of hostilities accompanied by a large degree of relief, and he was glad of it, for the main thing in his mind for some moments had been horror of the temporary agony. He did not wish to be hurt.

Presently he saw a man running along the shore. He was undressing with most remarkable speed. Coat, trousers, shirt, everything flew magically off him.

"Come to the boat," called the captain.

7 rural region in northwestern France.

"All right, captain." As the correspondent paddled, he saw the captain let himself down to the bottom and leave the boat. Then the correspondent performed his one little marvel of the voyage. A large wave caught him and flung him with ease and supreme speed completely over the boat and far beyond it. It struck him even then as an event in gymnastics, and a true miracle of the sea. An overturned boat in the surf is not a plaything to a swimming man.

The correspondent arrived in water that reached only to his waist, but his condition did not enable him to stand for more than a moment. Each wave knocked him into a heap, and the under-tow pulled at him.

235 Then he saw the man who had been running and undressing, and undressing and running, come bounding into the water. He dragged ashore the cook, and then waded towards the captain, but the captain waved him away, and sent him to the correspondent. He was naked, naked as a tree in winter, but a halo was about his head, and he shone like a saint. He gave a strong pull, and a long drag, and a bully heave at the correspondent's hand. The correspondent, schooled in the minor formulæ, said: "Thanks, old man." But suddenly the man cried: "What's that?" He pointed a swift finger. The correspondent said: "Go."

In the shallows, face downward, lay the oiler. His forehead touched sand that was periodically, between each wave, clear of the sea.

The correspondent did not know all that transpired afterward. When he achieved safe ground he fell, striking the sand with each particular part of his body. It was as if he had dropped from a roof, but the thud was grateful to him.

It seems that instantly the beach was populated with men with blankets, clothes, and flasks, and women with coffee-pots and all the remedies sacred to their minds. The welcome of the land to the men from the sea was warm and generous, but a still and dripping shape was carried slowly up the beach, and the land's welcome for it could only be the different and sinister hospitality of the grave.

When it came night, the white waves paced to and fro in the moonlight, and the wind brought the sound of the great sea's voice to the men on shore, and they felt that they could then be interpreters.

(1897)

James Joyce (1882–1941)

Although Dublin-born, James Joyce lived most of his adult life in Europe, including twenty years in Paris, where he wrote most of his books about Dublin and its people: *Dubliners*, a collection of short stories; and three novels, *A Portait of the Artist as a Young Man*, *Ulysses*, and *Finnegans Wake*. The first three of these were filled with minutely depicted presentations of scenes and characters of Dublin. In *Dubliners*, from which "Araby" is taken, the details are given symbolic meanings that transform specific aspects of late-nineteenth-century Irish life into the universal. Many of the characters experience what Joyce called an "epiphany," a moment of insight in which they understand the nature of their lives. At the edge of adolescence, the young narrator experiences a profound conflict between his emerging sexuality and his strict religious upbringing. From the opening sentence's reference to a "blind" street to the concluding one's references to the darkness of the bazaar, Joyce carefully selects and arranges details to emphasize the boy's movement from innocence and ignorance to insight.

ARABY[1]

North Richmond Street, being blind,[2] was a quiet street except at the hour when the Christian Brothers' School set the boys free. An uninhabited house of two storeys stood at the blind end, detached from its neighbours in a square ground. The other houses of the street, conscious of decent lives within them, gazed at one another with brown imperturbable faces.

The former tenant of our house, a priest, had died in the back drawing-room. Air, musty from having been long enclosed, hung in all the rooms, and the waste room behind the kitchen was littered with old useless papers. Among these I found a few paper-covered books, the pages of which were curled and damp: *The Abbot*,[3] by Walter Scott, *The Devout Communicant*[4] and *The Memoirs of Vidocq*.[5] I liked the last best because its leaves were yellow. The wild garden behind the house contained a central apple-tree and a few straggling bushes under one of which I found the late tenant's rusty bicycle-pump. He had been a very charitable priest; in his will he had left all his money to institutions and the furniture of his house to his sister.

When the short days of winter came dusk fell before we had well eaten our dinners. When we met in the street the houses had grown sombre. The space of sky above us was the colour of ever-changing violet and towards it the lamps of the street lifted their feeble lanterns. The cold air stung us and we played till our bodies glowed. Our shouts echoed in the silent street. The career of our play brought us through the dark muddy lanes behind the houses where we ran the gantlet of the rough tribes from the cottages, to the back doors

---

1 Dublin charity bazaar with a name evoking the romance and mystery of Arabia. 2 dead-end street.
3 in Sir Walter Scott's 1820 novel set in the sixteenth century, a young man loyally serves Mary Queen of Scots. 4 nineteenth-century religious tract. 5 François Vidocq was an early-nineteenth-century French thief turned detective.

of the dark dripping gardens where odours arose from the ashpits, to the dark odorous stables where a coachman smoothed and combed the horse or shook music from the buckled harness. When we returned to the street light from the kitchen windows had filled the areas. If my uncle was seen turning the corner we hid in the shadow until we had seen him safely housed. Or if Mangan's sister came out on the doorstep to call her brother in to his tea we watched her from our shadow peer up and down the street. We waited to see whether she would remain or go in and, if she remained, we left our shadow and walked up to Mangan's steps resignedly. She was waiting for us, her figure defined by the light from the half-opened door. Her brother always teased her before he obeyed and I stood by the railings looking at her. Her dress swung as she moved her body and the soft rope of her hair tossed from side to side.

Every morning I lay on the floor in the front parlour watching her door. The blind was pulled down to within an inch of the sash so that I could not be seen. When she came out on the doorstep my heart leaped. I ran to the hall, seized my books and followed her. I kept her brown figure always in my eye and, when we came near the point at which our ways diverged, I quickened my pace and passed her. This happened morning after morning. I had never spoken to her, except for a few casual words, and yet her name was like a summons to all my foolish blood.

5   Her image accompanied me even in places the most hostile to romance. On Saturday evenings when my aunt went marketing I had to go to carry some of the parcels. We walked through the flaring streets, jostled by drunken men and bargaining women, amid the curses of labourers, the shrill litanies of shop-boys who stood on guard by the barrels of pigs' cheeks, the nasal chanting of street-singers, who sang a *come-all-you* about O'Donovan Rossa,[6] or a ballad about the troubles in our native land. These noises converged in a single sensation of life for me: I imagined that I bore my chalice safely through a throng of foes. Her name sprang to my lips at moments in strange prayers and praises which I myself did not understand. My eyes were often full of tears (I could not tell why) and at times a flood from my heart seemed to pour itself out into my bosom. I thought little of the future. I did not know whether I would ever speak to her or not or, if I spoke to her, how I could tell her of my confused adoration. But my body was like a harp and her words and gestures were like fingers running upon the wires.

One evening I went into the back drawing-room in which the priest had died. It was a dark rainy evening and there was no sound in the house. Through one of the broken panes I heard the rain impinge upon the earth, the fine incessant needles of water playing in the sodden beds. Some distant lamp or lighted window gleamed below me. I was thankful that I could see so little. All my senses seemed to desire to veil themselves and, feeling that I was about to slip from them, I pressed the palms of my hands together until they trembled, murmuring: *O love! O love!* many times.

At last she spoke to me. When she addressed the first words to me I was so confused that I did not know what to answer. She asked me was I going to

6 popular street ballad about a nineteenth-century Irish revolutionary.

Araby. I forget whether I answered yes or no. It would be a splendid bazaar, she said; she would love to go.

— And why can't you? I asked.

While she spoke she turned a silver bracelet round and round her wrist. She could not go, she said, because there would be a retreat that week in her convent. Her brother and two other boys were fighting for their caps and I was alone at the railings. She held one of the spikes, bowing her head towards me. The light from the lamp opposite our door caught the white curve of her neck, lit up her hair that rested there and, falling, lit up the hand upon the railing. It fell over one side of her dress and caught the white border of a petticoat, just visible as she stood at ease.

10 — It's well for you, she said.

— If I go, I said, I will bring you something.

What innumerable follies laid waste my waking and sleeping thoughts after that evening! I wished to annihilate the tedious intervening days. I chafed against the work of school. At night in my bedroom and by day in the classroom her image came between me and the page I strove to read. The syllables of the word *Araby* were called to me through the silence in which my soul luxuriated and cast an Eastern enchantment over me. I asked for leave to go to the bazaar on Saturday night. My aunt was surprised and hoped it was not some Freemason[7] affair. I answered few questions in class. I watched my master's face pass from amiability to sternness; he hoped I was not beginning to idle. I could not call my wandering thoughts together. I had hardly any patience with the serious work of life which, now that it stood between me and my desire, seemed to me child's play, ugly monotonous child's play.

On Saturday morning I reminded my uncle that I wished to go to the bazaar in the evening. He was fussing at the hallstand, looking for the hat-brush, and answered me curtly:

— Yes, boy, I know.

15 As he was in the hall I could not go into the front parlour and lie at the window. I left the house in bad humour and walked slowly towards the school. The air was pitilessly raw and already my heart misgave me.

When I came home to dinner my uncle had not yet been home. Still it was early. I sat staring at the clock for some time and, when its ticking began to irritate me, I left the room. I mounted the staircase and gained the upper part of the house. The high cold empty gloomy rooms liberated me and I went from room to room singing. From the front window I saw my companions playing below in the street. Their cries reached me weakened and indistinct and, leaning my forehead against the cool glass, I looked over at the dark house where she lived. I may have stood there for an hour, seeing nothing but the brown-clad figure cast by my imagination, touched discreetly by the lamplight at the curved neck, at the hand upon the railings and at the border below the dress.

When I came downstairs again I found Mrs Mercer sitting at the fire. She was an old garrulous woman, a pawnbroker's widow, who collected used stamps for some pious purpose. I had to endure the gossip of the tea-table.

7 the Protestant Masons were considered enemies of Irish Roman Catholics.

The meal was prolonged beyond an hour and still my uncle did not come. Mrs Mercer stood up to go: she was sorry she couldn't wait any longer, but it was after eight o'clock and she did not like to be out late, as the night air was bad for her. When she had gone I began to walk up and down the room, clenching my fists. My aunt said:

— I'm afraid you may put off your bazaar for this night of Our Lord.

At nine o'clock I heard my uncle's latchkey in the halldoor. I heard him talking to himself and heard the hallstand rocking when it had received the weight of his overcoat. I could interpret these signs. When he was midway through his dinner I asked him to give me the money to go to the bazaar. He had forgotten.

20   — The people are in bed and after their first sleep now, he said.

I did not smile. My aunt said to him energetically:

— Can't you give him the money and let him go? You've kept him late enough as it is.

My uncle said he was very sorry he had forgotten. He said he believed in the old saying: *All work and no play makes Jack a dull boy.* He asked where I was going and, when I had told him a second time he asked me did I know *The Arab's Farewell to his Steed.*[8] When I left the kitchen he was about to recite the opening lines of the piece to my aunt.

I held a florin[9] tightly in my hand as I strode down Buckingham Street towards the station. The sight of the streets thronged with buyers and glaring with gas recalled to me the purpose of my journey. I took my seat in a third-class carriage of a deserted train. After an intolerable delay the train moved out of the station slowly. It crept onward among ruinous houses and over the twinkling river. At Westland Row Station a crowd of people pressed to the carriage doors; but the porters moved them back, saying that it was a special train for the bazaar. I remained alone in the bare carriage. In a few minutes the train drew up beside an improvised wooden platform. I passed out on to the road and saw by the lighted dial of a clock that it was ten minutes to ten. In front of me was a large building which displayed the magical name.

25   I could not find any sixpenny entrance and, fearing that the bazaar would be closed, I passed in quickly through a turnstile, handing a shilling to a weary-looking man. I found myself in a big hall girdled at half its height by a gallery. Nearly all the stalls were closed and the greater part of the hall was in darkness. I recognized a silence like that which pervades a church after a service. I walked into the centre of the bazaar timidly. A few people were gathered about the stalls which were still open. Before a curtain, over which the words *Café Chantant* were written in coloured lamps, two men were counting money on a salver. I listened to the fall of the coins.

Remembering with difficulty why I had come I went over to one of the stalls and examined porcelain vases and flowered tea-sets. At the door of the stall a young lady was talking and laughing with two young gentlemen. I remarked their English accents and listened vaguely to their conversation.

— Oh, I never said such a thing!

8 sentimental nineteenth-century poem about a man who, disconsolate at selling his horse, reclaims it.
9 two-shilling coin worth about 50 cents at that time.

— O, but you did!

— O, but I didn't!

30   — Didn't she say that?

— Yes. I heard her.

— O, there's a . . . fib!

Observing me the young lady came over and asked me did I wish to buy anything. The tone of her voice was not encouraging; she seemed to have spoken to me out of a sense of duty. I looked humbly at the great jars that stood like eastern guards at either side of the dark entrance to the stall and murmured:

— No, thank you.

35   The young lady changed the position of one of the vases and went back to the two young men. They began to talk of the same subject. Once or twice the young lady glanced at me over her shoulder.

I lingered before her stall, though I knew my stay was useless, to make my interest in her wares seem the more real. Then I turned away slowly and walked down the middle of the bazaar. I allowed the two pennies to fall against the sixpence in my pocket. I heard a voice call from one end of the gallery that the light was out. The upper part of the hall was now completely dark.

Gazing up into the darkness I saw myself as a creature driven and derided by vanity; and my eyes burned with anguish and anger.

(1914)

Katherine Mansfield (1888–1923)

Born in Wellington, New Zealand, Katherine Mansfield (the pseudonym of Kathleen Beauchamp) moved to London when she was twenty and shortly after began her career as a writer. Critics have compared her works to those of Russian author Anton Chekhov, whose ironic view of life and whose technical innovations, particularly the use of small details to reveal character, she greatly admired. In her collections of short stories, three of which — *In a German Pension*, *Bliss*, and *The Garden Party* — were published during her life, she examined the nature of childhood and the troubled relationships between men and women. The description of the heroine's activities in the early pages of "Bliss" reveals the happiness Bertha feels as she prepares for a dinner party, while later details indicate her changing emotions. Events of the narrative and her emotions and feelings subtly foreshadow the story's conclusion.

BLISS

Although Bertha Young was thirty she still had moments like this when she wanted to run instead of walk, to take dancing steps on and off the pavement, to bowl a hoop, to throw something up in the air and catch it again, or to stand still and laugh at — nothing — at nothing, simply.

What can you do if you are thirty and, turning the corner of your own street, you are overcome, suddenly, by a feeling of bliss — absolute bliss! — as though you'd suddenly swallowed a bright piece of that late afternoon sun and it burned in your bosom, sending out a little shower of sparks into every particle, into every finger and toe?...

Oh, is there no way you can express it without being "drunk and disorderly"? How idiotic civilization is! Why be given a body if you have to keep it shut up in a case like a rare, rare fiddle?

"No, that about the fiddle is not quite what I mean," she thought, running up the steps and feeling in her bag for the key — she's forgotten it, as usual — and rattling the letter-box. "It's not what I mean, because — Thank you, Mary" — she went into the hall. "Is nurse back?"

5   "Yes, M'm."

"And has the fruit come?"

"Yes, M'm. Everything's come."

"Bring the fruit up to the dining-room, will you? I'll arrange it before I go upstairs."

It was dusky in the dining-room and quite chilly. But all the same Bertha threw off her coat; she could not bear the tight clasp of it another moment, and the cold air fell on her arms.

10   But in her bosom there was still that bright glowing place — that shower of little sparks coming from it. It was almost unbearable. She hardly dared to breathe for fear of fanning it higher, and yet she breathed deeply, deeply. She hardly dared to look into the cold mirror — but she did look, and it gave her back a woman, radiant, with smiling, trembling lips, with big, dark eyes and an air of listening,

waiting for something…divine to happen…that she knew must happen…infallibly.

Mary brought in the fruit on a tray and with it a glass bowl, and a blue dish, very lovely, with a strange sheen on it as though it had been dipped in milk.

"Shall I turn on the light, M'm?"

"No, thank you. I can see quite well."

There were tangerines and apples stained with strawberry pink. Some yellow pears, smooth as silk, some white grapes covered with a silver bloom and a big cluster of purple ones. These last she had bought to tone in with the new dining-room carpet. Yes, that did sound rather far-fetched and absurd, but it was really why she had bought them. She had thought in the shop: "I must have some purple ones to bring the carpet up to the table." And it had seemed quite sense at the time.

15
When she had finished with them and had made two pyramids of these bright round shapes, she stood away from the table to get the effect — and it really was most curious. For the dark table seemed to melt into the dusky light and the glass dish and the blue bowl to float in the air. This, of course in her present mood, was so incredibly beautiful. . . . She began to laugh.

"No, no. I'm getting hysterical." And she seized her bag and coat and ran upstairs to the nursery.

Nurse sat at a low table giving Little B her supper after her bath. The baby had on a white flannel gown and a blue woollen jacket, and her dark, fine hair was brushed up into a funny little peak. She looked up when she saw her mother and began to jump.

"Now, my lovey, eat it up like a good girl," said Nurse, setting her lips in a way that Bertha knew, and that meant she had come into the nursery at another wrong moment.

"Has she been good, Nanny?"

20
"She's been a little sweet all the afternoon," whispered Nanny. "We went to the park and I sat down on a chair and took her out of the pram and a big dog came along and put his head on my knee and she clutched its ear, tugged it. Oh, you should have seen her."

Bertha wanted to ask if it wasn't rather dangerous to let her clutch at a strange dog's ear. But she did not dare to. She stood watching them, her hands by her side, like the poor little girl in front of the rich little girl with the doll.

The baby looked up at her again, stared, and then smiled so charmingly that Bertha couldn't help crying:

"Oh, Nanny, do let me finish giving her her supper while you put the bath things away."

"Well, M'm, she oughtn't to be changed hands while she's eating," said Nanny, still whispering. "It unsettles her; it's very likely to upset her."

25
How absurd it was. Why have a baby if it has to be kept — not in a case like a rare, rare fiddle — but in another woman's arms?

"Oh, I must!" said she.

Very offended, Nanny handed her over.

"Now, don't excite her after her supper. You know you do, M'm. And I have such a time with her after!"

Thank heaven! Nanny went out of the room with the bath towels.

30   "Now I've got you to myself, my little precious," said Bertha, as the baby leaned against her.

She ate delightfully, holding up her lips for the spoon and then waving her hands. Sometimes she wouldn't let the spoon go; and sometimes, just as Bertha had filled it, she waved it away to the four winds.

When the soup was finished Bertha turned round to the fire.

"You're nice — you're very nice!" said she, kissing her warm baby. "I'm fond of you. I like you."

And, indeed, she loved Little B so much — her neck as she bent forward, her exquisite toes as they shone transparent in the firelight — that all her feeling of bliss came back again, and again she didn't know how to express it — what to do with it.

35   "You're wanted on the telephone," said Nanny, coming back in triumph and seizing *her* Little B.

Down she flew. It was Harry.

"Oh, is that you, Ber? Look here. I'll be late. I'll take a taxi and come along as quickly as I can, but get dinner put back ten minutes — will you? All right?"

"Yes, perfectly. Oh, Harry!"

"Yes?"

40   What had she to say? She'd nothing to say. She only wanted to get in touch with him for a moment. She couldn't absurdly cry: "Hasn't it been a divine day!"

"What is it?" rapped out the little voice.

"Nothing. *Entendu*,"[1] said Bertha, and hung up the receiver, thinking how more than idiotic civilization was.

They had people coming to dinner. The Norman Knights — a very sound couple — he was about to start a theatre, and she was awfully keen on interior decoration, a young man, Eddie Warren, who had just published a little book of poems and whom everybody was asking to dine, and a "find" of Bertha's called Pearl Fulton. What Miss Fulton did, Bertha didn't know. They had met at the club and Bertha had fallen in love with her, as she always did fall in love with beautiful women who had something strange about them.

The provoking thing was that, though they had been about together and met a number of times and really talked, Bertha couldn't yet make her out. Up to a certain point Miss Fulton was rarely, wonderfully frank, but the certain point was there, and beyond that she would not go.

45   Was there anything beyond it? Harry said "No." Voted her dullish, and "cold like all blond women, with a touch, perhaps, of anaemia of the brain." But Bertha wouldn't agree with him; not yet, at any rate.

"No, the way she has of sitting with her head a little on one side, and smiling, has something behind it, Harry, and I must find out what that something is."

"Most likely it's a good stomach," answered Harry.

He made a point of catching Bertha's heels with replies of that kind…"liver frozen, my dear girl," or "pure flatulence," or "kidney disease,"…and so on. For some strange reason Bertha liked this, and almost admired it in him very much.

She went into the drawing-room and lighted the fire; then, picking up the cushions, one by one, that Mary had disposed so carefully, she threw them back

1 understood, agreed.

on to the chairs and the couches. That made all the difference; the room came alive at once. As she was about to throw the last one she surprised herself by suddenly hugging it to her, passionately, passionately. But it did not put out the fire in her bosom. Oh, on the contrary!

50   The windows of the drawing-room opened on to a balcony overlooking the garden. At the far end, against the wall, there was a tall, slender pear tree in fullest, richest bloom; it stood perfect, as though becalmed against the jade-green sky. Bertha couldn't help feeling, even from this distance, that it had not a single bud or a faded petal. Down below, in the garden beds, the red and yellow tulips, heavy with flowers, seemed to lean upon the dusk. A grey cat, dragging its belly, crept across the lawn, and a black one, its shadow, trailed after. The sight of them, so intent and so quick, gave Bertha a curious shiver.

"What creepy things cats are!" she stammered, and she turned away from the window and began walking up and down....

How strong the jonquils smelled in the warm room. Too strong? Oh, no. And yet, as though overcome, she flung down on a couch and pressed her hands to her eyes.

"I'm too happy — too happy!" she murmured.

And she seemed to see on her eyelids the lovely pear tree with its wide open blossoms as a symbol of her own life.

55   Really — really — she had everything. She was young. Harry and she were as much in love as ever, and they got on together splendidly and were really good pals. She had an adorable baby. They didn't have to worry about money. They had this absolutely satisfactory house and garden. And friends — modern, thrilling friends, writers and painters and poets or people keen on social questions — just the kind of friends they wanted. And then there were books, and there was music, and she had found a wonderful little dressmaker, and they were going abroad in the summer, and their new cook made the most superb omelettes....

"I'm absurd! Absurd!" She sat up; but she felt quite dizzy, quite drunk. It must have been the spring.

Yes, it was the spring. Now she was so tired she could not drag herself upstairs to dress.

A white dress, a string of jade beads, green shoes and stockings. It wasn't intentional. She had thought of this scheme hours before she stood at the drawing-room window.

Her petals rustled softly into the hall, and she kissed Mrs. Norman Knight, who was taking off the most amusing orange coat with a procession of black monkeys round the hem and up the fronts.

60   "... Why! Why! Why is the middle-class so stodgy — so utterly without a sense of humour! My dear, it's only by a fluke that I am here at all — Norman being the protective fluke. For my darling monkeys so upset the train that it rose to a man and simply ate me with its eyes. Didn't laugh — wasn't amused — that I should have loved. No, just stared — and bored me through and through."

"But the cream of it was," said Norman, pressing a large tortoiseshell-rimmed monocle into his eye, "you don't mind me telling this, Face, do you?" (In their home and among their friends they called each other Face and Mug.) "The cream of it was when she, being full fed, turned to the woman beside her and said: 'Haven't you ever seen a monkey before?'"

"Oh, yes!" Mrs. Norman Knight joined in the laughter. "Wasn't that too absolutely creamy?"

And a funnier thing still was that now her coat was off she did look like a very intelligent monkey — who had even made that yellow silk dress out of scraped banana skins. And her amber ear-rings; they were like little dangling nuts.

"This is a sad, sad fall!" said Mug, pausing in front of Little B's perambulator. "When the perambulator comes into the hall —" and he waved the rest of the quotation away.

The bell rang. It was lean, pale Eddie Warren (as usual) in a state of acute distress.

"It *is* the right house, *isn't* it?" he pleaded.

"Oh, I think so — I hope so," said Bertha brightly.

"I have had such a *dreadful* experience with a taxi-man; he was *most* sinister. I couldn't get him to *stop*. The *more* I knocked and called the *faster* he went. And *in* the moonlight this *bizarre* figure with the *flattened* head *crouching* over the *lit-tle* wheel...."

He shuddered, taking off an immense white silk scarf. Bertha noticed that his socks were white, too — most charming.

"But how dreadful!" she cried.

"Yes, it really was," said Eddie, following her into the drawing-room. "I saw myself *driving* through Eternity in a *timeless* taxi."

He knew the Norman Knights. In fact, he was going to write a play for N.K. when the theatre scheme came off.

"Well, Warren, how's the play?" said Norman Knight, dropping his monocle and giving his eye a moment in which to rise to the surface before it was screwed down again.

And Mrs. Norman Knight: "Oh, Mr. Warren, what happy socks?"

"I *am* so glad you like them," said he, staring at his feet. "They seem to have got so *much* whiter since the moon rose." And he turned his lean sorrowful young face to Bertha. "There *is* a moon, you know."

She wanted to cry: "I am sure there is — often — often!"

He really was a most attractive person. But so was Face, crouched before the fire in her banana skins, and so was Mug, smoking a cigarette and saying as he flicked the ash: "Why doth the bridegroom tarry?"

"There he is, now."

Bang went the front door open and shut. Harry shouted: "Hullo, you people. Down in five minutes." And they heard him swarm up the stairs. Bertha couldn't help smiling; she knew how he loved doing things at high pressure. What, after all, did an extra five minutes matter? But he would pretend to himself that they mattered beyond measure. And then he would make a great point of coming into the drawing-room, extravagantly cool and collected.

Harry had such a zest for life. Oh, how she appreciated it in him. And his passion for fighting — for seeking in everything that came up against him another test of his power and of his courage — that, too, she understood. Even when it made him just occasionally, to other people, who didn't know him well, a little ridiculous perhaps.... For there were moments when he rushed into battle where no battle was.... She talked and laughed and positively forgot until he had come in (just as she had imagined) that Pearl Fulton had not turned up.

"I wonder if Miss Fulton has forgotten?"

"I expect so," said Harry. "Is she on the 'phone?"

"Ah! There's a taxi, now." And Bertha smiled with that little air of propri-etorship that she always assumed while her women finds were new and mysteri-ous. "She lives in taxis."

"She'll run to fat if she does," said Harry coolly, ringing the bell for dinner. "Frightful danger for blond women."

85 "Harry — don't," warned Bertha, laughing up at him.

Came another tiny moment, while they waited, laughing and talking, just a trifle too much at their ease, a trifle too unaware. And then Miss Fulton, all in silver, with a silver fillet binding her pale blond hair, came in smiling, her head a little on one side.

"Am I late?"

"No, not at all," said Bertha. "Come along." And she took her arm and they moved into the dining-room.

What was there in the touch of that cool arm that could fan — fan — start blazing — blazing — the fire of bliss that Bertha did not know what to do with?

90 Miss Fulton did not look at her; but then she seldom did look at people directly. Her heavy eyelids lay upon her eyes and the strange half smile came and went upon her lips as though she lived by listening rather than seeing. But Bertha knew, suddenly, as if the longest, most intimate look had passed between them — as if they had said to each other: "You, too?" — that Pearl Fulton, stir-ring the beautiful red soup in the grey plate, was feeling just what she was feeling.

And the others? Face and Mug, Eddie and Harry, their spoons rising and falling — dabbing their lips with their napkins, crumbling bread, fiddling with the forks and glasses and talking.

"I met her at the Alpha shore — the weirdest little person. She'd not only cut off her hair, but she seemed to have taken a dreadfully good snip off her legs and arms and her neck and her poor little nose as well."

"Isn't she very *liée*[2] with Michael Oat?"

"The man who wrote *Love in False Teeth*?"

95 "He wants to write a play for me. One act. One man. Decides to commit suicide. Gives all the reasons why he should and why he shouldn't. And just as he has made up his mind either to do it or not to do it — curtain. Not half a bad idea."

"What's he going to call it —'Stomach Trouble'?"

"I *think* I've come across the *same* idea in a lit-tle French review, *quite* unknown in England."

No, they didn't share it. They were dears — dears — and she loved having them there, at her table, and giving them delicious food and wine. In fact, she longed to tell them how delightful they were, and what a decorative group they made, how they seemed to set one another off and how they reminded her of a play by Tchekof![3]

Harry was enjoying his dinner. It was part of his — well, not his nature, exactly, and certainly not his pose — his — something or other — to talk about food and to glory in his "shameless passion for the white flesh of the lobster" and "the green of pistachio ices — green and cold like the eyelids of Egyptian dancers."

100 When he looked up at her and said: "Bertha, this is a very admirable *soufflée*!" she almost could have wept with child-like pleasure.

2 attached (involved). 3 Anton Chekhov, nineteenth-century Russian writer of ironic dramas and short stories.

Oh, why did she feel so tender towards the whole world tonight? Everything was good — was right. All that happened seemed to fill again her brimming cup of bliss.

And still, in the back of her mind, there was the pear tree. It would be silver now, in the light of poor dear Eddie's moon, silver as Miss Fulton, who sat there turning a tangerine in her slender fingers that were so pale a light seemed to come from them.

What she simply couldn't make out — what was miraculous — was how she should have guessed Miss Fulton's mood so exactly and so instantly. For she never doubted for a moment that she was right, and yet what had she to go on? Less than nothing.

"I believe this does happen very, very rarely between women. Never between men," thought Bertha. "But while I am making the coffee in the drawing-room perhaps she will 'give a sign.'"

105   What she meant by that she did not know, and what would happen after that she could not imagine.

While she thought like this she saw herself talking and laughing. She had to talk because of her desire to laugh.

"I must laugh or die."

But when she noticed Face's funny little habit of tucking something down the front of her bodice — as if she kept a tiny, secret hoard of nuts there, too — Bertha had to dig her nails into her hands — so as not to laugh too much.

It was over at last. And: "Come and see my new coffee machine," said Bertha.

110   "We only have a new coffee machine once a fortnight," said Harry. Face took her arm this time; Miss Fulton bent her head and followed after.

The fire had died down in the drawing-room to a red, flickering "nest of baby phoenixes," said Face.

"Don't turn up the light for a moment. It is so lovely." And down she crouched by the fire again. She was always cold . . . "without her little red flannel jacket, of course," thought Bertha.

At that moment Miss Fulton "gave the sign."

"Have you a garden?" said the cool, sleepy voice.

115   This was so exquisite on her part that all Bertha could do was to obey. She crossed the room, pulled the curtains apart, and opened those long windows.

"There!" she breathed.

And the two women stood side by side looking at the slender, flowering tree. Although it was so still it seemed, like the flame of a candle, to stretch up, to point, to quiver in the bright air, to grow taller and taller as they gazed — almost to touch the rim of the round, silver moon.

How long did they stand there? Both, as it were, caught in that circle of unearthly light, understanding each other perfectly, creatures of another world, and wondering what they were to do in this one with all this blissful treasure that burned in their bosoms and dropped, in silver flowers, from their hair and hands?

For ever — for a moment? And did Miss Fulton murmur: "Yes. Just *that*." Or did Bertha dream it?

120   Then the light was snapped on and Face made the coffee and Harry said: "My dear Mrs. Knight, don't ask me about my baby. I never see her. I shan't feel the slightest interest in her until she has a lover," and Mug took his eye out of the conservatory for a moment and then put it under glass again and Eddie Warren drank his coffee and set down the cup with a face of anguish as though he had drunk and seen the spider.

"What I want to do is to give the young men a show. I believe London is simply teeming with first-chop, unwritten plays. What I want to say to 'em is: 'Here's the theatre. Fire ahead.'"

"You know, my dear, I am going to decorate a room for the Jacob Nathans. Oh, I am so tempted to do a fried-fish scheme, with the backs of the chairs shaped like frying pans and lovely chip potatoes embroidered all over the curtains."

"The trouble with our young writing men is that they are still too romantic. You can't put out to sea without being seasick and wanting a basin. Well, why won't they have the courage of those basins?"

"A *dreadful* poem about a *girl* who was *violated* by a beggar *without* a nose in a lit-tle wood...."

125   Miss Fulton sank into the lowest, deepest chair and Harry handed round the cigarettes.

From the way he stood in front of her shaking the silver box and saying abruptly: "Egyptian? Turkish? Virginian? They're all mixed up," Bertha realized that she not only bored him; he really disliked her. And she decided from the way Miss Fulton said: "No, thank you, I won't smoke," that she felt it, too, and was hurt.

"Oh, Harry, don't dislike her. You are quite wrong about her. She's wonderful, wonderful. And, besides, how can you feel so differently about some one who means so much to me. I shall try to tell you when we are in bed tonight what has been happening. What she and I have shared."

At those last words something strange and almost terrifying darted into Bertha's mind. And this something blind and smiling whispered to her: "Soon these people will go. The house will be quiet — quiet. The lights will be out. And you and he will be alone together in the dark room — the warm bed...."

She jumped up from her chair and ran over to the piano.

130   "What a pity some one does not play!" she cried. "What a pity somebody does not play."

For the first time in her life Bertha Young desired her husband.

Oh, she'd loved him — she'd been in love with him, of course, in every other way, but just not in that way. And, equally, of course, she'd understood that he was different. They'd discussed it so often. It had worried her dreadfully at first to find that she was so cold, but after a time it had not seemed to matter. They were so frank with each other — such good pals. That was the best of being modern.

But now — ardently! ardently! The word ached in her ardent body! Was this what that feeling of bliss had been leading up to? But then — then —

"My dear," said Mrs. Norman Knight, "you know our shame. We are the victims of time and train. We live in Hampstead. It's been so nice."

135   "I'll come with you into the hall," said Bertha. "I love having you. But you must not miss the last train. That's so awful, isn't it?"

"Have a whisky, Knight, before you go?" called Harry.

"No, thanks, old chap."

Bertha squeezed his hand for that as she shook it.

"Good night, good-bye," she cried from the top step, feeling that this self of hers was taking leave of them for ever.

When she got back into the drawing-room the others were on the move.

"...Then you can come part of the way in my taxi."

"I shall be *so* thankful *not* to have to face *another* drive *alone* after my *dreadful* experience."

"You can get a taxi at the rank just at the end of the street. You won't have to walk more than a few yards."

"That's comfort. I'll go and put on my coat."

Miss Fulton moved towards the hall and Bertha was following when Harry almost pushed past.

"Let me help you."

Bertha knew that he was repenting his rudeness — she let him go. What a boy he was in some ways — so impulsive — so — simple.

And Eddie and she were left by the fire.

"I *wonder* if you have seen Bilks' *new* poem called *Table d'Hôte*," said Eddie softly. "It's *so* wonderful. In the last Anthology. Have you got a copy? I'd *so* like to *show* it to you. It begins with an *incredibly* beautiful line: 'Why Must it Always be Tomato Soup?'"

"Yes," said Bertha. And she moved noiselessly to a table opposite the drawing-room door and Eddie glided noiselessly after her. She picked up the little book and gave it to him; they had not made a sound.

While he looked it up she turned her head towards the hall. And she saw. ..Harry with Miss Fulton's coat in his arms and Miss Fulton with her back turned to him and her head bent. He tossed the coat away, put his hands on her shoulders and turned her violently to him. His lips said: "I adore you," and Miss Fulton laid her moonbeam fingers on his cheeks and smiled her sleepy smile. Harry's nostrils quivered; his lips curled back in a hideous grin while he whispered: "Tomorrow," and with her eyelids Miss Fulton said "Yes."

"Here it is," said Eddie. "'Why Must it Always be Tomato Soup?' It's so *deeply* true, don't you feel? Tomato soup is so *dreadfully* eternal."

"If you prefer," said Harry's voice, very loud, from the hall, "I can 'phone you a cab to come to the door."

"Oh, no. It's not necessary," said Miss Fulton, and she came up to Bertha and gave her the slender fingers to hold.

"Good-bye. Thank you so much."

"Good-bye," said Bertha.

Miss Fulton held her hand a moment longer.

"Your lovely pear tree!" she murmured.

And then she was gone, with Eddie following, like the black cat following the grey cat.

"I'll shut up shop," said Harry, extravagantly cool and collected.

"Your lovely pear tree — pear tree — pear tree!"

Bertha simply ran over to the long windows.

"Oh, what is going to happen now?" she cried.

But the pear tree was as lovely as ever and as full of flower and as still.

(1918)

William Faulkner   (1897–1962)

In his 1950 acceptance speech for the Nobel Prize for literature, William Faulkner defined his subject matter as "the human heart in conflict with itself, which alone can make good writing because only that is worth writing about." Universal in their themes, most of his novels and short stories are set in Yoknapatawpha County, a fictionalized version of West Lafayette County, Mississippi, where he was born and lived most of his life. A major focus in many of his works is the central characters' awareness of the degeneration of their families from a once glorious past and their sense of imprisonment in memories of that past. In such novels as *Absalom, Absalom!* and *The Reivers*, Faulkner is as interested in attempts by the characters to understand the past as he is in that past itself. "A Rose for Emily," which begins after the death of the title character, presents an unnamed townsman's account and interpretation of details of Emily Grierson's life, many of which occurred before his birth, and the discovery he and the villagers make about her when they break into one of the rooms of her home after her funeral. With new knowledge, the narrator finally understands the recluse's character and her actions.

A ROSE FOR EMILY

I

When Miss Emily Grierson died, our whole town went to her funeral: the men through a sort of respectful affection for a fallen monument, the women mostly out of curiosity to see the inside of her house, which no one save an old man-servant — a combined gardener and cook — had seen in at least ten years.

It was a big, squarish frame house that had once been white, decorated with cupolas and spires and scrolled balconies in the heavily lightsome style of the seventies, set on what had once been our most select street. But garages and cotton gins had encroached and obliterated even the august names of that neighborhood; only Miss Emily's house was left, lifting its stubborn and coquettish decay above the cotton wagons and the gasoline pumps — an eyesore among eyesores. And now Miss Emily had gone to join the representatives of those august names where they lay in the cedar-bemused cemetery among the ranked and anonymous graves of Union and Confederate soldiers[1] who fell at the battle of Jefferson.[2]

Alive, Miss Emily had been a tradition, a duty, and a care; a sort of hereditary obligation upon the town, dating from that day in 1894 when Colonel Sartoris, the mayor — he who fathered the edict that no Negro woman should appear on the streets without an apron — remitted her taxes, the dispensation dating from the death of her father on into perpetuity. Not that Miss Emily

---

1 soldiers who fought for the North and South, respectively, during the American Civil War.
2 Civil War battle fought in Mississippi; Jefferson is Faulkner's fictional name for Oxford, Mississippi.

would have accepted charity. Colonel Sartoris invented an involved tale to the effect that Miss Emily's father had loaned money to the town, which the town, as a matter of business, preferred this way of repaying. Only a man of Colonel Sartoris' generation and thought could have invented it, and only a woman could have believed it.

When the next generation, with its more modern ideas, became mayors and aldermen, this arrangement created some little dissatisfaction. On the first of the year they mailed her a tax notice. February came, and there was no reply. They wrote her a formal letter, asking her to call at the sheriff's office at her convenience. A week later the mayor wrote her himself, offering to call or to send his car for her, and received in reply a note on paper of an archaic shape, in a thin, flowing calligraphy in faded ink, to the effect that she no longer went out at all. The tax notice was also enclosed, without comment.

5   They called a special meeting of the Board of Aldermen. A deputation waited upon her, knocked at the door through which no visitor had passed since she ceased giving china-painting lessons eight or ten years earlier. They were admitted by the old Negro into a dim hall from which a stairway mounted into still more shadow. It smelled of dust and disuse — a close, dank smell. The Negro led them into the parlor. It was furnished in heavy, leather-covered furniture. When the Negro opened the blinds of one window, they could see that the leather was cracked; and when they sat down, a faint dust rose sluggishly about their thighs, spinning with slow motes in the single sun-ray. On a tarnished gilt easel before the fireplace stood a crayon portrait of Miss Emily's father.

They rose when she entered — a small, fat woman in black, with a thin gold chain descending to her waist and vanishing into her belt, leaning on an ebony cane with a tarnished gold head. Her skeleton was small and spare; perhaps that was why what would have been merely plumpness in another was obesity in her. She looked bloated, like a body long submerged in motionless water, and of that pallid hue. Her eyes, lost in the fatty ridges of her face, looked like two small pieces of coal pressed into a lump of dough as they moved from one face to another while the visitors stated their errand.

She did not ask them to sit. She just stood in the door and listened quietly until the spokesman came to a stumbling halt. Then they could hear the invisible watch ticking at the end of the gold chain.

Her voice was dry and cold. "I have no taxes in Jefferson. Colonel Sartoris explained it to me. Perhaps one of you can gain access to the city records and satisfy yourselves."

"But we have. We are the city authorities, Miss Emily. Didn't you get a notice from the sheriff, signed by him?"

10   "I received a paper, yes," Miss Emily said. "Perhaps he considers himself the sheriff...I have no taxes in Jefferson."

"But there is nothing on the books to show that, you see. We must go by the —"

"See Colonel Sartoris. I have no taxes in Jefferson."

"But, Miss Emily —"

"See Colonel Sartoris." (Colonel Sartoris had been dead almost ten years.) "I have no taxes in Jefferson. Tobe!" The Negro appeared. "Show these gentlemen out."

II

15 So she vanquished them, horse and foot, just as she had vanquished their fathers thirty years before about the smell. That was two years after her father's death and a short time after her sweetheart — the one we believed would marry her — had deserted her. After her father's death she went out very little; after her sweetheart went away, people hardly saw her at all. A few of the ladies had the temerity to call, but were not received, and the only sign of life about the place was the Negro man — a young man then — going in and out with a market basket.

"Just as if a man — any man — could keep a kitchen properly," the ladies said; so they were not surprised when the smell developed. It was another link between the gross, teeming world and the high and mighty Griersons.

A neighbor, a woman, complained to the mayor, Judge Stevens, eighty years old.

"But what will you have me do about it, madam?" he said.

"Why, send her word to stop it," the woman said. "Isn't there a law?"

20 "I'm sure that won't be necessary," Judge Stevens said. "It's probably just a snake or a rat that nigger of hers killed in the yard. I'll speak to him about it."

The next day he received two more complaints, one from a man who came in diffident deprecation. "We really must do something about it, Judge. I'd be the last one in the world to bother Miss Emily, but we've got to do something." That night the Board of Aldermen met — three graybeards and one younger man, a member of the rising generation.

"It's simple enough," he said. "Send her word to have her place cleaned up. Give her a certain time to do it in, and if she don't . . ."

"Dammit, sir," Judge Stevens said, "will you accuse a lady to her face of smelling bad?"

So the next night, after midnight, four men crossed Miss Emily's lawn and slunk about the house like burglars, sniffing along the base of the brickwork and at the cellar openings while one of them performed a regular sowing motion with his hand out of a sack slung from his shoulder. They broke open the cellar door and sprinkled lime there, and in all the outbuildings. As they recrossed the lawn, a window that had been dark was lighted and Miss Emily sat in it, the light behind her, and her upright torso motionless as that of an idol. They crept quietly across the lawn and into the shadow of the locusts that lined the street. After a week or two the smell went away.

25 That was when people had begun to feel really sorry for her. People in our town, remembering how old lady Wyatt, her great-aunt, had gone completely crazy at last, believed that the Griersons held themselves a little too high for what they really were. None of the young men were quite good enough for Miss Emily and such. We had long thought of them as a tableau, Miss Emily a slender figure in white in the background, her father a spraddled silhouette in the foreground, his back to her and clutching a horsewhip, the two of them framed by the back-flung front door. So when she got to be thirty and was still single, we were not pleased exactly, but vindicated; even with insanity in the family she wouldn't have turned down all of her chances if they had really materialized.

When her father died, it got about that the house was all that was left to her; and in a way, people were glad. At last they could pity Miss Emily. Being left alone, and a pauper, she had become humanized. Now she too would know the old thrill and the old despair of a penny more or less.

The day after his death all the ladies prepared to call at the house and offer condolence and aid, as is our custom. Miss Emily met them at the door, dressed as usual and with no trace of grief on her face. She told them that her father was not dead. She did that for three days, with the ministers calling on her, and the doctors, trying to persuade her to let them dispose of the body. Just as they were about to resort to law and force, she broke down, and they buried her father quickly.

We did not say she was crazy then. We believed she had to do that. We remembered all the young men her father had driven away, and we knew that with nothing left, she would have to cling to that which had robbed her, as people will.

III

She was sick for a long time. When we saw her again, her hair was cut short, making her look like a girl, with a vague resemblance to those angels in colored church windows — sort of tragic and serene.

30   The town had just let the contracts for paving the sidewalks, and in the summer after her father's death they began the work. The construction company came with niggers and mules and machinery, and a foreman named Homer Barron, a Yankee — a big, dark, ready man, with a big voice and eyes lighter than his face. The little boys would follow in groups to hear him cuss the niggers, and the niggers singing in time to the rise and fall of picks. Pretty soon he knew everybody in town. Whenever you heard a lot of laughing anywhere about the square, Homer Barron would be in the center of the group. Presently we began to see him and Miss Emily on Sunday afternoons driving in the yellow-wheeled buggy and the matched team of bays from the livery stable.

At first we were glad that Miss Emily would have an interest, because the ladies all said, "Of course a Grierson would not think seriously of a Northerner, a day laborer." But there were still others, older people, who said that even grief could not cause a real lady to forget noblesse oblige[3] — without calling it noblesse oblige. They just said, "Poor Emily. Her kinsfolk should come to her." She had some kin in Alabama; but years ago her father had fallen out with them over the estate of old lady Wyatt, the crazy woman, and there was no communication between the two families. They had not even been represented at the funeral.

And as soon as the old people said, "Poor Emily," the whispering began. "Do you suppose it's really so?" they said to one another. "Of course it is. What else could ..." This behind their hands; rustling of craned silk and satin behind jalousies closed upon the sun of Sunday afternoon as the thin, swift clop-clop-clop of the matched team passed: "Poor Emily."

3 the responsibility of privileged, high-born people to be honourable.

She carried her head high enough — even when we believed that she was fallen. It was as if she demanded more than ever the recognition of her dignity as the last Grierson; as if it had wanted that touch of earthiness to reaffirm her imperviousness. Like when she bought the rat poison, the arsenic. That was over a year after they had begun to say "Poor Emily," and while the two female cousins were visiting her.

"I want some poison," she said to the druggist. She was over thirty then, still a slight woman, though thinner than usual, with cold, haughty black eyes in a face the flesh of which was strained across the temples and about the eye-sockets as you imagine a lighthouse-keeper's face ought to look. "I want some poison," she said.

"Yes, Miss Emily. What kind? For rats and such? I'd recom —"

"I want the best you have. I don't care what kind."

The druggist named several. "They'll kill anything up to an elephant. But what you want is —"

"Arsenic," Miss Emily said. "Is that a good one?"

"Is . . . arsenic? Yes, ma'am. But what you want —"

"I want arsenic."

The druggist looked down at her. She looked back at him, erect, her face like a strained flag. "Why, of course," the druggist said. "If that's what you want. But the law requires you to tell what you are going to use it for."

Miss Emily just stared at him, her head tilted back in order to look him eye for eye, until he looked away and went and got the arsenic and wrapped it up. The Negro delivery boy brought her the package; the druggist didn't come back. When she opened the package at home there was written on the box, under the skull and bones: "For rats."

IV

So the next day we all said, "She will kill herself"; and we said it would be the best thing. When she had first begun to be seen with Homer Barron, we had said, "She will marry him." Then we said, "She will persuade him yet," because Homer himself had remarked — he liked men, and it was known that he drank with the younger men in the Elks' Club — that he was not a marrying man. Later we said, "Poor Emily" behind the jalousies as they passed on Sunday afternoon in the glittering buggy, Miss Emily with her head high and Homer Barron with his hat cocked and a cigar in his teeth, reins and whip in a yellow glove.

Then some of the ladies began to say that it was a disgrace to the town and a bad example to the young people. The men did not want to interfere, but at last the ladies forced the Baptist minister — Miss Emily's people were Episcopal [4] — to call upon her. He would never divulge what happened during that interview, but he refused to go back again. The next Sunday they again drove about the streets, and the following day the minister's wife wrote to Miss Emily's relations in Alabama.

So she had blood-kin under her roof again and we sat back to watch developments. At first nothing happened. Then we were sure that they were

4 the Anglican Church in the United States.

to be married. We learned that Miss Emily had been to the jeweler's and ordered a man's toilet set in silver, with the letters H.B. on each piece. Two days later we learned that she had bought a complete outfit of men's clothing, including a nightshirt, and we said, "They are married." We were really glad. We were glad because the two female cousins were even more Grierson than Miss Emily had ever been.

So we were not surprised when Homer Barron — the streets had been finished some time since — was gone. We were a little disappointed that there was not a public blowing-off, but we believed that he had gone on to prepare for Miss Emily's coming, or to give her a chance to get rid of the cousins. (By that time it was a cabal, and we were all Miss Emily's allies to help circumvent the cousins.) Sure enough, after another week they departed. And, as we had expected all along, within three days Homer Barron was back in town. A neighbor saw the Negro man admit him at the kitchen door at dusk one evening.

And that was the last we saw of Homer Barron. And of Miss Emily for some time. The Negro man went in and out with the market basket, but the front door remained closed. Now and then we would see her at a window for a moment, as the men did that night when they sprinkled the lime, but for almost six months she did not appear on the streets. Then we knew that this was to be expected too; as if that quality of her father which had thwarted her woman's life so many times had been too virulent and too furious to die.

When we next saw Miss Emily, she had grown fat and her hair was turning gray. During the next few years it grew grayer and grayer until it attained an even pepper-and-salt iron-gray, when it ceased turning. Up to the day of her death at seventy-four it was still that vigorous iron-gray, like the hair of an active man.

From that time on her front door remained closed, save for a period of six or seven years, when she was about forty, during which she gave lessons in china-painting. She fitted up a studio in one of the downstairs rooms, where the daughters and granddaughters of Colonel Sartoris' contemporaries were sent to her with the same regularity and in the same spirit that they were sent to church on Sundays with a twenty-five-cent piece for the collection plate. Meanwhile her taxes had been remitted.

50 Then the newer generation became the backbone and the spirit of the town, and the painting pupils grew up and fell away and did not send their children to her with boxes of color and tedious brushes and pictures cut from the ladies' magazines. The front door closed upon the last one and remained closed for good. When the town got free postal delivery, Miss Emily alone refused to let them fasten the metal numbers above her door and attach a mailbox to it. She would not listen to them.

Daily, monthly, yearly we watched the Negro grow grayer and more stooped, going in and out with the market basket. Each December we sent her a tax notice, which would be returned by the post office a week later, unclaimed. Now and then we would see her in one of the downstairs windows — she had evidently shut up the top floor of the house — like the carven torso of an idol in a niche, looking or not looking at us, we could never tell which. Thus she passed from generation to generation — dear, inescapable, impervious, tranquil, and perverse.

And so she died. Fell ill in the house filled with dust and shadows, with only a doddering Negro man to wait on her. We did not even know she was sick;

we had long since given up trying to get any information from the Negro. He talked to no one, probably not even to her, for his voice had grown harsh and rusty, as if from disuse.

She died in one of the downstairs rooms, in a heavy walnut bed with a curtain, her gray head propped on a pillow yellow and moldy with age and lack of sunlight.

V

The Negro met the first of the ladies at the front door and let them in, with their hushed, sibilant voices and their quick, curious glances, and then he disappeared. He walked right through the house and out the back and was not seen again.

55   The two female cousins came at once. They held the funeral on the second day, with the town coming to look at Miss Emily beneath a mass of bought flowers, with the crayon face of her father musing profoundly above the bier and the ladies sibilant and macabre; and the very old men — some in their brushed Confederate uniforms — on the porch and the lawn, talking of Miss Emily as if she had been a contemporary of theirs, believing that they had danced with her and courted her perhaps, confusing time with its mathematical progression, as the old do, to whom all the past is not a diminishing road but, instead, a huge meadow which no winter ever quite touches, divided from them now by the narrow bottle-neck of the most recent decade of years.

Already we knew that there was one room in that region above stairs which no one had seen in forty years, and which would have to be forced. They waited until Miss Emily was decently in the ground before they opened it.

The violence of breaking down the door seemed to fill this room with pervading dust. A thin, acrid pall as of the tomb seemed to lie everywhere upon this room decked and furnished as for a bridal: upon the valance curtains of faded rose color, upon the rose-shaded lights, upon the dressing table, upon the delicate array of crystal and the man's toilet things backed with tarnished silver, silver so tarnished that the monogram was obscured. Among them lay a collar and tie, as if they had just been removed, which, lifted, left upon the surface a pale crescent in the dust. Upon a chair hung the suit, carefully folded; beneath it the two mute shoes and the discarded socks.

The man himself lay in the bed.

For a long while we just stood there, looking down at the profound and fleshless grin. The body had apparently once lain in the attitude of an embrace, but now the long sleep that outlasts love, that conquers even the grimace of love, had cuckolded him. What was left of him, rotted beneath what was left of the nightshirt, had become inextricable from the bed in which he lay; and upon him and upon the pillow beside him lay that even coating of the patient and biding dust.

60   Then we noticed that in the second pillow was the indentation of a head. One of us lifted something from it, and leaning forward, that faint and invisible dust dry and acrid in the nostrils, we saw a long strand of iron-gray hair.

(1930)

Ernest Hemingway (1899–1961)

Like Stephen Crane, whose short stories he admired, Ernest Hemingway, a native of Oak Park, Illinois, began his writing career as a newspaper correspondent. The short sentences, crisp description of settings and actions, and relative lack of authorial comment that are distinguishing features of his mature style no doubt reflect his background in journalism. Hemingway's experiences in Italy during World War I, where he was injured while serving as an ambulance driver, and in Paris during the 1920s, where he was a member of the so-called Lost Generation (individuals who no longer believed in absolute moral or religious values), contributed to the development of his major theme: the need of the individual to live with control and dignity in a violent world devoid of spiritual meaning. Most fully developed in *The Sun Also Rises* (1926) and *A Farewell to Arms* (1929), two of his finest novels, these ideas are also expressed in "A Clean, Well-Lighted Place." The prose, which at first appears simply reportorial, implicitly develops the themes and symbols of the story.

A CLEAN, WELL-LIGHTED PLACE

It was late and every one had left the café except an old man who sat in the shadow the leaves of the tree made against the electric light. In the day time the street was dusty, but at night the dew settled the dust and the old man liked to sit late because he was deaf and now at night it was quiet and he felt the difference. The two waiters inside the café knew that the old man was a little drunk, and while he was a good client they knew that if he became too drunk he would leave without paying, so they kept watch on him.

"Last week he tried to commit suicide," one waiter said.

"Why?"

"He was in despair."

5   "What about?"

"Nothing."

"How do you know it was nothing?"

"He has plenty of money."

They sat together at a table that was close against the wall near the door of the café and looked at the terrace where the tables were all empty except where the old man sat in the shadow of the leaves of the tree that moved slightly in the wind. A girl and a soldier went by in the street. The street light shone on the brass number on his collar. The girl wore no head covering and hurried beside him.

10   "The guard will pick him up," one waiter said.

"What does it matter if he gets what he's after?"

"He had better get off the street now. The guard will get him. They went by five minutes ago."

The old man sitting in the shadow rapped on his saucer with his glass. The younger waiter went over to him.

"What do you want?"

15 The old man looked at him. "Another brandy," he said.

"You'll be drunk," the waiter said. The old man looked at him. The waiter went away.

"He'll stay all night," he said to his colleague. "I'm sleepy now. I never get into bed before three o'clock. He should have killed himself last week."

The waiter took the brandy bottle and another saucer from the counter inside the café and marched out to the old man's table. He put down the saucer and poured the glass full of brandy.

"You should have killed yourself last week," he said to the deaf man. The old man motioned with his finger. "A little more," he said. The waiter poured on into the glass so that the brandy slopped over and ran down the stem into the top saucer of the pile. "Thank you," the old man said. The waiter took the bottle back inside the café. He sat down at the table with his colleague again.

20 "He's drunk now," he said.

"He's drunk every night."

"What did he want to kill himself for?"

"How should I know."

"How did he do it?"

25 "He hung himself with a rope."

"Who cut him down?"

"His niece."

"Why did she do it?"

"Fear for his soul."

30 "How much money has he got?"

"He's got plenty."

"He must be eighty years old."

"Anyway I should say he was eighty."

"I wish he would go home. I never get to bed before three o'clock. What kind of hour is that to go to bed?"

35 "He stays up because he likes it."

"He's lonely. I'm not lonely. I have a wife waiting in bed for me."

"He had a wife once too."

"A wife would be no good to him now."

"You can't tell. He might be better with a wife."

40 "His niece looks after him. You said she cut him down."

"I know."

"I wouldn't want to be that old. An old man is a nasty thing."

"Not always. This old man is clean. He drinks without spilling. Even now, drunk. Look at him."

"I don't want to look at him. I wish he would go home. He has no regard for those who must work."

45 The old man looked from his glass across the square, then over at the waiters.

"Another brandy," he said, pointing to his glass. The waiter who was in a hurry came over.

"Finished," he said, speaking with that omission of syntax stupid people employ when talking to drunken people or foreigners. "No more tonight. Close now."

"Another," said the old man.

"No. Finished." The waiter wiped the edge of the table with a towel and shook his head.

50 The old man stood up, slowly counted the saucers, took a leather coin purse from his pocket and paid for the drinks, leaving half a peseta tip.

The waiter watched him go down the street, a very old man walking unsteadily but with dignity.

"Why didn't you let him stay and drink?" the unhurried waiter asked. They were putting up the shutters. "It is not half-past two."

"I want to go home to bed."

"What is an hour?"

55 "More to me than to him."

"An hour is the same."

"You talk like an old man yourself. He can buy a bottle and drink at home."

"It's not the same."

"No, it is not," agreed the waiter with a wife. He did not wish to be unjust. He was only in a hurry.

60 "And you? You have no fear of going home before your usual hour?"

"Are you trying to insult me?"

"No, hombre, only to make a joke."

"No," the waiter who was in a hurry said, rising from pulling down the metal shutters. "I have confidence. I am all confidence."

"You have youth, confidence, and a job," the older waiter said. "You have everything."

65 "And what do you lack?"

"Everything but work."

"You have everything I have."

"No. I have never had confidence and I am not young."

"Come on. Stop talking nonsense and lock up."

70 "I am with those who like to stay late at the café," the older waiter said. "With all those who do not want to go to bed. With all those who need a light for the night."

"I want to go home and into bed."

"We are of two different kinds," the older waiter said. He was now dressed to go home. "It is not only a question of youth and confidence although those things are very beautiful. Each night I am reluctant to close up because there may be some one who needs the café."

"Hombre, there are bodegas open all night long."

"You do not understand. This is a clean and pleasant café. It is well lighted. The light is very good and also, now, there are shadows of the leaves."

75 "Good night," said the younger waiter.

"Good night," the other said. Turning off the electric light he continued the conversation with himself. It is the light of course but it is necessary that the place be clean and pleasant. You do not want music. Certainly you do not want music. Nor can you stand before a bar with dignity although that is all that is provided for these hours. What did he fear? It was not fear or dread. It was a nothing that he knew too well. It was all a nothing and a man was

nothing too. It was only that and light was all it needed and a certain clean-
ness and order. Some lived in it and never felt it but he knew it all was nada y
pues nada y nada y pues nada.[1] Our nada who art in nada, nada be thy name
thy kingdom nada thy will be nada in nada as it is in nada. Give us this nada
our daily nada and nada us our nada as we nada our nadas and nada us not into
nada but deliver us from nada; pues nada. Hail nothing full of nothing, nothing
is with thee. He smiled and stood before a bar with a shining steam pressure
coffee machine.

"What's yours?" asked the barman.

"Nada."

"Otro loco mas,"[2] said the barman and turned away.

80   "A little cup," said the waiter.

The barman poured it for him.

"The light is very bright and pleasant but the bar is unpolished," the
waiter said.

The barman looked at him but did not answer. It was too late at night for
conversation.

"You want another copita?"[3]

85   "No, thank you," said the waiter and went out. He disliked bars and
bodegas. A clean, well-lighted café was a very different thing. Now, without
thinking further, he would go home to his room. He would lie in the bed and
finally, with daylight, he would go to sleep. After all, he said to himself, it is
probably only insomnia. Many must have it.

(1933)

---

1 nothing, and therefore nothing. 2 another crazy one. 3 small cup.

Sinclair Ross   (1908–1996)

Born on a farm near Prince Albert, Saskatchewan, Sinclair Ross, in his novel *As For Me and My House* (1941) and his first collection of short stories, *The Lamp at Noon* (1968), portrays life on the Canadian prairies during the "Dust Bowl" era of the 1930s. In addition to depicting the hardship and isolation, courage, and loneliness of his characters, Ross emphasizes the power of the land, which, as Margaret Laurence noted, appears "almost as a chief protagonist." In "The Lamp at Noon," the contrasting reactions of a husband and wife to a three-day dust storm that all but destroys their farm are presented in part by Ross's careful selection of physical symbols: the storm, the barren landscape, the barn to which the husband retreats, and the kitchen feebly illuminated by the lamp.

THE LAMP AT NOON

A little before noon she lit the lamp. Demented wind fled keening past the house: a wail through the eaves that died every minute or two. Three days now without respite it had held. The dust was thickening to an impenetrable fog.

She lit the lamp, then for a long time stood at the window motionless. In dim, fitful outline the stable and oat granary still were visible; beyond, obscuring fields and landmarks, the lower of dust clouds made the farmyard seem an isolated acre, poised aloft above a sombre void. At each blast of wind it shook, as if to topple and spin hurtling with the dust-reel into space.

From the window she went to the door, opening it a little, and peering toward the stable again. He was not coming yet. As she watched there was a sudden rift overhead, and for a moment through the tattered clouds the sun raced like a wizened orange. It shed a soft, diffused light, dim and yellow as if it were the light from the lamp reaching out through the open door.

She closed the door, and going to the stove tried the potatoes with a fork. Her eyes all the while were fixed and wide with a curious immobility. It was the window. Standing at it, she had let her forehead press against the pane until the eyes were strained apart and rigid. Wide like that they had looked out to the deepening ruin of the storm. Now she could not close them.

5   The baby started to cry. He was lying in a homemade crib over which she had arranged a tent of muslin. Careful not to disturb the folds of it, she knelt and tried to still him, whispering huskily in a singsong voice that he must hush and go to sleep again. She would have liked to rock him, to feel the comfort of his little body in her arms, but a fear had obsessed her that in the dust-filled air he might contract pneumonia. There was dust sifting everywhere. Her own throat was parched with it. The table had been set less than ten minutes, and already a film was gathering on the dishes. The little cry continued, and with wincing, frightened lips she glanced around as if to find a corner where the air was less oppressive. But while the lips winced the eyes maintained their wide, immobile stare. "Sleep," she whispered again. "It's too soon for you to be hungry. Daddy's coming for his dinner."

He seemed a long time. Even the clock, still a few minutes off noon, could not dispel a foreboding sense that he was longer than he should be. She went to the door again — and then recoiled slowly to stand white and breathless in the middle of the room. She mustn't. He would only despise her if she ran to the stable looking for him. There was too much grim endurance in his nature ever to let him understand the fear and weakness of a woman. She must stay quiet and wait. Nothing was wrong. At noon he would come — and perhaps after dinner stay with her awhile.

Yesterday, and again at breakfast this morning, they had quarrelled bitterly. She wanted him now, the assurance of his strength and nearness, but he would stand aloof, wary, remembering the words she had flung at him in her anger, unable to understand it was only the dust and wind that had driven her.

Tense, she fixed her eyes upon the clock, listening. There were two winds: the wind in flight, and the wind that pursued. The one sought refuge in the eaves, whimpering, in fear; the other assailed it there, and shook the eaves apart to make it flee again. Once as she listened this first wind sprang inside the room, distraught like a bird that has felt the graze of talons on its wing; while furious the other wind shook the walls, and thudded tumbleweeds against the window till its quarry glanced away again in fright. But only to return — to return and quake among the feeble eaves, as if in all this dust-mad wilderness it knew no other sanctuary.

Then Paul came. At his step she hurried to the stove, intent upon the pots and frying pan. "The worst wind yet," he ventured, hanging up his cap and smock. "I had to light the lantern in the tool shed, too."

They looked at each other, then away. She wanted to go to him, to feel his arms supporting her, to cry a little just that he might soothe her, but because his presence made the menace of the wind seem less, she gripped herself and thought, "I'm in the right. I won't give in. For his sake, too, I won't."

He washed, hurriedly, so that a few dark welts of dust remained to indent upon his face a haggard strength. It was all she could see as she wiped the dishes and set the food before him: the strength, the grimness, the young Paul growing old and hard, buckled against a desert even grimmer than his will. "Hungry?" she asked, touched to a twinge of pity she had not intended. "There's dust in everything. It keeps coming faster than I can clean it up."

He nodded. "Tonight, though, you'll see it go down. This is the third day."

She looked at him in silence a moment, and then as if to herself muttered broodingly, "Until the next time. Until it starts again."

There was a dark resentment in her voice now that boded another quarrel. He waited, his eyes on her dubiously as she mashed a potato with her fork. The lamp between them threw strong lights and shadows on their faces. Dust and drought, earth that betrayed alike his labour and his faith, to him the struggle had given sternness, an impassive courage. Beneath the whip of sand his youth had been effaced. Youth, zest, exuberance — there remained only a harsh and clenched virility that yet became him, that seemed at the cost of more engaging qualities to be fulfilment of his inmost and essential nature. Whereas to her the same debts and poverty had brought a plaintive indignation, a nervous dread of what was still to come. The eyes were hollowed, the lips pinched dry and colourless. It was the face of a woman that had aged without maturing, that had loved the little vanities of life, and lost them wistfully.

15   "I'm afraid, Paul," she said suddenly. "I can't stand it any longer. He cries all the time. You will go, Paul — say you will. We aren't living here — not really living —"

The pleading in her voice now, after its shrill bitterness yesterday, made him think that this was only another way to persuade him. He answered evenly, "I told you this morning, Ellen; we keep on right where we are. At least I do. It's yourself you're thinking about, not the baby."

This morning such an accusation would have stung her to rage; now, her voice swift and panting, she pressed on, "Listen, Paul — I'm thinking of all of us — you, too. Look at the sky — what's happening. Are you blind? Thistles and tumbleweeds — it's a desert. You won't have a straw this fall. You won't be able to feed a cow or a chicken. Please, Paul, say we'll go away —"

"Go where?" His voice as he answered was still remote and even, inflexibly in unison with the narrowed eyes and the great hunch of muscle-knotted shoulder. "Even as a desert it's better than sweeping out your father's store and running his errands. That's all I've got ahead of me if I do what you want."

"And here —" she faltered. "What's ahead of you here? At least we'll get enough to eat and wear when you're sweeping out his store. Look at it — look at it, you fool. Desert — the lamp lit at noon —"

20   "You'll see it come back. There's good wheat in it yet."

"But in the meantime — year after year — can't you understand, Paul? We'll never get them back —"

He put down his knife and fork and leaned toward her across the table. "I can't go, Ellen. Living off your people — charity — stop and think of it. This is where I belong. I can't do anything else."

"Charity!" she repeated him, letting her voice rise in derision. "And this — you call this independence! Borrowed money you can't even pay the interest on, seed from the government — grocery bills — doctor bills —"

"We'll have crops again," he persisted. "Good crops — the land will come back. It's worth waiting for."

25   "And while we're waiting, Paul!" It was not anger now, but a kind of sob. "Think of me — and him. It's not fair. We have our lives, too, to live."

"And you think that going home to your family — taking your husband with you —"

"I don't care — anything would be better than this. Look at the air he's breathing. He cries all the time. For his sake, Paul. What's ahead of him here, even if you do get crops?"

He clenched his lips a minute, then, with his eyes hard and contemptuous, struck back, "As much as in town, growing up a pauper. You're the one who wants to go, it's not for his sake. You think that in town you'd have a better time — not so much work — more clothes —"

"Maybe —" She dropped her head defencelessly. "I'm young still. I like pretty things."

30   There was silence now — a deep fastness of it enclosed by rushing wind and creaking walls. It seemed the yellow lamplight cast a hush upon them. Through the haze of dusty air the walls receded, dimmed, and came again. At last she

raised her head and said listlessly, "Go on — your dinner's getting cold. Don't sit and stare at me. I've said it all."

The spent quietness in her voice was even harder to endure than her anger. It reproached him, against his will insisted that he see and understand her lot. To justify himself he tried, "I was a poor man when you married me. You said you didn't mind. Farming's never been easy, and never will be."

"I wouldn't mind the work or the skimping if there was something to look forward to. It's the hopelessness — going on — watching the land blow away."

"The land's all right," he repeated. "The dry years won't last forever."

"But it's not just dry years, Paul!" The little sob in her voice gave way suddenly to a ring of exasperation. "Will you never see? It's the land itself — the soil. You've plowed and harrowed it until there's not a root or fibre left to hold it down. That's why the soil drifts — that's why in a year or two there'll be nothing left but the bare clay. If in the first place you farmers had taken care of your land — if you hadn't been so greedy for wheat every year —"

35   She had taught school before she married him, and of late in her anger there had been a kind of disdain, an attitude almost of condescension, as if she no longer looked upon the farmers as her equals. He sat still, his eyes fixed on the yellow lamp flame, and seeming to know how her words had hurt him, she went on softly, "I want to help you, Paul. That's why I won't sit quiet while you go on wasting your life. You're only thirty — you owe it to yourself as well as me."

He sat staring at the lamp without answering, his mouth sullen. It seemed indifference now, as if he were ignoring her, and stung to anger again she cried, "Do you ever think what my life is? Two rooms to live in — once a month to town, and nothing to spend when I get there. I'm still young — I wasn't brought up this way."

"You're a farmer's wife now. It doesn't matter what you used to be, or how you were brought up. You get enough to eat and wear. Just now that's all I can do. I'm not to blame that we've been dried out five years."

"Enough to eat!" she laughed back shrilly. "Enough salt pork — enough potatoes and eggs. And look —" Springing to the middle of the room she thrust out a foot for him to see the scuffed old slipper. "When they're completely gone I suppose you'll tell me I can go barefoot — that I'm a farmer's wife — that it's not your fault we're dried out —"

"And what about these?" He pushed his chair away from the table now to let her see what he was wearing. "Cowhide — hard as boards — but my feet are so calloused I don't feel them any more."

40   Then he stood up, ashamed of having tried to match her hardships with his own. But frightened now as he reached for his smock she pressed close to him. "Don't go yet. I brood and worry when I'm left alone. Please, Paul — you can't work on the land anyway."

"And keep on like this? You start before I'm through the door. Week in and week out — I've troubles enough of my own."

"Paul — please stay —" The eyes were glazed now, distended a little as if with the intensity of her dread and pleading. "We won't quarrel any more. Hear it! I can't work — I just stand still and listen —"

The eyes frightened him, but responding to a kind of instinct that he must withstand her, that it was his self-respect and manhood against the fretful weakness of a woman, he answered unfeelingly, "In here safe and quiet — you don't know how well off you are. If you were out in it — fighting it — swallowing it —"

"Sometimes, Paul, I wish I was. I'm so caged — if I could only break away and run. See — I stand like this all day. I can't relax. My throat's so tight it aches —"

45   With a jerk he freed his smock from her clutch. "If I stay we'll only keep on all afternoon. Wait till tomorrow — we'll talk things over when the wind goes down."

Then without meeting her eyes again he swung outside, and doubled low against the buffets of the wind, fought his way slowly toward the stable. There was a deep hollow calm within, a vast darkness engulfed beneath the tides of moaning wind. He stood breathless a moment, hushed almost to a stupor by the sudden extinction of the storm and the stillness that enfolded him. It was a long, far-reaching stillness. The first dim stalls and rafters led the way into cavern-like obscurity, into vaults and recesses that extended far beyond the stable walls. Nor in these first quiet moments did he forbid the illusion, the sense of release from a harsh, familiar world into one of peace and darkness. The contentious mood that his stand against Ellen had roused him to, his tenacity and clenched despair before the ravages of wind, it was ebbing now, losing itself in the cover of darkness. Ellen and the wheat seemed remote, unimportant. At a whinny from the bay mare, Bess, he went forward and into her stall. She seemed grateful for his presence, and thrust her nose deep between his arm and body. They stood a long time motionless, comforting and assuring each other.

For soon again the first deep sense of quiet and peace was shrunken to the battered shelter of the stable. Instead of release or escape from the assaulting wind, the walls were but a feeble stand against it. They creaked and sawed as if the fingers of a giant hand were tightening to collapse them; the empty loft sustained a pipelike cry that rose and fell but never ended. He saw the dust-black sky again, and his fields blown smooth with drifted soil.

But always, even while listening to the storm outside, he could feel the tense and apprehensive stillness of the stable. There was not a hoof that clumped or shifted, not a rub of halter against manger. And yet, though it had been a strange stable, he would have known, despite the darkness, that every stall was filled. They, too, were all listening.

From Bess he went to the big grey gelding, Prince. Prince was twenty years old, with rib-grooved sides, and high, protruding hipbones. Paul ran his hand over the ribs, and felt a sudden shame, a sting of fear that Ellen might be right in what she said. For wasn't it true — nine years a farmer now on his own land, and still he couldn't even feed his horses? What, then, could he hope to do for his wife and son?

50   There was much he planned. And so vivid was the future of his planning, so real and constant, that often the actual present was but half felt, but half endured. Its difficulties were lessened by a confidence in what lay beyond them. A new house — land for the boy — land and still more land — or education, whatever he might want.

But all the time was he only a blind and stubborn fool? Was Ellen right? Was he trampling on her life, and throwing away his own? The five years since he married her, were they to go on repeating themselves, five, ten, twenty, until all the brave future he looked forward to was but a stark and futile past?

She looked forward to no future. She had no faith or dream with which to make the dust and poverty less real. He understood suddenly. He saw her face again as only a few minutes ago it had begged him not to leave her. The darkness round him now was as a slate on which her lonely terror limned itself. He went from Prince to the other horses, combing their manes and forelocks with his fingers, but always it was her face before him, its staring eyes and twisted suffering. "See Paul — I stand like this all day. I just stand still — My throat's so tight it aches —"

And always the wind, the creak of walls, the wild lipless wailing through the loft. Until at last as he stood there, staring into the livid face before him, it seemed that this scream of wind was a cry from her parched and frantic lips. He knew it couldn't be, he knew that she was safe within the house, but still the wind persisted as a woman's cry. The cry of a woman with eyes like those that watched him through the dark. Eyes that were mad now — lips that even as they cried still pleaded, "See, Paul — I stand like this all day. I just stand still — so caged! If I could only run!"

He saw her running, pulled and driven headlong by the wind, but when at last he returned to the house, compelled by his anxiety, she was walking quietly back and forth with the baby in her arms. Careful, despite his concern, not to reveal a fear or weakness that she might think capitulation to her wishes, he watched a moment through the window, and then went off to the tool shed to mend harness. All afternoon he stitched and riveted. It was easier with the lantern lit and his hands occupied. There was a wind whining high past the tool shed too, but it was only wind. He remembered the arguments with which Ellen had tried to persuade him away from the farm, and one by one he defeated them. There would be rain again — next year or the next. Maybe in his ignorance he had farmed his land the wrong way, seeding wheat every year, working the soil till it was lifeless dust — but he would do better now. He would plant clover and alfalfa, breed cattle, acre by acre and year by year restore to his land its fibre and fertility. That was something to work for, a way to prove himself. It was ruthless wind, blackening the sky with his earth, but it was not his master. Out of his land it had made a wilderness. He now, out of the wilderness, would make a farm and home again.

55   Tonight he must talk with Ellen. Patiently, when the wind was down, and they were both quiet again. It was she who had told him to grow fibrous crops, who had called him an ignorant fool because he kept on with summer fallow and wheat. Now she might be gratified to find him acknowledging her wisdom. Perhaps she would begin to feel the power and steadfastness of the land, to take a pride in it, to understand that he was not a fool, but working for her future and their son's.

And already the wind was slackening. At four o'clock he could sense a lull. At five, straining his eyes from the tool shed doorway, he could make out a neighbour's buildings half a mile away. It was over — three days of blight and havoc like a scourge — three days so bitter and so long that for a moment he stood still, unseeing, his senses idle with a numbness of relief.

But only for a moment. Suddenly he emerged from the numbness; suddenly the fields before him struck his eyes to comprehension. They lay black, naked. Beaten and mounded smooth with dust as if a sea in gentle swell had turned to stone. And though he had tried to prepare himself for such a scene, though he had known since yesterday that not a blade would last the storm, still now, before the utter waste confronting him, he sickened and stood cold. Suddenly like the fields he was naked. Everything that had sheathed him a little from the realities of existence: vision and purpose, faith in the land, in the future, in himself — it was all rent now, stripped away. "Desert," he heard her voice begin to sob. "Desert, you fool — the lamp lit at noon!"

In the stable again, measuring out their feed to the horses, he wondered what he would say to her tonight. For so deep were his instincts of loyalty to the land that still, even with the images of his betrayal stark upon his mind, his concern was how to withstand her, how to go on again and justify himself. It had not occurred to him yet that he might or should abandon the land. He had lived with it too long. Rather was his impulse still to defend it — as a man defends against the scorn of strangers even his most worthless kin.

He fed his horses, then waited. She too would be waiting, ready to cry at him, "Look now — that crop that was to feed and clothe us! And you'll still keep on! You'll still say 'Next year — there'll be rain next year'!"

But she was gone when he reached the house. The door was open, the lamp blown out, the crib empty. The dishes from their meal at noon were still on the table. She had perhaps begun to sweep, for the broom was lying in the middle of the floor. He tried to call, but a terror clamped upon his throat. In the wan, returning light it seemed that even the deserted kitchen was straining to whisper what it had seen. The tatters of the storm still whimpered through the eaves, and in their moaning told the desolation of the miles they had traversed. On tiptoe at last he crossed to the adjoining room; then at the threshold, without even a glance inside to satisfy himself that she was really gone, he wheeled again and plunged outside.

He ran a long time — distraught and headlong as a few hours ago he had seemed to watch her run — around the farmyard, a little distance into the pasture, back again blindly to the house to see whether she had returned — and then at a stumble down the road for help.

They joined him in the search, rode away for others, spread calling across the fields in the direction she might have been carried by the wind — but nearly two hours later it was himself who came upon her. Crouched down against a drift of sand as if for shelter, her hair in matted strands around her neck and face, the child clasped tightly in her arms.

The child was quite cold. It had been her arms, perhaps, too frantic to protect him, or the smother of dust upon his throat and lungs. "Hold him," she said as he knelt beside her. "So — with his face away from the wind. Hold him until I tidy my hair."

Her eyes were still wide in an immobile stare, but with her lips she smiled at him. For a long time he knelt transfixed, trying to speak to her, touching fearfully with his fingertips the dustgrimed cheeks and eyelids of the child. At last she said, "I'll take him again. Such clumsy hands — you don't know how to hold a baby yet. See how his head falls forward on your arm."

65   Yet it all seemed familiar — a confirmation of what he had known since noon. He gave her the child, then, gathering them up in his arms, struggled to his feet, and turned toward home.

It was evening now. Across the fields a few spent clouds of dust still shook and fled. Beyond, as if through smoke, the sunset smouldered like a distant fire.

He walked with a long dull stride, his eyes before him, heedless of her weight. Once he glanced down and with her eyes she still was smiling. "Such strong arms, Paul — and I was so tired just carrying him. . . ."

He tried to answer, but it seemed that now the dusk was drawn apart in breathless waiting, a finger on its lips until they passed. "You were right, Paul. . . ." Her voice came whispering, as if she too could feel the hush. "You said tonight we'd see the storm go down. So still now, and a red sky — it means tomorrow will be fine."

(1938)

Eudora Welty   (1909–2001)

Like fellow Mississippian William Faulkner, whose works she admired, Eudora Welty set most of her short stories in and around the city where she was born and lived most of her life: Jackson. Family and a sense of place are most important for her characters, for a place of one's own provides "a base of reference," and enables "individuals to put out roots." "Why I Live at the P.O.," which takes place on July 4, American Independence Day, traditionally a time of family reunions, focusses on the developing hostility the narrator feels toward her family and her own declaration of independence from them. Ironically, in its portrayal of the disintegrating interrelationships, the story provides a negative example of Welty's belief that "communication and hope of it are conditions of life itself."

WHY I LIVE AT THE P.O.

I was getting along fine with Mama, Papa-Daddy and Uncle Rondo until my sister Stella-Rondo just separated from her husband and came back home again. Mr. Whitaker! Of course I went with Mr. Whitaker first, when he first appeared here in China Grove,[1] taking "Pose Yourself" photos, and Stella-Rondo broke us up. Told him I was one-sided. Bigger on one side than the other, which is a deliberate, calculated falsehood: I'm the same. Stella-Rondo is exactly twelve months to the day younger than I am and for that reason she's spoiled.

She's always had anything in the world she wanted and then she'd throw it away. Papa-Daddy gave her this gorgeous Add-a-Pearl necklace when she was eight years old and she threw it away playing baseball when she was nine, with only two pearls.

So as soon as she got married and moved away from home the first thing she did was separate! From Mr. Whitaker! This photographer with the popeyes she said she trusted. Came home from one of those towns up in Illinois and to our complete surprise brought this child of two.

Mama said she like to made her drop dead for a second. "Here you had this marvelous blonde child and never so much as wrote your mother a word about it," says Mama. "I'm thoroughly ashamed of you." But of course she wasn't.

5   Stella-Rondo just calmly takes off this *hat*, I wish you could see it. She says, "Why, Mama, Shirley-T.'s adopted, I can prove it."

"How?" says Mama, but all I says was, "H'm!" There I was over the hot stove, trying to stretch two chickens over five people and a completely unexpected child into the bargain, without one moment's notice.

"What do you mean —'H'm!'?" says Stella-Rondo, and Mama says, "I heard that, Sister."

I said that oh, I didn't mean a thing, only that whoever Shirley-T. was, she was the spit-image of Papa-Daddy if he'd cut off his beard, which of course he'd never do in the world. Papa-Daddy's Mama's papa and sulks.

---

1 town in central Mississippi.

Stella-Rondo got furious! She said, "Sister, I don't need to tell you you got a lot of nerve and always did have and I'll thank you to make no future reference to my adopted child whatsoever."

"Very well," I said. "Very well, very well. Of course I noticed at once she looks like Mr. Whitaker's side too. That frown. She looks like a cross between Mr. Whitaker and Papa-Daddy."

"Well, all I can say is she isn't."

"She looks exactly like Shirley Temple[2] to me," says Mama, but Shirley-T. just ran away from her.

So the first thing Stella-Rondo did at the table was turn Papa-Daddy against me.

"Papa-Daddy," she says. He was trying to cut up his meat. "Papa-Daddy!" I was taken completely by surprise. Papa-Daddy is about a million years old and's got this long-long beard. "Papa-Daddy, Sister says she fails to understand why you don't cut off your beard."

So Papa-Daddy l-a-y-s down his knife and fork! He's real rich. Mama says he is, he says he isn't. So he says, "Have I heard correctly? You don't understand why I don't cut off my beard?"

"Why," I says, "Papa-Daddy, of course I understand, I did not say any such of a thing, the idea!"

He says, "Hussy!"

I says, "Papa-Daddy, you know I wouldn't any more want you to cut off your beard than the man in the moon. It was the farthest thing from my mind! Stella-Rondo sat there and made that up while she was eating breast of chicken."

But he says, "So the postmistress fails to understand why I don't cut off my beard. Which job I got you through my influence with the government. 'Bird's nest'— is that what you call it?"

Not that it isn't the next to smallest P.O. in the entire state of Mississippi.

I says, "Oh, Papa-Daddy," I says, "I didn't say any such of a thing, I never dreamed it was a bird's nest, I have always been grateful though this is the next to smallest P.O. in the state of Mississippi, and I do not enjoy being referred to as a hussy by my own grandfather."

But Stella-Rondo says, "Yes, you did say it too. Anybody in the world could of heard you, that had ears."

"Stop right there," says Mama, looking at *me*.

So I pulled my napkin straight back through the napkin ring and left the table.

As soon as I was out of the room Mama says, "Call her back, or she'll starve to death," but Papa-Daddy says, "This is the beard I started growing on the Coast when I was fifteen years old." He would of gone on till nightfall if Shirley-T. hadn't lost the Milky Way she ate in Cairo.[3]

So Papa-Daddy says, "I am going out and lie in the hammock, and you can all sit here and remember my words: I'll never cut off my beard as long as I live, even one inch, and I don't appreciate it in you at all." Passed right by me in the hall and went straight out and got in the hammock.

2 American child movie star of the 1930s. 3 town in southern Illinois.

It would be a holiday. I wasn't five minutes before Uncle Rondo suddenly appeared in the hall in one of Stella-Rondo's flesh-colored kimonos, all cut on the bias, like something Mr. Whitaker probably thought was gorgeous.

"Uncle Rondo!" I says. "I didn't know who that was! Where are you going?"

"Sister," he says, "get out of my way, I'm poisoned."

30 "If you're poisoned stay away from Papa-Daddy," I says. "Keep out of the hammock. Papa-Daddy will certainly beat you on the head if you come within forty miles of him. He thinks I deliberately said he ought to cut off his beard after he got me the P.O., and I've told him and told him and told him, and he acts like he just don't hear me. Papa-Daddy must of gone stone deaf."

"He picked a fine day to do it then," says Uncle Rondo, and before you could say "Jack Robinson" flew out in the yard.

What he'd really done, he'd drunk another bottle of that prescription. He does it every single Fourth of July as sure as shooting, and it's horribly expensive. Then he falls over in the hammock and snores. So he insisted on zigzagging right on out to the hammock, looking like a half-wit.

Papa-Daddy woke up with this horrible yell and right there without moving an inch he tried to turn Uncle Rondo against me. I heard every word he said. Oh, he told Uncle Rondo I didn't learn to read till I was eight years old and he didn't see how in the world I ever got the mail put up at the P.O., much less read it all, and he said if Uncle Rondo could only fathom the lengths he had gone to to get me that job! And he said on the other hand he thought Stella-Rondo had a brilliant mind and deserved credit for getting out of town. All the time he was just lying there swinging as pretty as you please and looping out his beard, and poor Uncle Rondo was *pleading* with him to slow down the hammock, it was making him as dizzy as a witch to watch it. But that's what Papa-Daddy likes about a hammock. So Uncle Rondo was too dizzy to get turned against me for the time being. He's Mama's only brother and is a good case of a one-track mind. Ask anybody. A certified pharmacist.

Just then I heard Stella-Rondo raising the upstairs window. While she was married she got this peculiar idea that it's cooler with the windows shut and locked. So she has to raise the window before she can make a soul hear her outdoors.

35 So she raises the window and says, "*Oh!*" You would have thought she was mortally wounded.

Uncle Rondo and Papa-Daddy didn't even look up, but kept right on with what they were doing. I had to laugh.

I flew up the stairs and threw the door open! I says, "What in the wide world's the matter, Stella-Rondo? You mortally wounded?"

"No," she says, "I am not mortally wounded but I wish you would do me the favor of looking out that window there and telling me what you see."

So I shade my eyes and look out the window.

40 "I see the front yard," I says.

"Don't you see any human beings?" she says.

"I see Uncle Rondo trying to run Papa-Daddy out of the hammock," I says. "Nothing more. Naturally, it's so suffocating-hot in the house, with all the windows shut and locked, everybody who cares to stay in their right mind will have to go out and get in the hammock before the Fourth of July is over."

"Don't you notice anything different about Uncle Rondo?" asks Stella-Rondo.

"Why, no, except he's got on some terrible-looking flesh-colored contraption I wouldn't be found dead in, is all I can see," I says.

45 "Never mind, you won't be found dead in it, because it happens to be part of my trousseau, and Mr. Whitaker took several dozen photographs of me in it," says Stella-Rondo. "What on earth could Uncle Rondo *mean* by wearing part of my trousseau out in the broad open daylight without saying so much as 'Kiss my foot,' *knowing* I only got home this morning after my separation and hung my negligee up on the bathroom door, just as nervous as I could be?"

"I'm sure I don't know, and what do you expect me to do about it?" I says. "Jump out the window?"

"No, I expect nothing of the kind. I simply declare that Uncle Rondo looks like a fool in it, that's all," she says. "It makes me sick to my stomach."

"Well, he looks as good as he can," I says. "As good as anybody in reason could." I stood up for Uncle Rondo, please remember. And I said to Stella-Rondo, "I think I would do well not to criticize so freely if I were you and came home with a two-year-old child I had never said a word about, and no explanation whatever about my separation."

"I asked you the instant I entered this house not to refer one more time to my adopted child, and you gave me your word of honor you would not," was all Stella-Rondo would say, and started pulling out every one of her eyebrows with some cheap Kress tweezers.

50 So I merely slammed the door behind me and went down and made some green-tomato pickle. Somebody had to do it. Of course Mama had turned both the niggers loose; she always said no earthly power could hold one anyway on the Fourth of July, so she wouldn't even try. It turned out that Jaypan fell in the lake and came within a very narrow limit of drowning.

So Mama trots in. Lifts up the lid and says, "H'm! Not very good for your Uncle Rondo in his precarious condition, I must say. Or poor little adopted Shirley-T. Shame on you!"

That made me tired. I says, "Well, Stella-Rondo had better thank her lucky stars it was her instead of me came trotting in with that very peculiar-looking child. Now if it had been me that trotted in from Illinois and brought a peculiar-looking child of two, I shudder to think of the reception I'd of got, much less controlled the diet of an entire family."

"But you must remember, Sister, that you were never married to Mr. Whitaker in the first place and didn't go up to Illinois to live," says Mama, shaking a spoon in my face. "If you had I would of been just as overjoyed to see you and your little adopted girl as I was to see Stella-Rondo, when you wound up with your separation and came on back home."

"You would not," I says.

55 "Don't contradict me, I would," says Mama.

But I said she couldn't convince me though she talked till she was blue in the face. Then I said, "Besides, you know as well as I do that that child is not adopted."

"She most certainly is adopted," says Mama, stiff as a poker.

I says, "Why, Mama, Stella-Rondo had her just as sure as anything in this world, and just too stuck up to admit it."

"Why, Sister," said Mama. "Here I thought we were going to have a pleasant Fourth of July, and you start right out not believing a word your own baby sister tells you!"

60   "Just like Cousin Annie Flo. Went to her grave denying the facts of life," I remind Mama.

"I told you if you ever mentioned Annie Flo's name I'd slap your face," says Mama, and slaps my face.

"All right, you wait and see," I says.

"I," says Mama, "I prefer to take my children's word for anything when it's humanly possible." You ought to see Mama, she weighs two hundred pounds and has real tiny feet.

Just then something perfectly horrible occurred to me.

65   "Mama," I says, "can that child talk?" I simply had to whisper! "Mama, I wonder if that child can be — you know — in any way? Do you realize," I says, "that she hasn't spoken one single, solitary word to a human being up to this minute? This is the way she looks," I says, and I looked like this.

Well, Mama and I just stood there and stared at each other. It was horrible!

"I remember well that Joe Whitaker frequently drank like a fish," says Mama. "I believed to my soul he drank *chemicals*." And without another word she marches to the foot of the stairs and calls Stella-Rondo.

"Stella-Rondo? O-o-o-o-o! Stella-Rondo!"

"What?" says Stella-Rondo from upstairs. Not even the grace to get up off the bed.

70   "Can that child of yours talk?" asks Mama.

Stella-Rondo says, "Can she what?"

"Talk! Talk!" says Mama. "Burdyburdyburdyburdy!"

So Stella-Rondo yells back, "Who says she can't talk?"

"Sister says so," says Mama.

75   "You didn't have to tell me, I know whose word of honor don't mean a thing in this house," says Stella-Rondo.

And in a minute the loudest Yankee voice I ever heard in my life yells out, "OE'm Pop-OE the Sailor-r-r-r Ma-a-an!" and then somebody jumps up and down in the upstairs hall. In another second the house would of fallen down.

"Not only talks, she can tap-dance!" calls Stella-Rondo. "Which is more than some people I won't name can do."

"Why, the little precious darling thing!" Mama says, so surprised. "Just as smart as she can be!" Starts talking baby talk right there. Then she turns on me. "Sister, you ought to be thoroughly ashamed! Run upstairs this instant and apologize to Stella-Rondo and Shirley-T."

"Apologize for what?" I says. "I merely wondered if the child was normal, that's all. Now that she's proved she is, why, I have nothing further to say."

80   But Mama just turned on her heel and flew out, furious. She ran right upstairs and hugged the baby. She believed it was adopted. Stella-Rondo hadn't done a thing but turn her against me from upstairs while I stood there

helpless over the hot stove. So that made Mama, Papa-Daddy and the baby all on Stella-Rondo's side.

Next, Uncle Rondo.

I must say that Uncle Rondo has been marvelous to me at various times in the past and I was completely unprepared to be made to jump out of my skin, the way it turned out. Once Stella-Rondo did something perfectly horrible to him — broke a chain letter from Flanders Field[4] — and he took the radio back he had given her and gave it to me. Stella-Rondo was furious! For six months we all had to call her Stella instead of Stella-Rondo, or she wouldn't answer. I always thought Uncle Rondo had all the brains of the entire family. Another time he sent me to Mammoth Cave,[5] with all expenses paid.

But this would be the day he was drinking that prescription, the Fourth of July.

So at supper Stella-Rondo speaks up and says she thinks Uncle Rondo ought to try to eat a little something. So finally Uncle Rondo said he would try a little cold biscuits and ketchup, but that was all. So *she* brought it to him.

85 "Do you think it wise to disport with ketchup in Stella-Rondo's flesh-colored kimono?" I says. Trying to be considerate! If Stella-Rondo couldn't watch out for her trousseau, somebody had to.

"Any objections?" asks Uncle Rondo, just about to pour out all the ketchup.

"Don't mind what she says, Uncle Rondo," says Stella-Rondo. "Sister has been devoting this solid afternoon to sneering out my bedroom window at the way you look."

"What's that?" says Uncle Rondo. Uncle Rondo has got the most terrible temper in the world. Anything is liable to make him tear the house down if it comes at the wrong time.

So Stella-Rondo says, "Sister says, 'Uncle Rondo certainly does look like a fool in that pink kimono!' "

90 Do you remember who it was really said that?

Uncle Rondo spills out all the ketchup and jumps out of his chair and tears off the kimono and throws it down on the dirty floor and puts his foot on it. It had to be sent all the way to Jackson to the cleaners and re-pleated.

"So that's your opinion of your Uncle Rondo, is it?" he says. "I look like a fool, do I? Well, that's the last straw. A whole day in this house with nothing to do, and then to hear you come out with a remark like that behind my back!"

"I didn't say any such of a thing, Uncle Rondo," I says, "and I'm not saying who did, either. Why, I think you look all right. Just try to take care of yourself and not talk and eat at the same time," I says. "I think you better go lie down."

"Lie down my foot," says Uncle Rondo. I ought to of known by that he was fixing to do something perfectly horrible.

95 So he didn't do anything that night in the precarious state he was in — just played Casino with Mama and Stella-Rondo and Shirley-T. and gave Shirley-T. a nickel with a head on both sides. It tickled her nearly to death, and she

4 in Belgium, site of graves of World War I soldiers. 5 popular tourist attraction in Kentucky.

called him "Papa." But at 6:30 A.M. the next morning, he threw a whole five-cent package of some unsold one-inch firecrackers from the store as hard as he could into my bedroom and they every one went off. Not one bad one in the string. Anybody else, there'd be one that wouldn't go off.

Well, I'm just terribly susceptible to noise of any kind, the doctor has always told me I was the most sensitive person he had ever seen in his whole life, and I was simply prostrated. I couldn't eat! People tell me they heard it as far as the cemetery, and old Aunt Jep Patterson, that had been holding her own so good, thought it was Judgment Day and she was going to meet her whole family. It's usually so quiet here.

And I'll tell you it didn't take me any longer than a minute to make up my mind what to do. There I was with the whole entire house on Stella-Rondo's side and turned against me. If I have anything at all I have pride.

So I just decided I'd go straight down to the P.O. There's plenty of room there in the back, I says to myself.

Well! I made no bones about letting the family catch on to what I was up to. I didn't try to conceal it.

100   The first thing they knew, I marched in where they were all playing Old Maid and pulled the electric oscillating fan out by the plug, and everything got real hot. Next I snatched the pillow I'd done the needlepoint on right off the davenport from behind Papa-Daddy. He went "Ugh!" I beat Stella-Rondo up the stairs and finally found my charm bracelet in her bureau drawer under a picture of Nelson Eddy.[6]

"So that's the way the land lies," says Uncle Rondo. There he was, piecing on the ham. "Well, Sister, I'll be glad to donate my army cot if you got any place to set it up, providing you'll leave right this minute and let me get some peace." Uncle Rondo was in France.

"Thank you kindly for the cot and 'peace' is hardly the word I would select if I had to resort to firecrackers at 6:30 A.M. in a young girl's bedroom," I says back to him. "And as to where I intend to go, you seem to forget my position as postmistress of China Grove, Mississippi," I says. "I've always got the P.O."

Well, that made them all sit up and take notice.

I went out front and started digging up some four-o'clocks to plant around the P.O.

105   "Ah-ah-ah!" says Mama, raising the window. "Those happen to be my four-o'clocks. Everything planted in that star is mine. I've never known you to make anything grow in your life."

"Very well," I says. "But I take the fern. Even you, Mama, can't stand there and deny that I'm the one watered that fern. And I happen to know where I can send in a box top and get a packet of one thousand mixed seeds, no two the same kind, free."

"Oh, where?" Mama wants to know.

But I says, "Too late. You 'tend to your house, and I'll 'tend to mine. You hear things like that all the time if you know how to listen to the radio. Perfectly marvelous offers. Get anything you want free."

6 popular American singer on radio programs of the 1930s.

So I hope to tell you I marched in and got that radio, and they could of all bit a nail in two, especially Stella-Rondo, that it used to belong to, and she well knew she couldn't get it back, I'd sue for it like a shot. And I very politely took the sewing-machine motor I helped pay the most on to give Mama for Christmas back in 1929, and a good big calendar, with the first-aid remedies on it. The thermometer and the Hawaiian ukulele certainly were rightfully mine, and I stood on the step-ladder and got all my watermelon-rind preserves and every fruit and vegetable I'd put up, every jar. Then I began to pull the tacks out of the bluebird wall vases on the archway to the dining room.

110   "Who told you you could have those, Miss Priss?" says Mama, fanning as hard as she could.

"I bought 'em and I'll keep track of 'em," I says. "I'll tack 'em up one on each side the post-office window, and you can see 'em when you come to ask me for your mail, if you're so dead to see 'em."

"Not I! I'll never darken the door to that post office again if I live to be a hundred," Mama says. "Ungrateful child! After all the money we spent on you at the Normal."[7]

"Me either," says Stella-Rondo. "You can just let my mail lie there and rot, for all I care. I'll never come and relieve you of a single, solitary piece."

"I should worry," I says. "And who you think's going to sit down and write you all those big fat letters and postcards, by the way? Mr. Whitaker? Just because he was the only man ever dropped down in China Grove and you got him — unfairly — is he going to sit down and write you a lengthy correspondence after you come home giving no rhyme nor reason whatsoever for your separation and no explanation for the presence of that child? I may not have your brilliant mind, but I fail to see it."

115   So Mama says, "Sister, I've told you a thousand times that Stella-Rondo simply got homesick, and this child is far too big to be hers," and she says, "Now, why don't you all just sit down and play Casino?"

Then Shirley-T. sticks out her tongue at me in this perfectly horrible way. She has no more manners than the man in the moon. I told her she was going to cross her eyes like that some day and they'd stick.

"It's too late to stop me now," I says. "You should have tried that yesterday. I'm going to the P.O. and the only way you can possibly see me is to visit me there."

So Papa-Daddy says, "You'll never catch me setting foot in that post office, even if I should take a notion into my head to write a letter some place." He says, "I won't have you reachin' out of that little old window with a pair of shears and cuttin' off any beard of mine. I'm too smart for you!"

"We all are," says Stella-Rondo.

120   But I said, "If you're so smart, where's Mr. Whitaker?"

So then Uncle Rondo says, "I'll thank you from now on to stop reading all the orders I get on postcards and telling everybody in China Grove what you think is the matter with them," but I says, "I draw my own conclusions and will continue in the future to draw them." I says, "If people want to write their

7 teachers' college.

inmost secrets on penny postcards, there's nothing in the wide world you can do about it, Uncle Rondo."

"And if you think we'll ever *write* another postcard you're sadly mistaken," says Mama.

"Cutting off your nose to spite your face then," I says. "But if you're all determined to have no more to do with the U.S. mail, think of this: What will Stella-Rondo do now, if she wants to tell Mr. Whitaker to come after her?"

"Wah!" says Stella-Rondo. I knew she'd cry. She had a conniption fit right there in the kitchen.

125 "It will be interesting to see how long she holds out," I says. "And now — I am leaving."

"Good-bye," says Uncle Rondo.

"Oh, I declare," says Mama, "to think that a family of mine should quarrel on the Fourth of July, or the day after, over Stella-Rondo leaving old Mr. Whitaker and having the sweetest little adopted child! It looks like we'd all be glad!"

"Wah!" says Stella-Rondo, and has a fresh conniption fit.

"*He* left *her* — you mark my words," I says. "That's Mr. Whitaker. I know Mr. Whitaker. After all, I knew him first. I said from the beginning he'd up and leave her. I foretold every single thing that's happened."

130 "Where did he go?" asks Mama.

"Probably to the North Pole, if he knows what's good for him," I says.

But Stella-Rondo just bawled and wouldn't say another word. She flew to her room and slammed the door.

"Now look what you've gone and done, Sister," says Mama. "You go apologize."

"I haven't got time, I'm leaving," I says.

135 "Well, what are you waiting around for?" asks Uncle Rondo.

So I just picked up the kitchen clock and marched off, without saying "Kiss my foot" or anything, and never did tell Stella-Rondo goodbye.

There was a nigger girl going along on a little wagon right in front.

"Nigger girl," I says, "come help me haul these things down the hill, I'm going to live in the post office."

Took her nine trips in her express wagon. Uncle Rondo came out on the porch and threw her a nickel.

140 And that's the last I've laid eyes on any of my family or my family laid eyes on me for five solid days and nights. Stella-Rondo may be telling the most horrible tales in the world about Mr. Whitaker, but I haven't heard them. As I tell everybody, I draw my own conclusions.

But oh, I like it here. It's ideal, as I've been saying. You see, I've got everything cater-cornered, the way I like it. Hear the radio? All the war news. Radio, sewing machine, book ends, ironing board and that great big piano lamp — peace, that's what I like. Butter-bean vines planted all along the front where the strings are.

Of course, there's not much mail. My family are naturally the main people in China Grove, and if they prefer to vanish from the face of the earth, for all the mail they get or the mail they write, why, I'm not going to open my mouth.

Some of the folks here in town are taking up for me and some turned against me. I know which is which. There are always people who will quit buying stamps just to get on the right side of Papa-Daddy.

But here I am, and here I'll stay. I want the world to know I'm happy.

And if Stella-Rondo should come to me this minute, on bended knees, and *attempt* to explain the incidents of her life with Mr. Whitaker, I'd simply put my fingers in both my ears and refuse to listen.

(1941)

Mavis Gallant (b. 1922)

Montreal-born novelist and short story writer Mavis Gallant has acknowledged the influence of James Joyce and Katherine Mansfield on both the style and themes of her short stories. Unlike most of her works, such as the stories in *The Other Paris*, which are set in Europe and often deal with rootless Canadian and American expatriates, "My Heart Is Broken" takes place in a remote construction camp in the Canadian bush. However, like her other stories, it deals with lonely individuals who feel alienated from the life around them. In the account of the short meeting between an older and a younger woman, Gallant's careful depiction of setting and presentation of the two people's emotionally intense dialogue reveals a great deal about their characters, their past lives, and their possible futures.

MY HEART IS BROKEN

"When that Jean Harlow[1] died," Mrs. Thompson said to Jeannie, "I was on the 83 streetcar with a big, heavy paper parcel in my arms. I hadn't been married for very long, and when I used to visit my mother she'd give me a lot of canned stuff and preserves. I was standing up in the streetcar because nobody'd given me a seat. All the men were unemployed in those days, and they just sat down wherever they happened to be. You wouldn't remember what Montreal was like then. *You* weren't even on earth. To resume what I was saying to you, one of these men sitting down had an American paper — the *Daily News*, I guess it was — and I was sort of leaning over him, and I saw in big print 'JEAN HARLOW DEAD.' You can believe me or not, just as you want to, but that was the most terrible shock I ever had in my life. I never got over it."

Jeannie had nothing to say to that. She lay flat on her back across the bed, with her head toward Mrs. Thompson and her heels just touching the crate that did as a bedside table. Balanced on her flat stomach was an open bottle of coral-pink Cutex nail polish. She held her hands up over her head and with some difficulty applied the brush to the nails of her right hand. Her legs were brown and thin. She wore nothing but shorts and one of her husband's shirts. Her feet were bare.

Mrs. Thompson was the wife of the paymaster in a road-construction camp in northern Quebec. Jeannie's husband was an engineer working on the same project. The road was being pushed through country where nothing had existed until now except rocks and lakes and muskeg. The camp was established between a wild lake and the line of raw dirt that was the road. There were no towns between the camp and the railway spur, sixty miles distant.

Mrs. Thompson, a good deal older than Jeannie, had become her best friend. She was a nice, plain, fat, consoling sort of person, with varicosed legs,

1 American movie star and sex symbol of the 1930s.

shoes unlaced and slit for comfort, blue flannel dressing gown worn at all hours, pudding-bowl haircut, and coarse gray hair. She might have been Jeannie's own mother, or her Auntie Pearl. She rocked her fat self in the rocking chair and went on with what she had to say: "What I was starting off to tell you is you remind me of her, of Jean Harlow. You've got the same teeny mouth, Jeannie, and I think your hair was a whole lot prettier before you started fooling around with it. That peroxide's no good. It splits the ends. I know you're going to tell me it isn't peroxide but something more modern, but the result is the same."

5   Vern's shirt was spotted with coral-pink that had dropped off the brush. Vern wouldn't mind; at least, he wouldn't say that he minded. If he hadn't objected to anything Jeannie did until now, he wouldn't start off by complaining about a shirt. The campsite outside the uncurtained window was silent and dark. The waning moon would not appear until dawn. A passage of thought made Mrs. Thompson say, "Winter soon."

Jeannie moved sharply and caught the bottle of polish before it spilled. Mrs. Thompson was crazy; it wasn't even September.

"Pretty soon," Mrs. Thompson admitted. "Pretty soon. That's a long season up here, but I'm one person doesn't complain. I've been up here or around here every winter of my married life, except for that one winter Pops was occupying Germany."

"I've been up here seventy-two days," said Jeannie, in her soft voice. "Tomorrow makes seventy-three."

"Is that right?" said Mrs. Thompson, jerking the rocker forward, suddenly snappish. "Is that a fact? Well, who asked you to come up here? Who asked you to come and start counting days like you was in some kind of jail? When you got married to Vern, you must of known where he'd be taking you. He told you, didn't he, that he liked road jobs, construction jobs, and that? Did he tell you, or didn't he?"

10   "Oh, he told me," said Jeannie.

"You know what, Jeannie?" said Mrs. Thompson. "If you'd of just listened to me, none of this would have happened. I told you that first day, the day you arrived here in your high-heeled shoes, I said, 'I know this cabin doesn't look much, but all the married men have the same sort of place.' You remember I said that? I said, 'You just get some curtains up and some carpets down and it'll be home.' I took you over and showed you my place, and you said you'd never seen anything so lovely."

"I meant it," said Jeannie. "Your cabin is just lovely. I don't know why, but I never managed to make this place look like yours."

Mrs. Thompson said, "That's plain enough." She looked at the cold grease spattered behind the stove, and the rag of towel over by the sink. "It's partly the experience," she said kindly. She and her husband knew exactly what to take with them when they went on a job, they had been doing it for so many years. They brought boxes for artificial flowers, a brass door knocker, a portable bar decorated with sea shells, a cardboard fireplace that looked real, and an electric fire that sent waves of light rippling over the ceiling and walls. A concealed gramophone played the records they loved and cherished — the good old tunes. They had comic records that dated back to the year 1, and sad soprano records about shipwrecks and broken promises and babies' graves. The first time Jeannie heard one of the funny records, she was scared to death. She was paying a formal call, sitting straight in her chair, with her skirt pulled around her knees. Vern and Pops Thompson were talking about the Army.

"I wish to God I was back," said old Pops.

15   "Don't I?" said Vern. He was fifteen years older than Jeannie and had been through a lot.

At first there were only scratching and whispering noises, and then a mosquito orchestra started to play, and a dwarf's voice came into the room. "Little Johnnie Green, little Sallie Brown," squealed the dwarf, higher and faster than any human ever could. "Spooning in the park with the grass all around."

"Where is he?" Jeannie cried, while the Thompsons screamed with laughter and Vern smiled. The dwarf sang on: "And each little bird in the treetop high / Sang 'Oh you kid!' and winked his eye."

It was a record that had belonged to Pops Thompson's mother. He had been laughing at it all his life. The Thompsons loved living up north and didn't miss cities or company. Their cabin smelled of cocoa and toast. Over their beds were oval photographs of each other as children, and they had some Teddy bears and about a dozen dolls.

Jeannie capped the bottle of polish, taking care not to press it against her wet nails. She sat up with a single movement and set the bottle down on the bedside crate. Then she turned to face Mrs. Thompson. She sat cross-legged, with her hands outspread before her. Her face was serene.

20   "Not an ounce of fat on you," said Mrs. Thompson. "You know something? I'm sorry you're going. I really am. Tomorrow you'll be gone. You know that, don't you? You've been counting days, but you won't have to any more. I guess Vern'll take you back to Montreal. What do you think?"

Jeannie dropped her gaze, and began smoothing wrinkles on the bedspread. She muttered something Mrs. Thompson could not understand.

"Tomorrow you'll be gone," Mrs. Thompson continued. "I know it for a fact. Vern is at this moment getting his pay, and borrowing a jeep from Mr. Sherman, and a Polack driver to take you to the train. He sure is loyal to *you*. You know what I heard Mr. Sherman say? He said to Vern, 'If you want to send her off, Vern, you can always stay,' and Vern said, 'I can't very well do that, Mr. Sherman.' And Mr. Sherman said, 'This is the second time you've had to leave a job on account of her, isn't it?,' and then Mr. Sherman said, 'In my opinion, no man by his own self can rape a girl, so there were either two men or else she's invented the whole story.' Then he said, 'Vern, you're either a saint or a damn fool.' That was all I heard. I came straight over here, Jeannie, because I thought you might be needing me." Mrs. Thompson waited to hear she was needed. She stopped rocking and sat with her feet flat and wide apart. She struck her knees with her open palms and cried, "I *told* you to keep away from the men. I told you it would make trouble, all that being cute and dancing around. I said to you, I remember saying it, I said nothing makes trouble faster in a place like this than a grown woman behaving like a little girl. Don't you remember?"

"I only went out for a walk," said Jeannie. "Nobody'll believe me, but that's all. I went down the road for a walk."

"In high heels?" said Mrs. Thompson. "With a purse on your arm, and a hat on your head? You don't go taking a walk in the bush that way. There's no place to walk *to*. Where'd you think you were going? I could smell Evening in Paris a quarter mile away."

25 "There's no place to go," said Jeannie, "but what else is there to do? I just felt like dressing up and going out."

"You could have cleaned up your home a bit," said Mrs. Thompson. "There was always that to do. Just look at that sink. That basket of ironing's been under the bed since July. I know it gets boring around here, but you had the best of it. You had the summer. In winter it gets dark around three o'clock. Then the wives have a right to go crazy. I knew one used to sleep the clock around. When her Nembutal[2] ran out, she took about a hundred aspirin. I knew another learned to distill her own liquor, just to kill time. Sometimes the men get so's they don't like the life, and that's death for the wives. But here you had a nice summer, and Vern liked the life."

"He likes it better than anything," said Jeannie. "He liked the Army, but this was his favorite life after that."

"There," said Mrs. Thompson, "you had every reason to be happy. What'd you do if he sent you off alone, now, like Mr. Sherman advised? You'd be alone and you'd have to work. Women don't know when they're well off. Here you've got a good, sensible husband working for you and you don't appreciate it. You have to go and do a terrible thing."

"I only went for a walk," said Jeannie. "That's all I did."

30 "It's possible," said Mrs. Thompson, "but it's a terrible thing. It's about the worst thing that's ever happened around here. I don't know why you let it happen. A woman can always defend what's precious, even if she's attacked. I hope you remembered to think about bacteria."

"What d'you mean?"

"I mean Javel,[3] or something."

Jeannie looked uncomprehending and then shook her head.

"I wonder what it must be like," said Mrs. Thompson after a time, looking at the dark window. "I mean, think of Berlin and them Russians and all. Think of some disgusting fellow you don't know. Never said hello to, even. Some girls ask for it, though. You can't always blame the man. The man loses his job, his wife if he's got one, everything, all because of a silly girl."

35 Jeannie frowned, absently. She pressed her nails together, testing the polish. She licked her lips and said, "I was more beaten up, Mrs. Thompson. It wasn't exactly what you think. It was only afterwards I thought to myself, Why, I was raped and everything."

Mrs. Thompson gasped, hearing the word from Jeannie. She said, "Have you got any marks?"

"On my arms. That's why I'm wearing this shirt. The first thing I did was change my clothes."

2 brand of sleeping pill. 3 bleach solution.

Mrs. Thompson thought this over, and went on to another thing: "Do you ever think about your mother?"

"Sure."

40 "Do you pray? If this goes on at nineteen —"

"I'm twenty."

"— what'll you be by the time you're thirty? You've already got a terrible, terrible memory to haunt you all your life."

"I already can't remember it," said Jeannie. "Afterwards I started walking back to camp, but I was walking the wrong way. I met Mr. Sherman. The back of his car was full of coffee, flour, all that. I guess he'd been picking up supplies. He said, 'Well, get in.' He didn't ask any questions at first. I couldn't talk anyway."

"Shock," said Mrs. Thompson wisely.

45 "You know, I'd have to see it happening to know what happened. All I remember is that first we were only talking..."

"You and Mr. Sherman?"

"No, no, before. When I was taking my walk."

"Don't say who it was," said Mrs. Thompson. "We don't any of us need to know."

"We were just talking, and he got sore all of a sudden and grabbed my arm."

50 "Don't say the name!" Mrs. Thompson cried.

"Like when I was little, there was this Lana Turner movie. She had two twins. She was just there and then a nurse brought her in the two twins. I hadn't been married or anything, and I didn't know anything, and I used to think if I just kept on seeing the movie I'd know how she got the two twins, you know, and I went, oh, I must have seen it six times, the movie, but in the end I never knew any more. They just brought her the two twins."

Mrs. Thompson sat quite still, trying to make sense of this. "Taking advantage of a woman is a criminal offense," she observed. "I heard Mr. Sherman say another thing, Jeannie. He said, 'If your wife wants to press a charge and talk to some lawyer, let me tell you,' he said, 'you'll never work again anywhere,' he said. Vern said, 'I know that, Mr. Sherman.' And Mr. Sherman said, 'Let me tell you, if any reporters or any investigators start coming around here, they'll get their... they'll never...' Oh, he was mad. And Vern said, 'I came over to tell you I was quitting, Mr. Sherman.'" Mrs. Thompson had been acting this with spirit, using a quiet voice when she spoke for Vern and a blustering tone for Mr. Sherman. In her own voice, she said, "If you're wondering how I came to hear all this, I was strolling by Mr. Sherman's office window — his bungalow, that is. I had Maureen out in her pram." Maureen was the Thompsons' youngest doll.

Jeannie might not have been listening. She started to tell something else: "You know, where we were before, on Vern's last job, we weren't in a camp. He was away a lot, and he left me in Amos, in a hotel. I liked it. Amos isn't all that big, but it's better than here. There was this German in the hotel. He was selling cars. He'd drive me around if I wanted to go to a movie or anything. Vern didn't like him, so we left. It wasn't anybody's fault."

"So he's given up two jobs," said Mrs. Thompson. "One because he couldn't leave you alone, and now this one. Two jobs, and you haven't been married five months. Why should another man be thrown out of work? We don't need to know a thing. I'll be sorry if it was Jimmy Quinn," she went on slowly. "I like that boy. Don't say the name, dear. There's Evans. Susini. Palmer. But it might have been anybody, because you had them all on the boil. So it might have been Jimmy Quinn — let's say — and it could have been anyone else, too. Well, now let's hope they can get their minds back on the job."

55   "I thought they all liked me," said Jeannie sadly. "I get along with people. Vern never fights with me."

    "Vern never fights with anyone. But he ought to have thrashed *you*."

    "If he . . . you know. I won't say the name. If he'd liked me, I wouldn't have minded. If he'd been friendly. I really mean that. I wouldn't have gone wandering up the road, making all this fuss."

    "Jeannie," said Mrs. Thompson, "you don't even know what you're saying."

    "He could at least have liked me," said Jeannie. "He wasn't even friendly. It's the first time in my life somebody hasn't liked me. My heart is broken, Mrs. Thompson. My heart is just broken."

60   She has to cry, Mrs. Thompson thought. She has to have it out. She rocked slowly, tapping her foot, trying to remember how she'd felt about things when she was twenty, wondering if her heart had ever been broken, too.

(1961)

Margaret Laurence (1926–1987)

Margaret Laurence's best-known novels and short stories are set in Manawaka, a fictionalized version of her home town of Neepawa, Manitoba. However, her first novel, *This Side Jordan* (1960), grew out of her experiences living in Africa during the 1950s and reflects her life-long concern with the repression of Native peoples. Later, in such novels as *The Stone Angel* (1964) and *A Jest of God* (1966), she depicted the social conflicts of the largely Scots-Presbyterian Manitoba community and the struggles of the women who grew up in it. "The Loons" is from *A Bird in the House* (1970), a collection of stories in which the portrayal of the maturation of Vanessa MacLeod is what Laurence called "fictionalized biography." In this story, the narrator examines the nature of her relationship to a Métis friend after the young woman's death.

THE LOONS

Just below Manawaka, where the Wachakwa River ran brown and noisy over the pebbles, the scrub oak and grey-green willow and chokecherry bushes grew in a dense thicket. In a clearing at the centre of the thicket stood the Tonnerre family's shack. The basis of this dwelling was a small square cabin made of poplar poles and chinked with mud, which had been built by Jules Tonnerre some fifty years before, when he came back from Batoche[1] with a bullet in his thigh, the year that Riel was hung and the voices of the Metis entered their long silence.[2] Jules had only intended to stay the winter in the Wachakwa Valley, but the family was still there in the thirties, when I was a child. As the Tonnerres had increased, their settlement had been added to, until the clearing at the foot of the town hill was a chaos of lean-tos, wooden packing cases, warped lumber, discarded car tyres, ramshackle chicken coops, tangled strands of barbed wire and rusty tin cans.

The Tonnerres were French halfbreeds, and among themselves they spoke a *patois* that was neither Cree nor French. Their English was broken and full of obscenities. They did not belong among the Cree of the Galloping Mountain reservation, further north, and they did not belong among the Scots-Irish and Ukrainians of Manawaka, either. They were, as my Grandmother MacLeod would have put it, neither flesh, fowl, or good salt herring. When their men were not working at odd jobs or as section hands on the C.P.R., they lived on relief. In the summers, one of the Tonnerre youngsters, with a face that seemed totally unfamiliar with laughter, would knock at the doors of the town's brick houses and offer for sale a lard-pail full of bruised wild strawberries, and if he got as much as a quarter he would grab the coin and run before the customer had time to change her mind. Sometimes old Jules, or his son Lazarus, would get mixed up in a Saturday-night brawl, and would hit out at whoever was nearest, or howl drunkenly among the offended shoppers on

---

1 near Prince Albert, Saskatchewan; in 1885, the site of a major battle in the Northwest Rebellion.
2 Louis Riel was the leader of the Métis people, who were of mixed white and Native blood.

Main Street, and then the Mountie would put them for the night in the barred cell underneath the Court House, and the next morning they would be quiet again.

Piquette Tonnerre, the daughter of Lazarus, was in my class at school. She was older than I, but she had failed several grades, perhaps because her attendance had always been sporadic and her interest in schoolwork negligible. Part of the reason she had missed a lot of school was that she had had tuberculosis of the bone, and had once spent many months in hospital. I knew this because my father was the doctor who had looked after her. Her sickness was almost the only thing I knew about her, however. Otherwise, she existed for me only as a vaguely embarrassing presence, with her hoarse voice and her clumsy limping walk and her grimy cotton dresses that were always miles too long. I was neither friendly nor unfriendly towards her. She dwelt and moved somewhere within my scope of vision, but I did not actually notice her very much until that peculiar summer when I was eleven.

"I don't know what to do about that kid," my father said at dinner one evening. "Piquette Tonnerre, I mean. The damn bone's flared up again. I've had her in hospital for quite a while now, and it's under control all right, but I hate like the dickens to send her home again."

5 "Couldn't you explain to her mother that she has to rest a lot?" my mother said.

"The mother's not there," my father replied. "She took off a few years back. Can't say I blame her. Piquette cooks for them, and she says Lazarus would never do anything for himself as long as she's there. Anyway, I don't think she'd take much care of herself, once she got back. She's only thirteen, after all. Beth, I was thinking — what about taking her up to Diamond Lake with us this summer? A couple of months rest would give that bone a much better chance."

My mother looked stunned.

"But Ewen — what about Roddie and Vanessa?"

"She's not contagious," my father said. "And it would be company for Vanessa."

10 "Oh dear," my mother said in distress, "I'll bet anything she has nits in her hair."

"For Pete's sake," my father said crossly, "do you think Matron would let her stay in the hospital for all this time like that? Don't be silly, Beth."

Grandmother MacLeod, her delicately featured face as rigid as a cameo, now brought her mauve-veined hands together as though she were about to begin a prayer.

"Ewen, if that half-breed youngster comes along to Diamond Lake, I'm not going," she announced. "I'll go to Morag's for the summer."

I had trouble in stifling my urge to laugh, for my mother brightened visibly and quickly tried to hide it. If it came to a choice between Grandmother MacLeod and Piquette, Piquette would win hands down, nits or not.

15 "It might be quite nice for you, at that," she mused. "You haven't seen Morag for over a year, and you might enjoy being in the city for a while. Well, Ewen dear, you do what you think best. If you think it would do Piquette some good, then we'll be glad to have her, as long as she behaves herself."

So it happened that several weeks later, when we all piled into my father's old Nash, surrounded by suitcases and boxes of provisions and toys for my ten-month-old brother, Piquette was with us and Grandmother MacLeod, miraculously, was not. My father would only be staying at the cottage for a couple of weeks, for he had to get back to his practice, but the rest of us would stay at Diamond Lake until the end of August.

Our cottage was not named, as many were, "Dew Drop Inn" or "Bide-a-Wee," or "Bonnie Doon." The sign on the roadway bore in austere letters only our name, MacLeod. It was not a large cottage, but it was on the lakefront. You could look out the windows and see, through the filigree of the spruce trees, the water glistening greenly as the sun caught it. All around the cottage were ferns, and sharp-branched raspberry bushes, and moss that had grown over fallen tree trunks. If you looked carefully among the weeds and grass, you could find wild strawberry plants which were in white flower now and in another month would bear fruit, the fragrant globes hanging like miniature scarlet lanterns on the thin hairy stems. The two grey squirrels were still there, gossiping at us from the tall spruce beside the cottage, and by the end of the summer they would again be tame enough to take pieces of crust from my hands. The broad moose antlers that hung above the back door were a little more bleached and fissured after the winter, but otherwise everything was the same. I raced joyfully around my kingdom, greeting all the places I had not seen for a year. My brother, Roderick, who had not been born when we were here last summer, sat on the car rug in the sunshine and examined a brown spruce cone, meticulously turning it round and round in his small and curious hands. My mother and father toted the luggage from car to cottage, exclaiming over how well the place had wintered, no broken windows, thank goodness, no apparent damage from storm-felled branches or snow.

Only after I had finished looking around did I notice Piquette. She was sitting on the swing, her lame leg held stiffly out, and her other foot scuffing the ground as she swung slowly back and forth. Her long hair hung black and straight around her shoulders, and her broad coarse-featured face bore no expression — it was blank, as though she no longer dwelt within her own skull, as though she had gone elsewhere. I approached her very hesitantly.

"Want to come and play?"

Piquette looked at me with a sudden flash of scorn.

"I ain't a kid," she said.

Wounded, I stamped angrily away, swearing I would not speak to her for the rest of the summer. In the days that followed, however, Piquette began to interest me, and I began to want to interest her. My reasons did not appear bizarre to me. Unlikely as it may seem, I had only just realised that the Tonnerre family, whom I had always heard called half-breeds, were actually Indians, or as near as made no difference. My acquaintance with Indians was not extensive. I did not remember ever having seen a real Indian, and my new awareness that Piquette sprang from the people of Big Bear and Poundmaker,[3] of Tecumseh,[4] of the Iroquois who had eaten Father Brebeuf's heart[5] — all this

20

3 nineteenth-century Cree chiefs who supported Louis Riel. 4 Shawnee chief, allied with the British in the War of 1812. 5 Jesuit missionary killed by Iroquois in 1649.

gave her an instant attraction in my eyes. I was a devoted reader of Pauline Johnson[6] at this age, and sometimes would orate aloud and in an exalted voice, *West Wind, blow from your prairie nest; Blow from the mountains, blow from the west*— and so on. It seemed to me that Piquette must be in some way a daughter of the forest, a kind of junior prophetess of the wilds, who might impart to me, if I took the right approach, some of the secrets which she undoubtedly knew — where the whippoorwill made her nest, how the coyote reared her young, or whatever it was that it said in Hiawatha.

I set about gaining Piquette's trust. She was not allowed to go swimming, with her bad leg, but I managed to lure her down to the beach — or rather, she came because there was nothing else to do. The water was always icy, for the lake was fed by springs, but I swam like a dog, thrashing my arms and legs around at such speed and with such an output of energy that I never grew cold. Finally, when I had had enough, I came out and sat beside Piquette on the sand. When she saw me approaching, her hand squashed flat the sand castle she had been building, and she looked at me sullenly, without speaking.

"Do you like this place?" I asked, after a while, intending to lead on from there into the question of forest lore.

Piquette shrugged. "It's okay. Good as anywhere."

"I love it," I said. "We come here every summer."

"So what?" Her voice was distant, and I glanced at her uncertainly, wondering what I could have said wrong.

"Do you want to come for a walk?" I asked her. "We wouldn't need to go far. If you walk just around the point, you come to a bay where great big reeds grow in the water, and all kinds of fish hang around there. Want to? Come on."

She shook her head.

"Your dad said I ain't supposed to do no more walking than I got to."

I tried another line.

"I bet you know a lot about the woods and all that, eh?" I began respectfully.

Piquette looked at me from her large dark unsmiling eyes.

"I don't know what in hell you're talkin' about," she replied. "You nuts or somethin'? If you mean where my old man, and me, and all them live, you better shut up, by Jesus, you hear?"

I was startled and my feelings were hurt, but I had a kind of dogged perseverance. I ignored her rebuff.

"You know something, Piquette? There's loons here, on this lake. You can see their nests just up the shore there, behind those logs. At night, you can hear them even from the cottage, but it's better to listen from the beach. My dad says we should listen and try to remember how they sound, because in a few years when more cottages are built at Diamond Lake and more people come in, the loons will go away."

Piquette was picking up stones and snail shells and then dropping them again.

"Who gives a good goddamn?" she said.

6 early-twentieth-century Native writer.

It became increasingly obvious that, as an Indian, Piquette was a dead loss. That evening I went out by myself, scrambling through the bushes that overhung the steep path, my feet slipping on the fallen spruce needles that covered the ground. When I reached the shore, I walked along the firm damp sand to the small pier that my father had built, and sat down there. I heard someone else crashing through the undergrowth and the bracken, and for a moment I thought Piquette had changed her mind, but it turned out to be my father. He sat beside me on the pier and we waited, without speaking.

At night the lake was like black glass with a streak of amber which was the path of the moon. All around, the spruce trees grew tall and close-set, branches blackly sharp against the sky, which was lightened by a cold flickering of stars. Then the loons began their calling. They rose like phantom birds from the nests on the shore, and flew out onto the dark still surface of the water.

No one can ever describe that ululating sound, the crying of the loons, and no one who has heard it can ever forget it. Plaintive, and yet with a quality of chilling mockery, those voices belonged to a world separated by aeons from our neat world of summer cottages and the lighted lamps of home.

"They must have sounded just like that," my father remarked, "before any person ever set foot here."

Then he laughed. "You could say the same, of course, about sparrows, or chipmunks, but somehow it only strikes you that way with the loons."

"I know," I said.

Neither of us suspected that this would be the last time we would ever sit here together on the shore, listening. We stayed for perhaps half an hour, and then we went back to the cottage. My mother was reading beside the fireplace. Piquette was looking at the burning birch log, and not doing anything.

"You should have come along," I said, although in fact I was glad she had not.

"Not me," Piquette said. "You wouldn' catch me walkin' way down there jus' for a bunch of squawkin' birds."

Piquette and I remained ill at ease with one another. I felt I had somehow failed my father, but I did not know what was the matter, nor why she would not or could not respond when I suggested exploring the woods or playing house. I thought it was probably her slow and difficult walking that held her back. She stayed most of the time in the cottage with my mother, helping her with the dishes or with Roddie, but hardly ever talking. Then the Duncans arrived at their cottage, and I spent my days with Mavis, who was my best friend. I could not reach Piquette at all, and I soon lost interest in trying. But all that summer she remained as both a reproach and a mystery to me.

That winter my father died of pneumonia, after less than a week's illness. For some time I saw nothing around me, being completely immersed in my own pain and my mother's. When I looked outward once more, I scarcely noticed that Piquette Tonnerre was no longer at school. I do not remember seeing her at all until four years later, one Saturday night when Mavis and I were having Cokes in the Regal Café. The jukebox was booming like tuneful thunder, and beside it, leaning lightly on its chrome and its rainbow glass, was a girl.

Piquette must have been seventeen then, although she looked about twenty. I stared at her, astounded that anyone could have changed so much. Her face, so stolid and expressionless before, was animated now with a gaiety that was almost violent. She laughed and talked very loudly with the boys around her. Her lipstick was bright carmine, and her hair was cut short and frizzily permed. She had not been pretty as a child, and she was not pretty now, for her features were still heavy and blunt. But her dark and slightly slanted eyes were beautiful, and her skin-tight skirt and orange sweater displayed to enviable advantage a soft and slender body.

She saw me, and walked over. She teetered a little, but it was not due to her once-tubercular leg, for her limp was almost gone.

"Hi, Vanessa." Her voice still had the same hoarseness. "Long time no see, eh?"

"Hi," I said. "Where've you been keeping yourself, Piquette?"

"Oh, I been around," she said. "I been away almost two years now. Been all over the place — Winnipeg, Regina, Saskatoon. Jesus, what I could tell you! I come back this summer, but I ain't stayin'. You kids goin' to the dance?"

55 "No," I said abruptly, for this was a sore point with me. I was fifteen, and thought I was old enough to go to the Saturday-night dances at the Flamingo. My mother, however, thought otherwise.

"Y'oughta come," Piquette said. "I never miss one. It's just about the on'y thing in this jerkwater town that's any fun. Boy, you couldn' catch me stayin' here. I don' give a shit about this place. It stinks."

She sat down beside me, and I caught the harsh over-sweetness of her perfume.

"Listen, you wanna know something, Vanessa?" she confided, her voice only slightly blurred. "Your dad was the only person in Manawaka that ever done anything good to me."

I nodded speechlessly. I was certain she was speaking the truth. I knew a little more than I had that summer at Diamond Lake, but I could not reach her now any more than I had then. I was ashamed, ashamed of my own timidity, the frightened tendency to look the other way. Yet I felt no real warmth towards her — I only felt that I ought to, because of that distant summer and because my father had hoped she would be company for me, or perhaps that I would be for her, but it had not happened that way. At this moment, meeting her again, I had to admit that she repelled and embarrassed me, and I could not help despising the self-pity in her voice. I wished she would go away. I did not want to see her. I did not know what to say to her. It seemed that we had nothing to say to one another.

60 "I'll tell you something else," Piquette went on. "All the old bitches an' biddies in this town will sure be surprised. I'm gettin' married this fall — my boyfriend, he's an English fella, works in the stockyards in the city there, a very tall guy, got blond wavy hair. Gee, is he ever handsome. Got this real classy name. Alvin Gerald Cummings — some handle, eh? They call him Al."

For the merest instant, then, I saw her. I really did see her, for the first and only time in all the years we had both lived in the same town. Her defiant face, momentarily, became unguarded and unmasked, and in her eyes there was a terrifying hope.

"Gee, Piquette —" I burst out awkwardly, "that's swell. That's really wonderful. Congratulations — good luck — I hope you'll be happy —"

As I mouthed the conventional phrases, I could only guess how great her need must have been, that she had been forced to seek the very things she so bitterly rejected.

When I was eighteen, I left Manawaka and went away to college. At the end of my first year, I came back home for the summer. I spent the first few days in talking non-stop with my mother, as we exchanged all the news that somehow had not found its way into letters — what had happened in my life and what had happened here in Manawaka while I was away. My mother searched her memory for events that concerned people I knew.

"Did I ever write you about Piquette Tonnerre, Vanessa?" she asked one morning.

"No, I don't think so," I replied. "Last I heard of her, she was going to marry some guy in the city. Is she still there?"

My mother looked perturbed, and it was a moment before she spoke, as though she did not know how to express what she had to tell and wished she did not need to try.

"She's dead," she said at last. Then, as I stared at her, "Oh, Vanessa, when it happened, I couldn't help thinking of her as she was that summer — so sullen and gauche and badly dressed. I couldn't help wondering if we could have done something more at that time — but what could we do? She used to be around in the cottage there with me all day, and honestly, it was all I could do to get a word out of her. She didn't even talk to your father very much, although I think she liked him, in her way."

"What happened?" I asked.

"Either her husband left her, or she left him," my mother said. "I don't know which. Anyway, she came back here with two youngsters, both only babies — they must have been born very close together. She kept house, I guess, for Lazarus and her brothers, down in the valley there, in the old Tonnerre place. I used to see her on the street sometimes, but she never spoke to me. She'd put on an awful lot of weight, and she looked a mess, to tell you the truth, a real slattern, dressed any old how. She was up in court a couple of times — drunk and disorderly, of course. One Saturday night last winter, during the coldest weather, Piquette was alone in the shack with the children. The Tonnerres made home brew all the time, so I've heard, and Lazarus said later she'd been drinking most of the day when he and the boys went out that evening. They had an old woodstove there — you know the kind, with exposed pipes. The shack caught fire. Piquette didn't get out, and neither did the children."

I did not say anything. As so often with Piquette, there did not seem to be anything to say. There was a kind of silence around the image in my mind of the fire and the snow, and I wished I could put from my memory the look that I had seen once in Piquette's eyes.

I went up to Diamond Lake for a few days that summer, with Mavis and her family. The MacLeod cottage had been sold after my father's death, and I did not even go to look at it, not wanting to witness my long-ago kingdom possessed now by strangers. But one evening I went down to the shore by myself.

The small pier which my father had built was gone, and in its place there was a large and solid pier built by the government, for Galloping Mountain was now a national park, and Diamond Lake had been re-named Lake Wapakata, for it was felt that an Indian name would have a greater appeal to tourists. The one store had become several dozen, and the settlement had all the attributes of a flourishing resort — hotels, a dance-hall, cafés with neon signs, the penetrating odours of potato chips and hot dogs.

I sat on the government pier and looked out across the water. At night the lake at least was the same as it had always been, darkly shining and bearing within its black glass the streak of amber that was the path of the moon. There was no wind that evening, and everything was quiet all around me. It seemed too quiet, and then I realized that the loons were no longer here. I listened for some time, to make sure, but never once did I hear that long-drawn call, half mocking and half plaintive, spearing through the stillness across the lake.

75   I did not know what had happened to the birds. Perhaps they had gone away to some far place of belonging. Perhaps they had been unable to find such a place, and had simply died out, having ceased to care any longer whether they lived or not.

I remembered how Piquette had scorned to come along, when my father and I sat there and listened to the lake birds. It seemed to me now that in some unconscious and totally unrecognised way, Piquette might have been the only one, after all, who had heard the crying of the loons.

(1966)

Alice Munro   (b. 1931)

Born in Wingham, Ontario, Alice Munro began writing short stories in high school but did not publish her first collection, *Dance of the Happy Shades*, winner of the Governor General's Award for fiction, until 1968. Like the American writer Eudora Welty, whose work she admires, Munro is essentially a regional writer, portraying girls and women from small-town western Ontario confronting the various stages of their lives and the nature of their relationships with other people. She has been praised for her precise depiction of the events and settings that are used to reveal aspects of the personalities of her characters. In "Wild Swans," from *Who Do You Think You Are?*, another winner of the Governor General's Award, a girl's first trip alone from her small southwestern Ontario town to the metropolis of Toronto is presented as a transition period in her coming of age. Rose's ambiguous response to the actions of the man next to her will have a lasting effect on her attitudes toward sexuality.

WILD SWANS

Flo said to watch out for White Slavers. She said this was how they operated: an old woman, a motherly or grandmotherly sort, made friends while riding beside you on a bus or train. She offered you candy, which was drugged. Pretty soon you began to droop and mumble, were in no condition to speak for yourself. Oh, Help, the woman said, my daughter (granddaughter) is sick, please somebody help me get her off so that she can recover in the fresh air. Up stepped a polite gentleman, pretending to be a stranger, offering assistance. Together, at the next stop, they hustled you off the train or bus, and that was the last the ordinary world ever saw of you. They kept you a prisoner in the White Slave place (to which you had been transported drugged and bound so you wouldn't even know where you were), until such time as you were thoroughly degraded and in despair, your insides torn up by drunken men and invested with vile disease, your mind destroyed by drugs, your hair and teeth fallen out. It took about three years, for you to get to this state. You wouldn't want to go home, then, maybe couldn't remember home, or find your way if you did. So they let you out on the streets.

Flo took ten dollars and put it in a little cloth bag which she sewed to the strap of Rose's slip. Another thing likely to happen was that Rose would get her purse stolen.

Watch out, Flo said as well, for people dressed up as ministers. There were the worst. That disguise was commonly adopted by White Slavers, as well as those after your money.

Rose said she didn't see how she could tell which ones were disguised.

Flo had worked in Toronto once. She had worked as a waitress in a coffee shop in Union Station. That was how she knew all she knew. She never saw sunlight, in those days, except on her days off. But she saw plenty else. She saw a man cut another man's stomach with a knife, just pull out his shirt and do a tidy cut, as if it was a watermelon not a stomach. The stomach's owner just saw looking down surprised, with no time to protest. Flo implied that that was nothing, in Toronto. She saw two bad women (that was what Flo called whores, running the two words together, like badminton) get into a fight, and a man laughed at them, other men stopped and laughed and egged them on, and they had their fists full of each other's hair. At last the police came and took them away, still howling and yelping.

She saw a child die of a fit, too. Its face was black as ink.

"Well I'm not scared," said Rose provokingly. "There's the police, anyway."

"Oh, them! They'd be the first ones to diddle you!"

She did not believe anything Flo said on the subject of sex. Consider the undertaker.

A little bald man, very neatly dressed, would come into the store sometimes and speak to Flo with a placating expression.

"I only wanted a bag of candy. And maybe a few packages of gum. And one or two chocolate bars. Could you go to the trouble of wrapping them?"

Flo in her mock-deferential tone would assure him that she could. She wrapped them in heavy-duty white paper, so there were something like presents. He took his time with the selection, humming and chatting, then dawdling for a while. He might ask how Flo was feeling. And how Rose was, if she was there.

"You look pale. Young girls need fresh air." To Flo he would say, "You work too hard. You've worked hard all your life."

"No rest for the wicked," Flo would say agreeably.

When he went out she hurried to the window. There it was — the old black hearse with its purple curtains.

"He'll be after them today!" Flo would say as the hearse rolled away at a gentle pace, almost a funeral pace. The little man had been an undertaker, but he was retired now. The hearse was retired too. His sons had taken over the undertaking and bought a new one. He drove the old hearse all over the country, looking for women. So Flo said. Rose could not believe it. Flo said he gave them the gum and the candy. Rose said he probably ate them himself. Flo said he had been seen, he had been heard. In mild weather he drove with the windows down, singing, to himself or to somebody out of sight in the back.

> Her brow is like the snowdrift
> Her throat is like the swan

Flo imitated him singing. Gently overtaking some woman walking on a back road, or resting at a country crossroads. All compliments and courtesy and chocolate bars, offering a ride. Of course every women who reported being asked said she had turned him down. He never pestered anybody, drove politely on. He called in at houses, and if the husband was home he seemed to like just as well as anything to sit and chat. Wives said that was all he ever did anyway but Flo did not believe it.

"Some women are taken in," she said. "A number." She liked to speculate on what the hearse was like inside. Plush. Plush on the walls and the roof and the floor. Soft purple, the color of the curtains, the color of dark lilacs.

All nonsense, Rose thought. Who could believe it, of a man that age?

Rose was going to Toronto on the train for the first time by herself. She had been once before, but that was with Flo, long before her father died. They took along their own sandwiches and bought milk from the vendor on the train. It was sour. Sour chocolate milk. Rose kept taking tiny sips, unwilling to admit that something so much desired could fail her. Flo sniffed it, then hunted up and down the train until she found the old man in his red jacket, with no teeth and the tray hanging around his neck. She invited him to sample chocolate milk. She invited people nearby to smell it. He let her have some ginger ale for nothing. It was slightly warm.

"I let him know," Flo said looking around after he had left. "You have to let them know."

A woman agreed with her but most people looked out the window. Rose drank the warm ginger ale. Either that, or the scene with the vendor, or the conversation Flo and the agreeing woman now got into about where they came from, why there were going to Toronto, and Rose's morning constipation which was why she was lacking color, or the small amount of chocolate milk she had got inside her, caused her to throw up in the train toilet. All day long she was afraid people in Toronto could smell vomit on her coat.

This time Flo started the trip off by saying, "Keep an eye on her, she's never been away from home before!" to the conductor, then looking around and laughing, to show that was jokingly meant. Then she had to get off. It seemed the conductor had no more need for jokes than Rose had, and no intention of keeping an eye on anybody. He never spoke to Rose except to ask for her ticket. She had a window seat, and was soon extraordinarily happy. She felt Flo receding, West Hanratty flying away from her, her own wearying self discarded as easily as everything else. She loved the towns less and less known. A woman was standing at her back door in her nightgown, not caring if everybody on the train saw her. They were traveling south, out of the snow belt, into an earlier spring, a tenderer sort of landscape. People could grow peach trees in their backyards.

25 Rose collected in her mind the things she had to look for in Toronto. First, things for Flo. Special stockings for her varicose veins. A special kind of cement for sticking handles on pots. And a full set of dominoes.

For herself Rose wanted to buy hair-remover to put on her arms and legs, and if possible an arrangement of inflatable cushions, supposed to reduce your hips and thighs. She thought they probably had hair-remover in the drugstore in Hanratty, but the woman in there was a friend of Flo's and told everything. She told Flo who bought hair dye and slimming medicine and French safes.[1] As for the cushion business, you could send away for it but there was sure to be a comment at the Post Office, and Flo knew people there as well. She also hoped to buy some bangles, and an angora sweater. She had great hopes of silver bangles and powder-blue angora. She thought they could transform her, make her calm and slender and take the frizz out of her hair, dry her underarms and turn her complexion to pearl.

The money for these things, as well as the money for the trip, came from a prize Rose had won, for writing an essay called "Art and Science in the World

---

1 condoms.

of Tomorrow." To her surprise, Flo asked if she could read it, and while she was reading it, she remarked that they must have thought they had to give Rose the prize for swallowing the dictionary. Then she said shyly, "It's very interesting."

She would have to spend the night at Cela McKinney's. Cela McKinney was her father's cousin. She had married a hotel manager and thought she had gone up in the world. But the hotel manager came home one day and sat down on the dining room floor between two chairs and said, "I am never going to leave this house again." Nothing unusual had happened, he had just decided not to go out of the house again, and he didn't, until he died. That had made Cela McKinney odd and nervous. She locked her doors at eight o'clock. She was also very stingy. Supper was usually oatmeal porridge, with raisins. Her house was dark and narrow and smelled like a bank.

The train was filling up. A Brantford a man asked if she would mind if he sat down beside her.

30 "It's cooler out than you'd think," he said. He offered her part of his newspaper. She said no thanks.

Then lest he think her rude she said it really was cooler. She went on looking out the window at the spring morning. There was no snow left, down here. The trees and bushes seemed to have a paler bark than they did at home. Even the sunlight looked different. It was as different from home, here, as the coast of the Mediterranean would be, or the valleys of California.

"Filthy windows, you'd think they'd take more care," the man said. "Do you travel much by train?"

She said no.

35 Water was lying in the fields. He nodded at it and said there was a lot this year.

"Heavy snows."

She noticed his saying *snows*, a poetic-sounding word. Anyone at home would have said *snow*.

"I had an unusual experience the other day. I was driving out in the country. In fact I was on my way to see one of my parishioners, a lady with a heart condition —"

She looked quickly at his collar. He was wearing an ordinary shirt and tie and a dark blue suit.

40 "Oh, yes," he said. "I'm a United Church minister. But I don't always wear my uniform. I wear it for preaching in. I'm off duty today."

"Well as I said I was driving through the country and I saw some Canada geese down on a pond, and I took another look, and there were some swans down with them. A whole great flock of swans. What a lovely sight they were. They would be on their spring migration, I expect, heading up north. What a spectacle. I never saw anything like it."

Rose was unable to think appreciatively of the wild swans because she was afraid he was going to lead the conversation from them to Nature in general and then to God, the way a minister would feel obliged to do. But he did not, he stopped with the swans.

"A very fine sight. You would have enjoyed them."

He was between fifty and sixty years old, Rose thought. He was short, and energetic-looking, with a square ruddy face and bright waves of gray hair combed straight up from his forehead. When she realized he was not going to mention God she felt she ought to show her gratitude.

She said they must have been lovely.

"It wasn't even a regular pond, it was just some water lying in a field. It was just by luck the water was lying there and I had to drive by there. And they came down and I came driving by at the right time. Just by luck. They come in at the east end of Lake Erie, I think. But I never was lucky enough to see them before."

She turned by degrees to the window, and he returned to his paper. She remained slightly smiling, so as not to seem rude, not to seem to be rejecting conversation altogether. The morning really was cool, and she had taken down her coat off the hook where she put it when she first got on the train, she had spread it over herself, like a lap robe. She had set her purse on the floor when the minister sat down, to give him room. He took the sections of the paper apart, shaking and rustling them in a leisurely, rather showy, way. He seemed to her the sort of person who does everything in a showy way. A ministerial way. He brushed aside the sections he didn't want at the moment. A corner of newspaper touched her leg, just at the edge of her coat.

She thought for some time that it was the paper. Then she said to herself, what if it is a hand? That was the kind of thing she could imagine. She would sometimes look at men's hands, at the fuzz on their forearms, their concentrating profiles. She would think about everything they could do. Even the stupid ones. For instance the driver-salesman who brought the bread to Flo's store. The ripeness and confidence of manner, the settled mixture of ease and alertness, with which he handled the bread truck. A fold of mature belly over the belt did not displease her. Another time she had her eye on the French teacher at school. Not a Frenchman at all, really, his name was McLaren, but Rose thought teaching French had rubbed off on him, made him look like one. Quick and sallow; sharp shoulders; hooked nose and sad eyes. She saw him lapping and coiling his way through slow pleasures, a perfect autocrat of indulgences. She had a considerable longing to be somebody's object. Pounded, pleasured, reduced, exhausted.

But what if it was a hand? What if it really was a hand? She shifted slightly, moved as much as she could towards the window. Her imagination seemed to have created this reality, a reality she was not prepared for at all. She found it alarming. She was concentrating on that leg, that bit of skin with the stocking over it. She could not bring herself to look. Was there a pressure, or was there not? She shifted again. Her legs had been, and remained, tightly closed. It was. It was a hand. It was a hand's pressure.

Please don't. That was what she tried to say. She shaped the words in her mind, tried them out, then couldn't get them past her lips. Why was that? The embarrassment, was it, the fear that people might hear? People were all around them, the seats were full.

It was not only that.

She did manage to look at him, not raising her head but turning it cautiously. He had tilted his seat back and closed his eyes. There was his dark blue suit sleeve, disappearing under the newspaper. He had arranged the paper so that it overlapped Rose's coat. His hand was underneath, simply resting, as if flung out in sleep.

Now, Rose could have shifted the newspaper and removed her coat. If he was not asleep, he would have been obliged to draw back his hand. If he was asleep, if he did not draw it back, she could have whispered, *Excuse me*, and set his hand firmly on his own knee. This solution, so obvious and foolproof, did not occur to her. And she would have to wonder, why not? The minister's hand was not, or not yet, at all welcome to her. It made her feel uncomfortable, resentful, slightly disgusted, trapped and wary. But she could not take charge of it, to reject it. She could not insist that it was there, when he seemed to be insisting that it was not. How could she declare him responsible, when he lay there so harmless and trusting, resting himself before his busy day, with such a pleased and healthy face? A man older than her father would be, if he were living, a man used to deference, an appreciator of Nature, delighter in wild swans. If she did say *Please don't* she was sure he would ignore her, as if over-looking some silliness or impoliteness on her part. She knew that as soon as she said it she would hope he had not heard.

But there was more to it than that. Curiosity. More constant, more imperious, than any lust. A lust in itself, that will make you draw back and wait, wait too long, risk almost anything, just to see what will happen. *To see what will happen.*

The hand began, over the next several miles, the most delicate, the most timid, pressures and investigations. Not asleep. Or if he was, his hand wasn't. She did feel disgust. She felt a faint, wandering nausea. She thought of flesh: lumps of flesh, pink snouts, fat tongues, blunt fingers, all on their way trotting and creeping and lolling and rubbing, looking for their comfort. She thought of cats in heat rubbing themselves along the top of board fences, yowling with their miserable complaint. It was pitiful, infantile, this itching and shoving and squeezing. Spongy tissues, inflamed membranes, tormented nerve-ends, shameful smells; humiliation.

All that was starting. His hand, that she wouldn't ever have wanted to hold, that she wouldn't have squeezed back, his stubborn patient hand was able, after all, to get the ferns to rustle and the streams to flow, to waken a sly luxuriance.

Nevertheless, she would rather not. She would still rather not. Please remove this, she said out the window. Stop it, please, she said to the stumps and barns. The hand moved up her leg past the top of her stocking to her bare skin, had moved higher, under her suspender, reached her underpants and the lower part of her belly. Her legs were still crossed, pinched together. While her legs stayed crossed she could lay claim to innocence, she had not admitted anything. She could still believe that she would stop this in a minute. Nothing was going to happen, nothing more. Her legs were never going to open.

But they were. They were. As the train crossed the Niagara Escarpment above Dundas, as they looked down at the preglacial valley, the silver-wooded rubble of little hills, as they came sliding down to the shores of Lake Ontario, she would make this slow, and silent, and definite, declaration, perhaps disappointing as much as satisfying the hand's owner. He would not lift his eyelids, his face would not alter, his fingers would not hesitate, but would go powerfully and discreetly to work. Invasion, and welcome, and sunlight flashing far and wide on the lake water; miles of bare orchards stirring round Burlington.

This was disgrace, this was beggary. But what harm in that, we say to ourselves at such moments, what harm in anything, the worse the better, as we ride the cold wave of greed, of greedy assent. A stranger's hand, or root vegetables or humble kitchen tools that people tell jokes about; the world is tumbling with innocent-seeming objects ready to declare themselves, slippery and obliging. She was careful of her breathing. She could not believe this. Victim and accomplice she was borne past Glassco's Jams and Marmalades, past the big pulsating pipes of oil refineries. They glided into suburbs where bedsheets, and towels used to wipe up intimate stains flapped leeringly on the clotheslines, where even the children seemed to be frolicking lewdly in the schoolyards, and the very truckdrivers stopped at the railway crossings must be thrusting their thumbs gleefully into curled hands. Such cunning antics now, such popular visions. The gates and towers of the Exhibition Grounds came to view the painted domes and pillars floated marvellously against her eyelids' rosy sky. Then flew apart in celebration. You could have had such a flock of birds, wild swans, even, wakened under one big dome together, exploding from it, taking to the sky.

60   She bit the edge of her tongue. Very soon the conductor passed through the train, to stir the travelers, warn them back to life.

In the darkness under the station the United Church minister, refreshed, opened his eyes and got his paper folded together, then asked if she would like some help with her coat. His gallantry was self-satisfied, dismissive. No, said Rose, with a sore tongue. He hurried out of the train ahead of her. She did not seem him in the station. She never saw him again in her life. But he remained on call, so to speak, for year and years, ready to slip into place at a critical moment, without even any regard, later on, for husband or lovers. What recommended him? She could never understand it. His simplicity, his arrogance, his perversely appealing lack of handsomeness, even of ordinary grown-up masculinity? When he stood up she saw that he was shorter even than she had thought, that his face was pink and shiny, that there was something crude and pushy and childish about him.

Was he a minister, really, or was that only what he said? Flo had mentioned people who were not ministers, dressed up as if they were. Not real ministers dressed as if they were not. Or, stranger still, men who were not real ministers pretending to be real but dressed as if they were not. But that she had come as close as she had, to what could happen, was an unwelcome thing. Rose walked through Union Station feeling the little bag with the ten dollars rubbing at her, knew she would feel it all day long, rubbing its reminder against her skin.

She couldn't stop getting Flo's messages, even with that. She remembered, because she was in Union Station, that there was a girl named Mavis working here, in the Gift Shop, when Flo was working in the coffee shop. Mavis had warts on her eyelids that looked like they were going to turn into sties but they didn't, they went away. Maybe she had them removed, Flo didn't ask. She was very good looking, without them. There was a movie star in those days she looked a lot like. The movie star's name was Frances Farmer.[2]

Frances Farmer. Rose had never heard of her.

2   an American actress popular in the 1930s and early 1940s.

65   That was the name. And Mavis went and bought herself a big hat that dipped over one eye and a dress entirely made of lace. She went off for the weekend to Georgian Bay, to a resort up there. She booked herself in under the name of Florence Farmer. To give everybody the idea she was really the other one, Frances Farmer, but calling herself Florence because she was on holidays and didn't want to be recognized. She had a little cigarette holder that was black and mother-of-pearl. She could have been arrested, Flo said. For the *nerve*.

Rose almost went over to the Gift Shop, to see if Mavis was still there and if she could recognize her. She thought it would be an especially fine thing, to manage a transformation like that. To dare it; to get away with it, to enter on preposterous adventures in your own, but newly named, skin.

(1978)

Jane Rule (b. 1931)

Born in Plainfield, New Jersey, Jane Rule taught creative writing for several years at the University of British Columbia, before moving to her present home on Galiano Island, British Columbia. Beginning with her first novel, *Desert of the Heart*, published in 1964, Rule has explored the complex nature of lesbian relationships. In novels, short stories, and critical essays, she examines not only the social pressures on such partnerships, but also the insecurities, vulnerabilities, and joys of the women involved. Her works have been praised for the sensitivity and compassion with which individuals are portrayed. Lesbianism is seen as a natural part of life, as are the relationships between other characters, often marginalized, that she creates. In "Inland Passage," a boat journey from Vancouver, through the narrow waterways between the British Columbia mainland and offshore islands, symbolizes the careful navigation two women who have recently lost loved ones must execute in the beginning stages of their new relationship. In the cramped quarters of their cabin, both Troy and Fido must "get [their] bearings" as individuals and potential partners.

INLAND PASSAGE

"The other lady..." the ship's steward began.

"We're not together," a quiet but determined female voice explained from the corridor, one hand thrust through the doorway insisting that he take her independent tip for the bag he had just deposited on the lower bunk.

There was not room for Troy McFadden to step into the cabin until the steward had left.

"It's awfully small," Fidelity Munroe, the first occupant of the cabin, confirmed, shrinking down into her oversized duffle coat.

5   "It will do if we take turns," Troy McFadden decided. "I'll let you settle first, shall I?"

"I just need a place to put my bag."

The upper bunk was bolted against the cabin ceiling to leave headroom for anyone wanting to sit on the narrow upholstered bench below.

"Under my bunk," Troy McFadden suggested.

There was no other place. The single chair in the cabin was shoved in under the small, square table, and the floor of the minute closet was taken up with life jackets. The bathroom whose door Troy McFadden opened to inspect, had a coverless toilet, sink and triangle of a shower. The one hook on the back of the door might make dressing there possible. When she stepped back into the cabin, she bumped into Fidelity Munroe, crouching down to stow her bag.

10   "I'm sorry," Fidelity said, standing up, "But I can get out now."

"Let's both get out."

They sidled along the narrow corridor, giving room to other passengers in search of their staterooms.

Glancing into one open door, Troy McFadden said, "At least we have a window."

"Deck?" Fidelity suggested.

"Oh, yes."

Neither had taken off her coat. They had to shoulder the heavy door together before they could step out into the moist sea air. Their way was blocked to the raised prow of the ship where they might otherwise have watched the cars, campers, and trucks being loaded. They turned instead and walked to the stern of the ferry to find rows of wet, white empty benches facing blankly out to sea.

"You can't even see the Gulf Islands this morning," Troy McFadden observed.

"Are you from around here?"

"Yes, from North Vancouver. We should introduce ourselves, shouldn't we?"

"I'm Fidelity Munroe. Everyone calls me Fido."

"I'm Troy McFadden, and nearly everyone calls me Mrs. McFadden."

They looked at each other uncertainly, and then both women laughed.

"Are you going all the way to Prince Rupert?" Fidelity asked.

"And back, just for the ride."

"So am I. Are we going to see a thing?"

"It doesn't look like it," Troy McFadden admitted. "I'm told you rarely do on this trip. You sail into mist and maybe get an occasional glimpse of forest or the near shore or an island. Mostly you seem to be going nowhere."

"Then why...?"

"For that reason, I suppose," Troy McFadden answered, gathering her fur collar more closely around her ears.

"I was told it rarely gets rough," Fidelity Munroe offered.

"We're in open sea only two hours each way. All the rest is inland passage."

"You've been before then."

"No," Troy McFadden said. "I've heard about it for years."

"So have I, but I live in Toronto. There you hear it's beautiful."

"Mrs. Munroe?"

"Only technically," Fidelity answered.

"I don't think I can call you Fido."

"It's no more ridiculous than Fidelity once you get used to it."

"Does your mother call you Fido?"

"My mother hasn't spoken to me for years," Fidelity Munroe answered.

Two other passengers, a couple in their agile seventies, joined them on the deck.

"Well..." Troy McFadden said, in no one's direction, "I think I'll get my bearings."

She turned away, a woman who did not look as if she ever lost her bearings.

You're not really old enough to be my mother, Fidelity wanted to call after her, *Why take offense?* But it wasn't just that remark. Troy McFadden would be as daunted as Fidelity by such sudden intimacy, the risk of its smells as much as its other disclosures. She would be saying to herself, *I'm too old for this. Why on earth didn't I spend the extra thirty dollars?* Or she was on her way to the purser to see if she might be moved, if not into a single cabin then into one with someone less... more...

Fidelity looked down at Gail's much too large duffle coat, her own jeans and hiking boots. Well, there wasn't room for the boots in her suitcase, and, ridiculous as they might look for walking the few yards of deck, they might be very useful for exploring the places the ship docked.

45   *Up yours, Mrs. McFadden, with your fur collar and your expensive, sensible shoes and matching bag. Take up the whole damned cabin!*

All Fidelity needed for this mist-bound mistake of a cruise was a book out of her suitcase. She could sleep in the lounge along with the kids and the Indians, leave the staterooms (what a term!) to the geriatrics and Mrs. McFadden.

Fidelity wrenched the door open with her own strength, stomped back along the corridor like one of the invading troops, and unlocked and opened the cabin door in one gesture. There sat Troy McFadden, in surprised tears.

"I'm sorry..." Fidelity began, but she could not make her body retreat. Instead she wedged herself around the door and closed it behind her. Then she sat down beside Troy McFadden, took her hand, and stared quietly at their unlikely pairs of feet. A shadow passed across the window. Fidelity looked up to meet the eyes of another pasenger glancing in. She reached up with her free hand and pulled the small curtain across the window.

50   "I simply can't impose..." Troy finally brought herself to say.

"Look," Fidelity said, turning to her companion, "I may cry most of the way myself... it doesn't matter."

"I just can't make myself... walk into those public rooms... alone."

"How long have you been alone?" Fidelity asked.

"My husband died nearly two years ago... there's no excuse."

55   "Somebody said to me the other day, 'Shame's the last stage of grief.' 'What a rotten arrangement then,' I said. 'To be ashamed for the rest of my life.'"

"You've lost your husband?"

Fidelity shook her head, "Years ago. I divorced him."

"You hardly look old enough..."

"I know, but I am. I'm forty-one. I've got two grown daughters."

60   "I have two sons," Troy said. "One offered to pay for this trip just to get me out of town for a few days. The other thought I should lend him the money instead."

"And you'd rather have?"

"It's so humiliating," Troy said.

"To be alone?"

"To be afraid."

65   The ship's horn sounded.

"We're about to sail," Troy said. "I didn't even have the courage to get off the ship, and here I am, making you sit in the dark..."

"Shall we go out and get our bearings together?"

"Let me put my face back on," Troy said.

Only then did Fidelity let go of her hand so that she could take her matching handbag into the tiny bathroom and smoothe courage back into her quite handsome and appealing face.

70   Fidelity pulled her bag out from under the bunk, opened it and got out her own sensible shoes. If she was going to offer this woman any sort of reassurance, she must make what gestures she could to be a bird of her feather.

The prow of the ship had been lowered and secured, and the reverse engines had ceased their vibrating by the time the two women joined the bundled passengers on deck to see, to everyone's amazement, the sun breaking through, an ache to the eyes on the shining water.

Troy McFadden reached for her sunglasses. Fidelity Munroe had forgotten hers.

"This is your captain," said an intimate male voice from a not very loud speaker just above their heads. "We are sailing into a fair day."

The shoreline they had left remained hidden in clouds crowded up against the Vancouver mountains, but the long wooded line of Galiano Island and beyond it to the west the mountains of Vancouver Island lay in a clarity of light.

75   "I'm hungry," Fidelity announced. "I didn't get up in time to have breakfast."

"I couldn't eat," Troy confessed.

When she hesitated at the entrance to the cafeteria, Fidelity took her arm firmly and directed her into the short line that had formed.

"Look at that!" Fidelity said with pleasure. "Sausages, ham, bacon, pancakes. How much can we have?"

"As much as you want," answered the young woman behind the counter.

80   "Oh, am I ever going to pig out on this trip!"

Troy took a bran muffin, apple juice and a cup of tea.

"It isn't fair," she said as they unloaded their contrasting trays at a window table. "My husband could eat like that, too, and never gain a pound."

Fidelity, having taken off her coat, revealed just how light-bodied she was.

"My kids call me bird bones. They have their father to thank for being human size. People think I'm their little brother."

85   "Once children tower over you, being their mother is an odd business," Troy mused.

"That beautiful white hair must help," Fidelity said.

"I've had it since I was twenty-five. When the boys were little, people thought I was their grandmother."

"I suppose only famous people are mistaken for themselves in public," Fidelity said, around a mouthful of sausage; so she checked herself and chewed instead of elaborating on that observation.

"Which is horrible in its way, too, I suppose," Troy said.

90   Fidelity swallowed. "I don't know. I've sometimes thought I'd like it: Mighty Mouse[1] fantasies."

She saw Troy try to smile and for a second lose the trembling control of her face. She hadn't touched her food.

"Drink your juice," Fidelity said, in the no-nonsense, cheerful voice of motherhood.

Troy's dutiful hand shook as she raised the glass to her lips, but she took a sip. She returned the glass to the table without accident and took up the much less dangerous bran muffin.

"I would like to be invisible," Troy said, a rueful apology in her voice.

95   "Well, we really are, aren't we?" Fidelity asked. "Except to a few people."

"Have you traveled alone a lot?"

---

1 cartoon character who uses super powers in his battles with cats.

"No," Fidelity said, "just about never. I had the girls, and they're still only semi-independent. And I had a friend, Gail. She and I took trips together. She died last year."

"I'm so sorry."

"Me, too. It's a bit like being a widow, I guess, except, nobody expects it to be. Maybe that helps."

100 "Did you live with Gail?"

"No, but we thought maybe we might...someday."

Troy sighed.

"So here we both are at someday," Fidelity said. "Day one of someday and not a bad day at that."

They both looked out at the coast, ridge after ridge of tall trees, behind which were sudden glimpses of high peaks of snow-capped mountains.

105 Back on the deck other people had also ventured, dressed and hatted against the wind, armed with binoculars for sighting of eagles and killer whales, for inspecting the crews of fishing boats, tugs, and pleasure craft.

"I never could use those things," Fidelity confessed. "It's not just my eyes. I feel like that woman in the Colville[2] painting."

"Do you like his work?" Troy asked.

"I admire it," Fidelity said. "There's something a bit sinister about it: all those figures seem prisoners of normality. That woman at the shore, about to get into the car..."

"With the children, yes," Troy said. "They seem so vulnerable."

110 "Here's Jonathan Seagull!" a woman called to her binocular-blinded husband, "Right here on the rail."

"I loathed that book," Troy murmured to Fidelity.

Fidelity chuckled. "In the first place, I'm no friend to seagulls."

Finally chilled, the two women went back inside. At the door to the largest lounge, again Troy hesitated.

"Take my arm," Fidelity said, wishing it and she were more substantial.

115 They walked the full length of that lounge and on into the smaller space of the gift shop where Troy was distracted from her nerves by postcards, travel books, toys and souvenirs.

Fidelity quickly picked up half a dozen postcards.

"I'd get home before they would," Troy said.

"I probably will, too, but everybody likes mail."

From the gift shop, they found their way to the forward lounge where tv sets would later offer a movie, on into the children's playroom, a glassed-in area heavily padded where several toddlers tumbled and stumbled about.

120 "It's like an aquarium," Fidelity said.

"There aren't many children aboard."

"One of the blessings of traveling in October," Fidelity said. "Oh, I don't feel about kids the way I do about seagulls, but they aren't a holiday."

"No," Troy agreed. "I suppose I really just think I miss mine."

Beyond the playroom they found the bar with only three tables of prelunch drinkers. Troy looked in, shook her head firmly and retreated.

2 twentieth-century Canadian artist whose paintings depict everyday events and scenes.

125   "Not a drinker?" Fidelity asked.

"I have a bottle of scotch in my case," Troy said. "I don't think I could ever...alone..."

"Mrs. McFadden," Fidelity said, taking her arm, "I'm going to make a hard point. You're not alone. You're with me, and we're both old enough to be grandmothers, and we're approaching the turn of the 21st not the 20th century, and I think we both could use a drink."

Troy McFadden allowed herself to be steered into the bar and settled at a table, but, when the waiter came, she only looked at her hands.

"Sherry," Fidelity decided. "Two sherries," and burst out laughing.

130   Troy looked over at her, puzzled.

"Sherry is my idea of what you would order. I've never tasted it in my life."

"You're quite right," Troy said. "Am I such a cliché?"

"Not a cliché, an ideal. I don't know, maybe they're the same thing when it comes down to it. You have style. I really admire that. If I ever got it together enough to have shoes and matching handbag, I'd lose one of the shoes."

"Is that really your coat?" Troy asked.

135   Fidelity looked down at herself. "No, it belonged to Gail. It's my Linus blanket."[3]

"I've been sleeping in my husband's old pajamas. I had to buy a night-gown to come on this trip," Troy confided. "I think it's marvelous the way you do what you want."

Fidelity bit her lip and screwed her face tight for a moment. Then she said, "But I don't want to cry any more than you do."

The waiter put their sherries before them, and Fidelity put a crumpled ten dollar bill on the table.

"Oh, you should let me," Troy said, reaching for her purse.

140   "Next round," Fidelity said.

Troy handled her glass more confidently than she had at breakfast, and, after her first sip, she said with relief, "Dry."

"This is your captain," the intimate male voice asserted again. "A pod of killer whales is approaching to starboard."

Fidelity and Troy looked out the window and waited. No more than a hundred yards away, a killer whale broke the water, then another, then another, their black backs arching, their bellies unbelievably white.

"They don't look real," Fidelity exclaimed.

145   Then one surfaced right alongside the ferry, and both women caught their breath.

"This trip is beginning to feel less like somebody else's day dream," Fidelity said. "Just look at that!"

For some moments after the whales had passed, the women continued to watch the water, newly interested in its possibilities for surprise. As if as a special reward for their attention, an enormous bird dropped out of the sky straight into the sea, then lifted off the water with a strain of great wings, a flash of fish in its talons.

---

3 security blanket clutched by a character in Charles Schultz's cartoon "Peanuts."

"What on earth was that?" Fidelity cried.

"A bald eagle catching a salmon," Troy replied.

150　　The ship had slowed to navigate a quite narrow passage between the mainland and a small island, its northern crescent shore fingered with docks, reached by flights of steps going back up into the trees where the glint of windows and an occasional line of roof could be seen.

"Do people live there all year long?" Fidelity asked.

"Not many. They're summer places mostly."

"How do people get there?"

"Private boats or small planes."

155　　"Ain't the rich wealthy?" Fidelity sighed.

Troy frowned.

"Did I make a personal remark by mistake?"

"Geoff and I had a place when the boys were growing up. We didn't *have* money, but he earned a good deal . . . law. He hadn't got around to thinking about . . . retiring. I'm just awfully grateful the boys had finished their education. It scares me to think what it might have been like if it had happened earlier. You just don't think . . . we didn't anyway. Oh, now that I've sold the house, I'm perfectly comfortable. When you're just one person . . ."

"Well, on this trip with the food all paid for, I'm going to eat like an army," Fidelity said. "Let's have lunch."

160　　Though the ship wasn't crowded, there were more people in the cafeteria than there had been for breakfast.

"Let's not sit near the Jonathan Seagulls," Fidelity said, leading the way through the tables to a quiet corner where they could do more watching than being watched. Troy had chosen a seafood salad that Fidelity considered a first course to which she added a plate of lamb chops, rice and green beans.

"I really don't believe you could eat like that all the time," Troy said.

"Would if I could."

Fidelity tried not to let greed entirely overtake her, yet she needed to eat quickly not to leave Troy with nothing to do.

165　　"See those two over there?" Fidelity said, nodding to a nondescript pair of middle-aged women. "One's a lady cop. The other's her prisoner."

"How did you figure that out?"

"Saw the handcuffs. That's why they're sitting side by side."

"They're both right handed," Troy observed critically.

"On their ankles."

170　　"What's she done?"

"Blown up a mortgage company," Fidelity said.

"She ought to get a medal."

"A fellow anarchist, are you?"

"Only armchair," Troy admitted modestly.

175　　"Mrs. McFadden, you're a fun lady. I'm glad we got assigned to the same shoe box."

"Do call me Troy."

"Only if you call me Fido."

"Will you promise not to bark?"

"No," Fidelity said and growled convincingly at a lamb chop but quietly enough not to attract attention.

180 "Fido, would it both antisocial and selfish of me to take a rest after lunch?"

"Of course not," Fidelity said. "I'll just come up and snag a book."

"Then later you could have a rest."

"I'm not good at them," Fidelity said. "I twitch and have horrible dreams if I sleep during the day. But, look, I do have to know a few intimate things about you, like do you play bridge or Scrabble or poker because I don't, but I could probably scout out some people who do..."

"I loathe games," Troy said. "In any case, please don't feel responsible for me. I do feel much better, thanks to you."

185 A tall, aging fat man nodded to Troy as they left the cafeteria and said, "Lovely day."

"Don't panic," Fidelity said out of the side of her mouth. "I bite too, that is, unless you're in the market for a shipboard romance."

"How about you?" Troy asked wryly.

"I'm not his type."

"Well, he certainly isn't mine!"

190 Fidelity went into the cabin first, struggled to get her case out from under the bunk and found her book, Alice Walker's[4] collection of essays.

"Is she good?" Troy asked, looking at the cover.

"I think she's terrific, but I have odd tastes."

"Odd?"

"I'm a closet feminist."

195 "But isn't that perfectly respectable by now?" Troy asked.

"Nothing about me is perfectly respectable."

"You're perfectly dear," Troy said and gave Fidelity a quick, hard hug before she went into the cabin.

Fidelity paused for a moment outside the closed door to enjoy that affectionate praise before she headed off to find a window seat in the lounge where she could alternately read and watch the passing scene. An occasional deserted Indian village was now the only sign of habitation on the shores of this northern wilderness.

The book lay instead neglected in her lap, and the scenery became a transparency through which Fidelity looked at her inner landscape, a place of ruins.

200 A man whose wife had died of the same cancer that had killed Gail said to Fidelity, "I don't even want to take someone out to dinner without requiring her to have a thorough physical examination first."

The brutality of that remark shocked Fidelity because it located in her her own denied bitterness, that someone as lovely and funny and strong as Gail could be not only physically altered out of recognition but so horribly transformed humanly until she seemed to have nothing left but anger, guilt, and fear, burdens she tried to shift, as she couldn't her pain, onto Fidelity's shoulders,

4 feminist African American writer.

until Fidelity found herself praying for Gail's death instead of her life. Surely she had loved before she grew to dread the sight of Gail, the daily confrontations with her appalled and appalling fear. It was a face looking into hell Fidelity knew did not exist, and yet her love had failed before it. Even now it was her love she mourned rather than Gail, for without it she could not go back to the goodness between them, believe in it and go on.

She felt herself withdraw from her daughters as if her love for them might also corrupt and then fail them. In the way of adolescents they both noticed and didn't, excused her grief and then became impatient with it. They were anyway perched at the edge of their own lives, ready to be free of her.

"Go," she encouraged them, and they did.

"I guess I only think I miss them," Troy said. Otherwise this convention of parent abandonment would be intolerable, a cruel and unusual punishment for all those years of intimate attention and care.

And here she was, temporarily paired with another woman as fragile and shamed by self-pity as she was. At least they wouldn't be bleeding all over the other passengers. If they indulged in pitying each other, well, what was the harm in it?

Fidelity shifted uncomfortably. The possibility of harm was all around her.

"Why did you marry me then?" she had demanded of her hostile husband.

"I felt *sorry* for you," he said.

"That's a lie!"

"It's the honest truth."

So pity, even from someone else, is the seed of contempt.

Review resolutions for this trip: be cheerful, eat, indulge in Mighty Mouse fantasies, and enjoy the scenery.

An island came into focus, a large bird perched in a tree, another eagle no doubt, and she would not think of the fish except in its surprised moment of flight.

"This is your captain speaking . . ."

Fidelity plugged her ears and also shut her eyes, for even if she missed something more amazing than whales, she wanted to see or not see for herself.

"Here you are," Troy said. "What on earth are you doing?"

"Do you think he's going to do that all through the trip?" Fidelity demanded.

"Probably not after dark."

"Pray for an early sunset."

It came, as they stood watching it on deck, brilliantly red with promise, leaving the sky christened with stars.

"Tell me about these boys of yours," Fidelity said as they sat over a predinner drink in the crowded bar. "We've spent a whole day together without even taking out our pictures. That's almost unnatural."

"In this den of iniquity," Troy said, glancing around, "I'm afraid people will think we're exchanging dirty post-cards."

"Why oh why did I leave mine at home?"

Fidelity was surprised that Troy's sons were not better looking than they were, and she suspected Troy was surprised at how much better looking her daughters were than she had any right to expect. It's curious how really rare a handsome couple is. Beauty is either too vain for competition or indifferent to itself. Troy would have chosen a husband for his character. Fidelity had fallen for narcissistic good looks, for which her daughters were her only and lovely reward.

225   "Ralph's like his father," Troy said, taking back the picture of her older son, "conservative with some attractive independence of mind. So many of our friends had trouble with first children and blame it on their own inexperience. Geoff used to say, 'I guess the more we knew, the worse we did.'"

"What's the matter with Colin?" Fidelity asked.

"I've never thought there was anything the matter with him," Troy said, "except perhaps the world. Geoff didn't like his friends or his work (Colin's an actor). It was the only hard thing between Geoff and me, but it was very hard."

The face Fidelity studied was less substantial and livelier than Ralph's, though it was easy enough to tell that they were brothers.

"We ought to pair at least two of them off, don't you think?" Fidelity suggested flippantly. "Let's see. Is it better to put the conservative, responsible ones together, and let the scallywags go off and have fun, or should each kite have a tail?"

230   "Colin won't marry," Troy said. "He's homosexual."

Fidelity looked up from the pictures to read Troy's face. Her dark blue eyes held a question rather than a challenge.

"How lucky for him that you're his mother," Fidelity said. "Did you realize that I am, too?"

"I wondered when you spoke about your friend Gail," Troy said.

"Sometimes I envy people his age," Fidelity said. "There's so much less guilt, so much more acceptance."

235   "In some quarters," Troy said. "Geoff let it kill him."

"How awful!"

"That isn't true," Troy said. "It's the first time I've ever said it out loud, and it simply isn't true. But I've been so afraid Colin thought so, so angry, yes, *angry*. I always thought Geoff would finally come round. He was basically a fair-minded man. Then he had a heart attack and died. If he'd had any warning, if he'd had time..."

Fidelity shook her head. She did not want to say how easily that might have been worse. Why did people persist in the fantasy that facing death brought out the best in people when so often it did just the opposite?

"How does Colin feel about his father?"

240   "He always speaks of him very lovingly, remembering all the things he did with the boys when they were growing up. He never mentions those last, awful months when Geoff was remembering the same things but only so that he didn't have to blame himself."

"Maybe Colin's learning to let them go," Fidelity suggested.

"So why can't I?" Troy asked.

There was Fidelity's own question in Troy's mouth. *It's because they're dead,* she thought. *How do you go about forgiving the dead for dying?* Then, because she had no answer, she simply took Troy's hand.

"Is that why your mother doesn't speak to you?" Troy asked.

"That and a thousand other things," Fidelity said. "It used to get to me, but, as my girls have grown up, I think we're all better off for not trying to please someone who won't be pleased. Probably it hasn't anything to do with me, just luck, that I like my kids, and they like me pretty well most of the time."

"Did they know about you and Gail?"

"Did and didn't. We've never actually talked about it. I would have, but Gail was dead set against it. I didn't realize just how much that had to do with her own hang-ups. Once she was gone, there didn't seem to be much point, for them."

"But for you?"

"Would you like another drink?" Fidelity asked as she signaled the waiter and, at Troy's nod, ordered two. "For myself, I'd like to tell the whole damned world, but I'm still enough of my mother's child to hear her say, 'Another one of your awful self-indulgences' and to think maybe she has a point."

"It doesn't seem to me self-indulgent to be yourself," Troy said.

Fidelity laughed suddenly. "Why that's exactly what it is! Why does everything to do with the *self* have such a bad press: self-pity, self-con-sciousness, self-indulgence, self-satisfaction, practices of selfish people, people being themselves?"

"The way we are," Troy said.

"Yes, and I haven't felt as good about myself in months."

"Nor I," Troy said, smiling.

"Are we going to watch the movie tonight, or are we going to go on telling each other the story of our lives?"

"We have only three days," Troy said. "And this one is nearly over."

"I suppose we'd better eat before the cafeteria closes."

They lingered long over coffee after dinner until they were alone in the room, and they were still there when the movie goers came back for a late night snack. Troy yawned and looked at her watch.

"Have we put off the evil hour as long as we can?" Fidelity asked.

"You're going to try to talk me out of the lower bunk."

"I may be little, but I'm very agile," Fidelity claimed.

The top bunk had been made up, leaving only a narrow corridor in which to stand or kneel, as they had to to get at their cases. Troy took her nightgown and robe and went into the bathroom. Fidelity changed into her flannel tent and climbed from the chair to the upper bunk, too close to the ceiling for sitting. She lay on her side, her head propped up on her elbow.

It occurred to her that this cabin was the perfect setting for the horrible first night of a honeymoon and she was about to tell Troy so as she came out of the bathroom but she looked both so modest and so lovely that an easy joke seemed instead tactless.

"I didn't have the courage for a shower," Troy confessed. "Really, you know, we're too old for this."

265 "I think that's beginning to be part of the fun."

When they had both settled and turned out their lights, Fidelity said, "Good night, Troy."

"Good night, dear Fido."

Fidelity did not expect to sleep at once, her head full of images and revelations, but the gentle motion of the ship lulled her, and she felt herself letting go and dropping away. When she woke, it was morning, and she could hear the shower running.

"You did it!" Fidelity shouted as Troy emerged fully dressed in a plum and navy pant suit, her night things over her arm.

270 "I don't wholeheartedly recommend it as an experience, but I do feel better for it."

Fidelity followed Troy's example. It seemed to her the moment she turned on the water, the ship's movement became more pronounced, and she had to hang onto a bar which might have been meant for a towel rack to keep her balance, leaving only one hand for the soaping. By the time she was through, the floor was awash, and she had to sit on the coverless toilet to pull on her grey and patchily soggy trousers and fresh wool shirt.

"We're into open water," Troy said, looking out their window.

"Two hours, you said?"

"Yes."

275 "I think I'm going to be better off on deck," Fidelity admitted, her normally pleasurable hunger pangs suddenly unresponsive to the suggestion of sausages and eggs. "Don't let me keep you from breakfast."

"What makes you think I'm such an old sea dog myself?"

Once they were out in the sun and air of a lovely morning, the motion of the open sea was exciting. They braced themselves against the railing and plunged with the ship, crossing from the northern tip of Vancouver Island to the mainland.

A crewman informed them that the ship would be putting in at Bella Bella to drop off supplies and pick up passengers.

"Will there be time to go ashore?" Fidelity asked.

280 "You can see everything there is to see from here," the crewman answered.

"No stores?"

"Just the Indian store . . . for the Indians," he said, as he turned to climb to the upper deck.

"A real, lived-in Indian village!" Fidelity said. "Do you want to go ashore?"

"It doesn't sound to me as if we'd be very welcome," Troy said.

285 "Why not?"

"You're not aware that we're not very popular with the Indians?"

Fidelity sighed. She resented, as she always did, having to take on the sins and clichés of her race, nation, sex, and yet she was less willing to defy welcome at an Indian village than she was at the ship's bar.

They were able to see the whole of the place from the deck, irregular rows of raw wood houses climbing up a hill stripped of trees. There were more dogs than people on the dock. Several family groups, cheaply but more formally dressed than most of the other passengers, boarded.

"It's depressing," Fidelity said.

290 "I wish we knew how to expect something else and make it happen."

"I'm glad nobody else was living on the moon," Fidelity said, turning sadly away.

The Indian families were in the cafeteria where Troy and Fidelity went for their belated breakfast. The older members of the group were talking softly among themselves in their own language. The younger ones were chatting with the crew in a friendly enough fashion. They were all on their way to a great wedding in Prince Rupert that night and would be back on board ship when it sailed south again at midnight.

"Do you work?" Troy suddenly asked Fidelity as she put a large piece of ham in her mouth.

Fidelity nodded as she chewed.

295 "What do you do?"

"I'm a film editor," Fidelity said.

"Something as amazing as that, and you haven't even bothered to tell me?"

"It's nothing amazing," Fidelity said. "You sit in a dark room all by yourself, day after day, trying to make a creditable half hour or hour and a half out of hundreds of hours of film."

"You don't like it at all?"

300 "Oh, well enough," Fidelity said. "Sometimes it's interesting. Once I did a film on Haida carving that was shot up here in the Queen Charlottes, one of the reasons I've wanted to see this part of the country."

"How did you decide to be a film editor?"

"I didn't really. I went to art school. I was going to be a great painter. Mighty Mouse fantasy number ten. I got married instead. He didn't work; so I had to. It was a job, and after a while I got pretty good at it."

"Did he take care of the children?"

"My mother did," Fidelity said, "until they were in school. They've had to be pretty independent."

305 "Oh, Fido, you've done so much more with your life than I have."

"Got divorced and earned a living because I had to. Not exactly things to brag about."

"But it's ongoing, something of your own to do."

"I suppose so," Fidelity admitted, "but you know, after Gail died, I looked around me and realized that, aside from my kids, I didn't really have any friends. I worked alone. I lived alone. I sometimes think now I should quit, do something entirely different. I can't risk that until the girls are really independent, not just playing house with Mother's off-stage help. Who knows? One of them might turn up on my doorstep as I did on my mother's."

"I'd love a job," Troy said, "but I'd never have the courage . . ."

310 "Of course you would," Fidelity said.

"Are you volunteering to take me by the hand as you did yesterday and say to the interviewer, 'This is my friend, Mrs. McFadden. She can't go into strange places by herself?'"

"Sure," Fidelity said. "I'll tell you what, let's go into business together."

"What kind of business?"

"Well, we could run a selling gallery and lose our shirts."

315 "Or a bookstore and lose our shirts . . . I don't really have a shirt to lose."

"Let's be more practical. How about a gay bar?"

"Oh, Fido," Troy said, laughing and shaking her head.

The ship now had entered a narrow inland passage, moving slowly and carefully past small islands. The captain, though he still occasionally pointed out a deserted cannery, village or mine site, obviously had to pay more attention to the task of bringing his ship out of this narrow reach in a nearly silent wilderness into the noise and clutter of the town of Prince Rupert.

A bus waited to take those passengers who had signed up for a tour of the place, and Troy and Fidelity were among them. Their driver and guide was a young man fresh from Liverpool, and he looked on his duty as bizarre, for what was there really to see in Prince Rupert but one ridge of rather expensive houses overlooking the harbor and a small neighborhood of variously tasteless houses sold to fishermen in seasons when they made too much money so that they could live behind pretentious front doors on unemployment all the grey winter long. The only real stop was a small museum of Indian artifacts and old tools. The present Indian population was large and poor and hostile.

320 "It's like being in Greece," Fidelity said, studying a small collection of beautifully patterned baskets. "Only here it's been over for less than a hundred years."

They ate delicious seafood at an otherwise unremarkable hotel and then skipped an opportunity to shop at a mall left open in the evening for the tour's benefit, business being what it was in winter. Instead they took a taxi back to the ship.

"I think it's time to open my bottle of scotch," Troy suggested.

They got ice from a vending machine and went back to their cabin, where Fidelity turned the chair so that she could put her feet up on the bunk and Troy could sit at the far end with her feet tucked under her.

"Cozy," Troy decided.

325 "I wish I liked scotch," Fidelity said, making a face.

By the time the steward came to make up the bunks, returning and new passengers were boarding the ship. Troy and Fidelity out on deck watched the Indians being seen off by a large group of friends and relatives who must also have been to the wedding. Fidelity imagined them in an earlier time getting into great canoes to paddle south instead of settling down to a few hours' sleep on the lounge floor. She might as well imagine herself and Troy on a sailing ship bringing drink and disease.

A noisy group of Australians came on deck.

"You call this a ship?" they said to each other. "You call those cabins?"

They had traveled across the States and had come back across Canada, and they were not happily prepared to spend two nights in cabins even less comfortable than Fidelity's and Troy's.

330   "Maybe the scenery will cheer them up," Fidelity suggested as they went back to their cabin.

"They sound to me as if they've already had more scenery than they can take."

True enough. The Australians paced the decks like prisoners looking at the shore only to evaluate their means of escape, no leaping whale or plummeting eagle compensation for this coastal ferry which had been described in their brochures as a "cruise ship." How different they were from the stoically settled Indians who had quietly left the ship at Bella Bella shortly after dawn.

Fidelity and Troy stayed on deck for the open water crossing to Port Hardy on Vancouver Island, went in only long enough to get warm, then back out into the brilliant sun and sea wind to take delight in every shape of island, contour of hill, the play of light on the water, the least event of sea life until even their cloud of complaining gulls seemed part of the festival of their last day.

"Imagine preferring something like The Love Boat,"[5] Troy said.

335   "Gail and I were always the ferry, barge, and freighter types," Fidelity said.

Film clips moved through her mind, Gail sipping ouso in a café in Athens, Gail hailing a cab in London, Gail...a face she had begun to believe stricken from her memory was there in its many moods at her bidding.

"What is it?" Troy asked.

"Some much better reruns in my head," Fidelity said, smiling. "I guess it takes having fun to remember how often I have."

"What time is your plane tomorrow?" Troy asked.

340   The question hit Fidelity like a blow.

"Noon," she managed to say before she excused herself and left Troy for the first time since she had pledged herself to Troy's need.

Back in their cabin, sitting on the bunk that was also Troy's bed, Fidelity was saying to herself, "You're such an idiot, such an idiot, such an idiot!"

Two and a half days playing Mighty Mouse better than she ever had in her life, and suddenly she was dissolving into a maudlin fool, into tears of a sort she hadn't shed since her delayed adolescence.

"I can't want her. I just can't," Fidelity chanted.

345   It was worse than coming down with a toothache, breaking out in boils, this stupid, sweet desire which she simply had to hide from a woman getting better and better at reading her face unless she wanted to wreck the last hours of this lovely trip.

Troy shoved open the cabin door.

"Did I say something...?"

Fidelity shook her head, "No, just my turn, I guess."

5 television series in which passengers on a cruise ship often discover romance.

"You don't want to miss your last dinner, do you?"

"Of course not," Fidelity said, trying to summon up an appetite she could indulge in.

They were shy of each other over dinner, made conversation in a way they hadn't needed to from the first few minutes of their meeting. The strain of it made Fidelity both long for sleep and dread the intimacy of their cabin where their new polite reserve would be unbearable.

"Shall we have an early night?" Troy suggested. "We have to be up awfully early to disembark."

As they knelt together, getting out their night things, Troy said, mocking their awkward position, "I'd say a prayer of thanks if I thought there was anybody up there to pray to."

Fidelity *was* praying for whatever help there was against her every instinct.

"I'm going to find it awfully hard to say good-bye to you, Fido."

Fidelity had to turn then to Troy's lovely, vulnerable face.

"I just can't . . ." Fidelity began.

Then, unable to understand that it could happen, Fidelity was embracing Troy, and they moved into love-making as trustingly as they had talked.

At six in the morning, when Troy's travel alarm went off, she said, "I don't think I can move."

Fidelity, unable to feel the arm that lay under Troy, whispered, "We're much too old for this."

"I was afraid you thought I was," Troy said as she slowly and painfully untangled herself, "and now I'm going to prove it."

"Do you know what I almost said to you the first night?" Fidelity asked, loving the sight of Troy's naked body in the light of the desk lamp she'd just turned on. "I almost said, 'what a great setting for the first horrible night of a honeymoon.'"

"Why didn't you?"

"You were so lovely, coming out of the bathroom," Fidelity explained, knowing it wasn't an explanation.

"You were wrong," Troy said, defying her painful stiffness to lean down to kiss Fidelity.

"Young lovers would skip breakfast," Fidelity said.

"But you're starved."

Fidelity nodded, having no easy time getting out of bed herself.

It occurred to her to disturb the virgin neatness of her own upper bunk only because it would have been the first thing to occur to Gail, a bed ravager of obsessive proportions. If it didn't trouble Troy, it would not trouble Fidelity.

As they sat eating, the sun rose over the Vancouver mountains, catching the windows of the apartment blocks on the north shore.

"I live over there," Troy said.

"Troy?"

"Will you invite me to visit you in Toronto?"

"Come with me."

"I have to see Colin . . . and Ralph. I could be there in a week."

"I was wrong about those two over there," Fidelity said. "They sit side by side because they're lovers."

"And you thought so in the first place," Troy said.

Fidelity nodded.

"This is your captain speaking..."

380 Because he was giving them instructions about how to disembark, Fidelity did listen but only with one ear, for she had to keep her own set of instructions clearly in her head. She, of course, had to see her children, too.

(1985)

Elizabeth McGrath   (b. 1932)

A native of St. John's, Newfoundland, short story writer and English professor Elizabeth McGrath grew up in St. John's, St. Mary's, Harbour Grace, and Montreal. She studied and taught at several Canadian universities before returning to Newfoundland to teach at Memorial University. In "Fogbound in Avalon," which first appeared in *The New Yorker* magazine, the narrator attempts, after the breakup of her marriage, to find focus in her life by returning to her home town and renewing old friendships. The fog that shrouds the airport and the rough landing it causes are physical foreshadowings of the psychological difficulties that the narrator will face.

FOGBOUND IN AVALON [1]

Neither Laurel nor I will ever be certifiable, I imagine, though, having put in, between us, going on a hundred years in this world, we have inevitably had a brush or two with the darker side of things. So this will not be a story of alienation. And to put your mind at rest, right from the beginning, we have never been in love with each other, in spite of having been reared in the most repressive of girls' schools from the ages of five to eighteen.

Laurel and I, middle-aged, neurotic, still thin, still suffering, still fascinated by the world and ourselves in it, are friends. We were born on this rock, Newfoundland, and are fixed in the cracks of it, through and beyond the sparse topsoil, in a way that makes us neither want to nor be able to free ourselves, ever. Laurel, except for holidays in Europe and the Caribbean and occasional forays into New York, has been here all her life. I, Anne-Marie, onetime academic — Presentation Convent, Collège Sophie-Barat, Memorial, Oxford — am another kettle of fish.

For about twenty years we circled each other, meeting once a year when I came back from wherever I had been, tentative, polite, mildly admiring of each other, gradually spilling a bean here and a bean there until so many beans had been spilled that there was no going back from it. And we found ourselves, not unhappily, in that giggling communion characteristic of the passionate friendships of thirteen and a half. What we don't know about each other now you could put in your eye. What is more, what she and I don't know about the others on this rock isn't worth knowing. When we put our heads together, and we frequently do, we can pool enough of everyone's tatty little secrets to blackmail all the professions, including the oldest, the civil service, the clergy, and every House of Assembly back to 1855.

Just about everybody here is related by blood, marriage, or sheer tomfoolery to everybody else, and we all know our cousins to the third and fourth degree. At the rate we reproduce, emigrate, wander the world, and keep in

1 the most southeasterly peninsula of Newfoundland. In Celtic mythology, the blessed island of Avalon was believed to be the final resting place of King Arthur.

touch, there is no secret service that can approach us. What may be called ESP elsewhere can be nailed down here by genealogy, and we are all expert. Yesterday morning Laurel was telling me that when they were five she and her twin brother took the diapers off the minister's daughter to get a look at what was so carefully concealed. In the afternoon I called her and said, "Hey, remember Daphne Green?" "Remember her?" said Laurel. "She's the one Leonard and I took the diapers off. What in God's name made you ask about her?" "I've been hearing little baby voices all day," I said, "whispering to me 'Daphne Green, Daphne Green.'"

5   The truth is, I'd been warming a bench at Canada Manpower most of the afternoon with one of the other rock-born overeducated, bilingual unemployed and Daphne's name came up, the way names do, because I'd asked who his wife was. All you need in this town to get a reputation for extraordinary powers is a large acquaintance, a few elementary research skills, and coincidence. Laurel, of course, being a thoroughgoing romantic, wants to believe in the spookies and so she does. I don't, but I like to cater to her. My own reluctant rationalism is one of the things that keep me from going mad, but I do break out from time to time.

Fern, Laurel's husband — surgeon, reliable backbencher, utterly devoted to her (christened, unfortunately, Ferdinand, because his mother was a great reader of the lesser works of Lord Beaconsfield)[2] — is the only one of us who can pass muster as a healthy, well-integrated, well-adjusted dealer with life. If he weren't there to remind us unremittingly of health, sanity, hard work, and the old-fashioned values of the Church of England in Canada, I don't know where we'd be. He and Laurel have lived amid her storms and his calms for twenty years, and their daughters, both at college on the mainland, are beautiful and bright and loving and a credit to them. Actually, all our children are pretty good.

Though the men on this island are great talkers — never shutting up, as the rest of the country has cause to know — they don't talk much about themselves to women. If they do talk to each other of how they feel, they certainly don't let on about it. As a charter member of the Status of Women Council I should, I suppose, hack away at that, but I don't and won't. I am concerned with what people do. What they think in the inner recesses of their own beings is their own damned business. Unless they are moved to tell me, I will never know, and it is better not to ask. It wasn't very long ago that my children's father, Con O'Neill, told me what was in his head, at my request. It took him four and a half days, at the end of which I prevailed upon him to buy me four plane tickets from Vancouver to St. John's. I then resigned from the only really good job I have ever had and launched myself back to the rock, the Public Service Commission, Canada Manpower, the vagaries of Memorial University, and a dilapidated three-story frame dwelling fifty yards from where I had been born forty-two years before.

*****

2 Benjamin Disraeli, nineteenth-century British prime minister and novelist. Ferdinand is the hero of his novel *Henrietta Temple* (1837).

Not five hours out of Vancouver, coincidence and further disaster overtook me in the person of Hugh Forbes, run into at Halifax Airport as I shepherded three dazed and baffled kids off one flight and onto another. Hugh, asking loudly, "Jesus, Annie, what have you got there, a traveling circus?" Hugh, whom I hadn't seen since the winter I was twenty-one, changed almost beyond recall but merging into himself, Cape Shore[3] voice and all, as we talked on the two-seat side of the DC-9 and the kids slept, across the aisle, on the three-seat side.

I had braced myself for what had appeared to be only the first of many awkward but insignificant encounters with my past. After the usual stylized exchanges, I realized I had miscalculated.

10   "Going home on holiday, Annie?" asked Hugh.

"Not exactly," I said.

The feeling of being at a disadvantage with Hugh was familiar. Even the setting was eerily appropriate — Hugh and I, side by side in some vehicle, each wondering who would be the first to break the silence. I plunged in. "As a matter of fact, I am right this moment *leaving* home. I'm a bit punchy, so don't expect me to make too much sense."

"Annie, I don't remember your ever making too much sense. But I think I get the message. You blew it."

Lack of directness had never been one of Hugh's failings. I must have looked stricken, for he was immediately contrite and slightly embarrassed.

15   "Annie, I'm sorry. I didn't mean to be quite so blunt."

"It's all right," I said, making a face at him. "I find it reassuring that you haven't changed all that much."

He still looked embarrassed.

"Perhaps I'd better go sit somewhere else." He started to unbuckle his seat belt. "You'd probably rather not be bothered with me right now."

"Hugh, no," I said. "I'd like to talk. Please."

20   I looked at him. He seemed solid and friendly and, in spite of being annoyed with himself for his blunder, amused and curious. So I gave him fifteen minutes of the story of my life.

He listened without interrupting. As I talked, I watched his hands rebuckling the seat belt, unbuttoning his jacket, adjusting the tray, reaching for coffee from the stewardess, scratching his head, using a handkerchief, twisting his ring. Guilt and nostalgia flooded over me.

"Your hands," I said, "your arms, they're all right!"

He turned his palms upward, flexed his fingers, stretched his arms. "Yes," he said. "Good enough."

"How did you do it?"

25   "On hate, mostly."

There was a long silence. Nineteen fifty-nine had been the year of the last St. John's polio epidemic. Hugh, home from McGill, engineer's iron ring on his finger, job offer in his pocket, had found himself one August morning, after a weekend of pain and fever, flat on his back in the Fever Hospital with both arms immovable.

---

3 residents of the area between Placentia and Cape St. Mary's speak with a distinctive, almost Irish, accent.

"September," he said quietly, looking at me with a face devoid of expression. "All September I spent two hours a day watching my girl Annie making a public spectacle of herself on bloody television. I told myself that I was going to get my hands and arms back, if only to wring your neck. I hated and Ma prayed. It worked like a charm. By Christmas I was going to dances. My arms were in slings, but the fingers were good. By spring I had the slings off. After eighteen months I was able to work. After two years I was ready to pick a fight with Con O'Neill and break his jaw. After that I packed my bags and lit out for Ontario, all cured."

"None of it had anything to do with Con," I said.

"As I perceived it, it had a great deal to do with Con. And apart from everything else I was disgusted with your whole carry on."

30 "I was afraid of you," I said. "You scared me to death. All I could see was you beating around while I minded youngsters and forgot how to read and write."

"It wouldn't have been like that."

"Don't tell me," I said. "Anyway, what about my neck?"

"What?" He was momentarily puzzled.

"Do you want to wring it?"

35 "Hell, no, girl. I never wring ladies' necks when they're down and out. I kiss them instead. Better for everybody."

He leaned across and kissed me. The tears stung in my eyes.

"Oh my God, Annie, you're not still at that!"

"I always get tears in my eyes when in the grip of strong feeling," I said in my lecture-room voice.

He looked at me in amazed disbelief, then looked again and exploded into laughter. I could feel the hot blush climbing to my hairline.

40 "Dear Lord above! Every time I'd put my arm around you, you'd start to bawl. I thought you were afraid for your virtue. Well, I'm damned."

I blinked, sniffed, and smiled at him. "Well, now you know," I said. "Better late than never."

Hugh smiled back. "Thanks, Annie."

Sweetest Mother, I thought, I love him. "Hugh," I said quietly, "I think we scuttled the ship."

"Yes," he said. "We sure as hell did."

45 He turned to look out the window, then adjusted his seat to the horizontal and closed his eyes.

"My son Gerald," he said. "My wife Clare."

Again there was silence. He readjusted his seat to the vertical and turned back to face me. "Gerald died one night when he was six months old. Crib death, they called it; no explanation, no one's guilt, they said. Still, Clare took to the bottle and after three years of it I took to the girls. And there we are. But we're still married and we're going to stay married. Make no mistake."

I said nothing. Hugh's forthrightness had left me stunned.

"One thing more, Annie. If you and I are going to be friends, you will never refer to any of it again. But I want you to keep it in mind."

50 He pointed a thumb across the aisle at the sleeping children. "What about them? Were you good at it?"

"Yes," I said, clutching at a subject I could at least talk about. "Like falling off a log. It's in the blood."

He looked at me speculatively. "I should have stuffed you full of babies and stuck you down with Mom on Cape St. Mary's.[4] She'd have learned you the five sorrowful mysteries[5] all right."

"I learned," I said.

"I don't know. Seems to me you could still use some toughening up."

55 He took my hand, called the stewardess, ordered a bottle of champagne, and told her we had just got engaged.

"Forbes," she said, "if you get engaged on my flight one more time, I will personally drown you in champagne."

The landing was the worst I have ever had, even in Torbay fog.[6] Passengers I recognized as old hands showed in the rigid set of their shoulders what I myself felt — too much airspeed, the runway overshot, and a violent touchdown with too many rebounds off the tarmac. I was trying to remember if the runway ended at a cliff, a hill, or the woods, when we came to a shuddering stop. There was absolute quiet and then the captain's voice: "Ladies and gentlemen, as you may have noticed, we have just landed at St. John's."

A ripple of laughter ran through the aircraft and an audible communal sigh of relief. Hugh stood up, collected his briefcase and raincoat, and touched my shoulder with his free hand. "That time, Annie, it almost ended happily ever after." He smiled bleakly. "I'll call you."

I watched him as he headed up the aisle, and then I busied myself with the children. My sister Catherine met me in the crowded terminal. We went to Mother's, put the still groggy children to bed, took care of half a bottle of Captain Morgan,[7] and turned in ourselves. The next morning I was going to have to turf my tenants out of my house on St. Columb's Street and start job hunting.

*****

60 What happens when you bolt after sixteen years, four universities, three kids, the whole of Eng. Lit. read together, Paris, Florence, London, Oxford, Toronto, Lisbon, Washington, Vancouver, and hundreds of friends held in common? What I did was stash my books in Vancouver and go back home. I went because I wanted to do nothing else. I didn't want to face another city, another group of strangers. My ears hungered for the accents of the island. I wanted the smells and sights and sounds of St. John's Harbor, my father's grave, my mother's tenacious grip on life, old people I had known when they were young, middle-aged people I had known when they were children. I wanted my house on St. Columb's Street, groceries from Belbin's, gas from Fred and Eric Adams, vitamins from Stowe's Pharmacy, understanding from Laurel and Fern, and the children of my friends for my children. I wanted to terrify myself climbing up Barter's Hill in the sleet, to drive to Corner Brook and back in a night and a day, seeing if I could still evade the Mounties and not kill myself, to lie

---

4 the most southwesterly tip of the Avalon Peninsula. 5 grief of the Virgin Mary for the sufferings of Christ. 6 Torbay Airport, St. John's, is noted for its dense fogs. 7 brand of rum.

on the grass listening to the blessed silence in St. Mary's, and to breathe on the embers of old friendships and see if the flames would light my way out of the dark.

In spite of the encounter with Hugh, I was in good shape when I arrived. "Am I not the very picture of the wronged wife?" I said to Fern, and he laughed and hugged me and we all had a drink to celebrate. Five months later I had lost twenty-five pounds I could ill afford losing, my temper was unreliable, and I was still unemployed, but my children were happy and my house was looking less like a slum.

St. Columb's Street used to be solidly middle-class, occupied by people associated with the ships and stores of the port. My own house once belonged to a ship's chandler.[8] Some of the others were built by captains and shipowners who lived here because of the incomparable view of the town and the harbor — every ship that comes and goes can be seen from my kitchen window. Now many of the bigger houses have become "multiple-family dwellings," the pretty, decrepit terraces are occupied by the poor, and some foreign entrepreneur has put up a yellow brick apartment house directly opposite me. The roadway is potholed, the sidewalks crumbling and cracked. Rough-looking teen-agers skylark and catcall outside the corner stores, speaking a dialect that suggests a lengthy inheritance of infected adenoids and bad teeth.

But at the top of the street is the hospital where I was born: farther down is St. Columb's Church, which my grandmother's grandfather helped build; and beside it is St. Columb's Convent, which houses an elderly nun who taught me to read and write and made me, over six years, memorize the whole of Butler's *Catechism* and MacLaren and Campbell's *Grammar*.[9] These are the things I think about on the days when I struggle with the idea that I do not really belong here. And, try as I may, I cannot see myself old, with my grandchildren visiting, in this house on St. Columb's Street. It makes me unbearably, unutterably, sad. The Heritage Foundation is interested in us now and determined to improve us. I am afraid I may have to move, along with the other poor, since I cannot afford to be improved any further. Sooner or later someone with the money to repair the roof flashings and the rotting window frames and the exterior paint and the leaking laundry room will make me an offer and I will have to accept it.

The house — my house for the moment — is a narrow, plain three-story with bow windows and a peaked roof. It must have been intended for a large family with no servants, for the kitchen is the biggest room and there is only one bathroom and no back stairs. Built the year that I was born, it just misses being good, even of its kind. I suppose the ship's chandler ran out of money, too. The house has that look. The exterior walls and the floors are sound and strong and draftproof; the fireplaces are pleasant thirties neoclassical; the doors are paneled and the windows big and generously framed. But the walls are surfaced with painted or papered fiberboard instead of plaster, and the wainscoting and the additions made over the years are ill-conceived and cheap, running to plywood and wood-grained Arborite and acoustic tile.

8 merchant who sells supplies and equipment to ships. 9 standard religious and grammar texts in Newfoundland Catholic schools of the 1940s and 1950s.

How I acquired the house at all is an earnest of the emotional myopia with which I am afflicted. My marriage to Con had gone through one of its intermittent crises following a move from Toronto to Vancouver. Con suggested that since we hadn't much capital, certainly not enough to buy a house in expensive Vancouver, it would be sensible to invest in a house in an older part of St. John's, live in it for a summer, and then rent it. Our children would then have a base of operations, a home that would exist in their minds wherever they happened to be in actuality. To me the proposal made perfect sense. I had never seen myself as an emigrant, merely a traveler. The idea of a home on the island appealed to me and I liked the implicit promise that we would eventually all return. When the break came, the house was there, with boxes of old toys and baby clothes in the attic, discarded prams and pushchairs in the cellar, clothes hooks with the children's names on them in the bathroom, and odds and ends of furniture from my own childhood home in the bedrooms and living room.

By then responsibility for the house, for keeping it insured and tenanted, had gradually devolved on me. I was mildly mystified but not displeased. I saw the process as being one with the independence I was gaining as the children grew older and I settled, once again, into a fulltime job at the university. The years during which I had been, uncomfortably and resentfully, a financial dependent faded away and I assumed, along with the house on St. Columb's Street, responsibility for paying almost everything to do with myself and the children, except keeping the Vancouver roof over our heads. Food, clothing, dentistry, toys, Christmas, birthdays came out of my income from my job. We had been setting the stage for years. When the curtain went up, I said my lines and made my moves. We all did, even the children. "We knew it was a matter of time," my daughter said. "We just didn't know when. We thought it wouldn't be so soon." Nor did I.

*****

My first morning in St. John's, Laurel met me at Mother's and came with me to look at the house. All my tenants had been university students, so I assumed that not much housekeeping had been done. They had rented rooms to one another in a complex set of permutations that I had never tried to keep track of as long as they paid the rent punctually. Time and the salt air had worked their will on the exterior paint of the house, but it had been fairly shabby to begin with. When I opened the door, Laurel went rigid with shock. An effluvium of Victorian dimensions asssaulted us. The hall was crammed with old boots and dust-laden cartons of empty beer bottles. The windows were opaque with dirt, and where the panes had been broken, on either side of the door, pieces of plastic had been stretched over them and secured with bits of rough lath nailed into the moldings. The walls and floors had not been washed since I had left. The carpets were stained and felted with dog hair. Filthy and half furnished, without curtains or pictures, with its paint scabby, its wallpaper peeling, and its plastic tile discolored, the house was tawdry. "You cannot propose to live in this," Laurel said flatly. But I could and I did.

The children, when I moved them in, wept over their shattered fantasies. I attacked what I could with bucket and mop, Glass Wax and cloth, crowbar and paintbrush. The children, after their initial distress, channeled their energies and their disappointment into working with me. They took apart the broken fences and cut them into kindling. They lugged out sheets of wallboard and plywood and eight-foot two-by-fours as my crowbar did its work. They carried mattresses and bedsteads down from the attic and up from the cellar. I had not realized how strong ten- and twelve-year-olds can be when they have a job they want to do. When a semblance of normality had been achieved, they just quit and concentrated once again on their private concerns — school, games, hobbies, squabbling, television, and eating.

They were puzzled by my evident lack of pleasure in just being alive, in having a house to live in and enough to eat and wear and them to love me. I overheard one saying, "Why is she unhappy?" and another answering, "Life gave her a raw deal." I felt ashamed of not being happier and tried to smile more, but they asked me why I had that funny look on my face. I opted for the truth, which they found odd but uninteresting.

The process of recovering the house was alternately uplifting and depressing. "I refuse to lie here and watch you seesaw," said my mother, but did it nonetheless. When I had got one room fit for human habitation I persuaded her to stop for lunch on her way back from a visit to her doctor. "This is perfectly respectable," she said, on looking around my sitting room. "I fail to see what you are making such a fuss about." At that point, I found myself wanting not even to think about another tin of paint. I let the brushes dry and the children revert to their usual slovenly practices. I began, in spite of myself, to think of what it was going to mean to be on my own with no one to bitch at, no one to protect the kids from my habitual anxieties, no one to lean on, no one to sleep with, and, above all, no one to tell me, perhaps for the rest of my life, that I was essential to his breathing and being. Hugh? It was two months before Hugh turned up.

I was hammering palings into the front fence when a Land-Rover stopped at the curb and Hugh got out. I wanted to put my arms around him, but he had a very don't-touch-me look about him, so I just said it was good to see him and held on to my hammer for security. He said that he had just swung by to see how I was getting on and that I should write or call if there was anything he could do to help. I replied dryly that there were more accessible sources of help than his sweet self but that I would be glad to see him any time he got tired of doing whatever it was he did. He gave me his card, said he'd be back to share a dinner the following weekend, got into his Land-Rover, saluted, and drove off. I looked at the card and put it in my pocket. It had a Toronto address, and I thought how for seven years we had probably lived no more than fifteen blocks from each other in Don Mills.[10]

I threw down the hammer and went into the house to make tea. I drank it too fast, burned my tongue, and fired the mug viciously against the fireplace, smashing it and splattering tea over the newly scrubbed hearthrug. The mug had had a motto painted on the side. Later, I fitted the bits together, and read, "A house is made of bricks and stone but a home is made of love alone." I put the pieces on the hearth and bashed them to powder with the poker.

10 district in the City of North York, Ontario.

Hugh then appeared out of nowhere every two or three weeks, only to disappear into nowhere again. It seemed he did something with fish and oil and airplanes for the federal government. That made for a connection with Fern and Laurel. Sometimes he arrived on my doorstep monumentally plastered,[11] mirthful and bawdy, two quintals[12] and a fathom of black-hearted, cod-fed bayman.[13] Sometimes, rarely, he was sober and subtle, all civil servant and about as friendly as a cobra. I would hear his acquired Toronto accent overpowering the dental *t*'s and fog-soft vowels of the Cape Shore, and it served to remind me of what I would have preferred to forget.

I didn't ask questions of Hugh. He was there or he wasn't. He was sober or he wasn't. He loved me or he didn't. When he was drunk, I told him how beautiful he was and how I adored him. When he was sober, we talked politics and oil and mutual friends; I was careful not to show temper, and we tacitly avoided discussing how we felt. Either way, I was put into a state of elevation that sometimes lasted for days. The rest of my life the cats could have. But what was there to do? Making things happen was not my line. I watched, I listened, I cared. Nothing else was possible for me. I was through with moral imperatives: I care, therefore I am. I think, therefore I will make mistakes.

Though jobless, I was neither idle nor solitary. There was, if anything, too much to do, too many obligations, hordes of visiting children, and endless chores. I was ruthless about protecting my privacy, however, and my three hours of peace after the children were in bed and before midnight had overtaken me. I did not, except on very rare occasions, turn on television or stereo or take to drink. Except for smoking, I tried to do myself as little physical and spiritual harm as possible. Sometimes I even went to mass at St. Columb's, just in case. But I did, all the same, spend many days and nights in domestic squalor and intellectual tedium. I would go as much as six or eight weeks without balancing my checkbook, reading nothing but old copies of the *Atlantic* and the *Saturday Review*, washing the children's clothes in the bathwater and hanging them to dry on the bannister rails because I couldn't be bothered calling the repairman to fix the washer and dryer. I was sick to death of being bullied by ambition, concepts of efficiency, the demands of an academic conscience, fear at being out of work or even my own convenience.

Laurel held Hugh responsible for my otherwise unaccountable behaviour. I was a veteran of unrequited love, though, and surely familiar with its symptoms. I diagnosed, rather, some unease of the soul. Muddled and grubby, I read third-rate fiction and fourth-rate biography, thought fifth-rate thoughts, and felt sixth-rate emotions. And I was not at home on St. Columb's Street. I was instead, like a bird on a bush, waiting for whatever would happen next so that I would know what to do.

I talked a lot to Laurel. We were on the phone for at least thirty minutes a day. She visited me only rarely, for both the house and the neighborhood were in a world she did not care to inhabit and they made her uneasy. More frequently I visited her, early in the morning after I left the children off at school. I entered her world more easily than she did mine. We would sit in her ordered

11 drunk. 12 in Newfoundland, a measure of 112 pounds, or about 50.8 kilograms, usually of dried and salted cod fish. 13 a rural or outport person.

living room (oh, the relief of it!), me in jeans and sweater, with untidy hair, she combed and brushed and tidily made up but in an ugly green fuzzy dressing gown, hands shaking from insomnia and cigarettes and not following the diet required by her mild diabetes. We would ask each other if we were, as people told us, eccentric or simply mad as hares. We considered our acquaintances and determined that by and large they were even more appalling than ourselves, apart from the few saints who were out of our league and therefore irrelevant to the discussion. We concluded that we did not want to be other than who we were. What we were was another question. We spent a scandalous amount of time talking it out. I talked about my past, my emotions, unemployment, the current state of my house, my mind, or my bank account. She talked about her depression, the causes of which had never emerged. I talked about my rages, the causes of which had been only too evident. We compared childhoods, holiday trips, attitudes, fantasies. I suggested that she got depressed because of hunger, perversity, boredom, and the indulgence of an excess of sensibility. She suggested that my malaise could be cured by Hugh. I told her that it was just as likely to be cured by the Atlantic Loto, the riding of Placentia-St. Mary's, or the Henrietta Harvey Professorship.[14] Even as I said it, I thought it was probably not true. But if I had lived my life as Hugh said I should have done, I should now be like Laurel and be hankering after the kind of life I had had and botched.

Laurel knows that everyone assumes that she is lazy and self-indulgent and ought to have a job to do. But I am aware of how scared she is and how her mind and energy are drained by fear, so that she stays in bed for days and weeks at a time. Her concern for Fern makes her come awake long enough to straighten the house and get the meals, and she always seems to deal with any emergencies, including the most trivial social ones. Her usual waking time, though, is between three and eight in the morning, when she reads, makes notes, writes letters and poems in her head that never see the light of day, thinks of killing herself, and tries to stop the shakes by force of will. Her will power is irresistible, and sooner or later anyone who has much to do with her will be made to dance to her tune. Though she has had virtually every psychogenic symptom known to medicine, she succeeds always in looking as healthy as a chestnut in blossom.

Once Laurel actually did swallow sleeping pills and then, in her wayward fashion, followed them with a tin of anchovies and was sick all over the kitchen. She cleaned up while Fern continued to sleep the sleep of the just. As she tells it, he had one of his rare fits of furious exasperation when she refused to get up and prepare his breakfast. There is no questioning that in Laurel's life the farcical element continually intrudes.

80   All the same, her headlong emotionalism may be one of the things that make Laurel a superb political wife. She and Fern attract a variegated tribe of friends, because he is true blue and she is beautiful and amusing and enormously sympathetic. Some of her enthusiasms have led to dinner parties that could bring the government down, and Fern has learned to keep a covert eye on their guest list. Because Laurel takes everyone at face value, she is the repository of a multitude of confidences, which frequently inspire her to quixotic

14 distinguished professorship in the English Department of Memorial University of Newfoundland.

action. One Saturday, early on, she dropped in at my house without calling first and encountered Hugh. Hugh will inflict his adventures on anyone he can pin down, but even when well oiled[15] he tends to keep himself to himself. Laurel got more out of him in ten minutes than I had done in as many weeks.

After she had left, he turned to me indignantly and said, "Why do I tell Laurel all that stuff? I must be cracked."

"People do," I said, and shrugged. "They spend five minutes with her or get her when they've dialed a wrong number and she has their life stories, just like that."

"I suppose she knows enough of both of us now to write the book."

"No," I said. "But she has eyes in her head. And she loves me. She may try to help things along. I can't stop her, you know."

85   He made a particularly vulgar comment.

*****

When Laurel gets upset and concerned about someone, she has the gall of a robber's horse. Last February, I had an especially trying couple of weeks, with frozen water pipes, an ill-functioning furnace, kids home from school with the flu, and three job interviews at which I had been told I was overqualified. I was tense and miserable and jumpy. I had been expecting Hugh and looking forward to seeing him, but he hadn't turned up. Laurel called to say that she and Fern had met Hugh at a government function the previous night and that he had been in great form. One of the crosses I was having to bear was being unable to prevent Laurel from reporting on Hugh's whereabouts. I heard her out and then I ventilated for an hour and used some fairly extravagant language, including a reference to slitting my wrists Roman style[16] so that I wouldn't leave too much mess behind.

That evening Hugh was at my door. I had temporarily dismissed him from my mind and had been attempting to concentrate on sick, crotchety children and on the dirt and snow and oil handprints left by furnace men and plumbers. I needed a bath and was red-eyed and sleepless from nights of keeping coal fires going in the bedroom grates and was in no mood for dealing with Hugh's usual attitude of detached amusement at my ridiculous plight.

"Come in," I said. "If you can get in." A gust of icy wind accompanied him — and more snow. "Don't bother taking off your boots. The mess is past the point where I even care about it."

"You're all right, though?" he asked, looking at me warily.

90   "Sure," I said. "Dandy." I jammed my coal-blackened hands into the pockets of my jeans and leaned against the newel post.

"You look done in," he said.

"Beat to a rag. Want some coffee?"

"No thanks. I just took a notion to stop by. I've got a meeting to get back to. You're sure you're all right?"

---

15 drunk. 16 Roman suicides often slit their wrists while bathing.

"Perfectly fine." I tried what I hoped was a cheerful grin. "I'm cold, I'm tired, I'm unemployed, and the house is falling down. Don't expect Pollyanna[17] in this climate."

95 "Kids O.K.?"

"Sick as pigs," I said. "And crooked as sin."

"Anything I can do? You've only to ask."

"I know," I said, "I know. But there isn't anything, truly. I just need some sleep and a change in the weather."

"Don't overdo it, Annie." He put his hand under my chin and made me look at him. "Anything on your mind? You're sure you're all right?"

100 This sort of solicitude was unheard of from Hugh, who would normally only inquire about my state of being if he found me with my head under my arm like the ghost of Anne Boleyn.[18] I had a sudden shattering glimmer of understanding.

"Have you seen Fern lately?" I hazarded.

"Not this trip," he replied blandly. "Too busy." He looked at his watch. "I'd better get back. Take care, Annie."

"Sure," I said. "Pray for a thaw."

As soon as I'd closed the door on Hugh, I called Laurel.

105 "What did you tell him, Laurel?" I said. "That I was about to hang myself in my garters because he done me wrong?"

"An-nie, you puz-zle me," she said in her most nervous and distinct Bishop Spencer College[19] accents.

"And you are a damned liar," I said.

"You know I ne-ver tell an untruth, An-nie."

"Laurel," I said, "I can tell when you're lying within five syllables. I'll see you in the morning if I don't die of shame first." I hung up.

110 After another night of sleeplessness, half a bottle of Irish whiskey, and a packet of lethal American cigarettes from our all-night pizza parlor, I went to Laurel's to tell her to get off my case. It wasn't easy. In twenty years we had never had a serious difference. With the help of a couple of pints of Strongbow,[20] I managed to enlighten her on the enormity of what she had done. By lunchtime, when Fern got home, I was wandering the house barefoot, hugging the cider mug and humming a dirty song that I'd learned from Hugh when I was a freshman. Fern patted me on the head, said it must be great to have nothing to do, and went back to the hospital to see someone whose legs were in traction. Laurel took her telling-off better than I dealt it out, and promised never to interfere again.

Then she asked me how my life was going and how I thought it would all work out. I turned the question back to her, and she said she should never have thrown up the pills. I said that perhaps she and Hugh would be killed in a car crash when they wickedly, and in heedless contravention of all the ground rules of friendship, slipped off to Clarenville for a weekend, leaving me and Fern, given a decent interval of mourning, to console each other. Her eyes widened and she laughed with delight.

17 optimistic heroine in early-twentieth-century children's novels written by Eleanor Porter. 18 the second wife of Henry VIII of England, she was beheaded in 1536. 19 Protestant high school in St. John's, generally attended by students of wealthier families. 20 brand of alcoholic cider.

"An-nie, you are naugh-ty," she said. "How per-fect!" And I knew I had not been all that far from the truth.

"It won't work," I said. "It's a horrible cliché."

"No, no," she said, and laughed again. "I can't wait to tell Fern."

What actually did occur was one night in early spring, having read myself into a stupor, fully clothed in my bed, along with dirty ashtrays, my accounts and calculator, carbons of job applications, the phone, an alarm clock, unanswered letters, unsent Christmas cards, *The Oxford Book of Oxford*, unread, *The Pauper's Cook Book*, and an illustrated essay on the paintings of Edvard Munch,[21] I fell asleep smoking a cigarette and woke at dawn to find that I had burned a hole through two carbons, a book bill from Blackwell's, and my only pair of sheets.

For some minutes I stared at the burn without moving, then I headed for the bathroom. My hands were shaking and my eyes were large and dark and frightened. My impulse was to wrap myself in a blanket, crawl back into bed, and go to sleep — deeply, deeply to sleep — when one of the children knocked at the door and asked the time. I snapped to attention, cleaned out the sink, called the others, and went downstairs. I made an unusually big breakfast and insisted that it be eaten. After I had taken the children to school, I returned home, washed the dishes, then gathered up all the loose papers I could find — the year's small collection of books and the 1669 Donne[22] I had brought in my pocket from Vancouver. I put them in the ashcan, and carried it out to the sidewalk. I washed my hair, had a bath, and dressed in a silk shirt and a suit. I called my mother's cleaning woman and arranged for three days of her time. As I left the house again, the phone rang, and while I stood in the doorway, not answering it, I saw that the ashmen had been and gone. I got into the car and drove slowly down St. Columb's Street.

The fog was coming in through the Narrows, but the sun was still shining and the town and the harbor were brilliant with color and beautiful beyond the reaches of fantasy. My throat hurt and I could hardly see. I thought about my grandmother's grandfather leaning out over the unfinished walls of St. Columb's, watching the arrival of the White Fleet.[23] I thought about Sister Columba in her convent and about the day I was born in the hospital at the top of the street. I thought about Hugh and Laurel and Fern and the Heritage Foundation. My heart was breaking, for I knew inescapably that I had already, once again, set out on my travels.

(1980)

---

21 early-twentieth-century Norwegian expressionist artist whose paintings explored the depths of human feelings. 22 early and therefore valuable edition of the works of English poet John Donne. 23 the white-painted boats of the Portuguese fishing fleet would sail into St. John's harbour for supplies or to escape bad weather.

Philip Roth   (b. 1933)

Philip Roth, a native of Newark, New Jersey, achieved international attention in 1959 with the publication of his first book, *Goodbye, Columbus,* a collection of short stories. In many of these stories, as in such later novels as *Portnoy's Complaint* and *The Ghost Writer,* Roth explores the attempts by Jewish boys and men to reconcile individual desires with the conflicting forces of contemporary American society and their religious heritage. "The Conversion of the Jews," from his first book, focuses on the religious earnestness and inner rebelliousness of Ozzie Freedman. As he confronts his mother and the rabbi, Ozzie seeks answers to questions that deeply puzzle him; he also looks to achieve a kind of heroism in the eyes of his fellow students. The title may have been taken from a line in Andrew Marvell's seventeenth-century poem "To His Coy Mistress," referring to an event many people believed would not occur until the end of time.

THE CONVERSION OF THE JEWS

"You're a real one for opening your mouth in the first place," Itzie said. "What do you open your mouth all the time for?"

"I didn't bring it up, Itz, I didn't," Ozzie said.

"What do you care about Jesus Christ for anyway?"

"I didn't bring up Jesus Christ. He did. I didn't even know what he was talking about. Jesus is historical, he kept saying. Jesus is historical." Ozzie mimicked the monumental voice of Rabbi Binder.

5   "Jesus was a person that lived like you and me," Ozzie continued. "That's what Binder said —"

"Yeah?... So what! What do I give two cents whether he lived or not. And what do you gotta open your mouth!" Itzie Lieberman favored closed-mouthedness, especially when it came to Ozzie Freedman's questions. Mrs. Freedman had to see Rabbi Binder twice before about Ozzie's questions and this Wednesday at four-thirty would be the third time. Itzie preferred to keep *his* mother in the kitchen; he settled for behind-the-back subtleties such as gestures, faces, snarls and other less delicate barnyard noises.

"He was a real person, Jesus, but he wasn't like God, and we don't believe he is God." Slowly, Ozzie was explaining Rabbi Binder's position to Itzie, who had been absent from Hebrew School the previous afternoon.

"The Catholics," Itzie said helpfully, "they believe in Jesus Christ, that he's God." Itzie Lieberman used "the Catholics" in its broadest sense — to include the Protestants.

Ozzie received Itzie's remark with a tiny head bob, as though it were a footnote, and went on. "His mother was Mary, and his father probably was Joseph," Ozzie said. "But the New Testament says his real father was God."

10   "His *real* father?"

"Yeah," Ozzie said, "that's the big thing, his father's supposed to be God."

"Bull."

"That's what Rabbi Binder says, that it's impossible —"

"Sure it's impossible. That stuff's all bull. To have a baby you gotta get laid," Itzie theologized. "Mary hadda get laid."

15 "That's what Binder says: 'The only way a woman can have a baby is to have intercourse with a man.'"

"He said *that*, Ozz?" For a moment it appeared that Itzie had put the theological question aside. "He said that, intercourse?" A little curled smile shaped itself in the lower half of Itzie's face like a pink mustache. "What you guys do, Ozz, you laugh or something?"

"I raised my hand."

"Yeah? Whatja say?"

"That's when I asked the question."

20 Itzie's face lit up. "Whatja ask about — intercourse?"

"No, I asked the question about God, how if He could create the heaven and earth in six days — the light especially, that's what always gets me, that He could make the light. Making fish and animals, that's pretty good —"

"That's damn good." Itzie's appreciation was honest but unimaginative: it was as though God had just pitched a one-hitter.[1]

"But making light...I mean when you think about it, it's really something," Ozzie said. "Anyway, I asked Binder if He could make all that in six days, and He could *pick* the six days He wanted right out of nowhere, why couldn't He let a woman have a baby without having intercourse."

"You said intercourse, Ozz, to Binder?"

25 "Yeah."

"Right in class?"

"Yeah."

Itzie smacked the side of his head.

"I mean, no kidding around," Ozzie said, "that'd really be nothing. After all that other stuff, that'd practically be nothing."

30 Itzie considered a moment. "What'd Binder say?"

"He started all over again explaining how Jesus was historical and how he lived like you and me but he wasn't God. So I said I under*stood* that. What I wanted to know was different."

What Ozzie wanted to know was always different. The first time he had wanted to know how Rabbi Binder could call the Jews "The Chosen People" if the Declaration of Independence claimed all men to be created equal. Rabbi Binder tried to distinguish for him between political equality and spiritual legitimacy, but what Ozzie wanted to know, he insisted vehemently, was different. That was the first time his mother had to come.

Then there was the plane crash. Fifty-eight people had been killed in a plane crash at La Guardia. In studying a casualty list in the newspaper his mother had discovered among the list of those dead eight Jewish names (his grandmother had nine but she counted Miller as a Jewish name); because of the eight she said the plane crash was "a tragedy." During free-discussion time on Wednesday Ozzie had brought to Rabbi Binder's attention this matter of "some of his relations" always picking out the Jewish names. Rabbi Binder had begun to explain cultural unity and some other things when Ozzie stood up at his seat

1 baseball game in which the pitcher yields only one base hit.

and said that what he wanted to know was different. Rabbi Binder insisted that he sit down and it was then that Ozzie shouted that he wished all fifty-eight were Jews. That was the second time his mother came.

"And he kept explaining about Jesus being historical, and so I kept asking him. No kidding, Itz, he was trying to make me look stupid."

"So what he finally do?"

"Finally he starts screaming that I was deliberately simple-minded and a wise guy, and that my mother had to come, and this was the last time. And that I'd never get bar-mitzvahed if he could help it. Then, Itz, then he starts talking in that voice like a statue, real slow and deep, and he says that I better think over what I said about the Lord. He told me to go to his office and think it over." Ozzie leaned his body towards Itzie. "Itz, I thought it over for a solid hour, and now I'm convinced God could do it."

*****

Ozzie had planned to confess his latest transgression to his mother as soon as she came home from work. But it was a Friday night in November and already dark, and when Mrs. Freedman came through the door she tossed off her coat, kissed Ozzie quickly on the face, and went to the kitchen table to light the three yellow candles, two for the Sabbath[2] and one for Ozzie's father.

When his mother lit the candles she would move her two arms slowly towards her, dragging them through the air, as though persuading people whose minds were half made up. And her eyes would get glassy with tears. Even when his father was alive Ozzie remembered that her eyes had gotten glassy, so it didn't have anything to do with his dying. It had something to do with lighting the candles.

As she touched the flaming match to the unlit wick of a Sabbath candle, the phone rang, and Ozzie, standing only a foot from it, plucked it off the receiver and held it muffled to his chest. When his mother lit candles Ozzie felt there should be no noise; even breathing, if you could manage it, should be softened. Ozzie pressed the phone to his breast and watched his mother dragging whatever she was dragging, and he felt his own eyes get glassy. His mother was a round, tired, gray-haired penguin of a woman whose gray skin had begun to feel the tug of gravity and the weight of her own history. Even when she was dressed up she didn't look like a chosen person. But when she lit candles she looked like something better; like a woman who knew momentarily that God could do anything.

After a few mysterious minutes she was finished. Ozzie hung up the phone and walked to the kitchen table where she was beginning to lay the two places for the four-course Sabbath meal. He told her that she would have to see Rabbi Binder next Wednesday at four-thirty, and then he told her why. For the first time in their life together she hit Ozzie across the face with her hand.

All through the chopped liver and chicken soup part of the dinner Ozzie cried; he didn't have any appetite for the rest.

*****

2 celebration of the Jewish Sabbath begins at sundown Friday.

On Wednesday, in the largest of the three basement classrooms of the synagogue, Rabbi Marvin Binder, a tall, handsome, broad-shouldered man of thirty with thick strong-fibered black hair, removed his watch from his pocket and saw that it was four o'clock. At the rear of the room Yakov Blotnik, the seventy-one-year-old custodian, slowly polished the large window, mumbling to himself, unaware that it was four o'clock or six o'clock, Monday or Wednesday. To most of the students Yakov Blotnik's mumbling, along with his brown curly beard, scythe nose, and two heel-trailing black cats, made him an object of wonder, a foreigner, a relic, towards whom they were alternately fearful and disrespectful. To Ozzie the mumbling had always seemed a monotonous, curious prayer; what made it curious was that old Blotnik had been mumbling so steadily for so many years, Ozzie suspected he had memorized the prayers and forgotten all about God.

"It is now free-discussion time," Rabbi Binder said. "Feel free to talk about any Jewish matter at all — religion, family, politics, sports —"

There was silence. It was a gusty, clouded November afternoon and it did not seem as though there ever was or could be a thing called baseball. So nobody this week said a word about that hero from the past, Hank Greenberg[3] — which limited free discussion considerably.

And the soul-battering Ozzie Freedman had just received from Rabbi Binder had imposed its limitation. When it was Ozzie's turn to read aloud from the Hebrew book the rabbi had asked him petulantly why he didn't read more rapidly. He was showing no progress. Ozzie said he could read faster but that if he did he was sure not to understand what he was reading. Nevertheless, at the rabbi's repeated suggestion Ozzie tried, and showed a great talent, but in the midst of a long passage he stopped short and said he didn't understand a word he was reading, and started in again at a drag-footed pace. Then came the soul-battering.

Consequently when free-discussion time rolled around none of the students felt too free. The rabbi's invitation was answered only by the mumbling of feeble old Blotnik.

"Isn't there anything at all you would like to discuss?" Rabbi Binder asked again, looking at his watch. "No questions or comments?"

There was a small grumble from the third row. The rabbi requested that Ozzie rise and give the rest of the class the advantage of his thought.

Ozzie rose. "I forget it now," he said, and sat down in his place.

Rabbi Binder advanced a seat towards Ozzie and poised himself on the edge of the desk. It was Itzie's desk and the rabbi's frame only a dagger's-length away from his face snapped him to sitting attention.

"Stand up again, Oscar," Rabbi Binder said calmly, "and try to assemble your thoughts."

Ozzie stood up. All his classmates turned in their seats and watched as he gave an unconvincing scratch to his forehead.

"I can't assemble any," he announced, and plunked himself down.

"Stand up!" Rabbi Binder advanced from Itzie's desk to the one directly in front of Ozzie; when the rabbinical back was turned Itzie gave it five-fingers

3 all-star player for the Detroit Tigers baseball team in the 1930s and 1940s.

off the tip of his nose, causing a small titter in the room. Rabbi Binder was too absorbed in squelching Ozzie's nonsense once and for all to bother with titters. "Stand up, Oscar. What's your question about?"

55   Ozzie pulled a word out of the air. It was the handiest word. "Religion."

"Oh, now you remember?"

"Yes."

"What is it?"

Trapped, Ozzie blurted the first thing that came to him. "Why can't He make anything he wants to make!"

60   As Rabbi Binder prepared an answer, a final answer, Itzie, ten feet behind him, raised one finger on his left hand, gestured it meaningfully towards the rabbi's back, and brought the house down.

Binder twisted quickly to see what had happened and in the midst of the commotion Ozzie shouted into the rabbi's back what he couldn't have shouted to his face. It was a loud, toneless sound that had the timbre of something stored inside for about six days.

"You don't know! You don't know anything about God!"

The rabbi spun back towards Ozzie. "What?"

"You don't know — you don't —"

65   "Apologize, Oscar, apologize!" It was a threat.

"You don't —"

Rabbi Binder's hand flicked out at Ozzie's cheek. Perhaps it had only meant to clamp the boy's mouth shut, but Ozzie ducked and the palm caught him squarely on the nose.

The blood came in a short, red spurt on to Ozzie's shirt front.

The next moment was all confusion. Ozzie screamed, "You bastard, you bastard!" and broke for the classroom door. Rabbi Binder lurched a step backwards, as though his own blood had started flowing violently in the opposite direction, then gave a clumsy lurch forward and bolted out the door after Ozzie. The class followed after the rabbi's huge blue-suited back, and before old Blotnik could turn from his window, the room was empty and everyone was headed full speed up the three flights leading to the roof.

*****

70   If one should compare the light of day to the life of man: sunrise to birth; sunset — the dropping down over the edge — to death; then as Ozzie Freedman wiggled through the trapdoor of the synagogue roof, his feet kicking backwards bronco-style at Rabbi Binder's outstretched arms — at that moment the day was fifty years old. As a rule, fifty or fifty-five reflects accurately the age of late afternoons in November, for it is in that month, during those hours, that one's awareness of light seems no longer a matter of seeing, but of hearing: light begins clicking away. In fact, as Ozzie locked shut the trapdoor in the rabbi's face, the sharp click of the bolt into the lock might momentarily have been mistaken for the sound of the heavier gray that had just throbbed through the sky.

With all his weight Ozzie kneeled on the locked door; any instant he was certain that Rabbi Binder's shoulder would fling it open, splintering the wood into shrapnel and catapulting his body into the sky. But the door did not move and below him he heard only the rumble of feet, first loud then dim, like thunder rolling away.

A question shot through his brain. "Can this be *me?*" For a thirteen-year-old who had just labeled his religious leader a bastard, twice, it was not an improper question. Louder and louder the question came to him — "Is it me?" "Is it me?" — until he discovered himself no longer kneeling, but racing crazily towards the edge of the roof, his eyes crying, his throat screaming, and his arms flying everywhichway as though not his own!

"Is it me? Is it me ME ME ME! It has to be me — but is it!"

It is the question a thief must ask himself the night he jimmies open his first window, and it is said to be the question with which bridegrooms quiz themselves before the altar.

In the few wild seconds it took Ozzie's body to propel him to the edge of the roof, his self-examination began to grow fuzzy. Gazing down at the street, he became confused as to the problem beneath the question: was it, is-it-me-who-called-Binder-a-bastard? or, is-it-me-prancing-around-on-the-roof? However, the scene below settled all, for there is an instant in any action when whether it is you or somebody else is academic. The thief crams the money in his pockets and scoots out the window. The bridegroom signs the hotel register for two. And the boy on the roof finds a streetful of people gaping at him, necks stretched backwards, faces up, as though he were the ceiling of the Hayden Planetarium. Suddenly you know it's you.

"Oscar! Oscar Freedman!" A voice rose from the center of the crowd, a voice that, could it have been seen, would have looked like the writing on scroll. "Oscar Freedman, get down from there. Immediately!" Rabbi Binder was pointing one arm stiffly up at him; and at the end of that arm, one finger aimed menacingly. It was the attitude of a dictator, but one — the eyes confessed all — whose personal valet had spit neatly in his face.

Ozzie didn't answer. Only for a blink's length did he look towards Rabbi Binder. Instead his eyes began to fit together the world beneath him, to sort out people from places, friends from enemies, participants from spectators. In little jagged starlike clusters his friends stood around Rabbi Binder, who was still pointing. The topmost point on a star compounded not of angels but of five adolescent boys was Itzie. What a world it was, with those stars below, Rabbi Binder below . . . Ozzie, who a moment earlier hadn't been able to control his own body, started to feel the meaning of the word control: he felt Peace and he felt Power.

"Oscar Freedman, I'll give you three to come down."

Few dictators give their subjects three to do anything; but, as always, Rabbi Binder only looked dictatorial.

"Are you ready, Oscar?"

Ozzie nodded his head yes, although he had no intention in the world — the lower one or the celestial one he'd just entered — of coming down even if Rabbi Binder should give him a million.

"All right then," said Rabbi Binder. He ran a hand through his black Samson hair as though it were the gesture prescribed for uttering the first digit. Then, with his other hand cutting a circle out of the small piece of sky around him, he spoke. "One!"

There was no thunder. On the contrary, at that moment, as though "one" was the cue for which he had been waiting, the world's least thunderous person appeared on the synagogue steps. He did not so much come out of the synagogue door as lean out, onto the darkening air. He clutched at the doorknob with one hand and looked up at the roof.

"Oy!"

85 Yakov Blotnik's old mind hobbled slowly, as if on crutches, and though he couldn't decide precisely what the boy was doing on the roof, he knew it wasn't good — that is, it wasn't-good-for-the-Jews. For Yakov Blotnik life had fractionated itself simply: things were either good-for-the-Jews or no-good-for-the-Jews.

He smacked his free hand to his in-sucked cheek, gently. "Oy, Gut!"[4] And then quickly as he was able, he jacked down his head and surveyed the street. There was Rabbi Binder (like a man at an auction with only three dollars in his pocket, he had just delivered a shaky "Two!"); there were the students, and that was all. So far it-wasn't-so-bad-for-the-Jews. But the boy had to come down immediately, before anybody saw. The problem: how to get the boy off the roof?

Anybody who has ever had a cat on the roof knows how to get him down. You call the fire department. Or first you call the operator and you ask her for the fire department. And the next thing there is great jamming of brakes and clanging of bells and shouting of instructions. And then the cat is off the roof. You do the same thing to get a boy off the roof.

That is, you do the same thing if you are Yakov Blotnik and you once had a cat on the roof.

*****

When the engines, all four of them, arrived, Rabbi Binder had four times given Ozzie the count of three. The big hook-and-ladder swung around the corner and one of the firemen leaped from it, plunging headlong towards the yellow fire hydrant in front of the synagogue. With a huge wrench he began to unscrew the top nozzle. Rabbi Binder raced over to him and pulled at his shoulder.

90 "There's no fire . . ."

The fireman mumbled back over his shoulder and, heatedly, continued working at the nozzle.

"But there's no fire, there's no fire . . ." Binder shouted. When the fireman mumbled again, the rabbi grasped his face with both his hands and pointed it up at the roof.

To Ozzie it looked as though Rabbi Binder was trying to tug the fireman's head out of his body, like a cork from a bottle. He had to giggle at the picture they made: it was a family portrait — rabbi in black skullcap, fireman in red fire hat, and the little yellow hydrant squatting beside like a kid brother, bareheaded. From the edge of the roof Ozzie waved at the portrait, a one-handed, flapping, mocking wave; in doing it his right foot slipped from under him. Rabbi Binder covered his eyes with his hands.

4 Yiddish expression signifying dismay.

Firemen work fast. Before Ozzie had even regained his balance, a big, round, yellowed net was being held on the synagogue lawn. The firemen who held it looked up at Ozzie with stern, feelingless faces.

95   One of the firemen turned his head towards Rabbi Binder. "What, is the kid nuts or something?"

Rabbi Binder unpeeled his hands from his eyes, slowly, painfully, as if they were tape. Then he checked: nothing on the sidewalk, no dents in the net.

"Is he gonna jump, or what?" the fireman shouted.

In a voice not at all like a statue, Rabbi Binder finally answered, "Yes, yes, I think so...He's been threatening to..."

Threatening to? Why, the reason he was on the roof, Ozzie remembered, was to get away: he hadn't even thought about jumping. He had just run to get away, and the truth was that he hadn't really headed for the roof as much as he'd been chased there.

100   "What's his name, the kid?"

"Freedman," Rabbi Binder answered. "Oscar Freedman."

The fireman looked up at Ozzie. "What is it with you, Oscar? You gonna jump, or what?"

Ozzie did not answer. Frankly, the question had just arisen.

"Look, Oscar, if you're gonna jump, jump — and if you're not gonna jump, don't jump. But don't waste our time, willya?"

105   Ozzie looked at the fireman and then at Rabbi Binder. He wanted to see Rabbi Binder cover his eyes one more time.

"I'm going to jump."

And then he scampered around the edge of the roof to the corner, where there was no net below, and he flapped his arms at his sides, swishing the air and smacking his palms to his trousers on the downbeat. He began screaming like some kind of engine, "Wheeeee...wheeeeee," and leaning way out over the edge with the upper half of his body. The firemen whipped around to cover the ground with the net. Rabbi Binder mumbled a few words to somebody and covered his eyes. Everything happened quickly, jerkily, as in a silent movie. The crowd, which had arrived with the fire engines, gave out a long, Fourth-of-July fireworks oooh-aahhh. In the excitement no one had paid the crowd much heed, except, of course, Yakov Blotnik, who swung from the door now counting heads. "Fier und tsvansik...finf und tsvansik.[5] Oy, Gut!" It wasn't like this with the cat.

Rabbi Binder peeked through his fingers, checked the sidewalk and net. Empty. But there was Ozzie racing to the other corner. The firemen raced with him but were unable to keep up. Whenever Ozzie wanted to he might jump and splatter himself upon the sidewalk, and by the time the firemen scooted to the spot all they could do with their net would be to cover the mess.

"Wheeeee...wheeeeee..."

110   "Hey, Oscar," the winded fireman yelled, "What the hell is this, a game or something?"

"Wheeeee...wheeeee..."

"Hey, Oscar —"

5 Twenty-four...twenty-five.

But he was off now to the other corner, flapping his wings fiercely. Rabbi Binder couldn't take it any longer — the fire engines from nowhere, the screaming suicidal boy, the net. He fell to his knees, exhausted, and with his hands curled together in front of his chest like a little dome, he pleaded, "Oscar, stop it, Oscar. Don't jump, Oscar. Please come down...Please don't jump."

And further back in the crowd a single voice, a single young voice, shouted a lone word to the boy on the roof.

115 "Jump!"

It was Itzie. Ozzie momentarily stopped flapping.

"Go ahead, Ozz — jump!" Itzie broke off his point of the star and courageously, with the inspiration not of a wise-guy but of a disciple, stood alone. "Jump, Ozz, jump!"

Still on his knees, his hands still curled, Rabbi Binder twisted his body back. He looked at Itzie, then, agonizingly, back to Ozzie.

"OSCAR, DON'T JUMP! PLEASE, DON'T JUMP...PLEASE, PLEASE..."

120 "Jump! This time it wasn't Itzie but another point of the star. By the time Mrs. Freedman arrived to keep her four-thirty appointment with Rabbi Binder, the whole little upside down heaven was shouting and pleading for Ozzie to jump, and Rabbi Binder no longer was pleading with him not to jump, but was crying into the dome of his hands.

*****

Understandably Mrs. Freedman couldn't figure out what her son was doing on the roof. So she asked.

"Ozzie, my Ozzie, what are you doing? My Ozzie, what is it?"

Ozzie stopped wheeeeeing and slowed his arms down to a cruising flap, the kind birds use in soft winds, but he did not answer. He stood against the low, clouded, darkening sky — light clicked down swiftly now, as on a small gear — flapping softly and gazing down at the small bundle of a woman who was his mother.

"What are you doing, Ozzie?" She turned towards the kneeling Rabbi Binder and rushed so close that only a paper-thickness of dust lay between her stomach and his shoulders.

125 "What is my baby doing?"

Rabbi Binder gaped up at her but he too was mute. All that moved was the dome of his hands; it shook back and forth like a weak pulse.

"Rabbi, get him down! He'll kill himself. Get him down, my only baby..."

"I can't," Rabbi Binder said, "I can't..." and he turned his handsome head towards the crowd of boys behind him. "It's them. Listen to them."

And for the first time Mrs. Freedman saw the crowd of boys, and she heard what they were yelling.

130 "He's doing it for them. He won't listen to me. It's them." Rabbi Binder spoke like one in a trance.

"For them?"

"Yes."

"Why for them?"

"They want him to..."

135   Mrs. Freedman raised her two arms upward as though she were conducting the sky. "For them he's doing it!" And then in a gesture older than pyramids, older than prophets and floods, her arms came slapping down to her sides. "A martyr I have. Look!" She tilted her head to the roof. Ozzie was still flapping softly. "My martyr."

    "Oscar, come down, *please*," Rabbi Binder groaned.

    In a startling even voice Mrs. Freedman called to the boy on the roof. "Ozzie, come down, Ozzie. Don't be a martyr, my baby."

    As though it were a litany, Rabbi Binder repeated her words. "Don't be a martyr, my baby. Don't be a martyr."

    "Gawhead, Ozz — *be* a Martin!" It was Itzie. "Be a Martin, be a Martin," and all the voices joined in singing for Martindom, whatever *it* was. "Be a Martin, be a Martin..."

*****

140   Somehow when you're on a roof the darker it gets the less you can hear. All Ozzie knew was that two groups wanted two new things: his friends were spirited and musical about what they wanted; his mother and the rabbi were eventoned, chanting, about what they didn't want. The rabbi's voice was without tears now and so was his mother's.

    The big net stared up at Ozzie like a sightless eye. The big, clouded sky pushed down. From beneath it looked like a gray corrugated board. Suddenly, looking up into that unsympathetic sky, Ozzie realized all the strangeness of what these people, his friends, were asking: they wanted him to jump, to kill himself; they were singing about it now — it made them happy. And there was an even greater strangeness: Rabbi Binder was on his knees, trembling. If there was a question to be asked now it was not "Is it me?" but rather "Is it us?... Is it us?"

    Being on the roof, it turned out, was a serious thing. If he jumped would the singing become dancing? Would it? What would jumping stop? Yearningly, Ozzie wished he could rip open the sky, plunge his hands through, and pull out the sun; and on the sun, like a coin, would be stamped JUMP or DON'T JUMP.

    Ozzie's knees rocked and sagged a little under him as though they were setting him for a dive. His arms tightened, stiffened, froze, from shoulders to fingernails. He felt as if each part of his body were going to vote as to whether he should kill himself or not — and each part as though it were independent of *him*.

    The light took an unexpected click down and the new darkness, like a gag, hushed the friends singing for this and the mother and rabbi chanting for that.

145   Ozzie stopped counting votes, and in a curiously high voice, like one who wasn't prepared for speech, he spoke.

    "Mamma?"

    "Yes, Oscar."

    "Mamma, get down on your knees, like Rabbi Binder."

    "Oscar —"

150   "Get down on your knees," he said, "or I'll jump."

    Ozzie heard a whimper, then a quick rustling, and when he looked down where his mother had stood he saw the top of a head and beneath that a circle of dress. She was kneeling beside Rabbi Binder.

He spoke again. "Everybody kneel." There was the sound of everybody kneeling.

Ozzie looked around. With one hand he pointed towards the synagogue entrance. "Make *him* kneel."

There was a noise, not of kneeling, but of body-and-cloth stretching. Ozzie could hear Rabbi Binder saying in a gruff whisper, " . . . or he'll *kill* himself," and when next he looked there was Yakov Blotnik off the doorknob and for the first time in his life upon his knees in the Gentile[6] posture of prayer.

155 As for the firemen — it is not as difficult as one might imagine to hold a net taut while you are kneeling.

Ozzie looked around again; and then he called to Rabbi Binder.

"Rabbi?"

"Yes, Oscar."

"Rabbi Binder, do you believe in God?"

160 "Yes."

"Do you believe God can do Anything?" Ozzie leaned his head out into the darkness. "Anything?"

"Oscar, I think —"

"Tell me you believe God can do Anything."

There was a second's hesitation. Then: "God can do Anything."

165 "Tell me you believe God can make a child without intercourse."

"He can."

"Tell me!"

"God," Rabbi Binder admitted, "can make a child without intercourse."

"Mamma, you tell me."

170 "God can make a child without intercourse," his mother said.

"Make *him* tell me." There was no doubt who *him* was.

In a few moments Ozzie heard an old comical voice say something to the increasing darkness about God.

Next, Ozzie made everybody say it. And then he made them all say they believed in Jesus Christ — first one at a time, then all together.

When the catechizing was through it was the beginning of evening. From the street it sounded as if the boy on the roof might have sighed.

175 "Ozzie?" A woman's voice dared to speak. "You'll come down now?"

There was no answer, but the woman waited, and when a voice finally did speak it was thin and crying, and exhausted as that of an old man who has just finished pulling the bells.

"Mamma, don't you see — you shouldn't hit me. He shouldn't hit me. You shouldn't hit me about God, Mamma. You should never hit anybody about God —"

"Ozzie, please come down now."

"Promise me, promise me you'll never hit anybody about God."

180 He had asked only his mother, but for some reason everyone kneeling in the street promised he would never hit anybody about God.

---

6 non-Jewish people; generally refers to Christians.

Once again there was silence.

"I can come down now, Mamma," the boy on the roof finally said. He turned his head both ways as though checking the traffic lights. "Now I can come down..."

And he did, right into the center of the yellow net that glowed in the evening's edge like an overgrown halo.

(1959)

Austin C. Clarke (b. 1934)

Barbadian-born novelist and short story writer Austin Clarke, who moved to Toronto in 1955, has chronicled the lives of his compatriots both in the Caribbean and in Canada, the latter often referred to as "that cold, ungodly place" by his characters. His acclaimed Toronto trilogy, *The Meeting Point, Storm of Fortune*, and *The Bigger Light*, portrays the tensions that exist among poor men and women who have travelled to Toronto in search of better lives and found low-paying jobs and racial prejudice. "The Motor Car" uses the familiar initiation journey structure, tracing the move of a young man from a small town to a big city. The result of Calvin's search for happiness, which involves an attempt to deny his past and to find materialistic well-being through ownership of an automobile, symbolizes the lot of the immigrant in modern Canadian society. The story exemplifies the author's sensitive understanding of his characters, the gentle humour with which he depicts their situations, and his accurate reproduction of the dialect and rhythms of Barbadian speech.

THE MOTOR CAR

That Canadian thing you see lying down there in that bed is Calvin woman, I mean *was* Calvin woman. Calvin wash motor cars back in Barbados till his back hurt and his belly burn, and when the pain stop in the body it start up fresh in his mind. Good thing Calvin was a God-faring man, cause if not he would have let go some real bad curse words that would have blow way the garage itself. But instead o' talking to the customers bout the hard work, instead o' talking to the boss bout the slave work he was making Calvin do in 1968 in these modern days, Calvin talk to God. Calvin didn' know if God did really hear him, cause the more he talk to God every morning before he went to work on his old Raleigh green three-speed bicycle, and after work when his head hit that pillow, the more the work did get harder. One day Calvin take in with a bout o' bad-feels, and the moment he come outta the fit or the trance, or the *hellucinations* as his boss call it, right that very second Calvin swear blind to God that he leffing Barbados. One time. For good. First chance. Is only the governorship or the governor-generalship that could get Calvin to stay in Barbados. That is the kind o' swearing he put pon God. And it ain't really clear, even at this time, if God really understand the kind o' message that Calvin put to him. But Calvin didn't care. Calvin decide already. Calvin start to work hard, more harder than he ever work in his life, from the very day after he decide that he pulling outta Barbados. And is to Canada he coming. Now the problems start falling pon top o' Calvin head like rainwater. First problem: he can't get a Canadian visa. He seeing Canadian tourisses morning noon and night all bout his island, walking bout like if they own the blasted place, and if you don't look out they getting on as if they want to own Calvin too. Calvin hit a low point o' studyation. The work done now and he pack already, two big big imitation leather valises; and he manage to buy the ticket too, although there is a regulation down there in the island that say a black man can't buy a ticket pon *Air Canada* saving he have a job and a roof to come to in Canada, or he have family here, or some kind o' support, cause Trudeau[1] get vex vex as hell bout supporting the boys when they come up here and can't find proper ployment. Calvin walking bout Bridgetown the capital all day telling people he pulling out next week for Canada. Next week come and he still walking bout Bridgetown. He ain't pull out in trute, yuh: he ain't like he pulling out at all, man; that is what the boys was beginning to think. They start laughing at Calvin behind his back, and Calvin grinning and telling them, "Gorblummuh, you laugh! *laugh*! he who laugh last, laugh…" And for purpose, he won't finish the saying at all, he only ordering a next round o' steam for his friends, and his mind focus-on pon a new shining motto-car that he going buy up in Canada before he even living there a year. He done make up his mind that he going work at two car-wash places, and if the Lord hear his prayers, and treat he nice, he going hustle a next job on top o' them two, too. Well, the more the boys laugh, the more Calvin decide with a piece o' real bad-mind that he going buy a brand-new Chevvy, perhaps even a custom-build *Galaxie*. And then, all of a sudden, one night when the fellas drink three free-round o' rum offa Calvin, Calvin really start to laugh. He push he hand inside his pocket, and he pull out a thing that look real important and official, and all he say is, "I taking off at nine in the morning." Calvin then throw a new-brand twenty dollar bill pon Marcus rum shop counter, and the fellas gone wild, be-Christ, cause is now real drinking going begin. Calvin stand up like a man. Every one that his best friend Willy fire, Calvin fire one, too. Willy, who didn' lick he mouth too much gainst Calvin going way, when he reach the fifth straight *Mount Gay*, Calvin was right there with him. Is rum for rum. Drink for drink. They start eating raw salt fish, and Calvin iamming the cod fish as if he catch it himself off the banks o' Newfoundland in the same Canada that he heading out to. The fellas eat off all o' Marcus bad half-rotten salt fish, and then start-on pon a tin o' corn beef and raw onions and you would have think that Calvin was pon a real religious fast during the time he was worrying bout the Canadian visa. "I going tell you fellas something," Willy say, for no conceivable reason at all, cause they just then telling Calvin that he ain' going see no good cricket when he get up in that cold ungodly place call Canada. "I going tell you fellas something now," Willy say, after he clear his throat for effect, and to make the fellas stop drinking and eating and listen to him. "Godblummuh! Calvin is the most luckiest one o' we, yuh! Calvin lucky-lucky-lucky as shite!" He say the last two "lucky" like if they was one word. Anyhow, he went on, "Calvin is a king to we!" Now, nobody ain' know what the arse Willy trying to say, cause Willy is a man who does try to talk big and talk a lot o' shite in the bargain. But this time, solemn occasion as it be, the fellas decide to give Willy a listen. "We lis'ning, man, so talk yuh talk. We lis'ning." Willy take a long pull pon the rum bottle, and he stuff bout a half-pound o' corn beef inside his mouth, with the biscuits flying bout the place like big drops o' spit. "You see that salt fish that we just put way? Well, it make up in Canada. Tha's where Calvin here going. Now understand this when I say it. I only say that to say this. Comprehend? The salt fish that we does

1 Pierre Elliott Trudeau, prime minister of Canada from 1968 to 1979 and 1980 to 1984.

get down here, send-down by Canada, is the same quality o' salt fish that they uses to send down here to feed we when we was slaves. It smell stink. You could tell when a woman cooking salt fish. We even invent a term to go long with this kind o' salt fish and this kind o' stinkingness. We does say to a person who uses *profine* words, 'Yuh mouth smell like a fucking salt-fish barrel,' Unnerstand? I going to lay a bet pon any one o' you bitches in here now, drinking this rum. I going wager five dollars gainst a quarter that the brand o' salt fish Calvin going get to buy and eat up in that place call Canada is a better quality o' salt fish. It rass-hole bound to be, cause that is where it produce. And if you ever study Marx, you would understand the kind o' socialism I talking bout." Nobody ain' answer Willy for a time, all they do is laugh. "Laugh! laugh!" Willy say with scorn, "cause godblindme!..." And then Calvin say, like if he didn' really want to say the words at-all, "Be-Jesus Christ, when you see me leff this blasted backwards place, call Barbados, that is the last time I eating salt fish. I eating steaks!"

Well, they poured Calvin on pon the *Air Canada*, next morning, nine sharp, drunk as a flying-fish. Good thing Calvin mother did pack the fry dolphin steak, a bottle o' Cod Liver Oil, in case the bowels do a thing and give trouble in that cold ungodly climate, as she call Canada; and she pack some Phensic for headache, just in case; she pack some miraculous bush, for medicine, "cause they ain' have doctor no place under the sun who know the goodness in this mirac'lous bush-tea as we does, so you tek it along with you, son; you going up in that strange savage place, and you far from me, and I ain' near enough no more to run to you and rub your face with a lime and some Limacol, and tie it up with oil-leaves and candle-grease..."; and she put in half dozen limes and two bottle o' Limacol; man, is a good-good thing that Calvin mother had the presence o' mind to pack these things for Calvin whilst Calvin was walking bout Broadstreet in Bridgetown like if he was one o' them Canadian tourisses. Calvin mother do a real good job, and when she done pack the things, and she inspect the clothes that Calvin carrying way, she tie-up the two valises with a strong piece o' string, although they had brand-new locks pon them. "Good!" is the last thing she say to Calvin, as she was holding over the kitchen door, whilst Willy was revving up the hired car and blowing the horn — which, of course, Calvin pay for, the hired car I mean — plus dropping a ten dollar bill inside Willy hand for old times sake. "Go long in the name o' the Lord, and make yuh fortune, son." A tear or two drop outta she eye, too; but she was glad-glad in she heart that she boy-child was leffing Barbados. "Too much foreigners and tourisses and crooks living here with we, now, son. Canada more brighter than here." Calvin get vex-vex when he see the water in his mother eye, and he was embarrass as hell, cause he always use to brag how nothing he do, or don't do, could make his mother belly burn she. Good thing Willy had the car motor revving, cause Calvin get in such a state over the tears and heart-break on the part of his mother that he almost forget that deep-down he is a christian-minded man and say a bad word, whiching as he did know full-well, God would be vex as hell with him for. The motto-car was making good time moving like hell going up the airport road, and everybody Calvin know, and everybody that he barely know in the twenty-nine years he born and living in Barbados, he hold half of his body out through the car window, and yell out, "Boy, I going this morning! Canada, in your arse!" All the people who see and hear, wave back and grin their teet', if they could hear from the distance and through the speed; and some o' them say, "Bless." If everybody in Barbados, down Broadstreet, at the airport didn' know that Calvin pulling out for Canada at quarter-to-nine that morning, by nine o'clock the whole world did know. Friend or no friend, every time he see a face, or a hand, he saying, "Well, I won't be see you for a while, man, I going up." And they did all know what he meant, cause it was a time when all the young boys and young girls was pulling outta the island and going to Amer'ca, Britain, although Britain begin to tighten up things for the fellas because o' Powell; and some o' them start running up in Canada. And they was more *Air Canada* planes all bout Seawell Airport in Barbados in them days that you would have think that Barbados did own *Air Canada*. But is the other way round. Anyhow, drunk as Calvin was when he step pon that plane, and the white lady smile at him and say, "Good morning, sir" — first time in Calvin life white woman ever call him that, that way — well, Calvin know long time that he make the right move. Canada nice, he say in his heart; and he end it up with "Praise God." Canada now gone straight to Calvin head, long time and with a kind o' power, that when the airplane start up Calvin imagine that he own the whole blasted plane along with the white ladies who tell him, "Good morning, sir"; he feel that the plane is the big motto-car he intend to own one year after he land pon Canadian soil. The plane making time fast fast, and Calvin drink rum after rum till he went fast asleep and didn' even know he was in Toronto. The white lady come close to him, and tap him soft soft pon his new tropical suit and say, "Sir?", like if she asking some important question, when all she want is to wake up Calvin outta the white man plane. Well, Calvin wake up. He stretch like how he uses to stretch when he wake up in his mother bed. He yawn so hard that the white lady move back a step or two, after she see the pink inside his mouth and the black and blue gums running round them white pearly teets. Calvin eyes red red as a cheery from lack o' sleep and too much rum drinking, and the body tired like how it uses to get tired and wrap-up like a old motto-car fender. But is Canada, old man, and in a jiffy, before the white lady get to the front o' the plane to put down the last glass, Calvin looking out through the window. "Toronto in your arse!" he went to say to himself, but it come out too loud, as if he was saying it to Willy and the boys who didn' think he was really going to come through. "Toronto in your arse, man!" The plane touch down, and the first man outta the plane is, well, no need to tell you who it was. Calfuckingvin! And he pass through the customs like if he was born in Toronto. The white man didn' even ask him a question. Something like it was wrong, cause Calvin did know as far away as in Barbados that the Immigration and Customs men in Toronto is the roughest in the world, when they see a black face in front o' them. But this white gentleman must have been down in the islands recently, cause all he tell Calvin was, "Don't tell me! Don't tell me! You're a Bajun!" For years after, Calvin wondering how the hell this white man know so much bout black people. Before the first week come and gone, Calvin take up pen and paper and send off a little thing to Willy and the boys: *. . . and I am going to tell you something, this place is the greatest place for a working man to live. I hear some things about this place, but*

I isn't a man to complain, because while I know I am a man, and I won't take no shit from no Canadian, white, black or red, I still have another piece of knowledge which says that I didn't born here. So I controls myself to suit, and make the white man money. The car only a couple of months off. I see one already that I got my eyes on. And if God willing, by the next two months, DV, I sitting down in the drivers seat. The car I got my eyes on is a red one, with white tires. The steering wheel as you know is on the left hand side, and we drives on the right hand side of the road up here, not like back in Barbados where you drive on the left hand. Next week, I taking out my licents. I not found a church I like yet, mainly because I see some strange things happening up here in churches. You don't know, man, Willy, but black people can't or don't go in the same church as white people. God must be have two colours then. One for black people and one for white people. And a next thing. There is some fellas up here from the islands who talking a lot of shite about Black Power, and I hear that one of them is a Barbadian. But I am one man who don't want to hear no shit about Black Power. I am here working for a living and a motor car and if my mother herself come in my way and be an obstacle against me getting them two things, a living and a motor car, I would kill her by Christ ... Calvin was going to write more: about the room he was renting for twenty dollars a week, which a white fellow tell him was pure robbery, because he was paying ten dollars for a more larger room on the ground floor in the same house; and he didn' write Willy bout the car-wash job he got the next day down Spadina Avenue, working for a dollar a hour, and when the first three hours pass he felt he been working for three days, the work was so hard; he didn' tell Willy that a certain kind of white people in Canada didn' sit too close to him on the street car, that they didn' speak to him on the street ... lots o' things he didn' worry to tell Willy, cause he did want Willy to think that he was really a king to the boys back home, a champion for emigrading to Canada. Willy send back a post card with a mauby[2] woman on the colour side selling mauby, and on the writing side, in his scribbly handwriting, "As man!" But be-Christ, Calvin didn' care what they do, he was here for two purpose; one, living, and number two, motto-car. If they touch my motto-car, now, well, that would be something else ... and Calvin work hard, man, Calvin work more harder than when he was washing-off cars back in Barbados. The money was good too. Sal'ry and tips. From the two car-wash jobs he uses to clear a hundred dollars a week, and that is two hundred back home, and not even Dipper does make that kind o' money, and he is the fucking prime minister! The third job, Calvin land like a dream; nightwatchman with a big big important company which put him in big big important uniform and thing, big leather belt like what he uses to envy the officers in the Volunteer Force back home wearing pon a Queen Birthday parade on the Garrison Savannah,[3] shoes the company people even provide, and the only thing that was missing, according to what Calvin figure out some months afterwards, was that the holster at his side, join-on to the leather belt, didn' have in no blasted gun. He tell it to a next Barbadian he make friends with, and the Bajan just laugh and say, "They think you going rass-hole shoot yourself, boy!" But Calvin did already become Canadified enough to know that the only people he see in them uniforms with guns in the leather

---

2 West Indian herbal beverage. 3 race track in Barbados.

holster was certain white people, and he know he wasn' Canadified so much that he did turn white overnight. "Once it don't stop me from getting that *Galaxie!*" Work work work, a occasional postcard to Willy, cause envelopes was costing too much all of a sudden, and postage stamps was going up too, no pleasure for Calvin: he went down by the *Tropics Club* where they play calypsoes and dance, one time, and he never went back cause the ugly Grenadian fellow at the door ask him for "Three dollars to come in!", and he curse the fellow and leff. But the bank account was mounting and climbing like a woman belly when she in the family-way. Quick-quick so, Calvin have a thousand dollars pon the bank. Fellas who get to know Calvin and who Calvin won't sociate with because "sociating does cost money, boy!", them fellas so who here donkey years, still borrowing money to help pay their rent, fellas gambling like hell, throwing dice every Fridee night right into Mondee morning early, missing work and getting fired from work, fellas playing poker and betting, "Forty dollars more for these two fours, in your rass, sah! I *raise!*", them brand o' Trinidadian, Bajan, Jamaican, Grenadian and thing, them so can't understand at-all how Calvin just land and he get rich so fast. "I bet all-yuh Calvin selling pussy!" one fella say. A next bad-minded fella say, "He peddling his arse to white boys down Yonge Street," and a third fella who did just bet fifty dollars 'pon a pair o' deuces, and get broke at the poker game, say quick-quick before the words fall-out o' the other fella mouth, "I going peddle mine too, then! Bread is bread." Calvin start slacking up on the first car wash work, and he humming as he shine the white people car, he skinning his teet in the shine and he smiling, and the white people thinking he smiling because he like the work and them, cause his hands never tarried whilst he was car-dreaming, they drop a little dollar bill pon Calvin as a tip, and a regular twenty-five cent piece, and Calvin pinching pon the groceries, eating a lotta pigs feet and chicken necks and salt fish . . . "I gotta write Willy and tell him bout the brand o' salt fish in this place. Willy was right!" . . . Calvin won't spend thirty cents pon a beer with a sinner, only time he even reading is when he clean out a car in the car wash and it happen to have a used paper inside it, or a throw-away paperback book. But Calvin decide long time that he didn' come here for eddication. He come for a living and a motto-car. A new one, too! And he intend to get both. And by the look o' things, be-Christ, both almost in his hand. Only now waiting to see the right model o' motor car, with the right colour inside it, and the right mileage and thing. The motto-car must have the right colour o' tires, right colour o' gear shift and in the handle too. And it have to have-in radio; and he see a fella in the car wash with a thing inside his Cadillac, and Calvin gone crazy over Cadillacs until he walk down by Bay Street and price the price of a old one. He bawl for murder. "Better stick to the *Galaxie*, boy!" he tell himself; and he do that. But he really like the thing inside the white man Cadillac and he ask the man one morning what it was, and the man tell Calvin. Now Calvin *must* have red *Galaxie*, with not more than 20,000 miles on the register, black upholstery, red gear shift, radio, AM *and FM and a tellyfone* . . . Them last three things is what the man had inside his Cadillac. Calvin working even on a Sundee, bank holidays ain' touching Calvin, and the Old Queen back home who send a occasional letter asking Calvin to remember the house rent and the Poor Box in the Nazarene Church where he was a testifying brother, preaching and thing, and also to remember "who birthed him", well, Calvin tell the Old Queen, his own-own mother; *Things hard up here, mother. Don't let nobody fool you that because a man emigrade it mean that he elevate. That isn't true. But I am sending this Canadian money order for five dollars, which is ten dollars back home, and I hope that next week I would find myself a nice job, and then I am going to send you a little something more. Your loving son, Calvin. P.S. Pray for me.* Calvin start thinking that maybe the Old Queen had a bad mind for him; he start one long stewpsing, and the fellas at work even had to ask him if he sick or something, he even stop laughing and chumming around with the Canadians at work; he refuse to play Frisbee and throw the ball in the other fellas mittens, he even stop begging the German fella for a lift home after work. Calvin start getting ingrown like a toenail: pressure in Calvin arse. The studyation take a hold o' him and one weekend it capsize him in bed, Fridee night, Sardah morning and Sardah night, Sundee and right into Mondee morning half hour before he is to leff for work. Landlady couldn' even come in and change the filthy linens and bed sheets. But Calvin make sure he went to work that Mondee. "Can't lose that money now, boy!" Willy was the next joker at this time o' hardship and studyation. Willy send a letter registered and thing, in a real pretty envelope with the colours o' the Union Jack, to Calvin: *... and if it isn't asking too much, Calvin, I wonder if you can see your way in sending me down a piece of change. I am thinking about emigrading too, because Barbados is at a standstill for people like me, people who don't have no high school education, no big kind of skills and no kiss-me-arse godfather in big jobs in the civil service. My kind of man in Barbados is loss. I hope I am not imposing when I ask you if you could see your way in lending me the passage money, one way, and I am going to open a new bank account with it and take a picture of it and show it to the Canadian immigration people down here, because another fellow promise to do the same thing for me with the return part of the passage money. The Canadian high commission place in Trinidad giving the fellows a hard time. But we smarter than any number of Canadian immigration people they send down here. So I asking this favour for old times sake, because not that I hard on you, but I don't want to remind you of the time when you had the accident with the motor car that didn't belongst to you, and you was in hospital, and you know who help you out, so ...* Calvin get in a bad bad mood straightaway, thinking that everybody back home think he is a millionaire, everybody back there getting on like crabs, willing to pull him down the moment he come up for breath. "Be-Christ, not me!" and in that frame o' mind Calvin take up a piece o' stationery he borrow from a Jamaican fellow who had a job in the General Hospital, and a envelope to match, with the hospital name on both, and he ask a next fellow who had a typewriter to write this letter back to Willy: *Dear Willy, I have been laid up in this hospital for two months now. I am getting a friend who is in the hospital too, but who is not confine to bed and who can barely walk around, to post this letter to you for me. Things really bad, man ...* because all my friends back home think I is a arse or something, they see me emigrade to this place and they think that I get rich overnight, or that I don't work hard as hell for my money, but that ain't true. Willy didn' answer back immediately, but a month and a half later, two days before Calvin decide he see the right automobile, a card drop through the door where Calvin living, address to Calvin: *What are you doing up there, then?*

Canadians buying out all the island. You standing for that? Send down a couple of *dollars and let me invest it in a piece of beach land for you, Brother. Power to the* *people! Salaam and love. Willy X.* Calvin get so blasted vex, so damn vex, cause he sure now that Willy gone mad too, like everybody else he been reading bout in the States and in England; black people gone mad, Calvin say; and he get more vex when he think that it was the landlady, Mistress Silvermann who take up the post card from the linoleum and hand it to him, and he swear blind that she hand it to him after she done read the thing: and now she must be frighten like hell for Calvin, cause Calvin getting letters from these polit-ical extremists, and birds of a feather does flock together, she thinking now that Calvin perhaps is some kind o' political maniac, crying Black Power! all this damn foolishness bout Power to the People, and signing his name Willy X, when everybody in Barbados know that that damn fool's name is really William Fortesque: Calvin get shame-shame-shame that the landlady thinking dif-ferent bout him, because sometimes she does be in the house alone all night with Calvin, and she must be even thinking bout giving him notice, which would be a damn bad thing to happen right now, cause the motto-car just two days off, the room he renting now is a nice one, the rent come down like the temperature in May when he talk plain to Mistress Silvermann bout how he paying twice as much as other tenants, but what really get Calvin really vex-vex-vex as hell is that a little Canadian thing in the room over his head come downstairs one night in a mini-dress and thing, bubbies jumping bout inside her bosom, free and thing and looking juicy, and giggling all the time and calling sheself a women liberation, all her skin at the door, and the legs nice and fat just as Calvin like his meats, and Calvin already gone thinking that this thing is the right woman to drive-bout in his new automobile with, this Canadian thing coming downstairs every night for the past month, and out of the blue asking him, "You'll like a coffee?" When she say so the first time, coffee was as far from Calvin mind as lending Willy twenty-five cents for the downpayment for the house spot pon the beach back home. Now, be-Christ, Willy X, or whatever the hell that bastard calling himself nowadays, is going to stay right there down in Barbados and mash up Calvin life so! Just so? Simple so? Oh God, no, man! But the landlady couldn' read English, she did only uses to pretend she is a genius; the Canadian girl is who tell Calvin not to worry; one night when they was drinking the regular coffee in the communal kitchen, the Canadian girl say, "Missis Silvermann is only a D.P.[4] She can't read English." Calvin take courage. The bank book walking bout with him, inside his trousers all the time, he counting the digits going to work, coming from work, in the back seat alone, pon the street car, while waiting for the subway early on a morning at the Ossington Station, and then he make a plan. He plan it down to a T. Every penny organize for the proper thing, every nickel with its own work to do: the bottle of wine that the Canadian girl gave him the name to; the new suit from Eaton's that he see in the display window one night when he get hold of the girl and he get bold bold as hell and decide to take she for a lover's walk down Yonge Street; the new shoes, brown-brown till they look red to match the car; and the shirt and tie — every-blasted-thing matching-up like if he is a new bride

---

4 displaced person; derogatory term for a post–World War II European refugee or immigrant.

stepping down the aisle to the wedding march. And he even have a surprise up his sleeve for the thing, too. He isn' no longer a stingy man, cause he see his goal; and his goal is like gold. The car delivery arrange for three o'clock, Sardah; no work; the ice box in his room have in a beer or two, plus the wine; and he have a extra piece o' change in his pocket ... "I going have to remember to change the money from this pocket," he tell himself, as if he was talking to somebody else in the room with him, "to the next pocket in the new suit" ... and he have Chinese food now on his mind because the Canadian thing mention a nice Chinese restaurant down in Chinatown near Elizabeth Street. Calvin nervous as arse all Fridee night; all Fridee night the thing in Calvin room (here of late she behaving as if she live in Calvin room!), and Calvin is a man with ambitions: one night she tantalize Calvin head so much that he start talking bout high-rise apartment; perhaps, if she behave sheself he might even put a little gold thing pon her pretty little pink finger ... the girl start asking Calvin if he want *some*; not in them exact words, but that is what she did mean; and Calvin turn shame-shame and nearly blush, only thing, as you know black people can't show really if they blushing or if they mad as shite with a white person, and Calvin turn like a virgin on the night before she getting hang in church and in marriage, and he saying all the time because his mind pon the mileage in the motto-car, "Want some o' what?" And the girl laugh, and she throw back she head and show she gold fillings and she pink tongue and the little speck o' dirt under she neck; and she laugh and say to sheself, "This one is a real gentleman, not like what my girlfriend say to expect from West Indian men, at all ...." And you know something? She start one big confessing: "... and do you know what, Calvin? Would you like to hear something that I been thinking ..." Calvin thinking bout motto-car and this blasted white woman humbugging him bout sex! Calvin get vex, he play he get vex bout something different from the woman and she sex, and he send she flying back upstairs to she own room. He get in bed too, but he ain' sleeping, he wide awake in the dark like a thief, and he eyes open wide-wide-wide like a owl eyes, and in that darkness in that little little room that only have one small window way up by the ceiling and facing the clothes-lines and the dingy sheets that the landlady does spend all week washing, Calvin see the whole o' Toronto standing up and watching him drive by in his new motto-car — with the Canadian thing beside o' him in the front seat! — dream turn into different dream that Fridee night, because he was free to dream as much as he like since Sardah wasn' no work. Sardah is car day. He have everything plan. Go for the motto-car, pick it up, drive it home, pick up the Canadian thing, go for a spin down Bloor as far as Yonge, swing back up by Harbord, turn left at Spadina, take in College Street, and every West Indian in Toronto bound to see him in new car, before he get back home. Park she in front o' the house, *let everybody see me getting outta she, come in, have a little bite, change, change into the new suit, give the Canadian thing the surprise, and whilst she dressing, I sit down in the car* ... "And I hope she take a long time dressing so I would have to press the car-horn, press the horn just a little, a soft little thing, and call she outside, to see me in the ..." Morning break nice. It was a nice morning round the middle o' September, fall time in the air, everybody stretching and holding up their head cause the weather nice.

Even the cops have a smile on their fissiogomy.[5] Calvin get up at five, take a quick look at the alarm clock, curse the clock for being so damn slow, went back to sleep, had a dream in which he see Willy as the garage mechanic at the car-place taking too long over the *Galaxie*; he curse Willy in the dream and nearly didn' get up in time, then turn round and curse Willy for coming into his dream; he left without tea, travelling with the Canadian thing half-sleep beside him, and gone fast pon the subway at Ossington down Danforth for the machine. The salesman-man smile and shake Calvin hand strong, and give Calvin the history of the bird although Calvin did already hear the bird history before. The salesman-man come outta the office still smiling, holding the motto-car keys between the index finger and the big thumb, and he drop them in Calvin hand. Calvin make a shiver. A shiver o' pride and ownership. "*Galaxie in your arse!*" He say that in his mind, and he thinking o' Willy and the boys back in Marcus rum shop. He get in the car. He shuffle bout a bit in the leather seat. He straighten he trouser seams. He touch the leather. He start up the motor. Listen to the motor. It ticking over like a fucking charm. He put the thing in gear. And he make a little thing through the car park, and he would have gone straight back up Danforth if the Canadian thing didn' wave she handbag to remind Calvin that she come with he, cause Calvin did forget she standing up there looking at a white convertible Cadillac, which she say is the car for Calvin, that there is lots o' "Negro-men driving cars, even in Nova Scotia where I come from," that Calvin should have buy one o' them. "You start spending my blasted money already, woman! This is *mine*!" He didn' tell she out loud in words what he was really thinking bout she, but he was thinking so, though. The Canadian gash get in the motto-car, cause driving in a *Galaxie* more better than walking behind a Cadillac, and she sit down so comfortable that it look like if she own the car and she was giving Calvin a chance to try she out, and that it wasn' Calvin own-own money that pay-down pon the car. Calvin didn't like that at all: he want she to sit down in the front seat like if *he* own the motto-car. But Calvin gone up Danforth with new motto-car and white woman beside o' him, like if he going to a funeral: "got to break she in gently, man"; and the Canadian thing not too please that Calvin didn' listen to her advice as a woman should advise a man, and buy the Cadillac, but she still please and proud that Calvin get the *Galaxie*. She sitting in it like if she belong there by birth. And Calvin don't really mind, cause he have the car, and it driving like oil pon a tar road back home. He make a thing along Danforth as far as Bloor, turn pon Yonge and gone as far as Harbord... the itinerry ain' exactly as he first think it out, but it would do... make a thing along Harbord and meet up with Spadina, and continue according to plan. And in all this time so, not one blasted West Indian or black person in sight to look at Calvin new car and make a thing with his head, or laugh, or wave. When he make a right pon College at the corner o' Spadina, a woman with a bag mark HONEST ED'S start walking through the green light, drop a tomato, and she bend down to pick it up, and Calvin now, whether he looking for the woman tomato or he looking the wrong way, nearly run-over she. Blam! Brakes on, and the Canadian thing nearly break she

5 physiognomy, or face.

blasted neck 'gainst the windshield. Calvin rattle bad like a snake. Police come. Police look inside the car, see Calvin, turn he eyes pon the Canadian thing who get frighten as hell, and he say, "Okay, move along now, buster!" Calvin shaking till he get the *Galaxie* in front o' the landlady rooming house, and he ain' remember nothing bout what he plan to do when he bring home the prize of a motto-car; the police upset him and he trembling bad. "Give me a drink o' water," he say to the Canadian thing. She rubbing she neck all the time like if it really break in truth, and she get out, and she didn' even look back at the new car, whiching as you would understand is what Calvin expect any man who just have a new motto-car, to do: yuh have to walk out of the door, close the door soft-soft because it ain' the same thing as getting out of a taxi, make sure the door close, and when you know it close, open it again to show yuhself that it close proper, and then really close it a next time; then walk off, look at the car, turn yuh head right and left like if you escaping from a light jab to the head, rub yuh hand over the chrome, walk round to the door where the passenger does sit down, open that door too, close it, and open it, and then, lock it. Then yuh does have to forget something inside the car, so yuh could have a chance to open the doors a next time and play with the car, hoping in the meantime that somebody who never see you before with a car, see you now with this new one and would say something like, "My! How much horsepower?", because according to Calvin, a "Car in some ways is like a woman, yuh does have to care she!" Calvin do all these things, and he didn't forget to walk to the back o' the *Galaxie*, stoop down and play he looking at the tires, give them a little kick with his shoes to see if they got in enough air, look under the car to see what the muffler look like, and things like that, although he know full-well that he don't know one blasted thing bout motto-cars except to wash them off, or that yuh does drive them. He do the same thing when he walk round to the front o' the car. The Canadian thing gone inside the house long time; and Calvin remember the glass o' water and he walking up the front steps. Not one blasted person on the whole street look out at Calvin new motto-car. Then the landlady, Mistress Silvermann walk out, "Don't forget Mr. Kingston, today your rent is due." Calvin tell her in his mind something bad, and she look at the car as she reach the sidewalk, without looking back, she say, "Do you know the owner of this car, Mr. Kingston? Tell him to move it please ... I don't want cars blocking my driveway ..." Well, Calvin gone mad now. He walk in the house, and he catch the Canadian thing sitting down in his room, with the glass o' water in she hand, as if she dreaming, just sitting and looking at the air. He drink the water, but it was like drinking miraculous bush-tea the Old Queen uses to make when the bowels was giving trouble back in Barbados. Calvin think bout the Old Queen, put the Old Queen outta his head, and start dressing. He noticed that something was wrong with his dresser: perhaps the landlady was looking for she rent; perhaps the Canadian thing was ... "That's why she didn' come back outside with the water! Anyhow ..." He put on his clothes, the new suit, shoes and tie and shirt new and matching the *Galaxie* outside shining in the sun, and meantime the Canadian thing gone upstairs. Calvin finish dress, take up a old kerchief ... "Gotta have a shammy-cloth, gotta buy one Mondee!" ... and he gone outside polishing the motto-car. Back inside, he gone up to the Canadian thing room, knock soft, the door open, and out from behind his back he take a thing, and say in a sweet loving voice, "I buy this for you." Ohhhhhhhh! Myyyyyyyyyyyyyyy! "You shouldn't realllllllyyyyyyy!" But all the time she did know it was dress Calvin buy for she for the occasion, cause when she went inside for the water, she start searching all the man things, and she had a nice peep at the dress. She even know it cost twenty-nine dollars without tax: and she wonder if Calvin really love she so much. Well, they dress-off and they coming out like husband and wife going to church. The *Galaxie* smiling so, like if the *Galaxie* itself in love with the two o' them, too. The dress nearly red like the car, everybody in red, and looking nice. Calvin steal a peep at the Canadian thing and she look good-good-good, like something to eat! He inspect the tires a next time, though he just done looking at them, but what the hell it is his motto-car; and then he check the gas tank and the tank say, "Let's go for a long one, man!", and Calvin get in, fix the seams in the new trousers, adjust the tie, look at the knot in the mirror, fix the mirror two times, and then ask the Canadian thing if she comfortable. "I'm fine, thank you!" Calvin rev-up the thing, she turn over nice, and he ready to go. "You not nervous?" She smile. A dimple and a gold filling show when she smile. Nice. She ain' nervous. "Don't mind what happen just now by Spadina, eh?" She smile nice again. She ain' mind what happen by Spadina. Darling come to she lips with the smile. Calvin happy as hell now. He think he might treat this Canadian thing nice, and do the right thing with a gold ring even. "I take those things in my stride usually, but now it seems like an omen," she say, just as they turn into Bloor. Calvin ain' thinking bout omen, cause the only omen he know bout is that he pray for a *Galaxie* and he get a *Galaxie*! And the horses under the bonnet roaring like hell. Well, they drive and drive like if they was two explorers exploring Toronto: through Rosedale where the Canadian thing say she would *just love* to own a house; and in his mind, Calvin promise she she going get one in Rosedale; through the Bridle Path where she say the cheapest house cost a million dollars; through Don Mills where they see the big tall Foresters' Building, all up there by IBM; "You should get a job at IBM, dear" ("Doing wha'? Cleaning out the closets?"... this Canadian thing like she is the wrong kind o' woman for me, Calvin thinking: I hads better get a black woman!); all this she talk as they driving back on the Don Valley Parkway. The highway nice. The motto-car open a new whole life to Calvin, and he love Canada even better. Damn good thing he left Barbados! The *Galaxie* like a horse, prancing pon the white man road. Night fall long time as they travelling, and Calvin experimenting with the dip-lights and the high beam. It nice to play with. The FM radio thing ain' working good, cause Calvin never play one o' them radios before, and he forget to practise pon it when he was visiting the car in the lot after he pay-down something pon it, so that the salesman would keep it for him. So he working the AM thing overtime. A nice tune come on. Before the tune come on, he thinking again that the Canadian thing maybe the right woman for him: she nice, she tidy and she quiet. And he raise-up liking quiet women; his mother tell him never married a woman who ain' quiet, and like church. The tune is a calypso, man. "It's a nice calypso," Calvin say. "Sparrow, in you arse!" he shout, and he beg the Canadian pardon, he excited because it is the first time he hear a calypso on the radio. He start liking Canada bad bad again. "Look at me, though! New car! A *Galaxie*, and you beside me..." The Canadian thing start working up she behind beside o' Calvin; she start saying she been going down in the islands for years now, that she have more calypso records than any white woman in Toronto, and she wish she had the money to take them outta storage and play one or two for Calvin. She start singing the tune, and Calvin vex as hell, cause he don't like no woman who does sing calypso, his Old Queen didn' even let him sing calypso when he was a boy in Barbados. And he was a *man*! Besides, the calypso that the Canadian thing singing now is a thing bout "...*three white women travelling through Africa!*", and something bout "*Uh never had a white meat, yet!*", and this nice woman, the simple-looking Canadian girl know all the words, and she enjoying sheself too, and Calvin thinking that Sparrow watching him from through the AM radio thing, and laughing at him, and he vex as shite, cause the calypso mean that certain white women like black men to lash them, and..."Don't sing that!" he order the thing, as if he talking to his wife; and the Canadian thing tell him, in a sharp voice, that she isn' his damn wife, so "Don't you be uppity with me, buster!" Well, who tell she she could talk-back to a Bajan man like Calvin? Calvin slam on the brakes. The motto-car cry out, *screeennnnchhhhhh*! The Canadian thing head hit the windshield, bram! and she neck like it break this time, in truth. The motto-car half-way in the middle o' the highway. Traffics whizzing by, and the wind from them like it want to smash-up Calvin new *Galaxie*. Calvin vex as shite but he can't do nothing cause he trembling like hell: the woman in the front seat turning white-white-white like a piece o' paper, and the blood gone outta she face; Calvin ain' see no dimples in she face; and she ain' moving, she ain' talking, not a muscle ain' shiver. Traffics whizzing by and one come so damn close that Calvin close he eyes, and pray. "Look my blasted crosses! And my *Galaxie* ain' a fucking day old yet!" He try to start-up the motor and the motor only coughing like it have consumption. The woman like she sleeping or dead or something. The calypso still blaring over the AM radio, and Calvin so jittery he can't find the right button to turn the blasted thing off. And sudden so, one of the traffics flying by is a police. Calvin hear, *weeeeeeeeeeeeeeeeeeennnnnnnnnnnnnnnnnnnnnnn*! Sirens! A police car in the rear-view mirror. Calvin stop shaking sudden-sudden. He start thinking. White woman deading in his new motto-car, the car new, and he is a stranger in Canada. He jump out, and lift-up the hood, and he back his new jacket, and he touching this and touching that, playing he is a mechanic. The police stop. He face red as a beet. "What's holding you up, boy!" Calvin hear the "boy," and he get vex, but he can't say nothing, cause they is two against his one, and he remember that he black. But he ain' no damn fool. He talk fast and sweet, and soft, and he impress the police: "...and officer I *just-now-now-now* give this lady a lift as I pass she on the highway, she say she feeling bad, and I was taking she to the hospital, cause as a West Indian I learn how to be a good samaritan, and..." The police ask for the licents, and when he see that the ownership papers say that Calvin only had the car this morning, he smile, and say, "Help me with her in the cruiser. You *are* a good samaritan, fellow. Wish our coloured people were more like you West Indians..." They lift the Canadian thing with she neck half-popped outta the *Galaxie*, and into the cruiser, and

Calvin even had a tear in his eye too. But the police take she way, and the sireen start-up again, weeeeeeennnnnnn... Calvin manage to get the *Galaxie* outta the middle o' the road, the traffics still flying by, but now the new motto-car safe at the side o' the road. He put back on his jacket, and he shrug the jacket in shape and in fit pon his shoulders, he turn off the AM radio thing with the calypso, another calypso it was playing now, and fix the seams in his trousers, look back on the highway in the rear view mirror, start-up the *Galaxie*. He driving slow slow on the highway and the traffics blowing their horn to tell him get the fuck outta the road, nigger, but all the time he smiling and holding his hand outta the window and waving them on. He hold over outta habit to say something to the Canadian thing beside him, forgetting that she ain' there no more, and he still say, "This *Galaxie* is car for so! And godblummuh, look what a close shave I had!" He see the Canadian thing handbag open on the seat beside o' him, and he run his hand through it, searching. It had in five single dollar bills. He snap the handbag shut, leaving the money, touch the automatic window-winder, and throw the blasted handbag out on the Don Valley Parkway road.

(1971)

Alistair MacLeod (b. 1936)

A professor of English and creative writing at the University of Windsor, MacLeod was born in North Battleford, Saskatchewan, but spent his later childhood and teenage years on Nova Scotia's Cape Breton Island, home of his coal miner father. He has published two collections of short stories, *The Lost Salt Gift of Blood* (1976), and *As Birds Bring Forth The Sun* (1986), and a novel, *No Great Mischief* (1999). Most of his stories are set on Cape Breton Island and examine the harsh landscape and the hard lives of coal miners and fishermen as they are remembered by the narrators who have frequently moved away from their childhood homes. "The Boat," MacLeod's first published story, is such a recollection, as a professor in a midwestern American University recalls his childhood and the drowning of his fisherman father. The story incorporates a series of opposites, including the attitudes of the mother and father and the father's life as a fisherman and his unfulfilled desire of attending university. MacLeod's treatment of the perils of being at sea in a small boat provides an interesting contrast to Crane's in "The Open Boat."

THE BOAT

There are times even now, when I awake at four o'clock in the morning with the terrible fear that I have overslept; when I imagine that my father is waiting for me in the room below the darkened stairs or that the shorebound men are tossing pebbles against my window while blowing their hands and stomping their feet impatiently on the frozen steadfast earth. There are times when I am half out of bed and fumbling for socks and mumbling for words before I realize that I am foolishly alone, that no one waits at the base of the stairs and no boat rides restlessly in the waters by the pier.

At such times only the grey corpses on the overflowing ashtray beside my bed bear witness to the extinction of the latest spark and silently await the crushing out of the most recent of their fellows. And then because I am afraid to be alone with death, I dress rapidly, make a great to-do about clearing my throat, turn on both faucets in the sink and proceed to make loud splashing ineffectual noises. Later I go out and walk the mile to the all-night restaurant.

In the winter it is a very cold walk and there are often tears in my eyes when I arrive. The waitress usually gives a sympathetic little shiver and says, "Boy, it must be really cold out there; you got tears in your eyes."

"Yes," I say, "it sure is; it really is."

And then the three or four of us who are always in such places at such times make uninteresting little protective chit-chat until the dawn reluctantly arrives. Then I swallow the coffee which is always bitter and leave with a great busy rush because by that time I have to worry about being late and whether I have a clean shirt and whether my car will start and about all the other countless things one must worry about when he teaches at a great Midwestern university. And I know then that that day will go by as have all the days of the past ten years, for the call and the voices and the shapes and the boat were not really there in the early morning's darkness and I have all kinds of comforting reality to prove it. They are only shadows and echoes, the animals a child's hands make on the wall by lamplight, and the voices from the rain barrel; the cuttings from an old movie made in the black and white of long ago.

I first became conscious of the boat in the same way and at almost the same time that I became aware of the people it supported. My earliest recollection of my father is a view from the floor of gigantic rubber boots and then of being suddenly elevated and having my face pressed against the stubble of his cheek, and of how it tasted of salt and of how he smelled of salt from his red-soled rubber boots to the shaggy whiteness of his hair.

When I was very small, he took me for my first ride in the boat. I rode the half-mile from our house to the wharf on his shoulders and I remember the sound of his rubber boots galumphing along the gravel beach, the tune of the indecent little song he used to sing, and the odour of the salt.

The floor of the boat was permeated with the same odour and in its constancy I was not aware of change. In the harbour we made our little circle and returned. He tied the boat by its painter, fastened the stern to its permanent anchor and lifted me high over his head to the solidity of the wharf. Then he climbed up the little iron ladder that led to the wharf's cap, placed me once more upon his shoulders and galumphed off again.

When we returned to the house everyone made a great fuss over my precocious excursion and asked, "How did you like the boat?" "Were you afraid in the boat?" "Did you cry in the boat?" They repeated "the boat" at the end of all their questions and I knew it must be very important to everyone.

10   My earliest recollection of my mother is of being alone with her in the mornings while my father was away in the boat. She seemed to be always repairing clothes that were "torn in the boat," preparing food "to be eaten in the boat" or looking for "the boat" through our kitchen window which faced upon the sea. When my father returned about noon, she would ask, "Well, how did things go in the boat today?" It was the first question I remember asking: "Well, how did things go in the boat today?" "Well, how did things go in the boat today?"

The boat in our lives was registered at Port Hawkesbury. She was what Nova Scotians called a Cape Island boat and was designed for the small inshore fishermen who sought the lobsters of the spring and mackerel of summer and later the cod and haddock and hake. She was thirty-two feet long and nine wide, and was powered by an engine from a Chevrolet truck. She had a marine clutch and a high speed reverse gear and was painted light green with the name *Jenny Lynn* stencilled in black letters on her bow and painted on an oblong plate across her stern. Jenny Lynn had my mother's maiden name and the boat was called after her as another link in the chain of tradition. Most of the boats that berthed at the wharf bore the names of some female member of their owner's household.

I say this now as if I knew it all then. All at once, all about the boat dimensions and engines, and as if on the day of my first childish voyage I noticed the difference between a stencilled name and a painted name. But of course it was not that way at all, for I learned it all very slowly and there was not time enough.

I learned first about our house which was one of about fifty which marched around the horseshoe of our harbour and the wharf which was its heart. Some of them were so close to the water that during a storm the sea spray splashed against their windows while others were built farther along the beach as was the case with ours. The houses and their people, like those of the neighbouring towns and villages, were the result of Ireland's discontent and Scotland's Highland Clearances and America's War of Independence. Impulsive emotional Catholic Celts who could not bear to live with England and shrewd determined Protestant Puritans who, in the years after 1776,[1] could not bear to live without.

The most important room in our house was one of those oblong old-fashioned kitchens heated by a wood- and coal-burning stove. Behind the stove was a box of kindlings and beside it a coal scuttle. A heavy wooden table with leaves that expanded or reduced its dimensions stood in the middle of the floor. There were five wooden home-made chairs which had been chipped and hacked by a variety of knives. Against the east wall, opposite the stove, there was a couch which sagged in the middle and had a cushion for a pillow, and above it a shelf which contained matches, tobacco, pencils, odd fish-hooks, bits of twine, and a tin can filled with bills and receipts. The south wall was dominated by a window which faced the sea and on the north there was a five-foot board which bore a variety of clothes hooks and the burdens of each. Beneath the board there was jumble of odd footwear, mostly of rubber. There was also, on this wall, a barometer, a map of the marine area and a shelf which held a tiny radio. The kitchen was shared by all of us and was a buffer zone between the immaculate order of ten other rooms and the disruptive chaos of the single room that was my father's.

15   My mother ran her house as her brothers ran their boats. Everything was clean and spotless and in order. She was tall and dark and powerfully energetic. In later years she reminded me of the women of Thomas Hardy, particularly Eustacia Vye,[2] in a physical way. She fed and clothed a family of seven children, making all of the meals and most of the clothes. She grew miraculous gardens and magnificent flowers and raised broods of hens and ducks. She would walk miles on berry-picking expeditions and hoist her skirts to dig for clams when the tide was low. She was fourteen years younger than my father, whom she had married when she was twenty-six and had been a local beauty for a period of ten years. My mother was of the sea as were all of her people, and her horizons were the very literal ones she scanned with her dark and fearless eyes.

Between the kitchen clothes rack and barometer, a door opened into my father's bedroom. It was a room of disorder and disarray. It was as if this wind which so often clamoured about the house succeeded in entering this single

1   after the American Declaration of Independence many British colonists moved to Nova Scotia.
2   the passionate and unhappy heroine of British novelist Thomas Hardy's *The Return of the Native* (1878) drowns.

room and after whipping it into turmoil stole quietly away to renew its knowing laughter from without.

My father's bed was against the south wall. It always looked rumpled and unmade because he lay on top of it more than he slept within any folds it might have had. Beside it, there was a little brown table. An archaic goose-necked reading light, a battered table radio, a mound of wooden matches, one or two packages of tobacco, a deck of cigarette papers and an overflowing ashtray cluttered its surface. The brown larvae of tobacco shreds and the grey flecks of ash covered both the table and the floor beneath it. The once-varnished surface of the table was disfigured by numerous black scars and gashes inflicted by the neglected burning cigarettes of many years. They had tumbled from the ashtray unnoticed and branded their statements permanently and quietly into the wood until the odour of their burning caused the snuffing out of their lives. At the bed's foot there was a single window which looked upon the sea.

Against the adjacent wall there was a battered bureau and beside it there was a closet which held his single ill-fitting serge suit, the two or three white shirts that strangled him and the square black shoes that pinched. When he took off his more friendly clothes, the heavy woollen sweaters, mitts and socks which my mother knitted for him and the woollen and doeskin shirts, he dumped them unceremoniously on a single chair. If a visitor entered the room while he was lying on the bed, he would be told to throw the clothes on the floor and take their place upon the chair.

Magazines and books covered the battered bureau and competed with the clothes for domination of the chair. They furthered overburdened the heroic little table and lay on top of the radio. They filled a baffling and unknowable cave beneath the bed, and in the corner by the bureau they spilled from the walls and grew up from the floor.

20   The magazines were the most conventional: *Time, Newsweek, Life, Maclean's, Family Herald, Reader's Digest.* They were the result of various cut-rate subscriptions or the gift subscriptions associated with Christmas, "the two whole years for only $3.50."

The books were more varied. There were a few hard-cover magnificents and bygone Book-of-the-Month wonders and some were Christmas or birthday gifts. The majority of them, however, were used paperbacks which came from those second-hand bookstores which advertise in the backs of magazines: "Miscellaneous Used Paperbacks 10¢ Each." At first he sent for them himself, although my mother resented the expense, but in later years they came more and more often from my sisters who had moved to the cities. Especially at first they were very weird and varied. Mickey Spillane and Ernest Haycox vied with Dostoyevsky and Faulkner, and the Penguin Poets edition of Gerard Manley Hopkins[3] arrived in the same box as a little book on sex technique called *Getting the Most Out of Love.* The former had been assiduously annotated by a very fine hand using a very blue-inked fountain pen while the latter had been studied by some with very large

---

3 Spillane and Haycox were writers of popular detectitve novels and westerns respectively; nineteenth-century Russian novelist Fyodor Dostoyevsky wrote *Crime and Punishment* and *The Brothers Karamazov;* Faulkner, twentieth-century American author, wrote novels about the American South (see page 144); Hopkins, nineteenth century English poet.

thumbs, the prints of which were still visible in the margins. At the slightest provocation it would open almost automatically to particularly graphic and well-smudged pages.

When he was not in the boat, my father spent most of his time lying on the bed in his socks, the top two buttons of his trousers undone, his discarded shirt on the ever-ready chair and the sleeves of the woollen Stanfield underwear, which he wore both summer and winter, drawn half way up to his elbows. The pillows propped up the whiteness of his head and the goose-necked lamp illuminated the pages in his hands. The cigarettes smoked and smouldered on the ashtray and on the table and the radio played constantly, sometimes low and sometimes loud. At midnight and at one, two, three and four, one could sometimes hear the radio, his occasional cough, the rustling thud of a completed book being tossed to the corner heap, or the movement necessitated by his sitting on the edge of the bed to roll the thousandth cigarette. He seemed never to sleep, only to doze, and the light shone constantly from his window to the sea.

My mother despised the room and all it stood for and she had stopped sleeping in it after I was born. She despised disorder in rooms and in houses and in hours and in lives, and she had not read a book since high school. There she had read *Ivanhoe*[4] and considered it a colossal waste of time. Still the room remained, like a solid rock of opposition in the sparkling waters of a clear deep harbour, opening off the kitchen where we really lived our lives, with its door always open and its contents visible to all.

The daughters of the room and of the house were very beautiful. They were tall and willowy like my mother and had her fine facial features set off the reddish copper-coloured hair that had apparently once been my father's before it turned to white. All of them were very clever in school and helped my mother a great deal about the house. When they were young they sang and were very happy and very nice to me because I was the youngest and the family's only boy.

My father never approved of their playing about the wharf like the other children, and they went there only when my mother sent them on an errand. At such times they almost always overstayed, playing screaming games of tag or hide-and-seek in and about the fishing shanties, the piled traps and tubs of trawl, shouting down to the perch that swam languidly about the wharf's algae-covered piles, or jumping in and out of the boats that tugged gently at their lines. My mother was never uneasy about them at such times, and when her husband criticized her she would say, "Nothing will happen to them there," or "They could be doing worse things in worse places."

By about the ninth or tenth grade my sisters one by one discovered my father's bedroom and then the change would begin. Each would go into the room one morning when he was out. She would go with the ideal hope of imposing order or with the more practical objective of emptying the ashtray, and later she would be found spellbound by the volume in her hand. My mother's reaction was always abrupt, bordering on the angry. "Take your nose out of that trash and come and do your work," she would say, and once I saw

4 Sir Walter Scott's 1819 novel of adventure is set in the early middle ages and was a standard English high school text in the first half of the twentieth century.

her slap my youngest sister so hard that the print of her hand was scarletly emblazoned upon her daughter's cheek while the broken-spined paperback fluttered uselessly to the floor.

Thereafter my mother would launch a campaign against what she had discovered but could not understand. At times although she was not overly religious she would bring in God to bolster her arguments, saying, "In the next world God will see to those who waste their lives reading useless books when they should be about their work." Or without theological aid, "I would like to know how books help anyone to live a life." If my father were in, she would repeat the remarks louder than necessary, and her voice would carry into his room where he lay upon his bed. His usual reaction was to turn up the volume of the radio, although that action in itself betrayed the success of the initial thrust.

Shortly after my sisters began to read the books, they grew restless and lost interest in darning socks and baking bread, and all of them eventually went to work as summer waitresses in the Sea Food Restaurant. The restaurant was run by a big American concern from Boston and catered to the tourists that flooded the area during July and August. My mother despised the whole operation. She said the restaurant was not run by "our people," and "our people" did not eat there, and that it was run by outsiders for outsiders.

"Who are these people anyway?" she would ask, tossing back her dark hair, "and what do they, though they go about with their cameras for a hundred years, know about the way it is here, and what do they care about me and mine, and why should I care about them?"

30   She was angry that my sisters should even conceive of working in such a place and more angry when my father made no move to prevent it, and she was worried about herself and about her family and about her life. Sometimes she would say softly to her sisters, "I don't know what's the matter with my girls. It seems none of them are interested in any of the right things." And sometimes there would be bitter savage arguments. One afternoon I was coming in with three mackerel I'd been given at the wharf when I heard her say, "Well I hope you'll be satisfied when they come home knocked up and you'll have had your way."

It was the most savage thing I'd ever heard my mother say. Not just the words but the way she said them, and I stood there in the porch afraid to breathe for what seemed like the years from ten to fifteen, feeling the damp moist mackerel with their silver glassy eyes growing clammy against my leg.

Through the angle in the screen door I saw my father who had been walking into his room wheel around on one of his rubber-booted heels and look at her with his blue eyes flashing like clearest ice beneath the snow that was his hair. His usually ruddy face was drawn and grey, reflecting the exhaustion of a man of sixty-five who had been working in those rubber boots for eleven hours on an August day, and for a fleeting moment I wondered what I would do if he killed my mother while I stood there in the porch with those three foolish mackerel in my hand. Then he turned and went into his room and the radio blared forth the next day's weather forecast and I retreated under the noise and returned again, stamping my feet and slamming the door too loudly to signal my approach. My mother was busy at the stove when I came in, and did not raise her head when I threw the mackerel in a pan. As I looked into my father's room, I said, "Well, how did things go in the boat today?" and he replied, "Oh not too badly, all things considered." He was lying on his back and lighting the first cigarette and the radio was talking about the Virginia coast.

All of my sisters made good money on tips. They bought my father an electric razor which he tried to use for a while and they took out even more magazine subscriptions. They bought my mother a great many clothes of the type she was very fond of, the wide-brimmed hats and the brocaded dresses, but she locked them all in trunks and refused to wear any of them.

On one August day my sisters prevailed upon my father to take some of their restaurant customers for an afternoon ride in the boat. The tourists with their expensive clothes and cameras and sun glasses awkwardly backed down the iron ladder at the wharf's side to where my father waited below, holding the rocking Jenny Lynn in snug against the wharf with one hand on the iron ladder and steadying his descending passengers with the other. They tried to look both prim and wind-blown like the girls in the Pepsi-Cola ads and did the best they could, sitting on the thwarts where the newspapers were spread to cover the splattered blood and fish entrails, crowding to one side so that they were in danger of capsizing the boat, taking the inevitable pictures or merely trailing their fingers through the water of their dreams.

35 All of them liked my father very much and, after he'd brought them back from their circles in the harbour, they invited him to their rented cabins which were located high on a hill overlooking the village to which they were so alien. He proceeded to get very drunk up there with the beautiful view and the strange company and the abundant liquor, and late in the afternoon he began to sing.

I was just approaching the wharf to deliver my mother's summons when he began, and the familiar yet unfamiliar voice that rolled down from the cabins made me feel as I had never felt before in my young life or perhaps as I had always felt without really knowing it, and I was ashamed yet proud, young yet old and saved yet forever lost, and there was nothing I could do to control my legs which trembled nor my eyes which wept for what they could not tell.

The tourists were equipped with tape recorders and my father sang for more than three hours. His voice boomed down the hill and bounced off the surface of the harbour, which was an unearthly blue on that hot August day, and was then reflected to the wharf and the fishing shanties where it was absorbed amidst the men who were baiting their lines for the next day's haul.

He sang all the old sea chanties which had come across from the old world and by which men like him had pulled ropes for generations, and he sang the East Coast sea songs which celebrated the sealing vessels of Northumberland Strait and the long liners of the Grand Banks, and of Anticosti, Sable Island, Grand Manan, Boston Harbor, Nantucket and Block Island. Gradually he shifted to the seemingly unending Gaelic drinking songs with their twenty or more verses and inevitable refrains, and the men in the shanties smiled at the coarseness of some of the verses and at the thought that the singer's immediate audience did not know what they were applauding nor recording to take back to staid old Boston. Later as the sun was setting he switched to the laments and the wild and haunting Gaelic war songs of those spattered Highland ancestors he had never seen, and when his voice ceased, the savage melancholy of three hundred years seemed to hang over the peaceful harbour and the quiet boats and the men leaning in the doorways of their shanties with their cigarettes glowing in the dusk and the women looking to the sea from their open windows with their children in their arms.

When he came home he threw the money he had earned on the kitchen table as he did with all his earnings but my mother refused to touch it and the next day he went with the rest of the men to bait his trawl in the shanties. The tourists came to the door that evening and my mother met them there and told them that her husband was not in although he was lying on the bed only a few feet away with the radio playing and the cigarette upon his lips. She stood in the doorway until they reluctantly went away.

40   In the winter they sent him a picture which had been taken on the day of the singing. On the back it said, "To Our Ernest Hemingway" and the "Our" was underlined. There was also an accompanying letter telling how much they had enjoyed themselves, how popular the tape was proving and explaining who Ernest Hemingway was. In a way it almost did look like one of those unshaven, taken-in-Cuba pictures of Hemingway. He looked both massive and incongruous in the setting. His bulky fisherman's clothes were too big for the green and white lawn chair in which he sat, and his rubber boots seemed to take up all of the well-clipped grass square. The beach umbrella jarred with his sunburned face and because he had already been singing for some time, his lips which chapped in the winds of spring and burned in the water glare of summer had already cracked in several places, producing tiny flecks of blood at their corners and on the whiteness of his teeth. The bracelets of brass chain which he wore to protect his wrists from chafing seemed abnormally large and his broad leather belt had been slackened and his heavy shirt and underwear were open at the throat revealing an uncultivated wilderness of white chest hair bordering on the semicontrolled stubble of his neck and chin. His blue eyes had looked directly into the camera and his hair was whiter than the two tiny clouds which hung over his left shoulder. The sea was behind him and its immense blue flatness stretched out to touch the arching blueness of the sky. It seemed very far away from him or else he was so much in the foreground that he seemed too big for it.

Each year another of my sisters would read the books and work in the restaurant. Sometimes they would stay out quite late on the hot summer nights and when they came up the stairs my mother would ask them many long and involved questions which they resented and tried to avoid. Before ascending the stairs they would go into my father's room and those of us who waited above could hear them throwing his clothes off the chair before sitting on it or the squeak of the bed as they sat on its edge. Sometimes they would talk to him a long time, the murmur of their voices blending with the music of the radio into a mysterious vapour-like sound which floated softly up the stairs.

I say this again as if it all happened at once and as if all my sisters were of identical ages and like so many lemmings going into another sea and, again, it was of course not that way at all. Yet go they did, to Boston, to Montreal, to New York with the young men they met during the summers and later married in those far-away cities. The young men were very articulate and handsome and wore fine clothes and drove expensive cars and my sisters, as I said, were very tall and beautiful with their copper-coloured hair and were tired of darning socks and baking bread.

One by one they went. My mother had each of her daughters for fifteen years, then lost them for two and finally forever. None married a fisherman. My mother never accepted any of the young men, for in her eyes they seemed always a combination of the lazy, the effeminate, the dishonest and the unknown. They never seemed to do any physical work and she could not comprehend their luxurious vacations and she did not know whence they came nor who they were. And in the end she did not really care, for they were not of her people and they were not of her sea.

I say this now with a sense of wonder at my own stupidity in thinking I was somehow free and would go on doing well in school and playing and helping in the boat and passing into my early teens while streaks of grey began to appear in my mother's dark hair and my father's rubber boots dragged sometimes on the pebbles of the beach as he trudged home from the wharf. And there were but three of us in the house that had at one time been so loud.

45   Then during the winter that I was fifteen he seemed to grow old and ill all at once. Most of January he lay upon the bed, smoking and reading and listening to the radio while the wind howled about the house and the needle-like snow blistered off the ice-covered harbour and the doors flew out of people's hands if they did not cling to them like death.

In February when the men began overhauling their lobster traps he still did not move, and my mother and I began to knit lobster trap headings in the evenings. The twine was as always very sharp and harsh, and blisters formed upon our thumbs and little paths of blood snaked quietly down between our fingers while the seals that had drifted down from distant Labrador wept and moaned like human children on the ice-floes of the Gulf.

In the daytime my mother's brother who had been my father's partner as long as I could remember also came to work upon the gear. He was a year older than my mother and was tall and dark and the father of twelve children.

By March we were very far behind and although I began to work very hard in the evenings I knew it was not hard enough and that there were but eight weeks left before the opening of the season on May first. And I knew that my mother worried and that my uncle was uneasy and that all of our very lives depended on the boat being ready with her gear and two men, by the date of May the first. And I knew then that *David Copperfield* and *The Tempest*[5] and all those friends I had dearly come to love must really go forever. So I bade them all good-bye.

·

5   published in 1849-50, *David Copperfield*, the semi-autobiographical novel by Charles Dickens, traces the hero's life from his poor and unhappy childhood to his success as an author; *The Tempest* is a play by William Shakespeare.

The night after my first full day at home and after my mother had gone upstairs he called me into his room where I sat upon the chair beside his bed. "You will go back tomorrow," he said simply.

50   I refused then, saying I had made my decision and was satisfied.

"That is no way to make a decision," he said, "and if you are satisfied I am not. It is best that you go back." I was almost angry then and told him as all children do that I wished he would leave me alone and stop telling me what to do.

He looked at me a long time then, lying there on the same bed on which he had fathered me those sixteen years before, fathered me his only son, out of who knew what emotions when he was already fifty-six and his hair had turned to snow. Then he swung his legs over the edge of the squeaking bed and sat facing me and looked into my own dark eyes with his crystal blue and placed his hand upon my knee. "I am not telling you to do anything," he said softly, "only asking you."

The next morning I returned to school. As I left, my mother followed me to the porch and said, "I never thought a son of mine would choose useless books over the parents that gave him life."

In the weeks that followed he got up rather miraculously and the gear was ready and the *Jenny Lynn* was freshly painted by the last two weeks of April when the ice began to break up and the lonely screaming gulls returned to haunt the silver herring as they flashed within the sea.

55   On the first day of May the boats raced out as they had always done, laden down almost to the gunwales with their heavy cargoes of traps. They were almost like living things as they plunged through the waters of the spring and manoeuvred between the still floating icebergs of crystal white emerald green on their way to the traditional grounds that they sought out every May. And those of us who sat that day in the high school on the hill, discussing the water imagery of Tennyson, watched them as they passed back and forth beneath us until by afternoon the piles of traps which had been stacked upon the wharf were no longer visible but were spread about the bottom of the sea. And the *Jenny Lynn* went too, all day, with my uncle tall and dark, like a latter-day Tashtego[6] standing at the tiller with his legs wide apart and guiding her deftly between the floating pans of ice and my father in the stern standing in the same way with his hands upon the ropes that lashed to the cargo to the deck. And at night my mother asked, "Well, how did things go in the boat today?"

And the spring wore on and the summer came and school ended in the third week of June and the lobster season on July first and I wished that the two things I loved so dearly did not exclude each other in a manner that was so blunt and too clear.

At the conclusion of the lobster season my uncle said he had been offered a berth on a deep sea dragger and had decided to accept. We all knew that he was leaving the *Jenny Lynn* forever and that before the next lobster season he would buy a boat of his own. He was expecting another child and would be supporting fifteen people by the next spring and could not chance my father against the family that he loved.

---

6   a Native American harpooner in American novelist Herman Melville's 1851 novel *Moby-Dick*.

I joined my father then for the trawling season, and he made no protest and my mother was quite happy. Through the summer we baited the tubs of trawl in the afternoon and set them at sunset and revisited them in the darkness of the early morning. The men would come tramping by our house at four A.M. and we would join them and walk with them to the wharf and be on our way before the sun rose out of the ocean where it seemed to spend the night. If I was not up they would toss pebbles to my window and I would be very embarrassed and tumble downstairs to where my father lay fully clothed atop his bed, reading his book and listening to his radio and smoking his cigarette. When I appeared he would swing off his bed and put on his boots and be instantly ready and then we would take the lunches my mother had prepared the night before and walk off toward the sea. He would make no attempt to wake me himself.

It was in many ways a good summer. There were few storms and we were out almost every day and we lost a minimum of gear and seemed to land a maximum of fish and I tanned dark and brown after the manner of my uncles.

60 My father did not tan — he never tanned — because of his reddish complexion, and the salt water irritated his skin as it had for sixty years. He burned and reburned over and over again and his lips still cracked so that they bled when he smiled, and his arms, especially the left, still broke out into the oozing saltwater boils as they had ever since as a child I had first watched him soaking and bathing them in a variety of ineffectual solutions. The chafe-preventing bracelets of brass linked chain that all the men wore about their wrists in early spring were his the full season and he shaved but painfully and only once a week.

And I saw then, that summer, many things that I had seen all my life as if for the first time and I thought that perhaps my father had never been intended for a fisherman either physically or mentally. At least not in the manner of my uncles; he had never really loved it. And I remembered that, one evening in his room when we were talking about *David Copperfield*, he had said that he had always wanted to go to the university and I had dismissed it then in the way one dismisses his father's saying he would like to be a tight-rope walker, and we had gone on to talk about the Peggottys and how they loved the sea.[7]

And I thought then to myself that there were many things wrong with all of us and all our lives and I wondered why my father, who was himself an only son, had not married before he was forty and then I wondered why he had. I even thought that perhaps he had had to marry my mother and checked the dates on the flyleaf of the Bible where I learned that my oldest sister had been born a prosaic eleven months after the marriage, and I felt myself then very dirty and debased for my lack of faith and for what I had thought and done.

And then there came into my heart a very great love for my father and I thought it was very much braver to spend a life doing what you really do not want rather than selfishly following forever your own dreams and inclinations. And I knew then that I could never leave him alone to suffer the iron-tipped harpoons which my mother would forever hurl into his soul because he

7 characters in *David Copperfield*.

was a failure as a husband and a father who had retained none of his own. And I felt that I had been very small in a little secret place within me and that even the completion of high school was for me a silly shallow selfish dream.

So I told him one night very resolutely and very powerfully that I would remain with him as long as he lived and we would fish the sea together. And he made no protest but only smiled through the cigarette smoke that wreathed his bed and replied, "I hope you will remember what you've said."

65   The room was now so filled with books as to be almost Dickensian, but he would not allow my mother to move or change them and he continued to read them, sometimes two or three a night. They came with great regularity now, and there were more hard covers, sent by my sisters who had gone so long ago and now seemed so distant and so prosperous, and sent also pictures of small red-haired grandchildren with baseball bats and dolls which he placed upon his bureau and which my mother gazed at wistfully when she thought no one would see. Red-haired grandchildren with baseball bats and dolls who would never know the sea in hatred or in love.

And so we fished through the heat of August and into the cooler days of September when the water was so clear we could almost see the bottom and the white mists rose like delicate ghosts in the early morning dawn. And one day my mother said to me, "You have given added years to his life."

And we fished on into October when it began to roughen and we could no longer risk night sets but took our gear out each morning and returned at the first sign of the squalls; and on into November when we lost three tubs of trawl and the clear blue water turned to a sullen grey and the trochoidal[8] waves rolled rough and high and washed across our bows and decks as we ran within their troughs. We wore heavy sweaters now and the awkward rubber slickers and the heavy woollen mitts which soaked and froze into masses of ice that hung from our wrists like the limbs of gigantic monsters until we thawed them against the exhaust pipe's heat. And almost every day we would leave for home before noon, driven by the blasts of the northwest wind, coating our eyebrows with ice and freezing our eyelids closed as we leaned into a visibility that was hardly there, charting our course from the compass and the sea, running with the waves and between them but never confronting their towering might.

And I stood at the tiller now, on these homeward lunges, stood in the place and in the manner of my uncle, turning to look at my father and to shout over the roar of the engine and the slop of the sea to where he stood in the stern, drenched and dripping with the snow and the salt and the spray and his bushy eyebrows caked in ice. But on November twenty-first, when it seemed we might be making the final run of the season, I turned and he was not there and I knew even in that instant that he would never be again.

On November twenty-first the waves of the grey Atlantic are very very high and the waters are very cold and there are no signposts on the surface of the sea. You cannot tell where you have been five minutes before and in the squalls of snow you cannot see. And it takes longer than you would believe to

8   rolling in circles.

check a boat that has been running before a gale and turn her ever so carefully in a wide and stupid circle, with timbers creaking and straining, back into the face of the storm. And you know it is useless and that your voice does not carry the length of the boat and that even if you knew the original spot, the relentless waves would carry such a burden perhaps a mile or so by the time you could return. And you know also, the final irony, that your father like your uncles and all the men that form your past, cannot swim a stroke.

The lobster beds off the Cape Breton coast are still very rich and now, from May to July, their offerings are packed in crates of ice, and thundered by the gigantic transport trucks, day and night, through New Glasgow, Amherst, Saint John and Bangor and Portland and into Boston where they are tossed still living into boiling pots of water, their final home.

And though the prices are higher and the competition tighter, the grounds to which the *Jenny Lynn* once went remain untouched and unfished as they have for the last ten years. For if there are no signposts on the sea in storm there are certain ones in calm and the lobster bottoms were distributed in calm before any of us can remember and the grounds my father fished were those his father fished before him and there were others before and before and before. Twice the big boats have come from forty and fifty miles, lured by the promise of the grounds, and strewn the bottom with their traps and twice they have returned to find their buoys cut adrift and their gear lost and destroyed. Twice the Fisheries Officer and the Mounted Police have come and asked many long and involved questions and twice they have received no answers from the men leaning in the doors of their shanties and the women standing at their windows with their children in their arms. Twice they have gone away saying: "There are no legal boundaries in the Marine area"; "No one can own the sea"; "Those grounds don't wait for anyone."

But the men and the women, with my mother dark among them, do not care for what they say, for to them the grounds are sacred and they think they wait for me.

It is not an easy thing to know that your mother lives alone on an inadequate insurance policy and that she is too proud to accept any other aid. And that she looks through her lonely window onto the ice of winter and the hot flat calm of summer and the rolling waves of fall. And that she lies awake in the early morning's darkness when the rubber boots of the men scrunch upon the gravel as they pass beside her house on their way down to the wharf. And she knows that the footsteps never stop, because no man goes from her house, and she alone of all the Lynns has neither son nor son-in-law that walks toward the boat that will take him to the sea. And it is not an easy thing to know that your mother looks upon the sea with love and on you with bitterness because the one has been so constant and the other so untrue.

But neither is it easy to know that your father was found on November twenty-eighth, ten miles to the north and wedged between two boulders at the base of the rock-strewn cliffs where he had been hurled and slammed so many many times. His hands were shredded ribbons as were his feet which had lost their boots to the suction of the sea, and his shoulders came apart in our hands when we tried to move him from the rocks. And the fish had eaten his testicles and the gulls had pecked out his eyes and the white-green stubble of his whiskers had continued to grow in death, like the grass on graves, upon the purple, bloated mass that was his face. There was not much left of my father, physically, as he lay there with the brass chains on his wrists and the seaweed in his hair.

(1968)

INTERVIEW
with Alistair MacLeod

Q. *It has been said that authors draw on the depths of their lives and on the literature that has become important in their lives. Do you agree with this statement and does it apply to your own writing?*

A. I think because I write in the first person, a lot of people think these stories are autobiographical. If you read a whole bunch of them, one is disabused of that notion. But none of them are; none of the events happened to me. But they sound autobiographical. I think that's a result of the technique; because obviously you want the reader to believe that such and such is true.

Q. *But readers do get a tremendous sense of the land and the people of Cape Breton Island; in that sense it could be said that the stories do come from you because you lived there so long.*

A. Well, I think that all authors come from some place; I am knowledgeable concerning that area of the country.

Q. *How about literature? Your characters talk a lot about literature in "The Boat" — Hemingway, Dickens, Haycox, Spillane. Literature seems to be very important to them.*

A. In "The Boat," literature isn't important to the mother, who once read *Ivanhoe* and decides never to do that again. But it is important to some of the characters; it's a kind of link to the larger world. In other cases, literature reinforces the kind of life that you lead. Sometimes it shows there are other ways of leading life than the way you are; and then sometimes it re-emphasizes the life you are leading. You see that the struggles you're going through aren't uniquely yours, or you're not the first person to deal with choice or loss or whatever.

Q. *How did you decide to become a writer? Was there a specific "moment of calling" or "epiphany?"*

A. No, I don't think so. I always liked to read. I think I was like someone with athletic or singing ability, who never took it seriously. In 1963, I went away to the United States to do a Ph.D. One of the things you do in studying for a

Ph.D. is read a lot of literature, study and analyze it. So I began to think then, that instead of analyzing other people's stories, perhaps I could write my own. The other thing was that when I was away from my particular Canadian land-scape, I began to think of it more carefully. If you're in something all the time, you just say this is the way it is. When you move away, you look back and notice that this was going on or that was going on. It's kind of like being a certain age and looking back on your childhood and realizing that there were more things going on than you recognized when you were in the midst of it all. I find that when I go to Europe I think of Canada in a different way. Maybe I make comparisons, or maybe I just become more thoughtful. As I said earlier, if you're just in the midst of your own kitchen all the time, you think of it as the world, and you don't think of it being interrelated to so many other things.

Q. *How did "The Boat" evolve?*

A. I wanted to write a story about choice, how sometimes choices are foisted upon you and sometimes you make your own. I was interested in the idea of the spider web, of all the things that go forward from a single action. I also wanted to write a story in which there were essentially no villains; I liked everybody in that story. I like to do that with all my work. I think that very often there are people who have good ideas as far as the individual's life is concerned, but these may not always be the best ideas for others. I thought about particular occupations, those that are hereditary occupations. And I thought about doing what you want to do yourself; or doing what your father wants you to do, what your mother wants you to do, and so on. So I was inter-ested in those kinds of issues. I was also interested in the gender and age of the people, because I thought it was important. Because fishing was then a man's job, I thought it was important that the narrator was born when the father was fifty-six and he was an only son and the last of his parents' children. All of this has a bearing, I hope, on the story. If his father were twenty when the boy was born, it would be very different, or if the boy were one of eleven sons it would be different instead of being the only son born into the relative old age of his parents.

Q. *There are a lot of dichotomies in the story: the boy versus sisters, Cape Breton contrasted to away, father and mother, land and sea, life and death. Is there any sense that these could be resolved? As I reread the stories in* Island *over the last couple of weeks, I felt that the tensions were stronger than the possibilities of resolution in the lives of the characters.*

A. There's a section in "The Boat" where the boy goes back to school and he thinks, "Well, maybe I could just stay studying the water imagery in Tennyson and fishing at the same time." But that's an impossible thing to do given his circumstances. The father is an example of someone like that. He fishes all his life and he doesn't like it, or he thinks he's not very good at it.

Maybe he should have been a literature professor. I think I was interested in looking at our parents' lives. When you're children, you just think, well, your parents are always there. You don't think of your parents as having been fourteen or fifteen because you come into their lives when they are adults. That's all you know of them. He has the chance to think, maybe his father wasn't always this way. Maybe his mother wasn't always that way. But maybe she was — I see her as being more consistent than the father, or more stable in some ways — whether that's good or bad — in her belief. I see her as someone who really knows how to lead a life.

Q. *She's a real pragmatist.*

A. Yes, she is. She does know how to live a life. But it may not be the life for everyone. She thinks of her children who want to lead a life different from hers as frivolous, or disloyal, or silly; but they're not.

Q. *You talked about water imagery in Tennyson. But there's a big difference between the Lady of Shalott floating down the river in a boat, and the fishing boat as a fragile thing and a vital link with the sea, a place so filled with danger.*

A. Young people at university or college, just study what's given them. And if they come from a certain background and they encounter this kind of water — Tennyson's water — they may say this is not the way I see it. But nonetheless, if you're going to pass the exam, this is what you study. I was interested in the irony of that.

Q. *You also refer to Shakespeare's* The Tempest. *And it seems there's a greater affinity to that work in "The Boat": the drowned sailor, the death by water in* The Tempest, *and the father-son relationship.*

A. I think that when you go to university, you are presented with this material and you say, oh, this is interesting, or not interesting or so on. But I think a lot of it does stick with you and becomes a part of your repertorie, your internal makeup, and then you apply it or don't apply it.

Q. *Did you write "The Boat" when you were still in Indiana?*

A. Yes, I was interested in some person who was a long way from where he came from — different landscape, different kind of people. I thought it was an interesting tension. One of the things I was interested in in that character was that he goes away and is successful. But it's not easy. If he'd stayed home — it wouldn't be easy either. It wasn't easy for the father. You pay a price for everything you do, no matter what the choice may be.

Q. *You mentioned how, when you were in Indiana, or Windsor, or Europe, you looked back and thought about where you had come from. There's a children's writer who uses the term "rememory" about her writing, and a lot of what the characters do are as much about remembering as about what they remember. I got a sense in reading "The Boat" that a lot was about remembering the past as a way of keeping it alive, as a way of understanding yourself.*

A. I was interested in that type of character. He's not particularly stupid. I just think that memory is with us a long time — with some people for a long time, certainly for him. And, in the end, he's never going to get over the fact that his mother thinks of him as not doing what she would want him to do, in fact none of her family — they've all gone into the larger world and she says: "None of my family want to do the right things." I think of her as someone — who tried to do her very best, and she feels a failure. But she's not. It's just that what she wants is not necessarily what others want. And I think that that kind of tension occurs when a new world comes into an older world. And no matter what way you go you're going to suffer some kind of pain. Given the way that story was set up — as I said before, if there were eleven sons in that family, maybe three would be happy in the boat and the other eight would be neurosurgeons or something like that. But that's not the kind of family they are, and that's not what's given them. They are unique in their own way.

Q. *The mothers and grandmothers are very strong in your stories.*

A. I think that they have a kind of certainty. And at certain stages in history, in that kind of landscape, women who stayed in the home were in control of their homes. When men went out they had to change their accent, change their language, had to learn new skills to stay alive. There would be a different kind of pressure on them. Maybe they wouldn't work as hard as the women, but they would be under a different kind of pressure. The man would go forth to do his work, not necessarily fishing, but in industry of some kind, at seven-thirty in the morning. He would go forth to a different kind of work than his wife and mother. One way of looking at that is in terms of tradition: women would be able to keep traditions longer than men because they would be in control of their own domains. If you go forth as a man, you would be more buffeted by the modern world.

Q. *Is that, perhaps, why the mother is so disgusted with the father when he sings for the tourists.*

A. She thinks of those summer people as frivolous. She's not given to artistic expression very much. And she sees them as tampering with her life in the same way that she sees the seafood restaurant as being not a great economic opportunity for her daughters, but as being a seductive force which will lead them away from what she has tried to teach them. And in those suspicions she is probably right.

Q. *I noticed in your stories a tremendous amount of love and respect for the people who stayed on Cape Breton Island and a more ambiguous attitude to those who moved away.*

A. I think people who stay there live a certain kind of life. You can live it well. People who go away, who become college professors or whatever, live different lives. Again, it's just people wanting different things, needing different things. I try to be as tolerant as I can. People who move inland to Toronto or Lincoln, Nebraska have different landscapes. Perhaps they have more security. Everything has a price.

Q. *What was there about the short story form that particularly appealed to you?*

A. One of the things I liked was that you could be intense with it. I think of it in track terms like a 100-metre dash; you just go as fast as you can. When you're dealing with a novel, you're more in a marathon mode; you have to conserve your energy. I like the intensity very much. It's good to be as intense as you can for twenty pages. Gradually, the short stories I was writing became forty pages; I just needed more space to say what I wanted to say. One of the limitations of the short story is that you can only have two or three characters, and your issues have to be very clear, only one or two of them. It's a different form — it's like comparing a lyric poem to a long narrative poem. You have just so much space to do what you want to do.

Margaret Atwood   (b. 1939)

Ottawa-born poet, novelist, short story writer, and critic Margaret Atwood is one of Canada's best-known authors, both at home and abroad. Such novels as *Surfacing* (1972) and *Cat's Eye* (1988) have been praised for their portrayal of introspective, contemporary women examining their pasts and their relationships as they search for new directions in their lives. In "The Resplendent Quetzal," the growing alienation between a childless husband and wife is revealed during a vacation tour of Mexico. Their separate reactions to a visit to ancient ruins emphasize the lovelessness of their relationship, which began to disintegrate when their baby died at birth.

THE RESPLENDENT QUETZAL

Sarah was sitting near the edge of the sacrificial well. She had imagined something smaller, more like a wishing well, but this was huge, and the water at the bottom wasn't clear at all. It was mud-brown; a few clumps of reeds were growing over to one side, and the trees at the top dangled their roots, or were they vines, down the limestone walls into the water. Sarah thought there might be some point to being a sacrificial victim if the well were nicer, but you would never get her to jump into a muddy hole like that. They were probably pushed, or knocked on the head and thrown in. According to the guidebook the water was deep but it looked more like a swamp to her.

Beside her a group of tourists were being rounded up by the guide, who obviously wanted to get the whole thing over with so he could cram them back onto their pink-and-purple-striped *turismo* bus and relax. These were Mexican tourists, and Sarah found it reassuring that other people besides Canadians and Americans wore big hats and sunglasses and took pictures of everything. She wished she and Edward could make these excursions at a less crowded time of year, if they had to make them at all, but because of Edward's teaching job they were limited to school holidays. Christmas was the worst. It would be the same even if he had a different job and they had children, though; but they didn't have any.

The guide shooed his charges back along the gravel path as if they were chickens, which was what they sounded like. He himself lingered beside Sarah, finishing his cigarette, one foot on a stone block, like a conquistador.[1] He was a small dark man with several gold teeth, which glinted when he smiled. He was smiling at Sarah now, sideways, and she smiled back serenely. She liked it when these men smiled at her or even when they made those juicy sucking noises with their mouths as they walked behind her on the street; so long as they didn't touch. Edward pretended not to hear them. Perhaps they did it so much because she was blonde: blondes were rare here.

1 Spanish invader of Mexico and Peru.

She didn't think of herself as beautiful, exactly; the word she had chosen for herself some time ago was "comely." Comely to look upon. You would never use that word for a thin woman.

The guide tossed his cigarette butt into the sacrificial well and turned to follow his flock. Sarah forgot about him immediately. She'd felt something crawling up her leg, but when she looked nothing was there. She tucked the full skirt of her cotton dress in under her thighs and clamped it between her knees. This was the kind of place you could get flea bites, places with dirt on the ground, where people sat. Parks and bus terminals. But she didn't care, her feet were tired and the sun was hot. She would rather sit in the shade and get bitten than rush around trying to see everything, which was what Edward wanted to do. Luckily the bites didn't swell up on her the way they did on Edward.

5   Edward was back along the path, out of sight among the bushes, peering around with his new Leitz binoculars. He didn't like sitting down, it made him restless. On these trips it was difficult for Sarah to sit by herself and just think. Her own binoculars, which were Edward's old ones, dangled around her neck; they weighed a ton. She took them off and put them into her purse.

His passion for birds had been one of the first things Edward had confided to her. Shyly, as if it had been some precious gift, he'd shown her the lined notebook he'd started keeping when he was nine, with its awkward, boyish printing — ROBIN, BLUE JAY, KINGFISHER — and the day and the year recorded beside each name. She'd pretended to be touched and interested, and in fact she had been. She herself didn't have compulsions of this kind; whereas Edward plunged totally into things, as if they were oceans. For a while it was stamps; then he took up playing the flute and nearly drove her crazy with the practising. Now it was pre-Columbian[2] ruins, and he was determined to climb up every heap of old stones he could get his hands on. A capacity for dedication, she guessed you would call it. At first Edward's obsessions had fascinated her, since she didn't understand them, but now they merely made her tired. Sooner or later he'd dropped them all anyway, just as he began to get really good or really knowledgeable; all but the birds. That had remained constant. She herself, she thought, had once been one of his obsessions.

It wouldn't be so bad if he didn't insist on dragging her into everything. Or rather, he had once insisted; he no longer did. And she had encouraged him, she'd let him think she shared or at least indulged his interests. She was becoming less indulgent as she grew older. The waste of energy bothered her, because it was a waste, he never stuck with anything, and what use was his encyclopaedic knowledge of birds? It would be different if they had enough money, but they were always running short. If only he would take all that energy and do something productive with it, in his job, for instance. He could be a principal if he wanted to, she kept telling him that. But he wasn't interested, he was content to poke along doing the same thing year after year. His Grade Six children adored him, the boys especially. Perhaps it was because they sensed he was a lot like them.

---

2 before Columbus arrived in the New World in 1492.

He'd started asking her to go birding, as he called it, shortly after they'd met, and of course she had gone. It would have been an error to refuse. She hadn't complained, then, about her sore feet or standing in the rain under the dripping bushes trying to keep track of some nondescript sparrow, while Edward thumbed through his Peterson's *Field Guide* as if it were the Bible or the bird were the Holy Grail.[3] She'd even become quite good at it. Edward was nearsighted, and she was quicker at spotting movement than he was. With his usual generosity he acknowledged this, and she'd fallen into the habit of using it when she wanted to get rid of him for a while. Just now, for instance.

"There's something over there." She'd pointed across the well to the tangle of greenery on the other side.

10   "Where?" Edward had squinted eagerly and raised his binoculars. He looked a little like a bird himself, she thought, with his long nose and stilt legs.

"That thing there, sitting in that thing, the one with the tufts. The sort of bean tree. It's got orange on it."

Edward focused. "An oriole?"

"I can't tell from here. Oh, it just flew." She pointed over their heads while Edward swept the sky in vain.

"I think it lit back there, behind us."

15   That was enough to send him off. She had to do this with enough real birds to keep him believing, however.

Edward sat down on the root of a tree and lit a cigarette. He had gone down the first side-path he'd come to; it smelled of piss, and he could see by the decomposing Kleenexes further along that this was one of the places people went when they couldn't make it back to the washroom behind the ticket counter.

He took off his glasses, then his hat, and wiped the sweat off his forehead. His face was red, he could feel it. Blushing, Sarah called it. She persisted in attributing it to shyness and boyish embarrassment; she hadn't yet deduced that it was simple rage. For someone so devious she was often incredibly stupid.

She didn't know, for instance, that he'd found out about her little trick with the birds at least three years ago. She'd pointed to a dead tree and said she saw a bird in it, but he himself had inspected that same tree only seconds earlier and there was nothing in it at all. And she was very careless: she described oriole-coloured birds behaving like kingbirds, woodpeckers where there would never be any woodpeckers, mute jays, neckless herons. She must have decided he was a total idiot and any slipshod invention would do.

But why not, since he appeared to fall for it every time? And why did he do it, why did he chase off after her imaginary birds, pretending he believed her? It was partly that although he knew what she was doing to him, he had no idea why. It couldn't be simple malice, she had enough outlets for that. He didn't want to know the real reason, which loomed in his mind as something formless, threatening and final. Her lie about the birds was one of the

3 sacred cup used by Christ at the Last Supper.

many lies that propped things up. He was afraid to confront her, that would be the end, all the pretences would come crashing down and they would be left standing in the rubble, staring at each other. There would be nothing left to say and Edward wasn't ready for that.

20   She would deny everything anyway. "What do you mean? Of course I saw it. It flew right over there. Why would I make up such a thing?" With her level gaze, blonde and stolid and immoveable as a rock.

Edward had a sudden image of himself, crashing out of the undergrowth like King Kong, picking Sarah up and hurling her over the edge, down into the sacrificial well. Anything to shatter that imperturbable expression, bland and pale and plump and smug, like a Flemish Madonna's.[4] Self-righteous, that's what it was. Nothing was ever her fault. She hadn't been like that when he'd met her. But it wouldn't work: as she fell she would glance at him, not with fear but with maternal irritation, as if he'd spilled chocolate milk on a white tablecloth. And she'd pull her skirt down. She was concerned for appearances, always.

Though there would be something inappropriate about throwing Sarah into the sacrificial well, just as she was, with all her clothes on. He remembered snatches from the several books he'd read before they came down. (And that was another thing: Sarah didn't believe in reading up on places beforehand. "Don't you want to understand what you're looking at?" he'd asked her. "I'll see the same thing in any case, won't I?" she said. "I mean, knowing all those facts doesn't change the actual statue or whatever." Edward found this attitude infuriating; and now that they were here, she resisted his attempts to explain things to her by her usual passive method of pretending not to hear.

("That's a Chac-Mool,[5] see that? That round thing on the stomach held the bowl where they put the hearts, and the butterfly on the head means the soul flying up to the sun."

("Could you get out the suntan lotion, Edward? I think it's in the tote bag, in the left-hand pocket."

25   And he would hand her the suntan lotion, defeated once again.)

No, she wouldn't be a fit sacrifice, with or without lotion. They only threw people in — or perhaps they jumped in, of their own free will — for the water god, to make it rain and ensure fertility. The drowned were messengers, sent to carry requests to the god. Sarah would have to be purified first, in the stone sweat-house beside the well. Then, naked, she would kneel before him, one arm across her breast in the attitude of submission. He added some ornaments: a gold necklace with a jade medallion, a gold circlet adorned with feathers. Her hair, which she usually wore in a braid coiled at the back of her head, would be hanging down. He thought of her body, which he made slimmer and more taut, with an abstract desire which was as unrelated as he could make it to Sarah herself. This was the only kind of desire he could feel for her any more: he had to dress her up before he could make love to her at all. He thought about their earlier days, before they'd married.

4 painting of the Virgin Mary in the style of sixteenth-century artists from Flanders, in Belgium.
5 Mayan and Toltec statues of the rain god.

It was almost as if he'd had an affair with another woman, she had been so different. He'd treated her body then as something holy, a white-and-gold chalice, to be touched with care and tenderness. And she had liked this; even though she was two years older than he was and much more experienced she hadn't minded his awkwardness and reverence, she hadn't laughed at him. Why had she changed?

Sometimes he thought it was the baby, which had died at birth. At the time he'd urged her to have another right away, and she'd said yes, but nothing had happened. It wasn't something they talked about. "Well, that's that," she said in the hospital afterwards. A perfect child, the doctor said; a freak accident, one of those things that happen. She'd never gone back to university either and she wouldn't get a job. She sat at home, tidying the apartment, looking over his shoulder, towards the door, out the window, as if she was waiting for something.

Sarah bowed her head before him. He, in the feathered costume and long-nosed, toothed mask of the high priest, sprinkled her with blood drawn with thorns from his own tongue and penis. Now he was supposed to give her the message to take to the god. But he couldn't think of anything he wanted to ask for.

And at the same time he thought: what a terrific idea for a Grade Six special project! He'd have them build scale models of the temples, he'd show the slides he'd taken, he'd bring in canned tortillas and tamales for a Mexican lunch, he'd have them make little Chac-Mools out of papier-mâché . . . and the ball game where the captain of the losing team had his head cut off, that would appeal to them, they were bloodthirsty at that age. He could see himself up there in front of them, pouring out his own enthusiasm, gesturing, posturing, acting it out for them, and their response. Yet afterwards he knew he would be depressed. What were his special projects anyway but a substitute for television, something to keep them entertained? They liked him because he danced for them, a funny puppet, inexhaustible and a little absurd. No wonder Sarah despised him.

Edward stepped on the remains of his cigarette. He put his hat back on, a wide-brimmed white hat Sarah had bought for him at the market. He had wanted one with a narrower brim, so he could look up through his binoculars without the hat getting in his way; but she'd told him he would look like an American golfer. It was always there, that gentle, patronizing mockery.

He would wait long enough to be plausible; then he would go back.

*****

Sarah was speculating about how she would be doing this whole trip if Edward had conveniently died. It wasn't that she wished him dead, but she couldn't imagine any other way for him to disappear. He was omnipresent, he pervaded her life like a kind of smell; it was hard for her to think or act except in reference to him. So she found it harmless and pleasant to walk herself through the same itinerary they were following now, but with Edward removed, cut neatly out of the picture. Not that she would be here at all if it wasn't for him. She would prefer to lie in a deck chair in, say, Acapulco, and drink cooling drinks. She threw in a few dark young men in bathing suits, but took them out: that would be too complicated and not relaxing. She had often thought about cheating on Edward — somehow it would serve him right, though she wasn't sure what for — but she had never actually done it. She didn't know anyone suitable, any more.

Suppose she was here, then, with no Edward. She would stay at a better hotel, for one thing. One that had a plug in the sink; they had not yet stayed in a hotel with a plug. Of course that would cost more money, but she thought of herself as having more money if Edward were dead: she would have all of his salary instead of just part of it. She knew there wouldn't be any salary if he really were dead, but it spoiled the fantasy to remember this. And she would travel on planes, if possible, or first-class buses, instead of the noisy, crowded second-class ones he insisted on taking. He said you saw more of the local colour that way and there was no point going to another country if you spent all your time with other tourists. In theory she agreed with this, but the buses gave her headaches and she could do without the closeup tour of squalor, the miserable thatched or tin-roofed huts, the turkeys and tethered pigs.

He applied the same logic to restaurants. There was a perfectly nice one in the village where they were staying, she'd seen it from the bus and it didn't look that expensive; but no, they had to eat in a seedy linoleum-tiled hutch, with plastic-covered tablecloths. They were the only customers in the place. Behind them four adolescent boys were playing dominoes and drinking beer, with a lot of annoying laughter, and some smaller children watched television, a program that Sarah realized was a re-run of *The Cisco Kid*, with dubbed voices.

35   On the bar beside the television set there was a crèche, with three painted plaster Wise Men, one on an elephant, the others on camels. The first Wise Man was missing his head. Inside the stable a stunted Joseph and Mary adored an enormous Christ Child which was more than half as big as the elephant. Sarah wondered how the Mary could possibly have squeezed out this colossus; it made her uncomfortable to think about it. Beside the crèche was a Santa Claus haloed with flashing lights, and beside that a radio in the shape of Fred Flintstone, which was playing American popular songs, all of them ancient.

"Oh someone help me, help me, plee-ee-ee-eeze . . ."

"Isn't that Paul Anka?"[6] Sarah asked.

But this wasn't the sort of thing Edward could be expected to know. He launched into a defence of the food, the best he'd had in Mexico, he said. Sarah refused to give him the consolation of her agreement. She found the restaurant even more depressing than it should have been, especially the crèche. It was painful, like a cripple trying to walk, one of the last spastic gestures of a religion no one, surely, could believe in much longer.

Another group of tourists was coming up the path behind her, Americans

6 popular Ottawa-born singer of the 1950s.

by the sound of them. The guide was Mexican, though. He scrambled up onto the altar, preparing to give his spiel.

40 "Don't go too near the edge, now."

"Who me, I'm afraid of heights. What d'you see down there?"

"Water, what am I supposed to see?"

The guide clapped his hands for attention. Sarah only half-listened: she didn't really want to know anything more about it.

"Before, people said they threw nothing but virgins in here," the guide began. "How they could tell that, I do not know. It is always hard to tell." He waited for the expected laughter, which came. "But this is not true. Soon, I will tell you how we have found this out. Here we have the altar to the rain god Tlaloc..."

45 Two women sat down near Sarah. They were both wearing cotton slacks, high-heeled sandals and wide-brimmed straw hats.

"You go up the big one?"

"Not on your life. I made Alf go up, I took a picture of him at the top."

"What beats me is why they built all those things in the first place."

"It was their religion, that's what he said."

50 "Well, at least it would keep people busy."

"Solve the unemployment problem." They both laughed.

"How many more of these ruins is he gonna make us walk around?"

"Beats me. I'm about ruined out. I'd rather go back and sit on the bus."

"I'd rather go shopping. Not that there's much to buy."

55 Sarah, listening, suddenly felt indignant. Did they have no respect? The sentiments weren't that far from her own of a moment ago, but to hear them from these women, one of whom had a handbag decorated with tasteless straw flowers, made her want to defend the well.

"Nature is very definitely calling," said the woman with the handbag. "I couldn't get in before, there was such a lineup."

"Take a Kleenex," the other woman said. "There's no paper. Not only that, you just about have to wade in. There's water all over the floor."

"Maybe I'll just duck into the bushes," the first woman said.

Edward stood up and massaged his left leg, which had gone to sleep. It was time to go back. If he stayed away too long, Sarah would be querulous, despite the fact that it was she herself who had sent him off on this fool's expedition.

60 He started to walk back along the path. But then there was a flash of orange, at the corner of his eye. Edward swivelled and raised his binoculars. They were there when you least expected it. It was an oriole, partly hidden behind the leaves; he could see the breast, bright orange, and the dark barred wing. He wanted it to be a hooded oriole, he had not yet seen one. He talked to it silently, begging it to come out into the open. It was strange the way birds were completely magic for him the first time only, when he had never seen them before. But there were hundreds of kinds he would never see; no matter how many he saw there would always be one more. Perhaps this was why he kept looking. The bird was hopping further away from him, into the

foliage. *Come back*, he called to it wordlessly, but it was gone.

Edward was suddenly happy. Maybe Sarah hadn't been lying to him after all, maybe she had really seen this bird. Even if she hadn't, it had come anyway, in answer to his need for it. Edward felt he was allowed to see birds only when they wanted him to, as if they had something to tell him, a secret, a message. The Aztecs thought hummingbirds were the souls of dead warriors, but why not all birds, why just warriors? Or perhaps they were the souls of the unborn, as some believed. "A jewel, a precious feather," they called an unborn baby, according to *The Daily Life of the Aztecs*. *Quetzal*, that was *feather*.

"This is the bird I want to see," Sarah said when they were looking through *The Birds of Mexico* before coming down.

"The Resplendent Quetzal," Edward said. It was a green-and-red bird with spectacular iridescent-blue tail plumes. He explained to her that Quetzal Bird meant Feather Bird. "I don't think we're likely to see it," he said. He looked up the habitat. "*Cloud forests*. I don't think we'll be in any cloud forests."

"Well, that's the one I want," Sarah said. "That's the only one I want."

Sarah was always very determined about what she wanted and what she didn't want. If there wasn't anything on a restaurant menu that appealed to her, she would refuse to order anything; or she would permit him to order for her and then pick around the edges, as she had last night. It was no use telling her that this was the best meal they'd had since coming. She never lost her temper or her self-possession, but she was stubborn. Who but Sarah, for instance, would have insisted on bringing a collapsible umbrella to Mexico in the dry season? He'd argued and argued, pointing out its uselessness and the extra weight, but she'd brought it anyway. And then yesterday afternoon it had rained, a real cloudburst. Everyone else had run for shelter, huddling against walls and inside the temple doorways, but Sarah had put up her umbrella and stood under it, smugly. This had infuriated him. Even when she was wrong, she always managed, somehow, to be right. If only just once she would admit...what? That she could make mistakes. This was what really disturbed him: her assumption of infallibility.

And he knew that when the baby had died she had blamed it on him. He still didn't know why. Perhaps it was because he'd gone out for cigarettes, not expecting it to be born so soon. He wasn't there when she was told; she'd had to take the news alone.

"It was nobody's fault," he told her repeatedly. "Not the doctor's, not yours. The cord was twisted."

"I know," she said, and she had never accused him; nevertheless he could feel the reproach, hanging around her like a fog. As if there was anything he could have done.

"I wanted it as much as you did," he told her. And this was true. He hadn't thought of marrying Sarah at all, he'd never mentioned it because it had never occurred to him she would agree, until she told him she was pregnant. Up until that time, she had been the one in control; he was sure he was just an amusement for her. But the marriage hadn't been her suggestion, it had

65

been his. He'd dropped out of Theology, he'd taken his public-school teaching certificate that summer in order to support them. Every evening he had
massaged her belly, feeling the child move, touching it through her skin.
To him it was a sacred thing, and he included her in his worship. In the
sixth month, when she had taken to lying on her back, she had begun to
snore, and he would lie awake at night listening to these gentle snores, white
and silver they seemed to him, almost songs, mysterious talismans.
Unfortunately Sarah had retained this habit, but he no longer felt the same
way about it.

70   When the child had died, he was the one who had cried, not Sarah.
She had never cried. She got up and walked around almost immediately,
she wanted to get out of the hospital as quickly as possible. The baby clothes
she'd been buying disappeared from the apartment; he never found out what
she'd done with them, he'd been afraid to ask.

Since that time he'd come to wonder why they were still married. It
was illogical. If they'd married because of the child and there was no child,
and there continued to be no child, why didn't they separate? But he wasn't
sure he wanted this. Maybe he was still hoping something would happen,
there would be another child. But there was no use demanding it. They
came when they wanted to, not when you wanted them to. They came when
you least expected it. A jewel, a precious feather.

"Now I will tell you," said the guide. "The archaeologists have dived down
into the well. They have dredged up more than fifty skeletons, and they
have found that some of them were not virgins at all but men. Also, most of
them were children. So as you can see, that is the end of the popular legend."
He made an odd little movement from the top of the altar, almost like a
bow, but there was no applause. "They do not do these things to be cruel,"
he continued. "They believe these people will take a message to the rain
god, and live forever in his paradise at the bottom of the well."

The woman with the handbag got up. "Some paradise," she said to her
friend. "I'm starting back. You coming?"

In fact the whole group was moving off now, in the scattered way they
had. Sarah waited until they had gone. Then she opened her purse and took
out the plaster Christ Child she had stolen from the crèche the night before.
It was inconceivable to her that she had done such a thing, but there it was,
she really had.

75   She hadn't planned it beforehand. She'd been standing beside the crèche
while Edward was paying the bill, he'd had to go into the kitchen to do it as
they were very slow about bringing it to the table. No one was watching
her: the domino-playing boys were absorbed in their game and the children
were riveted to the television. She'd just suddenly reached out her hand,
past the Wise Men and through the door of the stable, picked the child up
and put it into her purse.

She turned it over in her hands. Separated from the dwarfish Virgin
and Joseph, it didn't look quite so absurd. Its diaper was cast as part of it, more
like a tunic, it had glass eyes and a sort of pageboy haircut, quite long for a
newborn. A perfect child, except for the chip out of the back, luckily where

it would not be noticed. Someone must have dropped it on the floor.

You could never be too careful. All the time she was pregnant, she'd taken meticulous care of herself, counting out the vitamin pills prescribed by the doctor and eating only what the books recommended. She had drunk four glasses of milk a day, even though she hated milk. She had done the exercises and gone to the classes. No one would be able to say she had not done the right things. Yet she had been disturbed by the thought that the child would be born with something wrong, it would be a mongoloid or a cripple, or a hydrocephalic with a huge liquid head like the ones she'd seen taking the sun in their wheelchairs on the lawn of the hospital one day. But the child had been perfect.

She would never take that risk, go through all that work again. Let Edward strain his pelvis till he was blue in the face; "trying again," he called it. She took the pill every day, without telling him. She wasn't going to try again. It was too much for anyone to expect of her.

What had she done wrong? She hadn't done anything wrong, that was the trouble. There was nothing and no one to blame, except, obscurely, Edward; and he couldn't be blamed for the child's death, just for not being there. Increasingly since that time he had simply absented himself. When she no longer had the child inside her he had lost interest, he had deserted her. This, she realized, was what she resented most about him. He had left her alone with the corpse, a corpse for which there was no explanation.

80   "*Lost,*" people called it. They spoke of her as having lost the child, as though it was wandering around looking for her, crying plaintively, as though she had neglected it or misplaced it somewhere. But where? What limbo had it gone to, what watery paradise? Sometimes she felt as if there had been some mistake, the child had not been born yet. She could still feel it moving, ever so slightly, holding on to her from the inside.

Sarah placed the baby on the rock beside her. She stood up, smoothing out the wrinkles in her skirt. She was sure there would be more flea bites when she got back to the hotel. She picked up the child and walked slowly towards the well, until she was standing at the very brink.

Edward, coming back up the path, saw Sarah at the well's edge, her arms raised above her head. My God, he thought, she's going to jump. He wanted to shout to her, tell her to stop, but he was afraid to startle her. He could run up behind her, grab her . . . but she would hear him. So he waited, paralyzed, while Sarah stood immobile. He expected her to hurtle downwards, and then what would he do? But she merely drew back her right arm and threw something into the well. Then she turned, half stumbling, towards the rock where he had left her and crouched down.

"Sarah," he said. She had her hands over her face; she didn't lift them. He kneeled so he was level with her. "What is it? Are you sick?"

She shook her head. She seemed to be crying, behind her hands, soundlessly and without moving. Edward was dismayed. The ordinary Sarah, with all her perversity, was something he could cope with, he'd invented ways of coping. But he was unprepared for this. She had always been the one in control.

85   "Come on," he said, trying to disguise his desperation, "you need some

lunch, you'll feel better." He realized as he said this how fatuous it must sound, but for once there was no patronizing smile, no indulgent answer.

"This isn't like you," Edward said, pleading, as if that was a final argument which would snap her out of it, bring back the old calm Sarah.

Sarah took her hands away from her face, and as she did so Edward felt cold fear. Surely what he would see would be the face of someone else, someone entirely different, a woman he had never seen before in his life. Or there would be no face at all. But (and this was almost worse) it was only Sarah, looking much as she always did.

She took a Kleenex out of her purse and wiped her nose. It is like me, she thought. She stood up and smoothed her skirt once more, then collected her purse and her collapsible umbrella.

"I'd like an orange," she said. "They have them, across from the ticket office. I saw them when we came in. Did you find your bird?"

(1977)

Thomas King (b. 1943)

Thomas King, who is of Greek, German, and Cherokee ancestry, has taught at the University of Lethbridge and the University of Minnesota, where he was director of the Native Studies program. His fiction, in which, he says, comedy is used to present often tragic themes, is set in southern Alberta. "I am," he comments, "this Native writer who's out there in the middle, not of nowhere." This quality is found in many of his characters. *Medicine River*, a novel created out of the related stories of several people, focuses on a half-Blackfoot photographer who returns to his home town for his mother's funeral and discovers his own identity. In *Green Grass, Running Water*, five Native people engage in a similar quest. "Borders," from King's collection *One Good Story, That One*, presents the theme of Native people's situation in the modern world in the comic encounter between the narrator's proud mother and Canadian and American immigration officials. The invisible border dividing the two countries symbolizes the many divisions in the story among individuals and between cultures.

BORDERS

When I was twelve, maybe thirteen, my mother announced that we were going to go to Salt Lake City to visit my sister who had left the reserve, moved across the line, and found a job. Laetitia had not left home with my mother's blessing, but over time my mother had come to be proud of the fact that Laetitia had done all of this on her own.

"She did real good," my mother would say.

Then there were the fine points to Laetitia's going. She had not, as my mother liked to tell Mrs. Manyfingers, gone floating after some man like a balloon on a string. She hadn't snuck out of the house, either, and gone to Vancouver or Edmonton or Toronto to chase rainbows down alleys. And she hadn't been pregnant.

"She did real good."

5   I was seven or eight when Laetitia left home. She was seventeen. Our father was from Rocky Boy on the American side.

"Dad's American," Laetitia told my mother, "so I can go and come as I please."

"Send us a postcard."

Laetitia packed her things, and we headed for the border. Just outside of Milk River,[1] Laetitia told us to watch for the water tower.

"Over the next rise. It's the first thing you see."

10   "We got a water tower on the reserve," my mother said. "There's a big one in Lethbridge, too."

"You'll be able to see the tops of the flagpoles, too. That's where the border is."

---

1 river originating in northern Montana that flows north into Alberta before flowing south to the Missouri River.

When we got to Coutts, my mother stopped at the convenience store and bought her and Laetitia a cup of coffee. I got an Orange Crush.

"This is real lousy coffee."

"You're just angry because I want to see the world."

"It's the water. From here on down, they got lousy water."

"I can catch the bus from Sweetgrass. You don't have to lift a finger."

"You're going to have to buy your water in bottles if you want good coffee."

There was an old wooden building about a block away, with a tall sign in the yard that said "Museum." Most of the roof had been blown away. Mom told me to go and see when the place was open. There were boards over the windows and doors. You could tell that the place was closed, and I told Mom so, but she said to go and check anyway. Mom and Laetitia stayed by the car. Neither one of them moved. I sat down on the steps of the museum and watched them, and I don't know that they ever said anything to each other. Finally, Laetitia got her bag out of the trunk and gave Mom a hug.

I wandered back to the car. The wind had come up, and it blew Laetitia's hair across her face. Mom reached out and pulled the strands out of Laetitia's eyes, and Laetitia let her.

"You can still see the mountain from here," my mother told Laetitia in Blackfoot.

"Lots of mountains in Salt Lake," Laetitia told her in English.

"The place is closed," I said. "Just like I told you."

Laetitia tucked her hair into her jacket and dragged her bag down the road to the brick building with the American flag flapping on a pole. When she got to where the guards were waiting, she turned, put the bag down, and waved to us. We waved back. Then my mother turned the car around, and we came home.

We got postcards from Laetitia regular, and, if she wasn't spreading jelly on the truth, she was happy. She found a good job and rented an apartment with a pool.

"And she can't even swim," my mother told Mrs. Manyfingers.

Most of the postcards said we should come down and see the city, but whenever I mentioned this, my mother would stiffen up.

So I was surprised when she bought two new tires for the car and put on her blue dress with the green and yellow flowers. I had to dress up, too, for my mother did not want us crossing the border looking like Americans. We made sandwiches and put them in a big box with pop and potato chips and some apples and bananas and a big jar of water.

"But we can stop at one of those restaurants, too, right?"

"We maybe should take some blankets in case you get sleepy."

"But we can stop at one of those restaurants, too, right?"

The border was actually two towns, though neither one was big enough to amount to anything. Coutts was on the Canadian side and consisted of the convenience store and gas station, the museum that was closed and boarded up, and a motel. Sweetgrass was on the American side, but all you could see was an overpass that arched across the highway and disappeared into the prairies. Just hearing the names of these towns, you would expect that Sweetgrass, which is a nice name and sounds like it is related to other places such as

Medicine Hat and Moose Jaw and Kicking Horse Pass, would be on the Canadian side, and that Coutts, which sounds abrupt and rude, would be on the American side. But this was not the case.

Between the two borders was a duty-free shop where you could buy cigarettes and liquor and flags. Stuff like that.

We left the reserve in the morning and drove until we got to Coutts.

"Last time we stopped here," my mother said, "you had an Orange Crush. You remember that?"

"Sure," I said. "That was when Laetitia took off."

"You want another Orange Crush?"

"That means we're not going to stop at a restaurant, right?"

My mother got a coffee at the convenience store, and we stood around and watched the prairies move in the sunlight. Then we climbed back in the car. My mother straightened the dress across her thighs, leaned against the wheel, and drove all the way to the border in first gear, slowly, as if she were trying to see through a bad storm or riding high on black ice.

The border guard was an old guy. As he walked to the car, he swayed from side to side, his feet set wide apart, the holster on his hip pitching up and down. He leaned into the window, looked into the back seat, and looked at my mother and me.

"Morning, ma'am."

"Good morning."

"Where you heading?"

"Salt Lake City."

"Purpose of your visit?"

"Visit my daughter."

"Citizenship?"

"Blackfoot,"[2] my mother told him.

"Ma'am?"

"Blackfoot," my mother repeated.

"Canadian?"

"Blackfoot."

It would have been easier if my mother had just said "Canadian" and had been done with it, but I could see she wasn't going to do that. The guard wasn't angry or anything. He smiled and looked towards the building. Then he turned back and nodded.

"Morning, ma'am."

"Good morning."

"Any firearms or tobacco?"

"No."

"Citizenship?"

"Blackfoot."

He told us to sit in the car and wait, and we did. In about five minutes, another guard came out with the first man. They were talking as they came, both men swaying back and forth like two cowboys headed for a bar or a gunfight.

2 the Blackfoot Nation has reserves in both Alberta and Montana.

60 "Morning, ma'am."

"Good morning."

"Cecil tells me you and the boy are Blackfoot."

"That's right."

"Now, I know that we got Blackfeet on the American side and the Canadians got Blackfeet on their side. Just so we can keep our records straight, what side do you come from?"

65 I knew exactly what my mother was going to say, and I could have told them if they had asked me.

"Canadian side or American side?" asked the guard.

"Blackfoot side," she said.

It didn't take them long to lose their sense of humor, I can tell you that. The one guard stopped smiling altogether and told us to park our car at the side of the building and come in.

We sat on a wood bench for about an hour before anyone came over to talk to us. This time it was a woman. She had a gun, too.

70 "Hi," she said. "I'm Inspector Pratt. I understand there is a little misunderstanding."

"I'm going to visit my daughter in Salt Lake City," my mother told her. "We don't have any guns or beer."

"It's a legal technicality, that's all."

"My daughter's Blackfoot, too."

The woman opened a briefcase and took out a couple of forms and began to write on one of them. "Everyone who crosses our border has to declare their citizenship. Even Americans. It helps us keep track of the visitors we get from the various countries."

75 She went on like that for maybe fifteen minutes, and a lot of the stuff she told us was interesting.

"I can understand how you feel about having to tell us your citizenship, and here's what I'll do. You tell me, and I won't put it down on the form. No-one will know but you and me."

Her gun was silver. There were several chips in the wood handle and the name "Stella" was scratched into the metal butt.

We were in the border office for about four hours, and we talked to almost everyone there. One of the men bought me a Coke. My mother brought a couple of sandwiches in from the car. I offered part of mine to Stella, but she said she wasn't hungry.

I told Stella that we were Blackfoot and Canadian, but she said that that didn't count because I was a minor. In the end, she told us that if my mother didn't declare her citizenship, we would have to go back to where we came from. Then we got back in the car and drove to the Canadian border, which was only about a hundred yards away.

80 I was disappointed. I hadn't seen Laetitia for a long time, and I had never been to Salt Lake City. When she was still at home, Laetitia would go on and on about Salt Lake City. She had never been there, but her boyfriend Lester Tallbull had spent a year in Salt Lake at a technical school.

"It's a great place," Lester would say. "Nothing but blondes in the whole state."

Whenever he said that, Laetitia would slug him on his shoulder hard enough to make him flinch. He had some brochures on Salt Lake and some maps, and every so often the two of them would spread them out on the table.

"That's the temple. It's right downtown. You got to have a pass to get in."

"Charlotte says anyone can go in and look around."

"When was Charlotte in Salt Lake? Just when the hell was Charlotte in Salt Lake?"

"Last year."

"This is Liberty Park. It's got a zoo. There's good skiing in the mountains."

"Got all the skiing we can use," my mother would say. "People come from all over the world to ski at Banff. Cardston's got a temple, if you like those kinds of things."

"Oh, this one is real big," Lester would say. "They got armed guards and everything."

"Not what Charlotte says."

"What does she know?"

Lester and Laetitia broke up, but I guess the idea of Salt Lake stuck in her mind.

The Canadian border guard was a young woman, and she seemed happy to see us. "Hi," she said. "You folks sure have a great day for a trip. Where are you coming from?"

"Standoff."

"Is that in Montana?"

"No."

"Where are you going?"

"Standoff."

The woman's name was Carol and I don't guess she was any older than Laetitia. "Wow, you both Canadians?"

"Blackfoot."

"Really? I have a friend I went to school with who is Blackfoot. Do you know Mike Harley?"

"No."

"He went to school in Lethbridge, but he's really from Browning."[3]

It was a nice conversation and there were no cars behind us, so there was no rush.

"You're not bringing any liquor back, are you?"

"No."

"Any cigarettes or plants or stuff like that?"

"No."

"Citizenship?"

"Blackfoot."

"I know," said the woman, "and I'd be proud of being Blackfoot if I were Blackfoot. But you have to be American or Canadian."

---

3 town in northern Montana that is the American headquarters of the Blackfoot Nation.

When Laetitia and Lester broke up, Lester took his brochures and maps with him, so Laetitia wrote to someone in Salt Lake City, and, about a month later, she got a big envelope of stuff. We sat at the table and opened up all the brochures, and Laetitia read each one out loud.

"Salt Lake City is the gateway to some of the world's most magnificent skiing.

"Salt Lake City is the home of one of the newest professional basketball franchises, the Utah Jazz.

115   "The Great Salt Lake is one of the natural wonders of the world."

It was kind of exciting seeing all those color brochures on the table and listening to Laetitia read all about how Salt Lake City was one of the best places in the entire world.

"That Salt Lake City place sounds too good to be true," my mother told her.

"It has everything."

"We got everything right here."

120   "It's boring here."

"People in Salt Lake City are probably sending away for brochures of Calgary and Lethbridge and Pincher Creek right now."

In the end, my mother would say that maybe Laetitia should go to Salt Lake City, and Laetitia would say that maybe she would.

We parked the car to the side of the building and Carol led us into a small room on the second floor. I found a confortable spot on the couch and flipped through some back issues of *Saturday Night* and *Alberta Report*.

When I woke up, my mother was just coming out of another office. She didn't say a word to me. I followed her down the stairs and out to the car. I thought we were going home, but she turned the car around and drove back towards the American border, which made me think we were going to visit Laetitia in Salt Lake City after all. Instead she pulled into the parking lot of the duty-free store and stopped.

125   "We going to see Laetitia?"

"No."

"We going home?"

Pride is a good thing to have, you know. Laetitia had a lot of pride, and so did my mother. I figured that someday I'd have it, too.

"So where are we going?"

130   Most of that day, we wandered around the duty-free store, which wasn't very large. The manager had a name tag with a tiny American flag on one side and a tiny Canadian flag on the other. His name was Mel. Towards evening, he began suggesting that we should be on our way. I told him we had nowhere to go, that neither the Americans nor the Canadians would let us in. He laughed at that and told us that we should buy something or leave.

The car was not very comfortable, but we did have all that food and it was April, so even if it did snow as it sometimes does on the prairies, we wouldn't freeze. The next morning my mother drove to the American border.

It was a different guard this time, but the questions were the same. We didn't spend as much time in the office as we had the day before. By noon, we were back at the Canadian border. By two we were back in the duty-free shop parking lot.

The second night in the car was not as much fun as the first, but my mother seemed in good spirits, and, all in all, it was as much an adventure as an inconvenience. There wasn't much food left and that was a problem, but we had lots of water as there was a faucet at the side of the duty-free shop.

One Sunday, Laetitia and I were watching television. Mom was over at Mrs. Manyfingers's. Right in the middle of the program, Laetitia turned off the set and said she was going to Salt Lake City, that life around here was too boring. I had wanted to see the rest of the program and really didn't care if Laetitia went to Salt Lake City or not. When Mom got home, I told her what Laetitia had said.

135   What surprised me was how angry Laetitia got when she found out that I had told Mom.

"You got a big mouth."

"That's what you said."

"What I said is none of your business."

"I didn't say anything."

140   "Well, I'm going for sure, now."

That weekend, Laetitia packed her bags, and we drove her to the border.

Mel turned out to be friendly. When he closed up for the night and found us still parked in the lot, he came over and asked us if our car was broken down or something. My mother thanked him for his concern and told him that we were fine, that things would get straightened out in the morning.

"You're kidding," said Mel. "You'd think they could handle the simple things."

"We got some apples and a banana," I said, "but we're all out of ham sandwiches."

145   "You know, you read about these things, but you just don't believe it. You just don't believe it."

"Hamburgers would be even better because they got more stuff for energy."

My mother slept in the back seat. I slept in the front because I was smaller and could lie under the steering wheel. Late that night, I heard my mother open the car door. I found her sitting on her blanket leaning against the bumper of the car.

"You see all those stars," she said. "When I was a little girl, my grand-mother used to take me and my sisters out on the prairies and tell us stories about all the stars."

"Do you think Mel is going to bring us any hamburgers?"

150   "Every one of those stars has a story. You see that bunch of stars over there that look like a fish?"

"He didn't say no."

"Coyote[4] went fishing, one day. That's how it all started." We sat out under the stars that night, and my mother told me all sorts of stories. She was

---

4 trickster figure in the mythology of several Native peoples of the northern plains.

serious about it, too. She'd tell them slow, repeating parts as she went, as if she expected me to remember each one.

Early the next morning, the television vans began to arrive, and guys in suits and women in dresses came trotting over to us, dragging microphones and cameras and lights behind them. One of the vans had a table set up with orange juice and sandwiches and fruit. It was for the crew, but when I told them we hadn't eaten for a while, a really skinny blonde woman told us we could eat as much as we wanted.

They mostly talked to my mother. Every so often one of the reporters would come over and ask me questions about how it felt to be an Indian without a country. I told them we had a nice house on the reserve and that my cousins had a couple of horses we rode when we went fishing. Some of the television people went over to the American border, and then they went to the Canadian border.

155 Around noon, a good-looking guy in a dark blue suit and an orange tie with little ducks on it drove up in a fancy car. He talked to my mother for a while, and, after they were done talking, my mother called me over, and we got into our car. Just as my mother started the engine, Mel came over and gave us a bag of peanut brittle and told us that justice was a damn hard thing to get, but that we shouldn't give up.

I would have preferred lemon drops, but it was nice of Mel anyway.

"Where are we going now?"

"Going to visit Laetitia."

The guard who came out to our car was all smiles. The television lights were so bright they hurt my eyes, and, if you tried to look through the windshield in certain directions, you couldn't see a thing.

160 "Morning, ma'am."

"Good morning."

"Where you heading?

"Salt Lake City."

"Purpose of your visit?"

165 "Visit my daughter."

"Any tobacco, liquor, or firearms?"

"Don't smoke."

"Any plants or fruit?"

"Not any more."

170 "Citizenship?"

"Blackfoot."

The guard rocked back on his heels and jammed his thumbs into his gun belt. "Thank you," he said, his fingers patting the butt of the revolver. "Have a pleasant trip."

My mother rolled the car forward, and the television people had to scramble out of the way. They ran alongside the car as we pulled away from the border, and, when they couldn't run any farther, they stood in the middle of the highway and waved and waved and waved.

We got to Salt Lake City the next day. Laetitia was happy to see us, and, that first night, she took us out to a restaurant that made really good soups. The list of pies took up a whole page. I had cherry. Mom had chocolate. Laetitia said that she saw us on television the night before and, during the meal, she had us tell her the story over and over again.

Laetitia took us everywhere. We went to a fancy ski resort. We went to the temple. We got to go shopping in a couple of large malls, but they weren't as large as the one in Edmonton, and Mom said so.

After a week or so, I got bored and wasn't at all sad when my mother said we should be heading back home. Laetitia wanted us to stay longer, but Mom said no, that she had things to do back home and that, next time, Laetitia should come up and visit. Laetitia said she was thinking about moving back, and Mom told her to do as she pleased, and Laetitia said that she would.

On the way home, we stopped at the duty-free shop, and my mother gave Mel a green hat that said "Salt Lake" across the front. Mel was a funny guy. He took the hat and blew his nose and told my mother that she was an inspiration to us all. He gave us some more peanut brittle and came out into the parking lot and waved at us all the way to the Canadian border.

It was almost evening when we left Coutts. I watched the border through the rear window until all you could see were the tops of the flagpoles and the blue water tower, and then they rolled over a hill and disappeared.

(1993)

Alice Walker   (b. 1944)

Born in Eatonton in rural Georgia, where her parents were poor sharecrop-
pers, Alice Walker published her first book—a collection of poems entitled
Once—in 1968, shortly after graduating from Sarah Lawrence College in New
York. Active in Mississippi during the civil rights movement of the 1960s, she has
published several books: poetry, short stories, essays, and four novels, of which
the best known, *The Color Purple* (1982), was made into a motion picture. In all
her writing, Walker celebrates the lives of African-American women and their heritage. "Everyday Use" contrasts characters' attitudes toward an old quilt to
reveal the differences between, on the one hand, the narrator and her daughter Maggie, both of whom live simple lives close to the land, and, on the other,
Dee, who has developed a superficial sophistication. In her essay "In Search
of Our Mothers' Gardens," Walker writes of quilts, now often preserved in
museums, as creations of people who possessed "powerful imagination and
deep spiritual feeling."

EVERYDAY USE

FOR YOUR GRANDMAMA

I will wait for her in the yard that Maggie and I made so clean and wavy yesterday afternoon. A yard like this is more comfortable than most people know.
It is not just a yard. It is like an extended living room. When the hard clay is
swept clean as a floor and the fine sand around the edges lined with tiny,
irregular grooves, anyone can come and sit and look up into the elm tree and
wait for the breezes that never come inside the house.

Maggie will be nervous until her sister goes: she will stand hopelessly in
corners, homely and ashamed of the burn scars down her arms and legs, eying
her sister with a mixture of envy and awe. She thinks her sister has held life
always in the palm of one hand, that "no" is a word the world never learned to
say to her.

You've no doubt seen those TV shows where the child who has "made it" is confronted, as a surprise, by her own mother and father, tottering in weakly from
backstage. (A pleasant surprise, of course: What would they do if parent
and child came on the show only to curse out and insult each other?) On TV
mother and child embrace and smile into each other's faces. Sometimes the
mother and father weep, the child wraps them in her arms and leans across the
table to tell how she would not have made it without their help. I have seen
these programs.

Sometimes I dream a dream in which Dee and I are suddenly brought
together on a TV program of this sort. Out of a dark and soft-seated limousine
I am ushered into a bright room filled with many people. There I meet a
smiling, gray, sporty man like Johnny Carson who shakes my hand and tells me
what a fine girl I have. Then we are on the stage and Dee is embracing me with

tears in her eyes. She pins on my dress a large orchid, even though she has told me once that she thinks orchids are tacky flowers.

5   In real life I am a large, big-boned woman with rough, man-working hands. In the winter I wear flannel nightgowns to bed and overalls during the day. I can kill and clean a hog as mercilessly as a man. My fat keeps me hot in zero weather. I can work outside all day, breaking ice to get water for washing; I can eat pork liver cooked over the open fire minutes after it comes steaming from the hog. One winter I knocked a bull calf straight in the brain between the eyes with a sledge hammer and had the meat hung up to chill before nightfall. But of course all this does not show on television. I am the way my daughter would want me to be: a hundred pounds lighter, my skin like an uncooked barley pancake. My hair glistens in the hot bright lights. Johnny Carson has much to do to keep up with my quick and witty tongue.

But that is a mistake. I know even before I wake up. Who ever knew a Johnson with a quick tongue? Who can even imagine me looking a strange white man in the eye? It seems to me I have talked to them always with one foot raised in flight, with my head turned in whichever way is farthest from them. Dee, though. She would always look anyone in the eye. Hesitation was no part of her nature.

"How do I look, Mama?" Maggie says, showing just enough of her thin body enveloped in pink skirt and red blouse for me to know she's there, almost hidden by the door.

"Come out into the yard," I say.

Have you ever seen a lame animal, perhaps a dog run over by some careless person rich enough to own a car, sidle up to someone who is ignorant enough to be kind to him? That is the way my Maggie walks. She has been like this, chin on chest, eyes on ground, feet in shuffle, ever since the fire that burned the other house to the ground.

10   Dee is lighter than Maggie, with nicer hair and a fuller figure. She's a woman now, though sometimes I forget. How long ago was it that the other house burned? Ten, twelve years? Sometimes I can still hear the flames and feel Maggie's arms sticking to me, her hair smoking and her dress falling off her in little black papery flakes. Her eyes seemed stretched open, blazed open by the flames reflected in them. And Dee. I see her standing off under the sweet gum tree she used to dig gum out of; a look of concentration on her face as she watched the last dingy gray board of the house fall in toward the red-hot brick chimney. Why don't you do a dance around the ashes? I'd wanted to ask her. She had hated the house that much.

I used to think she hated Maggie, too. But that was before we raised the money, the church and me, to send her to Augusta[1] to school. She used to read to us without pity; forcing words, lies, other folks' habits, whole lives upon us two, sitting trapped and ignorant underneath her voice. She washed us in a river of make-believe, burned us with a lot of knowledge we didn't necessarily need to know. Pressed us to her with the serious way she read, to shove us away at just the moment, like dimwits, we seemed about to understand.

---

1 city in Georgia southeast of Atlanta.

Dee wanted nice things. A yellow organdy dress to wear to her graduation from high school; black pumps to match a green suit she'd made from an old suit somebody gave me. She was determined to stare down any disaster in her efforts. Her eyelids would not flicker for minutes at a time. Often I fought off the temptation to shake her. At sixteen she had a style of her own: and knew what style was.

I never had an education myself. After second grade the school was closed down. Don't ask me why: in 1927 colored asked fewer questions than they do now. Sometimes Maggie reads to me. She stumbles along good-naturedly but can't see well. She knows she is not bright. Like good looks and money, quickness passed her by. She will marry John Thomas (who has mossy teeth in an earnest face) and then I'll be free to sit here and I guess just sing church songs to myself. Although I never was a good singer. Never could carry a tune. I was always better at a man's job. I used to love to milk till I was hooked in the side in '49. Cows are soothing and slow and don't bother you, unless you try to milk them the wrong way.

I have deliberately turned my back on the house. It is three rooms, just like the one that burned, except the roof is tin; they don't make shingle roofs any more. There are no real windows, just some holes cut in the sides, like portholes in a ship, but not round and not square, with rawhide holding the shutters up on the outside. This house is in a pasture, too, like the other one. No doubt when Dee sees it she will want to tear it down. She wrote me once that no matter where we "choose" to live, she will manage to come see us. But she will never bring her friends. Maggie and I thought about this and Maggie asked me, "Mama, when did Dee ever *have* any friends?"

15   She had a few. Furtive boys in pink shirts hanging about on washday after school. Nervous girls who never laughed. Impressed with her they worshiped the well-turned phrase, the cute shape, the scalding humor that erupted like bubbles in lye. She read to them.

When she was courting Jimmy T she didn't have much time to pay to us, but turned all her faultfinding power on him. He *flew* to marry a cheap city girl from a family of ignorant flashy people. She hardly had time to recompose herself.

When she comes I will meet — but there they are!

Maggie attempts to make a dash for the house, in her shuffling way, but I stay her with my hand. "Come back here," I say. And she stops and tries to dig a well in the sand with her toe.

It is hard to see them clearly through the strong sun. But even the first glimpse of leg out of the car tells me it is Dee. Her feet were always neat-looking, as if God himself had shaped them with a certain style. From the other side of the car comes a short, stocky man. Hair is all over his head a foot long and hanging from his chin like a kinky mule tail. I hear Maggie suck in her breath. "Uhnnnh," is what it sounds like. Like when you see the wriggling end of a snake just in front of your foot on the road. "Uhnnnh."

20   Dee next. A dress down to the ground, in this hot weather. A dress so loud it hurts my eyes. There are yellows and oranges enough to throw back the

light of the sun. I feel my whole face warming from the heat waves it throws out. Earrings gold, too, and hanging down to her shoulders. Bracelets dangling and making noises when she moves her arm up to shake the folds of the dress out of her armpits. The dress is loose and flows, and as she walks closer, I like it. I hear Maggie go "Uhnnnh" again. It is her sister's hair. It stands straight up like the wool on a sheep. It is black as night and around the edges are two long pigtails that rope about like small lizards disappearing behind her ears.

"Wa-su-zo-Tean-o!"[2] she says, coming on in that gliding way the dress makes her move. The short stocky fellow with the hair to his navel is all grinning and he follows up with "Asalamalakim,[3] my mother and sister!" He moves to hug Maggie but she falls back, right up against the back of my chair. I feel her trembling there and when I look up I see the perspiration falling off her chin.

"Don't get up," says Dee. Since I am stout it takes something of a push. You can see me trying to move a second or two before I make it. She turns, showing white heels through her sandals, and goes back to the car. Out she peeks next with a Polaroid. She stoops down quickly and lines up picture after picture of me sitting there in front of the house with Maggie cowering behind me. She never takes a shot without making sure the house is included. When a cow comes nibbling around the edge of the yard she snaps it and me and Maggie *and* the house. Then she puts the Polaroid in the back seat of the car, and comes up and kisses me on the forehead.

Meanwhile Asalamalakim is going through motions with Maggie's hand. Maggie's hand is as limp as a fish, and probably as cold, despite the sweat, and she keeps trying to pull it back. It looks like Asalamalakim wants to shake hands but wants to do it fancy. Or maybe he don't know how people shake hands. Anyhow, he soon gives up on Maggie.

"Well," I say. "Dee."

25 "No, Mama," she says. "Not 'Dee,' Wangero Leewanika Kemanjo!"

"What happened to 'Dee'?" I wanted to know.

"She's dead," Wangero said. "I couldn't bear it any longer, being named after the people who oppress me."

"You know as well as me you was named after your aunt Dicie," I said. Dicie is my sister. She named Dee. We called her "Big Dee" after Dee was born.

"But who was *she* named after?" asked Wangero.

30 "I guess after Grandma Dee," I said.

"And who was she named after?" asked Wangero.

"Her mother," I said, and saw Wangero was getting tired. "That's about as far back as I can trace it," I said. Though, in fact, I probably could have carried it back beyond the Civil War through the branches.

"Well," said Asalamalakim, "There you are."

"Uhnnnh," I heard Maggie say.

35 "There I was not," I said, "before 'Dicie' cropped up in our family, so why should I try to trace it that far back?"

---

2 Islamic greeting popular among some African Americans in the 1960s. 3 Islamic greeting also popular during the 1960s.

He just stood there grinning, looking down on me like somebody inspecting a Model A car. Every once in a while he and Wangero sent eye signals over my head.

"How do you pronounce this name?" I asked.

"You don't have to call me by it if you don't want to," said Wangero.

"Why shouldn't I?" I asked. "If that's what you want us to call you, we'll call you."

40 "I know it might sound awkward at first," said Wangero.

"I'll get used to it," I said. "Ream it out again."

Well, soon we got the name out of the way. Asalamalakim had a name twice as long and three times as hard. After I tripped over it two or three times he told me to just call him Hakim-a-barber. I wanted to ask him was he a barber, but I didn't really think he was, so I didn't ask.

"You must belong to those beef-cattle peoples down the road," I said. They said "Asalamalakim" when they met you, too, but they didn't shake hands. Always too busy: feeding the cattle, fixing the fences, putting up salk-lick shelters, throwing down hay. When the white folks poisoned some of the herd the men stayed up all night with rifles in their hands. I walked a mile and a half just to see the sight.

Hakim-a-barber said, "I accept some of their doctrines, but farming and raising cattle is not my style." (They didn't tell me, and I didn't ask, whether Wangero (Dee) had really gone and married him.)

45 We sat down to eat and right away he said he didn't eat collards and pork was unclean. Wangero, though, went on through the chitlins and corn bread, the greens and everything else. She talked a blue streak over the sweet potatoes. Everything delighted her. Even the fact that we still used the benches her daddy made for the table when we couldn't afford to buy chairs.

"Oh, Mama!" she cried. Then turned to Hakim-a-barber. "I never knew how lovely these benches are. You can feel the rump prints," she said, running her hands underneath her and along the bench. Then she gave a sigh and her hand closed over Grandma Dee's butter dish. "That's it!" she said. "I knew there was something I wanted to ask you if I could have." She jumped up from the table and went over in the corner where the churn stood, the milk in it clabber by now. She looked at the churn and looked at it.

"This churn top is what I need," she said. "Didn't Uncle Buddy whittle it out of a tree you all used to have?"

"Yes," I said.

"Uh huh," she said happily. "And I want the dasher, too."

50 "Uncle Buddy whittle that, too?" asked the barber.

Dee (Wangero) looked up at me.

"Aunt Dee's first husband whittled the dash," said Maggie so low you almost couldn't hear her. "His name was Henry, but they called him Stash."

"Maggie's brain is like an elephant's," Wangero said, laughing. "I can use the churn top as a centrepiece for the alcove table," she said, sliding a plate over the churn, "and I'll think of something artistic to do with the dasher."

When she finished wrapping the dasher the handle stuck out. I took it for a moment in my hands. You didn't even have to look to see where hands pushing the dasher up and down to make butter had left a kind of sink in the wood. In fact, there were a lot of small sinks; you could see where thumbs and fingers had sunk into the wood. It was beautiful light yellow wood, from a tree that grew in the yard where Big Dee and Stash had lived.

After dinner Dee (Wangero) went to the trunk at the foot of my bed and started rifling through it. Maggie hung back in the kitchen over the dishpan. Out came Wangero with two quilts. They had been pieced by Grandma Dee and then Big Dee and me had hung them on the quilt frames on the front porch and quilted them. One was in the Lone Star pattern. The other was Walk Around the Mountain. In both of them were scraps of dresses Grandma Dee had worn fifty and more years ago. Bits and pieces of Grandpa Jarrell's Paisley shirts. And one teeny faded blue piece, about the size of a penny matchbox, that was from Great Grandpa Ezra's uniform that he wore in the Civil War.

"Mama," Wangero said sweet as a bird. "Can I have these old quilts?"

I heard something fall in the kitchen, and a minute later the kitchen door slammed.

"Why don't you take one or two of the others?" I asked. "These old things was just done by me and Big Dee from some tops your grandma pieced before she died."

"No," said Wangero. "I don't want those. They are stitched around the borders by machine."

"That'll make them last better," I said.

"That's not the point," said Wangero. "These are all pieces of dresses Grandma used to wear. She did all this stitching by hand. Imagine!" She held the quilts securely in her arms, stroking them.

"Some of the pieces, like those lavender ones, come from old clothes her mother handed down to her," I said, moving up to touch the quilts. Dee (Wangero) moved back just enough so that I couldn't reach the quilts. They already belonged to her.

"Imagine!" she breathed again, clutching them closely to her bosom.

"The truth is," I said, "I promised to give them quilts to Maggie, for when she marries John Thomas."

She gasped like a bee had stung her.

"Maggie can't appreciate these quilts!" she said. "She'd probably be backward enough to put them to everyday use."

"I reckon she would," I said. "God knows I been saving 'em for long enough with nobody using 'em. I hope she will!" I didn't want to bring up how I had offered Dee (Wangero) a quilt when she went away to college. Then she had told me they were old-fashioned, out of style.

"But they're *priceless*!" she was saying now, furiously; for she has a temper. "Maggie would put them on the bed and in five years they'd be in rags. Less than that!"

"She can always make some more," I said. "Maggie knows how to quilt."

Dee (Wangero) looked at me with hatred. "You just will not understand. The point is these quilts, *these* quilts!"

"Well," I said, stumped. "What would *you* do with them?"

"Hang them," she said. As if that was the only thing you *could* do with quilts.

Maggie by now was standing in the door. I could almost hear the sound her feet made as they scraped over each other.

"She can have them, Mama," she said, like somebody used to never winning anything, or having anything reserved for her. "I can 'member Grandma Dee without the quilts."

75   I looked at her hard. She had filled her bottom lip with checkerberry snuff and it gave her face a kind of dopey, hangdog look. It was Grandma Dee and Big Dee who taught her how to quilt herself. She stood there with her scarred hands hidden in the folds of her skirt. She looked at her sister with something like fear but she wasn't mad at her. This was Maggie's portion. This was the way she knew God to work.

When I looked at her like that something hit me in the top of my head and ran down to the soles of my feet. Just like when I'm in church and the spirit of God touches me and I get happy and shout. I did something I never had done before: hugged Maggie to me, then dragged her on into the room, snatched the quilts out of Miss Wangero's hands and dumped them into Maggie's lap. Maggie just sat there on my bed with her mouth open.

"Take one or two of the others," I said to Dee.

But she turned without a word and went out to Hakim-a-barber.

"You just don't understand," she said, as Maggie and I came out to the car.

80   "What don't I understand," I wanted to know.

"Your heritage," she said. And then she turned to Maggie, kissed her, and said, "You ought to try to make something of yourself, too, Maggie. It's really a new day for us. But from the way you and Mama still live you'd never know it."

She put on some sunglasses that hid everything above the tip of her nose and her chin.

Maggie smiled; maybe at the sunglasses. But a real smile, not scared. After we watched the car dust settle I asked Maggie to bring me a dip of snuff. And then the two of us sat there just enjoying, until it was time to go in the house and go to bed.

(1973)

Greg Hollingshead   (b. 1947)

A professor of eighteenth-century literature and creative writing at the University of Alberta, Greg Hollingshead was born in Toronto and studied at the universities of Toronto and London. In three collections of short stories and a novel, *Spin Dry*, Hollingshead examines the mystery and absurdity that lurk beneath the surface of apparently "ordinary" modern life. A student of the eighteenth-century philosopher George Berkeley, he considers writing "an ongoing perception of process and discovery. For me, narrative is philosophy as we actually live it, day by day, all our lives. Each event in a story conveys an understanding of those that precede it. Each raises and addresses the question 'Why?'" "The Naked Man" is from Hollingshead's most recent collection, *The Roaring Girl* (1995), winner of the Governor General's Award for fiction. Like "Rappaccini's Daughter" and "The Motor Car," its central character is a young man who has left his family home. Unlike Giovanni and Calvin, however, Dennis returns. The ambiguous feelings both he and his family experience are, in part, reflected in their attitudes toward his Studebaker, an ornate, chromium-decorated car popular in the 1950s.

THE NAKED MAN

By the time I was eighteen it was getting hard to live at home. Instead of moving out I bought a Studebaker. I loved the Studebaker, but it made no difference, so I left it with my parents and went to Australia. My parents had a double garage with so much junk in it there was hardly room for the family Chev. By stacking the junk higher up the walls I made room for a Studebaker too. This was fine with my parents, but I was uneasy for my car.

When I called home there was always some problem about it. Even just sitting in the garage. Of course, it made parking the Chev tighter, and I heard about that. A few times I hung up with the impression there had been some scraping. My father had talked me into leaving the keys for safety reasons. The first definite thing that happened was they lost the keys.

"Tell me again why you need them," I said to my father.

"Safety reasons," he replied.

5   Reluctantly I explained about the spare key under the front fender. He listened dubiously.

Another time I called he told me the Studebaker was leaking oil.

"It always did," I said. "It's not a leak. It's just a little drip."

"That car of yours is making a terrible mess out there," my mother said when she came on.

"So put a piece of carpeting under it," I said.

10   "A *what?*"

The next time I called they had got in a mechanic to see about the leak.

"He says you need a new clutch," my father told me. "He says you should have arranged to have it started at least every two weeks."

"What'd he say about the leak?"

"There's nothing he can do about the leak. The leak is the least of your worries. Do you realize what this car of yours is costing me?"

15   I told them to just leave the car alone.

After a while it stopped coming up. Sometimes this was how things would happen. Their lives had moved on. As a kind of joke I would say, "So how's my car?" and in a resigned voice my father would say, "Well, it's still there," or, "You realize your mother won't park in the garage any more, don't you."

When I got back from Australia it was six in the morning about a year later, and I had no money at all. But my parents lived twenty minutes from the airport, so I waited until seven and called home.

"Hello —" My father's voice was damaged and incredulous with sleep.

"Hi, Dad, it's Dennis."

20   There was a pause. "Dennis — ?"

"Your son, Dennis,"

"It's Dennis!" my mother cried in the background. She grabbed the phone. "Dennis, you sound so close! Where are you?"

An hour later the Chev pulled up at the Arrivals door with my father clinging to the wheel like a shipwreck victim. His hair fanned straight out at the side, and he was still breathing hard from sleep. I threw my bags in the back seat and got in beside him.

"So how was Australia?" he said. "Are they ahead of us or behind? It was dawn there too?"

25   "Australia was great. It's hard to know where to start —"

"Feed it out slowly, over time." And he told me how with the way interest rates were going it looked like we'd lose the house.

As we turned into the driveway I asked, "So how's the car?"

"It runs, doesn't it? It's not as if I could afford a new one."

My mother was at the foot of the driveway with her coat on, waiting impatiently for the Chev. She had an eight-thirty hair appointment and made us get out immediately.

30   We walked to the house. As soon as we were inside, my father called a cab. "Think I'll slide over to the track," he said, standing in the middle of the kitchen eating a bowl of cornflakes. "Now that I'm up."

As soon as he left I flopped down on the living-room chesterfield and passed out.

I woke up badly disoriented. I was on a different chesterfield, and for a long time I thought I was still in Australia, but I couldn't figure out which city. The only thing worse than waking up from sleeping too long at the wrong time is waking up in a different place from where you fell asleep.

It was my parents' main-floor guest room. When I tried to get up my body was completely without tonus. I fell back on the bed. "Hey Denny." It was my younger sister Sophie, passing the door. She shot me the six-gun salute.

"Sophie!" my mother called from the kitchen. "Why don't you give Dennis a tour of the house?"

35   "No time!" Sophie shouted from the bathroom. "Nothing ever changes!" She was washing her face.

I stepped out the French doors to the garage to take a look at my car. It was not there.

I checked the driveway and the other side of the house. From the darkness of the garage I watched Sophie's ride for work stop out front and pick her up. I waved, but she didn't see me. When I turned on the garage light I saw that I had tracked oil from the puddle where the Studebaker had been.

My mother was in the living room with her hair done, sitting next to a beautiful young woman I had never seen before. I said my name and we shook hands.

"You know Lori," my mother said.

40 "I never saw Lori before in my life."

"Get off it," my mother said.

Lori worked nearby with disturbed children.

"Lori's staying in the spare room downstairs," my mother explained.

"I didn't know there was a spare room downstairs," I said. There was only my room.

45 "Well, there isn't now," my mother said.

At that moment a naked man walked past the doorway down the hall between the main-floor bedrooms. A door closed.

"Excuse me," I said quietly, my heart going. "I think there's someone else in the house."

My mother was listing the people she had invited to a party we were having that night. She paused, looking at me. "I know," she said. "It can be kind of a Welcome Home Dennis party."

"What was it before?" I asked with a smile at Lori, who smiled back.

50 "A naked man just walked past the door," I said more loudly, pointing.

My mother was continuing with her list. "Susan and Ed, and Effie, and the Rauches (the Cy and Doris Rauches, that is), and Aunt B.J., and Wade of course, and the Chatterjees —"

"Who's Wade?" I asked.

"Lori's friend. And Dave Arkett, and Tony and his wife, and —"

I asked if there was a bed I could use.

55 "Of course there's a bed you can use," my mother said irritably. "Why do you have to put an edge on everything?" There was Dave's old room upstairs, she said. And could I please clear my bags out of the front hall. She didn't want our guests tripping over them.

Dave's bed was a double. I turned back the covers and checked around until I came up with two shades of pubic hair. I dropped these down behind the headboard and brushed away absently at the sheet. I sat on the edge of the mattress and rubbed my shanks. After a while I went to take a shower, but there was somebody in there.

I returned to the living room in Dave's dressing gown. Lori and my mother looked at me expectantly.

"I was going to take a shower, but there's somebody in there," I said.

"I thought you told us you were going to bed," my mother said.

60 "Can't I shower first?"

"Not if somebody's in there."

"It's not Sophie," I said. "Sophie went to work."

"Nonsense."

"I think she did, Mrs. Weatherall," Lori put in softly. "I heard the door."

65   "Well, I'm sure I don't know who it could be in that case," my mother said with impatience, refusing to be held accountable for strangers in the house.

"By the way," I said. "I've been meaning to ask. Where's my car?"

"What car?"

"The one I left in the garage."

"There's no car in the garage."

70   "That's what I'm saying. What did you do with it?"

"Why are you asking me? I haven't been able to park in my own garage for a year. You'll have to talk to your father."

"Well, I guess the bathroom's free now," I said, but it wasn't.

Instead of returning to the living room, I went on to the kitchen where I made myself a toasted bacon and tomato sandwich. I ate this standing in the middle of the kitchen like my father, I noticed, and then I went to bed.

When I came downstairs again it was dark. Lori was sitting in the same place in the living room, only now she was alone, smoking a cigarette and wearing a sequined gown with a generous neckline.

75   "Hi," I said.

"Hi."

"I guess I should change."

"You don't have to."

"I look like a bum."

80   "You look very nice."

My father entered from the kitchen with a couple of bowls of chips and dip. To Lori he said, "If that dress had slits you could call it a strange sequins of vents."

To me he said, "Help out a little."

In the kitchen my mother was mixing nuts in a bowl. She gave my father and me a look that said, *They'll be here any minute.*

"Right," my father said and rubbed his hands together while glancing around in vague anticipation.

85   She shot us another look that said, *You don't think you're greeting our guests dressed like that, do you?*

My father looked down at himself with his hands at his sides, spread and turned outward in a gesture that said, *What's wrong with the way I'm dressed?*

My mother made no reply.

My father grew silent as if musing. Finally he rubbed his jaw and murmured, "Maybe I'll shave."

An hour later my father had a bar set up on a card table in a corner of the dining room, telling women who ordered their drinks on the rocks, "I only have ice for you," and describing their Bristol Creams as rhapsodies in goo.

90   When he noticed me watching him, my father told me to take over. "Wade's shirking his responsibilities on all fronts," he said from the corner of his mouth.

"Which one's Wade?"

"The shifty one."

As soon as I was behind the bar, people started talking to me. Most of them when they heard I was a Weatherall thought I was my younger brother Dave, at that time in Hawaii. A few thought I was my dead brother Joe.

From behind the bar I could see Lori sitting completely alone in her place on the chesterfield, drinking soda water. As I poured my mother her usual — Silent Sam, a cloud of Pepsi, no ice — I asked what was wrong with Lori.

95   "It's Wade," my mother said, scarcely moving her lips. "He's ignored the poor kid all night. She's completely heartbroken."

"Which one is he?"

"Downstairs. Playing table tennis with Gwen Dermott."

"Who's Gwen Dermott?"

"You tell me. She tagged along with the Freibergs."

100   When the men had been drinking long enough to approach Lori and engage her in conversation, she talked and smiled but always sooner or later looked sadly into the distance as she took a long drag on her cigarette, and the men moved soberly away. A few minutes later, during a crush at the bar, as Lou Destaffo stepped in beside me to pour his own drink, I caught a glimpse of sequins in the hall.

"Thanks for taking over, Lou."

I was knocking on the main-floor guest-room door.

"Come in?"

Lori's voice was high and soft with expectation. When she saw who it was, her head pitched back onto the coats. She must have been lying on fifty coats, her body slightly arched. When I approached, she moved over a little to make room. I imagined her rolling down between the bed and wall and becoming lodged there. I took off my shoes and sat alongside her with my heels dug into the edge of the bed.

105   "Look," I said. "I'm really sorry about Wade."

"No, I'm the one who should be sorry."

"You don't have to be sorry."

There was a muffled crash at the door, and my mother rushed in with a cup and saucer. I could see it dripping across the floor. "Coffee!" she cried. "It's all right!" The cup and saucer clattered down on the bedside table and my mother dashed from the room.

"You must like him a lot," I said.

110   The front door slammed, hard. The blow of it shook the house.

"He's all right."

Suddenly there came a violent hammering on the window behind us. I twisted around to see. Nothing. More hammering. A fist! A flash of wild face at the window, mad-eyed and snarling. It fell away. Reappeared. Fell away. Reappeared. Heathcliff[1] on a trampoline. More hammering. For a better look, I turned off the bedside lamp. Immediately the frequency and violence of the hammering increased. At any moment a fist would smash through.

"You'd better turn the light back on," Lori said. "I think he's jealous."

As I switched on the lamp there was a knock at the door. It opened, and my father beckoned. When I went to the door he put an arm around my shoulder and walked me forcibly into the TV room and closed the door behind us.

---

1 the passionate and destructive central character in Emily Brontë's *Wuthering Heights*.

115 "Where's my car?" I said.

"Listen, Dennis. We've got a kid out here who's pretty much in love." My father looked away. The cartilage in his jaw danced. "Don't spoil it."

I shrugged out of his arm and went back to Lori. I asked her why she put up with it.

"Up with what?"

My mother rushed in holding an ashtray way out in front of her. "Ow by iddoo ums?" she cried breathlessly to no one. Keeping her face averted as if Lori and I were physically making love, she snatched up the unused ashtray from the bedside table and banged the other down in its place. She rushed away. Like a spun plate the ashtray took a long time to settle. *Wrowr wrowr wrowr wrowr* — I was stopping it with my hand when the window hammering resumed. And then my mother was back for the cup and saucer. "All right?" she cried on her way out, spilling coffee again. Immediately then, both my parents were at the door.

120 "Dennis!"

"No! Go away!"

But already they were inside the room, with people from the party peering over their shoulders like idle villagers. I sprang forward and tried to push everybody out, but once I got them into the hall my mother slipped past me into the guest room and locked the door.

"You're on the bar," my father said. His lips were thin and he was holding my arm in a vice grip.

My mother of course would not let me back into the guest room.

125 "My shoes are in there," I said.

"Socks are fine," my father said.

I returned to the bar, where people were helping themselves.

I was carrying more mix up from the basement when my father drew me aside, "Better come with me. We've got a major crisis on our hands out here."

Wade had disappeared.

130 "You check the driveway," my father said.

The driveway was all cars. It was a cold night, and I was wearing my father's galoshes without shoes. I didn't know what I was looking for.

When I got back to the house my father came around the corner. "Is it there?" he asked.

"Is what there?"

"His car."

135 "How would I know his car?"

"He's using the Studebaker."

"Who said you could lend out my car?" I cried.

"Relax," my father said. "We couldn't all use the Chev." He was looking over his shoulder into the darkness. "The river!" he cried suddenly and headed off at a jog across the lawn.

"Dad! The river's frozen!"

140 He stopped and walked back with his hands in his blazer pockets. "Let's go inside," he said. "It's cold out here."

In the kitchen my mother was waiting by the oven for a tray of hors d'oeuvres.

"Where's Lori?" I asked her.

"Where's that big platter? I want you to help me serve."

"Did you leave Lori alone?"

145 "Here it is. Never you mind about Lori. Lori's just fine." She handed me the platter. "Here. Arrange them nicely."

I passed around the platter, and then I started to drink. Eventually I went to bed. Some time in the night I staggered naked to the bathroom to throw up. The party was over. I slumped on the edge of the bed with my head in my hands, wondering if I was going to throw up again. But I must have thought I was sleeping in my old room and taken a wrong turn from the bathroom. I heard a stir behind me. I was practically sitting on my mother.

"Wade —" my father said.

"George, it's not Wade," my mother whispered. "I think it's Dave, I mean —"

"Dave, go back to your room."

150 "Dennis?" my mother said.

When I came downstairs the next day Lori was at her usual place. She was wearing jeans and a pale blue cashmere sweater. A cigarette was going in the ashtray alongside her hand.

"Is Wade still asleep?" I asked.

Lori shook her head. "Thanks for being so nice last night. Wade can be such a pain."

"Is he around? I never got a chance to meet him."

155 "I know. I think you'd really like each other, too. He was hoping he'd see you this morning, but he got a call first thing about his car."

"The Studebaker?"

"That's right. He lent it to somebody he didn't know all that well."

"Somebody who drove it drunk and stoned with a suspended licence and no insurance and the car's a write-off?"

"I think he might have still had his licence," Lori said.

(1995)

Lee Maracle (b. 1950)

Maracle, who is of Cree, Metis, and Coast Salish decent, grew up in Vancouver and studied at Simon Fraser University. Her works, all written from a Native and feminist perspective, include *Bobbi Lee: Indian Rebel* (1990), an autobiography; and *Sundogs* (1992), a novel. Maracle has stated that in her stories "all my characters live with both a condition and themselves." Frequently, the condition involves existing in a society in which the majority culture stereotypically defines minorities. However, as she explains, her central characters, frequently Native women, journey from the outside world to enact a "transformation of the internal." In "Too Much to Explain," the central character must deal with her painful memories of past tragedies and a deteriorating relationship. She ends her relationship near Vancouver's aptly named False Creek, an inlet of the sea surrounded by expensive condominiums.

TOO MUCH TO EXPLAIN

She sat on the upper level of the lounge, her chair up against the wall. She didn't want anyone behind her tonight. The table she leaned on was small and dark. There weren't many people in the room; it was, after all, a Tuesday night in October. He was late. It twisted her insides that he didn't have the decency to be on time. Just once, just once, you would think the bastard would be on time, she thought with more venom than was called for. She tapped her cigarette rapidly at the ashtray and scolded herself for smoking so much. She closed her eyes hard to shut out the hum that plagued her ears. The sound of the tapping did little to cancel the hum and closing her eyes did less. She knew both gestures were futile, even absurd, but she made them anyway.

He entered the room with grace and dignity, took a quick look around the room from the doorway before he recognized her tucked up in a corner. *He's probably sizing up the women*, and the humming grew sharp. She resisted putting her hands over her ears. He nodded in her direction, smiled and stroke over to the table.

From the door he had noted that she was thinner than when they first began seeing each other. Still, even thin she was lovelier than the other women he knew. He grinned at his own foolishness. It was not that she was so much lovelier but that he loved her; he liked the way his heart clouded his vision. She had been tense and inattentive lately. He wondered if this outing would suffer the same fate as the last two at Joe Kapp's. He tried to stop thinking about the harangues that had marred the last two occasions. Her smile quelled his momentary cynicism. He was embarrassed by his private recollection and his own suggestion that there might be a pattern developing here.

He stroked her hand lightly and pecked her cheek, then swung easily into the chair. She was nearly finished her margarita. His automatic display of affection did nothing for her. She feared that this exhibition was conducted more for everyone else's benefit — the way the lead wolf in a pack might covetously snuggle his females before younger hopefuls. She resented what might have been a perverse show of male possession. Her hand fidgeted slightly under his caress. A piece of her wanted to scream at him, but she knew that would not be rational. Rational people do not scream. The waiter came up just behind him and asked what they would like to order.

"Two margaritas," and he winked at her. She interpreted the wink and his sickening overconfidence as arrogance, mentally adding this to the list of his crimes. *Gawd, what am I doing? Don't blow this*, and she felt colour come involuntarily to her cheeks. The floor floated towards her as the humiliation she felt filled her face. She argued with herself. *He's taking me for granted ... Gawd, what a stupid catch-all phase that explains nothing and everything that goes wrong between people. The waiter probably thinks I'm one of those ridiculous women lapel-roses that can't speak for myself.* She ignored the fact that she was still toying with a margarita she had ordered earlier.

5   The waiter rested his eyes on her momentarily, awaiting confirmation. She felt his gaze but ceded nothing. Seeing that she was not going to look up, he shrugged and left.

When she looked at the floor her lover was not sure whether she was bored or angry. Then he flushed. He had answered for her again. The realization brought a knot of anxiety to his gut. He sighed annoyance and looked off into space, waiting for the barrel-load of condemnation that would assault his character, but it didn't come. He relaxed slightly, not bothering to reflect on his own internal need to eat up life's mundane and trivial decisions with his own decisiveness.

The pianist in the corner was plunking out a sad tune, "Moody River";[1] the sound was all the more melancholy in the absence of song and band. Just an old Black man, pecking at an even older piano. Pictures of her childhood home, the river and her solitary vigil next to it swam through her head. Her face wore a wistful smile when it turned to look at the piano player. Then her expression changed as she craned her neck to see.

"Dammit, the pole is blocking my view."

"Would you like to move?" he asked, trying to accommodate her. The question jarred her. A veil of darkness filmed her eyes.

10   "Why?"

Oh Christ, instant replay. When will I learn? Every time she invites me out like this, she gives me a hard time, but he didn't say that.

"Well, so you can see the piano player." He lit a cigarette. He rarely smoked and this little display of anxiety annoyed her.

"What do I want to look at some old man for?" She was rigid now, her words came out clipped into neat little pieces and were fed to him through tight lips. He sighed heavily, and even that she interpreted as male condescension in the face of a typical female airhead. The ringing hum in her ears gained volume as a steady stream of accusations whirled about insanely in her mind. Small bits of reason argued with the multitude of doubts until she finally regained her control.

He stared at the margarita in front of him and let his frustration drift

---

1   a 1961 hit song about a man mourning the drowning of his lover.

around the dimly lit bar while his fingers played with the salty ice ring on the glass. Fatigue crept up on him like a faithless companion. He had been through this before with other women. He was beginning to think that this affair was going nowhere. Age and passion kept him rooted to his chair. He felt weighed down by an anchor of his own making.

15   "How did your day go?" She carefully laminated the remark with layers of creamy sweetness. Surprised relief overtook him. *He knows I'm pissed, why doesn't he say something ... stop that ... Gawd*, and she recognized the voice that dominated her thoughts. She fought to still the voice, to stop the incessant humming. *Think of the river*. It swelled to a torrent and gave way to a memory she had thought dead. The flooding banks and the ranting of her mother returned to haunt her and she wanted to faint.

"Another day of make-work. If the new plans aren't ready soon, I think I'll lose my mind." Her glazed look did not escape him, despite her fawning attempt to disguise it. He ignored it. *What the hell am I supposed to do?* he asked himself. The question was in fact an old justification for doing nothing.

"Don't mock me." It slipped out too fast. *Oh Gawd, there it is, it's out, he'll guess*. Her fingers grabbed the napkin and tried to wring the thought out of her mind by twisting the paper into a white snake of anxiety. Far from surmising any hint of her mental turmoil, he was confused by her response. Neither confusion nor any of his other emotions had ever prompted him to self-examination or indecision before, and he didn't bother thinking about it now. The waiter rescued her with another useless interruption.

It looked like they would be harassed all night by the waiter's bored attentiveness. Her lover considered leaving but didn't want to ask. *No sense inviting trouble*, he told himself, and let the notion pass.

"I wasn't mocking you," he said with exaggerated warmth. The pianist had stopped to change songs, so his words echoed loudly across the emptiness, despite his effort to utter them softly. He reached for her hand. She feared that noncompliance with his overture would call attention to her near admission, but his hands inspired a feeling of revulsion that she could not let go of and so she dropped her hands to her lap. She concentrated on them guiltily.

20   "OK, what is it this time: my disgusting sexism, my appalling arrogance, or are you just generally dissatisfied with the meaninglessness of our relationship?" He laced the question with threat. His voice lied about the concern for his character that his question implied. The noise in her ears rose an octave. The pitch of it deafened her. It blocked out the reality of the bar. The roar of the river on top of the ringing in her ears distorted everything.

The table became a watery, seductive maw, the glass a slender woman staggering and begging to be let go. The weaving woman-glass swayed frantically in the clutches of her own liquid indecision, its every movement an accusatory cry to her for decisiveness. She threw the glass at the table. The margarita bled the content of her memory across the table and it leaked onto the floor. She jumped up babbling about stress, weakly trying to submerge her behaviour in neurotic nonsense. He signalled the waiter, relieved that he had not seen her throw the glass, and was sorry that his remark had been so harsh.

She stood aside while the waiter finished mopping up the drink with his rag. Her body hung limp against the wall. She knew she couldn't keep this façade up much longer. She wanted the floor to swallow her. She prayed that the river of her maddened mind would drown her. Anger abated, he looked at her more seriously now than he could remember doing. Her thinness took on dimensions of anorexic vulnerability. Her strangeness seemed less excusable.

"Is school getting to you?" he asked. She clasped her hands together with too much vigour. That voice, that "Nancy nursey" voice, drove her to the edge. She struggled to collect herself. She fought to rest her nameless agitation on something plausible.

"Don't patronize me. Who do you think you are? You just sit there like you are the only person in the world who can handle life. You don't think I can deal with anything, do you?" The words jerked out too fast between clenched teeth. Her eyes narrowed to slits. She would have said more but the stupid waiter was back again like a phantom, cajoling them to have another drink.

25   "A double daisy for me," she hissed.

"Huh?" The rude bugger didn't have the sense to say "pardon me." She didn't answer. She turned to face the wall and tugged at her cheek with tensed fingers.

"Two double margaritas," her lover said politely. The waiter sensed the tension and left quickly. She wanted to start in on him again, but scenes of the river broke her concentration. Instead of the usual hazy images of the past, the pictures took on a dangerous lucid clarity. *Maybe if I just let it happen ... maybe if I just lose myself in the lousy nightmare of it all instead of trying to stomp it out with rattling nonsense ...*

He was near the breaking point. *I'm just a gawdamn nail-pounder, not a fucking therapist. What the fuck do I know about her feminist anxieties*, and he closed his eyes. This was more than he could deal with. *Fuck yourself* was what he wanted to say, but he continued sitting there for reasons he could not adequately explain to himself.

The blood drained from her fingers and her hands shook from the loss. Weakly, she stood up and numbly walked to the bathroom. He paid the bill. When she returned they left.

30   The sound of the traffic failed to reach her and he had to hold her trembling body against him at the curb to prevent her from stepping out among the cars. He let her lead him into the blackness when the traffic cleared. The world was getting farther away from her. She needed to hear the water, it floated around in her head like a torrent of frustrated feminine rage, liquid unpredictability. They walked wordlessly forward and the hill rolled up behind their scurrying legs.

False Creek lurched into view at the bottom, a poorly lit facsimile of cultivated wild wood and trail. Over the hill of manicured lawn and untended brush the creek stretched out purple-black against a neon skyline. No other lovers were out. The night was cool and the city's citizenry were already asleep in anticipation of the morrow's work.

They climbed down the man-made stone embankment. At the bottom, she sat with knees up, her shins folded in her thin, shivering arms. She hugged herself, waiting for the ringing to subside so the pictures she had long suppressed could return. She forced herself, in the comfort of the night's quiet affection, to watch it all.

He wrapped her in his jacket and waited helplessly. He had no idea what was going to happen but his sense of chivalry and his knowledge of the city would not allow him to desert her. He resigned himself to a night of cold anticipation.

From the riverbank she saw her mother struggling with her husband, screaming at him to give her her papers ... silly little bits of brown bags and napkins that she had scribbled on. He had caught her scribbling poems again. Her six-year-old body watched him through her woman's mind, and the clarity of the moving picture in her mind surprised her. At the end of her memory's eye, her mother disappeared over the roar of the river and her drunken father staggered uselessly after her, calling her name as though she were deserting him and not perishing under the hands of his drunken rage.

35 "They said I was crazy, a bona fide nutcase." Her chuckle came out a murmur. It was the kind of chuckle women let out when they suddenly discover that the mysteries surrounding unplugging a toilet are pathetically simple and wonderment is unwarranted. Her lover lived quite outside her range of subtle emotional variance and so thought the chuckle evidence of the truth of the findings of whoever "they" were, rather than recognizing it as the "I'll be" chortle of realization. He didn't want to hear it. *Christ, what am I supposed to do with this?* He didn't move or answer her aloud. There must be more, and he waited for it. He stared at the lights reflected against the water and thought about how they, too, made a crazy dance pattern against its smooth surface. He rested his face against her neck, trying to search his mind for some hope.

"I spent most of my childhood yo-yoing between lonely foster homes and a mental ward ... Shit." She began to rock back and forth. Her memories rolled into the smooth lap of False Creek as the wall of fear and veil of confusion lifted. She couldn't leave the brutal trap her father had set for her. The little girl, traumatized by the scene, had jumped inside the same trap, running a marathon of imprisoning relationships because she had not wanted to remember. Now the trap sunk.

"The little girl just had no words." He couldn't accept that she was crazy, but this last remark wanted some point of reference to make it rational. If he accepted her insanity he would have to declare insane the hysteria of his mother, the violence of his sister and her breakdown and his own maddened binges of the past. He would have to condemn them all because he just wasn't cut out for looking inside at the why of himself or anyone else. He resigned himself to a crazy destiny, half wishing that he had been born snuggled up against the distant mountains of his ancestors a half millennium earlier.

"You don't have a monopoly on craziness," he said dully. She laughed at his flat sense of self, at the hopelessly two-dimensional perception that he clung to, and she wondered if the man who defined neurosis wasn't just a little like her lover. Without feeling the least bit guilty about the unfairness of leaving him like this, she handed him his jacket and left without saying goodbye.

He followed her up the hill and she left him there in a tangle of confused babbling while she climbed into a cab and drove out of his life. It was all too much to explain. How does one begin to unravel the accumulation of thousands of years of entrapment to a man bent on repairing the rents she occasionally made in the machinery of the trap.

40   "I just don't feel desperate anymore," was all she could come up with. As the cab sped away she could hear him holler in self-defence, "You really are crazy."

(1990)

Guy Vanderhaeghe   (b. 1951)

Born in Esterhazy, Saskatchewan, Guy Vanderhaeghe has twice won the Governor General's Award for fiction, for *Man Descending* (1982), a collection of short stories, and for *The Englishman's Boy* (1996), a novel. Influenced by the works of Margaret Laurence and Sinclair Ross, most of the short stories in *Man Descending* are about men and boys working on the Prairies. "What I Learned from Caesar" is an adult's reminiscence of his late childhood in a small Saskatchewan town during the Depression. The thirteen-year-old boy seeks a way of keeping faith in his Belgium-born father, who is suffering a mental breakdown, and finds it in the writings of Julius Caesar.

WHAT I LEARNED FROM CAESAR

The oldest story is the story of flight, the search for greener pastures. But the pastures we flee, no matter how brown and blighted — these travel with us; they can't be escaped.

My father was an immigrant. You would think this no penalty in a nation of immigrants, but even his carefully nurtured, precisely colloquial English didn't spare him much pain. Nor did his marriage to a woman of British stock (as we called it then, before the vicious-sounding acronym Wasp came into use). That marriage should have paid him a dividend of respectability, but it only served to make her suspect in marrying him.

My father was a lonely man, a stranger who made matters worse by pretending he wasn't. It's true that he was familiar enough with his adopted terrain, more familiar than most because he was a salesman. Yet he was never really of it, no matter how much he might wish otherwise. I only began to understand what had happened to him when I, in my turn, left for greener pastures, heading east. I didn't go so far, not nearly so far as he had. But I also learned that there is a price to be paid. Mine was a trivial one, a feeling of mild unease. At odd moments I betrayed myself and my beginnings; I knew that I lacked the genuine ring of a local. And I had never even left my own country.

Occasionally I return to the small Saskatchewan town near the Manitoba border where I grew up. To the unpractised eye of an easterner the countryside around that town might appear undifferentiated and monotonous, part and parcel of that great swath of prairie that vacationers drive through, pitying its inhabitants and deploring is restrooms, intent only on leaving it all behind as quickly as possible. But it is just here that the prairie verges on parkland, breaking into rolling swells of land, and here, too, that it becomes a little greener and easier on the eye. There is still more sky than any country is entitled to, and it teases the traveller into believing he can never escape it or find shelter under it. But if your attention wanders from that hypnotic expanse of blue and the high clouds drifting in it, the land becomes more comfortable as prospects shorten, and the mind rests easier on attenuated distances. There is cropland: fields of rye, oats, barley, and wheat; flat, glassy sloughs shining like mirrors in the sun; a solitary clump of trembling popular; a bluff that gently climbs to nudge the sky.

When I was a boy it was a good deal bleaker. The topsoil had blown off the fields and into the ditches to form black dunes; the crops were withered and burnt; there were no sloughs because they had all dried up. The whole place had a thirsty look. That was during the thirties when we were dealt a doubly cruel hand of drought and economic depression. It was not a time or place that was kindly to my father. He had come out of the urban sprawl of industrial Belgium some twenty-odd years before, and it was only then, I think, that he was beginning to come to terms with a land that must have seemed forbidding after his own tiny country, so well tamed and marked by man. And then this land played him the trick of becoming something more than forbidding; it became fierce, and fierce in every way.

5   It was in the summer of 1931, the summer that I thought was merely marking time before I would pass into high school, that he lost his territory. For as long as I could remember I had been a salesman's son, and then it ended. The company he worked for began to feel the pinch of the Depression and moved to merge its territories. He was let go. So one morning he unexpectedly pulled up at the front door and began to haul his sample cases out of the Ford.

"It's finished," he said to my mother as he flung the cases on to the lawn. "I got the boot. I offered to stay on — strictly commission. He wouldn't hear of it. Said he couldn't see fit to starve two men where there was only a living for one. I'd have starved that other sonofabitch out. He'd have had to hump his back and suck the hind tit when I was through with him." He paused, took off his fedora and nervously ran his index finger around the sweat-band. Clearing his throat, he said, "His parting words were, 'Good luck, Dutchie!' I should have spit in his eye. Jesus H. Christ himself wouldn't dare call me Dutchie. The bastard."

Offence compounded offence. He thought he was indistinguishable, that the accent wasn't there. Maybe his first successes as a salesman owed something to his naivety. Maybe in good times, when there was more than enough to go around, people applauded his performance by buying from him. He was a counterfeit North American who paid them the most obvious of compliments, imitation. Yet hard times make people less generous. Jobs were scarce, business was poor. In a climate like that, perceptions change, and perhaps he ceased to be merely amusing and became, instead, a dangerous parody. Maybe that district manager, faced with a choice, could only think of George Vander Elst as Dutchie. Then again, it might have been that my father just wasn't a good enough salesman. Who can judge at this distance?

But for the first time my father felt as if he had been exposed. He had never allowed himself to remember that he was a foreigner, or if he had, he persuaded himself he had been wanted. After all, he was a northern European, a Belgian. They had been on the preferred list.

He had left all that behind him. I don't even know the name of the town or the city where he was born or grew up. He always avoided my questions about his early life as if they dealt with a distasteful and criminal past that was best forgotten. Never, not even once, did I hear him speak Flemish. There were never any of the lapses you might expect. No pet names in his native language for my mother or myself; no words of endearment which would have had the comfort of childhood use. Not even when driven to one of his frequent rages did he curse in the mother tongue. If he ever prayed, I'm sure it was in English. If a man forgets the cradle language in the transports of prayer, love, and rage — well, it's forgotten.

10   The language he did speak was, in a sense, letter-perfect, fluent, glib. It was the language of wheeler-dealers, and of the heady twenties, of salesmen, high-rollers, and persuaders. He spoke of people as live-wires, go-getters, self-made men. Hyphenated words to describe the hyphenated life of the seller, a life of fits and starts, comings and goings. My father often proudly spoke of himself as a self-made man, but this description was not the most accurate. He was a remade man. The only two pictures of him which I have in my possession are proof of this.

The first is a sepia-toned photograph taken, as nearly as I can guess, just prior to his departure from Belgium. In this picture he is wearing an ill-fitting suit, round-toed, clumsy boots, and a cloth cap. The second was taken by a street photographer in Winnipeg. My father is walking down the street, a snap-brim fedora slanting rakishly over one eye. His suit is what must have been considered stylish then — a three-piece pin-stripe — and he is carrying an overcoat, casually over one arm. He is exactly what he admired most, a "snappy dresser," or since he always had trouble with his p's, a "snabby dresser." The clothes, though they mark a great change, aren't really that important. Something else tells the story.

In the first photograph my father stands rigidly with his arms folded across his chest, unsmiling. Yet I can see that he is a young man who is hesitant and afraid; not of the camera, but of what this picture-taking means. There is a reason why he is having his photograph taken. He must leave something of himself behind with his family so he will not be forgotten, and carry something away with him so that he can remember. That is what makes this picture touching; it is a portrait of a solitary, an exile.

In the second picture his face is blunter, fleshier: nothing surprising in that, he is older. But suddenly you realize he is posing for the camera — not in the formal, European manner of the first photograph but in a manner far more unnatural. You see, he is pretending to be entirely natural and unguarded; yet he betrays himself. The slight smile, the squared shoulder, the overcoat draped over the arm, all are calculated bits of a composition. He has seen the camera from a block away. My father wanted to be caught in exactly this negligent, unassuming pose, sure that it would capture for all time his prosperity, his success, his adaptability. Like most men, he wanted to leave a record. And this was it. And if he had coached himself in such small matters, what would he ever leave to chance?

That was why he was so ashamed when he came home that summer. There was the particular shame of having lost his job, a harder thing for a man than it might be today. There was the shame of knowing that sooner or later we would have to go on relief, because being a lavish spender he had no savings. But there was also the shame of a man who suddenly discovers that all his lies were transparent, and everything he thought so safely hidden had always been in plain view. He had been living one of those dreams. The kind of dream in which you are walking down the street, meeting friends and neighbours, smiling and nodding, and when you arrive at home and pass a mirror you see for the first time you are stark naked. He was sure that behind his back he had always been Dutchie. For a man with so much pride a crueller epithet would have been kinder; to be hated gives a man some kind of status. It was the condescension implicit in that diminutive, its mock playfulness, that made him appear so undignified in his own eyes.

15   And for the first time in my life I was ashamed of him. He didn't have the grace to bear an injustice, imagined or otherwise, quietly. At first he merely brooded, and then like some man with a repulsive sore, he sought pity by showing it. I'm sure he knew that he could only offend, but he was under a compulsion to justify himself. He began with my mother by explaining, where there was no need for explanation, that he had had his job taken from him for no good reason. However, there proved to be little satisfaction in preaching to the converted, so he carried his tale to everyone he knew. At first his references to his plight were tentative and oblique. The responses were polite but equally tentative and equally oblique. This wasn't what he had hoped for. He believed that the sympathy didn't measure up to the occasion. So his story was told and retold, and each time it was enlarged and embellished until the injustice was magnified beyond comprehension. He made a damn fool of himself. This was the first sign, although my mother and I chose not to recognize it.

In time everyone learned my father had lost his job for no good reason. And it wasn't long before the kids of the fathers he had told his story to were following me down the street chanting, "No good reason. No good reason." That's how I learned my family was a topical joke that the town was enjoying with zest. I suppose my father found out too, because it was about that time he stopped going out of the house. He couldn't fight back and neither could I. You never can.

After a while I didn't leave the house unless I had to. I spent my days sitting in our screened verandah reading old copies of *Saturday Evening Post*[1] and *Maclean's*. I was content to do anything that helped me forget the heat and the monotony, the shame and the fear, of that longest of summers. I was thirteen then and in a hurry to grow up, to press time into yielding the bounty I was sure it had in keeping for me. So I was killing time minute by minute with those magazines. I was to enter high school that fall and that seemed a prelude to adulthood and independence. My father's misfortunes couldn't fool me into believing that maturity didn't mean the strength to plunder at will. So when I found an old Latin grammar of my mother's I began to read that too. After all, Latin was the arcane language of the professions, of lawyers and doctors, those divinities owed immediate and unquestioning respect. I decided I would become either one, because respect could never be stolen from them as it had been from my father.

That August was the hottest I can remember. The dry heat made my nose bleed at night, and I often woke to find my pillow stiff with blood. The leaves

1 this popular American weekly magazine during the first half of the 20th century frequently pictured scenes of happy families on its cover.

of the elm tree in the front yard hung straight down on their stems; flies buzzed
heavily, their bodies tip-tapping lazily against the screens, and people passing
the house moved so languidly they seemed to be walking in water. My father,
who had always been careful about his appearance, began to come down for
breakfast barefoot, wearing only a vest undershirt and an old pair of pants.
He rarely spoke, but carefully picked his way through his meal as if it were a
dangerous obstacle course, only pausing to rub his nose thoughtfully. I noticed
that he had begun to smell.

One morning he looked up at me, laid his fork carefully down beside his
plate and said, "I'll summons him."

20   "Who?"

"Who do you think?" he said scornfully. "The bastard who fired me. He
had no business calling me Dutchie. That's slander."

"You can't summons him."

"I can," he said emphatically. "I'm a citizen. I've got rights. I'll go to law.
He spoiled my good name."

"That's not slander."

25   "It is."

"No, it isn't."

"I'll sue the bastard," he said vaguely, looking around to appeal to my mother,
who had left the room. He got up from the table and went to the doorway.
"Edith," he called, "tell your son I've got the right to summons that bastard."

Her voice came back faint and timid. "I don't know, George."

He looked back at me. "You're in the same boat, sonny. And taking sides
with them don't save you. When we drown we all drown together."

30   "I'm not taking sides," I said indignantly. "Nobody's taking sides. It's facts.
Can't you see …," but I didn't get a chance to finish. He left, walked out on me.
I could hear his steps on the stairway, tired, heavy steps. There was so much I
wanted to say. I wanted to make it plain that being on his side meant saving him
from making a fool of himself again. I wanted him to know he could never
win that way. I wanted him to win, not lose. He was my father. But he went up
those steps, one at a time, and I heard his foot fall distinctly, every time.
Beaten before he started, he crawled back into bed. My mother went up to him
several times that day, to see if he was sick, to attempt to gouge him out of that
room, but she couldn't. It was only later that afternoon, when I was reading in
the verandah, that he suddenly appeared again, wearing only a pair of under-
shorts. His body shone dully with sweat, his skin looked grey and soiled.

"They're watching us," he said, staring past me at an empty car parked in
the bright street.

Frightened, I closed my book and asked who was watching us.

"The relief people," he said tiredly. "They think I've got money hidden
somewhere. They're watching me, trying to catch me with it. The joke's on
them. I got no money." He made a quick, furtive gesture that drew attention
to his almost naked body, as if it were proof of his poverty.

"Nobody is watching us. That car's empty."

35   "Don't take sides with them," he said, staring through the screen. I thought
someone from one of the houses across the street might see him like that,
practically naked.

"The neighbours'll see," I said, turning my head to avoid looking at him.

"See what?" he asked, surprised.

"You standing like that. Naked almost."

"There's nothing they can do. A man's home is his castle. That's what the English say, isn't it?"

40   And he went away laughing.

Going down the hallway, drawing close to his door that always stood ajar, what did I hope? To see him dressed, his trousers rolled up to mid-calf to avoid smudging his cuffs, whistling under his breath, shining his shoes? Everything as it was before? Yes. I hoped that. If I had been younger then and still believed that frogs were turned into princes with a kiss,[2] I might even have believed it could happen. But I didn't believe. I only hoped. Every time I approached his door (and that was many times a day, too many), I felt the queasy excitement of hope.

It was always the same. I would look in and see him lying on the tufted pink bedspread, naked or nearly so, gasping for breath in the heat. And I always thought of a whale stranded on a beach because he was such a big man. He claimed he slept all day because of the heat, but he only pretended to. He could feel me watching him and his eyes would open. He would tell me to go away, or bring him a glass of water; or, because his paranoia was growing more marked, ask me to see if they were still in the street. I would go to the window and tell him, yes, they were. Nothing else satisfied him. If I said they weren't, his jaw would shift from side to side unsteadily and his eyes would prick with tears. Then he imagined more subtle and intricate conspiracies.

I would ask him how he felt.

"Hot," he'd say, "I'm always hot. Can't hardly breathe. Damn country," and turn on his side away from me.

45   My mother was worried about money. There was none left. She asked me what to do. She believed women shouldn't make decisions.

"You'll have to go to the town office and apply for relief," I told her.

"No, no," she'd say, shaking her head. "I couldn't go behind his back. I couldn't do that. He'll go himself when he feels better. He'll snap out of it. It takes a little time."

In the evening my father would finally dress and come downstairs and eat something. When it got dark he'd go out into the yard and sit on the swing he'd hung from a limb of our Manitoba maple years before, when I was a little boy. My mother and I would sit and watch him from the verandah. I felt obligated to sit with her. Every night as he settled himself onto the swing she would say the same thing. "He's too big. It'll never hold him. He'll break his back." But the swing held him up and the darkness hid him from the eyes of his enemies, and I like to think that made him happy, for a time.

He'd light a cigarette before he began to swing, and then we'd watch its glowing tip move back and forth in the darkness like a beacon. He'd flick it away when it was smoked, burning a red arc in the night, showering sparks briefly, like a comet. And then he'd light another and another, and we'd watch them glow and swing in the night.

2 in "The Frog Prince," a German folktale, only a princess's kiss can return the hero to his human form.

50   My mother would lean over to me and say confidentially, "He's thinking it all out. It'll come to him, what to do."

I never knew whether she was trying to reassure me or herself. At last my mother would get to her feet and call to him, telling him she was going up to bed. He never answered. I waited a little longer, believing that watching him I kept him safe in the night. But I always gave up before he did and went to bed too.

The second week of September I returned to school. Small differences are keenly felt. For the first time there was no new sweater, or unsharpened pencils, or new fountain pen whose nib hadn't spread under my heavy writing hand. The school was the same school I had gone to for eight years, but that day I climbed the stairs to the second floor that housed the high school. Up there the wind moaned more persistently than I remembered it had below, and intermittently it threw handfuls of dirt and dust from the schoolyard against the windows with a gritty rattle.

Our teacher, Mrs. MacDonald, introduced herself to us, though she needed no introduction since everyone knew who she was — she had taught there for over ten years. We were given our texts and it cheered me a little to see I would have no trouble with Latin after my summer's work. Then we were given a form on which we wrote a lot of useless information. When I came to the space which asked for Racial Origin I paused, and then, out of loyalty to my father, numbly wrote in "Canadian."

· After that we were told we could leave. I put my texts away in a locker for the first time — we had had none in public school — but somehow it felt strange going home from school empty-handed. So I stopped at the library door and went in. There was no school librarian and only a few shelves of books, seldom touched. The room smelled of dry paper and heat. I wandered around aimlessly, taking books down, opening them, and putting them back. That is, until I happened on Caesar's The Gallic Wars.[3] It was a small, thick book that nestled comfortably in the hand. I opened it and saw that the left-hand pages were printed in Latin and the right-hand pages were a corresponding English translation. I carried it away with me, dreaming of more than proficiency in Latin.

When I got home my mother was standing on the front step, peering anxiously up and down the street.

55   "Have you seen your father?" she asked.

"No," I said. "Why?"

She began to cry. "I told him all the money was gone. I asked him if I could apply for relief. He said he'd go himself and have it out with them. Stand on his rights. He took everything with him. His citizenship papers, baptismal certificate, old passport, bank book, everything. I said, 'Everyone knows you. There's no need.' But he said he needed proof. Of what? He'll cause a scandal. He's been gone for an hour."

We went into the house and sat in the living-room. "I'm a foolish woman," she said. She got up and hugged me awkwardly. "He'll be all right."

---

3 the military writings of Julius Caesar (100–44 B.C.) were standard reading in high school Latin courses.

We sat a long time listening for his footsteps. At last we heard someone come up the walk. My mother got up and said, "There he is." But there was a knock at the door.

60   I heard them talking at the door. The man said, "Edith, you better come with me. George is in some trouble."

My mother asked what trouble.

"You just better come. He gave the town clerk a poke. The constable and doctor have him now. The doctor wants to talk to you about signing some papers."

"I'm not signing any papers," my mother said.

"You'd better come, Edith."

65   She came into the living-room and said to me, "I'm going to get your father."

I didn't believe her for a minute. She put her coat on and went out.

She didn't bring him home. They took him to an asylum. It was a shameful word then, asylum. But I see it in a different light now. It seems the proper word now, suggesting as it does a refuge, a place to hide.

I'm not sure why all this happened to him. Perhaps there is no reason anyone can put their finger on, although I have my ideas.

But I needed a reason then. I needed a reason that would lend him a little dignity, or rather, lend me a little dignity; for I was ashamed of him out of my own weakness. I needed him to be strong, or at least tragic. I didn't know that most people are neither.

70   When you clutch at straws, anything will do. I read my answer out of Caesar's *The Gallic Wars*, the fat little book I had carried home. In the beginning of Book I he writes, "Of all people the Belgae are the most courageous...." I read on, sharing Caesar's admiration for a people who would not submit but chose to fight and see glory in their wounds. I misread it all, and bent it until I was satisfied. I reasoned the way I had to, for my sake, for my father's. What was he but a man dishonoured by faceless foes? His instincts could not help but prevail, and like his ancestors, in the end, on that one day, what could he do but make the shadows real, and fight to be free of them?

(1982)

Amy Tan   (b. 1952)

Born in Oakland, California, Amy Tan visited her ancestral homeland of China when she was 35. This visit, during which she met her sisters from her mother's first marriage, inspired the writing of her first book, *The Joy Luck Club*, a series of interrelated stories about Chinese mothers and their American-born daughters. "Two Kinds" depicts the conflicts, based on cultural differences and expectations, between one of these pairs when the young girl resists her mother's hopes of her achieving musical celebrity. The title, which refers explicitly to the piece the girl plays at the recital, implicitly refers to the many tensions the narrator feels within herself and between herself and her mother.

TWO KINDS

My mother believed you could be anything you wanted to be in America. You could open a restaurant. You could work for the government and get good retirement. You could buy a house with almost no money down. You could become rich. You could become instantly famous.

"Of course you can be prodigy, too," my mother told me when I was nine. "You can be best anything. What does Auntie Lindo know? Her daughter, she is only best tricky."

America was where all my mother's hopes lay. She had come here in 1949 after losing everything in China: her mother and father, her family home, her first husband, and two daughters, twin baby girls. But she never looked back with regret. There were so many ways for things to get better.

*****

We didn't immediately pick the right kind of prodigy. At first my mother thought I could be a Chinese Shirley Temple.[1] We'd watch Shirley's old movies on TV as though they were training films. My mother would poke my arm and say, "Ni kan" — You watch. And I would see Shirley tapping her feet, or singing a sailor song, or pursing her lips into a very round O while saying, "Oh my goodness."

5   "Ni Kan," said my mother as Shirley's eyes flooded with tears. "You already know how. Don't need talent for crying!"

Soon after my mother got this idea about Shirley Temple, she took me to a beauty training school in the Mission district[2] and put me in the hands of a student who could barely hold the scissors without shaking. Instead of getting big fat curls, I emerged with an uneven mass of crinkly black fuzz. My mother dragged me off to the bathroom and tried to wet down my hair.

"You look like Negro Chinese," she lamented, as if I had done this on purpose.

---

1 popular child actor in motion pictures of the 1930s. 2 fashionable residential district of San Francisco.

The instructor of the beauty training school had to lop off these soggy clumps to make my hair even again. "Peter Pan is very popular these days," the instructor assured my mother. I now had hair the length of a boy's, with straight-across bangs that hung at a slant two inches above my eyebrows. I liked the haircut and it made me actually look forward to my future fame.

In fact, in the beginning, I was just as excited as my mother, maybe even more so. I pictured this prodigy part of me as many different images, trying each one on for size. I was a dainty ballerina girl standing by the curtains, waiting to hear the right music that would send me floating on my tiptoes. I was like the Christ child lifted out of the straw manger, crying with holy indignity. I was Cinderella stepping from her pumpkin carriage with sparkly cartoon music filling the air.

10   In all of my imaginings, I was filled with a sense that I would soon become *perfect*. My mother and father would adore me. I would be beyond reproach. I would never feel the need to sulk for anything.

But sometimes the prodigy in me became impatient. "If you don't hurry up and get me out of here, I'm disappearing for good," it warned. "And then you'll always be nothing."

Every night after dinner, my mother and I would sit at the Formica kitchen table. She would present new tests, taking her examples from stories of amazing children she had read in *Ripley's Believe It or Not*, or *Good Housekeeping, Reader's Digest*, and a dozen other magazines she kept in a pile in our bathroom. My mother got these magazines from people whose houses she cleaned. And since she cleaned many houses each week, we had a great assortment. She would look through them all, searching for stories about remarkable children.

The first night she brought out a story about a three-year-old boy who knew the capitals of all the states and even most of the European countries. A teacher was quoted as saying the little boy could also pronounce the names of the foreign cities correctly.

"What's the capital of Finland?" my mother asked me, looking at the magazine story.

15   All I knew was the capital of California, because Sacramento was the name of the street we lived on in Chinatown. "Nairobi!" I guessed, saying the most foreign word I could think of. She checked to see if that was possibly one way to pronounce "Helsinki"[3] before showing me the answer.

The tests got harder — multiplying numbers in my head, finding the queen of hearts in a deck of cards, trying to stand on my head without using my hands, predicting the daily temperatures in Los Angeles, New York, and London.

One night I had to look at a page from the Bible for three minutes and then report everything I could remember. "Now Jehoshaphat[4] had riches and honor in abundance and . . . that's all I remember, Ma," I said.

And after seeing my mother's disappointed face once again, something inside of me began to die. I hated the tests, the raised hopes and failed expectations. Before going to bed that night, I looked in the mirror above the bathroom sink

---

3 Nairobi is the capital city of Kenya; Helsinki, the capital of Finland. 4 king of Judah in the ninth century B.C.

and when I saw only my face staring back — and that it would always be this ordinary face — I began to cry. Such a sad, ugly girl! I made high-pitched noises like a crazed animal, trying to scratch out the face in the mirror.

And then I saw what seemed to be the prodigy side of me — because I had never seen that face before. I looked at my reflection, blinking so I could see more clearly. The girl staring back at me was angry, powerful. This girl and I were the same. I had new thoughts, willful thoughts, or rather thoughts filled with lots of won'ts. I won't let her change me, I promised myself. I won't be what I'm not.

20   So now on nights when my mother presented her tests, I performed list-lessly, my head propped on one arm. I pretended to be bored. And I was. I got so bored I started counting the bellows of the foghorns out on the bay while my mother drilled me in other areas. The sound was comforting and reminded me of the cow jumping over the moon. And the next day, I played a game with myself, seeing if my mother would give up on me before eight bellows. After a while I usually counted only one, maybe two bellows at most. At last she was beginning to give up hope.

Two or three months had gone by without any mention of my being a prodigy again. And then one day my mother was watching The Ed Sullivan Show [5] on TV. The TV was old and the sound kept shorting out. Every time my mother got halfway up from the sofa to adjust the set, the sound would go back on and Ed would be talking. As soon as she sat down, Ed would go silent again. She got up, the TV broke into loud piano music. She sat down. Silence. Up and down, back and forth, quiet and loud. It was like a stiff embraceless dance between her and the TV set. Finally she stood by the set with her hand on the sound dial.

She seemed entranced by the music, a little frenzied piano piece with this mesmerizing quality, sort of quick passages and then teasing lilting ones before it returned to the quick playful parts.

"Ni kan," my mother said, calling me over with hurried hand gestures, "Look here."

I could see why my mother was fascinated by the music. It was being pounded out by a little Chinese girl, about nine years old, with a Peter Pan haircut. The girl had the sauciness of a Shirley Temple. She was proudly modest like a proper Chinese child. And she also did this fancy sweep of a curtsy, so that the fluffy skirt of her white dress cascaded slowly to the floor like the petals of a large carnation.

25   In spite of these warning signs, I wasn't worried. Our family had no piano and we couldn't afford to buy one, let alone reams of sheet music and piano lessons. So I could be generous in my comments when my mother bad-mouthed the little girl on TV.

"Play note right, but doesn't sound good! No singing sound," complained my mother.

"What are you picking on her for?" I said carelessly. "She's pretty good. Maybe she's not the best, but she's trying hard." I knew almost immediately I would be sorry I said that.

---

5 popular television variety show of the 1950s and 1960s.

"Just like you," she said. "Not the best. Because you not trying." She gave a little huff as she let go of the sound dial and sat down on the sofa.

The little Chinese girl sat down also to play an encore of "Anitra's Dance" by Grieg.[6] I remember the song, because later on I had to learn how to play it.

30   Three days after watching *The Ed Sullivan Show*, my mother told me what my schedule would be for piano lessons and piano practice. She had talked to Mr. Chong, who lived on the first floor of our apartment building. Mr. Chong was a retired piano teacher and my mother had traded housecleaning services for weekly lessons and a piano for me to practice on every day, two hours a day, from four until six.

When my mother told me this, I felt as though I had been sent to hell. I whined and then kicked my foot a little when I couldn't stand it anymore.

"Why don't you like me the way I am? I'm *not* a genius! I can't play the piano. And even if I could, I wouldn't go on TV if you paid me a million dollars!" I cried.

My mother slapped me. "Who ask you be genius?" she shouted. "Only ask you be your best. For you sake. You think I want you be genius? Hnnh! What for! Who ask you!"

"So ungrateful," I heard her mutter in Chinese. "If she had as much talent as she has temper, she would be famous now."

35   Mr. Chong, whom I secretly nicknamed Old Chong, was very strange, always tapping his fingers to the silent music of an invisible orchestra. He looked ancient in my eyes. He had lost most of the hair on top of his head and he wore thick glasses and had eyes that always looked tired and sleepy. But he must have been younger than I thought, since he lived with his mother and was not yet married.

I met Old Lady Chong once and that was enough. She had this peculiar smell like a baby that had done something in its pants. And her fingers felt like a dead person's, like an old peach I once found in the back of the refrigerator; the skin just slid off the meat when I picked it up.

I soon found out why Old Chong had retired from teaching piano. He was deaf. "Like Beethoven!" he shouted to me. "We're both listening only in our head!" And he would start to conduct his frantic silent sonatas.

Our lessons went like this. He would open the book and point to different things, explaining their purpose. "Key! Treble! Bass! No sharps or flats! So this is C major! Listen now and play after me!"

And then he would play the C scale a few times, a simple chord, and then, as if inspired by an old, unreachable itch, he gradually added more notes and running trills and a pounding bass until the music was really something quite grand.

40   I would play after him, the simple scale, the simple chord, and then I just played some nonsense that sounded like a cat running up and down on top of garbage cans. Old Chong smiled and applauded and then said, "Very good! But now you must learn to keep time!"

So that's how I discovered that Old Chong's eyes were too slow to keep up with the wrong notes I was playing. He went through the motions in half-time.

6 nineteenth-century Norwegian composer noted for his nationalistic music.

To help me keep rhythm, he stood behind me, pushing down on my right shoulder for every beat. He balanced pennies on top of my wrists so I would keep them still as I slowly played scales and arpeggios.[7] He had me curve my hand around an apple and keep that shape when playing chords. He marched stiffly to show me how to make each finger dance up and down, staccato like an obedient little soldier.

He taught me all these things, and that was how I also learned I could be lazy and get away with mistakes, lots of mistakes. If I hit the wrong notes because I hadn't practiced enough, I never corrected myself. I just kept playing in rhythm. And Old Chong kept conducting his own private reverie.

So maybe I never really gave myself a fair chance. I did pick up the basics pretty quickly, and I might have become a good pianist at that young age. But I was so determined not to try, not to be anybody different that I learned to play only the most ear-splitting preludes, the most discordant hymns.

Over the next year, I practiced like this, dutifully in my own way. And then one day I heard my mother and her friend Lindo Jong both talking in a loud bragging tone of voice so others could hear. It was after church, and I was leaning against the brick wall wearing a dress with stiff white petticoats. Auntie Lindo's daughter, Waverly, who was about my age, was standing farther down the wall about five feet away. We had grown up together and shared all the closeness of two sisters squabbling over crayons and dolls. In other words, for the most part, we hated each other. I thought she was snotty. Waverly Jong had gained a certain amount of fame as "Chinatown's Littlest Chinese Chess Champion."

45   "She bring home too many trophy," lamented Auntie Lindo that Sunday. "All day she play chess. All day I have no time do nothing but dust off her winnings." She threw a scolding look at Waverly, who pretended not to see her.

"You lucky you don't have this problem," said Auntie Lindo with a sigh to my mother.

And my mother squared her shoulders and bragged: "Our problem worser than yours. If we ask Jing-mei wash dish, she hear nothing but music. It's like you can't stop this natural talent."

And right then, I was determined to put a stop to her foolish pride.

A few weeks later, Old Chong and my mother conspired to have me play in a talent show which would be held in the church hall. By then, my parents had saved up enough to buy me a secondhand piano, a black Wurlitzer spinet with a scarred bench. It was the showpiece of our living room.

50   For the talent show, I was to play a piece called "Pleading Child" from Schumann's *Scenes from Childhood*.[8] It was a simple, moody piece that sounded more difficult than it was. I was supposed to memorize the whole thing, playing the repeat parts twice to make the piece sound longer. But I dawdled over it, playing a few bars and then cheating, looking up to see what notes followed. I never really listened to what I was playing. I daydreamed about being somewhere else, about being someone else.

---

7 playing the notes of a musical chord in succession instead of simultaneously; a standard exercise for piano students. 8 series of short, simple piano pieces by the nineteenth-century German composer Robert Schumann.

The part I liked to practice best was the fancy curtsy: right foot out, touch the rose on the carpet with a pointed foot, sweep to the side, left leg bends, look up and smile.

My parents invited all the couples from the Joy Luck Club to witness my debut. Auntie Lindo and Uncle Tin were there. Waverly and her two older brothers had also come. The first two rows were filled with children both younger and older than I was. The littlest ones got to go first. They recited simple nursery rhymes, squawked out tunes on miniature violins, twirled Hula Hoops, pranced in pink ballet tutus, and when they bowed or curtsied, the audience would sigh in unison, "Awww," and then clap enthusiastically.

When my turn came, I was very confident. I remember my childish excitement. It was as if I knew, without a doubt, that the prodigy side of me really did exist. I had no fear whatsoever, no nervousness. I remember thinking to myself, This is it! This is it! I looked out over the audience, at my mother's blank face, my father's yawn, Auntie Lindo's stiff-lipped smile, Waverly's sulky expression. I had on a white dress layered with sheets of lace, and a pink bow in my Peter Pan haircut. As I sat down I envisioned people jumping to their feet and Ed Sullivan rushing up to introduce me to everyone on TV.

And I started to play. It was so beautiful. I was so caught up in how lovely I looked that at first I didn't worry how I would sound. So it was a surprise to me when I hit the first wrong note and I realized something didn't sound quite right. And then I hit another and another followed that. A chill started at the top of my head and began to trickle down. Yet I couldn't stop playing, as though my hands were bewitched. I kept thinking my fingers would adjust themselves back, like a train switching to the right track. I played this strange jumble through two repeats, the sour notes staying with me all the way to the end.

55   When I stood up, I discovered my legs were shaking. Maybe I had just been nervous and the audience, like Old Chong, had seen me go through the right motions and had not heard anything wrong at all. I swept my right foot out, went down on my knee, looked up and smiled. The room was quiet, except for Old Chong, who was beaming and shouting, "Bravo! Bravo! Well done!" But then I saw my mother's face, her stricken face. The audience clapped weakly, and as I walked back to my chair, with my whole face quivering as I tried not to cry, I heard a little boy whisper loudly to his mother, "That was awful," and the mother whispered back, "Well, she certainly tried."

And now I realized how many people were in the audience, the whole world it seemed. I was aware of eyes burning into my back. I felt the shame of my mother and father as they sat stiffly throughout the rest of the show.

We could have escaped during intermission. Pride and some strange sense of honor must have anchored my parents to their chairs. And so we watched it all: the eighteen-year-old boy with a fake mustache who did a magic show and juggled flaming hoops while riding a unicycle. The breasted girl with white makeup who sang from *Madama Butterfly* [9] and got honorable mention.

---

9 early twentieth-century opera by Giacomo Puccini about a Japanese woman abandoned by her American husband.

And the eleven-year-old boy who won first prize playing a tricky violin song that sounded like a busy bee.

After the show, the Hsus, the Jongs, and the St. Clairs from the Joy Luck Club came up to my mother and father.

"Lots of talented kids," Auntie Lindo said vaguely, smiling broadly.

60 "That was somethin' else," said my father, and I wondered if he was referring to me in a humorous way, or whether he even remembered what I had done.

Waverly looked at me and shrugged her shoulders. "You aren't a genius like me," she said matter-of-factly. And if I hadn't felt so bad, I would have pulled her braids and punched her stomach.

But my mother's expression was what devastated me: a quiet, blank look that said she had lost everything. I felt the same way, and it seemed as if everybody were now coming up, like gawkers at the scene of an accident, to see what parts were actually missing. When we got on the bus to go home, my father was humming the busy-bee tune and my mother was silent. I kept thinking she wanted to wait until we got home before shouting at me. But when my father unlocked the door to our apartment, my mother walked in and then went to the back, into the bedroom. No accusations. No blame. And in a way, I felt disappointed. I had been waiting for her to start shouting, so I could shout back and cry and blame her for all my misery.

I assumed my talent-show fiasco meant I never had to play the piano again. But two days later, after school, my mother came out of the kitchen and saw me watching TV.

"Four clock," she reminded me as if it were any other day. I was stunned, as though she were asking me to go through the talent-show torture again. I wedged myself more tightly in front of the TV.

65 "Turn off TV," she called from the kitchen five minutes later.

I didn't budge. And then I decided. I didn't have to do what my mother said anymore. I wasn't her slave. This wasn't China. I had listened to her before and look what happened. She was the stupid one.

She came out from the kitchen and stood in the arched entryway of the living room. "Four clock," she said once again, louder.

"I'm not going to play anymore," I said nonchalantly. "Why should I? I'm not a genius."

She walked over and stood in front of the TV. I saw her chest was heaving up and down in an angry way.

70 "No!" I said, and I now felt stronger, as if my true self had finally emerged. So this was what had been inside me all along.

"No! I won't!" I screamed.

She yanked me by the arm, pulled me off the floor, snapped off the TV. She was frighteningly strong, half pulling, half carrying me toward the piano as I kicked the throw rugs under my feet. She lifted me up and onto the hard bench. I was sobbing by now, looking at her bitterly. Her chest was heaving even more and her mouth was open, smiling crazily as if she was pleased I was crying.

"You want me to be someone that I'm not!" I sobbed. "I'll never be the kind of daughter you want me to be!"

"Only two kinds of daughters," she shouted in Chinese. "Those who are obedient and those who follow their own mind! Only one kind of daughter can live in this house. Obedient daughter!"

75   "Then I wish I wasn't your daughter. I wish you weren't my mother," I shouted. As I said these things I got scared. It felt like worms and toads and slimy things crawling out of my chest, but it also felt good, as if this awful side of me had surfaced, at last.

"Too late change this," said my mother shrilly.

And I could sense her anger rising to its breaking point. I wanted to see it spill over. And that's when I remembered the babies she had lost in China, the ones we never talked about. "Then I wish I'd never been born!" I shouted. "I wish I were dead! Like them."

It was as if I had said the magic words. Alakazam! — and her face went blank, her mouth closed, her arms went slack, and she backed out of the room, stunned, as if she were blowing away like a small brown leaf, thin, brittle, lifeless.

*****

It was not the only disappointment my mother felt in me. In the years that followed, I failed her so many times, each time asserting my own will, my right to fall short of expectations. I didn't get straight As. I didn't become class president. I didn't get into Stanford. I dropped out of college.

80   For unlike my mother, I did not believe I could be anything I wanted to be. I could only be me.

And for all those years, we never talked about the disaster at the recital or my terrible accusations afterward at the piano bench. All that remained unchecked, like a betrayal that was now unspeakable. So I never found a way to ask her why she had hoped for something so large that failure was inevitable.

And even worse, I never asked her what frightened me the most: Why had she given up hope?

For after our struggle at the piano, she never mentioned my playing again. The lessons stopped. The lid to the piano was closed, shutting out the dust, my misery, and her dreams.

So she surprised me. A few years ago, she offered to give me the piano, for my thirtieth birthday. I had not played in all those years. I saw the offer as a sign of forgiveness, a tremendous burden removed.

85   "Are you sure?" I asked shyly. "I mean, won't you and Dad miss it?"

"No, this your piano," she said firmly. "Always your piano. You only one can play."

"Well, I probably can't play anymore," I said. "It's been years."

"You pick up fast," said my mother, as if she knew this was certain. "You have natural talent. You could been genius if you want to."

"No I couldn't."

90   "You just not trying," said my mother. And she was neither angry nor sad. She said it as if to announce a fact that could never be disproved. "Take it," she said.

But I didn't at first. It was enough that she had offered it to me. And after that, every time I saw it in my parents' living room, standing in front of the bay windows, it made me feel proud, as if it were a shiny trophy I had won back.

Last week I sent a tuner over to my parents' apartment and had the piano reconditioned, for purely sentimental reasons. My mother had died a few months before and I had been getting things in order for my father, a little bit at a time. I put the jewelry in special silk pouches. The sweaters she had knitted in yellow, pink, bright orange — all the colors I hated — I put those in moth-proof boxes. I found some old Chinese silk dresses, the kind with the little slits up the sides. I rubbed the old silk against my skin, then wrapped them in tissue and decided to take them home with me.

After I had the piano tuned, I opened the lid and touched the keys. It sounded even richer than I remembered. Really, it was a very good piano. Inside the bench were the same exercise notes with handwritten scales, the same secondhand music books with their covers held together with yellow tape.

I opened up the Schumann book to the dark little piece I had played at the recital. It was on the left-hand side of the page, "Pleading Child." It looked more difficult than I remembered. I played a few bars, surprised at how easily the notes came back to me.

95 And for the first time, or so it seemed, I noticed the piece on the right-hand side. It was called "Perfectly Contented." I tried to play this one as well. It had a lighter melody but the same flowing rhythm and turned out to be quite easy. "Pleading Child" was shorter but slower; "Perfectly Contented" was longer, but faster. And after I played them both a few times, I realized they were two halves of the same song.

(1989)

Rohinton Mistry (b. 1952)

Born and raised in Bombay, India, Mistry is a Parsi, a religious minority much favored by the British when they ruled in India. Mistry came to Canada in 1975 and began writing while attending the University of Toronto. *Tales from Firozsha Baag* (1987), his first book, is a collection of short stories about the frequently contentious interrelationships among the residents of a Bombay housing complex. His two novels, *Such a Long Journey* (1991), winner of the Governor General's Medal, and *A Fine Balance* (1995), are set in India during the country-wide political crises of the 1970s. "Squatter," the story of a Firozsha Baag resident's unfortunate immigration to Canada, plays on the pun of the title, which not only indicates his physical difficulties, but also his status as a new Canadian. The squatter's problems in an alien environment can be compared to those of Giovanni in Hawthorne's "Rappaccini's Daughter" and Calvin in Clarke's "The Motor Car." In addition to portraying the difficulties faced by immigrants, Mistry also examines the role of the storyteller, an old man who frequently recounts tales to an admiring audience of boys gathered outside his Bombay apartment.

SQUATTER

Whenever Nariman Hansotia returned in the evening from the Cawasji Framji Memorial Library in a good mood the signs were plainly evident.

First, he parked his 1932 Mercedes-Benz (he called it the apple of his eye) outside A Block, directly in front of his ground-floor veranda window, and beeped the horn three long times. It annoyed Rustomji who also had a ground-floor flat in A Block. Ever since he had defied Nariman in the matter of painting the exterior of the building, Rustomji was convinced that nothing the old coot did was untainted by the thought of vengeance and harassment, his retirement pastime.

But the beeping was merely Nariman's signal to let Hirabai inside know that though he was back he would not step indoors for a while. Then he raised the hood, whistling "Rose Marie,"[1] and leaned his tall frame over the engine. He checked the oil, wiped here and there with a rag, tightened the radiator cap, and lowered the hood. Finally, he polished the Mercedes star and let the whistling modulate into the march from *The Bridge on The River Kwai*.[2] The boys playing in the compound knew that Nariman was ready now to tell a story. They started to gather round.

"*Sahibji*,[3] Nariman Uncle," someone said tentatively and Nariman nodded, careful not to lose his whistle, his bulbous nose flaring slightly. The pursed lips had temporarily raised and reshaped his Clark Gable[4] moustache. More boys walked up. One called out, "How about a story, Nariman Uncle?" at which point Nariman's eyes began to twinkle, and he imparted increased energy to the polishing. The cry was taken up by others, "Yes, yes, Nariman Uncle, a story!"

---

1 title song from a 1954 Hollywood musical that depicted a romance between a Mountie and a French-Canadian girl. 2 1957 movie about a British colonel who, with his men, is imprisoned by the Japanese during World War II. 3 Sir, an expression of respect. 4 American movie star of the 1940s and 1950s.

He swung into a final verse of the march. Then the lips relinquished the whistle, the Clark Gable moustache descended. The rag was put away, and he began.

"You boys know the great cricketers: Contractor, Polly Umrigar, and recently, the young chap, Farokh Engineer. Cricket *aficionados*, that's what you all are." Nariman liked to use new words, especially big ones, in the stories he told, believing it was his duty to expose young minds to as shimmering and varied a vocabulary as possible; if they could not spend their days at the Cawasji Framji Memorial Library then he, at least, could carry bits of the library out to them.

The boys nodded; the names of the cricketers were familiar.

"But does any one know about Savukshaw, the greatest of them all?" They shook their heads in unison.

"This, then, is the story about Savukshaw, how he saved the Indian team from a humiliating defeat when they were touring in England." Nariman sat on the steps of A Block. The few diehards who had continued with their games could not resist any longer when they saw the gathering circle, and ran up to listen. They asked their neighbours in whispers what the story was about, and were told: Savukshaw the greatest cricketer. The whispering died down and Nariman began.

"The Indian team was to play the indomitable MCC as part of its tour of England. Contractor was our captain. Now the MCC being the strongest team they had to face, Contractor was almost certain of defeat. To add to Contractor's troubles, one of his star batsmen, Nadkarni, had caught influenza early in the tour, and would definitely not be well enough to play against the MCC. By the way, does anyone know what those letters stand for? You, Kersi, you wanted to be a cricketer once."

Kersi shook his head. None of the boys knew, even though they had heard the MCC mentioned in radio commentaries, because the full name was hardly ever used.

Then Jehangir Bulsara spoke up, or Bulsara Bookworm, as the boys called him. The name given by Pesi *paadmaroo*[5] had stuck even though it was now more than four years since Pesi had been sent away to boarding-school, and over two years since the death of Dr. Mody. Jehangir was still unliked by the boys in the Baag, though they had come to accept his aloofness and respect his knowledge and intellect. They were not surprised that he knew the answer to Nariman's question: "Marylebone Cricket Club."

"Absolutely correct," said Nariman, and continued with the story. "The MCC won the toss and elected to bat. They scored four hundred and ninety-seven runs in the first inning before our spinners could get them out. Early in the second day's play our team was dismissed for one hundred and nine runs, and the extra who had taken Nadkarni's place was injured by a vicious bumper that opened a gash on his forehead." Nariman indicated the spot and the length of the gash on his furrowed brow. "Contractor's worst fears were coming true. The MCC waived their own second inning and gave the Indian team a follow-on, wanting to inflict an inning's defeat. And this time he had to use the second extra. The second extra was as a certain Savukshaw."

5 lotus-boy, a mocking nickname.

The younger boys listened attentively; some of them, like the two sons of the chartered accountant in B Block, had only recently been deemed old enough by their parents to come out and play in the compound, and had not received any exposure to Nariman's stories. But the others like Jehangir, Kersi, and Viraf were familiar with Nariman's technique.

Once, Jehangir had overheard them discussing Nariman's stories, and he could not help expressing his opinion: that unpredictability was the brush he used to paint his tales with, and ambiguity the palette he mixed his colours in. The others looked at him with admiration. Then Viraf asked what exactly he meant by that. Jehangir said that Nariman sometimes told a funny incident in a very serious way, or expressed a significant matter in a light and playful manner. And these were only two rough divisions, in between were lots of subtle gradations of tone and texture. Which, then, was the funny story and which the serious? Their opinions were divided, but ultimately, said Jehangir, it was up to the listener to decide.

15   "So," continued Nariman, "Contractor first sent out his two regular openers, convinced that it was all hopeless. But after five wickets were lost for just another thirty-eight runs, out came Savukshaw the extra. Nothing mattered any more."

The street lights outside the compound came on, illuminating the iron gate where the watchman stood. It was a load off the watchman's mind when Nariman told a story. It meant an early end to the hectic vigil during which he had to ensure that none of the children ran out on the main road, or tried to jump over the wall. For although keeping out riff-raff was his duty, keeping in the boys was as important if he wanted to retain the job.

"The first ball Savukshaw faced was wide outside the off stump. He just lifted his bat and ignored it. But with what style! What panache! As if to say, come on, you blighters, play some polished cricket. The next ball was also wide, but not as much as the first. It missed the off stump narrowly. Again Savukshaw lifted his bat, boredom written all over him. Everyone was now watching closely. The bowler was annoyed by Savukshaw's arrogance, and the third delivery was a vicious fast pitch, right down on the middle stump.

"Savukshaw was ready, quick as lightning. No one even saw the stroke of his bat, but the ball went like a bullet towards the square leg.

"Fielding at square leg was giant fellow, about six feet seven, weighing two hundred and fifty pounds, a veritable Brobdingnagian,[6] with arms like branches and hands like a pair of huge *sapaat*,[7] the kind the Dr Mody used to wear, you remember what big feet Dr Mody had." Jehangir was the only one who did; he nodded. "Just to see him standing there was scary. Not one ball had got past him, and he had taken some great catches. Savukshaw purposely aimed his shot right at him. But he was as quick as Savukshaw, and stuck out his huge *sapaat* of a hand to stop the ball. What do you think happened then, boys?"

20   The older boys knew what Nariman wanted to hear at this point. They asked, "What happened, Nariman Uncle, what happened?" Satisfied, Nariman continued.

6 the giant people in Book II of Jonathan Swift's *Gulliver's Travels*. 7 boots.

"A howl is what happened. A howl from the giant fielder, a howl that rang through the entire stadium, that soared like the cry of a banshee right up to the cheapest seats in the furthest, highest corners, a howl that echoed from the scoreboard and into the pavilion, into the kitchen, startling the chap inside who was preparing tea and scones for after the match, who spilled boiling water all over himself and was severely hurt. But not nearly as bad as the giant fielder at square leg. Never at any English stadium was a howl heard like that one, not in the whole history of cricket. And why do you think he was howling, boys?"

The chorus asked, "Why, Nariman Uncle, why?"

"Because of Savukshaw's bullet-like shot, of course. The hand he had reached out to stop it, he now held up for all to see, and *dhur-dhur, dhur-dhur* the blood was gushing like a fountain in an Italian piazza, like a burst water-main from the Vihar-Powai reservoir, dripping onto his shirt and his white pants, and sprinkling the green grass, and only because he was such a giant of a fellow could he suffer so much blood loss and not faint. But even he could not last forever; eventually, he felt dizzy, and was helped off the field. And where do you think the ball was, boys, that Savukshaw had smacked so hard?"

And the chorus rang out again on the now dark steps of A Block: "Where, Nariman Uncle, where?"

25 "Past the boundary line, of course. Lying near the fence. Rent asunder. Into two perfect leather hemispheres. All the stitches had ripped, and some of the insides had spilled out. So the umpires sent for a new one, and the game resumed. Now none of the fielders dared to touch any ball that Savukshaw hit. Every shot went to the boundary, all the way for four runs. Single-handedly, Savukshaw wiped out the deficit, and had it not been for loss of time due to rain, he would have taken the Indian team to a thumping victory against the MCC. As it was, the match ended in a draw."

Nariman was pleased with the awed faces of the youngest ones around him. Kersi and Viraf were grinning away and whispering something. From one of the flats the smell of frying fish swam out to explore the night air, and tickled Nariman's nostrils. He sniffed appreciatively, aware that it was in his good wife Hirabai's pan that the frying was taking place. This morning, he had seen the pomfret[8] she had purchased at the door, waiting to be cleaned, its mouth open and eyes wide, like the eyes of some of these youngsters. It was time to wind up the story.

"The MCC will not forget the number of new balls they had to produce that day because of Savukshaw's deadly strokes. Their annual ball budget was thrown badly out of balance. Any other bat would have cracked under the strain, but Savukshaw's was seasoned with a special combination of oils, a secret formula given to him by a *sadhu*[9] who had seen him one day playing cricket when he was a small boy. But Savukshaw used to say his real secret was practice, lots of practice, that was the advice he gave to any young lad who wanted to play cricket."

The story was now clearly finished, but none of the boys showed any sign of dispersing. "Tell us about more matches that Savukshaw played in," they said.

8 a popular fish in India. 9 holy man.

"More nothing. This was his greatest match. Anyway, he did not play cricket for long because soon after the match against the MCC he became a champion bicyclist, the fastest human on two wheels. And later, a pole-vaulter — when he glided over on his pole, so graceful, it was like watching a bird in flight. But he gave that up, too, and became a hunter, the mightiest hunter ever known, absolutely fearless, and so skilful, with a gun he could have, from the third floor of A Block, shaved the whisker of a cat in the back-yard of C Block."

"Tell us about that," they said, "about Savukshaw the hunter!"

The fat ayah, Jaakaylee, arrived to take the chartered accountant's two children home. But they refused to go without hearing about Savukshaw the hunter. When she scolded them and things became a little hysterical, some other boys tried to resurrect the ghost she had once seen: "Ayah *bhoot*! Ayah *bhoot*!"[10] Nariman raised a finger in warning — that subject was still taboo in Firozsha Baag; none of the adults was in a hurry to relive the wild and ram-pageous days that Pesi *paadmaroo* had ushered in, once upon a time, with the *bhoot* games.

Jaakaylee sat down, unwilling to return without the children, and whis-pered to Nariman to make it short. The smell of frying fish which had tickled Nariman's nostrils ventured into and awakened his stomach. But the story of Savukshaw the hunter was one he had wanted to tell for a long time.

"Savukshaw always went hunting alone, he preferred it that way. There are many incidents in the life of Savukshaw the hunter, but the one I am telling you about involves a terrifying situation. Terrifying for us, of course; Savukshaw was never terrified of anything. What happened was, one night he set up camp, started a fire and warmed up his bowl of chicken-*dhansaak*."

The frying fish had precipitated famishment upon Nariman, and the subject of chicken-*dhansaak* suited him well. His own mouth watering, he elaborated: "Mrs. Savukshaw was as famous for her *dhansaak* as Mr. was for hunting. She used to put in tamarind and brinjal, coriander and cumin, cloves and cinnamon, and dozens of other spices no one knows about. Women used to come from miles around to stand outside her window while she cooked it, to enjoy the fragrance and try to penetrate her secret, hoping to identify the ingredients as the aroma floated out, layer by layer, growing more complex and delicious. But always, the delectable fra-grance enveloped the women and they just surrendered to the ecstasy, forget-ting what they had come for. Mrs. Savukshaw's secret was safe."

Jaakaylee motioned to Nariman to hurry up, it was past the children's dinner-time. He continued: "The aroma of savoury spices soon filled the night air in the jungle, and when the *dhansaak* was piping hot he started to eat, his rifle beside him. But as soon as he lifted the first morsel to his lips, a tiger's eyes flashed in the bushes! Not twelve feet from him! He emerged licking his chops! What do you think happened then, boys?"

"What, what, Nariman Uncle?"

Before he could tell them, the door of his flat opened. Hirabai put her head out and said, "*Chaalo ni*,[11] Nariman, it's time. Then if it gets cold you won't like it."

10 ghost. 11 let's go.

That decided the matter. To let Hirabai's fried fish, crisp on the outside, yet tender and juicy inside, marinated in turmeric and cayenne — to let that get cold would be something that *Khoedaiji*[12] above would not easily forgive. "Sorry boys, have to go. Next time about Savukshaw and the tiger."

There were some groans of disappointment. They hoped Nariman's good spirits would extend into the morrow when he returned from the Memorial Library, or the story would get cold.

40   But a whole week elapsed before Nariman again parked the apple of his eye outside his ground-floor flat and beeped the horn three times. When he had raised the hood, checked the oil, polished the star and swung into the "Colonel Bogie March,"[13] the boys began drifting towards A Block.

Some of them recalled the incomplete story of Savukshaw and the tiger, but they knew better than to remind him. It was never wise to prompt Nariman until he had dropped the first hint himself, or things would turn out badly.

Nariman inspected the faces: the two who stood at the back, always looking superior and wise, were missing. So was the quiet Bulsara boy, the intelligent one. "Call Kersi, Viraf, and Jehangir," he said. "I want them to listen to today's story."

Jehangir was sitting alone on the stone steps of C Block. The others were chatting by the compound gate with the watchman. Someone went to fetch them.

"Sorry to disturb your conference, boys, and your meditation, Jehangir," Nariman said facetiously, "but I thought you would like to hear this story. Especially since some of you are planning to go abroad."

45   This was not strictly accurate, but Kersi and Viraf did talk a lot about America and Canada. Kersi had started writing to universities there since his final high-school year, and had also send letters of inquiry to the Canadian High Commission in New Delhi and to the U.S. Consulate at Breach Candy.[14] But so far he had not made any progress. He and Viraf replied with as much sarcasm as their unripe years allowed, "Oh yes, next week, just have to pack our bags."

"Riiiight," drawled Nariman. Although he spoke perfect English, this was the one word with which he allowed himself to take liberties, indulging in a broadness of vowel more American than anything else. "But before we go on with today's story, what did you learn about Savukshaw, from last week's story?"

"That he was a very talented man," said someone.

"What else?"

"He was also a very lucky man, to have so many talents," said Viraf.

50   "Yes, but what else?"

There was silence for a few moments. Then Jehangir said, timidly: "He was a man searching for happiness, by trying all kinds of different things."

"Exactly! And he never found it. He kept looking for new experiences, and though he was very successful at everything he attempted, it did not bring him happiness. Remember this, success alone does not bring happiness.

12 God.   13 a marching tune whistled by captured British soldiers in *The Bridge on the River Kwai*.   14 an affluent, fashionable district of Bombay.

Nor does failure have to bring unhappiness. Keep it in mind when you listen to today's story."

A chant started somewhere in the back: "We-want-a-story! We-want-a-story!"

"Riiiight," said Nariman. "Now, everyone remembers Vera and Dolly, daughters of Najamai from C Block." There were whistles and hoots; Viraf nudged Kersi with his elbow, who was smiling wistfully. Nariman held up his hand: "Now now, boys, behave yourselves. Those two girls went abroad for studies many years ago, and never came back. They settled there happily.

55 "And like them, a fellow called Sarosh also went abroad, to Toronto, but did not find happiness there. This story is about him. You probably don't know him, he does not live in Firozsha Baag, though he is related to someone who does."

"Who? Who?"

"Curiosity killed the cat," said Nariman, running a finger over each branch of his moustache, "and what's important is the tale. So let us continue. This Sarosh began calling himself Sid after living in Toronto for a few months, but in our story he will be Sarosh and nothing but Sarosh, for that is his proper Parsi name. Besides, that was his own stipulation when he entrusted me with the sad but instructive chronicle of his recent life." Nariman polished his glasses with his handkerchief, put them on again, and began.

"At the point where our story commences, Sarosh had been living in Toronto for ten years. We find him depressed and miserable, perched on top of the toilet, crouching on his haunches, feet planted firmly for balance upon the white plastic oval of the toilet seat.

"Daily for a decade had Sarosh suffered this position. Morning after morning, he had no choice but to climb up and simulate the squat of our Indian latrines. If he sat down, no amount of exertion could produce success.

60 "At first, this inability was not more than mildly incommodious. As time went by, however, the frustrated attempts caused him grave anxiety. And when the failure stretched unbroken over ten years, it began to torment and haunt all his waking hours."

Some of the boys struggled hard to keep straight faces. They suspected that Nariman was not telling just a funny story, because if he intended them to laugh there was always some unmistakable way to let them know. Only the thought of displeasing Nariman and prematurely terminating the story kept their paroxysms of mirth from bursting forth unchecked.

Nariman continued: "You see, ten years was the time Sarosh had set himself to achieve complete adaptation to the new country. But how could he claim adaptation with any honesty if the acceptable catharsis continually failed to favour him? Obtaining his new citizenship had not helped either. He remained dependent on the old way, and this unalterable fact, strengthened afresh every morning of his life in the new country, suffocated him.

"The ten-year time limit was more an accident than anything else. But it hung over him with the awesome presence and sharpness of a guillotine. Careless words, boys, careless words in a moment of lightheartedness, as is so often the case with us all, had led to it.

"Ten years before, Sarosh had returned triumphantly to Bombay after fulfilling the immigration requirements of the Canadian High Commission in

New Delhi. News of his imminent departure spread amongst relatives and friends. A farewell party was organized. In fact, it was given by his relatives in Firozsha Baag. Most of you will be too young to remember it, but it was a very loud party, went on till late in the night. Very lengthy and heated arguments took place, which is not the thing to do at a party. It started like this: Sarosh was told by some what a smart decision he had made, that his whole life would change for the better; others said he was making a mistake, emigration was all wrong, but if he wanted to be unhappy that was his business, they wished him well.

65   "By and by, after substantial amounts of Scotch and soda and rum and Coke had disappeared, a fierce debate started between the two groups. To this day Sarosh does not know what made him raise his glass and announce: 'My dear family, my dear friends, if I do not become completely Canadian in exactly ten years from the time I land there, then I will come back. I promise. So please, no more arguments. Enjoy the party.' His words were greeted with cheers and shouts of hear! hear! They told him never to fear embarrassment; there was no shame if he decided to return to the country of his birth.

    "But shortly, his poor worried mother pulled him aside. She led him to the back room and withdrew her worn and aged prayer book from her purse, saying, 'I want you to place your hand upon the *Avesta*[15] and swear that you will keep that promise.'

    "He told her not to be silly, that it was just a joke. But she insisted. '*Kassum khà*[16]— on the *Avesta*. One last thing for your mother. Who knows when you will see me again?' and her voice grew tremulous as it always did when she turned deeply emotional. Sarosh complied, and the prayer book was returned to her purse.

    "His mother continued: 'It is better to live in want among your family and your friends, who love you and care for you, than to be unhappy surrounded by vacuum cleaners and dishwashers and big shiny motor cars.' She hugged him. Then they joined the celebration in progress.

    "And Sarosh's careless words spoken at the party gradually forged themselves into a commitment as much to himself as to his mother and the others. It stayed with him all his years in the new land, reminding him every morning of what must happen at the end of the tenth, as it reminded him now while he descended from his perch."

70   Jehangir wished the titters and chortles around him would settle down, he found them annoying. When Nariman structured his sentences so carefully and chose his words with extreme care as he was doing now, Jehangir found it most pleasurable to listen. Sometimes, he remembered certain words Nariman had used, or combinations of words, and repeated them to himself, enjoying again the beauty of their sounds when he went for his walks to the Hanging Gardens or was sitting alone on the stone steps of C Block. Mumbling to himself did nothing to mitigate the isolation which the other boys in the Baag had dropped around him like a heavy cloak, but he had grown used to all that by now.

15 sacred Zoroastrian (Parsi) text. 16 swear an oath.

Nariman continued: "In his own apartment Sarosh squatted barefoot. Elsewhere, if he had to go with his shoes on, he would carefully cover the seat with toilet paper before climbing up. He learnt to do this after the first time, when his shoes had left telltale footprints on the seat. He had had to clean it with a wet paper towel. Luckily, no one had seen him.

But there was not much he could keep secret about his ways. The world of washrooms is private and at the same time very public. The absence of his feet below the stall door, the smell of faeces, the rustle of paper, glimpses caught through the narrow crack between stall door and jamb — all these added up to only one thing: a foreign presence in the stall, not doing things in the conventional way. And if the one outside could receive the fetor of Sarosh's business wafting through the door, poor unhappy Sarosh too could detect something malodorous in the air: the presence of xenophobia and hostility."

What a feast, thought Jehangir, what a feast of words! This would be the finest story Nariman had ever told, he just knew it.

"But Sarosh did not give up trying. Each morning he seated himself to push and grunt, grunt and push, squirming and writhing unavailingly on the white plastic oval. Exhausted, he then hopped up, expert at balancing now, and completed the movement quite effortlessly.

75   "The long morning hours in the washroom created new difficulties. He was late going to work on several occasions, and one such day, the supervisor called him in: 'Here's your time-sheet for this month. You've been late eleven times. What's the problem?'"

Here, Nariman stopped because his neighbour Rustomji's door creaked open. Rustomji peered out, scowling and muttered, "Saala[17] loafers, sitting all evening outside people's houses, making a nuisance, and being encouraged by grownups at that."

He stood there a moment longer, fingering the greying chest hair that was easily accessible through his sudra,[18] then went inside. The boys immediately took up a soft and low chant: "Rustomji-the-curmudgeon! Rustomji-the-curmudgeon!"

Nariman held up his hand disapprovingly. But secretly, he was pleased that the name was still popular, the name he had given Rustomji when the latter had refused to pay his share for painting the building. "Quiet, quiet!" said he. "Do you want me to continue or not?"

"Yes, yes!" The chanting died away, and Nariman resumed the story.

80   "So Sarosh was told by his supervisor that he was coming late to work too often. What could poor Sarosh say?"

"What, Nariman Uncle?" rose the refrain.

"Nothing, of course. The supervisor, noting his silence, continued: 'If it keeps up, the consequences could be serious as far as your career is concerned.'

"Sarosh decided to speak. He said embarrassedly, 'It's a different kind of problem. I…I don't know how to explain…it's an immigration-related problem.'

"Now this supervisor must have had experience with other immigrants, because right away he told Sarosh, 'No problem. Just contact your Immigrant Aid Society. They should be able to help you. Every ethnic group has one:

17 dirty. 18 woolen shirt.

Vietnamese, Chinese — I'm certain that one exists for Indians. If you need time off to go there, no problem. That can be arranged, no problem. As long as you do something about your lateness, there's no problem.' That's the way they talk over there, nothing is ever a problem.

85 "So Sarosh thanked him and went to his desk. For the umpteenth time he bitterly rued his oversight. Could fate have plotted it, concealing the western toilet behind a shroud of anxieties which had appeared out of nowhere to beset him just before he left India? After all, he had readied himself meticulously for the new life. Even for the great, merciless Canadian cold he had heard so much about. How could he have overlooked preparation for the western toilet with its matutinal demands unless fate had conspired? In Bombay, you know that offices of foreign businesses offer both options in their bathrooms. So do all hotels with three stars or more. By practising in familiar surroundings, Sarosh was convinced he could have mastered a seated evacuation before departure.

"But perhaps there was something in what the supervisor said. Sarosh found a telephone number for the Indian Immigrant Aid Society and made an appointment. That afternoon, he met Mrs. Maha-Lepate at the Society's office.

Kersi and Viraf looked at each other and smiled. Nariman Uncle had a nerve, there was more *lepate* in his own stories than anywhere else.

"Mrs. Maha-Lepate was very understanding, and made Sarosh feel at ease despite the very personal nature of his problem. She said, 'Yes, we get many referrals. There was a man here last month who couldn't eat Wonder Bread — it made him throw up.'

"By the way, boys, Wonder Bread is a Canadian bread which all happy families eat to be happy in the same way; the unhappy families are unhappy in their own fashion by eating other brands." Jehangir was the only one who understood, and murmured, "Tolstoy,"[19] at Nariman's little joke. Nariman noticed it, pleased. He continued.

90 "Mrs. Maha-Lepate told Sarosh about that case: 'Our immigrant specialist, Dr. No-Ilaaz, recommended that the patient eat cake instead. He explained that Wonder Bread caused vomiting because the digestive system was used to Indian bread only, made with Indian flour in the village he came from. However, since his system was unfamiliar with cake, Canadian or otherwise, it did not react but was digested as a newfound food. In this way he got used to Canadian flour first in cake form. Just yesterday we received a report from Dr. No-Ilaaz. The patient successfully ate his first slice of whole-wheat Wonder Bread with no ill effects. The ultimate goal is pure white Wonder Bread.'

"Like a polite Parsi boy, Sarosh said, 'That's very interesting.' The garrulous Mrs. Maha-Lepate was about to continue, and he tried to interject: 'But I —' but Mrs. Maha-Lepate was too quick for him: 'Oh, there are so many interesting cases I could tell you about. Like the woman from Sri Lanka — referred to us because they don't have their own Society — who could not drink the water here. Dr. No-Ilaaz said it was due to the different mineral content. So he started her on Coca-Cola and then began diluting it with water, bit by bit. Six weeks later she took her first sip of unadulterated Canadian water and managed to keep it down.'

19 nineteenth-century Russian author of *War and Peace*; the lines about happy and unhappy families parody the opening of his novel *Anna Karenina*.

"Sarosh could not halt Mrs. Maha-Lepate as she launched from one case history into another: 'Right now, Dr. No-Ilaaz is working on a very unusual case. Involves a whole Pakistani family. Ever since immigrating to Canada, none of them can swallow. They choke on their own saliva, and have to spit constantly. But we are confident that Dr. No-Ilaaz will find a remedy. He has never been stumped by any immigrant problems. Besides, we have an information network with other third-world Immigrant Aid Societies. We all seem to share a history of similar maladies, and regularly compare notes. Some of us thought these problems were linked to retention of original citizenship. But this was a false lead.'

"Sarosh, out of his own experience, vigorously nodded agreement. By now he was truly fascinated by Mrs. Maha-Lepate's wealth of information. Reluctantly, he interrupted: 'But will Dr. No-Ilaaz be able to solve my problem?'

" 'I have every confidence that he will,' replied Mrs. Maha-Lepate in great earnest. 'And if he has no remedy for you right away, he will be delighted to start working on one. He loves to take up new projects.' "

95 Nariman halted to blow his nose, and a clear shrill voice travelled the night air of the Firozsha Baag compound from C Block to where the boys had collected around Nariman in A Block: "Jehangoo! O Jehangoo! Eight o'clock! Upstairs now!"

Jehangir stared at his feet in embarrassment. Nariman looked at his watch and said, "Yes, it's eight." But Jehangir did not move, so he continued.

"Mrs. Maha-Lepate was able to arrange an appointment while Sarosh waited, and he went directly to the doctor's office. What he had heard so far sounded quite promising. Then he cautioned himself not to get overly optimistic, that was the worst mistake he could make. But along the way to the doctor's, he could not help thinking what a lovely city Toronto was. It was the same way he had felt when he first saw it ten years ago, before all the joy had dissolved in the acid of his anxieties."

Once again that shrill voice travelled through the clear night: "Arré[20] Jehangoo! Muà,[21] do I have to come down and drag you upstairs!"

Jehangir's mortification was now complete. Nariman made it easy for him, though: "The first part of the story is over. Second part continues tomorrow. Same time, same place." The boys were surprised, Nariman did not make such commitments. But never before had he told such a long story. They began drifting back to their homes.

100 As Jehangir strode hurriedly to C Block, falsettos and piercing shrieks followed him in the darkness: "Arré Jehangoo! Muà, Jehangoo! Bulsara Bookworm! Eight o'clock Jehangoo!" Shaking his head, Nariman went indoors to Hirabai.

Next evening the story punctually resumed when Nariman took his place on the topmost step of A Block: "You remember that we left Sarosh on his way to see the Immigrant Aid Society's doctor. Well, Dr. No-Ilaaz listened patiently to Sarosh's concerns, then said, 'As a matter of fact, there is a remedy which is so new even the IAS does not know about it. Not even that Mrs. Maha-Lepate who knows it all,' he added drolly, twirling his stethoscope like a

20 oh. 21 a good-for-nothing.

stunted lasso. He slipped it on around his neck before continuing: 'It involves a minor operation which was developed with financial assistance from the Multicultural Department. A small device, *Crappus Non Interruptus*, or CNI as we call it, is implanted in the bowel. The device is controlled by an external handheld transmitter similar to the ones used for automatic garage door-openers — you may have seen them in hardware stores.'"

Nariman noticed that most of the boys wore puzzled looks and realized he had to make some things clearer. "The Multicultural Department is a Canadian invention. It is supposed to ensure that ethnic cultures are able to flourish, so that Canadian society will consist of a mosaic of cultures — that's their favourite word, mosaic — instead of one uniform mix, like the American melting pot. If you ask me, mosaic and melting pot are both nonsense, and ethnic is a polite way of saying bloody foreigner. But anyway, you understand Multicultural Department? Good. So Sarosh nodded, and Dr. No-Ilaaz went on: 'You can encode the hand-held transmitter with a personal ten-digit code. Then all you do is position yourself on the toilet seat and activate your transmitter. Just like a garage door, your bowel will open without pushing or grunting.'"

There was some snickering in the audience, and Nariman raised his eye-brows, whereupon they covered up their mouths with their hands. "The doctor asked Sarosh if he had any questions. Sarosh thought for a moment, then asked if it required any maintenance.

"Dr. No-Ilaaz replied: 'CNI is semi-permanent and operates on solar energy. Which means you would have to make it a point to get some sun peri-odically, or it would cease and lead to constipation. However, you don't have to strip for a tan. Exposing ten percent of your skin surface once a week during summer will let the device store sufficient energy for year-round operation.'

105   "Sarosh's next question was: 'Is there any hope that someday the bowels can work on their own, without operating the device?' at which Dr No-Ilaaz grimly shook his head: 'I'm afraid not. You must think very, very carefully before making a decision. Once CNI is implanted, you can never pass a motion in the natural way — neither sitting nor squatting.'

"He stopped to allow Sarosh time to think it over, then continued: 'And you must understand what that means. You will never be able to live a normal life again. You will be permanently different from your family and friends because of this basic internal modification. In fact, in this country or that, it will set you apart from your fellow countrymen. So you must consider the whole thing most carefully.'

"Dr. No-Ilaaz paused, toyed with his stethoscope, shuffled some papers on his desk, then resumed: 'There are other dangers you should know about. Just as a garage door can be accidentally opened by a neighbour's transmitter on the same frequency, CNI can also be activated by someone with similar apparatus.' To ease the tension he attempted to quick laugh and said, 'Very embarrassing, eh, if it happened at the wrong place and time. Mind you, the risk is not so great at present, because the chances of finding yourself within a fifty-foot radius of another transmitter on the same frequency are infinites-imal. But what about the future? What if CNI becomes very popular? Sufficient permutations may not be available for transmitter frequencies and you could be sharing the code with others. Then the risk of accidents becomes greater.'"

Something landed with a loud thud in the yard behind A Block, making Nariman startle. Immediately, a yowling and screeching and caterwauling went up from the stray cats there, and the *kuchrawalli's*[22] dog started barking. Some of the boys went around the side of A Block to peer over the fence into the backyard. But the commotion soon died down of its own accord. The boys returned and, once again, Nariman's voice was the only sound to be heard.

"By now, Sarosh was on the verge of deciding against the operation. Dr. No-Ilaaz observed this and was pleased. He took pride in being able to dissuade his patients from following the very remedies which he first so painstakingly described. True to his name, Dr. No-Ilaaz believed no remedy is the best remedy, rather than prescribing this-mycin and that-mycin for every little ailment. So he continued: 'And what about our sons and daughters? And the quality of their lives? We still don't know about the long-term effects of CNI. Some researchers speculate that it could generate a genetic deficiency, that the offspring of a CNI parent would also require CNI. On the other hand, they could be perfectly healthy toilet seat-users, without any congenital defects. We just don't know at this stage.'

110 "Sarosh rose from his chair: 'Thank you very much for your time, Dr. No-Ilaaz. But I don't think I want to take such a drastic step. As you suggest, I will think it over carefully.'

"'Good, good,' said Dr. No-Ilaaz, 'I was hoping you would say that. There is one more thing. The operation is extremely expensive, and is not covered by the province's Health Insurance Plan. Many immigrant groups are lobbying to obtain coverage for special immigration-related health problems. If they succeed, then good for you.'

"Sarosh left Dr. No-Ilaaz's office with his mind made up. Time was running out. There had been a time when it was perfectly natural to squat. Now it seemed a grotesquely aberrant thing to do. Wherever he went he was reminded of the ignominy of his way. If he could not be westernized in all respects, he was nothing but a failure in this land — a failure not just in the washrooms of the nation but everywhere. He knew what he must do if he was to be true to himself and to the decade-old commitment. So what do you think Sarosh did next?"

"What, Nariman Uncle?"

"He went to the travel agent specializing in tickets to India. He bought a fully refundable ticket to Bombay for the day when he would complete exactly ten immigrant years — if he succeeded even once before that day dawned, he would cancel the booking.

115 "The travel agent asked sympathetically, 'Trouble at home?' His name was Mr. Rawaana, and he was from Bombay too.

"'No,' said Sarosh, 'trouble in Toronto.'

"'That's a shame,' said Mr. Rawaana. 'I don't want to poke my nose into your business, but in my line of work I meet so many people who are going back to their homeland because of their problems here. Sometimes I forget I'm a travel agent, that my interest is to convince them to travel. Instead, I tell them: don't give up, God is great, stay and try again. It's bad for my profits

22 security guard.

but gives me a different, a spiritual kind of satisfaction when I succeed. And I succeed about half the time. Which means,' he added with a wry laugh, 'I could double my profits if I minded my own business.'

"After the lengthy sessions with Mrs. Maha-Lepate and Dr. No-Ilaaz, Sarosh felt he had listened to enough advice and kind words. Much as he disliked doing it, he had to hurt Mr. Rawaana's feelings and leave his predicament undiscussed: 'I'm sorry, but I'm in a hurry. Will you be able to look after the booking?'

"'Well, okay,' said Mr. Rawaana, a trifle crestfallen; he did not relish the travel business as much as he did counselling immigrants. 'Hope you solve your problem. I will be happy to refund your fare, believe me.'

120   "Sarosh hurried home. With only four weeks to departure, every spare minute, every possible method had to be concentrated on a final attempt at adaptation.

"He tried laxatives, crunching down the tablets with a prayer that these would assist the sitting position. Changing brands did not help, and neither did various types of suppositories. He spent long stretches on the toilet seat each morning. The supervisor continued to reprimand him for tardiness. To make matters worse, Sarosh left his desk every time he felt the slightest urge, hoping: maybe this time.

"The working hours expended in the washroom were noted with unflagging vigilance by the supervisor. More counselling sessions followed. Sarosh refused to extinguish his last hope, and the supervisor punctiliously recorded 'No Improvement' in his daily log. Finally, Sarosh was fired. It would soon have been time to resign in any case, and he could not care less.

"Now whole days went by seated on the toilet, and he stubbornly refused to relieve himself the other way. The doorbell would ring only to be ignored. The telephone went unanswered. Sometimes, he would awake suddenly in the dark hours before dawn and rush to the washroom like a madman."

Without warning, Rustomji flung open his door and stormed: "Ridiculous nonsense this is becoming! Two days in a row, whole Firozsha Baag gathers here! This is not Chaupatty beach, this is not a squatters' colony, this is a building, people want to live here in peace and quiet!" Then just as suddenly, he stamped inside and slammed the door. Right on cue, Nariman continued, before the boys could say anything.

125   "Time for meals was the only time Sarosh allowed himself off the seat. Even in his desperation he remembered that if he did not eat well, he was doomed — the downward pressure on his gut was essential if there was to be any chance of success.

"But the ineluctable day of departure dawned, with grey skies and the scent of rain, while success remained out of sight. At the airport Sarosh checked in and went to the dreary lounge. Out of sheer habit he started towards the washroom. Then he realized the hopelessness of it and returned to the cold, clammy plastic of the lounge seats. Airport seats are the same almost anywhere in the world.

"The boarding announcement was made, and Sarosh was the first to step onto the plane. The skies were darker now. Out of the window he saw a flash of lightning fork through the clouds. For some reason, everything he'd learned years ago in St. Xavier's about sheet lightning and forked lightning went through his mind. He wished it would change to sheet, there was something sinister and unpropitious about forked lightning."

Kersi, absorbedly listening, began cracking his knuckles quite unconsciously. His childhood habit still persisted. Jehangir frowned at the disturbance, and Viraf nudged Kersi to stop it.

"Sarosh fastened his seat-belt and attempted to turn his thoughts towards the long journey home: to the questions he would be expected to answer, the sympathy and criticism that would be thrust upon him. But what remained uppermost in his mind was the present moment — him in the plane, dark skies lowering, lightning on the horizon — irrevocably spelling out: defeat.

130 "But wait. Something else was happening now. A tiny rumble. Inside him. Or was it his imagination? Was it really thunder outside which, in his present disoriented state, he was internalizing? No, there it was again. He had to go.

"He reached the washroom, and almost immediately the sign flashed to 'Please return to seat and fasten seat-belts.' Sarosh debated whether to squat and finish the business quickly, abandoning the perfunctory seated attempt. But the plane started to move and that decided him; it would be difficult now to balance while squatting.

"He pushed. The plane continued to move. He pushed again, trembling with the effort. The seat-belt sign flashed quicker and brighter now. The plane moved faster and faster. And Sarosh pushed hard, harder than he had ever pushed before, harder than in all his ten years of trying in the new land. And the memories of Bombay, the immigration interview in New Delhi, the farewell party, his mother's tattered prayer book, all these, of their own accord, emerged from beyond the region of the ten years to push with him and give him new-found strength."

Nariman paused and cleared his throat. Dusk was falling, and the frequency of B.E.S.T. buses plying the main road outside Firozsha Baag had dropped. Bats began to fly madly from one end of the compound to the other, silent shadows engaged in endless laps over the buildings.

"With a thunderous clap the rain started to fall. Sarosh felt a splash under him. Could it really be? He glanced down to make certain. Yes, it was. He had succeeded!

135 "But was it already too late? The plane waited at its assigned position on the runway, jet engines at full thrust. Rain was falling in torrents and takeoff could be delayed. Perhaps even now they would allow him to cancel his flight, to disembark. He lurched out of the constricting cubicle.

"A stewardess hurried towards him: 'Excuse me, sir, but you must return to your seat immediately and fasten your belt.'

"'You don't understand!' Sarosh shouted excitedly. 'I must get off the plane! Everything is all right. I don't have to go anymore...'

"'That's impossible, sir!' said the stewardess, aghast. 'No one can leave now. Takeoff procedures are in progress!' The wild look in his sleepless eyes, and the dark rings around them scared her. She beckoned for help.

"Sarosh continued to argue, and a steward and the chief stewardess hurried over: 'What seems to be the problem, sir? You *must* resume your seat. We are authorized, if necessary, to forcibly restrain you, sir.'

"The plane began to move again, and suddenly Sarosh felt all the urgency leaving him. His feverish mind, the product of nightmarish days and tortuous nights, was filled again with the calm which had fled a decade ago, and he spoke softly now: 'That...that will not be necessary...it's okay, I understand.' He readily returned to his seat.

"As the aircraft sped down the runway, Sarosh's first reaction was one of joy. The process of adaptation was complete. But later, he could not help wondering if success came before or after the ten-year limit had expired. And since he had already passed through the customs and security check, was he really an immigrant in every sense of the word at the moment of achievement?

"But such questions were merely academic. Or were they? He could not decide. If he returned, what would it be like? Ten years ago, the immigration officer who had stamped his passport had said, 'Welcome to Canada.' It was one of Sarosh's dearest memories, and thinking of it, he fell asleep.

"The plane was flying about the rainclouds. Sunshine streamed into the cabin. A few raindrops were still clinging miraculously to the windows, reminders of what was happening below. They sparkled as the sunlight caught them."

Some of the boys made as if to leave, thinking the story was finally over. Clearly, they had not found this one as interesting as the others Nariman had told. What dolts, thought Jehangir, they cannot recognize a masterpiece when they hear one. Nariman motioned with his hand for silence.

"But our story does not end there. There was a welcome-home party for Sarosh a few days after he arrived in Bombay. It was not in Firozsha Baag this time because his relatives in the Baag had a serious sickness in the house. But I was invited to it anyway. Sarosh's family and friends were considerate enough to wait till the jet lag had worked its way out of his system. They wanted him to really enjoy this one.

"Drinks began to flow freely again in his honour: Scotch and soda, rum and Coke, brandy. Sarosh noticed that during his absence all the brand names had changed — the labels were different and unfamiliar. Even for the mixes. Instead of Coke there was Thums-Up, and he remembered reading in the papers about Coca-Cola being kicked out by the Indian Government for refusing to reveal their secret formula.

"People slapped him on the back and shook his hand vigorously, over and over, right through the evening. They said: 'Telling the truth, you made the right decision, look how happy your mother is to live to see this day;' or they asked: 'Well, bossy, what changed your mind?' Sarosh smiled and nodded his way through it all, passing around Canadian currency at the insistence of some of the curious ones who, egged on by his mother, also pestered him to display his Canadian passport and citizenship card. She had been badgering him since his arrival to tell her the real reason: 'Saachoo kahé, what brought you back?' and was hoping that tonight, among his friends, he might raise his glass and reveal something. But she remained disappointed.

"Weeks went by and Sarosh found himself desperately searching for his old place in the pattern of life he had vacated ten years ago. Friends who had organized the welcome-home party gradually disappeared. He went walking in the evenings along Marine Drive, by the sea-wall, where the old crowd used to congregate. But the people who sat on the parapet while waves crashed behind their backs were strangers. The tetrapods were still there, staunchly protecting the reclaimed land from the fury of the sea. He had watched as a kid when cranes had lowered these cement and concrete hulks of respectable grey into the water. They were grimy black now, and from their angularities rose the distinct stench of human excrement. The old pattern was never found by Sarosh; he searched in vain. Patterns of life are selfish and unforgiving.

"Then one day, as I was driving past Marine Drive, I saw someone sitting alone. He looked familiar, so I stopped. For a moment I did not recognize Sarosh, so forlorn and woebegone was his countenance. I parked the apple of my eye and went to him, saying, 'Hullo, Sid, what are you doing here on your lonesome?' And he said, 'No, no! No more Sid, please, that name reminds me of all my troubles.' Then, on the parapet at Marine Drive, he told me his unhappy and wretched tale, with the waves battering away at the tetrapods, and around us the hawkers screaming about coconut-water and sugar-cane juice and *paan*.

150

"When he finished, he said that he had related to me the whole sad saga because he knew how I told stories to boys in the Baag, and he wanted me to tell this one, especially to those who were planning to go abroad. 'Tell them,' said Sarosh, 'that the world can be a bewildering place, and dreams and ambitions are often paths to the most pernicious of traps.' As he spoke, I could see that Sarosh was somewhere far away, perhaps in New Delhi at his immigration interview, seeing himself as he was then, with what he thought was a life of hope and promise stretching endlessly before him. Poor Sarosh. Then he was back beside me on the parapet.

"'I pray you, in your stories,' said Sarosh, his old sense of humour returning as he deepened his voice for his favourite *Othello* lines"—and here, Nariman produced a basso profundo of his own—"'when you shall these unlucky deeds relate, speak of me as I am; nothing extenuate, nor set down aught in malice: tell them that in Toronto once there lived a Parsi boy as best as he could. Set you down this; and say, besides, that for some it was good and for some it was bad, but for me life in the land of milk and honey was just a pain in the posterior.'"[23]

And now, Nariman allowed his low-pitched rumbles to turn into chuckles. The boys broke into cheers and loud applause and cries of "Encore!" and "More!" Finally, Nariman had to silence them by pointing warningly at Rustomji-the-curmudgeon's door.

While Kersi and Viraf were joking and wondering what to make of it all, Jehangir edged forward and told Nariman this was the best story he had ever told. Nariman patted his shoulder and smiled. Jehangir left, wondering if Nariman would have been as popular if Dr. Mody was still alive. Probably, since the two were liked for different reasons: Dr. Mody used to be constantly jovial, whereas Nariman had his periodic story-telling urges.

23 based on the dying words of Othello, Shakespeare's tragic hero who was an African living in Venice.

Now the group of boys who had really enjoyed the Savukshaw story during the previous week spoke up. Capitalizing on Nariman's extraordinarily good mood, they began clamouring for more Savukshaw: "Nariman Uncle, tell the one about Savukshaw the hunter, the one you had started that day."

155

"What hunter? I don't know which one you mean." He refused to be reminded of it, and got up to leave. But there was a loud protest, and the boys started chanting, "We-want-Savukshaw! We-want-Savukshaw!"

Nariman looked fearfully towards Rustomji's door and held up his hands placatingly: "All right, all right! Next time it will be Savukshaw again. Savukshaw the artist. The story of Parsi Picasso."[24]

(1987)

---

24 twentieth-century Spanish artist who introduced and popularized many abstract styles.

Evelyn Lau (b. 1971)

A poet, short story writer, and autobiographer, Lau commented that she began writing for "the love and acceptance that presumably went along with it." Later, she sought to make "people think ... to have a clearer vision of their own emotional lives, their realities." In *Choose Me* (1999), many of the stories deal with middle-class men and women and the sexual tensions and conflicts that exist between what she has called individuals "walking emotional high wires." "Family" is the story of an outsider responding to a middle-class family. Zoe, a visiting poet, has been emotionally and physically attracted to her host, who invites her to live in his house while he and his family are away for the weekend. Alone, she feel apart from normal family life and often questions the reality of her existence.

FAMILY

Zoe stood in Douglas's bedroom, the one he shared with his wife. Outside the wood-framed window the afternoon was silver, the sky the shine of the inside of an oyster shell. Snow drifted through the air, and narrow icicles hung from the trees. The houses dwindling down the block were heritage properties, fronted in brick and stained glass; each resembled the house she was inside.

Douglas had invited her in so calmly. After she set down her bags in the hall with its high ceilings and polished floors, he pushed the keys to his home into her hand, two skeleton keys dangling from a loop of twisted wire. Then he motioned her back out onto the porch, where he wrapped his fingers around hers, demonstrating how to work the locks. Their breath showed in front of them, but his hand pulsed with warmth. She learned to shove the keys in smoothly, to jiggle them, to listen for the muffled internal click that signified the lock had been turned.

"Will you remember this?"

He repeated the code to the burglar alarm by the door, half-concealed by the winter coats hanging on the wooden rack.

"Yes. I think I'll remember."

His wife appeared on the landing at the top of the stairs.

5   "Ellen, this is our visiting poet, Zoe. She's been on campus all week working with the students, and I thought it'd be nice for her to stay in a real home before she leaves, especially since we won't be here."

Ellen came down the first flight of stairs, bending to extend her hand; her arm was long, her palm warm.

"Welcome."

Zoe held his wife's hand in her own and swallowed past the catch in her throat. His wife continued to lean down from the landing, bending her body from the waist, one hand holding the railing, the other clasping Zoe's as though to help her up. Douglas kept his eyes fastened on Ellen's face. Their two children were clamouring around her, tugging and demanding; the girl jumped up and down, whining, while the boy pulled down his trousers to reveal buttocks as smooth as cream.

"Jason, I said no. Look, we have a guest. Say hello, Jason, say hello to Zoe."

The boy ignored her, buying his face in his mother's thigh, squirming his bare bum in the air while his sister hid behind them both.

"Zoe will be staying here while we're at the cabin. You've got to be good and say hello."

After a while, just when it seemed he could not be persuaded, Jason lifted his face and grinned winningly. His eyes were like his father's, only clearer, the colour of amber.

"Hello. Hello!" he shouted.

Douglas pressed the keys once more into her palm. She looked at him then in a moment of terror, the weight and light of the house around her suddenly there for her to both protect and invade. He sensed her fear, mistook it for concern about burglar alarms, difficult locks, the house burning down.

"Got it?"

He repeated the code again.

"Is everything all right? Are you happy?"

He had given her the keys, his hands were empty. At the top of the stairs his wife was saying, "No, no, no," to the children. "No, you *can't* bring that. Look, you already have so much."

"I'm happy."

She stood in the doorway and watched him leave with his family. Ellen was weighted with the children's clothes, warm and puffy jackets that were awkward in her arms. Jason and Julie ran ahead, the tops of their heads bright and new in the winter light. Douglas paused before following them; he placed both his hands on Zoe's upper arms and kissed her on the cheek.

"One more."

He kissed her on the other cheek just as she was pulling away.

She looked over his shoulder and caught the blur of Ellen's face. She felt the sudden tension, her body electric with watchfulness. But the moment passed quickly — it was only a kiss, friendly, sociable. Ellen beamed and waved.

"Have a good time!"

"You too!"

She eased the door shut, the house was hers.

Zoe approached their bed as though it were an altar. It was smooth, flat, wide — a square of white in the room. She sat on its edge, where the comforter was folded back in a triangle, and the cotton sheet slid against her body. She could tell by the paraphernalia on the bedside table, the textbooks and manuscripts piled high, which side of the bed was his.

She wondered what Ellen looked like naked, how she approached him in the dark with the light from the window illuminating her body. Ellen had the figure of an adolescent, long and boyishly thin; her breasts would hardly be more than bumps on her chest, bare mouthfuls, and the bones in her hips and pubis would be prominent, traceable. The length of her would look like a white taper candle, if he opened his eyes in the night to watch her sleep.

Their bedroom was full of photographs — lined up on the mantel, jumbled above the chest of drawers, taped to the vanity mirror. The pictures were almost all of Douglas and the children; in the few where Ellen was present, her face was either obscured by her blowing hair or turned to one side, away from the camera. She appeared in the photos as a sort of ghost, rinsed of ego, her features blurred. It was Douglas who took centre stage, which was why Zoe had the impression when she saw them together on the stairs that he was the more attractive of the two. And yet when she looked again, objectively, she realized she was wrong — it was Ellen who was most attractive. Her face was white and well shaped, like a Madonna's, graceful and open. Her teeth glistened when she smiled. But Douglas had something she lacked, a force of personality that was revealed in the photographs, the same photos that revealed Ellen's downturned, devolving features.

30   Their family life was documented in the photographs. Douglas, Ellen and the children had taken summer holidays by the shore, stood in portals of museums and crumbling European buildings, hiked among shrub and rock and cliff. In one photograph he held his daughter spilling and giggling over his shoulder while he pointed, laughing, at the camera. In another his face was white with joy as he cradled a swaddled newborn in his arms. In a third he was naked to the waist at the beach, his feet buried in wet sand that flowered around his ankles; she saw the arc of his shoulders, the way he was shaped and curved, and the twin lines of his waist that sloped inwards. He was someplace where her own history was not, could never be.

When Zoe opened his wife's closet doors she saw loose, layered clothes in deep jewel colours. The surface of the vanity next to the closet was scattered with drugstore cosmetics and, incongruously, a shiny, unopened bottle of Chanel No. 5[1] which must have been a gift. Her eye pencils were worn down to blurred nubs, her tube of mascara was dusty, she owned only the palest of lipsticks. This was the sort of woman his wife was, Zoe realized — natural, unselfconscious, without guile.

The house was old enough to be draughty, the heaters thin and metallic and cool to the touch. The walls were papered in a pattern of wide bronze stripes; the floorboards were stained walnut. That night she woke in their bedroom, curled to Douglas's side of the bed, shivering. She tiptoed across the icy floor to the dresser where one of Ellen's nightshirts hung from a knob; its worn cotton, smelling faintly of soap, was soft against her skin when she pulled it over her head. She wondered how Douglas was sleeping in his cabin. Were his arms wrapped around his wife, her stomach, her breasts? He was the warmest man she had ever met — his mouth, his hands, the heat barely contained by the skin of his body. To kiss him was like leaning her face over a hot stove, or into a fire. By comparison, she was cold, or he said, cold-blooded.

"Now I know why you came wearing so few clothes, it's because you're cold-blooded."

But she wore few clothes so that when he touched her, it would be that much more. So that when he took her hand from her lap and lifted it to his mouth, or held it between his own hands, the shock of his heat would be greater. It was deliberate. She had been freezing the whole week, at all the places he had taken her when she was lecturing to students. When they had stood in the organic-foods market with their hands in their pockets, the

---

1 an expensive and popular brand of French perfume.

breath issuing whitely in front of them, watching the butcher in his bloody apron behind the counter. The chopping blade that fit so firmly into his hand it was like an extension of him. Turkeys, pheasants, a dead deer hung by their hind legs in front of the shop, freshly killed. She imagined their bodies still warm, hearts still beating, had to resist the urge to lean forward and stroke her fingertips down the grain of their feathers and fur, towards the belly warm as the belly of a sleeping man. They were so beautiful, content. The turkeys' creamy eyelids tugged down over their eyes, their closed beaks bearing tremblingly a single drop of blood. They had stood together, side by side, looking at the dead animals strung silently in front of them. To see then his breath steaming beside hers, to know his hands were warm and alive in his pockets, composed of skin and flesh and bone and circulating blood, to see the flicker of his eyelashes, to know he was swallowing and breathing and thinking and wondering, to know that if she leaned into his chest he would hear the pulse of his heart — it was almost more than she could bear.

35   To drive back to the campus at night with the whole of the highway before them, the planes skimming low with their lit wings towards the airport, the singing stream of traffic, the gas stations along the way with their pumps and phone booths and chocolate bars, the dense black tar of the road painted with lines and signals. His hands on the wheel and then his thumb on the fleshy pocket between her own thumb and forefinger, touching just that part of her, and the balletic perfection of the traffic around them, orange and red taillights sliding past, speeding forward, the coordination of motion, the sense of at least being a part of something whole, his hand wrapping around her hand.

One day they had stood in a church tower with many windows and walked around and around to take in each disparate view. From here the emerald sea shaking in the distance like a mirage, from here the city with its multiple windows gleaming in the golden light. It had taken them fifteen minutes to climb to the top of the tower, the stairs so steep they had had to twist their bodies nearly sideways, so sharply angled that the steps above bit into their shins. And then they had emerged onto the wooden platform with the light flooding in from all directions, and they had stepped from window to window as though they were dancing, and when they stood next to each other the fringe of his scarf touched the shoulder of her sweater.

Then they had paused in the entrance of the church, overwhelmed by a window of stained glass. They had whispered to each other and he had wanted to touch her, she saw that, the times when he wanted to touch her, the look that came over his face, how it was turned to her beneath the flood of coloured light and how she had seen the thought in his eyes, his eyes that moved back and forth when he was thinking as though he were scanning the lines of a secret text.

The weekend passed slowly. After Zoe had wandered all the rooms in the house, picking up objects here and there, inspecting and then setting them down again, there was nothing more for her to do. So she was grateful when Douglas's associate at the publishing company called to invite her for lunch. He took her to a Wolfgang Puck restaurant with slender cedar chairs, papaya-coloured walls and preternaturally beautiful women whose heels clicked across the granite floor. During lunch she observed this man's gentleness — his patience with the waiters, his smiling consideration of her — and it made her sad. He was someone she could trust, the way she never would be able to trust Douglas. As they ate their scallop salads, she thought of the afternoon in the French restaurant with the brown and yellow tiles on the floor, when Douglas had made her translate the entire menu. She knew only a little French and he had had to correct her and help her along, from the starters to the specials to the entrées to the desserts, all the way down the menu, not letting her stop.

"How will you know what you want if you don't know what there is?"

What he said was true, so she kept translating. The waiters came and he waved them away. The other diners must have thought they were lovers, because of the way they looked at each other. The tables were set close together, there was no privacy; the women around them had wide mouths and espresso-coloured hair, and the nails that tipped their long fingers were manicured. Cellular phones rang at the tables of the men, who wore suit jackets over jeans. They'd ordered a bottle of wine with their meal, and the first glass of it rushed to her head. She could not pick out her own face in the strip of mirror that ran along the wall above the booths, not among so many faces crowded together. Since childhood it had been necessary for Zoe to see her reflection at all times, as if to assure herself of her own existence. When she tried to find herself in the mirror in the restaurant and could not, she drank the wine instead, to calm herself.

"Zoe, everything I've done in my life has been like an experiment. It started when I was a child. The way I looked at the world was different from the children around me. I was very observant, and because of that I felt removed from everything. I began to direct my own life. As a teenager, I experimented with drugs because I wanted to understand what it was like to lose control. And then I made myself fall in love over and over, for the same reason."

She watched him; everything he said made sense to her. He might have been describing her own past. But it was what was familiar in him that was dangerous to her.

He had chosen this restaurant from all the restaurants that lined the busy, taxi-filled street. They had stood on the corner and he had looked in either direction and then he had chosen this place.

"I know where we'll go. Come, follow me."

They crossed the murderous intersection, shiny cars veering in front and behind them. The stores all along the street were glass-fronted, etched with the names of Italian designers and filled with expensive merchandise — leaden suits, transparent dresses, shoes built with as much attention as one would give to the building of houses.

He let the waiter show them to the table where he had begun and ended relationships with other women. Now she was sitting on the plump red banquette where his other women had fitted their hips.

He was still talking. The women at the next table turned and looked at them. Zoe smiled. The women blinked their heavy lashes and after a while turned back to their salads.

"You seem closed to me. I don't know how to get close to you, other than to become so important to you that you fall in love with me."

Zoe let him talk.

50 "You aren't like anyone who is close to me. The people I value don't have centres that are so solid. I can enter them, they're vulnerable to me."

But she still could not pick out her face in the mirror. Could it be that he was mistaken, that she had no centre, only a space?

After lunch he took her to the downtown publishing office where he worked part-time as an editor. Walking against the direction of the wind, they passed a vendor with his wheelbarrow of roses and carnations, and a café with wrought-iron chairs arranged in circles around outdoor tables. The door to his building was covered in stained glass. He pushed it open, and they walked across a cracked marble floor to the elevator. In the elevator she was struck by a desire to kiss him, but he was already thinking about the work that had accumulated while they were eating. She was drunk only in the way that wine can make you drunk at noon. The angles of the building seemed wrong. The surfaces of things — the metal of desks and elevator doors, the cloth-covered partitions, the lenses of a secretary's glasses as she walked past — all seemed exceptionally bright and sharp. She thought her intoxication must be evident to others, yet there was not a flicker of suspicion or concern in any of the faces that tilted at her, with their black pupils and razor-sharp hair-cuts. Meanwhile he had vanished into the maze of offices, and left her on her own. She wandered towards the reception area and sat on the couch that curved like a crescent moon. The receptionists were carrying on conversations about clothes and lovers, in between the ringing phones.

When he was with her at dinner, even when there were others at their table, academics and editors, he watched her constantly. She saw him always at the edge of her vision, a pale, intense man in a tailored coat. While she talked to others around her, drank a glass of wine, placed her order with the waiter, she felt his eyes upon her. When at last she raised her eyes to his, he would not flinch away, he would only slowly turn his head to the side — as if she had been merely an object in the way of his turning gaze, as if all along he had been meaning to look at the edge of the table, or the spoon that lay on his saucer, or at another woman. This was how the nights of the previous week had passed, in restaurants where the windows were frosted over so that the night outside looked like it was walled in fog, with only the faint light of streetlamps to mark the distances. At their table, there were always people who drank too much, and she was one of them. At the end of the evening they would be drinking flaming shooters and daring each other to keep up, and she would, because when she tried to back down, looking to Douglas for help, he would stir sugar into his coffee and look back at her and not say anything. When she swallowed the contents of a shot glass in one throw of the wrist, the sensation was like dropping through a hole that had suddenly opened up in the sidewalk. Tears would rise in her eyes and she would feel separated from herself. But when her vision cleared he would still be there at the table, his face empty of reproach or encour-agement, only mildly curious as to what she would do next. Later, he would tell her what she was like with other people.

"You manipulate them, you draw them along with you. There is something about you that people can't resist."

55 He would watch her until the early hours of the morning, when empty shooter glasses lined the tabletop and the party disbanded to stumble through the streets with the fog winding above, the thick heels of their shoes sounding on the cement.

In turn she wanted to believe he was the most genuine person she had ever met. In the market in front of the dead animals when his breath steamed out of him and he spread his arms in wonder. In the car when he sang along with the radio and thumped the wheel and then turned and looked at her as they sat stalled in the black, runny streets. The noises he made when he was thinking, his fingers on the PowerBook keyboard, his head cocked to one side.

"*Tinka tinka tinka. Vroom.*"

He was a grown man, but when he was working he sounded like a child shoving toy race cars down a rubber track. So that one afternoon when they were walking down the street, when for an instant the sun broke through the layers of cloud, she had been astonished to see that his hair was peppered with silver. It was as though someone had taken a handful of needles and scattered them through his dark hair.

He would talk to the words that appeared on his computer screen, give the desk a small slap, wheel around in his chair.

60 "Yes. Done. Now, where would you like to go for lunch? What would you most like to eat in the whole wide world?"

They would smile at each other and she would see him slowly grow back into himself, see the work fade from his eyes, one wave receding and a different one advancing. He would rise from his chair and stand for a moment with his feet pressed together and his hands clasped behind his back, like someone at the edge of a diving board gazing into the pool, puzzling the point of entry, the locus where his body would knife into the water. She would watch him slowly come back to life the way she had begun to feel her own body assume its life, starting at the nucleus where his hands lay hot on her skin.

During the hours when she was alone in the house, Zoe wondered why Douglas had brought her here, when so much could go wrong. Was it enough that she was in his house, even if he could not be there with her? It was possible he had invited her only out of kindness and affection; after all, he had kissed her boldly on both sides of her face while his wife had watched them from the cobblestone path. Perhaps he felt they had nothing to hide. But she felt that to believe that would be to believe the world itself lacking intelligence and motive. Perhaps he only wanted to see what would happen, to observe his own emotions, his capacity for betrayal or loyalty. And to learn about her capacity for transgression. She saw then that he was the sort of man a woman should never love. Yet she walked about his house in a sort of drunkenness, his home where he lived and ate and slept, and she could almost feel the air parting and streaming around her, the pattern of its current, like she was moving in the corridors of space he had created for her with his own movements. She stood by the sink where he shaved and brushed each morning. She saw his black suit hanging in the bedroom closet, his sneakers flung to the bottom of the wardrobe, the book he was reading lying open on the braided mat that covered the bedside table. Sitting on the edge of their white bed, she felt looming inside her the inevitability of betrayal. It rose in her like the tide, leaving her without will. She knew that as soon as she slept with Douglas in his own house, she would feel relief. She craved it like a junkie; she could taste in her mouth the effects of the drug before it was injected. It would be sweet, his caresses on her body, the pain they would inflict upon his wife.

Once during the weekend the telephone rang for Ellen. Zoe answered it in their bedroom.

"Hello?"

"Ellen? It's Diane. How are you?"

"No. No, Ellen is away for the weekend with the family. Could I take a message?"

When she put down the phone, Zoe rose from their bed and looked at her reflection in their vanity mirror. She put her hand on her neck, felt the shape of her throat with her fingers. Her voice when it came out in the cold room was still hers, accompanied by a thin jet of white breath. She was still herself. She was not his wife.

The day the family came home Zoe woke to the sound of church bells filling the air. The sky was blue and the house so icy she wandered the rooms in a daze, her fingers clenched, her lips chapped. In the bathroom mirror her skin appeared exceptionally pale, stretched over a framework of bone, and the backs of her hands were translucent. She went downstairs to the living room and opened the curtains to look out onto the street. The occupants of the neighbouring houses could be seen here and there in their weekend sweats and denims, climbing into cars, conversing on doorsteps, carrying plastic bins of garbage to the curb. She felt far away from the domestic lives locked within houses such as these and had to remind herself that today, at least, she was on the inside looking out. The hours passed, afternoon darkened into winter evening, and still she waited for Douglas and Ellen. When their car pulled up to the front of the house and they came out with the children, hurrying up the path, she went to the door and let them in as though they were her guests.

"Tell me all about it. What did you do while we were gone?"

His wife was upstairs, putting the children to bed. Zoe heard their footsteps back and forth between the rooms — Ellen's long, purposeful strides, the children's patter. Douglas rose from the sofa to shut the living-room door, and before returning to his seat he detoured to Zoe's chair and ruffled her hair with one hand. He laughed, a self-conscious sound that he bit off quickly. She was so nervous that her upper lip was slick with perspiration, but she said it anyway.

"I missed you horribly."

For the moment he said nothing, but he could not look at her, and that in itself seemed a declaration. They were both saved by the sound of his wife's footsteps down the long stairs, the turn of the doorknob, her presence in the room. Ellen chose the other armchair, the one identical to Zoe's, which also faced the sofa where Douglas sat. Zoe knew that at some point he would not be able to refrain from comparing them, and saw to her surprise that his wife knew this also, by the sudden sharpening of her eyes. Still, it was easy to start a conversation with Ellen. Zoe, to hide her panic, was vivacious and charming, and they talked comfortably about books, children, movies, travel. Douglas became superfluous; he sat back in the sofa and watched them, perhaps for the first time aware of who he had brought into his home, of what she was capable. He saw his own wife warm towards the other woman, saw her caution evaporate, her limbs relax and loosen. When he left the room to escape to his office upstairs, it seemed that neither woman would notice or miss him. But Zoe watched his exit with the care of someone who is making a plan.

"I've got a pile of unmarked essays sitting upstairs. I'll be back down in a while to say goodnight."

Ellen glanced up at her husband.

"I'm not planning to stay up late, Douglas. An hour at most, then I'm coming upstairs and falling into bed. You two can chat down here if you want."

Douglas and Zoe did not look at each other.

"Well, anyway. Don't worry about making noise, I'll be fast asleep."

Douglas left the room, closing the door behind him. Ellen turned towards Zoe, cradling her drink near her knee, her face lit by the lamp on the sidetable. They continued to talk for a while, and the conversation turned towards her marriage.

"I was looking at some of the photos in the house," Zoe said.

"The two of you, and the children — you have such a wonderful family. I couldn't believe how different Douglas looked when he was younger."

"Yes, I was so in love with him when we first got together. He was beautiful."

Her eyes wrinkled with the memory, and a distant pleasure swept over Ellen's face, softening it, making it vulnerable.

"I thought so, too."

"Did you? Well, he's older now. But you saw how he used to have the most beautiful long curls. He was a gorgeous young man, I can't tell you. Sometimes I have to remind myself of the way he used to be."

"But could you imagine yourself with anyone else? I mean, is he your great love, you grand passion?"

The moment of consideration was so slight as to not be there. Then his wife was nodding, smiling.

"Yes. Yes, he is. You know, once when we were still going out, he left me for a year. I couldn't eat, I couldn't sleep, I thought I was going to die. I heard through mutual friends that he was living with another woman, and I couldn't bear it. I wanted to have his children. I couldn't imagine my life without him."

They were silent for a while. On the back of her neck Zoe felt the heat of the lamp behind her chair, and a line of perspiration travelled down her temple. The rest of the room was still cold but she was burning up. The bottle of whisky on the occasional table between them was half empty, and she realized that she had been doing most of the drinking. Ellen gazed into her own glass, the thin, slippery line of alcohol left at its bottom.

"Anyway. I really must get to bed, it all starts again tomorrow. I have to be up early to make the children's breakfast and get them ready. I'll wake you if you want."

90   "Please. I don't want to miss my flight."

Ellen unfolded her legs and stood up. The skin around her eyes had crumpled with exhaustion. She smiled at her guest.

"Thank you. I've enjoyed our talk, Zoe. I feel as if I've made a new friend."

"Goodnight."

Zoe was left alone for a few moments in the living room. Upstairs she heard the toilet flush, and footsteps. She imagined Ellen washing her face, sighing at the feel of the wet washcloth against her skin, then her soft entry into the children's rooms to check on their sleep before she went to her own bed. Zoe drew a deep breath, aware of the pounding of her heart and the tingling in her hands and feet. She poured herself another whisky, neat in the glass. She tapped her foot on the floor, stood up, paced the length of the room twice. Then she heard his footfalls on the stairs; the doorknob turned and he walked into the room. He was carrying a fresh bottle of whisky and two glasses, and he was unsteady on his feet.

95   "Let me pour you a *real* drink."

He took the glass from her hand and set it down, wobbling, on the floor. He handed her the two empty glasses and filled the first one to the brim, the neck of the bottle swaying in his hand. He was not so successful in pouring the second drink; whisky splashed over the rim of the glass, ran down her fingers and onto the floor.

"Oh, I'm sorry."

He grabbed at her wrist in apology.

"No, it's fine."

100   Zoe raised her wet glass and drank from it, smiling to show him everything was all right. They were not, she realized, bad people, either of them. They could not do what they were about to do without getting drunk beforehand.

There was nothing that remained to separate them. When Douglas reached for her, when he kissed her, Zoe found that place inside herself that she had been anticipating all weekend. She found the feeling she remembered — radiant, explosive, obliterating her senses. When his arms went around her body, when his mouth closed over hers, it was like the plunger of the needle pushed home. The drug filled the cavity of her chest, flooded upwards to drown the inside of her mouth, saturated her brain.

The house stood around them, holding its breath, listening to them. The furniture itself seemed suddenly attentive, like spies sent out by Ellen to watch while she slept. Douglas lifted her sweater and touched her breasts, he drew her towards the sofa and closed his mouth over her nipple, so that she looked down upon his shorn dark curls, his bent head. The fabric covering the couch was embroidered with silken threads in a pattern of birds and blossoms; he laid her upon the cushions, knelt above her and touched her face. They were very quiet, barely whispering, both listening for his wife and his children, sleeping in their rooms above. His face leaning over hers was lined around the mouth, under the eyes, but his lips were soft. They kissed for so long that she felt herself disappear, and when he at last drew away she shook her head and pulled him closer. Zoe felt secure at last. His weight along the length of her body, his bones, his flesh, the fabric of his clothes against her clothes. She knelt in front of him and reached up beneath his shirt to find his nipples, the folds in his stomach of incipient fat. She felt the shape of his penis, stroked the length of it with her fingertips, its fevered heat, the slight jumping pulse of its response. What she felt then, what she was amazed to feel, was nothing at all, and she almost drew away. When they had stood shoulder to shoulder in front of the slaughtered animals she had felt the blood in both their bodies, an endless circulating river. But what she felt now, touching the most secret part of his body, was that they were dead. That there was nothing inside them.

It was then that they heard movement in the house. His wife, waking to use the bathroom, to check on the children? They grew still in their embrace, their lips on each other's, slightly parted, motionless. His hands were warm on her back under her sweater. He would keep holding on to her, she realized with amazement, he would push this moment as far as it could go. He didn't care if they were discovered, he wouldn't care about the shock and the pain on his wife's face when she turned the doorknob and opened the door and saw them together. Perhaps he needed the pain.

It was Zoe who pushed him away, scrambled off the couch. When Ellen had seen her earlier that evening, she had been wearing a dark lipstick. Now her lips were bare, blurred with kissing. The tube of lipstick was in her purse, upstairs in the spare room. If his wife walked in, there would be nothing she could say or do to conceal what had happened. She ran over to one of the lamps, switched it off, then realized it wouldn't help for Ellen to discover them in a dark room together at two in the morning, either. There was no escape. Douglas was standing in the corner, watching her. He had lit a cigarette and he was listening to his wife's footsteps upstairs. Zoe looked at him, wide-eyed, wrapping her arms around herself. He blinked and drew on his cigarette.

105   It was then that she knew her life was bound up with the lives of others, with actions that invited consequences. She knew this in a way she had not known when her hand had closed over Ellen's husband's penis. At any moment the door would open, Ellen would stand there outlined in lamplight, the gathered, insubstantial darkness of the hall and the staircase behind her, and she would see their eyes, the disarray of their clothing, Zoe's smeared mouth. She would see all this and her mirroring face and eyes would change.

The footsteps paused on the landing, then turned around and went back to the bedroom. There was silence once more. Zoe's arms dropped to her side. Douglas ground his cigarette clumsily into the ashtray; a plume of smoke continued to rise from the burning butt. It seemed to Zoe that there had existed an opportunity for the world to prove to her that goodness would always triumph, but nothing had happened, and she felt lost.

Douglas was the first to make a sound. He coughed, shook his head as though to clear it, came up to her and touched her arm. The shock of his wife's footsteps had sobered them both, so that they no longer looked or moved like people who had been drinking.

"We must go to bed now. You'll go to yours, and I'll go to mine."

"Will everything be all right?"

110   "Yes, of course. She'll be sleeping now. You got up first, I'll follow later."

In the bathroom as Zoe washed her face and dabbed moisturizer on her cheeks, she had the curious sensation that it was to someone else's face she was ministering. The disjuncture between herself and her body seemed complete, irreparable; she did not know how to climb back inside her own skin. The face in the mirror had nothing to do with who she was, or what she had ever thought or done. She thought that all she had to do was take a step to one side, and she would physically leave her own body standing next to her.

When she left the bathroom — his razor and tufted brush on the edge of the sink, the children's jelly-coloured toothbrushes in a plastic mug, his wife's sponges and herbal soaps in a tray by the tub — she saw him standing on the landing. He was waiting for her, faceless in the dark, his shirt a pale shimmer over his body.

"Goodnight."

They kissed, his mouth open and hot on hers. The tenderness of his mouth, at last opened something in her. She felt herself slide back inside her own body, felt herself fit and fill her own outline.

115   Only once, in the middle of the night, did she wake. Her heart was racing, and when she coughed she thought she tasted blood in the back of her throat. The formless dark increased her panic — the unfamiliar contours of the room, the distant ceiling, the ghostly high shape of the window with its drawn curtains. She thought of the man and his wife, sleeping only footsteps away, and the children who lay in their small beds. For a moment she imagined herself tiptoeing into the parents' room, easing open the door, fitting herself between their heavy, adult forms. They would each curve an arm around her and she would smell the musk of their skin and the cotton of their nightshirts, the comfort of the warm sheets and pillows, and she would sleep.

(1999)

WRITING ESSAYS ABOUT LITERATURE

PUTTING THE JOB IN PERSPECTIVE

Writing well on any academic subject is demanding work, and writing about literature is among the most demanding kinds of academic writing. It helps to remember, however, that confronting the task seriously will improve not only the way you express what you think but your ability to think, as well. Mastering the critical and interpretive essays required in English courses will prepare you to handle other writing jobs with comparative ease. Whether you are committed to specializing in English or interested mainly in doing as well as you can in a required English course before going on to other areas of study, the advice that follows will help you make your choices sensibly and get the most from the work you do.

Writing about literature often starts with a feeling — you either like something or not — or an intuition about how a piece of writing works. In expressing these inklings in writing, you clarify them for yourself, identify the assumptions behind them, and learn how well they are grounded in the work you are considering. In the process, you not only come to understand better how literature works, but you also discover a good deal about how you think. Writing about literature is challenging for the same reasons it is rewarding — because it requires you to confront yourself as well as what you read.

When you explore literature in essays, you will rarely be looking for answers that are absolutely right or wrong. Depending on the approach taken and the questions asked, a wide variety of conclusions can be drawn about an individual work of literature, and because of the personal element in responses, even writers approaching questions in similar ways will often come up with quite different answers. Think of your essays about literature as part of an ongoing search for understanding, a process that begins when an author, poet, or playwright confronts his or her perceptions about the world in writing and that continues as long as somebody is reading and writing about the original creation. Remembering that you are taking part in a continuing dialogue rather than solving a problem with a single, predetermined answer will help you resist obvious conclusions and make your confrontation with a demanding subject less intimidating.

But again, "less intimidating" does not mean easy. The lack of pat answers, though reassuring in some ways, is no excuse for either slack thinking or sloppy writing. On the contrary, because your essays will be judged more by the quality of thought and expression they demonstrate than by how close they come to some established position, care is especially important. Originality is a start, but your original perceptions have to be supported scrupulously with evidence from the work in question; you must impress your audience by convincing it.

PREPARING TO WRITE

An essay about a literary work should say something illuminating about it, and an illumination depends on focus as well as initial brilliance. Thoughtful insights take time to develop, and an essential step in writing about literature involves clarifying for yourself what it is you want to say. Only when you are sure of your message can you decide how best to present it clearly and convincingly to your readers. The work cannot be rushed at this stage, so it is essential to leave yourself adequate time, not only to draft and revise, but to think, to plan, and to criticize your own ideas, as well.

PROCESS IN SUMMARY

Preparing to Write

Step 1:   Prepare for writing assignments in advance by reading all assigned texts in a course as early as possible and by including speculation about potential lines of argument in your notes.

Step 2:   Once you receive a writing assignment, evaluate it carefully to determine special requirements and anticipate problems.

Step 3:   Choose a subject that interests you.

Step 4:   Choose a topic you can handle well in the time available.

Step 5:   If you are confused about any aspect of an assignment or if you anticipate deviating in any way from the directions, check with your instructor.

Step 6:   Review the primary works you are writing about carefully, taking notes and identifying key passages as you read.

Step 7:   Read whatever background material you consider necessary.

Drafting

Step 1:   Begin generating ideas in writing while you still have more time than you need to complete your essay.

Step 2:   Focus your ideas into a manageable thesis and state this thesis clearly in a single sentence.

Step 3:   Prepare a simple, tentative outline. Do not spend a lot of time on this outline because it will probably have to be modified later. Repeat Step 2 if necessary.

Step 4:   Working from your outline and keeping your thesis statement clearly in mind, complete a rough draft of the entire essay without stopping to revise.

(continued)

Revising and Editing

Step 1: Review your essay to identify any parts that do not relate clearly to your thesis; cut or adapt these as necessary.

Step 2: Add support at any point where your conclusions seem to need it.

Step 3: Revise your opening to ensure that the main points of your essay are clear and supply any additional information your reader may need to follow your approach.

Step 4: When you are satisfied with the content of your essay, continue revising it for clarity and style until you are satisfied that it is the best you can make it or until the deadline requires you to commit yourself to a final version.

Step 5: When you are rested and free from distractions, proofread your essay carefully, making neat changes on the manuscript where necessary.

Reading with Awareness

The most fundamental preparation for writing about literature is reading. Read the piece you intend to write about, and then reread it. Read not just superficially to get a basic idea of what the piece says, but carefully, with an awareness of implications beneath the surface and of how the way it is written determines the way it affects you. Taking English courses and studying what others write about literature will teach you the kinds of things to look for, but you will need more. Serious reading, like serious writing, takes practice and cannot be rushed: putting off thinking about literature in general until you are required to write about a particular piece is like putting off training for a race until just before you have to run it. Developing the habit of reading seriously will put you far ahead of students who read only when forced to by an assignment, and it will also yield a great deal of satisfaction in itself.

Taking Notes

While reading thoughtfully is essential, it is not enough. You will find that your reading translates more readily into essays if you record your responses. Take notes as you read, perhaps on the text itself if it is your own copy and an inexpensive one. Marking particularly interesting passages will be a great help when you come back later to sort out evidence for an idea you are developing in an essay. When taking notes in class, record not only what your instructor says but the ideas that occur to you as well. If what is said about one work suggests comparison with another, take note of the possibility. Remark contradictions and unanswered questions. Your dissenting opinions, which you might well forget if you neglected to write them down at the time, will often provide the foundation for your most original essays and may in the long run prove to be the most valuable material you record in class.

An excellent practice for bridging the gap between the sketchy notes you write in class and fully developed essays is to extend your notes in a journal. Rather than reviewing class notes only when you are preparing for an exam, take time between classes to review and expand on the ideas your notes record. Consider which of your ideas may yield topics for essays, and test the manageability of these topics by sketching outlines. Elaborate in a paragraph or two on ideas you have had time to record in only a sentence. If you have recorded questions in your notes, attempt to answer them yourself in writing. The best time to develop your notes into something more useful occurs when the ideas they record are still fresh in your mind. While keeping a literary journal is not so different from taking notes, it allows you time to develop your ideas more thoughtfully and provides practice that will help you become more comfortable with critical writing.

Evaluating Assignments

Before attempting a writing assignment, you must first determine exactly what it requires and whether you can carry out any approach you are considering in the time available. The time you invest in evaluating assignments is rarely wasted. However eager you may be to get started, be cautious; enthusiasm is great, but you will win few races by sprinting off in the wrong direction.

Be especially careful when choosing topics from a list, a point at which the work of a few minutes can make the difference between success and failure. While you can assume that your instructor considers all suggested topics suitable for some students in your class, you cannot assume that all the topics will be suitable for all the students. Resist the temptation to commit yourself to the first topic that catches your interest. Evaluate all your options, eliminating the obvious impossibilities first. It will usually be clear that some works and some approaches are too difficult for you to manage. Personal taste is also an important consideration: until you gain more experience as a critic, you will rarely write successful essays about literary works you dislike. Once you have narrowed the choice to a few possibilities, sketch brief outlines to give yourself a better idea of where you might go with each topic. Determine whether you can meet all the requirements in each case. For example, even though you admire a certain poem, you may not be capable of handling a topic that requires you to produce a successful essay about how that poem's metrical patterns reinforce its meaning. While there can be long-term benefits in taking the extra time required to prepare for specialized topics, be sure you can manage the workload. Be wary of ambitious failures.

Once you find an assignment you think you can handle well, consider its wording carefully. Are you sure what all the terms mean? If not, ask your instructor to explain. Is there anything about the approach you are considering that seems at odds with the assignment as stated? Perhaps, for example, an assignment asks you to compare characterization in two stories, only one of which particularly impresses you. It may be permissible to concentrate on the one you like while using the other to illuminate by contrast what you admire in your favourite, but, then again, your instructor may want a more balanced comparison. Find out before you devote a lot of time to a questionable approach. Similarly, even though you plan no deviations from the stated requirements, you may find an assignment ambiguous in some respect. If you are told to compare two poems, for example, does this mean you are obligated to consider all aspects of the two poems? Or will you be permitted to devote most of your comparison to some aspect that seems especially revealing? While the more focused approach may seem more interesting to you, your instructor may have left the comparison general to test your understanding of a variety of elements in the poems. Any number of misunderstandings can occur, and you will be wise to anticipate them while you still have plenty of time to adapt.

Think early. Check early. Doing so can save you time, effort, and disappointment.

Research

In a very limited sense, any essay you write on a literary subject will involve research: you will have to read the works you intend to write about very carefully, probably a number of times, and even with an assignment that does not formally require research, you will often read other works by the same writer and explore his or her personal and historical background.

In a formal research paper, however, you will also be expected to find and evaluate what others have written about your subject. In this case, finding and properly acknowledging your debt to secondary material — writings about literature rather than the literature itself — will be a major part of your job. A detailed explanation of research methods and the format for acknowledging sources is beyond the scope of this chapter, but most college-level writing textbooks cover such material thoroughly. If you plan to take more than a few English courses, *The MLA Handbook for Writers of Research Papers*, which provides an exhaustive guide to the standard format used in English essays, is a good investment. Here it will suffice to provide a few general hints that can save you a lot of time and trouble.

Many students get into difficulty by confusing random sampling with research. They find the call number of a book on their topic, go to the specified shelf in the library, pull out several books on the same general subject, and consider their search complete. The one advantage of this approach — speed — cannot compensate for the problems it will almost certainly create. Books chosen at random rarely provide more than brief, general comment on an essay topic; what relevant comment they do include is often slanted according to their focal concerns. In addition, books stay on library shelves long after what they say has been qualified by later observations, and the material you find in a random selection will certainly not be the most recent available. This is not to say that books are of no value; the point is that books must be chosen carefully and supplemented by reference to up-to-date articles from scholarly journals.

The annotated bibliographies and the periodical indexes available in reference libraries will allow you to find material relevant to your topic quickly, and they will also give you an overview of the kinds of approaches to the work in question that others have found useful. But, as valuable as they are in saving you the trouble of reviewing irrelevant or barely relevant material, these resources will not solve all your problems. Often, they will list far more apparently relevant resources than you have time to consult. How are you to choose? In some cases your instructor will make suggestions, but such advice may still leave you guessing about which comments are most important and influential. One of the easiest ways into ongoing critical debates is to look first at the most recent writings you can find on your topic, taking careful note of the earlier works these cite. When two or three recent sources refer to an older one, it will usually be worth your while to check what it says directly. No method of sampling is a substitute for an exhaustive review of criticism, but methods that allow you to make an informed selection should be sufficient for most of your essays. They will certainly serve you better than random choice.

Seeking out the most pertinent material is not the only challenge in research, however. When you set out to research critical comment, remember that you are in at least as much danger from what you find as from what you miss. Discovering a source that carries on your line of argument so well that it leaves you little to add will take the satisfaction out of your work as well as the challenge, and you will learn little from basing your essay on such a source. Moreover, depending heavily on a source increases the chances of unintentional plagiarism — not making it entirely clear which ideas are really yours and which are borrowed. Thus, finding a published essay that covers much of what you intend to say about a topic is a good reason to consider changing topics or at least modifying your approach.

Much more serious than occasional reliance on secondary sources for ideas is developing a habit of dependency. It is all too easy to drift into a pattern of reviewing criticism before you begin to form your own ideas, thereby allowing others to shape your views. Always keep in mind when dealing with critical opinions that they are just that — opinions. Be impressed if you like, but never be intimidated. Even the best critics are human and therefore fallible. They are influenced by the prevailing critical assumptions of their times and often by specific theoretical affiliations. You have every right to disagree with published critics or, for that matter, with your instructors, provided you state your case clearly and support it conscientiously with references to the text in question. Consider other views carefully and with the respect any honest effort to advance understanding deserves, but then, when writing your essays, think for yourself.

STARTING TO WRITE

In contrast with the many difficulties involved in completing a good critical essay on time, putting off getting started is one of the easiest things you will ever do — easy and risky. It is human nature to put off the more difficult of competing tasks until the straightforward ones are out of the way, but with writing, the difficult jobs are precisely the ones to start first. Start early. Leave yourself time to explore blind alleys and, when you feel you are getting nowhere, to allow your subconscious mind to work on the problem while you are consciously engaged with other concerns. You will almost always find that ten hours invested in a writing project over a week will yield better results than a single ten-hour stretch of writing immediately before the deadline for submission.

Writer's Block

Unfortunately, even when you are well aware of the advantages of an early start, you may be held up by a psychological quirk commonly referred to as "writer's block."

Writer's block usually sets in at the earliest stages of a project, making it impossible to begin writing at all or, at best, to carry on past the first page or two. Because fear of failure is part of the cause, writer's block often strikes when you can least afford it — when you are involved in an especially important project or working under pressure. If you have never experienced writer's block, you may find the idea amusing, but sooner or later it affects most writers, and when it does, it can be both unpleasant and costly. Moreover, the anxiety created by one experience can lead to others, creating a steadily worsening problem. It makes sense, therefore, to prepare for writer's block before it strikes by experimenting with methods of resistance in order to determine which work best for you.

The methods described below are primarily intended to help you generate and shape ideas, but because they also encourage you to start writing early, not just when you have time to complete a project but when you have time to waste, they help eliminate writer's block as well. So, even if you find it fairly easy to think of things to say without writing, writing will usually help, and it will certainly make your work no harder.

Questions

Perhaps the most straightforward way to clarify what you think about a subject is to ask yourself questions about it. In order to avoid writer's block, not to mention loss and confusion, keep a record of your questions and answers in writing.

Beginning with very general questions, such as why you like or dislike something, progress gradually to questions that are more specific, quickly abandoning lines of inquiry that lead away from manageable topics. If you need help devising questions, you will find the lists included in writing textbooks many and varied, and most of them will work adequately up to a point. Watch for that point. At first, any question that forces you to examine your ideas will be better than none, but the further you carry on with a ready-made list, the more likely the questions are to limit your answers. As soon as a suggested line of inquiry begins to get in the way of your developing ideas, abandon it and strike off on your own. Such lists are generally more useful for getting started than for leading you to conclusions.

Be wary also of lists of questions not designed for students of literature. For example, lists are often based on the journalistic standard: Who? What? Where? When? Why? How? While such lists encourage thoroughness in getting at the facts of a situation, an essay about literature is, of course, far more subtle than a news story. Normally, your readers will be familiar with the facts of the works you are discussing and will not require a review. Thus you will be wise to pass quickly over the Who? What? Where? and When? and concentrate on questions concerned with Why? and How? More often than not, you will begin forming a useful argument only when you begin addressing these last two.

Interaction

If asking and answering questions by yourself seems lonely work, you may prefer to involve others. Approaches vary according to circumstances and temperament.

One common method of generating ideas, sometimes called brainstorming, involves gathering a group together, with tape recorder running or one member taking notes, and throwing out ideas. The exchange is kept as informal as possible to avoid inhibiting creativity. This sort of exercise works better in developing advertising slogans than critical essays, and a lot of what results will be useless, but finding and rejecting inappropriate approaches to a subject will often help you progress toward forming better ones. At least such an exchange of ideas will get you started.

If you lack the informed group required for brainstorming, you can sometimes develop ideas and free yourself from writer's block by talking to a single listener. Even if this person knows little about your subject, his or her responses can help you decide where your views lack clarity or need support. Remember, however, that in the end it should be you who judges and refines the ideas: using another person as a sounding board for your own ideas is not the same thing as allowing another person to tell you what to think. For the sake of honesty and your development as a critical thinker, avoid working with someone whose superior knowledge of your subject may make it hard to rely on your own judgement.

Free Writing

One of the most reliable ways of breaking writer's block is called "free writing." Free writing is a way of freeing yourself from worry about imperfections in expression that can inhibit the flow of ideas early in a project. It involves committing yourself to writing for a predetermined period of time. You simply sit down in a place where you will not be interrupted and, keeping your subject in mind, write until the time is up. Resist pausing for reflection or stopping to revise. At best, you will be well into a rough draft by the time you finish. At worst, what you produce will be only vaguely relevant to your subject, but, even if the written result is of little value, you will still have broken your writer's block and moved closer to understanding what you want to say. You can always begin a second session of free writing by reacting to the shortcomings of your first.

FOCUSING

Once you put your early inhibitions behind you and begin accumulating ideas, you will soon find yourself with more than you can hope to bring together in a paper. This is the time to turn your attention from generating ideas to pruning and focusing. Handling the focusing stage of a writing project well can save you a great deal of time later on, but it takes discipline. Piling up ideas becomes so easy once you get started that it is tempting to carry on too long, deluding yourself that you are accomplishing something when in fact you are rambling out of control. While writing anything is better than writing nothing at the start of the writing process, this does not remain true throughout. Avoid the common mistake of trying to substitute quantity for quality.

You can approach the job of focusing from two general directions — working from a thesis or toward one. If you are lucky, you will discover one particularly interesting line of argument early along. Stating your main ideas as a proposition to be proved — a proposition often referred to as a "thesis" and commonly announced near the beginning of an essay in a sentence termed a "thesis statement"— will provide you with a guide as you write, a premise to refer to as you choose which of your secondary ideas to expand, which to subordinate, and which to cut. If no clear thesis has emerged by the time you are ready to start focusing, you can develop one by grouping the most promising ideas and then pruning obvious loose ends. The more loose ends you cut, the more clearly you will see the best potential lines of argument. By the time you have narrowed the possibilities to two or three, you will not only be in a good position to choose the best, but you will also have developed a general idea of how best to support the one you choose.

Be certain, however, that you do not stop before the job is done. Just as it is important to begin focusing before you are overwhelmed with an unmanageable accumulation of ideas, it is also vital to carry on to the desired end — a single, supportable thesis:

> **Not** "Although Andrew Marvell's 'To His Coy Mistress' is manipulative to some extent in taking advantage of flattery, sophistry, and shocking images of mutability, it sometimes reveals a genuine regard for the object of passion and leaves the reader wondering how fully the object of Marvell's affection — or lust — would be capable of appreciating what is going on in the poem."

> **But** "In 'To His Coy Mistress,' Andrew Marvell is addressing a well-educated woman whose intelligence he respects."

> **Or** "Andrew Marvell's most compelling means of seduction in 'To His Coy Mistress' is neither flattery nor shock, but logic."

The first statement above has more than its share of interesting ideas, but it would likely yield either two or three papers tacked loosely together or, worse still, a muddled blend. Parting with ideas can be hard, but attempting to fit more notions into an essay than you can explain and support adequately will be much harder. Saving a few minutes by rushing the focusing stage can cost you many hours later on.

Outlines

Quite a few writing textbooks advise preparing a detailed outline before attempting the first draft, a practice that is usually less effective for critical arguments than expository essays. In essays devoted mainly to reviewing large amounts of factual information, information that is readily gathered and organized in advance of writing, a detailed outline will prove an invaluable tool, one that can greatly speed the process of writing and revision. In more speculative essays, however, the kind of essays commonly written about literature, the difficulty of deciding what you are going to say, and in what order, without a certain amount of groping on paper will often make a detailed outline harder to produce than a draft.

Therefore, using outlines for essays on literature requires flexibility. If planning is one of your strengths, beginning your writing with an outline will definitely speed the work that follows. But if you find preparing outlines more difficult than diving in and writing a draft without one, you will be wise not to spend too much time struggling to follow advice that is more appropriate for some types of writers and for some types of writing than others. Do what works for you.

Tree-Diagramming

If you like working from an outline yet find outlines difficult to organize while you are still generating ideas, try "tree-diagramming," a method that can help you form an outline in something the same way free writing helps you progress toward a first draft. Place a word or phrase representing your central idea in the middle of a large sheet of paper and work outward, connecting related ideas through a series of branches. Though the result of this exercise will rarely resemble a tree, it will provide you with an overview of relationships, revealing both dead ends and useful lines of inquiry quickly. (See Figures 1 and 2.)

WRITING AND REVISING

If you start early and use your time efficiently, you should have developed and focused your ideas several days before your essay is due. At this point, you will have at least a general idea of how your essay will be organized to support your thesis, and you will probably have done some drafting. The next step, completing your first draft, should be fairly straightforward if you resist the temptation to stop and polish style.

Once you have a completed draft that makes sense and includes all your main points, distance yourself from what you have written by leaving it alone

Figure 1   Writer's Block: First Tree Diagram

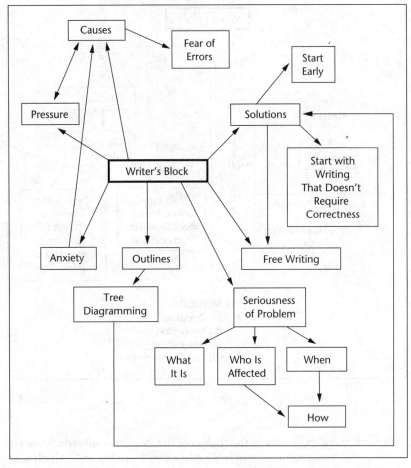

for a day or two. Then, coming back to the project relatively fresh, you will be able to decide more quickly and reliably whether what you have written needs cutting, expansion, or restructuring. After you are satisfied with the form and the essential content, it will be time for polishing style and fine-tuning your argument.

Remember: an essay you write over a week or ten days will almost always be better than one you produce in a single marathon effort, even though you invest the same number of hours in total.

Audience

As you revise your essay, you will have two main concerns — making your argument clear and forceful, and maintaining one consistent appropriate

Figure 2 Writer's Block: Second Tree Diagram

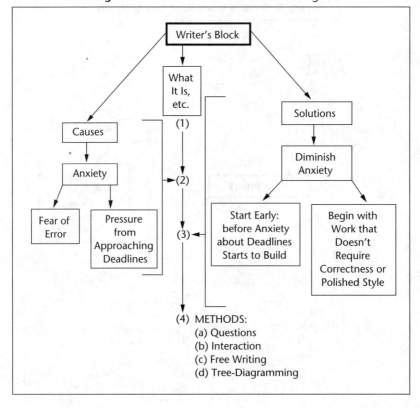

style throughout. Style can be the trickier of the two, especially when you try to affect it. Do not assume an overly sophisticated, erudite style which may not be appropriate even for literary critics. You will find that an unnatural style will be very difficult to maintain for an entire essay. A much easier and more reliable approach is to let your audience and your relationship with it control your style automatically, as they would your voice if you were speaking.

What audience do you write for? The answer is less obvious than you might think. While you probably want most to impress the instructor who will eventually give your work a grade, you may well find that writing with another audience in mind makes this easier. Consider the unnaturalness of explicating literature for someone who knows a great deal more about it than you and who has probably encountered views similar to yours many times before. Will this situation inspire you with confidence? Or is it more likely to make you adopt an apologetic tone and be slightly dismissive about your ideas? How do you feel about writing for someone who can be expected to note technical errors and lower your grade in consequence? Will this audience encourage a confident, forceful style? Hardly.

It makes more sense to write for an audience you can persuade and enlighten, one at about your own level of ability. An audience made up of the better students in your class is a sensible choice. You know this audience well, you can assume it will be familiar with the works you are considering, and you can be confident that it will find your insights fresh and interesting. Writing for an audience of equals will also make it easier for you to adopt a natural, unpretentious style — your own.

In addition to helping you find an appropriate style, writing for an audience of equals will also help you decide what needs to be explained and what does not. For example, since your audience has read and understood the surface meaning of the works you are writing about, you will not need to summarize plot or review other obvious facts. When you need to make specific references to plot or character in support of your developing argument, you will keep these references brief — reminders, rather than revelations. On the other hand, you cannot assume that your audience has seen reasoning similar to yours before, and you should therefore make your line of thinking and the connections between evidence and the conclusions you draw from it more explicit than you might if you were writing exclusively for your instructor.

Openings

Inexperienced writers often get into trouble by working on the assumption that the parts of an essay should be finished one at a time from first to last. This assumption is wrong on two counts. First, if you have the time, it is almost always easier to improve all the parts of an essay at about the same rate as you work through a series of drafts. Second, when lack of time makes a series of drafts impossible and you have to finish sections in sequence, it is usually easier to write the rest of the essay before you put the finishing touches on the opening.

If you are like most student writers, you have more difficulty with openings than with any other part of your essays. Your opening paragraphs may be wordy, vague, and repetitive, even though they receive more attention line for line than other sections. The problem is poor timing. While good essays generally require several drafts, inexperienced writers working under pressure hope to arrive at a final version in as few drafts as possible. In this hope, they attempt to produce a final, polished version when they have only an incomplete or very rough draft to revise, and they naturally start with the opening, struggling to introduce what they will say before they are sure of precisely what this will be. The time-consuming tinkering with wording and groping for ideas that ensue can take more time than revising the whole essay less meticulously. Even worse, having put so much effort into the opening, they are reluctant to make necessary changes once they finish the rest of the essay. The result: a vague, inflated introduction followed by a hastily composed argument that had to be dashed off because of all the time wasted in introducing it. There is nothing wrong with including an opening paragraph containing a clear thesis statement in your first draft; in fact it helps to keep your argument on topic. But, having done that, you will usually find it easiest to leave the opening rough until the rest of your essay is polished to its conclusion.

At this point, you will have a much more certain idea of what you want to introduce in the opening, and you will find writing it much easier in consequence.

Keep in mind as you complete your opening that it should actually accomplish something — excite your reader's interest, persuade your reader of the value of your approach, prepare your reader to grasp what follows. You can achieve these aims only when you yourself fully understand where your essay is going.

Revising for Correctness

While your first concerns throughout most of the writing process should be to make sense and express yourself in an appropriate, consistent style, you cannot afford to ignore correctness — following the accepted conventions of grammar, punctuation, and spelling. While correctness cannot in itself guarantee success, carelessness or incompetence in handling basic writing will certainly ensure failure.

Fortunately, whether they believe it or not, most students who are penalized for errors know enough about grammar and punctuation to write correctly. Attitude more than ignorance is the cause. If you tend to make a lot of mistakes, do not let discouragement or frustration exaggerate your weakness. Convincing yourself that you lack the ability to write correctly is simply an excuse for not investing the time and the work required to master correctness. Seriously confronted, the job of revising for correctness will become easier and less time-consuming with practice.

TEN COMMON MISTAKES TO AVOID IN WRITING ABOUT LITERATURE

Occasionally, even when you start early and work conscientiously, you will still get into difficulty in writing an essay about literature. More often than not this stems from one of the common errors below. While being on guard against these mistakes cannot guarantee success, it will greatly increase your chances.

1. Taking On Unrealistically Ambitious Projects
Be realistic in choosing topics. Avoid topics that will take more space, time, specialized knowledge, or research than you can put into them. If you are not sure whether your plans are manageable, check with your instructor.

2. Plagiarizing by Mistake
Be careful not to drift into plagiarism by keeping sloppy records of your research. Record complete information for references immediately upon

(continued)

encountering a source you may want to refer to later. When taking notes, make a clear distinction between recorded information, paraphrases, and quotations.

3. Retaining Irrelevant Material from Early Drafts
If sections of an essay seem loosely connected with each other or with the controlling thesis, try to put the essay in order by supplying clear transitions showing the reader how each part relates to the whole. If you find it difficult to justify a section, cut or shorten it. The ideas that could produce two or three good essays will usually make one bad one.

4. Attempting to Polish Style Too Early
Do not attempt to perfect style while you are still unsure of what you want to say. Be especially wary of polishing openings before you have a clear idea of what will follow.

5. Writing about Yourself Rather than Your Topic
Concentrate on your topic rather than your feelings, doubts, or difficulties as you write. Avoid such redundant insertions as "it seems to me that" and "I think that"; your reader will know you are doing the thinking that goes into your essay without constantly being reminded.

6. Summarizing Plot and Explaining the Obvious
Avoid boring your reader by summarizing what happens in literary works and reviewing obvious facts at length. Assume an audience of intelligent readers familiar with the works you are analyzing and supply only the information this audience will need to evaluate your argument.

Do not be influenced by the summaries provided in various publications termed "notes." These summaries do not constitute serious criticism and should not be imitated.

7. Confusing Verb Tenses
Keep the sequences of verb tenses within long sentences as simple as possible, and avoid shifting tenses unnecessarily. Using the conventional present tense to describe characters, circumstances, and events in literary works will help greatly.

8. Inflating Style
Inflated style is no substitute for good ideas. Impress your readers with the clarity and sense of your thinking rather than the sophistication of your presentation. Strive to write in your own voice; keep your sentence structure as straightforward as you can without being choppy and repetitive;

(continued)

use only those literary terms that you understand. If you work with a thesaurus, use it to find the most accurate and readily understood terms available rather than as a shortcut to pretentiousness and obscurity.

9. Failing to Follow Conventions of Manuscript Form

Follow the accepted conventions for presenting your work on the page and acknowledging sources. It helps to remember that these conventions are not merely decorative; rather, they are an essential code for communicating information efficiently and accurately.

10. Proofreading Inattentively

Proofread when you are rested, preferably after a good night's sleep, rather than immediately after you finish an essay. Proofread in a place free from distractions, and give the job the full attention it requires. The half hour or so you take to proofread an essay properly will often have more effect on the grade than any other half hour of work you invest in the project.

Time is the key factor. To write correctly you must know your limitations and allow yourself time to compensate for them. If you find yourself penalized for errors regularly, understand why. Is it carelessness in the final stages of writing? Or do you lack the background in the basics of writing? If you know what you are doing but make careless mistakes, you need merely improve your proofreading skills and find an appropriate proofreading time, which is to say a time when you will not be too tired to concentrate or likely to be distracted. If your problem is more serious and you are uncertain of what is correct in some cases, budget the extra time you will need to check. Checking your own work is a good way to learn, and you will probably find once you confront the problem of errors that you know more than you think you do. Like most students who are penalized for errors, you probably make the same types of errors again and again, although you handle most elements correctly. Take note of the types of things that go wrong and concentrate on these. Make a checklist of things to watch for. Review the relevant rules as you approach the final stages of writing. Ignorance, in this case, is no excuse: all the information you need about grammar and punctuation can be found easily in writing handbooks, and spelling can, of course, be checked in a dictionary — provided you allow yourself time to do the work.

Once you are satisfied that your own writing is correct, turn your attention to another aspect of your essay that requires care. Most instructors consider the format and accuracy of quotations and references to be just as important as the correctness of your own writing, so check these carefully before submitting your essay. Have you provided all the requirements, such as a title and title page, that are mentioned in the assignment? Are all your quotations recorded exactly? Have you consistently followed the correct format in supplying notes and bibliographical references? Taking care with such details shows that you are serious about your work; allowing even a few mistakes can call the accuracy of all your work into question.

One further word of warning, however: remember that timing is just as important as taking time in correcting your essays. It is as serious a mistake to let your concern with correctness preoccupy you during the earlier stages of writing as it is to neglect correctness later on. Worrying about errors early along will distract you from the important work of forming ideas, and it may also encourage you to adopt an overly cautious style aimed more at avoiding errors than communicating. So leave the job of checking for correctness till the end of your project, and then take it seriously.

*****

While you cannot avoid the basic fact that writing well about literature involves hard work, you can, by following the advice supplied here, avoid wasting the work you do and ensure that your hard work yields the good results it deserves. But be sceptical: this advice is a basis, not a formula, for success. Keep in mind that writing is a personal endeavour and that no one method will work best for every person and every occasion. Treat this and all advice on writing critically, measuring its usefulness against your experience of what works best for you as you continue to grow as a writer.

CREDITS

Atwood, Margaret "The Resplendent Quetzal" from *Dancing Girls and Other Stories*. Used by permission of the Canadian Publishers, McClelland & Stewart, Toronto.

Chopin, Kate "The Story of an Hour" from *The Complete Works of Kate Chopin, vol. 1* (Baton Rouge: Louisiana State University Press, 1969).

Clarke, Austin C. "The Motor Car" from *When He Was Free and Young and He Used to Wear Silks* (1971, House of Anansi). Published in Canada by Harcourt Canada.

Conrad, Joseph "An Outpost of Progress" from *The Medallion Edition of the Works of Joseph Conrad, vol. 1* (London: Gresham Publishing, 1925).

Faulkner, William "A Rose for Emily" from *Collected Stories of William Faulkner*. Copyright © 1930 and renewed 1958 by William Faulkner. Reprinted by permission of Random House, Inc.

Gallant, Mavis "My Heart Is Broken." Copyright © 1957 by Mavis Gallant. Reprinted by permission of Georges Borchardt, Inc. for the author.

Gilman, Charlotte Perkins "The Yellow Wallpaper" from *The Charlotte Perkins Gilman Reader, Volume 1* (New York: Pantheon, 1980). **Crane, Stephen** "The Open Boat" from *The Open Boat and Other Stories* (London: Heinemann, 1898).

Hemingway, Ernest "A Clean, Well-Lighted Place" from *The Complete Short Stories of Ernest Hemingway*. Copyright 1933 by Charles Scribner's Sons. Copyright renewed © 1961 by Mary Hemingway. Reprinted by permission of Scribner, a division of Simon & Schuster.

Hollingshead, Greg "The Naked Man" from *The Roaring Girl* (Toronto: Somerville House Books, 1995). Reprinted by permission of the author.

Joyce, James "Araby" from *Dubliners*. Copyright 1916 by B.W. Huebsch. Definitive text copyright © 1967 by the Estate of James Joyce. Reprinted by permission of Viking Penguin, a division of Penguin Books USA Inc.

King, Thomas "Borders" from *One Good Story, That One*, copyright © 1993 by Thomas King. Published in Canada by HarperCollins Publishers Ltd. Reprinted with permission.

Lau, Evelyn "Family" extracted from *Choose Me* by Evelyn Lau. Copyright © Evelyn Lau 1999. Reprinted by permission of Doubleday Canada, a division of Random House of Canada Limited.

Laurence, Margaret "The Loons" from *A Bird in the House*. Used by permission of the Canadian Publishers, McClelland & Stewart, Toronto.

MacLeod, Alistair "The Boat" from *Island*. Used by permission of the Canadian Publishers, McClelland & Stewart, Toronto.

Mansfield, Katherine "Bliss" from *Bliss and Other Stories* (New York: Alfred A. Knopf, 1931).

Maracle, Lee "Too Much to Explain" from *Sojourners and Sundogs: First Nations Fiction* (Vancouver: Press Gang Publishers, 1999). Reprinted by permission of Polestar/Raincoast and the author.

McGrath, Elizabeth "Fogbound in Avalon." Reprinted by permission of the author; © 1980.